Henry Ward Beecher

The Great Brooklyn Romance

All the Documents in the Famous Beecher-Tilton Case, Unabridged

Henry Ward Beecher

The Great Brooklyn Romance
All the Documents in the Famous Beecher-Tilton Case, Unabridged

ISBN/EAN: 9783337348526

Printed in Europe, USA, Canada, Australia, Japan

Cover: Foto ©Andreas Hilbeck / pixelio.de

More available books at **www.hansebooks.com**

THE

GREAT BROOKLYN ROMANCE.

ALL THE

DOCUMENTS IN THE FAMOUS BEECHER-TILTON CASE,

UNABRIDGED.

PORTRAITS AND FAC-SIMILES.

NEW YORK:

J. H. PAXON,

GRAPHIC BUILDING, 39 & 41 PARK PLACE, ROOM 5.

1874.

TABLE OF CONTENTS.

ILLUSTRATIONS.

TABLE OF CONTENTS.

LETTER-PRESS.

TABLE OF CONTENTS.

TABLE OF CONTENTS.

Brooklyn Jan 1/74
In trust with—
F. D. Moulton

My Dear Friend Moulton
I ask through
you Theodore Tilton's
forgiveness, and I
humble myself before
him as I do. before
my God, he would
have been a better man,
in my circumstances than
I have been — I can
ask nothing except
that he will remember
all the other hearts—
that would ache — I
will not further. I
Even with that I

...well, dead, but others must live and suffer. I will die before anyone but myself shall be inculcated. All my thoughts are running toward my friends. I spared the poor child lying there and praying with her folded hands; she is guiltless. I revolt against being the overthrow of another. Her forgiveness I have, I humbly pray to God that he may put into the heart of her husband to forgive me —

I have trusted this six months in confidence. H.W. Beecher

Dec 30. 1870

Wednesday.

My dear Friend,

Does your heart bound toward all, as it used? So does mine! I am myself again. I did not dare tell you till I was sure: but the bird has sung in my heart these four weeks & he has consented with me never again to leave. "Spring has come."* Because I thought it would gladden you to know this, & not to trouble or embarrass you in any way I now write. Of course I should like to share with you my joy: but can wait for the Beyond!

When dear Frank says I may see again go to old Plymouth, I will thank the dear Father.

Wearied with importunity, & weakened by sickness, I gave a letter inculpating my friend Henry Ward Beecher, under assurances that that would remove all difficulties between me & my husband. That letter I now revoke. I was persuaded to it almost forced when I was in a weakened state of mind I regret it & recall all its statements

E R Tilton

I desire to say explicitly Mr Beecher has never offered any improper solicitations, but has always treated me in a manner becoming a Christian & a gentleman

Elizabeth R. Tilton.

Mrs. Tilton's retraction of her recantation.

My Dear Husband,
Dec 30. 1870
Midnight

I desire to leave with you before going to sleep a statement that Mr Henry Ward Beecher called upon me this evening, asked me if I would defend him against any accusation in a <u>council of ministers,</u> & I replied solemnly that I would, in case the accuser was any other person than my husband. He (Dr W.B.) dictated a letter which I copied as my own, to be used by him as against any other accuser except my husband. This letter was designed to vindicate Mr Beecher against all other persons save only yourself.

I was ready to give him this letter because he said with pain that my letter in your hands addressed to him dated Dec 29. had struck him dead, & ended his usefulness.

You & I both are pledged to do our best to avoid publicity. God grant a speedy end to all further injuries.

Affectionately
Elizabeth.

Beecher to Moulton.

Monday July 5. 72

My dear friend:

I have torn to day, — & expect to pass this' f[or] Peekskill the Newhaven. Shall not be here till friday.

"Great Year of Sorrow", I would not have believed that any one could experience say pass this' my Sufferings & be alive, or sane —

I have been the center of three distinct circles, each one of which required clear-mindedness, and peculiar narrative, or originating power — viz.
1. The Great Church —
2. The Newspaper
3. The Book —

The first I could not then get out of, nor sleight. The sensitiveness of so many of my people would have made any appearance of trouble, on any remission of force, an occasion of alarm, and notice, & have excited, when it was important that minором all die & everything be quieted —

The Newspaper I did well off — doing but little & cept give general direction. & in so doing, I was continually spurred & exhorted, by those in interest. It could not be helped —

The Life of Christ, long delayed, had locked up the capital of the firm & was likely to sink them — I finished the manuscript be — the even book, born

of final sorrow as that was? —
The interior history of it will never be written —

During all this time, You, literally, have all my stay & comfort, I should have fallen in the way but for the courage & spirit which you inspired, & the hope which you breathed —

No man can see the difficulties that environ me, unless he stands where I do — To say that I have a Church on my hands is simple enough — but to have the hundreds & thousands of men, pressing me; each one with his keen suspicion, an anxiety, an zeal; to see tendencies which if not stopped would break out into a ruinous defence of me; to stop them without seeming to do it; to prevent any one questioning me; to meet and allay prejudices against T. which had their beginnings years before them; — to keep serene, as if I was not alarmed — & it is likely to be cheerful at home, & among friends, when I was suffering the torments of the damned. To pass sleepless nights often, yet, to come up fresh & full for Sunday, — all that I may be talked about; but the real thing cannot be understood fr. the outside, nor its wearing & grinding on the nervous system.

God knows that I have put more thought, & judgment, & earnest desire, into my efforts to prepare a way for T & E, than ever I did for myself — a hundred fold —

Act to the outside public—I have never lost an opportunity to soften prejudices, to refute falsehoods, & to excite kindly feeling among all those I meet, I am thrown among clergymen—public men—and generally, the makers of public opinion—and I have used my rational endeavor to repair the evils wh have been visited upon I. & will increasing success—

But, the roots of this prejudice are long. The catastrophe wh precipitated him from his place, only disclosed feeling that had existed long—Neither he, nor you, can be aware of the feelings of classes in Society, or other friends than little numers—I mention this to explain why I know will circumstance certainty—that no mere statement, letter, testimony, or affirmation, will reach the root of affairs & resistedly them. Some & when will that chinese will regain his ...

... Institution wh please here all will, that there but stand in the way. I am willing to obey chosen, & wait. No one can suffer more than truly. More I do affirm. Sacrifice now hesitation hesitation of your own already see. you may the love high & sufficing bleeding.

I do not think that any thing wh be gained by this—I should be destroyed, but he would not be saved—& the children would have their future clouded,—In one point of view, I should desire the sacrifice on my part. Nothing can possibly be so bad as the horror of great bankruptcy. In this I have had enough of my time. I look upon death as better faced than any friend I have in the world. Life would be pleasant, if I could see that ruin wh be in shattered. But to live on the sharp & ragged edge of anxiety, remorse, fear, despair, wept to put on all this appearance of serenity and happiness,—cannot be endured much longer.

I am well nigh discouraged. If you, too, cease to trust me—to love me—I am alone. I had not another person in the world to whom I could go.

Well—to God I commit all.—Whatever it may be here, it shall be well there—With sincere gratitude for your heroic friendship & with sincere affection even tho' your love see not, I am Yours (tho' unworthy to you)—HW

Brooklyn, Jan 1st 1871.

Mr. Henry C. Bowen,

Sir,

I received last evening your sudden notices breaking my two contracts, one with *The Independent* and the other with *The Brooklyn Union*.

With reference to this act of yours, I will make a plain statement of facts.

It was during the early part of the rebellion (if I recollect aright) when you first intimated to me that the Rev. Henry Ward Beecher had committed acts of adultery for which, if you should expose him, he would be driven from his pulpit.

From that time onward your references to this subject were frequent, and always accompanied with the exhibition of a deep-seated injury to your heart.

On the 26th day December, 1870, at an interview in your house, at which Mr. Oliver Johnson and I were present, you spoke freely and indignantly

against Mr. Beecher as an
unsafe relation among the
families of his congregation.
You alluded by name to a
woman, now a widow, whose
husband's death you had no
doubt was hastened by his
knowledge that Mr. Beecher had
maintained with her an improper
intimacy. You avowed your
knowledge of several other
cases of Mr. Beecher's adulteries.
Moreover, as if to leave no
doubt on the mind either of
Mr. Johnson or myself, you
informed us that Mr. Beecher
had made to you a confession
of his guilt, and had with tears
implored your forgiveness.

After Mr. Johnson
retired from this interview, you
related to me the case of a
woman whom you said (as
nearly as I can recall
your words) that Mr. Beecher
took in his arms by force,
threw down upon a sofa,
accomplished upon her his
deviltry, and

Tilton to Beecher.

Dec. 26, 1870
Brooklyn

Henry Ward Beecher,
Sir:

I demand
that, for reasons which you
explicitly understand, you immediately
cease from the ministry of
Plymouth Church and that you
quit the City of Brooklyn as a
residence.

Signed,

Theodore Tilton.

Mrs. Woodhull to Beecher.

48 Broad St. June 3d 1872

Rev. Henry Ward Beecher
My Dear Sir

The social
fight against me, being now waged in this
city, is becoming rather hotter than I can well
endure longer, standing unsupported and alone
as I have until now. Within the past two
weeks I have been shut out of Hotel after Hotel
and am now, after having obtained a place in
one, hunted down by a set of males & females, who
are determined that I shall not be permitted
to live, even if they can prevent it.

Now I want your assistance — I want to
be sustained in my position in the Gilsey House
from which I am ordered out, and from which
I do not wish to go — and all this simply because
I am Victoria C. Woodhull, the advocate of Social
Freedom. I have submitted to this persecution
just so long as I am able to. My business, my friends,
in fact everything for which I live, suffers from it, and
it must cease. Will you lend me your aid in this?

Yours very truly, Victoria C. Woodhull

Bessie Turner to Mrs. Tilton.

January 10th
1871

Brooklyn

My dear Mrs Tilton,

I regret to tell you something. Your Mother, Mrs Morse, has repeatedly attempted to hire me by offering me dresses & presents to go to certain persons and tell them ~~stories~~ injurious to the character of your husband ~~~~ I have been persuaded that the kind attentions shown me by Mr Tilton for years were dishonorable ~~demonstrations~~. I never at the time ~~thought~~ that Mrs Tilton's caresses were for such a purpose. I do not want to be made use of by Mrs Morse or any one else, to bring trouble on my two best friends you and your husband.

Byeby.

Bessie Turner.

Mrs. Tilton's Statement.

Dec 15. 1872.

In July 1871, prompted by my duty, I informed my husband that Mr H. W. Beecher, my friend & pastor had solicited me to be a wife to ~~him~~, together with all that this implies.

Six months afterward my husband felt impelled by the circumstances of a conspiracy against him in which Mrs Beecher had taken part to have an interview with Mr Beecher.

In order that Mr B— might know exactly what I had said to my husband, I wrote a brief statement (I have forgotten in what form) which my husband showed to Mr Beecher. Late the same evening Mr B— came to me (lying very sick at the time) & filled me with distress saying I had ruined him. — & wanting to know if I meant to appear against him. — This I certainly did not mean to do, & his thought was agonizing to me. I then signed a paper which he wrote, to clear him in case of a trial. In this instance, as in most others, when absorbed by one great interest or feeling, the harmony of my mind is entirely

destroyed, & I found an affliction that this paper and to leave it to place me most unjustly against my husband, & in the sight of all the Beecher. In order to refresh so cruel a blow to my long suffering husband I wrote an explanation of what first paper & my intention in both frames from Mr B—'s feelings & her in my infatuation & statement, & the letter I this and my connection with the case.

Elizabeth R. Tilton.

P.S. This statement ~~was~~ made at the request of Mr Carpenter that it may be shown confidentially to Mr Storrs & other friends with whom my husband & I are consulting.

Mrs. Hooker. to Beecher.

Hartford Wed. 27. 72

Dear Brother

Read the enclosed clipped from "The Times" of this city last evening.

I can endure no longer. — I must see you & persuade you & write a paper which I will read, going alone to your pulpit & taking sole charge of the service. I shall leave here on 8 A.M. train Friday morning — & unless you meet me at 42 St. Station shall go to Mrs Phelps house, opposite Young Mens Christian Assoc. No 49. 23rd St. Where I shall hope to see you during the day. Mrs Phelps kindly said to me when last in N. York — "My daughter & I are now alone — living quietly in one pleasant home & I want you to come there without warning whenever you are in N. York — unless you have other friends whom you prefer to visit".

So I shall go as if on a shopping trip: & stay as long as seems best.

Ever yrs in love.
unspeakable. Belle.

Thos. K. Beecher to Mrs. Hooker

Elmira Nov. 5. 1872

Dear Belle.

To allow the Devil himself to be crushed for speaking the truth is unspeakably cowardly & contemptible.

I respect, as at present advised Mrs Woodhull while I abhor her philosophy. She only carries out Henry's philosophy. against which I recorded my protest 10 years ago & parted (lovingly & achingly) from him. saying "We cannot work together." He has drifted & his heart hid like a crystal — till I am sharp cornered & exacting. I cannot help him except by prayer. I cannot help him this forward.

In my judgment — Henry in following his slippery doctrines of expediency & in his cry of progress & the nobleness of human nature has sacrificed clear exact ideal integrity.

Hands off — until he is down — & then my pulpit my home — my church & my purse & heart are at his service.

Of the two — Woodhull is my hero & Henry my coward. as at present advised. But I protest against the whole & all its belongings. — I was not anti-slavery — I am not anti-family. But. as I wrote years ago — whenever I assault & Henry because of it & above in authority I shall assail the church & the State — the family & all other institutions of selfish usage.

So item the papers. You cannot help Henry. You must be true to yourself. I am out of the circle & yet — & am glad of it. When the storm line inch me. I shall suffer as a christian — saying — Curse ye from man.

— Dont write to me. Follow the truth — I un you need me cry out.

Yours lovingly
Tom.

Brooklyn May 3/71

Mr Beecher,

My future either
for life or death, would be
happier, could I but feel that
you forgave while you forget
me. In all the sad com-
plications of the past year,
my endeavour was to entirely
keep from you all suffering;
bear myself alone, leaving
you forever ignorant of it.
My weapons were love, a larger
entering generosity & much
hiding! That I failed utterly,
we both know. But now I ask
forgiveness.

Mrs. Tilton to Mr. Moulton.

Dear Francis,
I did tell you
the falsehoods at your last
visit. I first I entirely misunderstood your question, thinking
it had reference to the

interview at your house the
day before. But when I withheld
gently replied to you, I replied
falsely. I wish now put myself on record truthfully.

I told Mr B— that at the
time of my confession, I—
had made similar confessions
to me of himself; but no
developments as to persons.

When you then asked for
your own satisfaction,
"Was it so!" I told my second
lie. After you had left
I said to T— You know I
was obliged to lie to Frank
and I now say rather than
make others suffer, as I now
do— I must lie; for it is a
physical impossibility for
me to tell the truth.

Yet I do think Francis
had not T—'s angry troubled
face been before me, I would
have told you the truth.

I am a perfect coward in his

forever not forgiving fault of his for-
getly, but from long habit of timidity;
I implore you all this be extreme
to be careful not to lead one into further
temptation.
You may show this to T— or to
B— or any one. An effort made for
truth.

Affectly Elizabeth

A HISTORY

OF THE

GREAT SCANDAL.

ACCORDING to Mr. Theodore Tilton's sworn statement, his wife informed him on the evening of the third of July, 1870—a little more than four years ago—that she had been overcome by the specious reasoning of the Rev. Henry Ward Beecher, and had yielded to him her person on several occasions. In November, 1872, Mrs. Woodhull published in her *Weekly* a long and circumstantial account of the alleged liaison between Mr. Beecher and Mrs. Tilton. This account was discussed and commented upon for some time, but as all the principal parties mentioned in it had preserved a wise reticence, the subject dropped out of the public mind. Mr. Tilton, after having been a member of Plymouth Church for a great number of years, ceased his attendance on the ministry of its pastor immediately after the discovery of his wife's faithlessness to him, and because of it, as he alleges. In August, 1873, about a year ago, a Mr. William F. West, a member of Plymouth Church, called upon Mr. Tilton, and informed him that he intended to cite him before the church for uttering slanders against its pastor. Mr. Tilton informed Mr. West that he was no longer a member of Plymouth Church; that he had withdrawn some years before, as its Clerk knew, and that he most peremptorily declined to go back to the church for any purpose whatsoever, and least of all for the insincere purpose of "investigating one man under pretence of investigating another." As Tilton's name was found upon the church books, Mr. West determined to push his charges against him. Messrs. Beecher, Moulton, and Tilton entered into an agreement to defeat West's object. On the morning of the day of the meeting for receiving the report of the committee on West's charges, Tilton heard that the subject was not to be disposed of according to agreement, but that he was to be made the scapegoat of the scandal. He determined to attend the meeting at Plymouth Church on that evening (October 31, 1873). Sure enough, the report alleged that he refused to answer certain charges made against him, and that therefore his name should be dropped from the church-roll. Tilton rose in the meeting and asked Mr. Beecher if he (Tilton) had ever slandered him (Beecher). Mr. Beecher replied that he had no charges whatever to make against Mr. Tilton. This ended the matter, and Tilton's name was dropped from the rolls of Plymouth Church. Drs. Storrs and Buddington, pastors of Congregational Churches in Brooklyn, criticised the action of Plymouth Church in dropping Tilton without investigating the charges which were said to emanate from him, and which compromised the Christian and moral character of its pastor. Out of this criticism grew the famous Congregational Council, which met in Dr. Storrs' church last spring, and which adjourned after much debate, without finding it expedient to do anything. Dr. Leonard Bacon, of Yale College, was Moderator of this Council. The Doctor found the Council a good subject for a lecture which he delivered in New Haven, and for a number of essays which appeared in the *Independent*. In these papers, Dr. Bacon took every opportunity of lauding Mr. Beecher to the skies, and denouncing Tilton as a "dog and a knave," the doctor reaching his climax by asserting that Tilton was the creature of Beecher's magnanimity.

> "Calmly he heard each calumny that rose,
> "And saw *his* agonies with such sublimity,
> "That all the world exclaimed 'What magnanimity!'"

Dr. Bacon's interference in a matter that did not belong to him, drove Tilton, so he alleges, to presenting the proofs that he was neither a dog nor a knave, and that, if there was magnanimity anywhere, he should be credited with it, and not Mr. Beecher. The result is the famous letter to Dr. Bacon, which called into existence the Plymouth Church committee for the investigation of the scandal, out of which has grown the separation of Mr. and Mrs. Tilton, and which may result in the ruin of Beecher, or in sending Tilton to States-prison.

Though the compiler has a very definite opinion on this sad case, he has not thought it worth while to mention it, nor yet to analyze the documents in the case. They are so grouped that the reader can form his own opinion of them.

The principal actors in this famous case are three in number, Rev. Henry Ward Beecher, Mr. Theodore Tilton, and Mrs. Theodore Tilton, all of Brooklyn. Sketches of the lives of these persons, accompanied by carefully worked-up portraits, from recent photographs, are given below. In order to make the narrative and illustrations as complete as possible, pictures of the exteriors of Plymouth Church and of the residences of Messrs. Beecher and Tilton are also given.

HOW THE SCANDAL CAME OUT.

As throwing some light on this unhappy affair, the following letter, signed "Inquirer," which appeared in the New York *Daily Graphic* of Saturday, July 24th, is inserted:

Please make room for the following points which may serve to throw a light upon the great scandal now agitating this community. In reciting them, I know fully whereof I speak:

1. Tilton was not acquainted with Mrs. Woodhull until nearly a year after the difficulty in his family. His acquaintance with her was due to the fact that it came to his knowledge that she was in possession of his family secret. His famous life of that woman was written in the endeavor to placate her and prevent the publication of the scandal.

2. The story of the scandal got to the public through the indiscretion of Mrs. Susan B. Anthony. She was a guest of the Tiltons when the alleged discovery was made by Mr. Tilton. Her story is that Mrs. Tilton came to her room one night complaining of the violence of "Theodore," and the matter was talked over fully at the breakfast-table the next morning.

3. The first person who communicated the alleged facts to Mrs. Woodhull was Mrs. Elizabeth Cady Stanton, who had received them in confidence from Miss Anthony, and of course they were told in the same way to all the family acquaintances of those two distinguished reformers.

4. It is understood that Mrs. Woodhull has in her possession a letter written by a brother of Miss Susan B. Anthony, a resident of Kansas, in which the whole story of the scene witnessed by his sister at the house of the Tiltons is told.

5. Tilton really tried to save his wife from this scandal. He did not confess the fact even to his most intimate friends, and did all that a man could do to keep it secret until he was fairly driven to the wall.

6. There is no doubt that at the time of this difficulty "free-love" doctrines had a great deal to do with the catastrophe; that they were held in a measure by all the parties to this unhappy scandal. The celebrated "free divorce" editorials in the *Independent* were written by Tilton subsequent to the discovery of the alleged scandal in his own family.

7. There is no allegation on record of any infidelity on Tilton's part before the discovery of the supposed guilt of his wife. Whatever charges are against him date from a subsequent period.

8. This was not a case of deliberate seduction on the part of Mr. Beecher, if the facts are as they are represented to me. She was angered at her husband for his self-sufficiency, his want of considera-

tion for her, and what seemed to her jealous mind his probable infidelities. She went to Mr. Beecher for counsel, and in the prolonged interviews which ensued the intimacy occurred—if the facts are as Tilton supposes them to be.

In closing I venture the prediction that it will be found at the bottom of this whole affair that Mr. Beecher held a sexual theory which he believes to be in advance of the present constitution of society, and that if the facts are as alleged he has fallen because of following out a higher law, as he supposed, than that which controls the conventions of our present society.

TILTON'S UNFAITHFULNESS.

The following letter also appeared in the "DAILY GRAPHIC." It was included in its issue of Thursday, July 23. It contains a "theory of the scandal" which may help to throw light on this painful subject. The letter is signed "Inquirer," and runs as follows :

Will you permit me to make a statement respecting this dep.orable Tilton-Beecher business which may throw some light upon it? I should never have felt moved to utter a word on the subject, were it not that the facts have now become public property, and the incidents I am about to relate may help to form what is greatly needed, a coherent theory of this great scandal. The country is likely to be divided into earnest partisans of Tilton on the one hand, and Beecher on the other ;—but surely there must be a large number of people who have no special partiality for either of those gentlemen, and who wish simply to get at the truth of the affair. The information came into my possession three years ago—how, it is needless to relate. My only object in giving it is to explain the relations of the parties to each other in a more judicial manner than would be the case if the *ex-parte* statements of either were taken as sole evidence.

When Mr. Tilton and his wife were first married, they lived together with a tolerable degree of happiness. But the conditions changed greatly within eight or ten years. The wife, who was an intelligent and clever woman, bore children very rapidly ; she has had seven, of whom four are now living. Immersed in maternal and household cares, Mrs. Tilton ceased to be attractive to her husband, over whom, in the meantime a great change had come. From the obscurity of a reporter on the *Tribune* he had become the celebrated editor of the greatest religious newspaper in the country ; he was moreover an admirable orator, and seemed to have a great and most brilliant career before him. With these changed conditions came changed deportment towards his wife. He manifested a remarkable degree of self-importance ; he treated her, my informant says, with great want of consideration, and it is further hinted, that he was by no means faithful to his marriage vows. Led away by the flattery of women he failed to observe that moral code without which the marriage bond loses its sanctity. All this, of course, was extremely mortifying to the high-spirited wife and mother. She resented such treatment. And here let me remark that Mrs. Tilton is said to possess in an unusual degree, that craving for sympathy and tenderness which is the marked characteristic of her sex. It is even said that her exactions in this respect amount almost to selfishness.

Thus, with extreme sensitiveness on both sides, the ill-feeling which Mrs. Tilton could not suppress was met on Mr. Tilton's part with a want of conciliation, which only tended to make matters worse. In this frame of mind Mrs. Tilton naturally turned for advice and sympathy to her pastor, to the friend of her husband, to the minister who had married her, to the man to whom she had always looked up with reverence and affection. It seems that Tilton had, about this time, been absent a great deal from home. It was in the winter, and he had seventy engagements for lectures, and consequently was travelling a great deal. Mrs. Tilton carried her bruised heart, her wounded pride, her unsatisfied longings to Mr. Beecher, and in him she found a warm sympathizer. Pity, as is well known, is near akin to love, and, if this theory is correct, it led the impulsive, warm-hearted preacher and the sympathetic, craving woman into an intimacy which it is alleged became criminal. This was kept up for some time with the results that are known to the world.

According to my information the explosion occurred in this wise : Miss Susan B. Anthony (through whom, it is alleged, the story subsequently became public, she relating it to all her female associates) was stopping at Mr. Tilton's house. Tilton had been unusually exasperating in his demeanor toward his wife, and it is said had given her renewed cause for jealousy. She was provoked beyond endurance, and, filled with a desire to humiliate him, in passionate utterances she told him, in the presence of the guest alluded to, that she had been as faithless to her marriage vows as he had been to his.

A tremendous scene followed. Tilton was furious. Finally the whole story of her intimacy with her pastor came out. The circumstances, as I have depicted them, explain how the story got abroad. The secret, which should have been guarded by Theodore Tilton, Henry Ward Beecher, Mrs. Tilton, and their mutual friend, Frank Moulton, was first of all babbled about in the clique of woman suffragists, and finally found its way to the public.

In justice to Mr. Tilton, however, it must be stated that up to the date of his last letter he invariably defended his wife. He had denied to everybody but Frank Moulton and Oliver Johnson that anything more occurred than an improper overture from Mr. Beecher to Mrs. Tilton.

The way in which the public regard Tilton is very curious. Everybody admitted that he was a young man of great promise, a fine orator, an able journalist. But somehow he was always the subject of unfavorable comment on the part of the press. He never did anybody any harm; he never spoke unkindly of any of his contemporaries; he engaged in no cabals. But somehow he impressed the public and, I am told, the editors as a man who possessed a great deal of self-consciousness and as assuming a position he was not entitled to. At any rate, he failed to make that favorable impression on his contemporaries which his talents certainly seemed to entitle him to. He possibly lacked a sense of humor, and often a want of tact in dealing with the outside public. But the fact remains that while he has a strong case as against Mr. Beecher, the press of this city is almost unanimously against him.

So here you have the story—the growing alienation between husband and wife, both of them strongly self-conscious, both craving sympathy, both failing to have due consideration for each other. Then comes the pastor, warm-blooded, exuberant, impulsive, and moreover, it is said, with an unhappy home of his own. Such a man dealing with such a woman—all parties being meanwhile infected more or less with the current sexual theories as to the right of individuals to bestow their affections on whom they please—such a man and such a woman, in such a frame of mind, are not at all unlikely to fall. How large a share the free-love doctrines had in this painful affair nobody will probably ever know; but that Henry Ward Beecher was deeply infected with these doctrines is no secret at all. Indeed, they were very plainly avowed by several members of his church to the writer as a positive defence of Mr. Beecher's slips when first this matter got into the papers; and I feel convinced that these pernicious doctrines have had much to do with this unhappy scandal.

I give the statement with the accompanying hypothesis, as it may probably afford a solution of this very painful affair. That Mr. Beecher is the treacherous seducer which Mr. Tilton tries to prove him, very few people will believe. Mr. Beecher fell, if this story is true, through his sympathy with a woman in distress, whom he believed was alienated from her husband by the cruelty of the latter. All this explicable, and the case affords another warning as to the misery which invariably results from the satisfaction of purely egotistic impulses.

HUSBAND AND WIFE TELL THE STORY TO LADY FRIENDS.

The facts stated in " Inquirer's " letter appear to be borne out by an interview which a reporter of the Brooklyn *Argus* had with Mrs. E. Cady Stanton. It appeared in its issue of July 26, and read as follows:

An *Argus* reporter called on Mrs. Elizabeth Cady Stanton, at her residence in Tenafly, N. J., this morning, for the purpose of eliciting facts in the great scandal.

" I am perfectly willing to be interviewed," remarked the lady, with a smile.

" Can you tell me when you first learned of this affair, Mrs. Stanton ? "

" I have shocking poor memory for dates, and will, therefore, not endeavor to fix the exact time. I think, however, it was a year before Mrs. Woodhull published her statement that I knew of the matter. Not all the details, you understand, which have since come to light, but the story in substance."

" And you are willing to tell in what manner you became possessed of this knowledge ? "

" Certainly. Some time—I think it was in the fall of the year, though I wont be positive—while Mrs. Bullard was still connected with the *Revolution*, Susan B. Anthony, Mr. and Mrs. Tilton, Mrs. Bullard and myself were in Brooklyn together. It was afternoon, and after calling at the office of the *Revolution*, Mr. Tilton and myself accompanied Mrs. Bullard to her residence, and remained to dinner. Through some misunderstanding Miss Anthony went with Mrs. Tilton, and dined with her instead of us. There was some feeling on the part of Mrs. Tilton in regard to this, although it was quite unintentional on my part. Well, at the table—no one was present but Mr. Bullard, Mr. Tilton and myself—Theodore told the whole story of his wife's faithlessness. As I before observed, he did not go into the details, but the sum and substance of the whole matter he related in the hearing of Mrs. Bullard and myself. We were reformers. He gave us the story as a phase of social life."

" This was the first you had heard of it ? "

" This was the first. The next evening, hearing that Miss Anthony was a little piqued at me for leaving her on the day before, I returned to my home here in Tenafly. To my surprise, I found Susan awaiting my arrival. That evening, when alone, I said to her :—' Theodore related a very strange story to Mrs. Bullard and me last evening.' Then I recounted to her all he had told us. Miss Anthony listened attentively to the end. Then she said :—' I have heard the same story from

Mrs. Tilton.' We compared notes, and found that by both man and wife the same story had indeed been told."

" What were the particulars of Mrs. Tilton's confession ?"

" I will tell you how it was made. When Mr. Tilton returned home that evening some angry words —growing out of the separation in the afternoon—passed between him and his wife. Both became intensely excited. In the heat of the passion and in the presence of Miss Anthony, each confessed to the other of having broken the marriage vow. In the midst of these startling disclosures Miss Anthony withdrew to her room. Shortly after she heard Mrs. Tilton come dashing up the stairs and Mr. Tilton following close after. She flung open her bedroom door and Elizabeth rushed in. The door was then closed and bolted. Theodore pounded on the outside and demanded admittance, but Miss Anthony refused to turn the key. So intense was his passion at that moment that she feared he might kill his wife' if he gained access to the room. Several times he returned to the door, and angrily demanded that it be opened. "No woman shall stand between me and my wife," he said. But Susan, who is as courageous as she is noble, answered him with the words, "If you enter this room it will be over my dead body !" And so the infuriated man ceased his demands and withdrew. Mrs. Tilton remained with Susan throughout the night. In the excitement of the hour, amid sobs and tears, she told all to Miss Anthony. The whole story of her own faithlessness, of Mr. Beecher's course, of her deception and of her anguish, fell upon the ears of Susan B. Anthony, and were spoken by the lips of Mrs. Tilton.

The next morning Mr. Tilton told Susan never to enter his house again. She told him she should enter whenever she chose; but I believe she did not go there again.

"By Mr. Tilton's cross-examination," observed the reporter, "It appears that Mrs. Tilton was far from friendly to Miss Anthony. How could she have made this confession to her?"

" On the contrary, Mrs. Tilton thought a great deal of Miss Anthony, of Mrs. Bullard, and all those ladies. I was very intimate with her before Mrs. Woodhull's thunderbolt. At the time of our first knowledge of the affair Mr. Wilkeson also heard of it. He besought the ladies not to make it public. To him it was a matter of money. He was a stockholder in Plymouth church, in the *Christian Union*, and in 'The Life of Christ.' Now, the destruction of Mr. Beecher would be the destruction of all these. As Mr. Wilkeson expressed it, 'It would knock "The Life of Christ" higher than a kite.' Hence his concern in keeping the matter secret."

FRANK B. CARPENTER ON THE SCANDAL.

Mr. Carpenter, now at the village of Homer, near Syracuse, at work on a picture of President Lincoln, was interviewed on Monday, July 27th. The following is the substance of his remarkable story :

Mr. Carpenter said :—I was first brought actively into this case by Mr. Beecher. On Sunday, May 25, 1873, Mr. Beecher sent Mr. H. M. Cleveland, his confidential friend and business partner, to my residence in Forty-fifth street, with a horse and carriage. Mr. Cleveland told me that Mr. Beecher wished me to come immediately to Brooklyn. On our way to Brooklyn, Mr. Cleveland said that Mr. Beecher had learned that Mr. Bowen had reasserted to me the charges against him (Beecher) which he had formerly made to Mr. Tilton, but which he had retracted in a written covenant, in the possession of Mr. H. B. Claflin. Mr. Beecher had learned that Mr. Bowen had said to myself, and also in the presence of Mr. E. D. Holton, a citizen of Milwaukee (in an interview at the *Independent* office), that he did not wish us to understand that he had made a retraction. Mr. Cleveland said Mr. Beecher wished me to confront Mr. Bowen on these points. He also said that the tripartite covenant was to be made public. Mr. Cleveland drove me to Mr. Moulton's house, in Remsen street. Mr. Beecher was not there, but Mr. Moulton said it was Mr. Beecher's wish that I should go to Mr. Bowen's house that evening, in company with Mr. Claflin and himself (Mr. Moulton), and repeat to them the substance of what Mr. Bowen had said to me. A few minutes later, Mr. Tilton came to Mr. Moulton's house ; I told him about making the covenant public. Mr. Tilton said that if Mr. Beecher's friends made that covenant public, it would be a very dangerous thing.

About eight o'clock Sunday evening Mr. Moulton and myself went to Mr. Claflin's house, in Pierrepont street, where we found Mr. Claflin, and then all proceeded to Mr. Bowen's residence, corner of Clark and Willow streets. There I recounted to Mr. Bowen, in the presence of Messrs. Claflin and Moulton, the statements made by Mr. Bowen to myself concerning Mr. Beecher. Mr. Bowen admitted all that I said, and Mr. Claflin expressed his astonishment that Mr. Bowen should have told those things after signing the covenant. Mr. Claflin was the man who induced Bowen to sign that covenant. Mr. Bowen said he protested against giving publicity to the covenant. I said to Mr. Bowen :—"The simplest justice to Mr. Beecher requires that, if your statements concerning Mr. Beecher are not true you should make the most unqualified public denial. But if they are true, stand by your statements. Mr. Bowen had said to me that Mr. Beecher had made a confession on his knees to him. Mr. Tilton and Mr. Moulton had been told by Mr. Beecher that this was a lie. I said, "Mr. Bowen, there is a direct lie between you and Mr. Beecher, and for once I want to know the truth."

Mr. Claflin said, "I think we had better have Mr. Beecher here to-night."

I said I would be glad to have Mr. Beecher present.

Mr. Bowen said, "I am willing to have Mr. Beecher come here and will confront him."

Mr. Claflin volunteered to go and get him, when Mr. Moulton started up and said :—

"Mr. Claflin, I will go."

He went out, and was gone fifteen or twenty minutes. He returned without Mr. Beecher, saying the house was closed and the windows darkened ; that he rung the bell, but couldn't raise anybody. This was about half-past ten o'clock. Mr. Claflin then said :—

"Well, I think it's very important that Mr. Bowen and Mr. Beecher should have a private interview before this matter goes any further."

Mr. Bowen pledged that he would be ready and willing to see Mr. Beecher the next day (Monday), any time between eight o'clock in the morning and ten o'clock at night.

Mr. Claflin said he would see Mr. Beecher the next morning and arrange such an interview, and a few minutes later, we left Mr. Bowen's residence.

A few days after this I saw Mr. Claflin, who told me that he had seen Mr. Beecher the next day, and that Mr. Beecher said :—

"There isn't force enough in Brooklyn to draw me into a private interview with Henry C. Bowen."

At this time I had never seen the tripartite covenant, but Mr. Claflin had told me the paper was in his hands.

In my business relations with Mr. Bowen we had frequent conversations in regard to his difficulty with Mr. Beecher. On one occasion Mr. Bowen told me that they first wanted him to sign a much more sweeping document, declaring his charges against Mr. Beecher to be untrue. This, he said, he had refused to do. Mr. Claflin then urged him to at least sign a paper withdrawing the charges, and he consented to do that. In regard to the second paper, Mr. Bowen subsequently said : "I made a mistake in signing that, but Mr. Claflin induced me to do it."

On the following Friday (May 30, 1873) the tripartite covenant was made public in the New York morning papers. The following Sunday night I went to Plymouth Church, and after the services I went up to have some conversation with Mr. Beecher in regard to his sending Mr. Cleveland for me the previous Sunday.

Mr. Carpenter here repeated to the writer the substance of the conversation which took place between Mr. Beecher and himself that evening. We can only say that the statements which Mr. Carpenter says Mr. Beecher made that evening are, if true, of the utmost significance and importance. Mr. Carpenter declares that he will not make public this conversation, unless he is called upon to testify before the proper tribunal. It was during this interview that Mr. Beecher told Mr. Carpenter that in case Theodore would make certain disavowals, he would share his fame and fortune with him, and pour in subscribers to the *Golden Age* by the thousand. The interview which Mr. Carpenter speaks of occurred on the evening of the same day when Mr. Beecher wrote his touching letter, dated Sunday, June 1, 1873. Great significance attaches to Mr. Carpenter's statement, from the fact that Mr. Beecher's card exonerating Mr. Tilton from being his slanderer and defamer was published the next day, June 2, 1873.

Reporter—How long have you been acquainted with Mr. Tilton?

Mr. Carpenter—Twenty years.

Reporter—Have you been intimate with him ?

Mr. Carpenter—I have.

Reporter—Has he ever evinced, either by word or manner, vindictiveness or malice against Henry Ward Beecher?

Mr. Carpenter—No, I never knew a man to bear so much. One of the editors of the *Eagle* told me that Theodore Tilton had suffered more than any man since Jesus Christ. Tilton told me the night he put the Bacon letter to press that he would rather take thirty-nine lashes in the flesh, and drawn blood every time, than have printed this thing against Mr. Beecher. Tilton further said :—

"Mr. Beecher has laid open his breast and told me to smite. His pleading face is before me now. But Dr. Bacon has put me in the attitude of a knave and a dog, and I must place myself right before the world." He also said, "This is no impersonal newspaper attack. Dr. Bacon was my senior on the *Independent*. He is a good and wise man, and if his statement goes forth uncontradicted I am disgraced before Christendom." The morning that Dr. Bacon's speech was published Mr. Beecher, Mr. Tilton, Mr. Moulton and Mr. Thomas G. Shearman were together in Mr. Moulton's study. Mr. Tilton took out of his pocket a New York paper containing a report of Dr. Bacon's speech. That part of the speech referring to Beecher's magnanimity and to Tilton's being a knave and a dog Mr. Tilton read to Mr. Beecher. He then said, "Mr. Beecher, you know that I have treated you with the utmost fairness, and that the statements of Dr. Bacon are untrue. I call upon you, as a simple act of justice, to make a correction of Dr. Bacon's charges. You have a newspaper of your own; you can do it without compromising yourself and without damage to yourself. If you do not correct the impression which Dr. Bacon has given the public I shall be compelled to do it myself, and if I do it, Mr. Beecher, it will be done with serious damage to you." Mr. Beecher made no reply.

Reporter—Have you regarded Theodore Tilton as a tale-bearer?

Mr. Carpenter—Theodore Tilton has striven to shield these parties. Dr. Storrs has frequently commented on his utter absence of vindictiveness and the sorrow-stricken air and attitude with which Mr. Tilton came to him to ask his advice.

Reporter—What was the character of Mr. Tilton's home?

Mr. Carpenter—It was one of the most delightful homes I ever knew.

Reporter—Are you prepared to say, from your own knowledge, that Mr. Tilton was disinclined to publish the letter to Dr. Bacon?

Mr. Carpenter—I am, and do so say. After Dr. Bacon had made that speech to the Divinity class, Mr. Tilton wrote him a private letter to correct the false impressions Dr. Bacon had formed up to three months after Mr. Tilton had called Mr. Beecher's attention to Dr. Bacon's open attack on him. Mr. Beecher had made no sign, had shown no intention of replying. Then Tilton wrote the Bacon letter, as the least he could do in justice to his own good name, to his children and to his friends. His intimate friends demanded that he should do it. They told Mr. Tilton that if he allowed such charges as Dr. Bacon had made concerning him to pass unrefuted he would forfeit the respect of everybody. Mr. Tilton asked me if I would take his letter to Dr. Bacon. I said I would. At my request he accompanied me to New Haven, as I thought Dr. Bacon, upon reading that letter, would wish to ask questions which I couldn't answer. Mr. Tilton finally consented to go with me. Dr. Bacon received us with courtesy and kindness. Mr. Tilton said:—"Dr. Bacon, I have come to you with my statement. You have represented me before the world as a bad man. You have not had the facts in this case on which to form a correct judgment. I have come here, believing you to be a wise and good man—incapable of doing any man wilful injustice. I do not want to make this case public, and I have come here with my friend Mr. Carpenter, who bears this letter, in the hope that your wisdom may devise a course by which my good name may be saved, without giving publicity to the facts in the case." He then read the letter to Mr. Bacon, with scarcely an interruption. When he finished, Dr. Bacon said:—"I have been thinking, Mr. Tilton, as you have been reading, whether this is a private communication?"

Mr. Tilton said:—"All I want is justice. I hope you will suggest some way by which justice may be done me without giving the case to the world."

A reference was then made to Mr. Bowen's part of the tripartite covenant, and Dr. Bacon said:—"I have observed that Mr. Bowen, in withdrawing his charges, does not say they are not true. He simply withdrew them."

Mr. Tilton spoke charitably and feelingly to Dr. Bacon with regard to Mr. Beecher, and did not show malice or vindictiveness. I call upon Dr. Bacon to testify to the truth of my statement. As we rose to take our leave, Dr. Bacon said he could not give advice on so important a matter without reflection. We bade him good-by and returned to New York the same evening. This was Friday, the 19th of last month.

The next evening Mr. Tilton asked me to write a note to Dr. Bacon, asking him if he could recommend any course by which publication could be avoided. In compliance with his request I wrote this note:—

MR. CARPENTER TO DR. BACON.

NEW YORK, June 20, 1874.

Rev. Dr. Bacon:—

MY DEAR SIR: I was at Mr. Tilton's office to-day and had a conversation with him concerning our recent interview at your study. The impression which you left on his mind was that of great fairness and candor towards his case and himself. This he expressed to me in still stronger terms than at first. He told me, furthermore, that, relying on your sense of justice, he would willingly forego the publication of his defence, if, in your judgment, the vindication of his course toward Plymouth church could be accomplished in some other way than in making painful references to the pastor.

Mr. Tilton's respect for your opinion as to the wisest course for him to pursue is so strong that I am sure he will either publish or suppress his letter, according as you shall advise. He said to-day, with great seriousness, "If I could see Dr. Bacon again I would ask him this question, 'Is there any reason, either of morals or of expediency, which should forbid me to publish this letter?' in other words, is the injury which this publication will inflict on Mr. Beecher too great to warrant my resort to so extreme a measure in self-defence?"

Mr. Tilton feels that the publication of his letter will strike a blow at Mr. Beecher from which he never can recover, and for this reason Mr. Tilton hopes you may be able to relieve him from his distressing public position without entailing distress upon Mr. Beecher. Mr. Tilton's continued silence, as you know, has been greatly misinterpreted by the public. The few who have stood faithfully through the storm of detraction are now urgent that he should speak.

Any communication from you to myself will be considered confidential in its character, should you so desire. I am, truly yours,

F. B. CARPENTER.

"This letter," said Mr. Carpenter, "I did not send, as I learned through Mr. C. C. Woolworth, of Brooklyn, that an esteemed mutual friend was going immediately to New Haven. I called on this friend (a Brooklyn gentleman esteemed for his piety and learning, whose name Mr. Carpenter desires to have suppressed for the present), and laid before him the points of my letter, asking him to have an interview with Dr. Bacon, and endeavor to arrange some settlement by which publicity could be avoided.

No word came, and after waiting until Wednesday afternoon, the letter was printed. My friend saw Dr. Bacon, as he had promised, and, in the course of the interview, Dr. Bacon said : "If Mr. Tilton publishes that letter, and Plymouth Church does not reply to it within twenty-four hours by a suit at law against Mr. Tilton, they will have no case before the Christian public."

THE ORIGINAL CHARGE AGAINST MR. BEECHER.

Mr. Carpenter continued :—

"In the original letter, as read to Dr. Bacon, the charge against Mr. Beecher was in these words: —'Knowledge came to me, in 1870, that he (Mr. Beecher) had committed against me and my family a revolting crime.' After the letter was in type and the proof was being corrected, one of Mr. Beecher's intimate friends implored Tilton to change this language, and make the charge in the words: 'An offence which I forbear to name or characterize.' This gentleman said to Mr. Tilton, in my presence: 'If you will so change this language, Mr. Beecher will make a public acknowledgment of an offence.' Mr. Tilton at first refused to so modify the expression, but was overruled by the pleadings of Mr. Beecher's friends. I consider this another proof that Theodore Tilton has acted without malice in this matter."

Reporter—Did not Mr. Tilton think that Mr. Beecher's apology bound him to silence?

Mr. Carpenter—He never revealed that apology either to Dr. Storrs or myself until after Mr. Beecher wrote the letter of defiance calling for an investigating committee.

Reporter—In what terms was Mrs. Tilton referred to by her husband ?

Mr. Carpenter—Always in the language of affection, and often with pride.

Reporter—Has Mr. Cleveland ever intimated to you that, in case of disclosure, other ladies would be involved?

Mr. Carpenter—He has repeatedly.

Reporter—Did he mention names ?

Mr. Carpenter—He did.

Reporter—Will you state them ?

Mr. Carpenter—I will not.

Reporter—Will you state them if called upon to give them before a court ?

Mr. Carpenter—I might then be compelled to. I will not do it voluntarily.

Reporter—Did you ever have any conversation with Oliver Johnson in reference to this case ?

Mr. Carpenter—Why do you ask this question?

Reporter—Mr. Johnson stated before the committee that Mr. Tilton had never, in conversation with him, accused Mr. Beecher of criminality. Did Mr. Johnson ever intimate to you that Mr. Tilton had charged criminality ?

Mr. Carpenter—He has. Mr. Johnson and myself, as the friends of Mr. Theodore Tilton, have frequently talked over this matter. I had reason to consider Mr. Johnson Mr. Tilton's most intimate friend next to Mr. Moulton. Mr. Johnson and myself often conversed about Mr. Tilton with mutual interest and sympathy for him. Mr. Johnson gave me my first absolute conviction that there was something criminally wrong between Mr. Beecher and Mrs. Tilton. Mr. Johnson distinctly told me that Mr. Tilton had charged adultery between Mr. Beecher and Mrs. Tilton. This statement was made to me in July, 1873, at the foot of the stairs leading to the office of the *Christian Union*.

I can prove that Oliver Johnson used these words : "My lips are sealed by a solemn promise ; but if I should disclose what I know, the roof of Plymouth Church would come right off." Another time, Mr. Johnson said to me, "I know a great deal more about this case than you do, and what you know is bad enough."

Reporter—Have you read Mrs. Tilton's statement ?

Mr. Carpenter—I have.

Reporter—Has Mrs. Tilton ever made any admissions to you compromising Mr. Beecher ?

Mr. Carpenter—Mrs. Tilton, in my presence, was asked by Mr. Tilton to put in writing something in reference to her relation with Mr. Beecher, that he could show to Dr. Storrs. This was in December, 1872, or January, 1873. Mrs. Tilton assented willingly, and, going to her room, returned in a few moments with a manuscript, on which was written, as near as I can remember, these words :

"On a certain occasion, Mr. Beecher solicited me to become a wife to him, with all that is implied in this relation. This proposition I communicated to my husband." Mr. Tilton took that writing to Rev. Dr. Storrs.

Reporter—How do you know this ?

Mr. Carpenter—I accompanied Mr. Tilton, and saw Theodore place this document in Dr. Storrs' hand.

Reporter—Why was Dr. Storrs called into this case ?

Mr. Carpenter—Mr. Tilton knew Dr. Storrs as an intimate friend of Mr. Beecher's, and he went to him for counsel soon after the Woodhull letter appeared. He said : "Dr. Storrs, I come to you for advice in regard to the proper action to be taken by myself in reference to the statements made in the Woodhull letter."

Dr. Storrs replied : "I have not read the statement made by Mrs. Woodhull, but if you think it is of sufficient importance to merit attention, I will do so."

Dr. Storrs read the remarkable Woodhull story, and a few days later, when Mr. Tilton visited him, said :

"Mr. Tilton, I have read this paper carefully, and if the statements are true, I draw from them four conclusions."

Mr. Tilton asked what the conclusions were.

Dr. Storrs then said :

First—That Mr. Beecher and Mrs. Tilton had criminal relations.

Second—That you discovered that.

Third—That Mr. Beecher received a paper from Mrs. Tilton denying that such relations had ever existed.

Fourth—That Mr. Moulton got that paper from Mr. Beecher.

Mr. Tilton said : "Dr. Storrs, what if those points can't be denied ?"

Dr. Storrs replied : "If those points cannot be denied, I have no advice to give. An evasion would be worse than silence."

Reporter—Did Mr. Tilton tell Dr. Storrs all the facts in the case ?

Mr. Carpenter—He did not. He told me he did not want to bring disgrace upon his wife, and, when he obtained from her the admission which he took to Dr. Storrs, he said he preferred that it should be made as delicate for Elizabeth as possible, but he could not bear to have the world think that he was attacking Mr. Beecher without just provocation, when the truth was exactly the opposite.

Reporter—Have you read Samuel Wilkeson's letter ?

Mr. Carpenter—Certainly. Mr. Wilkeson has surely been misinformed. The idea that Theodore Tilton attempted to blackmail anybody, I can dispose of in about five minutes; and I am glad you mentioned Wilkeson's communication. Mr. Bowen employed Mr. Tilton to edit the *Independent* and the *Union*, making a contract for five years. The contract provided that, in case Mr. Bowen should violate its terms, the forfeit should be six months' salary in advance. Mr. Tilton was discharged. He naturally expected that Mr. Bowen would, according to the contract, pay him six months' salary. The matter was left to arbitration. The gentlemen selected as arbitrators were James Freeland, Horace B. Claflin, and Charles Storrs. Both Mr. Bowen and Mr. Tilton declared that they would abide by the finding of these arbitrators. Messrs. Freeland, Claflin, and Storrs examined the contracts made between Mr. Tilton and Mr. Bowen, and, in a few moments, decided that Mr. Bowen ought to pay principal and interest to Mr. Tilton up to the last penny of the amount claimed. "This," said Mr. Carpenter, "is the truth about the so-called ' blackmailing' operation of Mr. Tilton's. It is just such abuse and misrepresentation of Tilton as this that has induced me to speak. I have felt and do feel very much as Frank Moulton does. Theodore Tilton is in the right in this matter. He should not be sacrificed. And I say this as an ardent admirer of Henry Ward Beecher. Frank Moulton was sincere when he said he loved Beecher, but beyond and above the love and admiration for that man, there is a controlling consideration of justice, and I know Frank Moulton too well to believe that he will think of shielding Henry Ward Beecher by wronging Theodore Tilton.

Reporter—Have you any statement or explanation to make concerning your affidavit charging that Mr. Beecher told you he would share his fame, fortune, and honor with Mr. Tilton, in case Tilton would do certain things ?

Mr. Carpenter—Only this : That I made that affidavit so that it would bear as lightly against Mr. Beecher as possible.

Reporter—Do you still refuse to give the substance of the conversation you had with Mr. Beecher on the evening of June 1, 1873 ?

Mr. Carpenter—I do. No power save a legal tribunal shall oblige me to make public the statements in that interview.

Reporter—In alluding to Mr. Tilton's character, you stated that Horace Greeley and Charles Sumner had both alluded to Mr. Tilton's case.

Mr. Carpenter—Yes, Horace Greeley said to me : "Nobody can make me believe Theodore Tilton is a corrupt man—no matter what Mrs. Woodhull says." In March, 1873, when Sumner was sitting to me for his portrait, he spoke of Tilton in these words : "Theodore Tilton is a great writer. He is a man of genius. In reference to his domestic troubles, I doubt the propriety of longer silence on his part. I think the thunderbolt ought to fall."

I said : "How can you say that, when such interests are involved ? "

Mr. Sumner replied : "I have been called into one such case, and I have seen the utter folly and futility of all measures to cover wrong."

Reporter—What is your opinion of Mrs. Tilton's statement?

Mr. Carpenter—I hesitate to express an opinion, for Mrs. Tilton has made such unaccountable statements to me. For instance, you remember I told you I was present when she put in writing the statement that Beecher had solicited her. Less than a year after, in conversation with her, she told me that her admission in that letter was untrue.

Reporter—Do you think Mr. Tilton published the Bacon letter because he thought it was Dr. Bacon's judgment that an investigation should be had ?

Mr. Carpenter—I do. He appealed to Dr. Bacon for advice, but waited in vain for a single word of counsel. Dr. Bacon did say, however, to the friend who called on him in Theodore's behalf, that if Mr. Tilton did not make that letter public, he should be inclined to do it himself. Dr. Bacon had the utmost confidence in Mr. Beecher's innocence, and, in the face of such serious charges, he very naturally and wisely wanted to see an issue made, and have the scandal settled finally and forever.

Reporter—It has been stated that Mr. Beecher did not think he could consistently defend Mr. Tilton until the latter renounced Mrs. Woodhull and her associates.

Mr. Carpenter—That is true. Mr. Beecher told me that if Theodore would take the public position he wanted him to, on the Woodhull question, he would pour subscriptions into the *Golden Age* office by the thousands. Oliver Johnson, at one time, prepared a statement for Tilton to sign in regard to Woodhull, but Tilton declined. Mr. Tilton asked his intimate friends not to lose sight of the fact that Mr. Beecher addressed to him the letter of apology six months before he (Tilton) ever saw Victoria C. Woodhull.

Reporter—You said that the phrase in Mr. Tilton's original letter to Dr. Bacon was one charging Mr. Beecher with a "revolting crime." You added that this phrase was modified so as to read, "an offence which I forbear to name or characterize." Who was the friend of Mr. Beecher who induced Mr. Tilton to modify the language of the charge ?

Mr. Carpenter—He was a friend of both Mr. Beecher and Mr. Tilton.

Reporter—Was it Frank Moulton ?

Mr. Carpenter—I decline to answer. But it was through his earnest pleading that the change was made. I remember he said :

"Theodore, don't put that word ' crime ' in there—make it easy for Beecher to explain."

Mr. Tilton assented, with the assurance from this friend that the modification would bring from Mr. Beecher a public acknowledgment of an offence.

Reporter—If Mr. Beecher knew of the existence of these letters, why did he challenge investigation?

Mr. Carpenter—There are several reasons which will answer that question. You know he had previously been sustained to a remarkable degree by his Church. He may have known that Mrs. Tilton would sustain him, if it came to the worst. He may have supposed that the most important documentary evidence was destroyed, as did Mrs. Tilton. Or, driven to desperation, he may have courted the worst, for you remember he declared in one of his letters to Mr. Moulton: "Nothing can possibly be so bad as the power of great darkness in which I spend much of my time. I look upon death as sweeter far than any friend I have in the world."

Reporter—What is your estimate of Theodore Tilton, as a moral man ?

Mr. Carpenter—I have scrutinized him for years, and I never could find in him, either in word or act, a suggestion of impurity. He is the cleanest man in his conversation I ever knew. Toward all women, Mr. Tilton is the most chivalrous of men. His references to his wife have invariably been of the most delicate and affectionate character. He has shielded her in every possible way.

Reporter—Mr. Carpenter, you have made some very important statements in regard to this scandal.

Mr. Carpenter—I have still more important ones in reserve. And in conclusion I want the *Argus* to understand that I am the friend of Theodore Tilton only so far as his position is one where he is fortified by truth. I have had an affection amounting to reverence for Henry Ward Beecher. But I am afraid this case has been taken out of Mr. Beecher's hands by his enthusiastic and over-zealous friends. The statements I have made I am prepared to make affidavit to. The dates and names I have quoted, I have mainly obtained from my written record, for I have kept a diary for many years.

In order to make his statement as complete and emphatic as possible, Mr. Carpenter sent the following telegram to the editor of the Brooklyn *Argus*, in which his interview was given :

HOMER, N. Y., July 29, 1874.

To the Editor of the Argus :

Please add to my statement to-day that Mr. Tilton told Rev. Dr. Storrs and myself, in December, 1872, that he had not told and could not tell us the whole truth.

Mr. Tilton never made a threat against Mr. Beecher.

He only spoke in self defence, and as a wronged and suffering man.

In all references to Mr. Beecher's apology, Mr. Tilton always omitted the most important part of it—shielding his wife, to Dr. Storrs, myself, and others.

FRANK B. CARPENTER.

OLIVER JOHNSON DENIES THE TRUTH OF CARPENTER'S STATEMENT.

A reporter of the New York *Tribune*, showed Mr. Carpenter's statement to Oliver Johnson on Tuesday, July 28th, when the following conversation ensued :

Q. Do you know anything of Mr. Carpenter's connection with the scandal, and the time it began ?

A. Yes, it began long before the time he names—May, 1873. He came to me about it as early, I think, as the latter part of 1871, or the beginning of 1872. He was a volunteer meddler and partisan of Mr. Tilton, and I heard of his gossiping on the subject in various quarters. He says he was first brought actively into the case by Mr. Beecher, but he had been actively in it for at least a year before the time he named, and seemed to enjoy nothing else so much as running about the city and talking to people on the subject. He has done more, I think, than any other man, save Mr. Tilton himself, to foster and propagate the scandal, and has been from the first a partisan rather than a true friend of Mr. Tilton, constantly lending himself to the plans devised by the latter to keep the scandal from dying out.

Q. Did you say in your testimony before the Committee that Mr. Tilton had never, in conversation with you, accused Mrs. Tilton of adultery ? A. I did not. I was not interrogated on that point, as the official report of the testimony must show. I was asked only to say what offence Mr. Tilton charged Mr. Beecher with in his interview with Mr. Bowen, December 26, 1870, and I said that he simply charged him on that occasion with having made improper advances to his wife, which she resisted. On other occasions he used language which I understood to imply something worse than than this ; but I do not remember that he ever used the word " adultery." He told me that he had forgiven Mr. Beecher, and sealed his forgiveness with a kiss ; and yet every now and then he spoke of Mr. Beecher to me in the most opprobious language, calling him more than once a " damned scoundrel," evincing a frightful bitterness and malignity. He told so many different and contradictory stories of the offense as to awaken a strong suspicion in my mind, at times, that he was either crazy or that the scandal had little or no foundation.

Q. What is your opinion as to Mr. Tilton's professed reluctance to publish the scandal ? A. I believe it to be entirely simulated. There is no possibility of explaining his conduct for the last three years without supposing him to have cherished the purpose to make the scandal public in such a form as would be likely to injure if not destroy Mr. Beecher. At every point where the public seemed to be forgetting it he always had some cunning device for reviving it ; and at every point he hypocritically set up the plea that it was Mr. Beecher who compelled him to speak. His treachery and perfidy, on his own showing, are simply indescribable. The ecclesiastical council was the result of his perfidy in propagating a scandal which he had solemnly professed to forgive. All the denunciations of his conduct by Dr. Bacon and others, of which he complained, were simply and solely the fruit of his own deliberate treachery. He knew that Mr. Beecher had no responsibility, or shadow of responsibility, for what Dr. Bacon had written on the subject, and that it was not within his province or power to silence him.

Q. Has Mr. Carpenter reported correctly what you said to him in July, 1873 ? A. He has not. Mr. Carpenter told me on that occasion Mr. Tilton had described Mr. Beecher's offense to him as nothing but an improper advance to Mrs. Tilton, and asked me if I knew of his ever having told a different story. I answered that I believed he had ; that he had used language at times implying something worse than an impropriety ; that, in short, he had told so many contradictory stories that it was impossible to tell which was true, or to be certain that either was. My conversation with Mr. Carpenter was confidential, but in accordance with his usual practice, he retailed it, with glosses to Mr. Tilton, with the apparent design of making all the mischief in his power and gratifying his prurient feelings.

THE TRIPARTITE CONVENTION.

The following is the text of the famous tripartite convention between Beecher, Tilton, and Bowen :

" We three men, earnestly desiring to remove all causes of offense existing between us, real or fancied, and to make Christian reparation for injuries done or supposed to be done, and to efface the disturbed past, and to provide concord, good will, and love for the future, do declare and covenant, each to the other, as follows :

" I. I, Henry C. Bowen, having given credit, perhaps without due consideration, to tales and innuendoes affecting Henry Ward Beecher, and being influenced by them, as was natural to a man who receives impressions suddenly, to the extent of repeating them (guardedly, however, and within limitations, and not for the purpose of injuring him, but strictly in the confidence of consultation), now feel that therein I did him wrong. Therefore I disavow all the charges and imputations that have been attributed to me as having been by me made against Henry Ward Beecher, and I declare fully and without reserve, that I know nothing which should prevent me from extending to him the most cordial friendship, confidence, and Christian fellowship. And I expressly withdraw all the charges, imputations, and innuendoes imputed as having been made and uttered by me, and set forth in a letter written by me to Theodore Tilton on the 1st of January, 1871 (a copy of which letter is hereto annexed), and I sincerely regret having made any imputations, charges, or innuendoes unfavorable to the Christian character of Mr. Beecher. And I covenant and promise that for all future time I will never, by word or deed, recur to, repeat, or allude to any or either of said charges, imputations, and innuendoes.

"II. And I, Theodore Tilton, do, of my free will and friendly spirit toward Henry Ward Beecher, hereby covenant and agree that I will never again repeat, by mouth or word or otherwise, any of the allegations, or imputations, or innuendoes contained in my letters hereunto annexed, or any other injurious imputations or allegations suggested by or growing out of these, and that I will never again bring up or hint at any difference or ground of complaint heretofore existing between the said Henry C. Bowen or myself, or the said Henry Ward Beecher.

"III. I, Henry Ward Beecher, put the past forever out of sight and out of memory. I deeply regret the causes for suspicion, jealousy and estrangement, which have come between us. It is a joy for me to have my old regard for Henry C. Bowen and Theodore Tilton restored, and a happiness to me to resume the old relations of love, respect and reliance, to each and both of them. If I have said anything injurious to the reputation of either, or have detracted from their standing and fame as Christian gentlemen and members of my church, I revoke it all, and heartily covenant to repair and reinstate them to the extent of my power.

(Signed,)

' BROOKLYN, April 2, 1872."

"H. C. BOWEN,
"THEODORE TILTON,
"H. W. BEECHER.

A FAITH-CONFESSION.

BY THEODORE TILTON.

As other men have creeds, so I have mine;
I keep the holy faith in God, in man,
And in the angels ministrant between.

I hold to one true church of all true souls;
Whose churchly seal is neither bread nor wine,
Nor laying on of hands, nor holy oil,
But only the anointing of God's grace.

I hate all kings, and caste, and rank of birth,
For all the sons of men are sons of God;
Nor limps a beggar but is nobly born;
Nor wears a slave a yoke, nor czar a crown,
That makes him less or more than just a man.

I love my country and her righteous cause;
So dare I not keep silent of her sin;
And after Freedom, may her bells ring Peace!

I love one woman with a holy fire,
Whom I revere as priestess of my house;
I stand with wondering awe before my babes,
Till they rebuke me to a nobler life;
I keep a faithful friendship with my friend,
Whom loyally I serve before myself;
I lock my lips too close to speak a lie;
I wash my hands too white to touch a bribe;
I owe no man a debt I cannot pay—
Except the love that man should always owe.

Withal each day, before the blessed heaven,
I open wide the chambers of my soul,
And pray the Holy Ghost to enter in.

Thus reads the fair confession of my faith,
So crossed with contradictions by my life,
That now may God forgive the written lie.
Yet still, by help of Him who helpeth men,
I face two worlds, and fear not life nor death!
O Father! lead me by thy hand! Amen.

MR THEODORE TILTON.

THEODORE TILTON.

Mr. Tilton, who figures as the accuser in this case, is still a young man, as he was born in New York, Oct. 2d, 1835. His father was a shoemaker, who made every sacrifice to give young Theodore a good education. He graduated from our public schools, and went to the Free Academy very early in its history. He continued a student only a couple of years—not long enough to obtain a degree. He became a reporter on the *Tribune* after leaving the Academy. He was a very good short-hand writer, and a careful, steady young man. An incident will show how strict he was in church matters. Mr. Hudson, of the New York *Herald*, who was constantly on the watch for young men of talent, offered Tilton a position on that paper, with a much higher salary than he was receiving from the *Tribune*. The offer was respectfully declined, because he would not work on Sunday. Theodore Tilton married Elizabeth Richards in 1855. Mr. Beecher performed the ceremony. Mr. and Mrs. Tilton are the parents of seven children, of whom four are now living.

Tilton began to report sermons for the *Independent* very early in his career as a short-hand reporter. He soon began to write articles for the same paper. In 1856, he became one of its editors, and he ultimately rose to be chief editor. In the latter position he continued for a number of years. Finally, five or six years ago, he and Mr. Bowen differed, and he resigned the editorial charge of the *Independent*, though he continued to write for it for some time thereafter. He also had an editorial writer's connection with the Brooklyn *Union*, which was severed about the same time as was that with the *Independent*. A couple of years ago Mr. Tilton started the *Golden Age*, a weekly paper, in which a great deal of money has been sunk, it is said, to no purpose. He continued the editorial supervision of this paper until the 27th of June, when it passed into other hands. Since the latter date his movements have been so public that they need not be recalled.

In personal appearance Mr. Tilton is very prepossessing. His face is a type of rather poetic manly beauty. His temperament is nervous. He is inclined to be proud, and there is no question that he holds a very high opinion of Mr. Theodore Tilton. As a lecturer he was very successful—that is, until this dreadful scandal began to be whispered about. Lecture committees for the last two years have been rather shy of Tilton, in consequence of it, no doubt. His style of oratory is said to be a mixture of the styles of Wendell Phillips and Henry Ward Beecher. He keeps the emotional side of his topics more in the background than the great pulpit orator does, though not as much as does the famous agitator. But if the present troubles do not end Tilton's career, his mark will be made as a writer. Already he has written better than he has ever spoken, though his turning the tables on Beecher himself in the famous home missionary case, when Tilton resisted the giving of the money of Plymouth Church to the Missionary Society, because some small part of its funds were donated to the slave-keeping Cherokees, and appealed with success to the Sharp's rifle, which Beecher himself had apostrophized with effect in the "Bleeding Kansas" days, shows that he possesses the oratorical faculty.

Many of Tilton's editorials in the *Independent* were very well writen. His late novel gives very great promise, and no reader of his contributions to the literature of this unhappy scandal can fail to recognize their rhetorical power and logical force. Mr. Tilton possesses considerable imagination. His vocabulary is rather extensive, and he chooses his words in many cases with great dexterity. He is in no sense a practical man. He is a poet and a writer, and it is unfortunate for him that he has had to figure in affairs that would have taxed the resources of any man, however thorough his training in the practical affairs of life. It is worthy of remark that Tilton's first platform hits were made in introducing Mr. Beecher to his lyceum audiences.

The accompanying portrait is from a recent photograph by Sarony.

SIR MARMADUKE'S MUSINGS.

BY THEODORE TILTON.

I won a noble fame,
But, with a sudden frown,
The people snatched my crown,
And in the mire trod down
My lofty name.

I bore a bounteous purse,
And beggars by the way
Then blessed me day by day,
But I, grown poor as they,
Have now their curse.

I gained what men call friends,
But now their love is hate,
And I have learned too late
How mated minds unmate,
And friendship ends.

I clasped a woman's breast,
As if her heart I knew,
Or fancied, would be true,
Who proved—alas, she too!
False like the rest.

I am now all bereft—
As when some tower doth fall,
With battlements and wall,
And gate and bridge and all—
And nothing left.

But I account it worth
All pangs of fair hopes crossed—
All loves and honors lost—
To gain the heavens at cost
Of losing earth.

So, lest I be inclined
To render ill for ill—
Henceforth in me instill,
O God, a sweet, good will
To all mankind.

SLEEPY HOLLOW, November 1, 1871.

TILTON AND BEECHER.

FULL TEXT OF THEODORE TILTON'S LETTER TO DR. BACON.

The New York *Golden Age*, of June 21, 1874, contained the following remarkable letter on "the Plymouth Church Case." It was addressed to Rev. Leonard Bacon, D. D., LL. D., ex-moderator of the Brooklyn Council. It is signed by Theodore Tilton, and runs as follows.

SIR :—I have carefully read your New Haven address concerning the late Council, and also your five essays on the same subject, just concluded in the *Independent*.

The numerous and extraordinary misrepresentations of my position which these writings of yours will perpetuate to my injury, if not corrected, compel me to lay before you the data for their correction : —misrepresentations which, on your part, are of course wholly unintentional, for you are incapable of doing any man a wilful wrong.

In producing to your inspection some hitherto unpublished papers and documents in this case, I need first to state a few facts in chronological sequence, sufficient to explain the documentary evidence which follows.

I. After I had been for fifteen years a member of Plymouth Church, and had become meanwhile an intimate friend of the pastor, knowledge came to me in 1870 that he had committed against me an offence which I forbear to name or characterize. Prompted by my self-respect, I immediately and forever ceased my attendance on his ministry. I informed him of this determination as early as January, 1871, in the presence of a mutual friend, Mr. Francis D. Moulton.

The rules of Plymouth Church afforded me a choice between two methods of retirement :—one to ask for a formal letter of dismissal ; the other, to dismiss myself less formally by prolonged absence. I chose the latter. In so doing, my chief desire was to avoid giving rise to curious inquiries into the reasons for my abandoning a church in which I had been brought up from boyhood ; and therefore I did not invite attention to the subject by asking for a dismissory letter, but adopted the alternative of silently staying away—relying on the rule that a prolonged absence would finally secure to me a dismissal involving no publicity to the case.

Several powerful reasons prompted me to the adoption of this alternative, among which were the following :—The pastor communicated to me in writing an apology signed by his name. He also appealed to me to protect him from bringing reproach to the cause of religion. He alleged that an exposure would forbid him to re-ascend his pulpit. These, and other similar reasons, I had no right or disposition to disregard ; and I acted upon them with a conscious desire to see Mr. Beecher protected rather than harmed.

II. At length my absence from the church—an absence of which not three members of the congregation, beside the pastor, knew the cause—began to excite comment in private circles.

Some of the members hinted that I had lapsed into a lamentable change of religious views—whereas my views continued to be the same as they had been for many years previous ; and though they had long before ceased to find their honest expression in the formal creed which I had professed in my childhood at the altar of Plymouth Church, yet my religious faith had not changed from that early original more than the views of some of the most honored members and officers of the same church had changed within the same time.

Other persons insinuated that I had adopted un-Christian tenets concerning marriage and divorce :— whereas, touching marriage, I have always held, and still hold, with ever-increasing firmness, the one and only view common to all Christendom ; and touching divorce, the substance of what I held was, and still is, the needful abrogation of our unjust New York code, and the substitution of the more humane legislation of New England and the West.

Other persons fancied that I had become a Spiritualist of an extravagant type :—whereas I have never yet seen my way clear to be a Spiritualist at all—certainly not to be so much a Spiritualist as some of the most prominent members of Plymouth Church are known to be.

All these suppositions, and many others, but never the right one, became current in the church (and still are) to explain my suddenly sundered membership ; the true reason for which has been understood always by the pastor, but never by his flock.

III. At length, after many calumnious whisperings, near and far (since evil tales magnify as they travel) a weekly paper in New York, in November, 1872, published a wicked and horrible scandal—a publication which some persons in the church ignorantly attributed in its origin and animus to me ; whereas I had previously spent many months of constant and unremitting endeavor to suppress it : an endeavor in which, with an earnest motive, but a foolish judgment, I made many ill-directed sacrifices of my reputation, position, money, and fair prospects in life ; for all which losses of things precious, since mine alone was the folly, let mine alone be the blame.

IV. In May, 1873, occurred the surreptitious publication of a tripartite agreement signed by H. C. Bowen, H. W. Beecher, and myself :—an agreement which, so far as I was concerned, had for its object to pledge me to silence against using or circulating charges which Mr. Bowen had made against Mr. Beecher. This covenant, as originally written, would have bound me never to speak, not only of Mr. Bowen's, but also of my own personal grievances against Mr. Beecher. I refused to sign the original paper. My position in the amended paper was this: Mr. Bowen had made grave charges against Mr. Beecher. These charges Mr. Bowen had been induced to recall in writing. I cheerfully agreed never to circulate the charges which Mr. Bowen had recalled.

V. In August, 1873, Mr. William F. West, a member of Plymouth Church, hitherto a stranger to me, came to my residence, accompanied (at his request) by my friend Mr. F. B. Carpenter, and told me that when the summer vacation was over he (Mr. W.) meant to cite me before the church on the charge of circulating scandals against the pastor ; declaring, in Mr. C.'s presence, that Mr. Beecher had acted as if the reported scandalous tales were true rather than false, and urging that I owed it to myself and the truth to go forward and become a willing witness in an investigation. I peremptorily declined to join Mr. West in his proposed investigation, and declared that as I had not been a member of Plymouth Church for several years, I could not be induced to return to that church for any purpose whatever, least of all for so distasteful a purpose as to participate in a scandal. Mr. West had meanwhile discovered that my name still remained on the church-roll ; from which circumstance he determined to assume that I was still a member, and to force me to trial. Accordingly, a few weeks later, he brought forward charges which were nominally made against myself but really against the pastor :—charges which, if I may characterize them by the recently-published language of the present clerk of Plymouth Church, were "an indirect and insincere method of investigating one man under the false pretense of investigating another."

Some leading members, including especially the pastor, desired my co-operation in defeating Mr. West, and I cheerfully gave it. To this end, I wrote—with their pre-knowledge and at their urgent desire—a letter declining to accept a copy of the charges addressed to me as a member, on the ground that I had, four years previously, ceased my connection with the church. For this letter, I received, on the next day after sending it, the pastor's prompt and hearty thanks. An understanding was then had between Mr. Beecher and myself, in an interview at the residence of Mr. Moulton, that Mr. West's indictment against me was to be disposed of in the following way, namely, by a simple resolution to the effect that, whereas I had, four years previously, terminated my membership ; and whereas by inadvertence my name still remained on the roll ; therefore resolved that the roll be amended in accordance with the fact. This was to put Mr. West's case quietly out of court without bringing up the scandal.

To my surprise and indignation, I learned on the morning of October 31, 1873, that the report which was to be presented at the church meeting to be held on that evening, would not be in the simple form already indicated, but would declare that whereas I had been charged with slandering the pastor ; and whereas I had been cited before the church to meet the charge ; and whereas I had pleaded non-membership as an excuse for not appearing for trial ; therefore resolved that I should be dropped, etc.

This gross imputation, thus foreshadowed to me, led me to appear in person at the church on that evening, there to await the reading of the forthcoming report. This report, when it came to be read, brought me the following novel intelligence, namely, "Whereas a copy of the charges was put into the hands of the said Tilton on the 17th of October, *and a request made of him that he should answer the same by the 23d of October,*" etc.

I do not know to this day whose hand it was that drew the above report, and therefore I am happily saved from an offensive personality when I say that the statement which I have here quoted is diametrically the opposite of the truth ; for instead of my having been requested to answer the charges, I had been requested *not* to answer them.

After the public reading of the above report I arose in the meeting and said in Mr. Beecher's presence, that if I had slandered him I would answer for it to his face ;—to which he replied in an equally public manner that he had no charge whatever to make against me.

VI. Next, growing out of the church's singular proceedings in this case, came the Congregational Council of which you were Moderator.

The above facts and events — which I have mentioned as briefly as possible, omitting their details—will serve as a sufficient groundwork whereon to base the correction of the unjust and injurious statements which you have unwittingly given of my participation and responsibility in the case. With the Congregational theories and usages which you have so ably discussed, I have no concern—you are probably right about them. But as to all the essential facts growing out of my relationship to Plymouth Church, you have been wholly misinformed—as you will see by the following proofs:

I. You say that I retired from the church, giving no announcement of my so doing to any proper officer; in other words, that I stole out secretly, letting no one in authority know of my purpose. Your language concerning me is as follows:

"His position was that he had terminated his membership four years previously—*not by requesting, the church* (as by its rules he might have done) *to drop his name from its roll,*" etc.

You then ask:

"Is this the beautiful non-stringency of the covenant which connects the members of that church with the body, and with each other? What sort of a covenant is that which can be dissolved at any moment, not merely by mutual consent, nor by either party giving notice to the other, but by a silent volition in the mind of either?"

The above is a thorough misstatement of the manner in which I left Plymouth Church.

On the very first occasion of my meeting the chief officer of the church, after my retirement from it, I gave notice to him of that retirement. At a later period, I repeated this notice to other officers of that body. In evidence of this fact I adduce the following extract from a recent card by Mr. Thomas S. Shearman, Clerk of Plymouth Church, published in *The Independent,* June 18, 1874. He says:

"Long before any charges were preferred against him, Mr. Tilton distinctly informed the clerk of the church and various other officers and members (myself included) *that he had withdrawn and that his name ought to be taken off the roll.*"

II. You say that I have either "a malicious heart," or "a crazy brain." I know the fountain-head of this opinion. While the Council was in session in Brooklyn, the following startling paragraph appeared in the Brooklyn *Union* of Saturday, March 28, 1874:

MR. SHEARMAN ON THE SITUATION.

"At the close of the services a *Union* reporter approached Mr. Beecher for the purpose of getting his views as to the Council, but he declined to be interviewed. Mr. Shearman, the Clerk of the church, however, was communicative. He said he had received no intimation as yet, what course the Council would pursue. In regard to the scandal on Mr. Beecher, he said so far as Tilton was concerned he (Tilton) was out of his mind, off his balance, and did not act reasonably. As for Mrs. Tilton, she had occasioned the whole trouble while in a half-crazed condition. She had mediumistic fits, and while under the strange power that possessed her, often spoke of the most incredible things, declared things possible that were impossible, and among the rest had slandered Mr. Beecher. Mr. Tilton himself had acknowledged that all the other things she had told him in her mediumistic trance were false and impossible; then why, asked Mr. Shearman, should the scandal on Mr. Beecher be the only truth in her crazy words?"

My attention was not called to the above paragraph until after the Council had adjourned, and its members had gone to their homes. At first, I was not willing to believe that the Clerk of Plymouth Church—the same officer whose name had been officially signed to all the documents which the church had just been sending to the Council—could have been guilty of such an outrage against truth and decency as the above paragraph contained :—particularly against a lady whose devout religious faith and life are at the farthest possible remove from spiritualism or fanaticism of any kind. Accordingly I procured the following sworn statement by the reporter certifying to the accuracy of his report:

Kings County, ss.,

Edwin F. Denyse, Reporter of the Brooklyn *Union,* being duly sworn, deposed as follows:

At the close of the Friday evening meeting in Plymouth Church, March 27, 1874, I, in company with another member of the press, requested Mr. Thomas G. Shearman, Clerk of the church, to communicate to us for publication any facts or comments or opinions which he might wish to make concerning the Congregational Council then in session: whereupon Mr. Shearman stated in our hearing, and for the purpose for which we asked him to do so, the allegations contained in the previous paragraph. And I do solemnly swear that this paragraph is a correct and moderate report of Mr. Shearman's statements, both in letter and spirit. And I further testify that I solicited as a reporter the above statement from Mr. Shearman because he was the Clerk of the church, whose name had been affixed in that capacity to the documents which Plymouth Church had sent to the Council, and because an opinion from such a high officer would have an official authenticity and importance.

Sworn to before me this 1st day of
April, 1874.
FRANK CROOKE, Justice of the Peace.

EDWIN F. DENYSE.

Shortly after the appearance of Mr. Shearman's reported interview in the *Union*, that gentleman sent to me through Mr. F. D. Moulton a letter the substance of which was that he (Mr. S.) had referred in the above conversation not to *me* or *my* family, but to other persons. This letter I declined to receive, and returned it to the writer, with a demand upon him to retract his untrue and unjust statements. Furthermore, I required as a condition of my accepting from Mr. Shearman any apology at all, that this apology should be presented to me in writing in the presence of the Rev. Henry Ward Beecher. This was promptly done at Mr. Moulton's house in Mr. Beecher's presence. Mr. Shearman's apologetic letter was as follows :

BROOKLYN, April 2, 1874.

DEAR SIR : Having seen a paragraph in the Brooklyn *Union* of Saturday last containing a report of a statement alleged to have been made by me concerning your family and yourself, I desire to assure you that this report is seriously incorrect, and that I have never authorized such a statement.

It is unnecessary to repeat here what I have actually said upon these subjects, because I am now satisfied that what I *did* say was erroneous, and that the rumors to which I gave some credit were without foundation.

I deeply regret having been mislead into an act of unintentional injustice, and am glad to take the earliest occasion to rectify it. I beg, therefore, to withdraw all that I said upon the occasion referred to as incorrect (although then believed by me), and to repudiate entirely the statement imputed to me as untrue and unjust to all parties concerned.

Yours obediently,

THEODORE TILTON, Esq.   T. G. SHEARMAN.

The above-named calumny, which Mr. T. G. Shearman thus retracted, is but one of several similar falsehoods against my wife and myself which have been fostered by interested parties to explain the action of Plymouth Church ; falsehoods which, in some instances, have been corrected in the same way, and which in others still await to be corrected either in this way, or in a court of justice.

III. You ask, "when did Mr. Tilton cease to be responsible to the Plymouth Church ?" I answer that I first ceased my responsibility to that church when I terminated my membership four years ago. I afterwards voluntarily renewed my responsibility to the church on the evening of Oct. 31, 1873, by appearing in person at one of its public meetings, and offering to answer then and there, in the pastor's presence, the charge that I had slandered him. Less than two months ago, I still further renewed my responsibility to Plymouth Church, as will appear by the following correspondence :

BROOKLYN, May 4, 1874.

Rev. Henry Ward Beecher, Pastor of Plymouth Church ; Rev. S. B. Halliday, Associate Pastor ; and Mr. Thomas G. Shearman, Clerk.

GENTLEMEN :—I address, through you, to the church of which you are officers, the following statement, which you are at liberty to communicate to the church through the Examining Committee, or in any other mode, private or public.

The Rev. Leonard Bacon, D.D., LL.D., Moderator of the recent Congregational Council, has seen fit, since the adjournment of that body, to proclaim, publish, and reiterate, with signal emphasis, and with the weight of something like official authority, a grave declaration which I here quote, namely:

"It was for the Plymouth Church," he says, "to vindicate its pastor against a damaging imputation from one of its members. But with great alacrity—the pastor himself consenting—IT THREW AWAY THE OPPORTUNITY OF VINDICATION" . . . "That act," he continued, "in which the PLYMOUTH CHURCH THREW AWAY THE OPPORTUNITY OF VINDICATING ITS PASTOR, was what gave occasion for remonstrances from neighboring churches" . . . "There are many," he says also, "not only in Brooklyn, but elsewhere, who felt that the church had not fairly met the question, and by evading the issue had THROWN AWAY THE OPPORTUNITY OF VINDICATING ITS PASTOR."

The Moderator's declaration is thus made three times over that the Plymouth Church, in dealing with my case, THREW AWAY ITS OPPORTUNITY OF VINDICATING THE PASTOR.

This declaration so emphatically repeated by the chief mouth-piece of the Council, and put forth by him apparently as an exposition of the Council's views compels me, as the third party to the controversy, to choose between two alternatives.

One of these is to remain contentedly in the dishonorable position of a man who denies to his former pastor an opportunity for the vindication of that pastor's character :—an offense the more heinous because an unsullied character and reputation are requisites to his sacred office.

The other alternative is for me to restore to his church their lost opportunity for his vindication by presenting myself voluntarily for the same trial to which the church would have power to summon me if I were a member :—a suggestion which (judging from my past experience) will subject me afresh to the unjust imputation of reviving a scandal for the suppression of which I have made more sacrifices than all other persons.

Between these two alternatives—which are all that the Moderator leaves to me—and which are both equally repugnant to my feelings—duty requires me to choose the second.

I therefore give you notice that if the Pastor, or the Examining Committee, or the Church as a body, desire to re-possess the opportunity which the Moderator laments that you have thrown away, I hereby restore to you this lost opportunity as freely as if you had never parted with it.

I authorize you (if such be your pleasure) to cite me at any time within the next thirty days to appear at the bar of Plymouth Church for trial on the charge heretofore made against me, namely, that of "circulating and promoting scandals derogatory to the Christian integrity of the pastor and injurious to the reputation of the church."

My only stipulation concerning the trial is that it shall not be held with closed doors, nor in the absence of the pastor.

I regret keenly that the Moderator has imposed on me the necessity for making this communication, for nothing but necessity would exhort it.

The practical good which I seek to achieve by this proposition is that, whether accepted or declined, it will in either case effectually put an end forever to the Moderator's grave charge that Plymouth Church has been deprived through me of an opportunity to vindicate its pastor, or that its pastor has been by any act of mine deprived of an opportunity to vindicate himself.

Truly yours, THEODORE TILTON.

To the above communication I received the following reply from the Clerk of the Church:

BROOKLYN, May 18, 1874.

DEAR SIR: Your note of the 4th inst., enclosing a letter addressed to Mr. Beecher, Mr. Halliday, and myself, was duly received.

This letter has been read by Mr. Halliday, with whose concurrence it has been submitted to the Examining Committee; and we all deem its contents to present a question which should be decided by that Committee, and which should not be submitted to the pastor of the church, to whom, therefore, the letter has not been advised of its substance.

Having consulted the members of the Committee, I am informed by them that they see no reason for accepting your proposition, or even laying it before the Church.

Whatever view may be taken of the case by others, the Examining Committee and the Church have seen no necessity for vindicating any member of the church from charges which no one has made, and the church has never in the twenty-seven years of its history adopted such a course. No one can, therefore, hold you responsible for the loss of an opportunity to the church to do that which it never yet has done, and probably never will do.

We do not understand your letter as implying that you have any charges to make, but to the contrary. If the Committee had so understood it, they would have readily entertained and fully investigated them.

It is proper to add that your name was dropped from the roll, not simply because of the statements made by you *after* charges had been preferred against you, but because months, if not years, *before* any charges were made you distinctly stated to various officers and members of the church that you had permanently abandoned your connection with it, thus bringing yourself expressly within the terms of our rule upon this subject.

Yours truly, THOMAS G. SHEARMAN.

MR. THEODORE TILTON.

As the above communication by Mr. Shearman seemed to bear no official but only a private signature, I addressed to him the following note:

174 LIVINGSTON STREET, Brooklyn, May 23, 1874.

Mr. Thomas G. Shearman, Clerk of Plymouth Church.

SIR: My recent communication addressed to the Pastor, the Associate Pastor, and the Clerk of Plymouth Church is acknowledged by you in a note which you seem to have signed merely as a private individual, and not as an officer of the church.

I call your attention to the fact that I did not address you in your private capacity but solely as the Clerk of Plymouth Church.

I therefore respectfully request to be informed by you, definitely and in writing, whether or not I am at liberty to regard your letter as an official reply to mine.

Yours truly, THEODORE TILTON.

Mr. Shearman's reply was as follows:

81 HICKS STREET, Brooklyn, May 29, 1874.

DEAR SIR: In reply to your inquiry whether my letter of 18th inst. was an official answer to yours of the 4th inst., I beg to say that I did not feel at liberty, without the express authority of the church itself, to sign that letter as its clerk.

In so far as the letter stated that your proposition of May 4 was declined, it was official; since as clerk of the church I declined then, and decline now, to lay the proposal before the church itself, holding myself responsible to the church for so doing.

The remainder of the letter of 18th inst. must be regarded as my individual statement of what I believe to be the unanimous opinion of the officers of the church.

Your obedient servant, THOMAS G. SHEARMAN.

MR. THEODORE TILTON.

It will thus be seen that Mr. Shearman, in answer to my inquiry, characterizes his previous letter to me as partly official and partly unofficial—though how he could originally have expected me to draw the dividing line between its two parts without this subsequent explanation, I am at a loss to understand. But the official portion of his letter (now that it has been pointed out to me) is sufficient to answer your query. "When did Mr. Tilton cease to be responsible to the Plymouth Church?" I respectfully submit that, setting aside all previous cavils and technicalities concerning the church-roll, I may be fairly said to have ceased my responsibility to Plymouth Church when the clerk of that church officially informed me that my voluntary offer to return and be tried was officially declined.

IV. In your five essays you were led, through ignorance of the facts, to make several other erroneous and injurious statements concerning my case; but the corrections and explanations which I have already given will of themselves correct the others.

It now remains for me to give you some reasons why I have been prompted, after years of reticence, to lay before you the grave matters contained in this communication. Nothing could induce me to make my present use of the foregoing facts except the conviction which the events of the last year, and particularly of the last half year, have forced upon my mind that Mr. Beecher, or his legal and other agents acting in his interest and by his consent, have shown themselves willing to sacrifice *my* good name for the maintenance of *his*. I have come slowly to this judgment—more slowly than my personal friends have done; but that I am not mistaken in it, you shall see by a few illustrative instances :

I. I have already shown you how the church, at a public meeting, on Friday evening, October 31, 1873, by an official document which was published the next morning in every leading journal in New York, gave the public falsely to understand that I had been cited to answer charges, when I had really been requested *not* to answer them :—a piece of ecclesiastical misrepresentation which was the more grievous to me because it was subsequently accepted by the Council as authentic, and because it is still widely believed by the public.

II. Mr. Beecher's journal, *The Christian Union*, published this official falsehood to a wide circle of readers, and took no notice of the correction which I addressed at the time in a brief note to the Council. Let me ask you to weigh the peculiar gravity of this omission by that journal. My case, as presented to the Council by the two protesting churches, was based by them, not on any private or accurate knowledge of the facts, but solely on the published misstatements of those facts by Plymouth Church. I was described by the two churches to the Council as follows :

"Specific charges of grossly un-Christian conduct are presented against him by a brother in the church, *to which charges he declines to answer*," etc.

You will remember that I promptly addressed to you a reply to the above, in which I used the following explicit words :

"Gentlemen of the Council, every man among you knows that I did *not* decline to answer."

You, as Moderator of the Council, courteously gave me the ecclesiastical reasons why my letters could not be officially laid before that body ; but can you give me any honorable reason why my defence should not have been published in *The Christian Union?* If every other American journal should be destroyed, and only the files of *The Christian Union* should remain, that journal's report of my case would represent me as a culprit, first, who had slandered a clergyman ; next, who had been summoned before the church to answer for this calumniation ; next, who had evaded this summons by resorting to the safe-shelter of non-membership ; and last, who on account of this moral poltroonery, had been dropped from the roll. Such is the record which Mr. Beecher's journal contains of my case, up to date.

III. During the Council, and when there seemed a probability that Plymouth Church would receive condemnation and be dis-fellowshipped by the neighboring churches, Mr. Beecher inspired a message from his church to the Council, closing with these words :

"We hold that it is our right, and may be our duty, to avoid the evils incident to a public explanation or a public trial ; and that such an exercise of our discretion furnishes us no good ground for the interference of other churches, *provided we neither retain within our fellowship, nor dismiss by letter, as in regular standing, persons who bring open dishonor upon the Christian name.*"

This adroit insinuation against me is what you, as Moderator of the Council, know to have been the turning point in the fortunes of Plymouth Church before that tribunal. The Council's verdict borrows almost these identical words. It says, "The accused person has not been retained in the church, nor commended to any other church." You, too, quote these words—borrowed thus doubly from the Church's plea and from the Council's verdict—and you then logically say, "Therefore the abnormal method in which the charges against him [me] were disposed of was overlooked."

In other words, the Council, on reading the above excusatory petition sent up to it by Plymouth Church, found in it the one and only ground for retaining that church within the Congregational fellowship ; and this one and only ground was because Mr. Beecher's final appeal to the Council represented me as a person who had neither been retained in his church, nor recommended to any other, but who was dropped from the roll for bringing "dishonor on the Christian name." This document—constituting Plymouth Church's ungenerous defence before the Council—was accepted by you in good faith, and has since led you to point against me the following cruel words :

"The Plymouth Church," you say, "made it known that they were no longer responsible for the dishonor which he has brought or may bring on the name of Christ. They dropped him from the roll of the church. In one word they excommunicated him, for such a dropping from the roll was excommunication from the church."

You never could have uttered the preceding injurious words against me had not Mr. Beecher and his church-agents given you the materials for so doing by ingeniously putting before the Council a document which you, as Moderator, interpreted as being only another way of Plymouth Church's saying that I had brought dishonor on the Christian name and had therefore been excommunicated.

Do not understand me. I will not say that, in my unsuccessful management of this unhappy scandal, I have brought no "dishonor on the Christian name :" the one name which, of all others, I most seek to honor. With infinite sorrow I look back through the last few years, and see instances in which, by the fatality of my false position, I have brought peculiar "dishonor on the Christian name :"—all which I freely acknowledge, and hope yet to repair. But I solemnly aver—and no man shall gainsay me —that the reason why Plymouth Church avoided an investigation into the scandal with which *I* was charged, was not because *I*, but another man, had "brought dishonor on the 'Christian name.'" And yet this other person, a clergyman, permitted his church to brand me before the Council with an accusation which, had I been in his place and he in mine, I would have voluntarily borne for myself instead of casting on another.

IV. I will adduce a further instance by a quotation from a letter which I had occasion to address to Mr. Beecher, dated May 1, 1874:

Henry Ward Beecher :

SIR : Mr. F. B. Carpenter mentions to me your saying to him that under certain conditions, involving certain disavowals by me, a sum of money would or could be raised to send me, with my family, to Europe for a term of years.
The occasion compels me to state explicitly that so long as life and self-respect continue to exist together in my breast. I shall be debarred from receiving, either directly or indirectly, any pecuniary or other favor at your hands.
The reason for this feeling on my part you know so well, that I will spare you the statement of it. Yours, truly,
THEODORE TILTON.

V. Take another instance. You will perceive that in Mr. Shearman's letter, given above, —the letter officially declining my offer to return to the church to be tried—he says, under date, May 18, 1874 :

"Your note of 4th inst. enclosing a letter addressed to Mr. Beecher, Mr. Halliday and myself was duly received. *This letter has been read by Mr. Halliday with whose concurrence it has been submitted to the Examining Committee.*"

And yet, a month and a half after Mr. Halliday saw this letter, and a month after Mr. Shearman had officially replied to it, the Brooklyn *Union* of June 19th contained the following singular statement, by a reporter who visited Mr. Halliday:

"In an extract," says the *Union*, "from a letter written to the Chicago *Tribune*, it is stated that Mr. Tilton had addressed a note to the 'Trustees of Plymouth Church.' The *Tribune's* correspondent declares that Mr. Tilton 'not only expresses his willingness but desire to answer any summons as a witness during the next thirty days.' A *Union* reporter (Mr. Tilton not being accessible), called on Rev. Mr. Halliday to-day, and, upon presenting the extract to him, was assured that the person who corresponded with the Chicago *Tribune* must have been misinformed. The very fact of his stating that the letter was addressed 'to the Trustees of the Church,' he said 'was an absurdity.' The trustees only attended to temporalities of the church. *If Mr. Tilton had written such a letter, of which, however, he had no knowledge, it would have been either addressed to the Church, to its pastor, or to some member or members.* At the last Friday evening meeting no such letter had been presented for consideration, and he was certain none had since been received, although he must say he had been absent in Massachusetts about a week. *He added that he had reason for believing that Mr. Tilton felt a little sore about what Rev. Mr. Bacon had said of him. But whether he would take to writing letters about it he couldn't say.*"

And yet Mr. Halliday, according to Mr. Shearman's testimony above given, had read my letter forty days before thus, denying that he had ever seen or heard of it.

A similar statement to the above appeared in the Brooklyn *Eagle*, at the same time (June 20), as follows:

"The trustees of Plymouth Church deny that Theodore Tilton has addressed a letter to them offering himself as a witness, and expressing a desire to answer certain charges against Mr. Beecher, during the next thirty days. They say that the whole story is false from beginning to end. " -

The above are recent specimens—not solitary or unique—of the manner in which Mr. Beecher's agents have not hesitated to use the Brooklyn press, on numerous occasions, to misrepresent and pervert my case to the community in which I reside, and to the public at large.

VI. Furthermore, I regret to point you to the evidence that Plymouth Church, or rather the attorney who now acts as its clerk, is attempting to make up a false but plausible record concerning this case, for the purpose of appealing to it in future to my disadvantage. It was to this end that Mr. Shearman ingeniously incorporated in his letter to me dated May 18, 1874, the following words :

"We do not understand your letter as implying that you have any charges to make, but the contrary. *If the Committee had so understood it, they would have readily entertained and fully investigated them.*"

The manifest object of the above record is to enable the church to say, a year or five years hence, that if I ever had any charges to make against Mr. Beecher, the church had long ago given me an abundant opportunity to make them. Mr. Shearman is still more bold in his communication to the *Independent*, dated June 18, 1874. He therein says of the church:

"Its officers have, in the proper way, without parade, *given every facility for investigation that could reasonably be desired, even by the most captious critics.*"

The above statement by Mr. Shearman is made in a letter which was put forth by him ostensibly in my interest, and which I am already accused of having inspired. This leads me to disavow the declaration which I have last quoted as insincere and at variance with the truth.

VII. Not to multiply instances needlessly, there is one other to which my self-respect compels me to allude with painful explicitness. In your New Haven speech you characterized Mr. Beecher as the most magnanimous of men, and in the context referred to me as a knave and dog. You left the public to infer that I had become in some despicable way the creature of Mr. Beecher's magnanimity. Early in April last I called Mr. Beecher's attention to the offensiveness and injuriousness of your statement, and informed him that I should insist on its correction either by him or me. In order to provide him with an easy way to correct it, involving no humiliation to his feelings I addressed to you the following letter:

BROOKLYN, April 3, 1874.

Rev. Leonard Bacon, D.D.:

MY DEAR SIR: I have just been reading the *Tribune's* report of your Yale speech on the Brooklyn Council, in which occurs the following paragraph:

"Another part of my theory is that Mr. Beecher's magnanimity is unspeakable. I never knew a man of a larger and more generous mind. One who was in relations to him the most intimate possible, said to me, 'If I wanted to secure his highest love, I would go into a church meeting and accuse him of crimes. This is his spirit. But I think he may carry it too far. A man whose life is a treasure to the Church Universal, to his country, to his age, has no right to subject the faith in it to such a strain. Some one has said that Plymouth Church's dealing with offenders is like Dogberry's. The comparison is apt: "If any one will not stand, let him go, and gather the guard, and thank God you are rid of such a knave.' So of Lance, who went into the stocks and the pillory to save his dog from execution for stealing puddings and geese. I think he would have done better to let the dog die. And I think Mr. Beecher would have done better to have let vengeance come on the heads of his slanderers." * * *

Setting aside the satire and mirth, if there be any criticism directed toward me in these words in sobriety and earnestness, then I beg you to do me the following act of justice:

Please forward to Mr. Beecher the letter I am now writing, and ask him to inform you, on his word of honor, whether I have been his slanderer—whether I have spoken against him falsely—whether I have evaded my just responsibility to Plymouth Church—whether I have treated him other than with the highest possible fairness—and whether he has not acknowledged to me, in large and ample terms, that *my* course towards *him* in this sorrowful business has been marked by the magnanimity which you apparently intimate has characterized *his* towards *me.*

If you write to Mr. Beecher as I have indicated, I will thank you for a line as the words or substance of his reply. With great respect I am truly yours,

THEODORE TILTON.

In reply to the above letter you sent me the following:

NEW HAVEN, April 10, 1874.

Theodore Tilton, Esq.:

DEAR SIR: Not being in Mr. Beecher's confidence, I have doubted what I ought to do with your letter written a week ago. I was not—and am not—willing to demand of him that he shall admit me to his confidence in a matter on which he chooses to be reticent. But as the letter seems to have been written for *him* quite as much as for *me,* I have now sent it to him without asking or expecting any reply.

* * * * * * *

With the best wishes for your welfare, I am, yours, truly,

LEONARD BACON.

It is now between two and three months since I received from you the foregoing letter; and as I have not heard that Mr. Beecher has made a reply, either to you or to me, I am at last forced to the disagreeable necessity of borrowing a reply in his own words, as follows:

BROOKLYN, Jan. 1, 1871.

I ask Theodore Tilton's forgiveness, and humble myself before him as I do before my God. He would have been a better man in my circumstances than I have been. I can ask nothing except that he will remember all the other breasts that would ache. I will not plead for myself. I even wish that I were dead.

* * * * * * *

H. W. BEECHER.

The above brief extract from Mr. Beecher's own testimony will be sufficient, without adducing the remainder of the document, to show that I have just ground to resist the imputation that I am the creature of his magnanimity.

In conclusion, the common impression that I have circulated and promoted scandals against Mr. Beecher is not true. I doubt if any other man in Brooklyn, during the whole extent of the last four years, has spoken to so few persons on this subject as I have done. A mere handful of my intimate friends—who had a right to understand the case—are the only persons to whom I have ever communicated the facts. To all other persons, I have been dumb—resisting all questions, and refusing all explanations.

If the public have heretofore considered my silence as inexplicable, let my sufficient motive be now seen in the just forbearance which I felt morally bound to show to a man who had sent me a written and absolute apology.

But my duty to continue this forbearance ceased when the spirit of that apology was violated to my injury by its author or his agents. These violations have been multitudinous already, and they threaten to multiply in the future—forcing me to protect myself against them in advance;—particu- larly against the cunning devices of the Clerk of the church who, acting as an attorney, appears to be conducting this business against me as if it were a case at law.

Had the fair spirit which I had a right to expect from Plymouth Church—at least for its pastor's sake—been shown toward me, I would have continued to rest in silence on Mr. Beecher's apology, and never during the remainder of my life would I have permitted any public word of mine to allude to the offence or the offender.

But the injurious measures which the author of this apology has since permitted his church to take against me without protest on his part—measures leading to the misrepresentation of my case and character by the church to the Council, and by the Council to the general public—involving gross injuries to me which have been greatly aggravated by your writings :—all these indictments, conjoin- ing to one end, have put me before my countrymen in the character of a base and bad man;—a character which, I trust, is foreign to my nature and life. Under the accumulating weight of this odium—unjustly bestowed on me—neither patience nor charity can demand that I keep silent.

In your capacity as ex-Moderator of the Council, and as its chief expositor, you have labelled the theme of your animadversions " the celebrated case of Theodore Tilton." You have declared that "the transaction with all its consequences belongs to history, and is in every way a legitimate sub- ject of public criticism." If, therefore, your estimate of the historic importance of the case is true (though I hope it is not) I now finally appeal to you as its chief historian not to represent me as playing an unmanly or dishonorable part in a case in which, so far as I can yet see, I have failed in no duty save to myself. Truly yours,

THEODORE TILTON.

BEECHER'S ALLEGED IMMORALITY.

On Monday, July 20, Mr. Tilton appeared before the Investigating Committee at the residence of Mr. Augustus Storrs, and read his sworn statement of charges against Mr. Beecher. He prefaced his statement by assigning the reasons for presenting the charges, and he added, as an epilogue, a restatement of what was implied in his preface—namely, that only Mr. Beecher and Mrs. Tilton could have wrung the statement from him.

WHY PRESENT THE CHARGES?

Before reading the "charges," Mr. Tilton addressed the Committee as follows :

GENTLEMEN OF THE COMMITTEE : In communicating to you the detailed statement of facts or evidences which you have had several days expecting at my hands, let me remind you of the circum- stances which call this statement forth. In my recent letter to Dr. Bacon, I alluded to an offence and an apology by the Rev. Henry Ward Beecher. To whomsoever else this allusion seemed indefinite, to Mr. Beecher it was plain. The offence was committed by him ; the apology was made by him ; both acts were his own, and were among the most momentous occurrences of his life. Of all men in Plymouth Church, or in the world, the Rev. Henry Ward Beecher was the one man who was best informed concerning this offence and apology, and the one man who least needed to inquire into either. Nevertheless, while possessing a perfect knowledge of both these acts done by himself, he has chosen to put on a public affectation of ignorance and innocence concerning them, and has conspicuously appointed a committee of six of the ablest men of his church, together with two attorneys, to inquire into what he leaves you to regard as the unaccountable mystery of this offence and apology, as if he had neither committed the one nor offered the other, but as if both were the mere figments of another man's imagination, thus adroitly prompting the public to draw the deduction that I am a person under some hallucination or delusion, living in a dream and forging a fraud. Furthermore, in order to cast over this explanation the delicate glamour which always lends a charm to the defence of a woman's honor, Mrs. Elizabeth R. Tilton, lately my wife, has been prompted away from her home to reside among Mr. Beecher's friends, and to co-operate with him in his ostensibly honest and laudable inquiry into facts concerning which she too, as well as he, has for years past had perfect and equal knowledge with himself.

The investigation, therefore, has been publicly pressed upon me by Mr. Beecher, seconded by Mrs. Tilton, both of whom, in so doing, have united in assuming before the public the non-existence of the grave and solemn facts into which they have conspired to investigate for the purpose, not of eliciting, but of denying the truth. This joint assumption by them, which has seemed to your Committee to be in good faith, has naturally led you into an examination in which you expect to find on their part nothing but innocence, and on my part nothing but slander. It is now my unhappy duty, from which I have in vain hitherto sought earnestly to be delivered, to give you the facts and evidences for reversing your opinion on this subject. In doing this painful, I may say heartrending duty, the responsibility for making the grave disclosures which I am about to lay before you belongs, not to me, but first to Mr. Beecher, who has prompted you to this examination, and next to Mrs. Tilton, who has joined him in a conspiracy which cannot fail to be full of peril and wretchedness to many hearts. I call you to witness that in my first brief examination by your Committee, I begged and implored you not to inquire into the facts of this case, but rather to seek to bury them beyond all possible revelation. Happy for all concerned had this entreaty been heeded! It is now too late. The last opportunity for reconciliation and settlement has passed. This investigation, undertaken by you in ignorance of dangers which Mr. Beecher should have warned you in advance, will shortly prove itself, to your surprise to have been an act of wanton and wicked folly, for which the Rev. Henry Ward Beecher, as its originator and public sponsor, will hereafter find no " space for repentance, though he seek it carefully and with tears." This desperate man must hold himself only, and not me, accountable for the wretchedness which these disclosures will carry to his own home and hearth, as they have already brought to mine. I will add that the original documents referred to in the ensuing sworn statement are, for the most part, in my possession ; but that the apology and a few other papers are in the hands of Mr. Francis D. Moulton.

Truly yours,   THEODORE TILTON.

THE SWORN STATEMENT.

Mr. Tilton then proceeded as follows :

Whereas, the Rev. Henry Ward Beecher has instigated the appointment of a committee consisting of six members of his church and society to inquire and report upon alleged aspersions upon his character by Theodore Tilton ; and, whereas, Mrs. Elizabeth R. Tilton, formerly the wife of Mr. Tilton, has openly deserted her home to co-operate with Mr. Beecher in a conspiracy to overthrow the credibility and good repute of her late husband as a man and citizen ; therefore, Theodore Tilton being thus authorized and required, and by the published demand made upon him by the Rev. Henry Ward Beecher, and being now and hereafter released by act of Mrs. Tilton from further responsibility for concealment of the truth touching her relations with Mr. Beecher—therefore Theodore Tilton hereby sets forth, under solemn oath, the following facts and testimony :

I. That on the second of October, 1855, at Plymouth Church, Brooklyn, a marriage between Theodore Tilton and Elizabeth M. Richards was performed by the Rev. Henry Ward Beecher, which marriage, thirteen years afterwards, was dishonored and violated by this clergyman, through the criminal seduction of this wife and mother, as hereinafter set forth.

II. That for a period of about fifteen years, extending both before and after this marriage, an intimate friendship existed between Theodore Tilton and the Rev. Henry Ward Beecher, which friendship was cemented to such a degree that in consequence thereof the subsequent dishonoring by Mr. Beecher of his friend's wife was a crime of uncommon wrongfulness and perfidy.

III. That about nine years ago the Rev. Henry Ward Beecher began, and thereafter continued, a friendship with Mrs. Elizabeth R. Tilton, for whose native delicacy and extreme religious sensibility he often expressed to her husband a high admiration ; visiting her from time to time for years, until the year 1870, when, for reasons hereinafter stated, he ceased such visits ; during which period, by many tokens and attentions, he won the affectionate love of Mrs. Tilton, whereby, after long moral resistance by her, and after repeated assaults by him upon her mind with overmastering arguments, accomplished the possession of her person ; maintaining with her thenceforward during the period hereinafter stated the relation called criminal intercourse ; this relation being regarded by her during that period as not criminal or morally wrong—such had been the power of his arguments as a clergyman to satisfy her religious scruples against such violation of virtue and honor.

IV. That on the evening of October 10, 1868, or thereabouts, Mrs. Elizabeth R. Tilton held an interview with the Rev. Henry Ward Beecher, at his residence, she being then in a tender state of mind, owing to the recent death and burial of a young child ; and during this interview an act of criminal commerce took place between this pastor and this parishioner, the motive on her part being, as hereinbefore stated, not regarded by her at the time criminal or wrong ; which act was followed by a similar act of criminality between these same parties at Mr. Tilton's residence during a pastoral visit paid by Mr. Beecher to her on the subsequent Saturday evening, followed also by other similar acts on various occasions from the autumn of 1868 to the spring of 1870, the places being the two residences aforesaid, and occasionally other places to which her pastor would invite and accompany her, or at which he would meet her by previous appointment ; these acts of wrong being on her part, from first to last, not wanton or consciously wicked, but arising through a blinding of her moral perceptions, occasioned by the powerful influence exerted on her mind at that time to this end by the Rev. Henry Ward Beecher, as her trusted religious preceptor and guide.

V. That the pastoral visits made by the Rev. Henry Ward Beecher to Mrs. Tilton during the year 1868 became so frequent as to excite comment, being in marked contrast with his known habit of making few pastoral calls on his parishioners, which frequency in Mrs. Tilton's case is shown in letters written to her husband during his absence in the West; these letters giving evidence that during the period of five or six weeks twelve different pastoral calls on Mrs. Tilton were made by the Rev. Henry Ward Beecher, which calls became noticeably infrequent on Mr. Tilton's return to his home.

VI. That previous to the aforesaid criminal intimacy, one of the reasons which Mrs. Tilton alleged for her encouragement of such exceptional attentions from the Rev. Henry Ward Beecher was the fact that she had been much distressed with rumors against his moral purity, and wished to convince him that she could receive his kindness, and yet resist his solicitations; and that she could inspire in him, by her purity and fidelity, an increased respect for the chaste dignity of womanhood. Previous to the autumn of 1868 she maintained with Christian firmness towards her pastor this position of resistance, always refusing his amorous pleas, which were strong and oft-repeated; and in a letter to her husband, dated February 3, 1868, she wrote as follows: "To love is praiseworthy, but to abuse the gift is sin. Here I am strong. No demonstrations or fascinations could cause me to yield my womanhood."

VII. That the first suspicion which crossed the mind of Theodore Tilton that the Rev. Henry Ward Beecher was abusing or might abuse the affection and reverence which Mrs. Tilton bore towards her pastor was an improper caress given by Mr Beecher to Mrs. Tilton by the * * * while seated by her side on the floor of his library, overlooking engravings. Mr. Tilton a few hours afterwards asked of his wife an explanation of her permission of such a liberty, whereat she at first denied the fact, but then confessed it, and said that she had spoken chidingly to Mr. Beecher concerning it. On another occasion Mr. Tilton, after leaving his house in the early morning, returned to it in the forenoon, and on going to his bedchamber found the door locked, and when on knocking the door was opened by Mrs. Tilton. Mr. Beecher was seen within apparently much confused and exhibiting a flushed face. Mrs. Tilton afterwards made a plausible explanation, which from the confidence reposed in her by her husband was by him deemed satisfactory.

VIII. That in the spring of 1870, on Mr. Tilton's return from a winter's absence, he noticed in his wife such evidences of the absorption of her mind in Mr. Beecher, that in a short time an estrangement took place between her husband and herself, in consequence of which she went into the country earlier than usual for a summer sojourn. After an absence of several weeks she voluntarily returned to her home in Brooklyn. On the evening of July 3, 1870, when, and then and there, within a few hours after her arrival, and after exacting from her husband a solemn promise that he would do the Rev. Henry Ward Beecher no harm, nor communicate to him what she was about to say, she made a circumstantial confession to her husband of the criminal facts hereinbefore stated, accompanied with citations from Mr. Beecher's arguments and reasonings with her to overcome her long-maintained scruple against yielding to his desires, and declaring that she had committed no wrong to her husband or her marriage vow, quoting, in support of this opinion, that her pastor had repeatedly assured her that she was spotless and chaste, which she believed herself to be. She further stated that her sexual commerce with him had never proceeded from low or vulgar thoughts either on her part or his, but always from pure affection and a high religious love. She stated, furthermore, that Mr. Beecher habitually characterized their intimacy by the term "nest hiding," and he would suffer pain and sorrow if his hidden secret were ever made known. She said that her mind was often burdened by the deceit necessary for her to practice in order to prevent discovery, and that her conscience had many times impelled her to throw off this burden of enforced falsehood by making a full confession to her husband, so that she would no longer be living before him a perpetual lie. In particular she said that she had been on the point of making this confession a few months previously, during a severe illness, when she feared she might die. She affirmed also that Mr. Beecher had assured her repeatedly that he loved her better than he had ever loved any other woman, and she felt justified before God in her intimacy with him, save the necessary deceit which accompanied it, and at which she frequently suffered in her mind.

IX. That after the above-named confession by Mrs. Elizabeth R. Tilton she returned to the country to await such action by her husband as he might see fit to take, whereupon, after many considerations, the chief of which was that she had not voluntarily gone astray, but had been artfully misled through religious reverence for the Rev. Henry Ward Beecher as her spiritual guide, together, also, from a desire to protect the family from open shame, Mr. Tilton condoned the wrong, and he addressed to his wife such letters of affection, tenderness, and respect, as he felt would restore her wounded spirit, and which did partially produce that result.

X. That in December, 1870, differences arose between Theodore Tilton and Henry C. Bowen, which were augmented by the Rev. Henry Ward Beecher and Mrs. Beecher, in consequence whereof and at the wish of Mrs. Elizabeth R. Tilton expressed in writing in a paper put into the hands of Francis D. Moulton, with a view to procure a harmonious interview between Mr. Tilton and Mr. Beecher, such an interview was arranged and carried out by Mr. Moulton at his then residence on Clinton street, Mr. Beecher and Mr. Tilton meeting and speaking then and there for the first time since Mrs. Tilton's confession of six months before. The paper in Mr. Moulton's hands was a statement by Mrs. Tilton of the substance of the confession which she had before made, and of her wish and prayer for reconciliation and peace between her pastor and her husband. This paper furnished to Mr. Beecher the first knowledge which he had as yet received that Mrs. Tilton had made such a confession. At this interview between Mr. Beecher and Mr. Tilton, permission was sought by Mr. Beecher to consult with Mrs. Tilton on that same evening. This permission being granted, Mr. Beecher departed from Mr. Moulton's house, and in about half an hour returned thither, expressing his remorse and shame, and declaring that his life and work seemed brought to a sudden end. Later in the same evening Mr. Tilton, on returning to his house, found his wife weeping and in great distress, saying that what she had meant for peace had only given pain and anguish ; that Mr. Beecher had just called on her, declaring that she had slain him, and that he would probably be tried before a Council of Ministers, unless she would give him a written paper for his protection. Whereupon she said he dictated to her, and she copied in her own handwriting, a suitable paper for him to use to clear himself before a Council of Ministers. Mrs. Tilton having kept no copy of this paper, her husband asked her to make a distinct statement in writing of her design and meaning in giving it, whereupon she wrote as follows :

DECEMBER 30, 1870—Midnight.

MY DEAR HUSBAND :—I desire to leave with you, before going to bed, a statement that Mr. Henry Ward Beecher called upon me this evening, and asked me if I would defend him against any accusation in a Council of Ministers ; and I replied solemnly that I would, in case the accuser was any other person than my husband. He (H. W. B.) dictated a letter, which I copied as my own, to be used by him as against any other accuser except my husband. This letter was designed to vindicate Mr. Beecher against all other persons save only yourself. I was ready to give him this letter because he said with pain that my letter in your hands addressed to him, dated December 29, "had struck him dead, and ended his usefulness." You and I are pledged to do our best to avoid publicity. God grant a speedy end to all further anxieties. Affectionately,

ELIZABETH.

On the next day, namely, December 31, 1870, Mr. Moulton, on being informed by Mr. Tilton of the above-named transaction by Mr. Beecher, called on him (Mr. Beecher) at his residence, and told him that a reconciliation seemed suddenly made impossible by Mr. Beecher's nefarious act in procuring the letter which Mrs. Tilton had thus been improperly persuaded to make falsely. Mr. Beecher promptly, through Mr. Moulton, returned the letter to Mr. Tilton, with an expression of shame and sorrow for having procured it in the manner he did. The letter was as follows :

DECEMBER 30, 1870.

Wearied with importunity and weakened by sickness, I gave a letter implicating my friend Henry Ward Beecher under the assurances that that would remove all difficulties between me and my husband. That letter I now revoke. I was persuaded to it—almost forced—when I was in a weakened state of mind. I regret it, and recall all its statements. E. R. TILTON.

I desire to say explicitly Mr. Beecher has never offered any improper solicitation, but has always treated me in a manner becoming a Christian and a gentleman. ELIZABETH R. TILTON.

At the time of Mr. Beecher's returning the above document to Mr. Tilton through Mr. Moulton, Mr. Beecher requested Mr. Moulton to call at his residence, in Columbia street, on the next day, which he did on the evening of January 1, 1871. A long interview then ensued, in which Mr. Beecher expressed to Mr. Moulton great contrition and remorse for his previous criminality with Mrs. Tilton ; taking to himself shame for having misused his sacred office as a clergyman to corrupt her mind, expressing a determination to kill himself in case of exposure, and begging Mr. Moulton to take a pen and receive from his (Mr. Beecher's) lips an apology to be conveyed to Mr. Tilton, in the hope that such an appeal would secure Mr. Tilton's forgiveness. The apology which Mr. Beecher dictated to Mr. Moulton was as follows :

MR. BEECHER'S APOLOGY.

[In trust with F. D. Moulton.]

MY DEAR FRIEND MOULTON :—I ask through you Theodore Tilton's forgiveness, and I humble myself before him as I do before my God. He would have been a better man in my circumstances than I have been. I can ask nothing, except that he will remember all the other breasts that would ache. I will not plead for myself. I even wish that I were dead. But others must live to suffer. I will die before any one but myself shall be inculpated. All my thoughts are running out towards my friends, and toward the poor child lying there, and praying, with her folded hands. She is guiltless, sinned against, bearing the transgression of another. Her forgiveness I have. I humbly pray to God to put it into the heart of her husband to forgive me. I have trusted this to Moulton, in confidence.

H. W. BEECHER.

In the above document, the last sentence and the signature are in the handwriting of the Rev. Henry Ward Beecher.

XI. That Mrs. Tilton wrote the following letter to a friend :

174 LIVINGSTON STREET,
BROOKLYN, January 5, 1871.

DEAR FRIEND :—A cruel conspiracy has been formed against my husband, in which my mother and Mrs. Beecher have been the chief actors. * * * Yours, truly, ELIZABETH R. TILTON.

XII. That in the following month Mr. Moulton, wishing to bind Mr. Tilton and Mr. Beecher by mutual expressions of a good spirit, elicited from them the following correspondence :

MR. TILTON TO MR. MOULTON.

BROOKLYN, February 7, 1871.

MY DEAR FRIEND :—In several conversations with you you have asked about my feelings toward Mr. Beecher, and yesterday you said the time had come when you would like to receive from me an expression of this kind in writing. I say, therefore, very cheerfully, that notwithstanding the great suffering which he has caused to Elizabeth and myself, I bear him no malice, shall do him no wrong, shall discountenance every project (by whomsoever proposed) for any exposure of his secret to the public, and (if I know myself at all) shall endeavor to act to Mr. Beecher as I would have him in similar circumstances act toward me. I ought to add, that your own good offices in this case have led me to a higher moral feeling than I might otherwise have reached.
Ever yours, affectionately, THEODORE.

To Frank Moulton.

On the same day Mr. Beecher wrote to Mr. Moulton the following :

MR. BEECHER TO MR. MOULTON.

February 7, 1871.

MY DEAR FRIEND MOULTON :—I am glad to send you a book, etc.
* * * * * * * *
Many, many friends has God raised up to me, but to no one of them has he ever given the opportunity and the wisdom so to serve me as you have. You have also proved Theodore's friend and Elizabeth's. Does God look down from heaven on three unhappier creatures that more need a friend than these ? Is it not an intimation of God's intent of mercy to all that each one of these has in you a tried and proved friend ? But only in you are we thus united. Would to God, who orders all hearts, that by his kind mediation Theodore, Elizabeth, and I could be made friends again. Theodore will have the hardest task in such a case; but has he not proved himself capable of the noblest things ? I wonder if Elizabeth knows how generously he has carried himself toward me. Of course I can never speak with her again without his permission, and I do not know, even then, it would be best. * * *

Mr. Moulton on the same day asked Mr. Tilton if he would permit Mr. Beecher to address a letter to Mrs. Tilton, and Mr. Tilton replied in the affirmative, whereupon Mr. Beecher wrote as follows :

MR. BEECHER TO MRS. TILTON.

BROOKLYN, February 7, 1871.

MY DEAR MRS. TILTON.—When I saw you last I did not expect ever to see you again. or to be alive many days. God was kinder to me than were my own thoughts. The friend whom God sent to me, Mr. Moulton, has proved, above all friends that I ever had, able and willing to help me in this terrible emergency of my life. His hand it was that tied up the storm that was ready to burst on our heads. You have no friend (Theodore excepted) who has it in his power to serve you so vitally, and who will do it with such delicacy and honor. It does my sore heart good to see in Mr. Moulton an unfeigned respect and honor for you. It would kill me if I thought otherwise. He will be as true a friend to your honor and happiness as a brother could be to a sister's. In him we have a common ground. You and I may meet in him. The past is ended. But is there no future ? No wiser, higher, holier future ? May not this friend stand as a priest in the new sanctuary of reconciliation, and mediate and bless Theodore and my most unhappy self ? Do not let my earnestness fail of its end. You believe in my judgment. I have put myself wholly and gladly in Moulton's hand, and there I must meet you. This is sent with Theodore's consent, but he has not read it. Will you return it to me by his own hand ? I am very earnest in this wish for all our sakes, as such a letter ought not to be subject to even a chance of miscarriage.
Your unhappy friend, H. W. BEECHER.

XIII. That about a year after Mrs. Tilton's confession her mind remained in the fixed opinion that her criminal relations with Mr. Beecher had not been morally wrong, so strongly had he impressed her to the contrary ; but at length a change took place in her convictions on this subject, as noted in the following letter addressed by her to her husband :

MRS. TILTON TO MR. TILTON.

SCHOHARIE, June 29, 1871.

MY DEAR THEODORE : To-day through the ministry of Catherine Gaunt, a character of fiction, my eyes have been opened for the first time in my experience, so that I see clearly my sin. It was when I knew that I was loved, to suffer it to grow to a passion. A virtuous woman should check instantly an absorbing love. But it appeared to me in such false light. That the love I felt and received could harm no one, not even you, I have believed unfalteringly until four o'clock this afternoon, when the heavenly vision dawned upon me. I see now, as never before, the wrong I have done you, and hasten immediately to ask your pardon, with a penitence so sincere that henceforth (if reason remains) you may trust me implicitly. Oh! my dear Theodore, though your opinions are not restful or congenial to my soul, yet my own integrity and purity are a sacred and holy thing to me. Bless God, with me, for Catharine

3

Gaunt, and for all the sure leadings of an all-wise and loving Providence. Yes; now I feel quite prepared to renew my marriage vow with you, to keep it as the Saviour requireth, who looketh at the eye and the heart. Never before could I say this. When you yearn toward me with true feeling, be assured of the tried, purified, and restored love of

ELIZABETH.

Mrs. Tilton followed the above letter with these:

MRS. TILTON TO MR. TILTON.

JULY 4, 1871.

O, my dear husband, may you never need the discipline of being misled by a good woman, as I was by a good man.

[No Date.]

I would mourn greatly if my life was to be made known to father. His head would be bowed indeed to the grave.

[No Date.]

Do not think my ill health is on account of my sin and its discovery. My sins and life-record I have carried to my Saviour. No; my prostration is owing to the suffering I have caused you.

XIV. That about one year after Mrs. Tilton's confession, and about a half year after Mr. Beecher's confirmation of the same, Mrs. V. C. Woodhull, then a total stranger to Mr. Tilton, save that he had been presented to her in a company of friends, a few days previous, wrote in the *World*, Monday, May 22, 1871, the following statement, namely:

I know of one man, a public teacher of eminence, who lives in concubinage with the wife of another public teacher of almost equal eminence. All three concur in denouncing offences against morality. I shall make it my business to analyze some of these lives,

VICTORIA C. WOODHULL.

New York, May 20, 1871.

On the day of the publication of the above card in the *World*, Mr. Tilton received from Mrs. Woodhull a request to call on imperative business at her office; and, on going thither, a copy of the above card was put into his hand by Mrs. Woodhull, who said that "the parties referred to therein were the Rev. Henry Ward Beecher and the wife of Theodore Tilton." Following this announcement, Mrs. Woodhull detailed to Mr. Tilton, with vehement speech, the wicked and injurious story which she published in the year following. Meanwhile, Mr. Tilton, desiring to guard against any possible temptation to Mrs. Woodhull to publish the grossly distorted version which she gave to Mr. Tilton (and which she afterwards attributed to him), he sought by many personal services and kindly attentions to influence her to such a good will towards himself and family as would remove all disposition or desire in her to afflict him with such a publication. Mr. Tilton's efforts and association with Mrs. Woodhull ceased in April, 1872, and six months afterwards, namely, November 2, 1872, she published the scandal which he had labored to suppress.

XV. That on the third day thereafter the Rev. Thomas K. Beecher, of Elmira, N. Y., wrote as follows:

ELMIRA, November 5, 1872.

"Mrs. Woodhull only carries out Henry's philosophy, against which I recorded my protest twenty years ago."

XVI. That in May, 1873, the publication by one of Mr. Beecher's partners of a tripartite covenant between H. C. Bowen, H. W. Beecher, and Theodore Tilton led the press of the country to charge that Mr. Tilton had committed against Mr. Beecher some heinous wrong, which Mr. Beecher had pardoned; whereas the truth was the reverse. To remedy this false public impression, Mr. Moulton requested Mr. Beecher to prepare a suitable card, relieving Mr. Tilton of this injustice. In answer to this request Mr. Beecher pleaded his embarrassments, which prevented his saying anything without bringing himself under suspicion. Mr. Tilton then proposed to prepare a card of his own, containing a few lines from the recently quoted apology, for the purpose of showing that Mr. Beecher, instead of having had occasion to forgive Mr. Tilton, had had occasion to be forgiven by him. Mr. Beecher then wrote a letter to Mr. Moulton, which, on being shown to Mr. Tilton, was successful in appealing to Mr. Tilton's feelings. Mr. Beecher said in it, under date of Sunday morning, June 1, 1873:

MR. BEECHER TO MR. MOULTON.

MY DEAR FRANK: I am determined to make no more resistance. Theodore's temperament is such that the future, even if temporarily earned, would be absolutely worthless, and rendering me liable at any hour of the day to be obliged to stultify all the devices by which we saved ourselves. It is only fair that he should know that the publication of the card which he proposes would leave him worse off than before. The agreement (viz., the "tripartite covenant") was made after my letter through you to him (viz. "the apology") was written. He had had it a year. He had condoned his wife's fault. He had enjoined upon me, with the utmost earnestness and solemnity not to betray his wife, nor leave his children to a blight. * * * With such a man as T. T., there is no possible salvation for any that depend upon him. With a strong nature, he does not know how to govern it. * * * * There is no use in trying further. I have a strong feeling upon me, and it brings great peace, that I am spending my last Sunday, and preaching my last sermon.

The hopelessness of spirit which the foregoing letter portrayed on the part of its writer led Mr. Tilton to reconsider the question of defending himself at the cost of producing misery to Mr. Beecher; which determination by Mr. Tilton to allow the prevailing calumnies against himself to go unanswered was further strengthened by the following note received by him two days thereafter from the office editor of Mr. Beecher's journal:

OLIVER JOHNSON TO THEODORE TILTON.

128 East Twelfth Street, June 4, 1873.

My Dear Theodore : May I tell you frankly that when I saw you last you did not seem to me to be the noble young man who inspired my warm affection so many years ago. You were yielding to an act which I could not help thinking would be dishonorable and perfidious ; and, although it is easy for me to make every allowance for the circumstances that had wrought you to such a frenzy, I was dreadfully shocked. My dear Theodore, let me as an old friend whose heart is wrung by your terrible suffering and sorrow tell you that you were then acting ignobly, and that you can never have true peace of mind till you conquer yourself and dismiss all purpose and thought of injuring the man who has wronged you. Of all the promises our lips can frame none are so sacred as those we make to those who have injured us, and whom we have professed to forgive : and they are sacred just in proportion as their violation would work injury to those to whom they are made. You cannot paint too blackly the wrongs you have suffered. On that point I make no plea in abatement, but I beg you to remember that nothing can change the law which makes forgiveness noble and godlike. I have prayed for you night and day, with strong crying and tears, beseeching God to restrain you from wronging yourself by violating your solemn engagements. To-night I am happy in the thought that you have been preserved from committing the act which I so much dreaded.

In a letter written by Mr. Beecher, in order to be shown to Mr. Tilton, Mr. Beecher spoke as follows :

MR. BEECHER TO MR. MOULTON.

No man can see the difficulties that environ me unless he stands where I do. To say that I have a church on my hands is simply enough, but to have the hundreds and thousands of men pressing me, each one with his keen suspicion, or anxiety, or zeal, to see the tendencies which, if not stopped, would break out into a ruinous defence of me ; to stop them without seeming to do it ; to prevent any one questioning me; to meet and allay prejudices against T., which had their beginning years before; to keep serene as if I was not alarmed or disturbed ; to be cheerful at home and among friends when I was suffering the torments of the damned ; to pass sleepless nights often, and yet to come up fresh and fair for Sunday—all this may be talked about, but the real thing cannot be understood from the outside, nor its wearing and grinding on the nervous system.

In still another letter, written for the same purpose as the above, Mr. Beecher said :

MR. BEECHER TO MR. MOULTON.

If my destruction would place him (Mr. Tilton) all right, that shall not stand in the way ; I am willing to step down and out. No one can offer more than that. That I do offer. Sacrifice me without hesitation if you can clearly see your way to his safety and happiness thereby. In one point of view I could desire the sacrifice on my part. Nothing can possibly be so bad as the power of great darkness in which I spend much of my time. I look upon death as sweeter far than any friend I have in the world. Life would be pleasant if I could see that rebuilt which is shattered. But to live on the sharp and ragged edge of anxiety, remorse, fear, despair, and yet to put on an appearance of serenity and happiness cannot be endured much longer. I am well nigh discouraged. If you cease to trust me, to love me, I am alone ; I do not know any person in the world to whom I could go.

Mr. Tilton yielded to the above quoted and other similar letters, and made no defence of himself against the public odium which attached to him unjustly.

XVII. That the marriage union between Mr. and Mrs. Tilton, until broken by Mr. Beecher, was more than common harmony, affection, and mutual respect. Their house and household were regarded for years, by all their guests, as an ideal home. As evidence of the feeling and spirit which this wife entertained for her husband, up to the time of her corruption by Mr. Beecher, the following letters by Mrs. Tilton, written only a few months before her loss of honor, will testify :

MRS. TILTON TO MR. TILTON.

Tuesday Morning, January 23, 1868.

My Beloved : Don't you know the peculiar phase of Christ's character as a lover is so precious to me because of my consecration and devotion to you ? I learn to love you from my love to him. I have learned to love him from loving you. Nor do I feel it one whit irreverent. And as every day I adorn myself consciously, as a bride to meet her bridegroom, so in like manner I lift imploring hands that my soul's love may be prepared. I, with the little girls, after you left us, with overflowing eyes and hearts, consecrated ourselves to our work and to you. My waking thoughts last night were of you. My rising thoughts this morning were of you. I bless you; I honor you; I love you. God sustain us and help us both to keep our vows.

MRS. TILTON TO MR. TILTON.

Saturday Evening, February 1, 1868.

O, well I know, as far as I am capable, I love you. Now to keep this fire high and generous is the ideal before me. I am only perfectly contented and restful when you are with me. These latter months I have thought, looked, and yearned for the hour when you would be at home with longings unutterable.

MRS. TILTON TO MR. TILTON.

MONDAY, February 3, 1868—9 o'clock A. M.

What may I bring to my beloved, this bright morning ? A large, throbbing heart, full of love, single in its aim and purpose to bless and cheer him ? Is it acceptable, sweet one ?

MRS. TILTON TO MR. TILTON.

MONDAY MORNING, February 24, 1868.

Do you wonder that I couple your love, your presence and relation to me with the Saviour's ? I lift you up sacredly and keep you in that exalted and holy place where I reverence, respect, and love you with the fervency of my whole being. Whatever capacity I have I offer to you. The closing lines of your letter are these words: " I shall hardly venture again upon a great friendship—your love shall be enough for the remaining days." That word " enough " 'seems a stoicism on which you have resolved to live your life ; but I pray God he will supply you with friendships pure and with wifely love, which your great heart demands withholding not himself as the chief love, which consumeth not though it burn, and whose effects are always perfect rest and peace. Again, in one of your letters you close with " Faithfully yours." That word " faithfully " means a great deal. Yes, darling, I believe it, trust it, and give you the same surety with regard to myself. I am faithful to you, have been always, and shall forever be, world without end. Call not this assurance impious ; there are some things we *know*. Blessed be God !

MRS. TILTON TO MR. TILTON.

HOME, February 29, 1868. }
SATURDAY EVENING. }

Ah, did ever man ever love so grandly as my Beloved ? Other friendships, public affairs, all " fail to nought " when I come to you. Though you are in Decorah, to-night, yet I have felt your love, and am very grateful for it. I had not received a line since Monday, and was so hungry and lonesome that I took out all your letters and indulged myself as at a feast, but without satiety. And now I long to pour out into your heart, of my abundance. I am conscious of three jets to the fountain of my soul—to the Great Lover and yourself—to whom as *one* I am eternally wedded ; my children ; and the dear friends who trust and love me. I do not want another long separation. While we are in the flesh, let us abide together.

MRS. TILTON TO MR. TILTON.

WEDNESDAY MORN., March, 1868.

O how almost perfectly could I minister to you, this winter, my heart glows so perpetually. I am conscious of great inward awakening toward you. If I live, I shall teach my children to *begin* their loves, where now I am. I cannot conceive of anything more delicious than a life consecrated to a faithful love. I insist that I miss you more than you do me, but soon I shall see my Beloved.

YOUR OWN DEAR WIFE.

In addition to the above, many other letters by Mrs. Tilton to her husband prior to her corruption by Mr. Beecher, served to show that a Christian wife, loving her husband to the extreme degree above set forth, could only have been swerved from the path of rectitude by artful and powerful persuasions, clothed in the phrases of religion and enforced by strong appeals from her chief Christian teacher and guide.

XVIII. That the story purporting to explain Mr. Beecher's apology as having been written because he had offended Mr. Tilton by engaging his wife in the project of a separation from her husband is false, as will be seen by the following letter written only three days after the date of the apology :

MRS. TILTON TO MR. TILTON.

174 LIVINGSTON STREET, BROOKLYN, January 4, 1871.

Mr. Francis D. Moulton :

MY DEAR FRIEND :—In regard to your question whether I have ever sought a separation from my husband, I indignantly deny that such was ever the fact, as I have denied it a hundred times before. The story that I wanted a separation was a deliberate falsehood, coined by my poor mother, who said she would bear the responsibility of this and other statements she might make, and communicated to my husband's enemy, Mrs. H. W. Beecher, and by her communicated to Mr. Bowen. *I feel outraged* by the whole proceeding, and am now suffering in consequence more than I am able to bear.

I am yours very truly,   ELIZABETH R. TILTON.

XIX. That during the first week in January, 1871, a few days after the apology was written, Mr. Beecher communicated to Mr. Tilton, through Mr. Moulton, an earnest wish that he (Mr. Tilton) would take his family to Europe and reside there for a term of years at Mr. Beecher's expense. Similar offers have been since repeated by Mr. Beecher to Mr. Tilton through the same channel. A message of kindred tenor was brought from Mr. Beecher to Mr. Tilton last summer, by Mr. F. B. Carpenter, as will appear from the following affidavit:

AFFIDAVIT OF F. B. CARPENTER.

HOMER, N. Y., July 18, 1874.

On Sunday, June 1, 1873, two days after the surreptitious publication of the tripartite covenant between H. W. Beecher, H. C. Bowen, and Theodore Tilton, I walked with Mr. Beecher from Plymouth Church to the residence of Mr. F. D. Moulton, in Remsen street. On the way to Mr. Moulton's house Mr. Beecher said to me that if Mr. Tilton would stand by him he would share his fame, his fortune, and everything he possessed with him (Tilton).　　　　　FRANCIS B. CARPENTER.

Sworn to and subscribed before me this eighteenth day of July, 1874.

　　　　　　　　　　　　　　　WILLIAM T. HICOK, Notary Public.

Mr. Carpenter, in communicating to Mr. Tilton the above affidavit, says in a letter accompanying it, "I have no hesitation in giving you the statement, as I understood at the time that it was for me to repeat in substance to you, and I did so repeat it. It was at this interview Mr. Beecher spoke to me of his apology to you." The charge that Mr. Tilton ever attempted to levy blackmail on Mr. Beecher is false ; on the contrary, Mr Tilton has always resented every attempt by Mr. Beecher to put him under pecuniary obligation.

XX. Not long after the scandal became public, Mrs. Tilton wrote on a slip of paper, and left on her husband's writing-desk, the following words : "Now that the exposure has come, my whole nature revolts to join with you or standing with you." Through the influence of Mr. Beecher's friends, the opinion has long been diligently propagated that the scandal was due to Mr. Tilton, and that the alleged facts were malicious inventions by him to revenge himself for supposed and imaginary wrongs done to him by Mr. Beecher. Many words were spoken from time to time by Mrs. Tilton to the praise and eulogy of Mr. Beecher, which being extensively quoted through his congregation, heightened the impression that Mr. Tilton was Mr. Beecher's slanderer, Mrs. Tilton being herself the authority for the statement. In this way Mrs. Tilton and one of her relatives have been the chief causes of the great difficulty of suppressing the scandal. They have had a habit of saying, "Mr. Tilton believes such and such things," and their naming of these things by way of denial has been a mischievous way of circulating them broadcast. In this way Mr. Tilton has been made to appear a defamer, whereas he has made every effort in his power to suppress the injurious tales which he has been charged with propagating. On all occasions he has systematically referred to his wife in terms favorable to her character. Further, Mr. Tilton would not have communicated to the Committee the facts contained in this statement except for the perverse course of Rev. Henry Ward Beecher and Mrs. Elizabeth R. Tilton to degrade and destroy him in the public estimation.

XXI. That one evening, about two weeks after the publication of Mr. Tilton's letter to Dr. Bacon, Mrs. Tilton, on coming home at a late hour, informed her husband that she had been visited at a friend's house by a committee of investigation, and had given sweeping evidence acquitting Mr. Beecher of every charge. This was the first intimation that Mr. Tilton received that any such committee was then in existence. Furthermore, Mrs. Tilton stated that she had done this by advice of a lawyer whom Mr. Beecher had sent to her, and who, in advance of her appearing before the Committee, arranged with her the questions and answers which were to constitute her testimony in Mr. Beecher's behalf. On the next day, after giving this untrue testimony before the Committee, she spent many hours of extreme suffering from pangs of conscience at having testified falsely. She expressed to her husband the hope that God would forgive her perjury, but that the motive was to save Mr. Beecher and her husband, and also to remove all reproach from the cause of religion. She also expressed similar contrition to one of her intimate friends.

XXII. Finally, that in addition to the foregoing facts and evidences, other confirmations could be adduced if needed to prove the following recapitulated statement, namely : that the Rev. Henry Ward Beecher, as pastor and friend of Mr. Tilton and family, trespassed upon the sanctity of friendship and hospitality in a long endeavor to seduce Mrs. Elizabeth R. Tilton ; that by the artful use of his priestly authority with her, she being his pupil in religion, he accomplished this seduction ; that for a period of a year and a half, or thereabout, he maintained criminal intercourse with her, overcoming her previous modest scruples against such conduct by investing it with a false justification as sanctioned by love and religion : that he then participated in a conspiracy to degrade Theodore Tilton before the public, by loss of place, business and repute ; that he abused Mr. Tilton's forgiveness and pledge of protection by thereafter authorizing a series of measures by Plymouth Church, having for their object the putting of a stigma upon Mr. Tilton before the church, and also before an ecclesiastical council, insomuch that the moderator of that council, interpreting these acts by Mr. Beecher and his church, declared publicly that they showed Mr. Beecher to be the most magnanimous of men, and Mr. Tilton to be a knave and a dog ; that when Mr. Tilton thereafter, not in malice, but for self-protection, wrote a letter to Dr. Bacon, alluding therein to an offence and apology by the Rev. Henry Ward Beecher, he (Mr. Beecher) defiantly appointed a committee of his church members to inquire into the injury done him by Mr. Tilton by the aforesaid allusion, and implying that he (Mr. Beecher) had never been the author of such offence and apology, and that Mr. Tilton was a slanderer ;

that to make this inquiry bear grievously against Mr. Tilton he (Mr. Beecher) previously connived with Mrs. E. R. Tilton to give false testimony in his (Mr. Beecher's) behalf ; that Mr. Beecher's course towards Mr. Tilton and family has at last resulted in the open destruction of Mr. Tilton's household and home, and in the desolation of his heart and life.   THEODORE TILTON.

Sworn to before me this twentieth day of July, 1874.

THEO. BURGMYER, Notary Public.

ONLY MR. BEECHER AND MRS. TILTON COULD HAVE EXTRACTED THIS STATEMENT.

Mr. Tilton read to the committee this supplementary note :

GENTLEMEN OF THE COMMITTEE : Having laid before you the above sworn statement, which I have purposely restricted to relations of Mr. Beecher with Mrs. Tilton only, and with no other person or persons, I wish to add an explanation due to yourselves. In the *Golden Age*, lately edited by me, a suggestion was made, not with my knowledge or consent, that your Committee, in order to be justly constituted, should comprise, in addition to the six members appointed by Mr. Beecher, six others appointed by myself. To no such proposal would I have consented, for I have never wanted any tribunal whatever for the investigation of this subject. Neither your Committee, as at present constituted, nor an enlarged committee on the plan just mentioned, nor any other committee of any kind, could in and of itself have persuaded or compelled me to lay before you the facts contained in the preceding statement. Distinctly be it understood that these facts have not been evoked by your Committee because of any authority which I recognize in you as a tribunal of inquiry. Nor would they have been yielded up to any other committee or board of reference, however constituted (except a court of law) ; but, on the contrary, I have divulged the above statement solely because of the openly-published demand for it made directly to me by the Rev. Henry Ward Beecher, aided and abetted by Mrs. Elizabeth R. Tilton. These two parties—these alone, and not your Committee—have by their action prevailed with me. No other authorities or influences (except a court of law) could have been powerful enough to have extorted from me the above disclosure. For the sake of one of these parties gladly would I have continued to hide these facts in the future as I have incessantly striven to do in the past. But, by the joint action of Mr. Beecher and Mrs. Tilton, I can withhold the truth only at the price of perpetual infamy to my name in addition to the penalty which I already suffer in the destruction of a home once as pleasant as any in which you yourselves dwell.

Respectfully,   THEODORE TILTON.

TILTON'S CROSS-EXAMINATION.

In view of the publication of Mr. Tilton's statement, the Investigating Committee published on Monday, July 27th, Mr. Tilton's cross-examination, which extended over two days, and was conducted for the most part by Gen. Tracy, Mr. Beecher's lawyer. The first day's cross-examination occurred on July 20, and reads as follows :

General Tracy—Are you able to give the date of the transaction which you say you witnessed at Mr. Beecher's house at the time of the examination of the engraving? A. I cannot state the date.

Q. At the time you received the information you speak of from your wife you were the editor of the *Independent* and of the Brooklyn *Union*, I believe ? A. I was.

Q. Did your wife continue to attend Plymouth Church after that information ? A. Yes, sir ; that was in the summer time ; she went into the country and was absent a long time ; she has always continued to attend once or twice a year ; she is a member of Plymouth Church.

Q. Did she attend regularly after returning from the country ! A. No, sir ; she attended occasionally for communion service, and would steal in quietly at the corner of the building so as to be unobserved.

Q. Previous to announcing your discovery or pretended discovery to Mr. Beecher you had fallen into trouble with Henry C. Bowen, had you not? A. Yes, sir.

Q. How long before? A. Two days.

Q. You had ceased to be the editor of the *Independent* when you made this announcement ? A. No, sir. I ceased to be the editor of the *Independent* on the 1st day of January.

Q. Was not your valedictory published on the 22d of December. A. Yes, sir, but my engagement ended on the 31st.

Q. Had you not entered into a contract with Mr. Bowen to be the editor of the *Union* and contributor to the *Independent* before you made any announcement to Mr. Beecher of this pretended discovery, and had not Mr. Bowen discovered immoralities on your part, and did he not threaten to break the engagement with you ? A. No, he did not.

Q. Did he not make such allegations against you, and did not you and he appoint a day of meeting at his house, when, in the presence of a mutual friend, the allegations against you should be stated, and you should make an explanation, and did not you meet in the presence of a mutual friend for that purpose? A. No, sir; Mr. Johnson wished me, about Christmas time to see Mr. Bowen; he said there was some story afloat concerning me; I think Christmas was Sunday and I went to see him on Monday; we had a few words concerning the matter; he did not tell me what the story was; I said, "If there is any story afloat bring the author of it here and let us see what it is;" we then went on in a conversation concerning Mr. Beecher.

Q. Did not you and Mr. Bowen meet on that day, and did not Mr. Bowen begin to repeat the charges against you, and did not you, while listening to those charges break out against the Rev. Henry Ward Beecher? A. I did not; I never heard of those charges until after that interview, when Mr. Bowen went from it to bear the letter to Mr. Beecher; I never knew that Mr. Beecher or Mrs. Beecher had anything to do with Mr. Bowen's feelings.

Q. Did not you make an allegation against Mr. Beecher? A. No, sir; after Mr. Johnson went out he made an allegation.

Q. Did you not make an allegation? A. I did toward the end of the interview.

Q. You made a very distinct allegation to Mr. Bowen, did you not, against Mr. Beecher, of the offence that he had committed against you? A. Yes.

Q. It was on that occasion, was it not, that the letter was agreed upon between you and Mr. Bowen demanding that Mr. Beecher should quit Plymouth pulpit? A. I remember a letter.

Q. Was it on that occasion that that letter was agreed upon between you and Mr. Bowen? A. Yes, it was.

Q. And was that agreement the result of his statement of the offences against Mr. Beecher which he and you knew of? A. On the part of Mr. Bowen, yes.

Q. On your part? A. I made one statement and he made many.

Q. Will you state what offence you stated against Mr. Beecher to Mr. Bowen on that occasion? A. Mr. Johnson having introduced the subject to Mr. Bowen said to me, "Mr. Tilton, you do not say as much of Plymouth Church as a Brooklyn paper should; you do not go there; why do you not go?"

Q. I asked what offence you stated against Mr. Beecher to Mr. Bowen? A. I must answer your question in my own way. I came to tell you the truth and not fragments of the truth. Mr. Bowen wanted me to speak more in the paper of Plymouth Church. Mr. Johnson said, "Perhaps Mr. Tilton has a reason for not going to Plymouth Church." And thereupon Mr. Bowen was curious to know the reason. I, in a solitary phrase, said that there was a personal domestic reason why I could not go there consistently with my self-respect—that Mr. Beecher had been unhandsome in his approaches to my wife. That is the sum and substance of all I have ever said on this subject to the very few people to whom I have spoken of it.

Q. It was on that occasion that you agreed upon the letter which demanded Mr. Beecher to leave the pulpit? A. Yes, sir, that was the precise occasion.

Q. You think that was on the 26th December? A. I have no recollection of dates; the only identification I have in my mind is that it was near Christmas.

Q. When were you dismissed from the *Union?* A. The last night of the year, I think.

Q. The 31st, was it? A. Yes, sir.

Q. When did you first learn that Mr. or Mrs. Beecher had in any way communicated facts to Mr. Bowen which inflamed him in the matter of your dismissal? A. I learned that from Mr. Beecher himself on the day after his apology was written; it was the 2d, possibly the 3d, of January; it was in Mr. Moulton's front room; Mr. Beecher came in, it was an unexpected meeting; he burst out into an expression of great sorrow to me, and said he hoped the communication he had sent to me by Mr. Moulton was satisfactory to me; he then and there told Mr. Moulton he had done wrong, not so much as some others had (referring to his wife, who had made statements to Mr. Bowen that ought to be unmade), and he there volunteered to write a letter to Mr. Bowen concerning the facts which he had misstated.

Q. Do you say that that was the first time that you knew that Mr. Beecher or Mrs. Beecher had given Mr. Bowen any information or had had any conversation with him on the subject? A. Yes, sir; I did not know that Mr. Beecher had given Mr. Bowen any such information; Mrs. Tilton had intimated to me that there was something.

Q. When did Mrs. Tilton intimate that to you? A. In December she told me of visits which Mrs. Beecher had made to her, and of testimony which they wanted to get.

Q. What time in December? A. I do not know.

Q. Was it before or after the publication of your valedictory in the *Independent?* A. I do not remember; Mrs. Tilton spoke to me a number of times of the enmity which Mrs. Beecher had, for some strange reason, connected with Mrs. Morse (Mrs. Tilton's mother); there was a conspiracy between Mrs. Morse and Mrs. Beecher before September; the truth is that Mrs. Tilton's confession was made also to her mother, and the mother naturally wanted to protect the daughter, and she made a kind of alliance with Mr. Beecher, and Mrs. Beecher took part in it; there was a desire on their part to protect Elizabeth.

Q. You say that Mrs. Tilton referred some time in December to the fact that Mrs. Beecher had interfered in your matters? A. Not that she had interfered in my matters, but that Mrs. Morse and Mrs. Beecher were colleaguing together with reference to me.

Q. Are you able to fix that date? A. It was many times.

Q. Was any of it before the 22d of December, think you? A. Yes, I think early in the summer, but do not know.

Q. Any time in December was Mrs. Tilton separated from you with her family? A. Not that I remember; Mrs. Tilton went a few weeks to make a visit at her mother's.

Q. Do you remember the occasion of sending for your wife to come to the *Union* office while she was separated from you? A. Yes, she was at her mother's.

Q. Do you remember telling her that you were about to be dismissed from the *Union*, and that she must return to you and live with you to prevent it? Did you tell her anything of that? A. Not a shadow; it would have made no difference one way or the other.

Q. Did you on that day send a letter by a servant by the name of Ellen, directing the person in whose house she was to return your children to your house in her absence? A. I do not recollect it; Mrs. Morse had the children, and I told Ellen Dennis to bring them home; I do not remember the time.

Q. Did you send a note by her? A. I sent quite a peremptory message.

Q. And the children came? A. Yes, or were brought; I think there was only one.

Q. Did your wife come late in the evening after that? A. I do not remember; I think I went personally for Elizabeth, and told her she was doing wrong in staying away; I have no distinct recollection of so many details.

Q. How long after that return was it that this statement, which you say she made, and which was placed in Mr. Moulton's hands, was written? A. I do not know; I have no means of knowing; the date of her giving the letter for the interview with Mr. Beecher I think was on the 29th of December.

Q. The object of giving the letters was to bring about an interview between you and Mr. Beecher that there might be a reconciliation, and that Mr. Beecher might aid in saving you from dismissal from the *Independent?* A. No. Mrs. Tilton thought that my retirement from the papers was due in some way to Mr. and Mrs. Beecher, and she thought, as I was very indignant against Mr. Bowen, unless there was some reconciliation between Mr. Beecher and myself, her secret would be exposed, and she begged me to have an interview with him, and wrote a note to that effect.

Q. Have you that note? A. I decline to answer.

Q. Will you produce it? I decline to answer. I decline to answer because you know the fact already.

Q. You say that note was written on the 29th day of December? A. I think there is a record on the subject here (in the statement which he had read) somewhere.

By Mr. Hill—Can you refer to a note written by you to Ellen? Do you think that had a date attached which would fix the time? A. I do not know; I remember Ellen to have had something to do with the return of one of the children; I think that note was written to Mrs. Morse.

Q. Was not the subject of the interview between you and Mr. Beecher for the purpose of inducing him to aid in preventing your dismissal? A. No more than it had with this investigation; the sole purpose of that interview was this; Mrs. Tilton felt that Mr. Beecher and I were in danger of coming into collision; for her sake, at her request, I had this interview; it was solely in reference to Mrs. Tilton.

Q. It was two days before your final dismissal, and pending the question whether you should be retained or not? A. My dismissal from the *Union* came after that interview; it took effect the last night of the year; my interview with Mr. Beecher had nothing to do with that.

By General Tracy—It was two days before it, and pending the question of whether you would be dismissed or retained was it not? A. No, sir; these documents themselves, I think, show that my interview with Mr. Beecher was after my dismissal from the *Union*.

Q. That interview was on the 29th, and your dismissal was on the 31st. Then that interview was before your dismissal, and pending the question whether you would be retained or dismissed, was it not? A. The question of my dismissal was decided in the flash of an eye; I never knew that there was any such question; I, two or three days previous to the interview with Mr. Beecher, had filled up contracts, one to be editor of the *Union* for five years, and the other to be chief contributor of the *Independent*, and there was no pending question.

Q. Was not your contract to be editor of the *Union* for five years, and to be chief contributor of the *Independent*, signed previous to the publication of your valedictory in the *Independent?* A. They were signed very near that time.

Q. Was not the interview, at which Mr. Johnson was present, at Mr. Bowen's house on the 26th of December? A. Yes, sir.

Q. The interview with Mr. Beecher was on the 29th? A. I cannot say precisely.

Q. Your final dismissal from the *Union* was on the 31st? A. I cannot say yes, unless the letters will show.

Q. Will you tell us why it was that having been possessed of this information for six months without any desire to communicate it to Mr. Beecher, you were seized with a desire to communicate that information to him on or about the 29th of December? A. Yes, sir; because Mrs. Tilton feared that Mr. Beecher, Mr. Bowen and I were in danger of such a clash and collision that the family secret would be exposed, and felt that there was a necessity for a reconciliation, and she begged and prayed me to be reconciled with Mr. Beecher; and on her account and for her sake I said I would have an interview with him.

Q. Will you explain why the difficulty you had with Mr. Bowen in regard to the *Independent* and the *Union* would involve the necessity of your exposing the family secret which you obtained from Mrs. Tilton six months before? A. It was not through fear of my exposing it; Mrs. Morse and Mrs. Beecher were sometimes in collision, and Mrs. Tilton always made me believe that Mr. Beecher knew this secret, until in December, when she told me, I took it for granted, all summer long, that she had told him what she had told me, and what she had told her mother, and I supposed that Mrs. Beecher was co-operating with Mrs. Morse.

Q. Did you complain of Mr. Beecher for not aiding you to remain in the *Independent?* A. No, sir; I would have scorned it.

Q. You have read Mr. Wilkeson's statement? A. I have not.

Q. You know Samuel Wilkeson? A. Yes.

Q. Did you say to him about that time that Mr. Beecher had not befriended you in that matter? A. I did not, and Mr. Wilkeson will not dare to say that under oath.

Q. You say you never complained of Mr. Beecher for not helping you? A. No, not for not helping me, but for being unjust to me and saying that I ought to be turned out; I understood that he said to Dr. Spear that they were going to have Mr. Tilton out of the *Independent;* Mr. Charles Briggs told me that; he said, "I know something about this thing; I heard some such thing."

Q. You say that Mr. Beecher apologized and that you accepted the apology? A. I read the account of that in the document.

Q. Did you, or did you not, as a matter of fact, accept the apology which Mr. Beecher made, and forgive the offence? A. I accepted the apology and forgave the offence with as much largeness as I thought it was possible for a Christian man to assume.

Q. Friendly relations continued after that between you and Mr. Beecher? A. Well, not friendly; you can understand what such relations would be; they were not hostile; they were relations which Mr. Moulton forced with an iron hand; he compelled them.

Q. Did you or not, after or about the time of the tripartite agreement, express friendly sentiments in regard to him? A. I have taken pains to make it appear in all quarters that Mr. Beecher and I were not in hostility, and I have suppressed my self-respect many times in doing it.

Q. Did you ever state this offence of Mr. Beecher as committed against you to Mr. Storrs? A. I never did.

Q. Was it ever stated in your presence to him? A. No, sir; he read a statement that Mrs. Tilton made, and that I helped her to make.

Q. Did you go with her when she made that statement to Dr. Storrs? A. I did not.

Q. Did you ever state or read to Dr. Storrs any statement of the offences which you charged against Mr. Beecher? A. No; I showed Dr. Storrs a letter which Elizabeth and myself wrote and which I still preserve; Mr. Carpenter and I went to Dr. Storrs as counsellor; my intention was to have Elizabeth go, but she preferred to write a few lines.

Q. You took what she wrote and what you helped her to write to Dr. Storrs, and showed it to him as the statement of the offence which you charged Mr. Beecher with? No; I did not charge Mr. Beecher with any offence at all.

Q. I am trying to get at what offence you stated against Mr. Beecher? A. Elizabeth stated that.

Q. And you have it and gave it to Dr. Storrs to read? A. Yes, sir.

Q. How was the offence stated? A. It began in this way, that on a certain day, in the summer of 1870, she had informed her husband that Mr. Beecher had asked her to be a wife to him together with all that this implies; she was very solicitous to make it appear that she did not accept his proposition, and, happily, in reading it, those who saw it naturally inferred that she did not accept his proposition; it was a perfectly correct statement.

Q. You and she wrote it? A. She wrote it with my assistance.

Q. You took that statement to Dr. Storrs, and it was read by him in your presence? A. Yes, sir.

Q. It was read also to Mr. Beecher? A. I read it to him myself. Mr. Beecher objected to it, and I made no further use of it.

Q. You prepared a document, did you not, giving a history of this case? A. No, not in this case, but of my relations to Mr. Bowen.

Q. It was stated in that document? A. Yes, this letter of Elizabeth's was quoted in it.

Q. And it was read to Dr. Storrs? A. Yes.

Q. Did you also quote the letter of apology in it? A. Just as I did in the letter to Dr. Bacon.

Q. You quoted the apology as an apology for the offence? You stated and cited it as proof that he had apologized for that offence? A. Yes, I put that in, not wishing to make the offence more than that; I was solicitous not to have the worst of the case shown.

Q. You went voluntarily to Dr. Storrs, did you not? A. I did, in great distress, wanting counsel.

Q. And so as to get correct counsel you misstated the case? A. Yes, as you did in your statement in the *Union;* it was a statement necessary to be made; after Mrs. Woodhull's statement I was out of town, and the thing had filled the country, and Mr. Beecher had taken no notice of it; it was seven or eight days old, and I went to Dr. Storrs for counsel; he asked me about the story; I said, "Do not ask me for that;" he said, "Give me some facts by which I can judge; give me that which can be proved;" so I gave an account of my affairs very largely, about Mrs. Woodhull, and so on; the origin of that document was a seeking for something that would put before the public a plausible answer to the Woodhull tale, and I conceived that by a chain of facts we might, perhaps, explain it away. I read it to Mr. Beecher and he burst into a long sigh, and I saw that he would not or could not stand upon it; and Elizabeth burned it or tore it in pieces.

Q. You showed it to others did you not? A. To a few friends.

Q. To whom besides Dr. Storrs? A. I think that I showed it to George Bell; I showed it to one or two.

Q. Did you show it to Mr. Beecher? A. No; I think not; I think I showed him the document in the tripartite confession.

Q. You have known Mr. Beecher many years? A. Yes, sir.

Q. Is he your personal friend? A. I used to regard him as such.

Q. You remember showing him something on this subject? A. I remember showing him the letter in proof which explained my going out of the *Independent* and the *Union;* whether I showed him the document I cannot say; I showed it to a number of people, hoping that it would do good; but it did not, so it disappeared.

Q. You say Mr. Beecher refused to stand upon it? A. No; Mr. Moulton asked Mr. Beecher to come and hear me read it; I was in hopes Mr. Beecher might not feel bad at such a document, but he felt slain by it.

Q. And, just as on other occasions, he refused to stand by a statement of the offence? A, No; he drew a long sigh.

Q. You understood him as refusing? A. No; I did not understand that.

Q. Why did you abandon the document? A. Because there was no success in it.

Q. Why was there no success in it? Was it not because he did not accept it? A. Because he did not accept or reject it; he wanted that no statement should be made, and so the thing was buried.

Q. Did you ever state the offence to Dr. Buddington? A. I never saw him until within two weeks; I heard that he went to see Dr. Bacon, and I went to see him.

Q. Have you not frequently asserted the purity of your wife? A. No; I have always had a strange technical use of words; I have always used words that conveyed that impression; I have taken pains to say that she was a devoted Christian woman; that necessarily carried the other; it was like the statement that I carried to Dr. Storrs; I do not think he caught the idea of the statement; as he took it I do not think that it covered the whole; I have said that Elizabeth was a tender, delicate, kindly, Christian woman, which I think she is.

Q. Have not you stated that she was pure? A. No.

Q. Have you not stated that she was as pure as an angel? A. No; Mr. Halliday says I said that; he asked me in Mrs. Bradshaw's presence whether or not I had not said that my wife was as pure as gold, "No," I said, "Mr. Halliday, because the conversation to which you allude was this: I said 'Go and ask Mr. Beecher himself and he will say that she is as pure as gold;'" it is an expression which he used; I have sought to give Elizabeth a good character; I have always wanted to do so; I think she deserves a good character; I think she is better than most of us—better than I am; I do not believe in point of actual moral goodness, barring some drawbacks, that there is in this company so white a soul as Elizabeth Tilton.

Q. Did you not state that, in substance, to one or more of the gentlemen with whom you were lunching? A. In substance, yes; and I state it now, but I did not use the phrase that she had never violated her chastity.

Q. Did you not say that she was pure? A. No.

Q. Did you not use expressions which you intended to be understood as meaning the purity of the woman? A. I did, exactly. There are many ways in which you can produce such impressions, and I have written this document to produce the same impression.

By Mr. White.—Mr. Wilkeson in his testimony testified in substance that he had a long conversation with you in regard to Mr. Beecher's offences, and that in answer to his inquiry as to what these offences consisted of you said that he had made improper addresses to your wife, and that he then said to you that he had heard from another person, whom he named to you, that it referred to more than the implication that it referred to adultery, which you denied. Is that true? A. No; the conversation was about Mr. Bowen; he came to me with a finished and rose-colored eulogy on Mr. Beecher for me to sign. It was desired that Mr. Bowen's charges should be withdrawn, and it was said to me, "Suppose Mr. Bowen is willing to blot this out, you have no interest to keep it afloat?" "No," I said. "Well if Mr. Bowen will withdraw those charges will you agree to consider them blotted out?" I said "Certainly." I was exceedingly glad to have it done, for I thought that every charge against Henry Ward Beecher endangered my wife; I said that I would sign it twenty times over, or conveyed such an idea: but when the paper was brought to me to sign, it was a compliment to Mr. Beecher, rose-colored, in which I was to look up to him with filial respect. I said, "I won't sign that to the end of the world," and I cut out a few lines and would not use them.

Q. It is not with reference to the circumstances of signing the paper that I am speaking, but in reference to the question which he put to you as to the offence. A. He did not put to me any such question; Mr. Wilkeson is too much of a gentleman to ask a man whether his wife had committed adultery.

Q. Mr. Wilkeson says you took the paper away to make such emendations as you chose before signing it, and that after, perhaps the second night, on its return, you said to him that you never would sign anything that required you to let up on Henry Ward Beecher? A. I said that my self-respect would not permit me to do it; I told him also, or I told other persons, that I would keep to the line of that necessary reconciliation which Mr. Moulton had planned, but that, as for going to Mr. Beecher's church, or signing such a letter, I would wait to the end of the world first, and I did not think Mr. Bowen would sign it.

By Mr. Cleveland.—You expressed confidence in the paper you signed in Mr. Beecher, did you not? A. No; I expressed friendliness toward him.

By Mr. White—Mr. Wilkeson says in substance, that in speaking of your dismissal from the *Union* you spoke of Mr. Beecher as not assisting you, and said that you would follow him to his grave? A. If Mr. Wilkeson communicates the impression that I ever wanted money from Henry Ward Beecher, it is false; Mr. Beecher has communicated, through Mr. Moulton, requests that I be assisted by him, but I would not take a penny of Mr. Beecher's money if I suffered from hunger or thirst; and I said that if directly or indirectly he (Mr. Moulton) communicated to me any of his (Mr. Beecher's) money it would break our friendship; Wilkeson was very friendly to me; he is a sweet, lovable man, and it is an unaccountable thing that his memory is so bad: he is getting old; I have a letter in which he wants that apology delivered up.

Q. I will read to you from Mr. Wilkeson's testimony: "His next complaint was that Mr. Beecher did not help him in his troubles." A. That's a lie: my complaint was that Mr. Beecher had been unjust to me, not that he had not helped me; I would not have taken his help.

By General Tracy—I ask you whether your relations and feelings toward Mr. Beecher, since January 1, 1871, have not been friendly? A. Yes, sir; my relations and feelings toward him since January, 1871, when he made the apology, down to the time when the church began to put out its right hand and take me by the throat, were friendly.

Q. They are not now friendly, but they were friendly up to the beginning of the action of the church in this matter? A. Yes, sir; that is to say, they were friendly in the sense that we were not in collision with each other.

Q. Were they not those of friendship? A. No, they were not.

Q. What did you mean by saying, after that apology was made, that you desired to see Mr. Beecher protected, rather than harmed, for his offence against you? A. So I did.

Q. Do you mean to say that that sentence expressed your real feelings toward a man who, you believed had seduced your wife? A. Yes: I was under obligation; I had taken his apology and I had given my word that I would not have him exposed.

Q. Is it your sentiment that there is an offence for which one man can apologize to another? A. I know there is a code of honor among gentlemen that a man cannot condone such an offence; but I cannot see what offence a man cannot forgive, where an apology is made by the person committing it to the person against whom it is committed; if a man believes in the Christian religion he ought to; I sometimes forgave and sometimes I did not; I do know the line of difference.

Q. Is that your handwriting (showing a slip of paper on which was written "H. W. B.—Grace, mercy, and peace. Sunday morning. T. T." A. I remember that; one morning Mr. Beecher met me in the street and told me how much pleasure it gave him; I have sent kindlier things than that to him.

Q. Did you feel as you spoke? A. I did; Mr. Moulton said two or three times, "Mr. Beecher is in great depression; can't you do something to cheer him?" One morning I walked to the church with him; in many circumstances I manifested feelings of kindness toward him; it would be a lie for me to say that I had a warm friendship for Mr. Beecher, and that I felt as kindly to him as if the offence had not been committed; if I had been a man morally great, I would have blotted it out and trodden it under foot; I was competent to forgive in a large degree; I forgave him in my best moods, but at other times I did not; I am not a very large man.

Q. You have quoted extensively the letters of your wife written prior to the time you say that she said this intercourse began—have you not her letters written to you also since that time and during that time? A. No; because at that time I came home to be editor of the *Union*, and have not lectured since.

Q. I ask you whether you have not letters from her written during the time that you say this was going on and since then? A. No, not written since; because I have not had occasion since to have letters; I have been at home.

Q. I understand you to say that these relations went on during your absence; have you any letters that were written by your wife at that time? A. No.

Q. Have you not letters from her that were written to you between 1868 and 1870? A. I think I have.

Q. Will you be kind enough to produce them to the committee? A. I do not know whether I will or not.

Q. Have you any letters from Mrs. Tilton complaining to you? A. Yes, I have.

Q. Have you not many letters from her stating forth her complaints and her grievances? A. No: she very rarely wrote such letters; she used occasionally to write me letters begging intercession in regard to her mother, and complaining of my views in theology.

Q. Did you never receive letters from her complaining in other respects? A. In what respects?

Q. Well, in regard to people who were in the habit of frequenting your house at your solicitation? A. I have had letters from her mother, complaining of Susan Anthony and Mrs. Stanton; Mrs. Tilton thought Mr. Johnson and others were leading me astray; she is very orthodox; and she wrote me letters expressing strong and earnest hopes that I would be intensely orthodox.

Q. Did she complain of any female society on that ground, or in any way? A. No.

Q. Did she never complain of the presence of any ladies at your house? A. I do not think of any.

Q. Not of Mrs. Stanton nor Susan Anthony? A. She said she would consider it an insult if they came to the house; I do not remember of any others.

Q. Mrs. Woodhull came a great deal, didn't she? A. She was three times in my house, once to meet Mr. Beecher, and on two other occasions.

Q. Only three times? A. Three only.

Q. You say she came to see Mr. Beecher? A. She did, on Sunday afternoon, at my house.

Q. Do you know when that was? A. I think Mr. Moulton made that interview; it must have been in 1871 or 1872, because my acquaintance with Mrs. Woodhull began in May, 1871; my impression is that it was warm weather; Mrs. Woodhull and her husband came; she always came with her husband.

Q. Did your wife complain of her being at your house? A. Yes, my wife came home, and Mrs. Woodhull and Mr. Moulton were there sitting in the front parlor.

Q. What happened? A. Oh, nothing, except that Elizabeth expressed her indignation against the woman; I told Elizabeth that she was too dangerous a woman, and that too much of the welfare of our family depended on her; Elizabeth was wiser than I was.

Q. Did you excuse your acquaintance with Mrs. Woodhull to your wife by exciting her fears? A. I did not; I explained that acquaintance; I told her the way to get along with Mrs. Woodhull and prevent this coming out was to keep friendly with her. It was a fatal policy, but then it seemed the only thing that we could do.

Q. Was the time that Mrs. Tilton expressed her indignation at Mrs. Woodhull's being at your house the first time that she had seen Mrs. Woodhull, to your knowledge? A. My impression is that she saw her in *The Golden Age* office once. It may have been before or after. I think Mrs. Woodhull came in to see me while Mrs. Tilton was there.

Q. With that exception, was the time when Mrs. Tilton expressed her indignation at Mrs. Woodhull's being at your house the first time that she had seen her? A. I do not know. Oh, no; Mrs. Woodhull and Colonel Blood had taken tea at our house.

Q. Before Mrs. Tilton came in and found her there? A. Yes.

Q. At whose invitation did they take tea there? A. At mine.

Q. Was it the first time Mrs. Tilton saw Mrs. Woodhull? A. I do not know.

Q. Mrs. Tilton always expressed her indignation at her being there, did she not? A. Yes, she had a violent feeling against her; she had a woman's instinct that Mrs. Woodhull was not safe; the mistake was not being friendly with Blood instead of Mrs. Woodhull; that was the blunder; I was at fault for that; nobody else.

Q. Did Mrs. Tilton continue her expressions of indignation at your acquaintance with Mrs. Woodhull? A. Yes; Mrs. Tilton always felt that the policy was a mistaken one of undertaking to do anything with Mrs. Woodhull; Mrs. Tilton objected violently to my writing the sketch of Mrs. Woodhull; I read part of it to her; Mrs. Woodhull's husband wrote a biography about her, and wanted me to rewrite it, because my style was more vivid; Mrs. Tilton said she thought I would rue the day; she was far wiser than I was.

Q. Then you never succeeded in convincing your wife that it was necessary to placate Mrs. Woodhull? A. No, she had the opposite opinion; Mrs. Tilton had a strong repugnance to Mrs. Woodhull, and two or three other public women—Mrs. Stanton and Susan Anthony; she would not permit them to come into the house, and some of her letters were very violent against them; she was frequently with them for a long time and took part with them in woman's meetings, and then she took a violent antagonism to them after her troubles came on.

Q. Did Mrs. Woodhull know of the antipathy of Mrs. Tilton to her? A. Yes; you could see it in the woman's eyes; they flashed fire: the moment they saw each other their eyes flashed fire.

Q. It was perfectly evident, then, when the women came together, that they were thoroughly antagonistic? A. Oh, yes; thoroughly.

Q. Bitterly so? A. I cannot say that Elizabeth had bitterness; she had a certain strong moral and religious repugnance.

Q. Did she not discard Mrs. Woodhull's sentiments and denounce them? A. Mrs. Woodhull had not then expressed her sentiments.

Q. Not in 1872? This was not in 1872; when I wrote the sketch of Mrs. Woodhull she had never said anything on the subject of free love; her ideas were spiritualism and woman's suffrage.

THE SECOND DAY'S CROSS-EXAMINATION OCCURRED ON JULY 22, AND WAS AS FOLLOWS:

By General Tracy—Q. Mr. Tilton, on page 51 of your manuscript, in subdivision X, you say, "In December, 1870, differences arose between Theodore Tilton and Henry C. Bowen, which were augmented by the Rev. Henry Ward Beecher and Mrs. Beecher, in consequence whereof, and at the wish of Mrs. Elizabeth R. Tilton, expressed in writing, in a paper put into the hands of," etc., you do not state then in whose handwriting it was. A. It was Mrs. Tilton's.

Q. Was it not in your handwriting? A. It was not, sir.

Q. Did you not write that statement and get her to sign it? A. No, sir.

Q. Did you dictate it in any manner? A. I did not.

Q. Did you write the original? A. I did not.

Q. Was she well or sick at the time? A. She was neither the one nor the other; she was ailing.

Q. Had not she suffered a miscarriage just previous? A. Well, I do not know how long before; I cannot tell the date; whether it came before or after I do not know; she was ill, I know.

Q. Was she not in bed? A. Most of the time.

Q. Was she not in bed at the time of the writing of this paper? A. I do not remember.

Q. Do not you remember whether she wrote it in bed or not? A. I do not.

Q. Do not you know that she had suffered a miscarriage a few days before? A. No; I knew she had suffered a miscarriage before.

Q. Before the 24th day of December? A. I do not remember the date.

Q. Do not you know that she was very sick, and sick unto death? A. No, I do not know that she was sick unto death; she was ill, but not dangerously so.

Q. Who suggested to her the writing of that letter? A. She did it herself.

Q. Was she conversant with the particular state of your difficulty with Mr. Bowen from time to time, and from day to day? A. It was not from day to day; I always informed her what troubles I had.

Q. You say this letter was written in consequence of the interference of Mr. and Mrs. Beecher? A. No, not precisely; I say that the letter was written through her desire that he and I should be reconciled.

Q. When you say that "In December, 1870, differences arose between Theodore Tilton and Henry C. Bowen, which were augmented by the Rev. Henry Ward Beecher and Mrs. Beecher; in consequence whereof, and at the wish of Mrs. Elizabeth R. Tilton, expressed in writing in a paper put into the hands of Mr. Francis D. Moulton," why do you say that it was in consequence of that difficulty being augmented by Mr. and Mrs. Beecher that this letter was written or this writing was made? A. Mrs. Tilton's confession to me was in the middle of the summer; she informed me shortly afterward that she had taken occasion to let Mr. Beecher know that she had made this confession, but she did not do that; I supposed that he knew of her confession, but he did not know of it. I met Mr. Beecher in the street, and he was about to speak to me; I did not speak to him; that excited my suspicion of the fact he could not have known of Mrs. Tilton's confession; so I said to her, "Elizabeth, did not you tell me that Mr. Beecher knew what you had told me; to my mind he don't know it;" she then informed me that she could not bear to let him know that she had confessed; then, I think, her sickness came, though my recollection of dates, as I have said, is very poor; toward the close of the year, or very near the close of the year, Mr. Bowen wanted to make a change in the editorship of the *Inde-*

pendent; Mrs. Tilton was at Mrs. Morse's; she had gone to stay there a little while; Mr. Bowen sent me a notice, or letter, saying that he wanted the termination of my contract as editor of the *Independent* to take place six months subsequently; I said to myself instantly,."If Mr. Bowen wishes me to terminate the *Independent,* I must give him notice to terminate the *Union;* but before that I will send to Elizabeth to come to the *Union* office and state this proposition to her;" she came down and I informed her; I said, "Now, I cannot afford to edit only one of these papers; if I am to give up one I cannot keep the other;" when Mr. Bowen proposed that I should give up one and retain the other I instantly said, "As he proposes that I shall give up the *Independent* I will give up the *Union,* and that will leave me free to lecture." After that, about the 23d or 24th of December, Mr. Bowen came to have a consultation with me and make new contracts, by which he should be editor of the *Independent* and I a special contributor of the *Independent* and for five years editor of the *Union;* that contract was signed during the last week or ten days of 1870, and I published a valedictory in the *Independent,* speaking well of Mr. Bowen, and he spoke well of me. Somewhere about the 23d or 24th or 25th—between the publishing of that valedictory and the making of those two or three contracts—Mr. Johnson came to my house and said, "Mr. Bowen has heard something prejudicial concerning you; I think you had better go and see him." It was Saturday night. I went plump to his house and saw him, and said, "Mr. Bowen, Mr. Johnson says that you know something prejudicial to me." Mr. Bowen said, "I have my new editors in consultation and it is Saturday night; come on Monday." Monday was a holiday. Either Sunday was the actual Christmas or else Monday was, I do not remember which. I went on Monday with Mr. Johnson. I think this was on the 25th. We had a little talk. It was mentioned that some story had come to Mr. Bowen. I said, "Bring the person who told it into my presence and we will have the matter settled." I then went on talking about the new contract which I was to enter upon two or three days hence, as the editor of the *Union* for five years; he said that I ought to make more of Plymouth Church, and go to Plymouth Church. Mr. Johnson said : "Perhaps this young man has a reason for not going to Plymouth Church:" I gave him in a line to understand that I had lost my respect for Mr. Beecher, and could not, as a man maintaining my pride and self-respect, go there; at that, Mr. Bowen stated all the particulars that I chronicled of Mr. Beecher in that letter, only more vividly; at that Mr. Bowen made a challenge that Mr. Beecher would retire from the ministry, and said he would bear it and fortify it with facts, and I signed it ; nd he carried it; in a few hours Mr. Moulton came in and I told him what I had done, and he said, "You are a damned fool, Mr. Bowen should have signed the letter as well as yourself;" the next morning I went to the *Union* office, and perhaps the morning after, I wrote a little note to Mr. Bowen, the substance of which was that I was going to have a personal interview with Mr. Beecher; that I thought was the manly thing; Mr. Bowen, the next morning, after he had instituted this demand for the retirement of Mr. Beecher, and after saying that he would fortify it with facts, came to the *Union* office and said. "Sir, if you ever reveal to Mr. Beecher the things that I told you and Mr. Johnson, it will cashier you;" it went through my blood ; I said, "I will, at my discretion, utterly uninfluenced by you," and he was in a rage; then, after two or three days, and while I was writing my first article for the *Independent* under this new arrangement, as contributor instead of editor, there came (I guess it was the last night of the year) notices breaking my two contracts; those two contracts had been made within a week, and were not to take effect until the first of the year and they were broken the last night of the year, or the night before; I went around to Frank with them, and showed them to him immediately; the next day I wrote my letter to Mr. Bowen; events came crowding together pell-mell, so thick and fast that I do not know how to disentangle them.

Q. Why do you say that it was in consequence of the difficulty being augmented by Mr. and Mrs. Beecher ? A. Elizabeth saw that Mr. Bowen and I were in collision; she was afraid that the collision would extend to Mr. Beecher and me, and she wished me, if possible, to make peace with him; that peace could be brought about only by his knowing what I knew of his relations with Mrs. Tilton ; therefore she wrote a womanly, kindly letter to him; I do not remember the phraseology ; I remember only one phrase ; it was peculiarly hers; she said she loved her husband with her maiden flame; Mr. Moulton will probably recall the whole phraseology.

Q. What was the substance of the letter? A. The substance of the letter I do not recall; the letter was returned to her; whether she has it or not I do not know; the object of the letter was to make peace ; she felt that if Mr. Beecher and I could be reconciled, she herself and I would be more reconciled ; there was a sort of mountain of clouds overcoming us.

Q. Who had reported to her the fact that your difficulty was being augmented by Mr. and Mrs. Beecher ? A. I do not know ; she reported it to me; it was through her that I learned that Mrs. Beecher was interfering with my affairs ; it was through Mrs. Tilton that I learned of Mrs. Beecher's antagonism to me; I do not think Mr. Beecher was so largely involved in it as his wife was.

Q. Had you known of Mrs. Beecher's interference with your affairs prior to that? A. I cannot say with my affairs—not with my business affairs ; with my domestic affairs ; no, as I recollect, Elizabeth went sometimes to the Health Lift, and Mrs. Beecher came there and saw her one day.

Q. What date was that ? A. I do not know ; Mrs. Beecher, through Mrs. Morse, got the idea that I was Mr. Beecher's enemy ; therefore Mrs. Beecher was very violently my enemy ; Mrs. Beecher being my enemy, and feeling that I was bent on a battle against her husband, sought to make an alliance with Elizabeth, and, as I understand, wanted Elizabeth to go away from me and part company, and she would not do it—the trouble having hinged on the fact that Elizabeth had made me and Mrs. Morse a confession, but had not told Mr. Beecher that she had done so ; I said there was only one way out of the difficulty, and that was that Mr. Beecher must know it.

Q. Did you say that to Elizabeth ? A. I do not know about that.

Q. Had you said it previous to that ? A. I do not know ; I felt greatly chagrined at her not having told him, as she said she had ; I could not understand why Mr. Beecher should speak to me in the street, and I instantly said, " He does not know it.".

Q. You do not know when it was that he spoke to you in the street ? A. My impression is that it could not have been much later than his first coming back from the country.

Q. When was that ? A. All I can remember of that is the picture of the man with a kind of sunburn on him ; if you will ask Elizabeth all of these things she can tell you ; there was a large mass of complications that were afterward explained.

Q. Was not Mrs. Tilton sick on the evening of the 30th December and in bed ? A. I do not know whether she was or not.

Q. Do not you know that one of your allegations or complaints was that he obtained that retraction from her when she was sick in bed ? A. I know that she was lying in bed.

Q. Did you not charge him with imposing upon her because she was sick ? A. Yes.

Q. And was she not sick ? A. I remember the picture of her lying ailing on the bed.

Q. What physician attended her ? A. I think Dr. Parker ; it may have been Dr. Stiles ; he was subsequently our physician.

Q. This first letter which you quote from Mrs. Tilton, on page 35, in which she says :—" Love is praiseworthy, but to abuse the gift is sin ; here I am strong ; no temptations or fascinations," etc., what did you understand by that ? A. I understood this—that she was in the receipt of visits from him, and that she had once or twice felt that perhaps he was exercising an undue influence upon her ; I know that once I was afraid she did not give me a correct account of his visits ; there were a great many visits mentioned in her correspondence.

Q. Have you the letters here ? A. No.

Q. I thought that you were to bring them ? A. All the originals from which I have quoted I will carry before Judge Reynolds, or any judge, in the presence of General Tracy ; I have great confidence in you, gentlemen, but I do not propose to produce the originals here ; if you will release one of your number to go with me before any magistrate, I will produce them ; Mr. Moulton will, of course, be asked to produce his for examination, line for line ; I do not suppose you would snatch them away or keep them, but at the same time I propose that if you would see the originals, General Tracy should go with me.

Q. Do you refuse to produce the originals before this committee ? A. I do not refuse to produce them to the committee in the presence of some outside parties.

Q. Do you refuse to produce them to the committee alone ? A. Yes, unless I can have some friend here with me.

Q. Why did you not take that position yesterday ? A. Because yesterday we had only a chat.

Q. Yes, but did you not promise to produce them ? A. Yes, and I do now.

Q. But you decline except in the presence of an officer ? A. I decline unless I can be perfectly certain that they will be returned to me ; I don't want you to consider that as a disparagement ; it is only a necessary element in this discussion ; you shall see the originals, but I will only show them under safeguards.

Q. Why do you make that qualification ? A. For this reason ; you are six gentlemen, determined if possible, not to find the facts, but to vindicate Mr. Beecher, and I am alone. There are eight of you and I am a single man, and if I should hand over to you now, Mr. Beecher's apology perhaps you would not return it to me. Though I do not mean to make that implication, I do not mean to give you the chance. That is frank.

Mr. Hill.—Let me say kindly, speaking on behalf of both the counsel—the committee may speak for themselves—that the suggestion of such a theory is altogether groundless.

General Tracy.—It is not only groundless, but outrageous.

Mr. Hill.—I think you are unjust.

Mr. Tilton.—I have been informed that this is a matter of life and death.

Mr. Claflin.—This committee could not afford to take that position. It would not do to take those letters from you.

Mr. Tilton—I am perfectly willing to bring several friends of mine and make an examination of these letters ; you shall see them ; but under proper safeguards—that is all ; if Mr. Tracy was in my position he would take the same ground.

General Tracy.—No he would not, I beg your pardon.

Q. At the beginning of the acquaintance of Mr. Beecher with your family—not with you or your wife, but with your family—did not you invite him frequently to your house? A. Yes, sir; and I was always very proud when he came.

Q. Did you not say to him frequently that you desired him to visit your house frequently? A. I did, and always scolded him because he did not come oftener; during the first part of our life we were in Oxford street, so far away that he very rarely came; the frequency of his visits took place after I purchased the house in Livingston street.

Q. When was that? A. I have forgotten the year; I should say it was seven, or eight, or nine, or ten years ago.

Q. Did you not say that there was a little woman at your house, that loved him dearly? A. I did, many a time; I always wanted him to come oftener.

Q. You frequently spoke to him of the high esteem and affection that your wife bore to him, did you not? A. I did; he knew it and I knew it.

Q. You always knew it? A. I cannot say that I always did, because at first, during the early years of my married life, I felt that Mr. Beecher rather slighted my family; he was intimate with me, and I think loved me; but he did not use to come very often to my house, and it did not please me; I wanted him to come oftener.

Q. And it wounded you, did it not? A. I cannot say that I was wounded; I was a mere boy; it was a matter of pride to have him there; Elizabeth at first was modest and frightened; she did not know how to talk with him, or how to entertain him, and it was a slow process by which he obtained her confidence so that she could talk with him; it was the same with Mr. Greeley; he had great reverence for her, and had an exalted opinion of her; I do not think there was a woman that he had a higher regard for than for Mrs. Tilton.

Q. And did she not have a high regard for him also? A. Yes.

Q. And that was known to you too? A. That was known to me, and I was very glad of it.

Q. Mr. Greeley came to your house often? A. He used to come and stay sometimes in the summer a week or two at a time; we kept bachelors' hall; yes, he came often; it was always a white day when Mr. Greeley came; he used to say that he never would come in my absence; he said it was not a good habit.

Q. Did you urge him to come when you were off lecturing? A. I did.

Q. Did not you impress upon Mr. Beecher the necessity and desire that you had that he would call upon your family and see your wife frequently during your absence? A. I did.

Q. Now, Mr. Tilton, you have stated the religious character of your wife; will you describe it again? A. My wife's religious character I have, if you will pardon the allusion, undertaken to set forth in the book that I have spent a year in writing—a work of fiction called "Tempest Tossed"—a name strangely borrowed from my own heaving breast; in that novel is a character, Mary Vail; I do not want to say vainly before the public that I drew that character for Elizabeth, but I did; there is a chapter—the ninth, I think (I won't be certain about the number)—which is called "Mary Vail's Journal;" I know it is good, because I made it up from Elizabeth's letters, and my heart was cleft in twain to find in these letters some of the same sentences that crept into this chapter; I changed them considerably, to make them conform to the story; I had this feeling, that if in this novel I could, as a more subordinate part of the story, paint that character, and have it go quietly, in an underhand way, forth, that that was Elizabeth (for I think I drew it faithfully), it would be a very thorough answer, as coming from me, to the scandals in the community, and that people would say, "Theodore respects his wife," as I do to-day.

Q. Was it a truthful character of Elizabeth? A. It was; it was not drawn as well as the original would warrant.

Q. You say it was not drawn as well as the original would warrant; then her devotion and purity of life would warrant a higher character than you have given "Mary Vail" in that book! A. Yes, unless you attach a technical meaning to the word purity; she was made a victim.

Q. You say that that character in that book falls below the original? A. Yes, because I did not make it a prominent, but a subordinate character.

Q. Are there any other persons that figure in this drama who are described in that book "Tempest Tossed?" A. No, except by mere suggestions.

Q. Is not your true friend described there?

Mr. Tilton—You mean Mr. Moulton?

General Tracy—Yes. A. No; of the characters in "Tempest Tossed" Mary Vail is the only one that is true to life; the character of the colored woman was partly suggested by a colored woman that I knew.

Q. You have brought forward the letter of your wife where she describes herself as having received new light, as having read the character of Catharine Gaunt in "Griffith Gaunt;" have you read the character of Catharine Gaunt? A. Yesterday I said no, but I have an impression that I have; a friend of mine yesterday morning said that it is a singular result from "A Terrible Temptation;" Charles Reade has written a book called "A Terrible Temptation:" I have never read that book, but on second thought I think I have read "Griffith Gaunt;" my impression is that I read it on a journey, and that I wrote something to Elizabeth about it, and asked her to read it.

Q. Did you think that the guilt of "Catherine Gaunt" was that of adultery? A. I have no idea that I did.

Q. Has there been a change in your religious views since you were married? A. Yes, sir, very decided, I am happy to say; I think there is in every sensible man's.

Q. Do you know whether the change in your religious convictions was a source of great grief and sorrow to your wife? A. It was a great source of tears and anguish to her; she said to me once that denying the divinity of Christ, in her view, nullified our marriage almost; and I think next to the sorrow of this scandal it has caused that woman to sorrow more than anything else she has suffered; because I cannot look upon the Lord Jesus Christ as the Lord God; I think her breast has been wrenched with it; she is almost an enthusiast on the subject of the divinity of her Saviour.

Q. You think her a Christian, do you? A. Yes; she is the best Christian I know of, barring her faults; better than any minister.

Q. Well, on the whole, do you not think that she is about as white as most Christians? A. Yes, whiter than ourselves.

Q. Then you would not qualify the expression when you say that she is the best Christian you know, barring her faults? Do not you think that she is the best Christian you know with her faults? A. No, I would not say that, because there has been a strong deceit wrought out in Elizabeth that comes from the weakness of her character; she has had three strong persons to circulate among—Mr. Beecher, her mother and me; in sentiment she outdoes us all; her life is shipwrecked, but she is not to blame; I will maintain that to my dying day.

Q. Do not you know that in these exigencies she sought consolation from her pastor? A. I think she did, and he took advantage of her orthodox views to make them the net and the mesh in which he ensnared her, and for which I hold him in a contempt which no English words can describe.

Q. The change of your religious views has been the subject of a great deal of conversation and anguish and labor on her part, has it not? A. Oh, yes—of letters, and prayers, and tears, and entreaties, many a time and oft.

Q. When you say that this has been the thing which has enabled her to be ensnared, do you mean by that that you think that was the cause why, in some degree, her confidence in the judgment and advice of her pastor was increased, and why your influence over her was lessened? A. Oh, yes; largely so; thoroughly so.

Q. Then when you found that she was leaning more strongly than formerly on the advice and consolation of her pastor, and less on your own, you attributed it naturally to your change in religious sentiments? A. Yes; at the same time I did not want Elizabeth to hold my view; I said that she might be a Catholic or a Mohammedan.

Q. Did she not feel that your views were a source of danger to the children? A. Yes; she would not let the children have playthings on Sunday; John G. Whittier came to our house (he appointed the time), and Mr. Greeley, and met Mr. Johnson; and it almost broke Elizabeth's heart to think that the best man in New England, whom she reverenced, should have appointed Sunday night; she never received visitors on Sunday.

Q. Is it not a feature in her character that she has great reverence for those men whom she believes to be pure in life and noble in thought and spirit? A. Yes; she would'kiss the hem of their garments.

Q. That is a marked feature of her character, is it not? A. Uncommonly so.

Q. Does it not almost go to the extent of idolatry in one sense? A. Well, no; there are a great many women who look upon a man with a sense of worship; Elizabeth never did that; Elizabeth is the peer of any man; at the same time she reverences; it was not vanity—it was reverence; she never regarded Mr. Beecher as a silly woman regards him; she was not a silly woman taken captive; she was a wise, good woman taken captive; there are a great many people, particularly women, who, if President Grant should call on them, would feel greatly flattered; I do not think she would; but if she regarded President Grant as a man of high religious nature, coming with the Gospel in his hand and devoted to the evangelical religion, then, whether he were famous or lowly, she would reverence him.

Q. So must there not be connected with her reverence the idea of absolute purity of life, as well as of religious character? A. Yes. I think Elizabeth regarded Mr. Beecher in early days, as the essence of all that was religious, apostolic; I think she looked upon him very much as she would look upon the Apostle Paul.

Q. And you understood that? A. Yes, and in fact looked upon him so in my early life; I loved that man as well as I ever loved a woman.

Q. And is it not true that there is nothing that your wife so much abhors in man or woman as impurity? A. Exactly so.

4

Q. The fact that she believed that any persons were impure, however, if it were otherwise, she might reverence them, would destroy her respect and reverence for them, would it not? A. It would in those days. [Here Mr. Tilton gave in illustration the instance of a gentleman who his wife felt had insulted her by saying that he sympathized with her, and hoped that she would lift up her head in self respect, remarking that Tilton's chief temptation had been temptation to the sin of the sexes.] Mr. Tilton resuming: I do not think he did it vindictively, but the fact that he could have done it at all burned in her blood.

Q. Was she not distressed at any suggestion of impropriety? A. She was particularly so; and she is more so now than ever, because in her early days such a thought was never in her mind; but when it had passed through her experience it came out with this contrition; I think that hers is one of the white souls; that is the truth of the case; she never ought to have been taken away from her home; you gentlemen did it; you did it, Mr. Tracy; "Thou art the man."

Q. Will you state more distinctly than you have done what you understood by that letter of February 3, 1868, in which she says:—"Love is praiseworthy, but to abuse the gift is sin. There I am strong. No temptation or fascination could cause me to yield my womanhood?" A. I quoted that letter to show how strong her views were at that time.

Q. Did you quote it for the purpose of showing that at that time she was being tempted? A. I have heard her say the substance of that over and over again.

· Q. When? A. I do not know when; a long time ago, years ago, when he (Mr. Beecher) used to go there; it was not because I had any suspicion of him then; Elizabeth always felt that when Mr. Beecher went to such and such a place there were women that would flatter him; I do not think she did at all; she has always been a stickler for the honor of her sex; she said to herself, "I will represent my sex."

Q. In other words she wanted to show him purity of sentiment, and of communion of mind without passion? A. That is what she meant, I think.

Q. That is what you understood her to mean? A. That is exactly what I understood her to mean.

Q. For years? A. Yes, sir.

Q. That is the way you looked upon the relation between them for years? A. I ought to say for the earlier years.

Q. When did you first bring to your wife's attention the fact that you feared that there was something wrong? A. Elizabeth so blotted that out of my mind, that I did not think of it again.

Q. How long ago was it? Years ago? A. Yes, as I recollect it, it must have been during the early years, when we lived in Livingston street, in our present house.

Q. How long have you lived there? A. I do not know.

Mr. Winslow—About ten years, I remember.

General Tracy—It was a great many years ago? A. Yes.

Q. Was it before 1868? A. Long before.

Mr. Claflin—In '64, probably.

General Tracy—Was it before 1865? A. About 1862.

Q. Where did you live at the beginning of the war? A. I am very much ashamed that I am never able to answer such a question.

Q. You say that it was in the early years of your living at No. 174 Livingston street? A. Yes; pictures are vivid to me, and I remember where Elizabeth was sitting in the corner of my parlor; I spoke to her about it when we came home.

Q. How long since was it that you have mentioned that subject to any one until you put it in this communication? A. She blotted it out of my mind.

Q. Did you ever speak of it to any one? A. She blotted out all wrong as concerning her in the circumstance.

Q. You never mentioned it to Mr. Beecher? A. I was very young in those days, and utterly unsuspicious of such things, and when I spoke to her about it she was a little confused and denied it; and then said it was so, but that she had said "You must not do that;" I had in those days something of the same reverence for Mr. Beecher that I have since so eminently lost.

THE LIBRARY SCENE.

· Q. Do you know who was present besides your wife and Mrs. Beecher? A. Nobody.

Q. There was nobody there but you three—you were looking at engravings? A. Yes.

By Mr. Winslow—Were you sitting on the floor? A. Not the whole of the time; I remember that those two were sitting down on the floor with the pictures; I am a restless sort of man, and I do not know where I was; it was a long time ago.

Q. Do you say that you saw it with your own eyes? A. With my own eyes.

Q. Do you remember whether Mr. Beecher looked at you first? A. No; he did not know that I noticed it; I was standing up, I think; I have to bring up the picture in my mind; I do not remember exactly whether I was standing or sitting; perhaps I was in a chair; I know that there was a kind of portfolio folded out and that the pictures were folded down (indicating with the hands); she was sitting on the floor or on a stool, and he on the floor.

Q. Where you were he could see you? A. He was looking at the pictures.

Q. If he had looked up would he have seen you? A. Yes.

By General Tracy—You were looking at some pictures in the room? A. Yes; these things were on her lap.

Q. What part of her person did he touch? A. Her ankles and lower limbs.

By Mr. Winslow—Not above the knee? A. No. If he had he probably would have been struck; it was a question in my mind whether a minister could consider that a proper sort of caress.

Q. Was it done slyly? A. Yes, very slyly; his right or left arm was under her dress.

By General Tracy—How were they sitting? A. My impression is that she was sitting on some little stool and he on the floor by her side, and that some pictures were, perhaps, put up against the chair and folded, and that it was by an accidental brushing up of her dress that I saw his hand on her ankle.

Q. Do you know whether it was accidental or casual with him? A. I only know that I asked her.

Q. Could you know whether it was accidental or intentional? A. I spoke of it to her; she at first denied it and then confessed it, and said that she had chidden him; I did not attach much importance to it after the explanation was made.

Q. You were in doubt whether it was intentional or accidental? A. It was merely a suspicion.

THE BED-CHAMBER SCENE.

Q. How about the bedchamber scene? A. That was a long while ago, and that was blotted out of my mind too.

Q. When was it? A. I do not remember the year; it was a good while ago.

By Mr. Winslow—Before or after the ankle scene? A. Before.

Q. How long? A. I do not know

Q. Before 1868? A. I do not know.

Q. After you were living in Livingston street? A. Yes; I remember the room; again, I identify it by the picture; it was in the left hand room; I have two front rooms on the second story, and it was the left hand of these two rooms; I knocked at the door and Elizabeth came; I was surprised that it was locked; she was surprised at finding me; Mr. Beecher was sitting in a red plush rocking chair—a sort of Ottoman chair—with his vest unbuttoned; his face colored like a rose when I saw him.

Q. How long ago was that? A. I do not know.

Q. How long had you lived in Livingston street at this time? A. Do not remember.

Q. Had you lived there for two or three years? A. That I do not know; I should say I had lived there, perhaps, two years.

Q. Was it during the war? A. That I do not know.

Q. Do you know whether it was before or after your visit to Fort Sumter? A. No.

Q. The explanation was satisfactory to you on that occasion? A. Entirely so.

Q. So that you let it be, and attributed nothing to it? A. Yes, I attributed nothing to it; if the door had been simply shut, I should have thought nothing of it, but the door being locked I wondered at it.

Q. Was there more than one door leading to that room? A. One door comes in from the hall.

Q. Was there any other door leading into the room from the other room? A. There is a middle door communicating between the two rooms.

Q. Two sliding doors? A. Yes.

Q. And was there a door leading from the hall to the other room? A. Yes, that is the plan of the house.

Q. And the room that Mr. Beecher and your wife were in was a room communicating with another room with sliding doors? A. Yes.

Q. What was that room used for that Mr. Beecher was in? A. A bedroom.

Q. Was there a bed in it? A. Yes, sir.

Q. Is the other room a sitting room? A. It is.

Q. Did you try that door which led into the sitting room? A. No.

Q. Why? A. Because I came and knocked at the hall door.

Q. For aught you know, they had gone into the sitting room from the hall, and from there Mr. Beecher may have gone into the bedroom? A. Yes; I will give them the benefit of the doubt.

THE SATISFACTORY EXPLANATION.

Q. Was it explained to your satisfaction ? A. Yes.

Q. What was the explanation that satisfied you ? A. The annoyance of the children; my wife said that our children and some of the neighbors' children were making a noise, and she wanted to have a quiet talk with Mr. Beecher, and so she locked herself in.

Q. That satisfied you ? A. That satisfied me ; it was entirely reasonable ; I only quote it as a suspicion.

Q. Do you remember whether the sliding doors leading from this room to the sitting room were open ? A. They were shut ; I remember it because I looked in; I saw the two white doors coming together; the picture is distinct to my mind; I do not forget pictures.

By Mr. Claflin.—Was the door opened immediately ? A. Yes; I do not want you to think that I thought there was anything wrong at that interview at all.

Q. The picture of the room was the only reason you have for believing that the sitting room door was shut ? A. Yes, sir.

Q. Did the explanation so satisfy you that that thing was blotted from your remembrance ? A. Yes.

Q. So you have never regarded that circumstance as evidence of wrong in any one ? A. No.

Q. Have you ever mentioned that ? A. I rather think I have.

Q. Why ? A. Because afterwards there arose circumstances which made me feel that the explanation which she had given of these two events was not true.

By Mr. Winslow.—To whom did you state it ? A. I think to my mother ; I do not recollect ; I never made any blazonry of it, you know, abroad ; I never thought, really, that there was any wrong in it until in the light of subsequent events ; I do not say now that there was any wrong in it ; Elizabeth always denied stoutly to me that anything wrong had taken place at that time.

Q. What kind of a room was that sitting room ? A. It was the common sitting room of the house.

Q. The right hand part was the sitting room, and the left hand part was a bedroom communicating with it by sliding doors ? A. Yes.

Q. That is where you receive your intimate friends ? A. Yes.

Q. If you had found Mr. Beecher with your wife in the sitting room you would have found him where you should have expected to find him, would you not ? A. Yes.

Q. If the door had not been locked you would not have thought anything of it ? A. No ; I should have been happy to have seen him ; we were in the best possible relations in those days ; nobody was a more welcome guest at our house than he.

Q. Now, Mr. Tilton, can you say whether this scene was before the date of that letter of February 3, 1868 ? A. Yes, it must have been a long time before that, I think ; I won't be certain ; it must have been a long time before 1868.

Q. You say that her letters informed you that Mr. Beecher had made twelve pastoral visits at your house in five weeks ? A. I have those letters.

By Mr. Hill—You have all the letters from which you say you discovered that the twelve visits were made when you were away ? A. Yes.

Q. And those you will produce ? A. I think that perhaps I will.

By General Tracy—It was written here (in Mr. Tilton's communication) six and changed to five weeks--which is correct ? A. (After some explanations.) It is correct as it is there.

Q. You say, Mr. Tilton, for a year after what you state as Mrs. Tilton's confession, she insisted to you that she had not violated her marriage vow ? A. Yes; Elizabeth was in a sort of vaporous-like cloud; she was between light and dark ; she could not see that it was wrong; she maintained to her mother in my presence that she had not done wrong; she cannot bear to do wrong; a sense of having done wrong is enough to crush her; she naturally seeks for her own peace a conscientious verdict; she never would have had these relations if she had supposed at the time that they were wrong; Elizabeth never does anything that at the time seems wrong; for such a large moral nature, there is a lack of a certain balance and equipoise ; she had not a will that guides and restrains; but Elizabeth never does at any time that which does not have the stamp of her conscience at the time upon it.

Q. Do you say that she did or did not insist that she had violated her marriage vows ? A. She always was saying that "it never seemed to her wrong;" and "Theodore, I do not now see that I have wronged you."

Q. What do you understand her as meaning by "To love is praiseworthy, but the abuse of love is sin ?" A. I rather think she meant carrying love to too great an extent.

Q. Would not that include criminal relations ? A. Yes.

Q. Then you understand her, as early as 1868, as saying that the abuse of the gift of love by adultery would be a sin ? A. Yes.

Q. She is a lady of intelligence, is she not ? A. She is in some respects a lady of extraordinary intelligence ; she has a remarkable gift at times which anybody might envy. There is nothing low about Elizabeth.

Q. Is she a lady of large reading? A. There are very few ladies of larger reading; she was educated at the Packer Institute; I do not think she took quite a full course; she reads much to her blind aunt and to the children; I used to read a good deal to her; she was a good critic; Mr. Beecher carried to her sheets of his "Life of Christ" and many chapters of "Norwood;" I used to read to her many things.

Q. What do you say about the "Life of Christ" and "Norwood"—that he carried them to her to criticise? A. Yes, or not exactly to criticise; she is not a critique in the sense that she can take a particular phrase and change the language of it; but she could tell whether a little speech put into Rose Wentworth's mouth was one a woman would be likely to say.

Q. He took those chapters to read to her for that purpose, having a high regard for her opinion in that matter—not as high regard for her opinion in a strictly critical sense? A. No; but in the sense whether it was womanly, and larger than that, whether it touched human sympathy or not. I remember that he took her the first sheet of the "Life of Christ;" she wrote to me saying, "He said he had not read it to anybody else."

Q. When did he write "Norwood?" A. I do not know.

Q. When did he write his first volume of his "Life of Christ?" A. It was after "Norwood," I think.

Q. It was published after "Norwood?" A. I do not know about that.

Q. You know he took it to her to read? A. I know, because she wrote it in her letters; I believe she told the truth; you ask about "Norwood" and the "Life of Christ;" he had brought the opening part of the "Life of Christ," and I think also chapters of "Norwood."

Q. You understand that he brought them to her for the purpose of criticism? A. Yes.

Q. You yourself would regard her as an admirable critic? A. Oh, yes; I always liked to take everything I wrote to Elizabeth; sometimes when I thought I had written anything particularly nice I ran down and read it to her; she was one of the best of critics; she never praised an article because it was mine or his, but only when she liked it.

Q. You found her judgment not warped by her affections in that? A. No, that is the particular feature of her character; if a lady were sitting at the piano and playing, and Elizabeth loved that lady very much, she would tell her about the playing—that it was good, or that it was not—but she would not say that the playing was good because she loved the woman; she would not say so unless it was good; I was always quite certain that if Elizabeth liked what I wrote, she did not like it on my account, though she was glad when I wrote a good thing; it was an honest criticism; if I had been a minister, none of this trouble would have come; she was always in sorrow that I was not a minister—which is the only virtue that I possess; thank God I do not belong to the priesthood or the Church; it may not be an acceptable statement to the Committee.

Q. Do you mean by that, Mr. Tilton, that the want of strong religious feature in your character was what she missed in you? A. No, Mr. Tracy, it was not that; because, though I should not like to say it of myself; yet I am a more religious man than most men of my acquaintance—that is, I am a man of religious sympathies, who thoroughly hates and despises religious creeds; I do not believe in one of the Thirty-nine Articles, nor in either of the Catechisms, nor in the divinity injunction of the Scriptures, nor in the divinity of Christ, in the sense in which it is held. I believe his writings to be enflooded by the Divine breath. It was not that I lack religious spirit. A man ought not to say that, perhaps, of himself, but I do not lack the religious spirit; I love God, and am fond of religious sentiment, but I hate the creeds; I was taught to hate them during the anti-slavery controversy; I saw the churches selling the negroes, and I despise a church; now put it down there (to a reporter); say that I despise the church, and generally despise ministers.

Q. Well, it was that lack of reverence for the church and its ordinances, and your lack of belief in the divinity of Christ, as she held it, that she missed in you? A. Yes.

Q. And she grieved over it? A. Oh yes, indeed; grieved over it with tears.

Q. And what she found wanting in you she found in Mr. Beecher, did she not? A. Yes, she did, and he took advantage of it; that is why I say he ought to spend the rest of his life in penitence and anguish; if Mr. Beecher had held the same religious views that I hold, and gone to that house denying the divinity of Christ, he never could have made any approach to her, and the affection and love which she bore to him would never have existed—I mean the strong affection—it could not possibly have done so.

Q. The enthusiasm for him which she felt would never have existed in that case? A. No.

Q. You have no doubt that it was that feature in his character which roused her enthusiasm and made him to her a sort of poem, did it not? A. Yes, a sort of apostle; I think she regarded Mr. Beecher almost as though Jesus Christ himself had walked in; that is an extravagant expression, but you must not take it literally; I know that she wanted to make the children look upon the clergy with reverence: she ought to be an intense Roman Catholic, like Mme. Guion—a mystic; I think she certainly spends hours on her knees some days; I don't suppose a day ever passes over Elizabeth that the sun, if he could peep through the windows, would not see her on her knees, and my oldest daughter, Florence, though she looks like me, is like her mother; here has come this great calamity on my house; there was that publication last night; she saw it; and this morning what did she do? I heard a noise in the house, and found that she was down in the front parlor playing on the melodeon like a heroine, standing in the midst of this calamity like a rock in the sea; she gets that somewhat from me; I can stand all storms; she gets also from her mother the religious inspiration. Florence, this morning, had a genius for religion, when you would suppose that she would have been crushed; you (General Tracy) are not stronger in the court-room than she was this morning at that musical instrument.

Q. You use the expression, in regard to your daughter, "genius for religion;" does not that express the character of your wife? A. Yes—even more so; my daughter is more intellectual; she is an abler and more stable woman, though not so sentimental, and less demonstrative; they are both great characters.

Q. Well, she is a character who could have an intimacy and reverence and enthusiasm for a man of Mr. Beecher's temperament and religious convictions and teaching, and carry it to an extreme length, without the thought of passion or criminality? A. I do not think the thoughts of passion and of criminality were in her breast at all; I think they were altogether in his; I think she thought only of her love and reverence.

Q. Such a character would not excite the thought of jealousy as to her? A. Not in the slightest; I never had the slightest feeling of jealousy in regard to Elizabeth.

Q. The fact that she was manifesting this enthusiasm, and all that, would not lead you to suspect her motives and purity originally? A. It would not; later it did.

Q. For how long a period? A. I do not know; I remember I wrote her some letters which, if she has kept them, would fix the date; there was a time when I felt that Mr. Beecher was using his influence greatly upon her.

Q. To control her in her domestic relations with you? A. No, but to win her; he was always trying to get her to say that she loved him better than me.

Q. She never would say it? A. I don't think she ever did.

Q. You do not believe she ever felt or believed it, do you? A. No; that is to say, in one sense she loved him; she loved his religious views; she loved him as an evangelical minister; but I don't think that on the whole he was as much to her as I was; still, of course, Mr. Tracy, I cannot question her motives; if she should say he was more to her than I was, I cannot dispute it.

Q. You set out a letter that she wrote on the night of December 30, after you returned to your house, referring to the retraction she had given to Mr. Beecher; did she write that letter, or did you? A. She wrote it.

Q. Did you dictate it? A. No.

Q. Why did she write it? A. Because I asked her to make a calm statement of what she had designed in this letter to Mr. Beecher. She was in such a state of agony that she told me she could not read her letter to him; she said she had given him this letter that he might fortify himself in a council of ministers; I asked her to take a pen at the end of the evening and give the exact circumstances, and explain what she meant by it, and she wrote that letter; it was only the next day that the other letter came back, and then this one ceased to be of any importance; what struck me in that business as so damnable to Mr. Beecher was, that after coming and confessing to me and Mr. Moulton his criminal relations with Mrs. Tilton, and then asking to see her a few minutes, and going around the corner to see her, he should have come back again in half an hour, expressing his absolute heart-brokenness, whereas he had in his pocket this retraction from her; I say it was damnable and nefarious.

Q. Do you say that when you saw Mr. Beecher at Mr. Moulton's house Mr. Moulton was present? A. Yes, he was present in this way—I wanted a lengthy interview with Mr. Beecher alone, and when he came into the room I locked the door and put the key in my pocket, and narrated in order Elizabeth's confession; it was a long one, and it would have been indelicate for me to touch it with any more elaboration than I have here; I do not wish to be questioned about it; it was a long story.

Q. Was Mr. Moulton present? A. Not at that part of the interview; after the door was opened he was; the interview that we three together had was very short; I was on the stairs while Mr. Beecher talked with Mr. Moulton on the stairs; that interview was to bring me and Mr. Beecher together; the next time we all three had an interview.

Q. This retraction, you say in your communication, Mr. Beecher returned to you through Mr. Moulton; is that true? A. Yes, sir.

Q. Was that retraction ever delivered to you? A. I have got it now.

Q. Is it not in the possession of Mr. Moulton? A. Yes; but it belongs to me. Mr. Moulton had a safe place and I had not, and he has some of my papers.

Q. Do you mean to say that Mr. Moulton delivered that retraction to your actual keeping, and that you have had possession of it for any length of time? A. He did deliver it to me, and it was sent back to him.

Q. I ask you whether Mr. Moulton delivered that retraction to you and you kept it. A. Mr. Moulton put that retraction into my hand; exactly what I did with it—whether I carried it to my safe or not—I do not remember; I took a number of papers and put them in his keeping because I had no safe place.

Q. How long, do you think, had you possession of that paper? A. I do not remember; I never saw the retraction till it was brought back to me; then I read it; it may be that I never took it away from Mr. Moulton's house; it was sent back to me; it was put into my hand; I read it, and I made a copy of it.

Q. In shorthand? A. Yes.

Q. Did you ever have it longer than that? A. Yes; long enough to make forty copies in shorthand.

Q. But you returned it to Mr. Moulton, and he has kept it and has it now? A. Yes, unless he has been robbed.

Q. The letter which you say Mr. Beecher wrote Mrs. Tilton, with your permission, I see, as published, directs her to return it to him through your hands? A. Yes.

Q. Was it returned to him through your hands? A. It was returned to Mr. Moulton by me.

Q. Did you make a copy of it? A. I did.

Q. Then you took advantage of Mr. Beecher's direction to have that letter returned to him through your hands, to make a copy, and you made and preserved a copy of the letter? A. I did, exactly; and I have found a very good use for it in this late emergency.

Q. What you call the "apology"—is that in Mr. Beecher's handwriting? A. It is not.

Q. In whose handwriting is it? A. In Francis D. Moulton's, except the last sentence, which is Mr. Beecher's.

Q. "I trust this to Moulton in confidence," is in Mr. Beecher's handwriting, is it not? A. Yes.

Q. The words "in confidence" are underscored, are they not? A. I do not know.

Q. That document is written on how many half sheets of paper? A. I do not think on any; it is on sheets as big as that (legal cap).

Q. On how many—two or three? A. Yes—large sheets.

Q. Do you know whether the last sentence, "I trust this to Moulton in confidence," is separated by a wide space from the rest? A. I do not know; Frank can show it to you.

Q. Is it not separated by a wide space? A. No, not by a wide space.

Q. I ask you whether the last sentence of the letter is not here somewhere (indicating with the hand), and the line, "I trust this to Moulton in confidence, H. W. Beecher," down there (indicating)? A. No; it is not.

Q. Is it not at the bottom of the page? A. It may be at the bottom of the page.

Q. Is it not away from the writing? A. No; it is not; it is a part of the letter.

Q. You were not present when it was written? A. No; otherwise, it would not have been written.

Q. Because it would have been spoken? A. Yes; the substance was spoken to me a day or two afterwards in Mr. Moulton's bedchamber.

Q. You say, if you had been present, it would not have been written? A. Yes.

Q. That letter is not addressed to you, is it? A. It was addressed to Mr. Moulton, but it was brought to me on the authority of Mr. Beecher, himself; it was brought to me greatly to my surprise; Mr. Moulton put it before me as evidence that I should maintain peace; I did not ask for it; it came unsolicited.

Q. You quote a letter dated on the 7th of January to you from Mr. Beecher. Was your suit with Bowen then pending? A. My suit with Bowen was pending from the 1st of January to the middle of the next year; I think it was in April, 1872; I never sued him; Mr. Moulton wanted to assume the management of my affairs with Mr. Bowen; Mr. Moulton, when sick, summoned us to him, and said "I want to keep you on record and bind you to good will."

Q. You had a controversy? A. I had a controversy; I agreed not to do anything but at Mr. Moulton's discretion; Mr. Bowen owed me $7,000, and Frank said, "He has got to pay that; but I would rather pay it myself that that it should bring Mr. Beecher in collision, and I will agree that you shall have it, if I have to pay it myself; therefore, let this thing remain with me as long as I like—a year or ten years;" Frank was determined that peace should be kept.

Q. Were there any proceedings to perpetuate testimony taken? A. Frank thought that Mr. Bowen ought to come to a settlement, and said, "I think I will put this in court;" and Mr. Ward instituted some proceedings; it was the mere suggestion of a suit, done without my knowledge; I think it was to perpetuate Mr. Johnson's testimony; I have forgotten.

Q. That was in 1872? A. Yes; it must have been in March.

Q. You say you put the management of your matter against Bowen in the hands of Moulton? A. I did.

Q. Did not he represent to you that it was absolutely indispensable or material that you and Mr. Beecher should keep on friendly terms in reference to this controversy with Bowen? A. No. The sum and essence of his management was the management of my relations to Mr. Beecher; he regarded Mr. Bowen as an incident; I could not afford to lose my office, and Mr. Moulton said, "You have got to keep peace with Mr. Beecher for the sake of yourself and family;" Mr. Moulton always made Mr. Bowen subsidiary to Mr. Beecher—and me also, till I revolted, after Dr. Bacon's letter.

Q. Do you mean to say that it was never regarded as important that friendly relations should be maintained between you and Mr. Beecher, having reference to your difficulty with Bowen? A. Not a particle ; the more I quarrelled with Mr. Beecher, the better Mr. Bowen liked it ; if, as a result of the controversy, Mr. Beecher should be dead, Mr. Bowen would not be one of the mourners, but one that would uplift the horn of gladness ; he never wanted peace with Mr. Beecher ; he always wanted war with Mr. Beecher ; he is an enemy of Mr. Beecher, and would rejoice in his downfall ; perhaps I ought not to say that ; it is speaking of the motives of people, but it is true.

Q. The tripartite treaty was not signed until after February 7, 1871 ? A. No.

Q. Was not your letter to Mr. Moulton of that date written for the purpose of calling out a reply from him ? A. No ; I wrote it because Frank insisted upon it ; Frank had the idea that if I gave my word he would have me bound ; he wanted me to write the utmost of what I could of good-will in this letter.

Q. And did he get a corresponding answer from Mr. Beecher ? A. Perhaps so ; I do not think that he informed me that he was going to get an answer from Mr. Beecher.

Q. He informed you that he had got an answer from him afterward, did he not ? A. Yes, he showed it to me and I copied it.

Q. Do you say that your letter was not written in order to draw out an answer from Mr. Beecher ? A. No, I wrote it to please Frank, because he wanted me to ; perhaps there may be a sense in which I was to write what I could of good will, and Mr. Beecher what he could of good will ; perhaps there may be correctness in your phrase ; there was no collusion on my part with Mr. Beecher ; it was Mr. Moulton's iron-like way of compelling things to go on in peace and harmony ; he is a man of desperate strength of will.

Q. Now, will you produce all the letters which you quote on pages 113 and 114 of your communication, beginning, " My dear Frank, I am determined to make. no more resistance. Theodore's temperament is such that the future, even if temporarily earned, would be absolutely worthless, and rendering me liable at any time of day ? " A. I cannot ; Mr. Moulton can.

Q. Have you a copy of it ? A. Yes, I think I am not wrong.

Q. Can you produce a copy ? A. I do not know ; I am sorry I cannot tell you ; I have a mass of phonographic notes ; whenever these letters came, whenever there was anything in them that Frank wanted me to see, he would read them to me ; whenever Mr. Beecher said anything that he thought, being read to me, would gratify my feelings and conduce to a compromise or peace between us, speaking of the kindness with which I treated him, or of his difficulties, Frank read them to me, and as I wrote shorthand, I always used to make a copy of them.

Q. And is that the only copy that you have of these papers ? A. It is the only copy I have of Frank's papers.

Q. Copies in shorthand being read and never being compared with the originals ? A. When Frank read to me three or four or five sentences I could write them down.

By Mr. Hall—Did you compare them with the originals ? A. What do you mean by comparing them with the originals ?

Q. Do you know that they are an exact transcript of the originals ? A. Yes.

Q. You wrote them from your phonographic notes ? A. You will find these extracts all perfectly correct—every one, absolutely.

By Mr. Winslow—Do you remember the purport of what you left out ? A. My impression is that this one of Mr. Beecher's letters to Frank was very long; it would certainly occupy four pages of a sheet of foolscap; there was a long argument in it to show the difficulties that he was in ; if I had quoted the whole it would have this statement much stronger, but it would have made it a cumbered document.

Q. Is there something that you have not quoted ? A. A great deal ; but there is nothing in that quotation that violates the whole spirit of the letter.

Q. Had you no reason for omitting what you did except to avoid length ? A. No ; only it alluded to interviews ; for instance, in this way :—" I am greatly distressed with what the deacon said," or " The Brooklyn *Eagle* must not go on in this way ; " many things might be added that are unimportant in this exhibit but that were important at the time.

Q. On page 103, " No man can see the difficulties that environ me," etc., did you quote the whole of that letter ? A. Only a fragment of it ; there is not a whole letter in all these quotations.

Q. In making these quotations I see no stars ? A. I do not know whether it is the omission of the printer, but I put in stars to show where the connection was broken off ; where I took a paragraph which was long and it was continuous from beginning to end there is no need of stars.

Q. Your letter, " To a Complaining Friend," that was published, to whom was that written ? A. That was written to nobody ; everybody was saying, " You ought to answer the scandal," and I put my wits together to frame a possible answer.

Q. Then you say that the letter " To a Complaining Friend," was a fiction ? A. Yes, it was written on purpose as a public card.

Q. How long after the Woodhull scandal was that ? A. It was published a long time after that date ; not longer than two or three weeks, I think, perhaps not ten days ; my impression is that it was not published until a long time after; I thought I had written an ingenious card, but it did not amount to anything; Wendell Phillips said, "It is said that your wife was not guilty;" but I could not say that, and the card went for nothing; it was one of a number of ingenious subterfuges; I wrote it thinking that it would please Elizabeth; I read it to her before it was printed and she liked it; afterward she spoke to me violently about it, and said it was another way of perpetuating the scandal.

Q. And charged you with publishing it for that purpose? A. No, not that.

Q. But did not she say that the effect of that publication would be to perpetuate the scandal and revive it? A. Yes, after it was published.

Q. The Woodhull scandal was dying out of the minds of the people, was it not, then, when that was published? A. I think not; I did not know the time when it was; it is a death of which I have had no notice yet; I thought I did a crafty thing in that card, but it failed.

Q. I asked whether the Woodhull scandal was not dying out of the minds of the people, and whether it would not have died out but for that? A. Well, I don't know; you are a better judge of that than I am; I think I heard less of it.

Q. Do you not know that the publication of that letter revived the talk and the scandal? A. Yes, yes; everything revives the talk; the appointment of an investigating committee revived it in the same way, in general terms.

Q. What other publications have you made since the publication of the Woodhull scandal and the letter "To a Complaining Friend," and the Bacon letter and letters to the Council? A. The letter "To a Complaining Friend" was put in the *Eagle* with a ferocious comment; if it had not been printed with a bad comment, I think it would have had a good effect; but that letter did harm.

Q. Do you mean to say that it revived or perpetuated the scandal instead of allaying it? A. It did harm in the sense that it purported to be a denial; looked as if it was meant for a denial which did not deny, and it left about this impression—that Mr. Tilton, a direct man, who knows what he means and could say it, if he could have denied this squarely would have done it; the impression was that it was written to deny, but that it did not deny.

Q. Did it not carry in it a strong implication of guilt? A. Well, perhaps in a sense you might inferentially say so; I think you might say that; I think if I had never said a word on the subject at all, from the beginning down, it would have been a great deal better.

Q. The scandal would have died out long ago, would it not? It has only been kept alive by your writings? A. I have acted like a fool, I admit.

By Mr. Tracy—We all concede that, and do not need to call witnesses to prove it.

Q. Now, when the council was in session, that took the form, did it not, of an ecclesiastical controversy, in which the scandal proper dropped out of sight? A. There is no scandal proper.

Q. Well, this scandal itself dropped out of sight, and the controversy was over an ecclesiastical question was it not? A. In a technical sense; but everybody said that that council revived the business.

Q. Did not you know that your letters revived the scandal? A. Yes; or it did not need reviving—it had life in it.

Q. Did not your letters to the council largely call out the letters by Dr. Bacon? A. I think Dr. Bacon took a sublime indifference to my letters in the first place; he sent them back from the council; I do not now recollect that there was any extract from my letters to the council that were introduced at all by Dr. Bacon; perhaps there was; if he made any allusion at all to them it was a most unimportant one.

Q. You knew that the effect of your letters to the council would be to revive the scandal, did you not? A. No, I did not: I wrote them to vindicate myself; I did not care whether they revived the scandal or not.

Q. Did not you know what the effect would be? A. I thought of vindicating myself; I had been attacked, and I wrote a defence; the scandal had to take care of itself; I was not so tender toward the scandal that I should refrain from defending myself if it would revive it even.

Q. That is evident. Mrs. Tilton's letter to you, quoted February 9, 1868, and commencing, "Ah I did angel ever love so grandly as my beloved." In that letter, on page 164, this sentence occurs, "And the dear friends who love us." You originally wrote it, and you have erased "us" and put in "me." Do you know which is correct? What is in the original? A. I think it is "me;" it is "me" (examining the first draft of the communication).

Q. How came Mrs. Tilton to write that letter to Moulton, denying that she had ever thought of separating from you? A. Frank, as soon as he undertook to make the compromise between us, undertook to straighten out whatever was wrong; there was a story which Mrs. Morse set afloat about my being divorced, and Frank wrote a note to her, or went to see her, and she wrote this note.

Q. Did not she write it at your suggestion? A. I do not think she did; I think she wrote it at Frank's suggestion; I had forgotten that letter until I found it among the papers.

Mr. Hill—Did not you make any suggestion to her about writing that letter? A. I do not recollect distinctly; it may be that I did; I do not know; I co-operated with Frank.

General Tracy—Has she not, during this controversy, signed letters that you have written for her? A. No; she wrote a letter to Dr. Storrs, a part of which I suggested the phraseology, of a delicate statement of her relations to Mr. Beecher, which, while it was not false, did not convey more than half of the truth; the remainder she wrote herself: she was going to state too much in it.

Q. Is there any other letter that she has ever written at your dictation, and signed after you had written it, in this controversy? A. Well, I do not know; I do not recollect any at present.

Q. Do you remember a letter that she wrote to Mr. Moulton, commencing, "Dear Francis, I told you a falsehood last night?" A. I never saw it.

Q. Do you remember that Mr. Moulton reported to you, on any occasion, that she had made a statement that what you claimed was her confession she had made at your solicitation and instance, and at a time when you were also confessing to her, or anything of that description, and that you were angry about it, and took Moulton to your house to have him see whether she would make such a statement or not, and that Mr. Moulton coming in and repeating the statement in your presence, you asked her whether she had ever said so, and she said she had not, and you turned to Moulton and said, "Then you see who is the liar?" A. I do not remember any such phrase as that; Frank Moulton said to me, as nearly as I can recollect (his memory is better than mine), that Elizabeth, in a mood of criticism on me (which she did not very often have), had said that I had made to her confessions against myself, corresponding with the confession which she had made to me against herself, which was not true; and Frank asked her squarely if it was so.

Q. Did he ask her or did you? A. I do not remember.

Q. What did she say? A. She said, "No," and then Frank afterwards told me she said the opposite.

Q. Now, did you not know that the very next morning she wrote to Mr. Moulton a letter beginning, "Dear Francis, I told you two falsehoods," and proceeded to say in substance, "The fact is, that when I am in the presence of Mr. Tilton he has such a control over me that I am not responsible for what I say," or, "I am obliged to say whatever he wills that I should say; but the truth is that I had reported the story just as you had heard it." A. I do not; I know that she had some conversations with him, which she reported to me as being greatly like a see-saw—saying one thing and unsaying it.

Q. Have you ever had doubts of her sanity? A. No.

Q. Never? No, sir.

Q. Have you ever threatened to put her in an asylum? A. No, sir.

Q. Have you ever circulated the story among her acquaintances or friends that she was becoming insane? A. No, but that her mother was; there was one time about then when she was a little delirious.

Q. When? A. I do not remember; her mind wandered a little in sickness; she has never had a taint of insanity; you know we have a customary phrase, "You say an extravagant thing, my friend, you are insane;" that is the only possible way in which Elizabeth has been insane; she is not insane at all.

Q. Mr. Tilton, you have quoted the letters of your wife here to prove what the character of your home was in the beginning of 1868 and through 1868? A. I quoted them to show what it was previous to her surrender to him.

Q. You have stated, Mr. Tilton, that there were acts of criminality, first at Mr. Beecher's house, and secondly, at your own house; do you pretend to have a personal knowledge of those acts? A. Only the knowledge of Mrs. Tilton's confession—that is all; I was absent at the time.

Q. Mr. Moulton was in college with you? A. Yes, sir.

Q. He has always been your friend from your college days? A. Yes, sir; and I hope he will be to the end of my life.

Q. Your novel is dedicated to him? A. Yes, but he has not done me the honor of reading it; I will never dedicate another.

Q. You say that you had not reported this scandal to the Woodhull women or woman; but you do not deny that you had frequently spoken harshly of Mr. Beecher to her? A. Oh, not harshly; I have spoken often critically of him, but always with a view to have her do no harm to him; I expressed my opinion about him.

Q. How came she and Mr. Beecher to have an interview? A. I do not remember the circumstances; I think Frank Moulton devised it; Mr. Beecher had a number of interviews with her at Frank's house, and one at mine.

Q. Was not the object to get Mr. Beecher committed to her views of free love? A. No; to her views of the fourteenth and fifteenth amendments of woman's suffrage; Mr. Butler and I championed it, and we wanted Mr. Beecher to do the same.

Q. Was it not to get him to preside at Steinway Hall ? A. That was not at my house, but at Frank's; I think at mine it was in regard to the fourteenth and fifteenth amendments.

Q. Well, an effort was made to get him to preside there and introduce her at Steinway Hall, and an exposition of this scandal was threatened if he did not preside there ? A. Frank received a letter from Colonel Blood that he thought was a threat ; it angered Frank a good deal.

By Mr. Winslow—Did you see the letter from Colonel Blood, in which it was threatened that this scandal would be exposed if Mr. Beecher did not preside at the Steinway Hall meeting ? A. I do not think that is so ; if it was I did not know it ; I do not think there was any truth.in it.

Q. Mr. Beecher had been importuned to preside, had he not ? A. Yes ; there came a note from Colonel Blood about the Woodhulls not being received in some hotel ; they said it was because they were unpopular, and they wanted Mr. Beecher's help ; there was something in the letter which Frank regarded as unhandsome, and I knew he was angry and expressed himself strongly about it, and said it looked like blackmail ; it was one of the first indications of their attempting to use us.

Q. Do you not know that Mr. Beecher was threatened that in case he did not preside at that meeting this scandal should be published ? A. It is the first time that I have ever heard it suggested.

Q. Was he not threatened by Mrs. Woodhull ? A. Not that I have any knowledge of.

Q. Was not the very object of soliciting Mr. Beecher to preside at the Steinway Hall meeting on the part of you and Mr. Moulton in order to place Mrs. Woodhull under obligation, so that she should not make the publication ? A. Precisely so ; we did not know that there was to be a publication ; we wanted to keep her on our side, and wanted to take every possible occasion to do it ; her husband had spent a considerable length of time to devise this Steinway Hall speech ; what it was about I do not know ; she gave me and Frank the proofs, and he put them in his drawer. I never looked at them ; it was our folly that we did not, for I might have known what was in that speech ; she wanted Mr. Beecher to preside ; I told Mr. Beecher, that however unpopular she was he might go and preside, and I sketched a little sort of a speech (and I think Frank sketched one) that, if he could see his way to do it, he might make :—"Fellow citizens—Here is a woman who is going to speak. She will probably speak on what you do not believe ; but that is no reason why she should not be heard. It is because I disagree with her that I would introduce her. I like free speech. I have the honor of presenting her." I said to him that he was able to carry a little speech of that sort, and I felt that if he went and presided it would put her under the same obligation to him, as I fancied I had put her under to me in writing her biography ; I considered that I had secured her good-will by writing that and other things, and I thought that if Mr. Beecher would do some signal service of that kind, which he could do, and which would be noted as such, it would fix her under gratitude, and we would all be fixed ; Frank had done her some service ; Frank had been very friendly to her ; he had done her many services, and he had great respect for her.

Q. You pressed that argument on Mr. Beecher ? A. Yes, and Frank also.

Q. As a matter of safety ? A. Yes ; I said " Think it over, and if you find that you can, go and do it."

Q. Do you know whether the letter from Colonel Blood had been received at that time ? A. I do not know.

Q. Mr. Beecher rejected your arguments and refused to preside ? A. He did not refuse, but said that if he saw his way clear he would come and let us know.

Q. But he did not let you know ? A. He did not let us know.

Q. And you presided instead ? A. I did not want to ; but I had no idea what the speech was going to be.

Q. Although the proofs were in your hands and you might have known ? A. Yes ; but I never did know ; the proofs had been brought to Frank's study ; I may have had the idea that they were for Mr. Beecher to see the speech ; but it was not the printed speech that did the damage, it was the interjected remarks in response to the audience ; she said violent things.

Q. Had you written her life at that time ? A. Yes, I had ; I am pretty certain of it.

Q. What other things had you done to put her under obligations ? A. I will tell you what I did ; I wrote that idea of the Fourteenth and Fifteenth amendments and spent three of the solidest weeks of my life in working it into an argument and printing it into a tract ; it was her idea, but she did not know how to expose it, and I worked it up in one of the most elaborate pieces of writing that I ever did ; that was one of the great services ; the second was the writing of a sketch ; then, also, when Senator Carpenter attacked that proposition I made an elaborate reply.

Q. You went to the meeting yourself, and deliberately intended to go ? A. No, I did not ; Frank came to the *Golden Age* office ; it rained, and it was late, half-past seven o'clock, and I went to see who was to preside ; there was no expectation that I would preside at all ; we got there at ten minutes to eight o'clock, and the crowd was so great that we could not get in at the front way, and we went to the rear and went into a large ante-room, and there was Mrs. Woodhull, flushed and excited because there was not a brave man in the circle of the two cities to preside at her meeting ; Mr. Beecher did not come, and one or two others who had been invited were not there ; she felt that there was no courage in men, and she was going on alone, and I said, "I will preside at your meeting ; " it was not more than ten minutes ; I do not believe five minutes, forethought ; I went on the platform and made a few remarks and introduced her ; that was the way it came about.

Q. You quote letters from your wife in 1868 to show the affection she bore you at that time, and then say that in 1870 you thought you discovered that her mind was absorbed in Mr. Beecher to too great an extent. Between the beginning of 1868 and the spring of 1870 had there been any act on your part calculated to disturb the happiness of your home or alienate the affections of your wife ? A. Not that I remember.

Q. Had there been no affection of a marked character existing between you and another lady which was calculated to disturb the happiness of a wife ? A. No, I think not.

[Here followed a series of circumstantial inquiries concerning Mr. Tilton's relations with different women, and equally circumstantial denials on his part of anything improper, or of any connection between these stories and his wife's estrangement from him.]

Q. Do you know that —— made charges against you, and that that was one of the reasons why Mr. Bowen discharged you ? A. I cannot say what operated on Mr. Bowen.

Q. That was one of the things discussed, was it not ? A. Yes, the only thing discussed; but, Mr. Tracy, I decline this examination; you have introduced names here, and you must take the consequences; there are charges against one of the names; I took pains to introduce no names; there are written charges made and filed concerning a lady whom you have named; now, I do not take the responsibility of reviving it.

General Tracy—We have to mention names here, but I think they won't be mentioned in the record.

Q. What was the character of the charges that —— made against you ? A. I never knew that —— made any until afterwards; Mr. Bowen said there had been a story told prejudicial to me: he would not tell me by whom, and he would not tell me the story; I said, "If there is any story prejudicial to me, bring the person who tells the story face to face with me; " Mr. Bowen said, "That is fair; " after that I heard that she wrote a letter.

Q. Was there any other lady that was in the habit of seeing you at your house ? A. If there was, do you suppose I would be little enough, as a gentleman, to name it ? I am not a minister.

General Tracy—Then perhaps you might mention it ? A. I should not; there are ladies that I know and honor and I should scorn to answer such a question.

Q. I asked you whether there were any other ladies who were in the habit of visiting your house, and whose visits disturbed the quiet and happiness of your wife ? A. You may ask her and take her answer; I scorn to answer; Elizabeth shall have the benefit of any statement she pleases to make concerning any names; this examination I understand the point of perfectly well; there is no woman that I have respected or honored whom I have not brought to my house, which is not the practice always of men in their relations with ladies; if Elizabeth has been troubled concerning my attentions to any lady take her testimony upon that subject.

General Tracy—I will do that, and I shall do it, because you have brought into the controversy the character of your home; you have said that her affections were alienated, and it is proper and essential that we should show that that was not the cause to which you attributed it.

Mr. Tilton—I say if Elizabeth's change of mind was due in her opinion to the fact that I had loves and affections for other ladies, take her testimony for that fact; I will not deny her.

Q. You are confident she will state the truth of that ? A. She will state what she wants to have appear, and that she is welcome to.

By Mr. Hill—Won't you say generally whether you had affections for other ladies which your wife knew of ? No answer.

By General Tracy—Do you refuse to be examined on that point ? A. No ; I don't refuse to be examined on that point.

Q. Then state whether there are not other ladies who have been intimate with you, and in your society at your house, often and repeatedly, and in a manner calculated to disturb the quiet and peace of mind of your wife. A. I think I brought Mrs. Stanton and Miss Anthony there ; she hated them, but it was because she thought they were radicals, and so on.

Q. Did you ever hear it stated or intimated that you had undue familiarities with those ladies at your house ? A. No, no.

General Tracy—I don't mean criminal familiarities, but undue familiarities, such as visiting their room or appearing in their room before they were dressed ? A. No, I didn't ; I cannot imagine any reason why anybody should.

Q. Was there any other lady besides the two that you have mentioned who annoyed Elizabeth ? A. Mrs. Woodhull always annoyed her when she came ; Elizabeth always took fire at every person who did not come within the limit of the orthodox ordinances ; she always loved all the women who were connected with the church ; my life was outside, and it generally happened that nearly all my public friends were radical in one way or another, and she could not bear it and it annoyed her.

Q. Don't you know of the visits and attentions of another lady that disturbed your wife very much ? A. No.

[A series of questions then followed concerning another lady, which Mr. Tilton answered at first frankly, and afterward with anger, claiming that the lady was an intimate and valued friend of his wife as well as himself.]

General Tracy—Do you know that about the time of your quitting the *Union*, in 1869, your name and ———'s were associated together by public rumor ? A. By Henry Ward Beecher ; and he wrote an apology to Mr. Bowen, which I possess, recalling it ; it was his slander and I can produce it ; the first thing Mr. Beecher did, within a week after his apology on the 4th of January, was to write to Mr. Bowen a retraction of what he had said in regard to ———.

Q. When was it that he said it ? A. I never heard of it until he had unsaid it ; it was a voluntary thing ; in making his retraction he confessed the fact ; I had never heard that he had spoken unhandsomely until he apologized to me and wrote the retraction ; that retraction was put into my hands.

Q. You mean to say that public rumor did not connect your name and ———'s at the time you were on the *Union*, or about that time ?

[Mr. Tilton admitted that there was a paragraph in one of the New York papers that they were go-. ing to elope together. He was then on the *Union*. Other questions followed concerning his visits to the lady, etc., which he explained as natural and proper.]

Q. Did it come to the knowledge of your wife ? A. I carried it to the knowledge of my wife ; it was during the summer of 1870, when I edited the *Union ;* I only edited it eight months ; it never was a good paper before or since—begging pardon for improprieties.

Q. Afterwards you made the acquaintance of Mrs. Woodhull, did you not ? A. The next year, 1871.

Q. Did you ever express your attachment for ——— in the presence of your wife ? A. Ask my wife; take her answer; you may depend that I never said to ———, or any other lady, in the absence of my wife, what I would not have said in her presence ; I have no secrets from Mrs. Tilton ; I never had any, and never should have had any but for this break-up ; I never had any secrets from Mrs. Tilton until within this last year or two, during which we have not harmonized as in former years.

Q. Have you ever admitted to her that you had committed adultery ? A. I never admitted to her anything of the kind.

Q. But you don't mean to say that you have not, do you ? A. Mr. Tracy, talk to me as one gentleman to another.

General Tracy—You charge your wife with having committed adultery ; I mean to ask you whether you have or not ? A. I say let my wife make the charge if she wishes to.

Q. I ask you the question. A. You may ask it till doomsday.

Q. You decline to answer ? A. I do not ; I say I will take my wife's answer.

Q. How could she know that you had, if you had not confessed it to her ? I ask you whether you have not been guilty of the crime ? A. I decline to hold a conversation with you on such a subject.

Q. Have you not admitted to others your commission of adultery ? A. Mr. Tracy, have you committed adultery ?

General Tracy—I have not charged my wife with that crime.

Mr. Tilton—If I am to be charged with the crime of adultery in this business, I wish to know it. I wish my wife, in whose interest you speak, to make the charge, if she chooses. Now let her choose. If you, gentlemen, suppose that you are to fight this battle in reference to my character, I will make it ten times harder than you see. Yesterday we were on the edge of peace; but if you mean to draw the sword, the sword shall be drawn.

Mr. Hill—Don't you think it is pretty well out ?

Mr. Tilton—There was one thing I was born for, and that is war.

Q. Did you make the acquaintance of Mrs. Woodhull in the absence of ——— ? A. I don't remember whether she was absent or present.

Q. Don't you remember whether it was while she was at home or not that you were associating with Mrs. Woodhull ? A. I knew Mrs. Woodhull a whole year.

Q. [After several questions interjected, involving reference to another woman.] Do you know whether or not information was communicated to your wife that you were living with Mrs. Woodhull ? A. I never lived with her.

Q. Do you remember whether your wife was told that you were living with her ? A. I never heard of it till now; I saw something the day before yesterday in a salacious newspaper.

Q. The *Chicago Times ?* A. Yes.

Q. Have you read it ? A. Yes.

Q. Don't you know that information of precisely the character then published was communicated to your wife by the mother of Mrs. Woodhull, during your intimacy with Mrs. Woodhull ? A. I never heard of such a thing ; I remember that Mrs. Morse was with Mrs. Claflin; the old crazy woman came at the foot of her stairs one night and made a hideous racket of some sort of trash ; Mrs. Morse quoted that, and got quite frightened about it.

General Tracy—I hope all the mothers of your friends are not insane. Don't you know that Mrs. Claflin at the same time communicated that to your wife ? A. I did not know that she saw my wife ; I understood that that woman made a visit at Mrs. Morse's ; it may be, perhaps, that Mrs. Tilton was there at the time.

Q. Don't you know that your wife's mind has been disturbed in regard to your own infidelity to her by your associations with public women ? A. No, sir ; if that pretence is made, Mr. Tracy, on your part, it is unmanly ; if it is made on her part it is false ; I have never associated with public women.

General Tracy—I don't mean prostitutes ; I mean reformers. A. Oh, yes ; I said before that Elizabeth had been annoyed, over and over again, by my associations with all persons out of the realm of religious orthodox ideas.

Q. In that class of people whom among your lady acquaintances do you include ? A. I include Mrs. Stanton and Miss Anthony, though I have not seen those people since Elizabeth ordered them out of the house ; beyond those persons I don't know ; Lucy Stone was one ; she lived in Boston ; she did not come very often ; Elizabeth was a reformer at one time, and had the getting up of women's rights meetings, and had the children take the tickets ; she arranged the campaign, but now she cannot endure them.

SESSION OF JULY 23, 1874.

At the session all the members were present and examined, with Mr. Tilton, who was also present, with the letter from his wife which he had quoted in his statement. The other letters which he had quoted from he said were in the hands of Mr. Frank Moulton. After some conversation the Committee-adjourned.

AN OMISSION FROM THE REPORT OF THE CROSS-EXAMINATION.

On the afternoon of the day of the publication by the Investigating Committee of his cross-examination—namely, Monday, July 27—Mr. Tilton published the following card, which explains itself :—

I respectfully call public attention to the fact that though the Plymouth Church Committee have this morning published eight or ten columns of the irrelevant and desultory conversation between Mr. Beecher's counsel and myself in the committee-room, yet this voluminous report strangely omits the most important part of my testimony, namely, that my criminality which my sworn statement charged upon the Rev. Henry Ward Beecher and his religious victim was confessed to me not only by herself but by Mr. Beecher : furthermore. that it was confessed by her and him to Mr. Moulton, as the friend and counsellor of both ; and still further, that Mr. Moulton's office as mediator for four years between Mr. Beecher and me was based on the one sole fact of this pre-existing criminality between Mr. Beecher and Mrs. Tilton. This statement I made to the Committee with my utmost plainness of speech.

I furthermore stated to the Committee that Mr. Beecher's apology to me, instead of growing out of any circumstances with which Mrs. Woodhull was connected, was communicated to me by Mr. Beecher nearly six months before I ever met, knew, or saw Mrs. Woodhull.

The omission of these facts from the Committee's report forces me to lay them before the public as a necessary part of my case.

(Signed) THEODORE TILTON.

Monday, July 27, 1874, No. 174 Livingston street, Brooklyn.

TILTON'S TWO-EDGED SWORD.

The Brooklyn *Daily Argus* of July 24th, 1874, contained a remarkable interview with Mr. Tilton. Mr. Tracy, Mr. Beecher's lawyer, had called the roll of Tilton's female acquaintance, asking him, as he named each one, if he had committed adultery with her. This mode of examination the witness resented, and threatened if it were kept up to call the roll on the other side. The interview is as follows :

A gentleman called on Mr. Tilton, this morning, at his residence in Livingston street, and asked him if his examination before the Committee had been concluded. Mr. Tilton replied that he did not know. He had promised to go before the Committee as often as they sent for him. He had been before them already four times. Whether they would want him any more, he could not say, but he said he had never failed to respond to their summons, and if they should ask for him forty times in succession he would be certain to appear. Upon being asked whether the reports which have appeared, pretending to give accounts of his cross-examinations before the Committee, were correct, Mr. Tilton said :

"I have never yet seen one that was correct. They all bear evidence of being one-sided and half malicious presentations of my examination, furnished to the reporters by the counsel to the Committee. The Committee themselves are not responsible for these misrepresentations. I am a journalist, and know the reporters. The reporters themselves have informed me that these travesties of the truth come to them by design from Mr. Tracy and Mr. Hill. These two gentlemen would deny this fact ; but a number of my friends on the press have communicated to me in confidence that Mr. Tracy and Mr. Hill are directly responsible for these misrepresentations of my examination. Please do not understand that I object, at this juncture, to be misrepresented either by the press or by Mr. Beecher's counsel. The more I am misrepresented, the more right I have to defend myself. Mr. Tracy and Mr. Hill, the counsel for Mr. Beecher, already have as little influence with the Committee as they have with the public. I have just ground of accusation against Mr. Tracy, and have been advised by far more eminent counsel than himself, that his course would not be sustained if submitted to the Bar. I do not wish to press it, because the Committee themselves—or, at least, a few of them—are men of too much dignity of character and moral integrity to be tossed up and down like a ball on a fountain, by the gushing leakages of Mr. Tracy and Mr. Hill. The Committee themselves have a grave case on their hands, and they are men wise enough to acknowledge its gravity ; but the Committee's counsel are full of tricks and stratagems to belittle it, to distort it, and to play upon the public with it.

So far as the Committee themselves are concerned—I mean the six men who compose it—they exhibit a sad and grieved willingness to listen to the truth. The substance of the examination up to the present time, so far as I am concerned, is briefly this : General Tracy asked me if I committed adultery. I asked General Tracy if he committed adultery. But neither General Tracy, nor Mr. Hill, nor anybody in the Committee has yet asked me whether Mr. Beecher committed adultery.

Reporter—These reports, then, seem to misrepresent you ?

Mr. Tilton—Yes, but do not misunderstand me. There are certain gentlemen on this Committee who would not willingly misrepresent any one ; but the counsel are playing a mad frolic with the facts, and will in the end be the two worst beaten attorneys who ever conducted a case.

Reporter—You think, then, that they have made blunders ?

Mr. Tilton—Yes ; and they have made one hideous blunder.

Reporter—What is it ?

Mr. Tilton—They have diverted their examination from the facts at issue into an inquiry into the names and characters of my female acquaintance—particularly those who, as writers or speakers on various reforms, have attained eminence in public life. The animus of this inquiry was obvious ; its design was to associate me with the extreme and radical sentiment against which the conservative class in the community are arrayed in large majority. I, myself, did not object to this inquiry, though I, myself, would not have begun any such line of policy in this case. General Tracy's supreme blunder has been that, in instituting an inquiry into the standing of the ladies of my acquaintance he gives me the right to institute a counter-inquiry into the standing of the ladies of Mr. Beecher's acquaintance. I informed the Committee yesterday that I deprecated such a plan of battle, but that, if it was forced upon me by the Committee's counsel, I could draw a sword with two edges to their one. If this new aspect, which General Tracy flings upon the case like a shadow, is to characterize the remainder of the controversy, it will be the better for General Tracy's chief client that he had never been born.

Reporter—I perceive that Mr. Tracy questioned you concerning your acquaintance with Mrs. Woodhull ?

Mr. Tilton—Yes ; but Mr. Tracy was careful not to elicit the fact that Mr. Beecher's apology. addressed to me through Mr. Moulton, was written half a year before I ever saw the face of Mrs. Woodhull. He was careful, also, not to elicit the fact that Mr. Beecher himself had had private interviews with Mrs. Woodhull, and that that lady had taken far more pains to associate himself with him and he with her than ever I had done.

Reporter—In what other respects have reports of your examination misrepresented you ?

Mr. Tilton—Well, on the day after I presented my sworn statement, I met the committee and held an interview with them, which was described in the next day's journals as a pitiful spectacle—my having broken down under cross-examination. The truth is, there was no cross-examination whatever on that day by the counsel, and nothing but a kindly interchange of talk between the committee and myself. I have my faults, and many of them, but I have never used the sentimental, declamatory, and ungrammatical English which Gen. Tracy and Mr. Hill have emitted to their reportorial friends as coming from me. The report which I am criticising, says that I admitted that I was the author of the Woodhull scandal—which was a falsehood. Have you a knife in your pocket ?

Reporter—Yes.

Mr. Tilton—Please cut out the following extract.

The reporter then took his penknife, and cut out the following paragraphs :

The following question was put to Tilton by Mr. Tracy :

Mr. Tilton, have you any evidence of Mr. Beecher's adultery, except what you say your wife told you ?

Tilton—I have none whatever.

I wish you would do me the favor to say through the columns of the *Argus*, that though I have hitherto declined being interviewed concerning my appearance before the Committee, and having steadfastly remained silent concerning the proceedings in the Committee, yet the above report, coming as it does from the Committee's counsel, is an absolute fabrication. I told the Committee distinctly that

Mr. Beecher had confessed his adultery to me ; that he had confessed it to Mr. Moulton; that he had confessed it to other persons whom I named, and, furthermore, I gave the names of several persons who for the last four years have been perfectly well aware that Mr. Moulton's entire connection with this case from beginning to end, has been based on the one and only corner-stone of Mr. Beecher's criminality. I ask that all these persons be produced before the Committee. I ask, furthermore, for the privilege of being present to cross-examine Mr. Beecher and the other witnesses. I still further suggested that the case had come to be of such magnitude that it would be better for the Committee to dismiss this informal examination in which no one but myself had thus far spoken under oath, and adjourn to meet in court. I expressed a willingness to be sued for libel, or to be put in any other way before a tribunal which could compel witnesses to testify under oath, and which could punish perjury with the State Prison. If this case, with all the facts which lie behind it, revealed and unrevealed, were now before a Criminal Court instead of a voluntary committee, and if Mr. Beecher's printed statement had been made under oath, subject to cross-questioning and overthrow, he would indeed be compelled to "step down and out." I feel at liberty to speak freely, because Mr. Beecher's counsel have falsified me to the world, and I have no recourse but to smite them in the face.

MR. TILTON'S LETTER TO A " COMPLAINING FRIEND."

In December, 1872, Mr. Tilton wrote the following letter :

No. 174 LIVINGSTON STREET,
BROOKLYN, December 27, 1872.

My Complaining Friend :

Thanks for your good letter of bad advice. You say, " How easy to give the lie to the wicked story and thus end it forever !" But stop and consider. The story is a whole library of statements—a hundred or more—and it would be strange if some of them were not correct, though I doubt if any are. To give a general denial to such an encyclopædia of assertions would be as vague and irrelevant as to take up the *Police Gazette*, with its twenty-four pages of illustrations, and say, "This is a lie." So extensive a libel requires, if answered at all, a special denial of its several parts ; and, furthermore, it requires, in this particular case, not only a denial of things misstated, but a truthful explanation of the things that remain unstated and in mystery. In other words, the false story, if met at all, should be confronted and confounded by the true one. Now, my friend, you urge me to speak ; but when the truth is a sword, God's mercy sometimes commands it sheathed. If you think I do not burn to defend my wife and little ones, you know not the fiery spirit within me. But my wife's heart is more a fountain of charity, and quenches all resentments. She says, "Let there be no suffering, save to ourselves alone," and forbids a vindication to the injury of others. From the beginning, she has stood with her hand on my lips, saying, "Hush !" So, when you prompt me to speak for her, you countervail her more Christian mandate of silence. Moreover, after all, the chief victim of the public displeasure is myself alone, and, so long as this is happily the case, I shall try with patience to keep my answer within my own breast, lest it shoot forth like a thunderbolt through other hearts.

Yours, truly,

THEODORE TILTON.

PLYMOUTH CHURCH, ORANGE STREET, BROOKLYN.

REV. HENRY WARD BEECHER.

Mr. Beecher, who stands charged before the bar of public opinion with the seduction of his friend's wife and, by implication, with numerous prevarications, was born at Litchfield, Ct., June 24, 1813. He is now, consequently, in the sixty-first year of his age. Mr. Beecher belongs to a very remarkable family—perhaps, excepting the Adamses, the most remarkable family in our annals. He is a son of Lyman Beecher, who carried for years all New England's orthodoxy in his hand, and he is the brother of Mrs. Harriet Beecher Stowe, whose literary achievements need not be particularized. And yet, though Henry and Harriet are the best known of the large family, all of the children possessed, and possess, rare abilities. They had all very original ways of thinking on many subjects, and rarely lacked the courage to express their thoughts. It is sad to think that this family, unlike the Adamses, will die out with the second generation.

Having completed his studies at Amherst College in 1834, Henry Ward Beecher became a preacher. He went "West," and was pastor of a church in Indianapolis, Ind., from 1839 to 1847, when the call of a small congregation in Brooklyn reached him. He accepted the call, and for more than a quarter of a century he has labored very successfully to build up Plymouth Church. With the true instinct of the man of genius, Mr. Beecher said that there were enough churches founded upon hard and fast dogmas. He determined that the creed of his church should be sufficiently elastic to meet the wants of the cultured middle classes. He perceived early that latitudinarianism was the tendency of the day in theology, as liberty was in politics, and that both grew out of the same root, the doctrine of extreme individualism. Though Plymouth Church has always been open—at least, until these latter days—for the advocacy of "reform" and the cause of the oppressed, as in the days of slavery, though it re-echoed to shouts of "bleeding Kansas," and stepped rather boldly to the tune of "John Brown's body," it has never been in any strict sense a church of the poor. A middle-class gospel was preached there, and the middle classes—shrewd business men, subtle lawyers, "able editors," and the like, composed, and compose, its membership. It has been a great success, because Mr. Beecher was the greatest and most famous preacher in America, and one of the great pulpit orators of the world; but, if Mr. Beecher should "step down and out," Plymouth Church would suffer greatly. Beecher made it; it is the child of his genius, and not an unworthy child either. Mr. Beecher married early in life, and by his wife, who still lives, he has had a number of children, most of whom are grown to manhood and womanhood.

When Mr. Beecher came to Brooklyn, he was poor and unknown. With fame has come money. His original salary as pastor of Plymouth Church was small. It is now $25,000 per annum. He lectures during a part of the year. He obtains in this way $10,000 per annum, so it is said ; and when it is remembered the audiences he can command, the sum does not seem extravagant. Exactly what he receives for editing the *Christian Union*, and for the copyright of the books published by J. B. Ford & Co., is not definitely known, but it is stated to be $25,000 per annum. His current literary work outside of all this is worth about $5,000 more. Taken all together, it would seem that Mr. Beecher has an income from his literary, platform and pulpit work of over $60,000 per annum. If this be so, he can afford to live comfortably, and lay by " a little " for a rainy day. Besides his house in Brooklyn, Mr. Beecher has a fine farm at Peekskill, on the Hudson, where he spends considerable of his time.

Though Mr. Beecher has written books which have had a large sale—his novel, "Norwood," and the first volume of his "Life of Christ," for instance—it is as an orator that he will be remembered. To none of the great orators of ancient or modern times was an audience more necessary than to Beecher. He lacks the imagination to create an ideal audience, and hence his books are devoid of that healthy glow which irradiates the sermons and lectures. That he is a master of the choice of words, and that he can transfer them to paper as well as he could deliver them from the pulpit or the rostrum, is clearly shown in the sad letters to Tilton. But this apparent exception but proves the rule, as the audience was there, and, though small, was very earnest. Mr. Beecher's great success may be attributed to his extraordinary common sense. Destitute of the imagination to conceive the future as if present, he is liable, in dealing with coming events, to do things that will have to be undone. But, in dealing with present emergencies, his tact is surprising, and his success is of course commensurate with it. Mr. Beecher's success in politics has not been great, though on several occasions he has intervened in that field ; most notably in 1864, when the opposition elements in the Republican Party endeavored to run Gen. Fremont as a candidate for the presidency, on a thoroughly anti-slavery platform. One reason, doubtless, why Mr. Beecher—whose words had a modifying effect in his party—has had little influence in its councils, was that he is not a party man. His early dislike of theological dogmas has gone with him into the political camp. Even for a purpose, he finds it difficult, if not impossible, to accept the utterances of the party mouth-pieces.

In presence, Mr. Beecher is imposing. In manners, he is affable and kind. He is beloved by his congregation as few men ever were beloved—a fact that speaks volumes in his favor, for a man is not worshipped by those around him unless he deserves it. In the pulpit or on the platform, his address is very easy, and his flow of words smooth, though at times he expresses his naturally strong feelings in more forcible language than some critics think proper.

The accompanying portrait is from a recent photograph by Warren, of Boston.

THE COMMITTEE OF INVESTIGATION.

On Thursday, June 25th, Mr. Tilton's letter to Dr. Bacon was published. On the following Saturday Mr. Beecher addressed the following note to the persons named therein :

BROOKLYN, June 27, 1874.

GENTLEMEN : In the present state of the public feeling, I owe it to my friends and to the Church and Society over which I am pastor, to have some proper investigation made of the rumors, insinuations, or charges made respecting my conduct, as compromised by the late publication made by Mr. Tilton.

I have thought that both the Church and Society should be represented, and I take the liberty of asking the following gentlemen to serve in this inquiry, and to do that which truth and justice may require. I beg that each of the gentlemen named will consider this letter as if it had been separately and personally sent to him, namely : From the Church—Henry W. Sage, Augustus Storrs, Henry M. Cleveland. From the Society—Horace B. Claflin, John Winslow, S. V. White. I desire you, when you have satisfied yourselves by an impartial and thorough examination of all sources of evidence, to communicate to the Examining Committee, or to the Church, such action as may then seem to you right and wise.

HENRY WARD BEECHER.

The men who compose this Committee are very well known in Brooklyn, and two of them at least are favorably known all over the country. We append short sketches of their lives.

HENRY W. SAGE, the Chairman, is a Deacon of the Church and a Trustee of the Society. As a business man and a citizen he is widely known. He is an extensive dealer in lumber; a man of unbending integrity and recognized business sagacity. His liberality is known by his acts, he having given $10,000 to found the "Lyman Beecher Lectureship on Preaching" in Yale College, $300,000 to found the "Sage College for Women" in Cornell University, and $40,000 toward the building of a church in Ithaca, N. Y., his former home.

AUGUSTUS STORRS, of the commission house of Storrs Brothers, is a man known and respected in Brooklyn and in business circles in New York. He is a member of the Plymouth Church Board of Trustees, Treasurer of the Society; a man of ample means, and kind, charitable disposition and clear sens.

HENRY M. CLEVELAND was originally a Connecticut man, and all intelligent people of that State will remember his eminent services a few years since on the State Board of Education. He has been a member of Plymouth Church some fourteen years, is a member of the Examining Committee, and is known as a keen-sighted, genial, honorable man. In business, he is a member of the large paper house of H. C. Hulbert & Co., of New York.

HORACE B. CLAFLIN, of New York, one of the Trustees of the Society (and, with the exception of its President, James Freeland, the oldest member of that Board—in service, not in years), has always been known as one of the foremost men in the affairs of the Society, and as a business man, ranks as one of the largest dry goods dealers in the world—a man whose uniform courtesy, generosity, integrity, and ability are facts of public knowledge.

JOHN WINSLOW is the District Attorney for Kings County, appointed by Gov. Dix, and is a member of the law firm of Winslow & Van Cott, in Brooklyn. He is a sound lawyer, and a respected citizen. His partner, Judge Van Cott, is a leading member of the Church of the Pilgrims (Dr. Storrs), and was on the Special Committee calling the late Congregational Council.

S. V. WHITE, the Church Treasurer, is prominently active in all the Plymouth Church and Sabbath School work. He is a well-known banker and broker in New York, a man of high reputation for ability and success.

On the seventh of July Mr. Beecher addressed a letter to the Examining Committee of this Church, telling its members of his action in naming this Committee, and asking their approval. It was unanimously given, and Mr. Beecher's action in this regard fully endorsed. The meetings of this Committee have been held for the most part at the residence of Mr. Augustus Storrs, in Monroe Place, Brooklyn.

BEECHER'S DENIAL.

Mr. Tilton read his sworn statement to the Investigating Committee on Monday evening, July 20. On Tuesday afternoon it appeared in the Brooklyn *Argus*. On the same night Mr. Beecher wrote the following general denial of Tilton's statement as regards his own conduct and defence of Mrs. Tilton from her husband's assaults. This denial and defence reads as follows:

I do not propose at this time a detailed examination of the remarkable statement of Mr. Theodore Tilton, made before the Committee of Investigation, and which appeared in the Brooklyn *Argus* of July 21, 1874. I recognize the many reasons which make it of transcendent importance to myself, the Church, and the cause of public morality, that I shall give a full answer to the charges against me. But having requested the Committee of Investigation to search this matter to the bottom, it is to them that I must look for my vindication.

But I cannot delay for an hour to defend the reputation of Mrs. Elizabeth R. Tilton, upon whose name, in connection with mine, her husband has attempted to pour shame.

One less deserving of such disgrace I never knew. From childhood she has been under my eye, and since reaching womanhood she has had my sincere admiration and affection. I cherish for her a pure feeling, such as a gentleman might honorably offer to a Christian woman, and which she might receive and reciprocate without moral scruple. I reject with indignation every imputation which reflects upon her honor or my own.

My regard for Mrs. Tilton was perfectly well known to her family. When serious difficulties sprang up in her household it was to my wife that she resorted for counsel; and both of us, acting from sympathy, and, as it subsequently appeared, without full knowledge, gave unadvised counsel which tended to harm.

I have no doubt that Mr. Tilton found that his wife's confidence and reliance on my judgment had greatly increased, while his influence had diminished, in consequence of a marked change in his religious and social views which were taking place during those years. Her mind was greatly exercised lest her children should be harmed by views which she deemed vitally false and dangerous.

I was suddenly and rudely aroused to the reality of impending danger by the disclosure of domestic distress, of sickness, perhaps unto death, of the likelihood of separation and the scattering of a family, every member of which I had tenderly loved. The effect upon me of the discovery of the state of Mr. Tilton's feelings and the condition of his family surpassed in sorrow and excitement anything that I had ever experienced in my life. That my presence, influence, and counsel, had brought to a beloved family sorrow and alienation gave, in my then state of mind, a poignancy to my suffering which I hope no other man may feel.

Even to be suspected of having offered, under the privileges of a peculiarly sacred relation, an indecorum to a wife and mother could not but deeply wound any one who is sensitive to the honor of womanhood.

There were peculiar reasons for alarm in this case on other grounds, inasmuch as I was then subject to certain malignant rumors, and a flagrant outbreak in this family would bring upon them an added injury, derived from these shameless falsehoods.

Believing at the time that my presence and counsels had tended, however unconsciously, to produce a social catastrophe, represented as imminent, I gave expression to my feelings in an interview with a mutual friend, not in cold and cautious self-defending words, but eagerly taking blame upon myself, and pouring out my heart to my friend in the strongest language, overburdened with the exaggerations of impassioned sorrow. Had I been the evil man Mr. Tilton now represents I should have been calmer and more prudent. It was my horror of the evil imputed that filled me with morbid intensity at the very shadow of it.

Not only was my friend affected generously, but he assured me that such expressions, if conveyed to Mr. Tilton, would soothe wounded feeling, allay anger and heal the whole trouble. He took down sentences and fragments of what I had been saying, to use them as a mediator. A full statement of the circumstances under which this memorandum was made I shall give to the Investigating Committee.

That these apologies were more than ample to meet the facts of the case is evident, in that they were accepted, that our intercourse resumed its friendliness, that Mr. Tilton subsequently ratified it in writing and that he has continued for four years and until within two weeks to live with his wife.

Is it conceivable, if the original charge had been what is now alleged, that he would have condoned the offence, not only with the mother of his children, but with him whom he believed to have wronged them? The absurdity as well as the falsity of this story is apparent, when it is considered that Mr. Tilton now alleges that he carried this guilty secret of his wife's infidelity for six months locked up in his own breast, and that then he divulged it to me only that there might be a reconciliation with me! Mr. Tilton has since, in every form of language, and to a multitude of witnesses, orally, in written statements, and in printed documents, declared his faith in his wife's purity.

After the reconciliation of Mr. Tilton with me every consideration of propriety and honor demanded that the family trouble should be kept in that seclusion which domestic affairs have a right to claim as a sanctuary, and to that seclusion it was determined that it should be confined.

Every line and word of my private and confidential letters which have been published is in harmony with the statements which I now make. My published correspondence on this subject comprises but two elements—the expression of my grief and that of my desire to shield the honor of a pure and innocent woman.

I do not purpose to analyze and contest at this time the extraordinary paper of Mr. Tilton; but there are two allegations which I cannot permit to pass without special notice. They refer to the only two incidents which Mr. Tilton pretends to have witnessed personally—the one an alleged scene in my house while looking over engravings, and the other a chamber scene in his own house. His statements concerning these are absolutely false. Nothing of the kind ever occurred nor any semblance of any such things. They are now brought to my notice for the first time.

To every statement which connects me dishonorably with Mrs. Elizabeth R. Tilton? or which in any wise would impugn the honor and purity of this beloved Christian woman, I give the most explicit, comprehensive, and solemn denial.   HENRY WARD BEECHER.

BROOKLYN, July 22, 1874.

BEECHER'S DENIAL OF THE WOODHULL STORY.

The following is the text of Mr. Beecher's denial of the story of his alleged immorality, when published in November, 1872, by Mrs. Woodhull: .

"To the Editor of the Brooklyn Eagle:

"SIR—In a long and active life in Brooklyn, it has rarely happened that the *Eagle* and myself have been in accord on questions of common concern to our fellow-citizens. I am for this reason compelled to acknowledge the unsolicited confidence and regard of which the columns of the *Eagle* of late bear testimony. I have just returned to the city to learn that application has been made to Mrs. Victoria Woodhull for letters of mine supposed to contain information respecting certain infamous stories against me. I have no objection to have the *Eagle* state, in any way it deems fit, that Mrs. Woodhull, or any other person or persons, who may have letters of mine in their possession, have my cordial consent to publish them. In this connection, and at this time, I will only add, that the stories and rumors which have, for some time past, been circulated about me are untrue, and I stamp them in general, and in particular, as utterly untrue.

         "Respectfully,   HENRY WARD BEECHER."

MRS. ELIZABETH R. TILTON.

MRS. ELIZABETH R. TILTON.

Mrs. Elizabeth R. Tilton, whose name has become unfortunately conspicuous in connection with the great Brooklyn scandal, is a lady of about forty years of age. She is under medium height, with black hair and eyes, a face that is interesting, though not beautiful, with an expression that indicates unusual sensibility and sentimentality rather than intellectual force or refinement. Her appearance is modest, and her air peculiarly sincere and confiding. Her manners are easy and natural, with a simple grace which is more pleasing than what passes for elegance in polite society. Her prevailing mood is profoundly serious, lit up with occasional gleams of joy, and sometimes breaking into a beautiful playfulness. At times, when her feelings are pleasantly excited, and her face glows with expression, she appears really handsome; at other times, when depressed, or wearied, or unexcited, her eye is lustreless, and her face is dull and unattractive. She is a good house-keeper, and an excellent mother, devotedly fond of her children, and doing more for them, and spending more time in reading to them and talking with them than most mothers. Her tastes and habits are domestic, sentimental, and religious, rather than æsthetic or literary; her reading has not been extensive, and her favorite pictures are valuable for their sentiment rather than artistic excellence or imaginative power. She has had seven children, four of whom are living. The eldest is a daughter of more than ordinary maturity of mind and force of character. She resembles her father much more than the other children—so much that she would be recognized as his daughter by those who are familiar with his features. The two youngest children are boys. Mrs. Tilton's former home, on Livingston street, was once peculiarly attractive and charming by affection that filled its rooms with a climate of summer and a fragrance as of blooming roses; it was tastefully furnished, graced with exquisite pictures, made poetic by the disposition and arrangement of its contents, and the ideal element visible and palpable in every apartment. It seemed to realize the ideal of home.

Elizabeth Richards was a New York girl, but early in her life her mother, then a widow, removed to Brooklyn. Elizabeth, or Lizzie, as she was then called, after attending in succession several private schools, was sent, to complete her education, to the Packer Institute. She was as *good* a girl as she is a woman. In deportment, her "marks" were nearly always higher than those of any of her classmates. Her scholarship, too, was of the highest grade; and the oldest and most advanced girls in her class never thought it beneath them to seek aid in the performance of their tasks from little Lizzie Richards. She was a strangely earnest little brunette, that inspired the kindest regards in her teachers, and a kind of awe in her schoolmates. She graduated at the age of eighteen, and at once came to the aid of her mother, who was then keeping a boarding house on Livingston street, a little below the pleasant frame cottage where she so lately lived, with the same energy and self-devotion that she had displayed in conquering her school tasks. It was here that she met Mr. Tilton. He was a *protegé* of Mr. Beecher, and hence came to her with the best of earthly recommendations. Mr. Beecher had known her from a child. She had sat upon his knee; and when she at last became acquainted with the tall, handsome, enthusiastic young writer, who carried his indorsement, she was not disinclined to receive his attentions. He became a boarder at her mother's house. When she was twenty-two years old they were married. This was in 1855. Her life now

MRS. ELIZABETH R. TILTON.

MRS. ELIZABETH R. TILTON.

Mrs. Elizabeth R. Tilton, whose name has become unfortunately conspicuous in connection with the great Brooklyn scandal, is a lady of about forty years of age. She is under medium height, with black hair and eyes, a face that is interesting, though not beautiful, with an expression that indicates unusual sensibility and sentimentality rather than intellectual force or refinement. Her appearance is modest, and her air peculiarly sincere and confiding. Her manners are easy and natural, with a simple grace which is more pleasing than what passes for elegance in polite society. Her prevailing mood is profoundly serious, lit up with occasional gleams of joy, and sometimes breaking into a beautiful playfulness. At times, when her feelings are pleasantly excited, and her face glows with expression, she appears really handsome; at other times, when depressed, or wearied, or unexcited, her eye is lustreless, and her face is dull and unattractive. She is a good house-keeper, and an excellent mother, devotedly fond of her children, and doing more for them, and spending more time in reading to them and talking with them than most mothers. Her tastes and habits are domestic, sentimental, and religious, rather than æsthetic or literary ; her reading has not been extensive, and her favorite pictures are valuable for their sentiment rather than artistic excellence or imaginative power. She has had seven children, four of whom are living. The eldest is a daughter of more than ordinary maturity of mind and force of character. She resembles her father much more than the other children—so much that she would be recognized as his daughter by those who are familiar with his features. The two youngest children are boys. Mrs. Tilton's former home, on Livingston street, was once peculiarly attractive and charming by affection that filled its rooms with a climate of summer and a fragrance as of blooming roses ; it was tastefully furnished, graced with exquisite pictures, made poetic by the disposition and arrangement of its contents, and the ideal element visible and palpable in every apartment. It seemed to realize the ideal of home.

Elizabeth Richards was a New York girl, but early in her life her mother, then a widow, removed to Brooklyn. Elizabeth, or Lizzie, as she was then called, after attending in succession several private schools, was sent, to complete her education, to the Packer Institute. She was as *good* a girl as she is a woman. In deportment, her "marks" were nearly always higher than those of any of her classmates. Her scholarship, too, was of the highest grade ; and the oldest and most advanced girls in her class never thought it beneath them to seek aid in the performance of their tasks from little Lizzie Richards. She was a strangely earnest little brunette, that inspired the kindest regards in her teachers, and a kind of awe in her schoolmates. She graduated at the age of eighteen, and at once came to the aid of her mother, who was then keeping a boarding house on Livingston street, a little below the pleasant frame cottage where she so lately lived, with the same energy and self-devotion that she had displayed in conquering her school tasks. It was here that she met Mr. Tilton. He was a *protegé* of Mr. Beecher, and hence came to her with the best of earthly recommendations. Mr. Beecher had known her from a child. She had sat upon his knee ; and when she at last became acquainted with the tall, handsome, enthusiastic young writer, who carried his indorsement, she was not disinclined to receive his attentions. He became a boarder at her mother's house. When she was twenty-two years old they were married. This was in 1855. Her life now became wholly domestic. A talent for writing, which she displayed in early youth, remained uncultivated.

Of Mrs. Tilton's married life it is obviously indelicate and unbecoming to say much. She was naturally religious, and united with the church when young, and had a class in the Sunday-school. She was attached to all persons of a religious cast of mind, and particularly friendly to her pastor, to whom she seems to have gone for counsel, and on whom she leaned perhaps more than was well for either. The last evidence of her religious sincerity is furnished by her husband's long defence of her, as well as his emphatic statements before the committee. If she has sinned, he contends that, it was through the blinding of her conscience and the misleading of her mind, and he acquits her of guilt while he accuses her of crime. "I have taken pains to say that she was a devoted Christian woman," said Mr. Tilton on examination; a tender, delicate, kindly Christian woman. Hers is one of the white souls."

" There are a great many women who look upon a man with a sense of worship; Elizabeth never did that; Elizabeth is the peer of any man; at the same time she reverences; it was not vanity—it was reverence; she never regarded Mr. Beecher as a silly woman regards him; she was not a silly woman taken captive; she was a wise good woman taken captive. Elizabeth was in a sort of vaporous-like cloud. She was between light and dark. She could not see that it was wrong. She maintained to her mother in my presence that she had not done wrong; she cannot bear to do wrong; a sense of having done wrong is enough to crush her; she naturally seeks for her own peace a conscientious verdict; she never would have had these relations if she had supposed at the time that they were wrong; Elizabeth never does anything that at the time seems wrong; for such a large moral nature, there is a lack of a certain balance and equipoise; she has not a will that guides and restrains; but Elizabeth never does at any time that which does not have the stamp of her conscience at the time upon it. I think she certainly spends hours on her knees some days; I don't suppose a day ever passes over Elizabeth that the sun, if he could peep through the windows, would not see her on her knees."

Testimony like this from an accusing husband invests the character of the wife with peculiar interest, if not with mystery. It is hard for a majority of people to comprehend such perplexity. But it is not difficult to see that such a woman as he has described could hardly enjoy his eccentricities of belief, his intimate relations with reformers of all kinds, his severe criticisms of the church she regarded as so sacred She naturally recoiled from much that he loved, and wanted to hide her face from the pictures he hung on the wall. His friends she looked upon as the foes of religion, and the more firmly he set his face towards freedom the more resolutely she hid hers in the tradition of her childhood. He says: "She would not let the children have playthings on Sunday. John G. Whittier came to our house one Sunday night, and Mr. Greeley, and met Mr. Johnson; and it almost broke Elizabeth's heart to think that the best man in New England, whom she reverenced, should have appointed Sunday night; she never received visitors on Sunday." His change of religious views was a great source of tears and anguish to her; she said to me once that denying the divinity of Christ nullified our marriage almost; and I think next to the sorrow of this scandal it has caused that woman to sorrow more than anything else; she has suffered because I cannot look upon the Lord Jesus Christ as the Lord God. I think her breast has been wrenched with it.

About five years ago, William Page, late President of the National Academy of Design, painted two portraits, one of her and one of her husband. The latter hangs now in the back parlor of Mr. Francis D. Moulton's house. The former is in the parlor of the now famous cottage, No. 174 Livingston Street. It is just over the head of a sofa on which Mr. Tilton habitually reclines when he is tired.

Mrs. Tilton's maiden name was Elizabeth M. Richards. Her mother is now the wife of Judge Nathan D. Morse, a wealthy lawyer of Brooklyn. Her brother Joseph is engaged in the advertising business in New York. She, herself, has no money, and her husband has little, but it is highly improbable that either her stepfather, or her brother, would ever permit her to lack the ordinary comforts of a cultivated life. The house on Livingston Street, Mr. Tilton says, shall be hers and the children's.

MRS. TILTON'S REPLY.

On Thursday, July 23d, Mrs. Elizabeth R. Tilton wrote the following letter, which is intended as her part of the answer to her husband's sworn statement. It reads as follows:

To pick up anew the sorrows of the last ten years, the stings and pains I had daily schooled myself to bury and forgive, makes this imperative duty, as called forth by the malicious statement of my husband, the saddest act of my life. Beside, my thought of following the Master contradicts this act of my pen, and a sense of the perversion of my life-faith almost compels me now to stand aside, till God himself delivers.

Yet, I see in this wanton act an urgent call and privilege from which I shrink not. To reply in detail to the twenty-two articles of arraignment I shall not attempt at present, yet if called upon to testify to each and all of them I shall not hesitate to do so. Suffice it for my purpose now that I reply to one or more of the most glaring charges.

Touching the feigned sorrow of my husband's compulsory revelations, I solemnly avow that long before the Woodhull publication I knew him, by insinuation and direct statement, to have repeated to my very near relative and friend the substance of these accusations which shock the moral sense of the entire community this day. Many times, when hearing that certain persons had spoken ill of him, he has sent me to chide them for so doing; and then and there I learned he had been before me with his calumnies against myself, so that I was speechless.

The reiteration in his statement that he had "persistently striven to hide" these so-called facts is utterly false, as his hatred to Mr. Beecher has existed these many years and the determination to ruin Mr. Beecher has been the one aim of his life.

Again, the perfidy with which the holiest love a wife ever offered has been recklessly discovered in this publication reaches well-nigh to sacrilege; and, added to this, the endeavor, like the early scandal of Mrs. Woodhull, to make my own words condemn me, has no parallel.

Most conspicuously, my letter quoting the reading of "Griffith Gaunt." Had Mr. Tilton read the pure character of Catharine, he would have seen that I lifted myself beside it—as near as any human may affect an ideal. But it was her character, and not the incidents of fiction surrounding it, to which I referred. Hers was no sin of criminal act or thought.

A like "confession" with hers I had made to Mr. Tilton in telling of my love to my friend and pastor one year before. And I now add that, notwithstanding all misrepresentations and anguish of soul, I owe to my acquaintance and friendship with Mr. Beecher, as to no other human instrumentality, that encouragement in my mental life and that growth toward the Divine nature which enables me to walk daily in a lively hope of the life beyond.

The shameless charges in articles seven, eight, and nine, are fearfully false in each and every particular.

The letter referred to in Mr. Tilton's tenth paragraph was obtained from me by importunity, and by representations that it was necessary for him to use in his then pending difficulties with Mr. Bowen. I was then sick, nigh unto death, having suffered a miscarriage only four days before. I signed whatever he required, without knowing or understanding its import. The paper I have never seen, and do not know what statements it contained.

In charge eighteen, a letter of mine addressed to Mr. Francis Moulton, quoted to prove that I never desired a separation or was advised by Mr. or Mrs. Beecher to leave my husband. I reply, the letter was of Mr. Tilton's own concocting, which he induced me to copy and sign as my own—an act which, in my weakness and mistaken thought to help him, I have done too often during these unhappy years.

The implication that the harmony of the home was unbroken till Mr. Beecher entered it as a frequent guest and friend, is a lamentable satire upon the household where he himself, years before, laid the corner-stone of Free Love, and desecrated its altars up to the time of my departure; so that the atmosphere was not only godless, but impure for my children. And in this effort and throe of agony I would fain lift my daughters and all womanhood from the insidious and diabolical teachings of these latter days.

His frequent efforts to prove me insane, weak minded, insignificant, of mean presence, all rank in the category of heartlessness, selfishness, and falsehood, having its climax in his present endeavor to convince the world that I am or ever have been unable to distinguish between an innocent or a guilty love.

In summing up the whole matter I affirm myself before God to be innocent of the crimes laid upon me; that never have I been guilty of adultery with Henry Ward Beecher in thought or deed; nor has he ever offered to me an indecorous or improper proposal.

To the further charge, that I was led away from my home by Mr. Beecher's friends, and by the advice of a lawyer whom Mr. Beecher had sent to me, and who, in advance of my appearing before the Committee, arranged with me the questions and answers which are to constitute my testimony in

Mr. Beecher's behalf, I answer that this is again untrue, having never seen the lawyer until introduced to him, a few moments before the arrival of the Committee, by my step-father, Judge Morse; and in further reply I submit the following statement of my action before the Committee, and the separation from my husband :

The publication of Mr. Tilton's letter in answer to Dr. Bacon I had not known nor suspected, when on Wednesday evening he brought home the *Golden Age*, handing it to me to read. Looking down its columns I saw, well-nigh with blinding eyes, that he had put into execution the almost daily threat of his life—" that *he* lived to crush out Mr. Beecher ; that the God of battles was in *him ;* he had always been Mr. Beecher's superior, and all that lay in his path—wife, children, or reputation, if need be—should fall before this purpose."

I did not read it. I saw enough without reading. My spirit rose within me as never before.

"Theodore," I said, "tell me what means this quotation from Mr. Beecher ? Two years ago you came to me at midnight, saying : 'Elizabeth, *all* letters and papers concerning my difficulties with Mr. Beecher and Mr. Bowen are burned, destroyed : now don't *you* betray me, for I have nothing to defend myself with.—" ·

"Did you believe that ?" said he.

"I certainly did, implicitly," I said.

"Well, let me tell you they all *live ;* not one is destroyed."

If this was said to intimidate me it had quite the contrary effect. I had never been so fearless, nor seen so clearly before with whom I was dealing.

Coming to me a little later, he said, "I want you to read it ; you will find it a vindication of *yourself.* You have not stood before the community for five years as you do now."

Roused still further by the wickedness hid behind so false a mask, I replied, "Theodore, understand me, this is the last time you call me publicly to walk through this filth. My character needs no vindication at this late hour from *you.* There was a time, had you spoken out clearly, truthfully, and manfully for me, I had been grateful, but now I shall speak and act for myself. Know, also, that if in the future I see a scrap of paper referring to any human being, however remote, which it seems to me you might use or pervert to your own ends, I will destroy it."

"This means battle on your part, then ?" said he.

"Just so far," I replied.

I write this because these words of mine he has since used to my harm.

The next morning I went to my brother and told him that now I had decided to act in this matter : that I had been created by my husband as a nonentity from the beginning—a plaything, to be used or let alone at will ; that it had always seemed to me I was a party not a little concerned. I then showed him a card I had made for publication.

He respected the motive, but still advised silence on my part. I yielded to him thus far, as to appearing in the public prints ; but counselling with myself *and no other*, it occurred to me, that among the brethren of my own communion I might be heard.

Not knowing of any Church Committee, I asked the privilege of such an interview in the parlors of those who had always been our mutual friends. Mr. and Mrs. Ovington then learned for the first time that the Committee would meet that night, and advised me to see *those* gentlemen, as perhaps the goodliest persons I could select. This I accordingly did.

There, *alone*, I pleaded the cause of my husband and my children, the result being that their hearts were moved in sympathy for my family—a feeling their pastor had shared for years, and for which he was now suffering.

On going home, I found my husband reading in bed. I told him where I had been, and that I did not conceal anything from him, as his habit was from me. He asked who the gentlemen were ; said no more ; rose, dressed himself, and bade me good-by forever.

The midnight following, I was awakened by my husband standing by my bed. In a very tender, kind voice, he said he wished to see me. I rose instantly, followed him into his room, and, sitting on the bed-side, he drew me into his lap, said " he was proud of me, loved me ; that nothing ever gave him such real peace and satisfaction as to hear me well spoken of ; that, meeting one of the Committee, he had learned that he had been mistaken as to my motive in seeing the Committee, and had hastened to assure me that he had been thoroughly wretched since his rash treatment of me the night before," etc.

Then and there we covenanted sacredly our hearts and lives—I most utterly ; renewing my trust in the one human heart I loved.

The next day, how happy we were ! Theodore wrote a statement to present to the Committee when they should call upon him, to all of which I heartily acceded. This document, God knows, was a true history of this affair, completely vindicating my honor and the honor of my pastor. In the afternoon he left me to show it to his friends.

He returned home early in the evening, passing the happiest hours I had known for years, renewedly assuring me that there was no rest for him away from me. So in grateful love to the dear Father I slept. Oh, that the end had then come ! I would not then have received the cruel blow ' which made a woman mad outright."

The next morning he called upon our friends, Mr. and Mrs. Ovington, and there, with a shocking bravado, began a wicked tirade, adding with oath and violence the shameless slanders against Mr. Beecher, of which I now believe him to be the author.

The fearful scene I learned next day. In the afternoon he showed me his invitation from the Committee to meet them that evening. I did not then show my hurt, but carried it heavily within, but calmly without, all night, till early morning.

Reflection upon this scene at Mr. Ovington's convinced me that, notwithstanding my husband's recent professions to me, his former spirit was unchanged ; that his declarations of repentance and affection were only for the purpose of gaining my assistance to accomplish his ends in his warfare upon Mr. Beecher. In the light of these conclusions, my duty appeared plain.

I rose quietly, and, having dressed, roused him only to say, "Theodore, I will never take another step by your side. The end has indeed come !"

He followed me to Mrs. Ovington's to breakfast, saying I was unduly excited, and that he had been misrepresented perhaps, but leaving me determined as before.

How to account for the change which twenty-fours have been capable of working in his mind these many years past I leave for the eternities with their mysteries to reveal. That he is an unreliable and unsafe guide, whose idea of truth-loving is self-loving, it is my misfortune in this late, sad hour to discover.   ELIZABETH R. TILTON.

July 23, 1874.

FRANK MOULTON'S LAST EFFORT FOR COMPROMISE.

Mr. Tilton read Mr. Beecher's note appointing an "Investigating Committee" as a direct challenge to him to tell all he knew, and do his worst. Mr. Francis D. Moulton so regarded it also, it would seem. As the common friend of both the parties and the depositary of their confidential secrets, he appeared before the Committee on Monday, July 13th, and made one last appeal for compromise. The tone of this appeal shows that Moulton believed publicity hazardous if not ruinous. The Committee refused to act on his suggestion, and as a consequence Tilton's sworn statement was read to the Committee the following Monday evening. This is the only statement that Mr. Moulton has made, up to time of going to press. It reads as follows :

Gentlemen of the Committee :

I appear before you, at your invitation to make a statement which I have read to Mr. Tilton and Mr. Beecher, which both deem honorable, and in the fairness and propriety of which, so far as I am concerned, they both concur. The parties in this case are personal friends of mine, in whose behalf I have endeavored to act as the umpire and peacemaker for the last four years, with a conscientious regard for all the interests involved.

I regret for your sakes the responsibility imposed on me of appearing here to-night. If I say anything, I must speak the truth. I do not believe that the simple curiosity of the world at large, or even of this Committee, ought to be gratified through any recitation by me of the facts which are in my possession, necessarily in confidence, through my relations to the parties. The personal differences of which I am aware, as the chosen arbitrator, have once been settled honorably between the parties, and would never have been revived except on account of recent attacks, both in and out of Plymouth Church, made upon the character of Theodore Tilton, to which he thought a reply necessary. If the present issue is to be settled, it must be, in my opinion, by the parties themselves, either together or separately, before your Committee, each taking the responsibility of his own utterance. As I am fully conversant with the facts and evidences, I shall, as between these parties, if necessary, deem it my duty to state the truth, in order to final settlement, and that the world may be well informed before pronouncing its judgment with reference to either. I therefore suggest to you that the parties first be heard ; that if then you deem it necessary that I should appear before you, I will do so, to speak the truth, the whole truth, and nothing but the truth. I hold to-night, as I have held hitherto, the opinion that Mr. Beecher should frankly state that he had committed an offense against Mr. Tilton, for which it was necessary to apologize, and for which he did apologize in the language of the letter, part of which has been quoted ; that he should have stated frankly that he deemed it necessary for Mr. Tilton to have made the defense against Dr. Leonard Bacon which he did make, and that he (Mr. Beecher) should refuse to be a party to the re-opening of this painful subject. If he had made this statement, he would have stated no more than the truth, and it would have saved him and you the responsibility of a further inquiry. It is better now that the Committee should not report ; and, in place of a report, Mr. Beecher himself should make the statement which I have suggested ; or that if the committee does report, the report should be a recommendation to Mr. Beecher to make such a statement.

GEN. BUTLER ON THE SCANDAL.

The Daily Graphic of Saturday, July 25, contained the following interesting account of a conversation with Gen. Butler, on the great scandal.

General Benjamin F. Butler has recently been prominently mentioned in connection with the Beecher-Tilton scandal as having said that Mr. Tilton had a "case," and as having advised Mr. Beecher's counsel to present the presentation of the proofs to the investigating committee. This advice, it was asserted, was given after General Butler had made an examination of the letters and document upon which the charges are based. General Butler was visited this morning by a representative of *The Daily Graphic* at the Fifth Avenue Hotel. The visitor's card was received by Mr. Butler's private secretary at the door of parlor 1, who requested him, with two other visitors, to wait in the general hotel parlor, as Mr. Butler was engaged. The representative of *The Daily Graphic* had scarcely entered the parlor, however, before the secretary touched him upon the shoulder and said the General would receive him at once. General Butler was found in his apartment standing near the window.

"The public, General Butler, is interested in your connection with the Beecher-Tilton matter, and, as you know, several stories have been published associating your name with those of Mr. Moulton, Mr. Tilton, and General Tracy. I wish to know the plain truth."

"The simple fact is," was the reply, "that Frank Moulton is a warm personal friend of mine, and previously to the recent publications he laid the case before me, asking my advice: This was purely on the basis of personal friendship. I have in no sense of the word been retained in the case."

"When did this interview between you and Mr. Moulton take place?"

"It was just after the publication of the Bacon letter. I had had some knowledge of the circumstances before, and knew enough about the case to advise that it should be settled by all means without publicity. This was the one piece of advice that I gave in the matter, and that is what I hold to yet. I never had anything to do with the case. You may be sure that if I had it would never have been made public."

"But Mr. Tilton claims it was made public in an entirely accidental manner. How could you have prevented that?"

"I don't think the accident would have occurred [with an expressive smile] if I had had the case. But what I mean is that a compromise could have been brought about. Mr. Tilton made his complaint that he had been placed in a false light by Mr. Beecher's friends; that he had been represented as a dog. Now at this stage the trouble might have been avoided by a prompt disclaimer on Mr. Beecher's part of any such intention. The summation of the whole matter is," continued General Butler, "that it is a miserable exhibition to the world of a quarrel that ought, above all things, to have been kept concealed. I don't care who is right or who is wrong, this exposure will work harm. What right-minded man is there who will say there can possibly be a balance of good to the world from the publication by the parties to this trouble of all this repulsive combination of details. The thing to be advised in the case was to keep it hidden, and that advice I strongly pressed. Now, however, the explosion has come. The details will be read by all men. It will go into every quarter of the world, into every family, into every boarding-school, and it is hard to estimate the balance of evil that will result, no matter who is right or who is wrong. I wish [earnestly] the whole matter were sunk four thousand fathoms deep in the sea."

"Did you advise General Tracy to prevent a meeting of the investigating committee on Monday night?"

"General Tracy is smart enough, I think, to advise himself. I have had nothing to do with him."

"But it was said your suggestion was carried to him to prevent there being a quorum of the committee present.

"Yes; so the newspapers said. They also said that I was closeted all day yesterday with Frank Moulton, when my private secretary distinctly told all inquirers the facts in the case—that from twelve o'clock until half-past five I was engaged at this table with three lawyers, making a deposition in a certain railroad case, the circumstances of which they thought I knew something about. Besides that they reported that I dined with Theodore Tilton and Frank Moulton on Tuesday evening at

Delmonico's. Now, as to that, I wish it to be distinctly understood that it is nobody's business whom I dine with. No matter who they might have been, I certainly did no worse than our Saviour, who dined with publicans and sinners."

"May I ask you what Frank Moulton's course in this matter is likely to be?"

"That I cannot answer. It should be remembered that he occupies a very peculiar position. He was the friend of Mr. Beecher and also of Mr. Tilton. Both intrusted him with secrets. He has no right to betray either without his consent."

"Do you mean to say that Mr. Beecher, for example, could now close the lips of Mr. Moulton and prevent him from testifying before the committee?"

"Certainly. That point does not seem to have been thought of."

"But have not both parties made in reality a public call for all the evidence in the case?"

"Yes; but that would not prevent the sealing of Moulton's lips if either party chooses to do so. This public call for evidence, for instance, would not justify the lawyers in the case in telling to the committee all they had learned in confidence from the parties at war with each other."

"Have you talked with Mr. Moulton since you have been in New York this time?"

"Yes. He came to see me, and I talked with him as a friend, but I am not his counsel."

"Is it at all likely that you will be engaged in the case?"

"It is not. Of course, if I were asked to do so, I might take up this case the same as any other."

"Did you ever say that Theodore Tilton had a case?"

"No. After looking over the matter, as it was explained to me by Mr. Moulton, I thought, and probably said, that Mr. Tilton could make a strong presentation, and it was with this knowledge in mind that I advised that every effort be made to bury the matter as privately as possible."

"I see Mrs. Woodhull is in town. Do you suppose that she or any other person besides Mr. Moulton has any very valuable testimony to offer?"

"I don't know; I have not seen Mrs. Woodhull. When a case of this kind is once opened, there is no telling where it will stop. It never should have been opened. That was the fatal step. The remarkable thing about this whole affair [speaking slowly, and gesticulating with his right forefinger] was, that when the scandal was broached by Mrs. Woodhull long ago, nobody paid any attention to it; but now, when these men [throwing his hands upward and outward] repeat the story, it at once engages the attention of everybody connected with it, and a defence is at once entered into."

THE CASE IN THE COURTS.

THEODORE TILTON was arrested on Tuesday, July 24, on a charge of libel. The person through whose instrumentality the arrest was made was one William J. Gaynor, a lawyer, who claims that as a citizen of Brooklyn he has a right to cause this arrest in the interest of public morality, and in order that the full light of truth may be thrown on this now much mixed question. It having been ascertained that Mr. Frank Moulton would not make a statement before the Investigating Committee without the consent of all the parties concerned, the lawyer referred to conceived the idea of proceeding to a police court and obtaining a warrant for the arrest of Mr. Tilton, on a charge of libel, with the view of eliciting at a preliminary examination the sworn statements of all concerned. He accordingly went before Judge Riley, at three o'clock yesterday afternoon, and presented the following affidavits.

STATE OF NEW YORK, KINGS COUNTY, ss.—William J. Gaynor, of 38 First Place, being duly sworn, deposes and says that on the 20th day of July Theodore Tilton did falsely, maliciously, and scandalously frame, make, write, compose, and cause to be published in the Brooklyn *Daily Eagle*, published in the City of Brooklyn, in the said county, on the 20th day of July, 1874, a certain, false, scandalous and libellous writing, of, concerning and against Henry Ward Beecher, of the City of Brooklyn, in the said county, to the purport and effect following, to wit :—

"2. That for a period of about fifteen years, extending both before and after this marriage, an intimate friendship existed between Theodore Tilton and the Rev. Henry Ward Beecher, which friendship was cemented to such a degree that in consequence thereof the subsequent dishonoring by Mr. Beecher of his friend's wife was a crime of uncommon wrongfulness and perfidy.

"3. That about nine years ago the Rev. Henry Ward Beecher began, and thereafter continued, a friendship with Mrs. Elizabeth Tilton, for whose native delicacy and extreme religious sensibility he often expressed to her husband a high admiration ; visiting her from time to time for years until the year 1870, when, for reasons hereinafter stated, he ceased such visits, during which period, by many tokens and attentions, he won the affectionate love of Mrs. Tilton, whereby after long moral resistance by her, and after repeated assaults by him upon her mind with overmastering arguments, accomplished the possession of her person, maintaining with her thenceforward during the period hereinafter stated the relation called criminal intercourse, this relation being regarded by her during that period as not criminal or morally wrong, such had been the power of his arguments as a clergyman to satisfy her religious scruples against such violation of virtue and honor."

Wherefore deponent prays that the defendant may be apprehended and dealt with according to law.
Sworn to before me this 24th day of July, 1874, THOMAS M. RILEY,
Justice of the Peace of the City of Brooklyn.

A second affidavit is as follows :

STATE OF NEW YORK, KINGS COUNTY, ss.—William J. Gaynor, of No. 38 First Place, being duly sworn, deposes and says, that on the 20th of July, 1874, Theodore Tilton did falsely, maliciously, and scandalously frame, make, write, compose, and publish in the Brooklyn *Daily Eagle* and the Brooklyn *Daily Argus*, newspapers published in the city of Brooklyn, in the said county, on the 20th day of July, 1874, a certain false, scandalous, and libellous writing, of, concerning and against Henry Ward Beecher, of the city of Brooklyn, in the said county, to the purport and effect following, to wit :—

The warrant on which the arrest was made reads as follows :

STATE OF NEW YORK, KINGS COUNTY, ss.—W. J. Gaynor, of No. 38 First Place, deposes and says that on the 20th day of July, 1874, at the said city of Brooklyn, in the said county of Kings, Theodore Tilton did falsely, maliciously, and scandalously frame, make, write, compose, and publish in the Brooklyn *Daily Eagle*, a newspaper published in the city of Brooklyn, in said county, a certain false, scandalous, and libellous writing of, concerning and against Henry Ward Beecher, of the city of Brooklyn, in the said county, of the effect and purport that the said Henry Ward Beecher had confessed to him, the said Tilton, and to one Mr. Moulton, that the said Beecher had had criminal intercourse or adultery with one Elizabeth R. Tilton, all with intent to scandalize and disgrace said Henry Ward Beecher.

Whereupon deponent prays that defendant may be apprehended and dealt with according to law.
Sworn to before me this 28th day of July, 1874. THOMAS M. RILEY,
Justice of the Peace.

This warrant was also sworn to, and the two gentlemen left.

This document was intrusted to the hands of Deputy Sheriff Thomas Shaughnessy, who, without much ado, proceeded to Mr. Tilton's residence, where he arrived about four o'clock.

"Is Mr. Tilton at home?" asked Mr. Shaughnessy, who, being answered in the affirmative, stepped in, with his hat in his hand.

"I am Mr. Tilton," answered that gentleman, rising from the sofa and coming forward to receive his visitor.

"Well, sir," said the officer, "I have a warrant for your arrest. I belong to the Third District Court."

"What! a warrant for my arrest?" said Mr. Tilton, laughing.

"Yes, sir," remarked the officer of the law; "here it is," at the same time handing it to Mr. Tilton, who smiled as he read it over.

"And must I go with you now?" asked Mr. Tilton.

"The Judge is waiting for you," said the officer; whereupon Mr. Tilton asked him to wait until he wrote a note to a friend with whom he had intended to go to Coney Island, and having finished the note, turned around to some parties in the room, observing, "Now, gentlemen, will you accompany me to the jail?"

Mr. Tilton then put on his hat, and quitting the house in charge of the officer, proceeded to the Third District Court, Brooklyn.

It was now nearly five o'clock, and but few persons—not more than ten—were in the court when Mr. Tilton walked boldly toward the bench, upon which Justice Riley had already taken his seat. Mr. Tilton seemed to be in rather a pleasant frame of mind. He asked the Judge, smilingly, whether he wanted him, and the following conversation then ensued:

"Well, Mr. Tilton," observed the Judge, "there is a charge of libel against you," and the affidavits and warrants were therefore read in open Court, after which the Judge made the following inquiries:

"What do you say to that, Mr. Tilton?"

Mr. Tilton inquired whether it was possible for him to obtain copies of the documents, to which the Judge replied in the affirmative.

"Now, then, Mr. Tilton," asked the judge, "do you plead guilty?"

"Well," replied Mr. Tilton, "I am not well posted in legal matters; I will have to ask your opinion on the subject."

"I must ask you," said the judge, "whether you plead guilty or not guilty?"

"Everything is true," replied Mr. Tilton. "One of these statements was published without my knowledge. The other was published with my knowledge and consent."

"What do you plead, Mr. Tilton, guilty or not guilty?"

Mr. Tilton.—"Well, not guilty. Before you take that, I would ask if it makes any difference in regard to the case as to the way I plead?"

"If you plead not guilty," remarked the judge, "you are entitled to a judgment and a hearing."

"Not guilty, then," said Mr. Tilton, and, taking his hat, was about to walk away, thinking the preliminaries had been arranged.

"Mr. Tilton," exclaimed the Judge, "I will have to hold you in $2,500 bail."

"Oh," said Mr. Tilton, musingly, "bail—you want bail. Well, sir, I give you my word of honor I will be here to-morrow morning at ten o'clock with my bail."

"Very well, Mr. Tilton, you can go until to-morrow morning, when you will appear and give bail to the extent of $2,500."

"Very well, sir," said Mr. Tilton good-humoredly, and having mentioned the fact that he would employ counsel, entered a carriage with a friend and drove to Coney Island.

In conversation with a reporter, Mr. Tilton said that he had never heard of Mr. Gaynor before his arrest. The Plymouth Church leaders and the Investigating Committee were astonished at the arrest.

THE SCENE IN COURT ON WEDNESDAY, JULY 29

Long before ten o'clock on Wednesday morning, Justice Riley's court-room on Myrtle avenue and Adelphi street, Brooklyn, was crowded. The news that Theodore Tilton was to appear to answer the charge of libel against Henry Ward Beecher drew a crowd that threatened even to fill the sidewalks, half-way down to Willoughby avenue. Many women were present. Some were well-dressed, and some had evidently thrown on bonnets and shawls hastily to run in from neighboring houses. "Now the matter will be settled," was an expression frequently heard. "Will Mrs. Woodhull be there?" "Do you suppose he had himself arrested?" "What do you suppose Beecher is going to make out of this?" and a hundred other questions exhibited the conjectures of the throng, or their ignorance of the matter in hand.

Judge Thomas M. Riley was promptly on the bench. He called a number of minor cases with much judical energy and precision. At ten minutes past ten o'clock Theodore Tilton entered. He was preceded by ex-Judge Samuel D. Morris, his counsel. The crowd pressed against them. Judge Morris shouldered his way through, two court officers acting as advance guard. The crowd vainly attempted to fall back to get a fair view of Mr. Tilton. His head and flowing hair rose nearly a foot above the mean level of heads in the court-room. He looked self-possessed, but wore his almost habitual expression of heroic, long suffering. A pause was made just inside of the bar. Judge Riley never looked up. He was busy trying a case. The machinery of the law did not stop for an instant. Mr. Tilton paused to look for a seat. It was just behind the chair of William J. Gaynor, who obtained the warrant for his arrest.

The complainant, Mr. Gaynor, is a solemn-looking young man, with a literary cast in his countenance, and reddish whiskers and moustache. At this juncture he looked so very unconcerned and so very much as if he were unaware of Mr. Tilton's presence that his solemn face came to wear an air of positive melancholy. There was a moment of painful interest to the newspaper representatives and legal gentlemen inside the bar, and then Judge Morris exclaimed in a loud whisper:

"This way Mr. Tilton."

"This way" led through a narrow passage into a room directly in rear of the court. In this room Mr. Tilton sat with Judge Morris and a half dozen other gentlemen, who had pressed their way in, until after eleven o'clock. He discoursed only in brief replies, and was vigorously reticent in relation to the details of the scandal.

"Did you see Gaynor?" Mr. Tilton was asked.

"No; I don't know him. Is he here?"

"Yes; he is in the court-room. He says that he called on you during the existence of the present trouble as a representative of a certain newspaper."

"I suppose," said Mr. Tilton, "that I have been called upon by forty different newspaper representatives recently, and though I think I should know each one of them if I should meet him alone, yet I probably should not be able to pick each of them out in a throng of people."

"What motive could he have had, do you think, for making this complaint?"

"I do not know. I do not understand what right he had to do so. I can readily understand how Mr. Beecher, if he believes as he professes to, could swear to such a complaint, but how this man could have become possessed of facts sufficient to warrant him to do so is a mystery to me."

Judge Morris sat near Mr. Tilton, but spoke to him only once or twice during the whole time of waiting. He is a rather stern gentleman, with short-cropped black whiskers and moustache. When asked questions, he says he really doesn't know, in a chilling sort of a way.

At a quarter past eleven, Justice Riley came into the waiting-room. He had finished his morning's calendar. He addressed Judge Morris :

Justice Riley—I came in to suggest a discontinuance of this case. I do not know what grounds there are for pressing it, and I have no doubt that the complainant would consent to a discontinuance. Or, if this won't do, suppose you agree to an adjournment of the case until Monday. You can see the complainant and arrange the matter with him.

Judge Morris—We are placed in such a peculiar situation that it won't do for us to see (emphasizing the word) this complainant.

Justice Riley—Well, then I suggest that I talk with him. I think the case ought to be broached to the District Attorney.

Here Judge Morris went to the sofa which Mr. Tilton had been reclining on at full length (his favorite posture), and held a short conversation with him. Justice Riley retired for a minute, and when he returned, spoke in a low tone to Judge Morris. Then it was announced that the case would go on.

As soon as the last case on the calendar had been passed up, the Judge said : "Will Mr. Gaynor step inside?" Mr. Gaynor accordingly arose and walked into the Judge's parlor at the back of the bench. Immediately it was intimated that the case was to be heard privately, and there was a great rush of reporters and artists, and the little room was soon most inconveniently crowded and unbearably hot. It is impossible to say who suggested that the hearing should be private. But Mr. Gaynor very soon backed out of the room, and informed Judge Riley, who was still sitting on the bench, that he would decline to conduct the hearing in private. The Judge accordingly opened the door and said : "The complainant declines to agree to a private hearing of this case."

Then there was a rush of the reporters and artists again back to the court-room. As soon as order was restored, the Judge, addressing counsel for Mr. Tilton, said: Have you any suggestion to make?

Mr. Morris—Yes, sir, I have a suggestion to offer. I have spoken to the complainant here, asking him whether this complaint was made at the suggestion of the party alleged to have been libelled, and I am informed that he has made it on his own responsibility and entirely without the knowledge of the person alleged to have been libelled, or any friend of his. Now, your Honor is aware that complaints of this kind are usually and properly made by the person alleged to have been libelled, or by some friend of that person, with his knowledge and consent. It is not in harmony with the judicial procedure of this State that a complaint of this kind should be made by a stranger, without the knowledge of the party libelled or of the friends of the party ; and, while Mr. Tilton is ready and willing to meet any charge preferred against him at any time and in any place, when properly presented, I submit that the forms of law and judicial procedure should not be called into requisition for the mere purpose of gratifying idle curiosity or giving cheap cheap notoriety to any person. I therefore submit, in view of the status of this case—Mr. Tilton, be it understood, comes forward quite ready and willing to meet the charge—I submit whether, in view of the status of this case, the ends of justice would not be best served by its terminating here. If your honor is of a different opinion I move the adjournment of the case till Monday, and in the meantime I shall see the legal representative of the people of this county and take his view as to what should be done.

Judge Riley—I think myself it would be a good thing for the complainant to allow the case to discontinue here. I cannot tell what good end would be served by a hearing of the case before me. I haven't any idea what caused him to come and make the complaint here.

Mr. Gaynor—What the counsel has stated with regard to the propriety or right which I had to make the complaint against Mr. Tilton I think is entirely without foundation, and when he says that your Honor knows that my action is not in accordance with the judicial procedure of the State, and that I am acting unwarrantably, I reply that your Honor knows, and counsel knows, and every member of the community knows, that whenever a violation of the laws of the State is committed it is the option of any member of that community to make a complaint, and cause such violation of its laws to be punished. If this man has been guilty of libel, he has been guilty of a violation of the laws of the State, and he deserves punishment, and I have a right to come forward and bring him to justice. If he had committed murder it is my duty, it is the duty of every member of the community, to bring him to justice. If a man steals a horse it is my duty, it is the duty of every member of the community who is aware of the fact, to bring him to justice. If a man libels one of his fellow-citizens he violates the law the same as the murderer or the horse-thief, and it is my duty to endeavor to bring him to justice. It may be a little unusual; it may be more usual to bring such cases before a Grand Jury, where probably nothing at all would be done with the case. But I have a right to have him arrested on this charge, and it is his privilege if he choses to waive an examination and wait for a Grand Jury.

The speaker was greeted with a round of applause as he closed.

Mr. Morris—I would ask again whether the complainant represents the party alleged to have been libelled ; or whether, as I am informed, he has caused this warrant to be issued on his own responsibility.

Mr. Gaynor—I have come forward of my own free will, as a member of the community who is interested in the observance of the laws of the State, and I am here to see that the laws of the State are applied. I am in collusion with nobody. I have consulted nobody. I wish to ascertain whether the laws of the State have been violated.

Mr. Morris—I deny that any of the laws of the State have been violated, but that is not the suggestion which I have made to your Honor. I am very glad to see that the complainant is so anxious to see the laws of the State upheld. But it must be perfectly manifest to your Honor, and will be manifest to the public, that that is not the motive of this complainant. His motive is simply notoriety.

Judge Riley—Do not impute motives. That is improper. I think the case must be heard.

Mr. Morris—Then I ask that the case stand over till Monday, until I can consult with the legal representative of the people of this county.

Mr. Gaynor—I wish to have Mr. Beecher and all the other parties subpœnaed. I am willing to let the case rest till then.

Judge Riley—The case is adjourned until ten o'clock on Monday morning next.

MR. TILTON AND MRS. WOODHULL.

In 1871, Mr. Theodore Tilton published a biography of Mrs. Victoria Woodhull. According to the recent story, Mr. Tilton did this to disarm Mrs. Woodhull—to prevent her from publishing his family secret. According to the original story, he never wrote anything under such inspiration. It was printed in his own office, with the following title-page :

The Golden Age Tracts.—No. 3. Victoria C. Woodhull. A Biographical Sketch by Theodore Tilton.

"He that uttereth a slander is a fool."—Solomon, Prov. x. 18.

Published at the office of *The Golden Age*, 9 Spruce street, New York, 1871.

Entered according to Act of Congress, in the year 1871, by Theodore Tilton, in the Office of the Librarian of Congress at Washington.

MR. TILTON'S ACCOUNT OF MRS. WOODHULL.

The following is a literal reprint of the main portions of this tract :

I shall swiftly sketch the life of Victoria Claflin Woodhull, a young woman whose career has been as singular as any heroine's in a romance ; whose ability is of a rare and whose character of the rarest type ; whose personal sufferings are of themselves a whole drama of pathos ; whose name (through the malice of some and the ignorance of others) has caught a shadow in strange contrast with the whiteness of her life ; whose position, as a representative of her sex in the greatest reform of modern times, renders her an object of peculiar interest to her fellow-citizens, and whose character (inasmuch as I know her well) I can portray without color or tinge from any other partiality save that I hold her in uncommon respect.

In Homer, Ohio, in a small cottage, white-painted and high-peaked, with a porch running round it and a flower-garden in front, this daughter, the seventh of ten children of Roxana and Buckman Claflin, was born September 23, 1838. As this was the year when Queen Victoria was crowned, the new-born babe, though clad neither in.purple nor fine linen, but comfortably swaddled in respectable poverty, was immediately christened (though without chrism) as the Queen's namesake, her parents little dreaming that her daughter would one day aspire to a higher seat than the English throne. The Queen, with that early matronly predilection which her subsequent life did so much to illustrate, foresaw that many glad mothers, who were to bring babes into the world during that coronation year, would name them after the chief lady of the earth, and accordingly she ordained a gift to all her little namesakes of Anno Domini 1838. As Victoria Claflin was one of these, she has lately been urged to make a trip to Windsor Castle, to see the illustrious giver of these gifts, and to receive the special souvenir which the Queen's bounty is supposed to hold still in store for the Ohio babe that uttered its first cry as if to say, "Long Live the Queen !" Mrs. Woodhull, who is now a candidate for the Presidency of the United States, should defer this visit till after her election, when she will have a beautiful opportunity to invite her elder sister in sovereignty—the mother of our mother country--to visit her fairest daughter, the Republic of the West.

* *   I must now let out a secret. She acquired her studies, performed her work, and lived her life by the help (as she believes) of heavenly spirits. From her childhood till now (having reached her thirty-third year), her anticipation of the other world has been more vivid than her realization of this. She has entertained angels, and not unawares. These gracious guests have been her constant companions. They abide with her night and day. They dictate her life with daily revelation; and, like St. Paul, she is "not disobedient to the heavenly vision." She goes and comes at their behest. Her enterprises are not the coinage of her own brain, but of their divine invention. Her writings and speeches are the.products, not only of their indwelling in her soul, but of their absolute control of her brain and tongue. Like a Greek of the olden time, she does nothing without consulting her oracles. Never, as she avers, have they deceived her, nor ever will she neglect their decrees. One-third of human life is passed in sleep; and in her case a goodly fragment of this third is spent in trance. Seldom a day goes by but she enters into this fairy-land, or rather into this spirit-realm. In pleasant weather she has a habit of sitting on the roof of her stately mansion on Murray Hill, and there communing hour by hour with the spirits. She is a religious devotee—her simple theology being an absorbing faith in God and the angels.

Moreover, I may as well mention here as later, that every characteristic utterance which she gives to the world is dictated while under spirit-influence, and most often in a totally unconscious state. The words that fall from her lips are garnered by the swift pen of her husband, and published almost verbatim as she gets and gives them. To take an illustration, after her recent nomination to the Presidency by "The Victoria League," she sent to that committee a letter of superior dignity and moral weight. It was a composition which she had dictated while so outwardly oblivious to the dictation, that when she ended and awoke, she had no memory at all of what she had just done. The product of that strange and weird mood was a beautiful piece of English not unworthy of Macaulay; and to prove what I say, I adduce the following eloquent passage, which (I repeat) was published without change as it fell from her unconscious lips:

"I ought not to pass unnoticed," she says, "your courteous and graceful allusion to what you deem the favoring omen of my name. It is true that a Victoria rules the great rival nation opposite to us on the other shore of the Atlantic, and it might grace the amity just sealed between the two nations, and be a new security of peace, if a twin sisterhood of Victorias were to preside over the two nations. It is true, also, that in its mere etymology the name signifies Victory! and the victory for the right is what we are bent on securing. It is again true, also, that to some minds there is a consonant harmony between the idea and the word, so that its euphonious utterance seems to their imaginations to be itself a genius of success. However this may be, I have sometimes imagined that there is perhaps something providential and prophetic in the fact that my parents were prompted to confer on me a name which forbids the very thought of failure; and, as the great Napoleon believed the star of his destiny, you will at least excuse me, and charge it to the credulity of the woman, if I believe also in fatality of triumph as somehow inhering in my name."

HER SPIRIT VISITORS—DEMOSTHENES.

The chief among her spiritual visitants, and one who has been a majestic guardian to her from the earliest years of her remembrance, she describes as a matured man of stately figure, clad in a Greek tunic, solemn and graceful in his aspect, strong in his influence, and altogether dominant over her life. For many years, notwithstanding an almost daily visit to her vision, he withheld his name, nor would her most importunate questionings induce him to utter it. But he always promised that in due time he would reveal his identity. Meanwhile, he prophesied to her that she would rise to great distinction; that she would emerge from her poverty and live in a stately house; that she would win great wealth in a city which he pictured as crowded with ships; that she would publish and conduct a journal; and that, finally, to crown her career, she would become the ruler of her people. At length, after patiently waiting on this spirit guide for twenty years, one day in 1868, during a temporary sojourn in Pittsburg, and while she was sitting at a marble table, he suddenly appeared to her, and wrote on the table, in English letters, the name "Demosthenes." At first the writing was indistinct, but grew to such a luster that the brightness filled the room. The apparition, familiar as it had been before, now affrighted her to trembling. The stately and commanding spirit told her to journey to New York, where she would find, at No. 17 Great Jones Street, a house in readiness for her, equipped in all things to her use and taste. She unhesitatingly obeyed, although she never before had heard of Great Jones Street, nor until that revelatory moment had entertained an intention of taking such a residence. On entering the house, it fulfilled in reality the picture which she saw of it in her vision—the self-same hall, stairways, rooms, and furniture. Entering with some bewilderment into the library, she reached out her hand by chance, and, without knowing what she did, took up a book, which, on idly looking at its title, she saw (to her blood-chilling astonishment) to be "The Orations of Demosthenes." From that time onward the Greek statesman has been, even more palpably than in her earlier years, her prophetic monitor, mapping out the life which she must follow, as a chart for the ship sailing the sea. She believes him to be her familiar spirit, the author of her public policy, and the inspirer of her published words. Without intruding my own opinion as to the authenticity of this inspiration, I have often thought that, if Demosthenes could arise and speak English, he could hardly excel the fierce light and heat of some of the sentences which I have heard from this singular woman in her glowing hours.

THE DEAD RETURNED TO LIFE.

Previous to this crisis, there had occurred a remarkable incident which more than ever confirmed her faith in the guardianship of spirits. One day, during a severe illness of her son, she left him to visit her patients, and on her return was startled with the news that the boy had died two hours before. "No," she exclaimed, "I will not permit his death." And with frantic energy she stripped her bosom naked, caught up his lifeless form, pressed it to her own, and sitting thus, flesh to flesh, glided insensibly into a trance, in which she remained seven hours, at the end of which time she awoke; a perspiration started from his clammy skin, and the child that had been thought dead was brought back again to life, and lives to this day in sad half death. It is her belief that the spirit of Jesus Christ brooded over the lifeless form, and rewrought the miracle of Lazarus for a sorrowing woman's sake.

HER SECOND MARRIAGE MADE IN HEAVEN.

But, even against the Scripture, it is safe to say that Victoria's second marriage was made in heaven ; that is, it was decreed by the self-same spirits whom she is ever ready to follow, whether they lead her for discipline into the valley of the shadow of death or for comfort in those ways of pleasantness which are paths of peace. Colonel James H. Blood, Commander of the Sixth Missouri Regiment, who, at the close of the war, was elected City Auditor of St. Louis, who became President of the Society of Spiritualists in that place, and who had himself been, like Victoria, the legal partner of a morally sundered marriage, called one day on Mrs. Woodhull to consult her as a Spiritualistic physician (having never seen her before), and was startled to see her pass into a trance, during which she announced, unconsciously to herself, that his future destiny was to be linked with hers in marriage. Thus, to their mutual amazement, but to their subsequent happiness, they were betrothed on the spot by "the powers of the air." The legal tie by which at first they bound themselves to each other was afterward, by mutual consent, annulled—the necessary form of Illinois law being complied with to this effect. But the marriage law stands on its merits, and is to all who witness its harmony known to be a sweet and accordant union of congenial souls.

Col. Blood is a man of a philosophical and reflective cast of mind, an enthusiastic student of the higher lore of spiritualism, a recluse from society, and an expectant believer in a stupendous destiny for Victoria. A modesty not uncommon to men of intellect, prompts him to sequester his name in the shade rather than to see it glittering in the sun. But he is an indefatigable worker—driving his pen through all hours of the day and half of the night. He is an active editor of *Woodhull and Claflin's Weekly*, and one of the busy partners in the firm of Woodhull, Claflin & Co., brokers at No. 44 Broad Street, New York. His civic views are (to use his favorite designation of them) cosmopolitical ; in other words he is a radical of extreme radicalism—an internationalist of the most uncompromising type—a communist who would rather have died in Paris than be the President of a pretended republic whose first official act has been the judicial murder of the only Republicans in France. His spiritualistic habits he describes in a letter to his friend, the writer of this memorial, as follows: " At about 11 or 12 o'clock at night, two or three times a week, and sometimes without nightly intervals, Victoria and I hold parliament with the spirits. It is by this kind of study that we both have learned nearly all the valuable knowledge that we possess. Victoria goes into a trance, during which her guardian spirit takes control of her mind, speaking audibly through her lips, propounding various matters for our subsequent investigation and verification, and announcing principles, detached thoughts, hints of systems and suggestions for affairs. In this way and in this spiritual night-school began that process of instruction by which Victoria has arisen to her present position as a political economist and politician. During her entranced state, which generally lasts about an hour, but sometimes twice as long, I make copious notes of all she says, and when her speech is unbroken I write down every word, and publish it without correction or amendment. She and I regard all the other portion of our lives as almost valueless as compared with these midnight hours." The preceding extract shows that this fine-grained transcendentalist is a reverent husband to his spiritual wife, the sympathetic companion of her entranced moods, and their faithful historian to the world.

After a union with Col. Blood, instead of changing her name to his, she followed the example of many actresses, singers, and other professional women whose names have become a business property to their owners, and she still continues to be known as Mrs. Woodhull.

MAKING CLAIRVOYANCE PAY.

Hitherto her clairvoyant faculty has been put to no pecuniary use, but she was now directed by the spirits to repair to Indianapolis, there to announce herself as a medium, and to treat patients for the cure of disease. Taking rooms in the Bates House, and publishing a card in the journals, she found herself able, on saluting her callers, to tell by inspiration their names, their residences, and their maladies. In a few days she became the town's talk. Her marvelous performances in clairvoyance being noised abroad, people flocked to her from a distance. Her rooms were crowded and her purse grew fat. She reaped a golden harvest—including as its worthiest part, golden opinions from all sorts of people. Her countenance would often glow as with a sacred light, and she became an object of religious awe to many wonder-stricken people whose inward lives she had revealed. Moreover, her unpretentious modesty, and her perpetual disclaimer of any merit or power of her own, and the entire crediting of this to spirit influence, augmented the interest with which all spectators regarded the amiable prodigy. First at Indianapolis, and afterward at Terre Haute, she wrought some apparently miraculous cures. She straightened the feet of the lame, she opened the ears of the deaf, she detected the robbers of a bank. she brought to light hidden crimes, she solved physiological problems, she unvailed business secrets, she prophesied future events. Knowing the wonders which she wrought, certain citizens disguised themselves and came to her, purporting to be strangers from a distant town, but she instantly said, "Oh, no ; you all live here." "How can you tell ?" they asked. "The spirits say so," she replied.

Benedictions followed her, gifts were lavished upon her, money flowed in a stream toward her. Journeying from city to city in the practice of her spiritual art, she thereby supported all her relatives far and near. Her income in one year reached nearly a hundred thousand dollars. She received in one day, simply as fees for cures which she had wrought, $5,000. The sum total of the receipts of her practice, and of her investments growing out of it, up to the time of its discontinuance by direction of the spirits in 1869, was $700,000. The age of wonders has not ceased !

HER FIRST HUSBAND RECOVERED.

One night, about half a year after their marriage, she and her husband were awakened at midnight, in Cincinnati, by the announcement that a man by the name of Dr. Woodhull had been attacked with delirium tremens at the Burnet House, and in a lucid moment had spoken of the woman from whom he had been divorced, and begged to see her. Colonel Blood immediately took a carriage, drove to the hotel, brought the wretched victim home, and jointly with Victoria took care of him with life-saving kindness for six weeks. On his going away they gave him a few hundred dollars of their joint property to make him comfortable in another city. He departed full of gratitude, bearing with him the assurance that he would always be willing to come and go as a friend of the family. And from that day to this the poor man, dilapidated in body and emasculated in spirit, has sojourned under Victoria's roof, and sometimes elsewhere, according to his whim or will. In the present ruin of the young gallant of twenty years ago there is more manhood (albeit an expiring spark like a candle in its socket) than during any of the former years ; and to be now turned out of doors by the woman he wronged, but who would not wrong him in return, would be an act of inhumanity which it would be impossible for Mrs. Woodhull and Colonel Blood either jointly or separately to commit. For this piece of noble conduct—what is commonly called her living with two husbands under one roof—she has received not so much censure on earth as I think she will receive reward in heaven. No other passage of her life more singularly illustrates the nobility of her moral judgments, or the supernal courage by which she stands by her convictions. Not all the clamorous tongues in Christendom, though they should simultaneously cry out against her, "Fie, for shame !" could persuade her to turn this wretched wreck from her home. And I say she is right ; and I will maintain this opinion against the combined Pecksniffs of the whole world.

PROPHECIES FULFILLED.

This act, and the malice of enemies, together with her bold opinions on social questions, have combined to give her reputation a stain. But no slander ever fell on any human soul with greater injustice. A more unsullied woman does not walk the earth. She carries in her very face the fair legend of a character kept pure by a sacred fire within. She is one of those aspiring devotees who tread the earth merely as a stepping-stone to heaven, and whose chief ambition is finally to present herself at the supreme tribunal, "spotless, and without wrinkle, or blemish, or any such thing." Knowing her as well as I do, I cannot hear an accusation against her without recalling Tennyson's line of King Arthur,

> "Is thy white blamelessness accounted blame !"

Fulfilling a previous prophecy, and following a celestial mandate, in 1869 she founded a bank and published a journal. These two events took the town by storm. When the doors of her office in Broad street were first thrown open to the public, several thousand visitors came in a flock on the first day. The "lady brokers," as they were called (a strange confession that brokers are not always gentlemen), were besieged like lionesses in a cage. The daily press interviewed them ; the weekly wits satirized them ; the comic sheets caricatured them ; but like a couple of fresh young dolphins, breasting the sea side by side, they showed themselves native to the element, and cleft gracefully every threatening wave that broke over their heads. The breakers could not dash the brokers. Indomitable in their energy, the sisters won the good graces of Commodore Vanderbilt—a fine old gentleman of comfortable means, who of all the lower animals prefers the horse, and of all the higher virtues admires pluck. Both with and without Commodore Vanderbilt's help, Mrs. Woodhull has more than once shown the pluck that has held the rein of the stock market as the Commodore holds his horse.

DEMOSTHENES AT IT AGAIN.

One night in December, 1869, while she lay in deep sleep, her Greek guardian came to her, and sitting transfigured by her couch, wrote on a scroll (so that she could not only see the words, but immediately dictated them to her watchful amanuensis) the memorable document now known in history as "The Memorial of Victoria C. Woodhull"—a petition addressed to Congress, claiming under the Fourteenth Amendment the right of women às of other "citizens of the United States," to vote in "the States wherein they reside"—asking; moreover, that the State of New York, of which she was a citizen, should be restrained by Federal authority from preventing the exercise of this constitutional right. As up to this time neither she nor her husband had been greatly interested in women suffrage, he had no sooner written this manifesto from her lips than he awoke her from the trance, and protested against the communication as nonsense, believing it to be a trick of some evil-disposed spirits. In the morning the document was shown to a number of friends, including one eminent judge, who ridiculed its logic and conclusions. But the lady herself, from whose sleeping and yet unsleeping brain the strange document had sprung like Minerva from the head of Jove, simply answered that her antique instructor, having never misled her before, was guiding her aright then. Nothing doubting, but much wondering, she took the novel demand to Washington, where, after a few days of laughter from the shallow minded, and of neglect from the indifferent, it suddenly burst upon the Federal Capitol like a storm, and then spanned it like a rainbow. She went before the Judiciary Committee, and delivered an argument in support of her claim to the franchise under the new amendments, which some who heard it pronounced one of the ablest efforts which they had ever heard on any subject. She caught the listening ears of Senator Carpenter, Gen. Butler, Judge Woodward, George W. Julian, Gen. Ashley, Judge Longhridge, and other able statesmen in Congress, and harnessed these gentlemen as steeds to her chariot. Such was the force of her appeal that the whole city rushed together to hear it, like the Athenians to the market place when Demosthenes stood in his own and not a borrowed clay. A great audience, one of the finest ever gathered in the capitol, assembled to hear her defend her thesis in the first public speech of her life. At the moment of rising her face was observed to be very pale, and she appeared about to faint. On being afterward questioned as to the cause of her emotion, she replied that during the first prolonged moment she remembered an early prediction of her guardian spirit, until then forgotten, that she would one day speak in public, and that her first discourse would be produced in the Capital of her country. The sudden fulfillment of this prophecy smote her so violently that for a moment she was stunned into apparent unconsciousness. But she recovered herself, and passed through the ordeal with great success—which is better luck than happened to the real Demosthenes, for Plutarch mentions that his maiden speech was a failure, and that he was laughed at by the people.

INDESCRIBABLE BEAUTY.

I must say something of her personal appearance, although it defies portrayal, whether by photograph or pen. Neither tall nor short, stout nor slim, she is of medium stature, lithe and elastic, free and graceful. Her side face, looked at over her left shoulder, is of perfect aquiline outline, as classic as ever went into a Roman marble, and resembles the mask of Shakespeare taken after death; the same view, looking from the right, is a little broken and irregular; and the front face is broad, with prominent cheek-bones, and with some unshapely nasal lines. Her countenance is never twice alike, so variable is its expression and so dependent are her moods. Her soul comes into it and goes out of it, giving her at one time the look of a superior and almost saintly intelligence, and at another leaving her dull, commonplace, and unprepossessing. When under a strong spiritual influence, a strange and mystical light irradiates from her face, reminding the beholder of the Hebrew Lawgiver, who gave to men what he received from God, and whose face during the transfer shone. Tennyson, as with the hand of a gold-beater, has beautifully gilded the same expression in his stanza of St. Stephen the Martyr in the article of death :

> And looking upward, full of grace,
> He prayed, and from a happy place,
> God's glory smote him on the face.

In conversation, until she is somewhat warmed with earnestness, she halts, as if her mind were elsewhere; but the moment she brings all her faculties to her lips for the full utterance of her message, whether it be of persuasion or indignation, and particularly when under spiritual control, she is a very orator for eloquence—pouring forth her sentences like a mountain stream, sweeping away everything that frets its flood.

Her hair, which, when left to itself is as long as those tresses of Hortense in which her son Louis Napoleon used to play hide and seek, she now mercilessly cuts close like a boy's, from impatience at the daily waste of time in suitably taking care of this prodigal gift of nature.

She can ride a horse like an Indian, and climb a tree like an athlete; she can swim, row a boat, play billiards, and dance ; moreover, as the crown of her physical virtues, she can walk all day like an Englishwoman.

POLITICS AND PRINCIPLES.

In making an epitome of her views, I may say that in politics she is a downright democrat, scorning to divide her fellow-citizens into upper and lower classes, but ranking them all in one comprehensive equality of right, privilege, and opportunity ; concerning finance, which is a favorite topic with her, she holds that gold is not the true standard of money value, but that the Government should abolish the gold standard, and issue its notes instead, giving to those a fixed and permanent value, and circulating them as the only money ; on social questions, her theories are similar to those which have long been taught by John Stuart Mill and Mrs. H. B. Stanton, and which are styled by some as free love doctrines, while others reject this appellation on account of its popular association with the idea of a promiscuous intimacy between the sexes—the essence of her system being that marriage is of the heart and not of the law, that when love ends marriage should end with it, being dissolved by nature, and that no civil statute should outwardly bind two hearts which have been inwardly sundered ; and, finally, in religion, she is a spiritualist of the most mystical and ethereal type.

In thus speaking of her views, I will add to them another fundamental article of her creed, which an incident will best illustrate. Once a sick woman who had been given up by the physicians, and who had received from a Catholic priest extreme unction in expectation of death, was put into the care of Mrs. Woodhull, who attempted to lure her back to life. This zealous physician, unwilling to be baffled, stood over her patient day and night, neither sleeping nor eating for ten days and nights, at the end of which time she was gladdened not only at witnessing the sick woman's recovery, but at finding her own body, instead of weariness or exhaustion from the double lack of sleep and food, was more fresh and bright than at the beginning. Her face, during this discipline, grew uncommonly fair and ethereal ; her her flesh wore a look of transparency ; and the ordinary earthiness of mortal nature began to disappear from her physical frame and its place to be supplied with what she fancied were the foretokens of a spiritual body. These phenomena were so vivid to her own consciousness and to the observation of her friends, that she was led to speculate profoundly on the transformation from our mortal to our immortal state, deducing the idea that the time will come when the living human body, instead of ending in death by disease, and dissolution in the grave, will be gradually refined away until it is entirely sloughed off, and the soul only, and not the flesh, remains. It is in this way that she fulfills to her daring hope the prophecy that "the last enemy to be destroyed is death."

Engrossed in business affairs, nevertheless at any moment she would rather die than live, such is her infinite estimate of the outer world over this. But she disdains all commonplace parleyings with the spirit realm such as are had in ordinary spirit manifestations. On the other hand, she is passionately eager to see the spirits face to face, to summon them at her will and commune with them at her pleasure. Twice, as she unshakingly believes, she has seen a vision of Jesus Christ, honored thus doubly over St. Paul, who saw his Master but once, and then was overcome by the sight. She never goes to any church, save to the solemn temple whose starry arch spans her housetop at night, where she sits like Simeon Stylites on his pillar, a worshiper in the sky. Against the inculcations of her childish education the spirits have taught her that He whom the Church' calls the Saviour of the world is not God but man. But her reverence for Him is supreme and ecstatic. The Sermon on the Mount fills her eyes with tears. The exulting exclamations of the Psalmist are her familiar outbursts of devotion. For two years, as a talisman against any temptation toward untruthfulness (which, with her, is the unpardonable sin), she wore, stitched into the sleeve of every one of her dresses, the second verse of the 120th Psalm, namely, "Deliver my soul, O Lord, from lying lips, and from a deceitful tongue." Speaking the truth punctiliously, whether in great things or small, she rigorously exacts the same of others, that a deceit practiced upon her enkindles her soul to a flame of fire ; and she has acquired a clairvoyant or intuitive power to detect a lie in the moment of its utterance, and to smite the liar in his act of guilt. She believes that intellectual power had its fountains in spiritual inspiration. And once when I put to her the searching question, "What is the greatest truth that has ever been expressed in words ?" she thrilled me with the sudden answer, "Blessed are the pure in heart, for they shall see God."

As showing that her early clairvoyant power still abides, I will mention a fresh instance. An eminent judge in Pennsylvania, in whose court-house I had once lectured, called lately to see me at the office of *The Golden Age*. On my inquiring after his family, he told me that a strange event had just happened in it. "Three months ago," said he, "while I was in New York, Mrs. Woodhull said to me, with a rush of feeling, 'Judge, I foresee that you will lose two of your children within six weeks.'" This announcement, he said, wounded him as a tragic sort of trifling with life and death. "But," I asked, "did anything follow the prophecy ?" "Yes," he replied, "fulfillment ; I lost two children within six weeks." The Judge, who is a Methodist, thinks that Victoria the clairvoyant is like "Anna the prophetess."

RELIGIOUS PEACE OF MIND.

Her enemies (save those of her own household) are strangers. To see her is to respect her—to know her is to vindicate her. She has some impetuous and headlong faults, but were she without the same traits which produce these she would not possess the mad and magnificent energies which (if she lives) will make her a heroine of history.

In conclusion, amid all the rush of her active life, she believes with Wordsworth that

> " The gods approve the depth and not
> The tumult of the soul."

So, whether buffeted by criticism, or defamed by slander, she carries herself in that religious peace which, through all turbulence, is a "measureless content." When apparently about to be struck down, she gathers unseen strength and goes forward conquering and to conquer. Known only as a rash iconoclast, and ranked even with the most uncouth of those noise-makers who are waking a sleepy world before its time, she beats her daily gong of business and reform with notes not musical but strong, yet, mellows the outward rudeness of the rhythm by the inward and devout song of one of the sincerest, most reverent, and divinely gifted of human souls.

THE ORIGINAL WOODHULL STATEMENT.

Mrs. Victoria C. Woodhull published in *Woodhull & Claflin's Weekly* of November 2, 1872, a long article signed with her name, in which she gave an account of the scandal which has been denounced as an "infamous libel" by all the principal persons compromised by it. We cut out such portions of this article as are irrelevant to its assumed conclusions. The parts bearing on the Beecher-Tilton case are as follows:

I propose, as the commencement of a series of aggressive moral warfare on the social question, to begin in this article by ventilating one of the most stupendous scandals which has ever occurred in any community. I refer to that which has been whispered broadcast for the last two or three years through the cities of New York and Brooklyn, touching the character and conduct of the Rev. * * * * * * in his relations with the family of Mr. T * .* ' *   I intend that this article shall burst like a bombshell into the ranks of the moralistic social camp.

Here follows a long account of why the writer has adopted a mode of warfare in the campaign for free love that would be considered nefarious elsewhere. She continues:

More than two years ago these two cities—New York and Brooklyn—were rife with rumors of an awful scandal in * * * Church. These rumors were whispered and covertly' alluded to in almost every circle. But the very enormity of the facts, as the world views such matters, hushed the agitation and prevented exposure. The press, warned by the laws of libel, and by a tacit and in the main honorable *consensus* to ignore all such rumors until they enter the courts, or become otherwise matters of irrepressible notoriety, abstained from any direct notice of the subject, and the rumors themselves were finally stifled or forgotten. A few persons only knew something directly of the facts, but among them, situated as I was, I happened to be one. In June, 1870, *Woodhull & Claflin's Weekly* published an article in reply to Mr. H. C. B.'s attack on myself in the columns of the *Independent*, the editorship of which had just been vacated by Mr. T * * * In this article the following paragraph occurred: "At this very moment awful and herculean efforts are being made in a neighboring city to suppress the most terrific scandal which has ever astonished and convulsed any community. Clergy, congregation and community will be alike hurled into more than all the consternation which the great explosion in Paris carried to that unfortunate city if this effort at suppression fail." Subsequently I published a letter in both *World* and *Times*, in which was the following sentence: "I know a clergyman of eminence in Brooklyn who lives in concubinage with the wife of another clergyman of equal eminence." It was generally and well understood, among the people of the press especially, that both of these references were to this case of Mr. * * * * and it came to be generally suspected that I was better informed regarding the facts of the case than others, and was reserving publicity of my knowledge for a more convenient season. This suspicion was heightened nearly into conviction when it transpired that Mr. T * * * was an earnest and apparently conscientious advocate of many of my radical theories, as appeared in his far-famed biography of me, and in numerous other publications in the *Golden Age* and elsewhere. Mr. T * * *'s warmest friends were shocked at his course, and when he added to his remarkable proceedings his brilliant advocacy of my Fourteenth Amendment theory, in his letters to Horace Greeley, Charles Sumner and Matt Carpenter, they considered him irremediably committed to the most radical of all radicals. Assurance was made doubly sure when he presided at Steinway Hall, when I, for the first time, fully and boldly advanced my free-love doctrines. It was noted, however, that this man who stood before the world so fully committed to the broadest principles of liberty, made it convenient to be conspicuously absent from the convention of the Women Suffragists at Washington last January.

About this time rumors floated out that Mrs. Woodhull, disgusted at the recent conduct of Mr. T * * *, and the advice given him by certain of his friends, was animadverting in not very measured terms upon their conduct. An article specifying matters involving several of these persons obtained considerable circulation, and with other circumstances, such as the definite statement of facts, with names and places, indicated that the time was at hand, nigh even unto the door, when the things that had remained hidden should be brought to light, and the whole affair be made public.

And let me now take occasion to affirm, that all the, otherwise viewed, terrible events which I am about to recite as having occurred in * * * Church, are merely parts of a drama which have been cautiously and laboriously prepared to astound men into the consciousness of the possibilities of a better life; and that I believe all the parties to this *imbroglio* have been throughout the unconscious agents of the higher powers. It is this belief, more than anything else, which finally reconciles me to enact my part in the matter, which is that of the mere *nuncia* to the world of the facts which have happened, and so of the new step in the dissolution of the Old and the inauguration of the New. Circumstances being in this state, the year rolled round, and the annual convention of the National Association of Spiritualists occurred in September, 1872, at Boston. I went there—dragged by the sense of duty—tired, sick and discouraged as to my own future, to surrender my charge as President of the Association, feeling as if I were distrusted and unpopular, and with no consolation but the consciousness of having striven to do right, and my abiding faith in the wisdom and help of the spirit world. Arrived at the great assemblage, I felt around me everywhere, not indeed a positive hostility, not even a fixed spirit of unfriendliness, but one of painful uncertainty and doubt. I listened to the speeches of others, and tried to gather the sentiment of the great meeting. I rose finally to my feet, to render an account of my stewardship, to surrender the charge, and retire. Standing there before that audience, I was seized by one of those overwhelming gusts of inspiration which sometimes come upon me, from I know not where; taken out of myself; hurried away from the immediate question of discussion, and made, by some power stronger than I, to pour out into the ears of that assembly, and, as I was told subsequently, in a rhapsody of indignant eloquence, with circumstantial detail, the whole history of the * * * and T * * * scandal in * * * Church, and to announce in prophetic terms something of the bearing of those events upon the future of Spiritualism. I know perhaps less than any of those present all that I did actually say. They tell me that I used some naughty words upon that occasion. All that I know is, that if I swore, *I did not swear profanely.* Some said, with the tears streaming from their eyes, *that I swore divinely.* That I could not have shocked or horrified the audience was shown by the fact that in the immense hall, packed to the ceiling, and as absolutely to my own surprise as at my first election at Troy, I was re-elected President of the Association. Still impressed by my own previous convictions, that my labors in that connection were ended, I promptly declined the office. The convention, however, refused to accept my declinature. The public press of Boston professed holy horror at the freedom of my speech, and restricted their reports to the narrowest limits, carefully suppressing what I had said of the conduct of the great clergyman. The report went forward, however, through various channels, in a muffled and mutilated form, the general conclusion being, probably, with the uninformed, simply that *Mrs. Woodhull had publicly slandered Rev. * * **

Mrs. Woodhull then gives an interview, or a supposed interview, with a reporter, which interview, be it understood, never appeared until Mrs. Woodhull published it. It runs as follows :

Reporter.—"Mrs. Woodhull, I have called to ask if you are prepared and willing to furnish a full statement of the * * * for publication in the city papers ?"

Mrs. Woodhull.—"I do not know that I ought to object to repeating whatever I know in relation to it. You understand, of course, that I take a different view of such matters from those usually avowed by other people. Still, I have good reason to think that far more people entertain views corresponding to mine than dare to assert them or openly live up to them."

Reporter.—"How, Mrs. Woodhull, would you state in the most condensed way your opinions on this subject, as they differ from those avowed and ostensibly lived by the public at large ?"

Mrs. Woodhull.—"I believe that the marriage institution, like slavery and monarchy, and many other things which have been good or necessary in their day, is now *effete*, and in a general sense injurious, instead of being beneficial to the community, although of course it must continue to linger until better institutions can be formed. I mean by marriage, in this connection, any *forced* or *obligatory tie* between the sexes; any *legal intervention* or *constraint* to prevent people from adjusting their love relations precisely as they do their religious affairs in this country, in complete personal freedom ; changing and improving them from time to time, and according to circumstances."

Reporter.—"I confess, then, I cannot understand why you of all persons should have any fault to find with Mr. * * * even assuming everything to be true of him which I have hitherto heard only vaguely hinted at."

Mrs. Woodhull.—" *I* have no fault to find with him in any such sense as you mean, nor in any such sense as that in which the world will condemn him. I have no doubt that he has done the very best which he could do under all the circumstances—with his demanding physical nature, and with the terrible restrictions upon a clergyman's life, imposed by that ignorant public opinion about physiological laws, which they, nevertheless, more, perhaps, than any other class, do their best to perpetuate. The fault I find with Rev. * * * is of a wholly different character, as I have told him repeatedly and frankly, and as he knows very well. It is, indeed, the exact opposite to that for which the world will condemn him. I condemn him because I know, and have had every opportunity to know, that he entertains, on conviction, substantially the same views which I entertain on the social question; that, under the influence of these convictions, he has lived for many years, perhaps for his whole adult life, in a manner which the religious and moralistic public ostensibly, and to some extent really, condemn; that he has permitted himself, nevertheless, to be overawed by public opinion, to profess to believe otherwise than as he does believe, to have helped to maintain for these many years that very social slavery under which he was chafing, and against which he was secretly revolting both in thought and practice; and that he has, in a word, consented, and still consents to be a hypocrite. The fault with which I, therefore, charge him, is not infidelity to the old ideas, but unfaithfulness to the new. He is in heart, in conviction and in life, an ultra socialist reformer; while in seeming and pretension he is the upholder of the old social slavery, and, therefore, does what he can to crush out and oppose me and those who act and believe with me in forwarding the great social revolution. I know, myself, so little of the sentiment of fear, I have so little respect for an ignorant and prejudiced public opinion, I am so accustomed to say the thing that I think and do the thing that I believe to be right, that I doubt not I am in danger of having far too little sympathy with the real difficulties of a man situated as Mr. * * * has been, and is, when he contemplates the idea of facing social opprobrium. Speaking from my feelings, I am prone to denounce him as a poltroon, a coward and a sneak; not, as I tell you, for anything that he has done, and for which the world would condemn him, but for failing to do what it seems to me so clear he ought to do; for failing, in a word, to stand shoulder to shoulder with me and others who are endeavoring to hasten a social regeneration which he believes in."

Reporter.—" You speak very confidently, Mrs. Woodhull, of Mr. * * *'s opinions and life. Will you now please to resume that subject, and tell me exactly what you know of both?"

Mrs. Woodhull.—" I had vaguely heard rumors of some scandal in regard to Rev. * * * which I put aside as mere rumor and idle gossip of the hour, and gave to them no attention whatever. The first serious intimation I had that there was something more than mere gossip in the matter came to me in the committee room at Washington, where the suffrage women congregated during the Winter of 1870, when I was there to urge my views on the Fourteenth Amendment. It was hinted in the room that some of the women, Mrs. H * * * a sister of Mr. * * * among the number, would snub Mrs. Woodhull on account of her social opinions and antecedents. Instantly a gentleman, a stranger to me, stepped forward and said: 'It would ill become these women, and especially a * * * to talk of antecedents, or to cast any smirch upon Mrs. Woodhull, for I am reliably assured that Mr. * * * preaches to at least twenty of his *mistresses* every Sunday.' "I paid no special attention to the remark at the time, as I was very intensely engaged in the business which had called me there; but it afterward forcibly recurred to me, with the thought also that it was strange that such a remark, made in such a presence, had seemed to have a subduing effect instead of arousing indignation. The women who were there could not have treated me better than they did. Whether this strange remark had any influence in overcoming their objections to me I do not know, but it is certain they were not set against me by it; and, all of them, Mrs. H * * * included, subsequently professed the warmest friendship for me."

Reporter—" After this I presume you sought for the solution of the gentleman's remark?"

HOW WOODHULL HEARD THE FULL STORY.

Mrs. Woodhull.—" No, I did not. It was brought up subsequently, in an intimate conversation between her and me, by Mrs. Pauline Wright Davis, without any seeking on my part, and to my very great surprise. Mrs. Davis had been, it seems, a frequent visitor at Mr. T * * *'s house in Brooklyn—they having long been associated in the Woman's Rights movement—and she stood upon certain terms of intimacy in the family. Almost at the same time to which I have referred, when I was in Washington, she called, as she told me, at Mr. T * * *. Mrs. T * * * met her at the door, and burst into tears, exclaiming : 'Oh, Mrs. Davis ! have you come to see me? For six months I have been shut up from the world, and I thought no one would ever come again to visit me.' In the interview that followed, Mrs. * * * spoke freely of a long series of intimate and so-called criminal relations on her part with a certain clergyman; of the discovery of the facts by Mr. T * * *; of the abuse she had suffered from him in consequence, and of her heart-broken condition. She seemed to allude to the whole thing as something already generally known, or known in a considerable circle, and impossible to be concealed, and attributed the long absence of Mrs. Davis from the house to her knowledge of the facts. She was, as she stated at the time, recovering from the effects of a miscarriage of a child of six months. The miscarriage was induced by the ill-treatment of Mr. T * * * in his rage at the discovery of such intimacy, and, as he believed, the great probability that she was *enciente*, but not by him. Mrs. T * * * confessed to Mrs. Davis the intimacy with this clergyman, and that it had been of years' standing. She also said that she loved him before she married Mr. T * * *, and that now the burden of her sorrow was greatly augmented by the knowledge that the clergyman was untrue to her. She had not only to endure the rupture with her husband, but also the certainty that, notwithstanding his repeated assurance of his faithfulness to her, he had recently had illicit intercourse, under most extraordinary circumstances, with another person. Said Mrs. Davis : 'I came away from that house, my soul bowed down with grief at the heart-broken condition of that poor woman, and I felt that I ought not to leave Brooklyn until I had stripped the mask from that infamous, hypocritical scoundrel.' In May, after returning home, Mrs. Davis wrote me a letter, from which I will read a paragraph to show that we conversed on this subject.

EXTRACT FROM A LETTER.

" 'DEAR VICTORIA :—I thought of you half of last night, dreamed of you, and prayed for you.
" 'I believe you are raised up of God to do a wonderful work, and I believe that you will unmask the hypocrisy of a class that none others dare touch. God help you and save you. The more I think of that *mass of clerical corruption* the more I desire its opening. Ever yours, lovingly.
" 'PAULINA WRIGHT DAVIS.

" 'Providence, R. I., May, 1871.' "

Reporter.—" Did you inform Mrs. Davis of your intention to expose this matter, as she intimates in the letter ? "

Mrs. Woodhull.—" I said in effect to her, that the matter would become public, and that I felt that I should be instrumental in making it so. But I was not decided about the course I should pursue. I next heard the whole story from Mrs. Elizabeth Cady Stanton."

Reporter.—" Indeed ! Is Mrs. Stanton also mixed up in this affair? Does she know the facts ? How could the matter have been kept so long quiet, when so many people are cognizant of it ? "

Mrs. Woodhull.—" The existence of the skeleton in the closet may be very widely known, and many people may have the key to the terrible secret, but still hesitate to open the door for the great outside world to gaze in upon it. This grand woman did indeed know the same facts, and from Mr. T * * * himself. I shall never forget the occasion of her first rehearsal of it to me at my residence, 15 East Thirty-eighth street, in a visit made to me during the Apollo Hall Convention, in May, 1871. It seems that Mr. T * * *, in agony at the discovery of what he deemed his wife's perfidy and his pastor's treachery, retreated to Mrs. Stanton's residence at Tenafly, where he detailed to her the entire story. Said Mrs. Stanton, 'I never saw such a manifestation of mental agony. He raved and tore his hair and seemed upon the very verge of insanity.' ' Oh,' said he, ' that that damned lecherous scoundrel should have defiled my bed for ten years, and at the same time have professed to be my best friend ! Had he come like a man to me and confessed his guilt, I could perhaps have endured it, but to have him creep like a snake into my house, leaving his pollution behind him, and I so blind as not to see, and esteeming him all the while as a saint—oh ! it is too much. And when I think how for years she upon whom I had bestowed all my heart's love, could have lied and deceived me so, I lose all faith in humanity. I do not believe there is any honor, any truth left in anybody in the world.' Mrs. Stanton continued, and repeated to me the sad story, which it is unnecessary to recite, as I prefer giving it as Mr. T * * * himself told it to me, subsequently, with his own lips."

Reporter—" Is it possible that Mr. T * * * confided this story to you ? It seems too monstrous to be believed ! "

Mrs. Woodhull—" He certainly did. And what is more, I am persuaded that in his inmost mind he will not be otherwise than glad when the skeleton in his closet is revealed to the world, if thereby the abuses which lurk like vipers under the cloak of social conservatism may be exposed and the causes removed. Mr. T * * * looks deeper into the soul of things than most men, and is braver than most."

Reporter—" How did your acquaintance with Mr. T * * * begin ? "

HOW TILTON AND WOODHULL GOT ACQUAINTED.

Mrs. Woodhull—" Upon the information received from Mrs. Davis and Mrs. Stanton I based what I said in the *Weekly*, and in the letters in the *Times* and *World* referring to the matter, I was nearly determined—though still not quite so—that what I, equally with those who gave me the information, believed, but for wholly other reasons, to be a most important social circumstance, should be exposed, my reasons being, as I have explained to you, not those of the world, and I took that method to cause inquiry and create agitation regarding it. The day that the letter appeared in the *World* Mr. * * * came to my office, No 44 Broad street, and showing me the letter, asked : 'Whom do you mean by that?' 'Mr. T * * *,' said I, 'I mean you and Mr. * * *.' I then told him what I knew, what I thought of it, and that I felt that I had a mission to bring it to the knowledge of the world, and that I had nearly determined to do so. I said to him much else on the subject; and he said: 'Mrs. Woodhull, you are the first person I have ever met who has dared to, or else who could, tell me the truth.' He acknowledged that the facts, as I had heard them, were true, but declared that I did not yet know the extent of the depravity of that man—meaning Rev. * * *. 'But,' said he, 'do not take any steps now. I have carried my heart as a stone in my breast for months, for the sake of * * *, my wife, who is broken-hearted as I am. I have had courage to endure rather than to add more to her weight of sorrow. For her sake I have allowed that rascal to go unscathed. I have curbed my feelings when every impulse urged me to throttle and strangle him. Let me take you over to my wife, and you will find her in no condition to be dragged before the public; and I know you will have compassion on her.' And I went and saw her, and I agreed with him on the propriety of delay."

Reporter—"Was it during this interview that Mr. T * * * explained to you all that you now know of the matter?"

Mrs. Woodhull—"Oh, no. His revelations were made subsequently at sundry times, and during months of friendly intercourse, as occasion brought the subject up. I will, however, condense his statements to me, and state the facts as he related them, as consecutively as possible. I kept notes of the conversations as they occurred from time to time, but the matter is so much impressed on my mind that I have no hesitation in relating them from memory."

Reporter—"Do you not fear that by taking the responsibility of this *exposé* you may involve yourself in trouble? Even if all you relate should be true, may not those involved deny it *in toto:* even the fact of their having made the statements?"

Mrs. Woodhull—"I do not fear anything of the sort. I know this thing must come out, and the statement of the plain ungarnished truth will outweigh all the perjuries that can be invented, if it come to that pass. I have been charged with attempts at blackmailing, but I tell you, sir, there is not money enough in these two cities to purchase my silence in this matter. I believe it is my duty and my mission to carry the torch to light up and destroy the heap of rottenness, which, in the name of religion, marital sanctity, and social purity, now passes as the social system. I know there are other churches just as false, other pastors just as recreant to their professed ideas of morality—by their immorality you know I mean their hypocrisy. I am glad that just this one case comes to me to be exposed. This is a great congregation. He is a most eminent man. When a beacon is fired on the mountain the little hills are lighted up. This exposition will send inquisition through all the churches and what is termed conservative society."

Reporter—"You speak like some weird prophetess, madam."

Mrs. Woodhull.—"I am a prophetess—I am an evangel—I am a saviour, if you would but see it, but I too come not to bring peace, but a sword."

TILTON IN A RAGE.

Mrs. Woodhull then resumed, saying: "Mr. T * * * first began to have suspicions of Mr. * * * on his own return from a long lecturing tour through the West. He questioned his little daughter privately, in his study, regarding what had transpired in his absence. 'The tale of iniquitous horror that was revealed to me was,' he said, 'enough to turn the heart of a stranger to stone, to say nothing of a husband and father.' It was not the fact of the intimacy alone, but in addition to that, the terrible orgies—so he said—of which his house had been made the scene, and the boldness with which matters had been carried on in the presence of his children—'These things drove me mad,' said he, 'and I went to my wife and confronted her with the child and the damning tale she had told me. My wife did not deny the charge nor attempt any palliation. She was then *enciente;* and I felt sure that the child would not be my child. I stripped the wedding ring from her finger. I tore the picture of Mr. * * * from the wall and stamped it in pieces. Indeed, I do not know what I did not do. I only look back to it as a time too horrible to retain any exact remembrance of it. She miscarried the child and it was buried. For two weeks, night and day, I might have been found walking to and fro from that grave, in a state bordering on distraction. I could not realize the fact that I was what I was. I stamped the ring with which we had plighted our troth deep into the soil that covered the fruit of my wife's infidelity. I had friends, many and firm, and good, but I could not go to them with this grief, and I suppose I should have remained silent through life had not an occasion arisen which demanded that I should seek counsel. Mr. * * * learned that I had discovered the fact, and what had transpired between my wife and myself, and when I was absent he called at my house and compelled or induced his victim to sign a statement he had prepared, declaring that so far as he, Mr. * * *, was concerned, there was no truth in my charges, and that there had never been any criminal intimacy between them. Upon learning this, as I did, I felt, of course, again outraged and could endure secrecy no longer. I had one friend who was like a brother, Mr. Frank Moulton. I went to him and stated the case fully. We were both members of * * * Church. My friend took a pistol, went to Mr. * * *, and demanded the letter of Mrs. T * * * under penalty of instant death." (Mrs. Woodhull here remarked that Mr. Moulton had himself, also since, described to her this interview, with all the piteous and abject beseeching of Mr. * * * not to be exposed to the public.) "Mr. Moulton obtained the letter," said Mrs. W., "and told me that he had it in his safe, where he should keep it until required for further use. After this, Mr. T * * *'s house was no house for him, and he seldom slept or eat there, but frequented the house of his friend Moulton, who sympathized deeply with him. Mrs. T * * * was also absent days at a time, and, as Mr. T * * * informed me, seemed bent on destroying her life. I went as I have said to see her, and found her indeed a wretched wreck of a woman, whose troubles were greater than she could bear. She made no secret of the facts before me. Mr. * * *'s selfish, cowardly cruelty in endeavoring to shield himself and create public opinion against Mr. T * * * added poignancy to her anxieties. She seemed indifferent as to what should become of herself, but labored under fear that murder might be done on her account.

WOODHULL AS AN ADVISER.

"This was the condition of affairs at the time that Mr. T * * * came to me. I attempted to show him the true solution of the embroglio, and the folly that it was for a man like him, a representative man of the ideas of the future, to stand whining over inevitable events connected with this transition age and the social revolution of which we are in the midst. I told him that the fault and the wrong were neither in * * * nor in Mrs. T * * *, nor in himself; but that it was in the false social institutions under which we still live, while the more advanced men and women of the world have outgrown them in spirit; and that, practically, everybody is living a false life by professing a conformity which they do not feel and do not live, and which they cannot feel and live any more than the grown boy can re-enter the clothes of his early childhood. I recalled to his attention splendid passages of his own rhetoric, in which he had unconsciously justified all the freedom that he was now strongly condemning, when it came home to his own door, and endeavoring, in the spirit of a tyrant, to suppress. I ridiculed the maudlin sentiment and mock heroics and 'dreadful suzz' he was exhibiting over an event the most natural in the world, and the most intrinsically innocent; having in it not a bit more of real criminality than the awful wickedness of 'negro stealing' formerly charged, in perfect good faith, by the slaveholders, on every one who helped the escape of a slave. I assumed at once, and got a sufficient admission, as I always do in such cases, that he was not exactly a vestal virgin himself; that his real life was something very different from the awful 'virtue' he was preaching, especially for women, as if women could 'sin' in this matter without men, and men without women, and which, he pretended, even to himself, to believe in the face and eyes of his own life, and the lives of nearly all the greatest and best men and women that he knew; that the 'dreadful suzz' was merely a bogus sentimentality, pumped in his imagination, because our sickly religious literature, and Sunday-school morality, and pulpit phariseeism had humbugged him all his life into the belief that he ought to feel and act in this harlequin and absurd way on such an occasion—that, in a word, neither Mr. * * * nor Mrs. T * * * had done any wrong, but that it was he who was playing the part of a fool and a tyrant; that it was he and the factitious or manufactured public opinion back of him, that was wrong; that his babyish whining and stage-acting were the real absurdity and disgrace—the unmanly part of the whole transaction, and that we only needed another Cervantes to satirize such stuff as it deserves, to squelch it instantly and forever. I tried to show him that a true manliness would protect and love to protect; would glory in protecting the absolute freedom of the woman who was loved, whether called wife, mistress, or by any other name, and that the true sense of honor in the future will be, not to know even what relations our lovers have with any and all other persons, than ourselves—as true courtesy never seeks to spy over or to pry into other people's private affairs. I believe I succeeded in pointing out to him that his own life was essentially no better than Mr. * * *, and that he stood in no position to throw the first stone at Mrs. T * * * or her reverend paramour. I showed him again and again that the wrong point, and the radically wrong thing, if not, indeed, quite the only wrong thing in the matter, was the idea of ownership in human beings, which was essentially the same in the two institutions of slavery and marriage. Mrs. T * * * had in turn grown increasingly unhappy when she found that Mr. * * * had turned some part of his exuberant affections upon some other object. There was in her, therefore, the same sentiment of the real slaveholder. Let it be once understood that whosoever is true to himself or herself is thereby, and necessarily, true to all others, and the whole social question will be solved. The barter and sale of wives stands on the same moral footing as the barter and sale of slaves. The god-implanted human affections cannot, and will not, be any longer subordinated to these external, legal restrictions and conventional engagements. Every human being belongs to himself or herself by a higher title than any which, by surrenders or arrangements or promises, he or she can confer upon any other human being. Self-ownership is inalienable. These truths are the latest and greatest discoveries in true science. "Perhaps Mr. * * * knows and feels all this, and if so, iu that knowledge consists his sole and his real justification, only the world around him has not yet grown to it ; institutions are not yet adapted to it ; and he is not brave enough to bear his open testimony to the truth he knows. All this I said to Mr. T * * * ; and I urged upon him to make this providential circumstance in his life the occasion upon which he should, himself, come forward to the front and stand with the true champions of social freedom."

REPORTER—"Then Mr. * * * became, as it were, your pupil, and you instructed him in your theories?"

MRS. WOODHULL.—"Yes, I suppose that is a correct statement ; and the verification of my views, springing up before my eyes upon this occasion, out of the very midst of religious and moral prejudices, was, I assure you, an interesting study for me, and a profound corroboration of the righteousness of what you call 'my Theories.' Mr. T * * *'s conduct toward Mr. * * * and toward his wife began from that time to be magnanimous and grand—by which I mean simply just and right—so unlike that which most other men's would have been, that it stamped him, in my mind, as one of the noblest souls that lived, and one capable of playing a great role in the social revolution, which is now so rapidly progressing. I never could, however, induce him to stand wholly and unreservedly, and on principle, upon the free-love platform ; and I always, therefore, feared that he might for a time vacillate or go backward. But he opened his house to Mr. * * * , saying to him, in the presence of Mrs. T * * * : 'You love each other. Mr. * * * , this is a distressed woman ; if it be in your power to alleviate her condition and make her life less a burden than it now is, be yours the part to do it. You have nothing to fear from me.' From that time Mr. * * * , was, so to speak, the slave of Mr. T * * * and Mr. Moulton. He consulted them in every matter of any importance. It was at this time that Mr. T * * * introduced Mr. * * * , to me, and I met him frequently both at Mr. T * * *'s and Mr. Moulton's. We discussed the social problem freely in all its varied bearings, and I found that Mr. * * * agreed with nearly all my views upon the question."

Reporter—"Do you mean to say that Mr. * * * disapproves of the present marriage system ?"

Mrs. Woodhull—"I mean to say just this—that Mr. * * * told me that marriage is the grave of love, and that he never married a couple that he did not feel condemned."

Reporter—"What excuse did Mr. * * * give for not avowing these sentiments publicly ?"

Mrs. Woodhull—' Oh, the moral coward's inevitable excuse—that of inexpediency. He said he was twenty years ahead of his church ; that he preached the truth just as fast as he thought his people could bear it. I said to him, 'Then Mr. * * * , you are defrauding your people. You confess that you do not preach the truth as you know it, while they pay for and persuade themselves you are giving them your best thought.' He replied : 'I know that our social system is corrupt. I know that marriage, as it exists to-day is the curse of society. We shall never have a better state until children are begotten and bred on the scientific plan. Stirpiculture is what we need.' 'Then,' said I, 'Mr. * * * , why do you not go into your pulpit and preach that science ?' He replied : 'If I were to do so I should preach to empty seats. It would be the ruin of my church.' 'Then,' said I, 'you are as big a fraud as any time-serving preacher, and I now believe you are all frauds. I gave you credit for ignorant honesty, but I find you all alike—all trying to hide, or afraid to speak the truth. A sorry pass has this Christian country come to, paying 40,000 ministers to lie to it from Sunday to Sunday, to hide from them the truth that has been given them to promulgate.'"

Reporter—"It seems you took a good deal of pains to draw Mr. * * * out."

Mrs. Woodhull—"I did. I thought him a man who would dare a good deal for the truth, and that, having lived the life he had, and entertaining the private convictions he did, I could perhaps persuade him that it was his true policy to come out and openly avow his principles, and be a thorough, consistent radical, and thus justify his life in some measure, if not wholly to the public."

Reporter—"Was Mr. * * * aware that you knew of his relations to Mrs. T. * * * ?"

Mrs. Woodhull—"Of course he was. It was because that I knew of them that he first consented to meet me. He could never receive me until he knew that I was aware of the real character he wore under the mask of his reputation. Is it not remarkable how a little knowledge of this sort brings down the most top-lofty from the stilts on which they lift themselves above the common level."

Reporter—"Do you still regard Mr. * * * as a moral coward ?"

BEECHER DECLINES TO DRAG THE WOODHULL CAR.

Mrs. Woodhull—"I have found him destitute of moral courage enough to meet this tremendous demand upon him. In minor things, I know that he has manifested courage. He could not be induced to take the bold step I demanded of him, simply for the sake of truth and righteousness. I did not entirely despair of him until about a year ago. I was then contemplating my Steinway Hall speech on Social Freedom, and prepared it in the hope of being able to persuade Mr. * * * to preside for me and thus make a way for himself into a consistent life on the radical platform. I made my speech as soft as I conscientiously could. I toned it down in order that it might not frighten him. When it was in type, I went to his study and gave him a copy and asked him to read it carefully and give me his candid opinion concerning it. Meantime, I had told Mr. T * * * and Mr. Moulton that I was going to ask Mr. * * * to preside, and they agreed to press the matter with him. I explained to them that the only safety he had was in coming out as soon as possible an advocate of social freedom, and thus palliate, if he could not completely justify, his practices by founding them at least on principle. I told them that this introduction of me would bridge the 'way. Both the gentlemen agreed with me in this view, and I was for a time almost sure that my desire would be accomplished. A few days before the lecture, I sent a note to Mr. * * * asking him to preside for me. This alarmed him. He went with it to Messrs. T * * * and Moulton, asking advice. They gave it in the affirmative, telling him they considered it eminently fitting that he should pursue the course indicated by me as his only safety, but it was not urged in such a way as to indicate that they had known the request was to have been made. Matters remained undecided until the day of the lecture, when I went over again to press Mr. * * * to a decision. I had then a long private interview with him, urging all the arguments I could to induce him to consent. He said he agreed perfectly with what I was to say, but that he could not stand on the platform of Steinway Hall and introduce me. He said, 'I should sink through the floor. I am a moral coward on this subject, and I know it, and I am not fit to stand by you, who go there to speak what you know to be the truth ; I should stand there a living lie.' He got upon the sofa on his knees beside me, and taking my face between his hands, while the tears streamed down his cheeks, begged me to let him off. Becoming thoroughly disgusted with what seemed to me pusillanimity, I left the room under the control of a feeling of contempt for the man, and reported to my friends what he had said. They then took me again with them and endeavored to persuade him. Mr. T * * * said to him : 'Mr. * * *, some day you have got to fall ; go and introduce this woman and win the radicals of the country, and it will break your fall.' 'Do you think,' said Mr. * * *, 'that this thing will come out to the world ?' Mr. T * * * replied : 'Nothing is more certain in earth or heaven, Mr. * * *; and this may be your last chance to save yourself from complete ruin. Mr. * * * replied : 'I can never endure such a terror. Oh ! if it must come, let me know of it twenty-four hours in advance, that I may take my own life. I cannot, cannot face this thing !' Thoroughly out of all patience, I turned on my heel and said : 'Mr. * * *, if I am compelled to go upon that platform alone, I shall begin by telling the audience why I am alone, and why you are not with me,' and I again left the room. I afterward learned that Mr. * * *, frightened at what I had said, promised, before parting with Mr. T * * *, that he would preside if he could bring his courage up to the terrible ordeal.

TILTON TO THE RESCUE.

"It was four minutes of the time for me to go forward to the platform at Steinway Hall when Mr. T * * * and Mr. Moulton came into the ante-room asking for Mr. * * *. When I told them he had not come they expressed astonishment. I told them I should faithfully keep my word, let the consequences be what they might. At that moment word was sent me that there was an organized attempt to break up the meeting, and that threats were being made against my life if I dared to speak what it was understood I intended to speak. Mr. T * * * then insisted on going on the platform with me and presiding, to which I finally agreed, and that I should not at that time mention Mr. T * * *. I shall never forget the brave words he uttered in introducing me. They had a magic influence on the audience, and drew the string of those who intended to harm me. However much Mr. T * * * may have regretted his course regarding me, and whatever he may say about it, I shall always admire the moral courage that enabled him to stand with me on that platform, and face that, in part, defiant audience. It is hard to bear the criticisms of vulgar minds, who can see in social freedom nothing but licentiousness and debauchery, and the inevitable misrepresentation of the entire press, which is as perfectly subsidized against reason and common sense, when social subjects are discussed, as is the religious press when any other science is discussed which is supposed to militate against the Bible as the direct word of God to man. The editors are equally bigots, or else as dishonest as the clergy. The nightmare of public opinion, which they are still professionally engaged in making, enslaves and condemns them both." Mrs. Woodhull concludes by saying that since her Steinway Hall speech she has surrendered all hope of easing the fall of Mr. * * *, that she had not attempted to see him, and had not in fact seen him. She only added one other fact, which was, that Mr. * * * endeavored to induce Mr. T * * * to withdraw from his membership in P * * * Church, to leave him, Mr. * * *, free from the embarrassment of his presence there ; and that Mr. T * * * had indignantly rejected the proposition, determined to hold the position with a view to such contingencies as might subsequently occur.

WAR AND PRIVACY.

"So much for the interviewing which was to have been published some months ago ; but when it failed or was suppressed, I was still so far undecided that I took no steps in the matter, and had no definite plan for the future in respect to it, until the events as I have recited them, which occurred at Boston. Since then I have not doubted that I must make up my mind definitely to act aggressively in this matter, and to use the facts in my knowledge to compel a more wide-spread discussion of the social question. I take the step deliberately, as an agitator and social revolutionist, which is my profession. I commit no breach of confidence, as no confidences have been made to me, except as I have compelled them, with a full knowledge that I was endeavoring to induce or to force the parties to come to the front along with me, in the announcement and advocacy of the principles of social revolution. Messrs. * * * and T * * *, and other half-way reformers, are to me like the border States in the great rebellion. They are liable to fall, with the weight of their influence, on either side in the contest, and I hold it to be legitimate generalship *to compel* them to declare on the side of truth and progress.

"My position is justly analogous to that of warfare. The public, Mr. * * * included, would gladly crush me if they could—will do so if they can—to prevent me from forcing on them considerations of the utmost importance. My mission is, on the other hand, to utter the unpopular truth, and to make it efficient by whatsoever legitimate means; and means are legitimate as a war measure, which would be highly reprehensible in a state of peace. I believe, as the law of peace, *in the right of privacy*, in the sanctity of individual relations. It is nobody's business but their own, in the absolute view, what Mr. * * * and Mrs. T * * * have done, or may choose at any time to do, as between themselves. And the world needs, too, to be taught just that lesson. I am the champion of that very right of privacy and of individual sovereignty. But that is only one side of the case. I need and the world needs Mr. * * * powerful championship of this very right. The world is on the very crisis of its final fight for liberty. The victory may fall on the wrong side, and his own liberty, and mine, and the world's, be again crushed out, or repressed for another century, for the want of fidelity in him to the new truth. It is not, therefore, Mr. * * * as the individual, that I pursue, but Mr. * * * as the representative man; Mr. * * * as a power in the world; and Mr. * * * as my auxiliary in a great war for freedom, or Mr. * * * as a violent enemy and a powerful hindrance to all that I am bent on accomplishing. To Mr. * * *, as the individual citizen, I tender, therefore, my humble apology, meaning and deeply feeling what I say, for this or any interference on my part with his private conduct. I hold that Mr. T * * * himself, that Mrs. * * * herself, have no more right to inquire, or to know or to spy over, with a view to knowing what has transpired between Mr. * * * and Mrs. T * * * than they have to know what I ate for breakfast, or where I shall spend my next evening; and that Mr. * * * 's congregation and the public at large have just as little right to know or to inquire. I hold that the so-called morality of society is a complicated mass of sheer impertinence, and a scandal on the civilization of this advanced century; that the system of social espionage under which we live is damnable, and that the very first axiom of a true morality is for the people *to mind their own business*, and learn to respect religiously the social freedom and the sacred social privacy of all others; but it was the paradox of Christ that, as the Prince of Peace, he still brought on earth not *peace*, but a *sword*. It is the paradox of life that, in order to have peace, we must first have war; and it is the paradox of my position that, believing in the right of privacy, and in the perfect right of Mr. * * *, socially, morally, and divinely, to have sought the embraces of Mrs. T * * *, or of any other woman or women whom he loved and who loved him, and being a promulgator and a public champion of those very rights, I still invade the most secret and sacred affairs of his life, and drag them to the light, and expose him to the opprobrium and vilification of the public. But the case is exceptional, and what I do I do for a great purpose. The social world is in the very agony of its new birth—or, to resume the warlike simile, the leaders of progress are in the very act of storming the last fortress of bigotry and error. Somebody must be hurled forward into the gap. I have the power, I think, to compel Mr. * * * to go forward and do the duty for humanity from which he shrinks; and I should, myself, be false to the truth if I were to shrink from compelling him.

"Of all the centers of influence on the great broad planet, the destiny that shapes our ends, bent on breaking up an old civilization and ushering in a new one, could have found no such spot for its vantage ground as * * * Church, no such man for the hero of the plot as its reverend pastor, and it may be, no such heroine as the gentle, cultured, and, perhaps, hereafter to be sainted wife of * * * Church's most distinguished layman. Indeed I think that Mrs. T * * * has had, at least at times, a clearer intuition guiding her, a better sense of right, and more courage than her reverend lover! for, on one occasion, Mr. T * * * told me that he took home to her one of my threatening notices, and told her that that meant her and Mr. * * *, and that the exposure must and would come; and he added that she calmly replied: "I am prepared for it. If the new social gospel must have its martyrs, and I must be one of them, I am prepared for it."

"Still, in conclusion, let me add, that in my view, and in the view of others who think with me, and of all, as I believe, who think rightly on the subject, Mr. * * * is to day, and after all that I have felt called upon to reveal of his life, as good, as pure and as noble a man as he ever was in the past, or as the world has held him to be, and that Mrs. * * * is still the pure, charming, cultured woman. It is, then, the public opinion that is wrong, and not the individuals, who must, nevertheless, for a time suffer its persecution.

"Mrs. H. * * * has, from the time that I met her in Washington, stood my fast friend, and given me manifold proofs of her esteem, knowing, as she did, both my radical opinions and my free life. I have been told, not by her, but upon what I believe to be perfectly good authority, that she has for months. perhaps for years past, known the life of her brother, and urged on him to announce publicly his radical convictions, and assured him that if he would do so she, at least, would stand by him. I know, too, by intimate intercourse, the opinions, and, to a great extent, the lives of nearly all the leading reformatory men and women in the land; and I know that Mr. * * *, passing through this crucial ordeal, retrieving himself and standing upon the most radical platform, need not stand alone for an hour, but that an army of glorious and emancipated spirits will gather spontaneously and instantaneously around him, and that the new social republic will have been forever established.

"VICTORIA C. WOODHULL."

MRS. WOODHULL AND MRS. TILTON.

The following interesting "Reminiscences of the Beecher-Tilton Scandal," from the pen of Mrs. Victoria C. Woodhull, has appeared in *Woodhull and Claflin's Weekly* for August 15th (published August 5th):

Before I had ever seen Mrs. Tilton I had come to entertain a deep respect for her for the faithfulness which she exhibited to what I then believed were her convictions upon the great social issues which at that time were just beginning to ruffle the waves of public thought. I believed that she considered the law which attempts to bind two human souls together whom the higher law of divine attraction had severed, was obsolete, and that she was merely waiting for some occasion to drop even her seeming allegiance to the old, and to publicly give in her adhesion to the new; and so indeed did I regard all of the persons connected with the now great social convulsion. I believe, too, that Mrs. Tilton felt in her soul that she had done no wrong; that, however much she might be condemned by those who profess to represent the old order of things, in the sight of God and Nature, and in her own conscience, she was pure; and I have always spoken of her from this conviction. I believe even now, although pressed by the exigencies of the situation to entirely different action, that she is fully convinced in her heart that she has done nothing but what she had a perfect right to do, and I venture to prophesy that it will so come out, when the convulsive struggles that are now rending the community shall have subsided, and the real sentiments and convictions that have produced them shall have risen to the surface. It is proper for me to say that, after the knowledge of this scandal came to me, I determined to make such use of it as the cause of social reform should seem to demand. I desire that the public shall fully realize my motives for what I have done, and I therefore repeat again that they were wholly the reverse of those with which I am generally credited. I had no ill-will toward any of the parties. Nor had I any desire to use their names for the purpose of a vulgar notoriety; but I believed by ventilating this case that I should be rendering humanity the greatest possible benefit, and eventually that the parties themselves would frankly acknowledge that the results were such as to justify this belief; and I may state frankly and truthfully that all the parties involved have time and again assented to the proposition that it would come out some time, let whatever might be done to suppress it; and the most that any of them can say is that I precipitated it sooner than it would otherwise have come.

THE SCANDAL IN TYPE—REMEMBER MY GRAY HAIRS.

I learned in my investigations that the scandal had already been put in type in the offices of no less than four prominent and influential papers. There were the facts of the scandal, or some of them, in the possession of half the newspaper offices in the country. Wherever I went I found something was known about them, and Mr. Beecher knew this was true to a certain extent, if not to the whole. He knew that some one of the papers was liable to publish the scandal any day. Is there any wonder that he lived constantly "on the sharp and ragged edge of anxiety, remorse, fear, and despair," as he says he lived, in his letter to Mr. Moulton? For instance, had a detailed statement of the scandal been made in the Brooklyn *Eagle*—as it was fully known to Mr. Kinsella, and so stated by him to me— or in any of the great New York journals, it would have fallen upon Mr. Beecher with such tremendous force that he could not have survived it, and undoubtedly he would have committed suicide, as he declared he would. That such a publication had been threatened seems evident, or why should Mr. Beecher have been to Mr. Kinsella imploring him "to remember his gray hairs and his twenty-five years' service in Brooklyn, and not expose him," as stated that he was by Mr. Kinsella to me, in presence of another person, who will confirm my statement at any time, and who has reminded me frequently of the circumstance.*

But to make the matter public in a paper already under the ban of the expressed public opinion was altogether a different thing. It was certain that the press would at once rush, as it did, almost unanimously, to the defense of Mr. Beecher, and it was certain that it would result, as it did, in shifting whatever odium there was attached to the case from him upon those who should publish the scandal.

It will be remembered that immediately after the publication of Mr Tilton's letter to Dr. Bacon, Mr. Beecher's theory of defense was foreshadowed by his friends, and widely published in the press. It was said that Mrs. Tilton, becoming annoyed and exasperated by Mr. Tilton's association with Victoria Woodhull, had sought the advice of Mr. Beecher, and that he had advised a separation; but afterward, finding that Mr. Tilton's story put altogether another light upon the subject, he apologized to Mr. Tilton in the language published by Mr. Tilton. This explanation was persistently alleged and eagerly seized upon by everybody who was prejudiced against me, or in favor of Mr. Beecher. But, in their eagerness to make me the cause of the estrangement between Mr. and Mrs. Tilton, they had entirely overlooked the fact that my acquaintance with Mr. Tilton only began fully three months after the date of Mr. Beecher's letter of apology. When this fact dawned upon them there came the necessity of bringing in the other women reformers as being the cause instead of me.

WHO BROKE UP THE "IDEAL HOME."

In Mrs. Tilton's statement to the Committee there is the following language:

The implication (in Mr. Tilton's affidavit) that the harmony of the home was unbroken till Mr. Beecher entered it as a frequent guest and friend, is a lamentable satire upon the household where he himself years before laid the corner-stone of free-love and desecrated its altars up to the time of my departure.

Now, who were his companions with whom Mr. Tilton laid the corner-stone of free-love, and desecrated the altars of the household ? Why, they were—as stated by Mr. Tilton in his cross-examination and by Mrs. Stanton in her letter—herself, Susan B. Anthony, Annie Dickinson, Laura Curtis Bullard, Celia Burleigh, Lucretia Mott, Martha Wright, Lucy Stone, Grace Greenwood, Paulina W. Davis, or other prominent women of the same character. Nobody pretends, Mrs. Tilton herself does not pretend, that Mr. Tilton ever brought home to her household any woman of any other sort of public notoriety than these. These, then, were the women who had helped him to desecrate the altars of her household ; these were they who with him had laid the corner-stone of free-love in her home, since, it must be remembered, it was not until all this bad been done that I entered her house. But having begun their defense by the statement that it was the doing of these things by me that brought out the advice and apology of Mr. Beecher, it was necessary, after finding that they could not apply it to me on account of my non-acquaintance at the time, to substitute these other women reformers for me in their story ; for to abandon the theory was to leave nothing to stand upon. So they were forced to assert, in amendment of their first story, that it was these women who had caused the trouble in the Tilton family. Now what are the facts in the case ? Why, precisely the opposite. Not only were these women constant visitors at Mrs. Tilton's, but they were her intimate and acknowledged friends, with whom she visited, attended public places, and associated at woman-suffrage meetings, herself being an enthusiastic advocate of that reform. Will these women, or such of them as are involved, remain quiet under such an impeachment from Mrs. Tilton ; even those who two years ago boasted in Steinway Hall that " they followed in the steps of such men as Henry Ward Beecher ? " Will they be willing to have it go to the country that it was with them that Mr. Tilton laid the corner-stone of free-love and desecrated the altars of Mrs. Tilton's household ? Mrs. Tilton says so, and Mr. Beecher's friends say that her word is not to be questioned in this connection ; that it is to be received as against Mr. Tilton's statement made under oath, and as against the statements of all other people whatsoever, when confirmed by Mr. Beecher's denial. But this is all too preposterous to merit the serious consideration of any one who has the capacity to put this and that together and to draw the logical deduction. Alone, it vitiates the truth of her whole statement ; and, if this were testimony made under oath before a jury, it would be thrown out as unworthy of belief upon this evident falsity.

MRS. WOODHULL MAKES MRS. TILTON'S ACQUAINTANCE.

But, seemingly bent on utter destruction, Mrs. Tilton hastens to volunteer other and equally transparent stories. Oblivious to everything except the assurance of friends that her statements will be believed as against everybody else's, she again appears before the Committee on the evening of August 1st, when she is reported, among other things, as making the following statement :

---

* The reference in the above statement, in which is used the name of the editor of this paper, was submitted to Mr. Kinsella, and, in response to it, that gentleman would say : "That if the statement were made by a man he would pronounce it a lie ; being made by a woman, he will simply declare that it is ' conspicuously inexact.' "—*Brooklyn Eagle, Aug. 5th.*

When he (Mr. Tilton) brought the Woodhulls to her house and imposed these harlots upon her, she used every means in her power to induce them to leave, but they would not go. She finally, in despair, sent for the police to remove them, and when the Woodhulls heard that, they left.

From the caution with which I proceeded in the development of this scandal, it will be seen that I saw the necessity of keeping minute records of everything that occurred with all of the principals. Every important word and act I have carefully noted down, which, if ever made public, as circumstances now seem to indicate may become a necessity, the most remarkable view of the internal operations of modern society will be seen that has ever been presented. By means of this record, when my memory fails me, I am able to judge of the truth or falsity of every statement that is made about this case by any of the parties involved; and when it shall come to the "summing-up," many "lapses of memory," on the part of those who are taking part in it, will be pointed out. Upon the day when Mr. Tilton came to my office bringing a New York *World*, and asked me who I meant when I said that "I knew of a public teacher of eminence who lives in concubinage with the wife of another public teacher of almost equal eminence," he said, "Let me take you over to see Elizabeth." On being introduced to Mrs. Tilton, she was evidently surprised, and only recovered when Mr. Tilton said:

"Elizabeth, Mrs. Woodhull knows all."

"All, do you say?" replied Elizabeth, with great alarm.

"Yes, Mrs. Woodhull knows everything." Whereupon she received me, and after a while relaxed into a friendly, and finally into a confidential manner. The subject of our conversation was the scandal, of course; how I had become informed, and what I knew about it. She conversed with and treated me frankly, and while she did not at that time affirm or deny the fact of sexual intercourse with Mr. Beecher, the whole conversation was based upon that fact and the further fact of her continued love for him, for all of which I fully justified her, and said "that it was such a revolution in society as would permit the peaceable adjustment of such cases that I was working to inaugurate." She invited me to remain and take tea with them, and I did so; and when I left she pressed me to come again, and I promised to do so. I left feeling that I had done her good, and that in her, at least, I should find no objections, at the right time, to make use of the scandal for reformatory purposes. I even hoped from some of her expressions that she might join with me in making the statement, and all my future intercourse with her was directed to this end.

THE BEST OF FRIENDS.

My visits to her continued at intervals during the whole time of Mr. Tilton's associations with me, Mrs. Tilton fully understood the object of this association, and she will well remember the occasion of my last visit. Certainly up to that time she will scarcely assume that she endeavored to get rid of me, or that, failing to do so, she called the police to aid her. On this occasion she will remember, upon second thought, that our conversation was anything but such as would lead to an expulsion from the house. She will remember that it was upon an afternoon, and that we were in a room upon the upper floor, adjoining Mr. Tilton's study, and that Mr. Tilton was in his study laboring upon one of his elaborate articles. She will remember that she sat sewing upon a dress for one of her daughters—a small checked, light silk pattern—and that I sat at her side upon a low chair, by her own request, in the most familiar converse—so familiar that several times she dropped her work, and, putting her arms around my neck, kissed me. And when she recalls all this she will not be able to forget the beautiful book of poems she presented me, in which she wrote with her own hand:

"*To my friend Victoria C. Woodhull.*

"Elizabeth R. Tilton."

Was it upon this occasion, Mrs. Tilton, that you called the police to expel me from your house? It must have been at this time, if at all, since this was my last visit to you. And then that you learned that I was a harlot? Oh, for shame, Mrs. Tilton, to resort to opprobrious epithets to pander to a supposed public opinion, with the hope that it may help you in the acceptance of your other stories! A cause that requires such means to support it is weak indeed, and that such resort is made shows the desperate condition to which its advocates are driven.

Finally, I deny Mrs. Tilton's statement regarding my visits to her house point-blank. The "Woodhull sisters" were never at her house. I never visited her house in company with my sister; and my sister never visited her house, either with me or with anybody else, or alone; and Mrs. Tilton never, at any of my visits, manifested any desire to have me retire, and never called the police to remove me; and Mrs. Tilton knew that she was telling a deliberate untruth when she so testified before the Committee. But the responsibility of this falsehood does not lie upon Mrs. Tilton. It is a part of the general theory of defense that Mr. Beecher's counsel have constructed for him. Having no valid defense based on ability to disprove Mr. Tilton's impeachment, they resort to blackguardism of everybody who is supposed to be against their theory of Mr. Beecher's innocence; Mr. Tilton is insane. Mr. Carpenter is a tattler, and Mrs. Woodhull is a harlot, say the friends of Mr. Beecher; and these allegations, they hold, are proofs that Mr. Beecher and Mrs. Tilton never committed legal adultery; or, if they did, that the wrong did not consist in the doing of it, and does not rest upon them, but in the telling of it, and rests with those who told. Mr. Beecher and Mrs. Tilton are innocent; while Mr. Tilton, Miss Anthony, Mrs. Stanton, and Mrs. Woodhull have committed all the crime there has been committed. They are the ravens and cormorants who have ruthlessly coupled the names of two pure and innocent people with what is made a crime by both the Christian and the statute law. Such is the morality, such the Christian virtue, that prevail in this day and age.

TILTON AND PLYMOUTH CHURCH.

On October 6th, 1873, Mr. Wm. F. West charged Mr. Theodore Tilton, "a member of the church," with having circulated and promoted scandals derogatory to the Christian character of Mr. Beecher and injurious to the reputation of Plymouth Church. After examination and negotiation, the Examining Committee of the church officially recommended after the prayer-meeting on Friday evening, October 31st, that Tilton's name "be dropped from the roll of membership of this church." After debate Mr. Tilton said:

LADIES AND GENTLEMEN:—Twenty-three years ago, I joined this church, and many of the most precious memories of my life cluster around these walls. Four years ago, I ceased my membership, nor have I ever been, from that time until to-night, once under this roof. Retiring from Plymouth Church, I did not ask for the erasure of my name from the roll, because the circumstances were such that I could not publicly state them without wounding the feelings of others beside myself. During these years of my absence, a story has filled the land, covering it like a mist, that I have slandered the minister of this church.

The speaker was interrupted by cries from two or three of " Order! order ! " Mr. Shearman stated the point of order to be that there was no question of slander before them. The Moderator decided that Mr. Tilton was in order, and the latter resumed :

WAS BEECHER SLANDERED BY TILTON ?

Last summer, Mr. Beecher published an explicit card exempting me from this injustice. Notwithstanding this public document in my behalf, a committee of this church, by its action, has given rise to injurious statements in the public press that my claim of non-membership is made by me in order to evade my just responsibility to the church as a member. I, therefore, come here to-night, not from any obligation of membership, since I am not a member, and not examined by any committee, for no committee has examined me, but of my free will, prompted by my self-respect, and as a matter vital to my life, and in order to say, in Mr. Beecher's presence, surrounded here by his friends, that if I have slandered him I am ready to answer for it to the man whom I have slandered. If, therefore, the minister of this church has anything whereof to accuse me, let him now speak, and I shall answer, as God is my judge.

Mr. Tilton spoke slowly and with feeling. He retired from the platform, and was given a chair close to its side. Mr. Beecher then said :

Mr. Tilton has been absent for four years. It has not been for the sake of excusing himself, or evading any process, or avoiding any proper responsibility. To my personal knowledge he was absent because he believed that his relation to the church had been separated by his own act. It cannot have been regular, but it was valid. The Roman Church holds that a child cannot die and go to heaven without it be baptized, except that it go to purgatory, and yet irregular baptism is allowed to be valid. Persons honestly believing themselves to be married are considered married, if they show good intention in the matter. For four years past Mr. Tilton has not been present at any of our meetings. You have known it and never protested against it in any meeting or social gathering. With the distinct knowledge that for nearly four years he had assumed the position of a man that had withdrawn from the church, you have permitted it to go on. It is substantially a sanction of his action ; and now to go back of your own action, for the sake of drawing into the church a troublesome case of discipline, is neither wise nor according to the spirit and administration of this church. I desire to say further, that I don't believe that Mr. Tilton has desired in any way whatever to shirk his proper responsibility, or to avoid or evade any proper charge that might be made by the church. He asks if I have any charge to make against him. I have none. Whatever differences have been between us, have been amicably adjusted ; and, so far as I am concerned, buried.

I HAVE NO CHARGES.

This whole matter has not been with my consent. This whole matter has been against my judgment. I have said to the brethren who were interested in it, but who have acted sincerely and bonestly, I believe, "You will only, to take up this matter, stop the proper business of the church, and reach a point at which you can do nothing. You will end just where you began, and I hold it not to be wise, not to be called for, certainly not to be, according to my judgment, the matter of the church." That which I held from the beginning I hold still. (Applause.)

Mr. Beecher was vigorously applauded on retiring from the platform. After several motions, a vote was taken on the question of dropping Mr. Tilton from the roll of members, and 201 members voted yea and 13 nay.

DR. BACON'S DOGBERRY SPEECH.

The following is the passage in Dr. Bacon's speech, delivered in New Haven, April 2, which more especially stung Tilton into writing his famous letter to the ex-Moderator of the Brooklyn Council :

"My theory of all these transactions and troubles proceeds on a belief in the highest Christian integrity of Mr. Beecher. I believe that the infamous women who have started this scandal have no basis for it. (Applause.) If it was their testimony alone, it would not be worth kicking a dog for. But I doubt not that he has his infirmity, which is to let unprincipled men know too much of him. I object not to his being a friend to publicans and sinners. Our Lord was. But the harlot who washed his feet with her tears, and wiped them with her tresses, was a repentant harlot. So one must hedge himself in a little. And you, as you go out to preach, be on your guard, lest, in your anxiety to do good to the low, you become liable to be charged with their sins. Another part of my theory is that Mr. Beecher's magnanimity is unspeakable. I never knew a man of a larger and more generous mind. One who was in relations to him the most intimate possible said to me, 'If I wanted to secure his highest love, I would go into a church meeting and accuse him of crimes.' This is his spirit, but I think he may carry it too far. A man whose life is a treasure to the Church Universal, to his country, to his age, has no right to subject the faith in it to such a strain. Some one has said that Plymouth Church's dealings with offenders is like Dogberry's. The comparison was apt: 'If any one will not stand, let him go and gather the guard and thank God that you are rid of such a knave.' So of Launce, who went into the stocks and the pillory to save his dog from execution for stealing puddings and geese. I think he would have done better to let the dog die. And I think Mr. Beecher would have done better to have let vengeance come on the heads of his slanderers.

"But he stands before his Master, and not before men. I hope ever to feel

THE FULLEST CONFIDENCE IN HIS CHARACTER,

and to see his influence enlarge and round out more and more. No one could give such a course of lectures as this last one of his here—which was the best—and show unconsciously such a reach of spiritual experience and growth, without being pure and noble. (Applause.) And in this feeling the Council shared. Dr. * * * himself said to me, as we went out of the church after Dr. Storrs's address, in which he paid high tribute to Mr. Beecher's character and work, 'That passage should be saved to be Mr. Beecher's funeral eulogy, for it could never be excelled.'"

IS TILTON INSANE?

The question of the mental condition of Theodore Tilton has professedly been investigated by the Brooklyn *Eagle*. A reporter was sent to Keyport, on Raritan Bay, the home of Tilton's family, where from conversation had with persons who have known the family for many years he learned something of its history. The following is a synopsis of the report of his antecedents :

ABOUT HIS FAMILY.

The Tilton family have always been considered a "queer" set. Theodore's father was originally a shoemaker, and was in the business in Greenwich street, New York, acquired some means, increased his property by a life insurance on the life of the lunatic son who was treated at Flatbush, and now is quite well to do in the world. The grandfather of Theodore, on his father's side, died many years ago. Of his sons—Theodore's father and uncles—Theodore's father was considered to be the "soundest" mentally. One of his uncles traveled about, shoemaking a little, and playing on the fiddle a great deal. Another was a carpenter. Another, "Zekiel," as he was familiarly termed, now dead, had two sons, George and Benjamin, by one wife, and a daughter, Mary, by another. George now lives in Keyport. Before going to New York, Benjamin got in a "queer" way. It is believed that Benjamin's mind is right now. George has been "in a queer way for years back."

One lady asserted that George Tilton, the cousin of Theodore and son of Ezekiel, was mentally defective. His half sister, Mary, by the same father, married a gentleman by the name of Carter. This cousin of Theodore became insane ten years ago on the occasion of a religious revival, when quite a young woman. She was sent to an asylum, and was supposed to be cured. She had separated from her husband; Mr. Carter instituted proceedings for divorce, but was defeated; they never lived together again, he practically deserting her. A year ago last winter, at another religious revival, Mary Carter again became insane. As she had been a schoolmate of the informant, and as her insanity appeared to be of a mild type, Mrs. —— provided assistance for her, and Mary was for some time in Mrs. ——'s family. The form of her derangement related to her religious life. She believed that she had lost her soul when a girl, and had never possessed one since. She could not work, she said, on that account.

ABOUT HIMSELF.

The state of Mr. Tilton is thus summarized:

For twelve years he has shown an inability to get to sleep without being read to by the hour or more.

He would drink ale and porter after retiring, and then read himself to sleep.

He often complained of distress in his head, and of heat in the top of his head. He would often get up and walk the house, in order to induce sleep, or he would walk the streets for hours, sometimes returning as late as three or four o'clock in the morning.

He would say all manner of cruel, insulting things to his wife, and then wonder that she felt badly, and would express his surprise that she should feel badly.

He has developed the peculiarity of frequently repeating the same story to the same person, who would be supposed to know the story in the first instance.

To these facts were added others which have appeared in the course of the investigation; the unaccountable eccentricities manifested; the contradictions, apparently without motive; the strange behavior in writing two irreconcilable statements; his strange conduct in leaving his wife, returning, then leaving her again; his conduct in regard to the proposed transfer of the property to his wife, and his subsequent refusal to do so; his proffer to permit his wife to take away her personal effects, and his sudden and causeless refusal to permit it, and the language he then made use of; his strange and persistent attempts to see his wife at Mrs. Ovington's, after having been refused, and without apparent motive for seeing her; his statements to Mrs. Ovington, Sunday evening last, that he had come to see what he could do for his wife, and his threatening and abuse of her almost in the same breath; and the fact that he has recently asserted that neither himself, nor Mrs. Tilton, nor Mr. Beecher, would live a year.

Several medical experts were questioned upon the bearing of these facts on Tilton's probable predisposition to insanity. The first of these gentlemen stated in reply that the belief had for some time been growing upon him that Theodore Tilton is not in his right mind. He had felt serious apprehensions on the subject, and had privately conversed with reference to it with other gentlemen. The family history was a remarkable one, the blood of two families in which there was insanity uniting in Tilton. He believed that Tilton's actions could not be explained on any other theory. He believed him to be insane.

The second of these gentlemen said that there was no doubt the family "was saturated with insanity. I am of the opinion that Theodore Tilton is insane."

The third of these gentlemen expressed his opinion in the most decided terms. He had been watching the case with deep interest, having had beforehand a partial knowledge of the mental history of Tilton's family. He believed Theodore Tilton to be afflicted with "emotional insanity, not yet developed into a homicidal tendency, but liable to be so at any moment."

This gentleman particularly expressed himself as believing that both Mr. Beecher and Mrs. Tilton were in danger, and that the greatest care should be exercised, or the end of the Beecher-Tilton case would be a tragedy. He also said that he believed the insanity of Theodore Tilton to be the true solution of the Beecher-Tilton case.

It should be known that both the friends of Mr. Beecher and Mrs. Tilton have been warned to take measures of safety against any possible outbreak on the part of Mr. Tilton.

MRS. TILTON'S TROUBLES.

On Tuesday, August 4th, "The Plymouth Church Investigating Committee" gave to the press the report of Mrs. Tilton's examination before the committee, as written out from their stenographer's notes. It appeared in the New York newspapers of August 5th; the names of several persons are suppressed. In other regards, the committee vouch for the correctness of the report, which runs as follows:

MRS. TILTON'S CROSS-EXAMINATION.

BROOKLYN, July 31.

By Mr. Hill—You stated, I think, the date of your marriage in your former examination? A. I believe so—1855.

Q. Did you begin your married life housekeeping or boarding? A. Boarding with my mother, on Livingston street.

Q. About how long did you remain boarding with her? A. My first housekeeping was in Oxford street; I think that was in the spring of 1860.

Q. How long did you remain in Oxford street? A. Nearly three years, I think.

Q. And then where did you go? A. We went to board with mother again, about three years, and then from there I went to my own house, in Livingston street, where I remained until within a few weeks.

Q. Please state to the committee what Mr. Tilton's conduct was toward you in the early part of your married life, so far as personal attention was concerned, in sickness or in health? A. I wish these gentlemen to understand that to a very large extent I take the blame upon myself of the indifference that my husband has shown to me in all my life; at first I understood very well that I was not to have the attention that many wives have; I realized that his talent and genius must not be narrowed down to myself; that I made him understand also; to a very large extent I attribute to that the later sorrows of my life; I gave him to understand that what might be regarded as neglect under other circumstances would not be regarded by me as neglect in him, owing to his business and to his desire to make a name for himself and to rise before the world.

NEGLECT.

Q. To what extent was that attention to outside matters carried by him to the neglect of his family? A. At the birth of the first three children I had very severe and prolonged sicknesses; but when he saw me he never felt that I was sick, because on seeing him I always tried to seem well; I felt so desirous of his presence; it was charged upon me many a time by my mother and my brother, "When Theodore or the doctor comes you are never sick;" they said of me, "She has never a genius for being sick?"

Q. Will you state just what attention your husband bestowed upon you in case of sickness during your confinement or any other illnesses, if you had them? A. Well, I had no attention whatever, I may truthfully say, from him any more than a stranger would give; I do not think it was from neglect so much as from an inability on his part to understand that I was sick and suffering, though, in fact, I was very seriously ill.

Q. Please give the committee some idea of the length and severity of your illnesses in these three instances, or in any one of them? A. At the birth of my second little girl I was sick from the middle of April until September, confined to my bed; I sat up for the first time in the middle of September a little while.

Q. Who was your physician? A. Dr. Morrill; Theodore, I can truthfully tell you, in that time never gave me any sympathy at all; he called to see how I did in the morning and in the evening, or late at night; at this period he was absorbed in chess to such a degree that he would sometimes be up all night; I have known him to stand up at night, ready for bed, engaged upon a problem in chess, and to be found in that same condition in the morning, without having gone to bed at all.

Q. Was his conduct in that respect the subject of remonstrance on the part of your mother and others? A. Frequently by my mother.

Q. Ever in your presence ? A. Yes, sir; and also by my nurse, who was a faithful woman; she would often speak to him and of him in his presence as thoughtless and heartless; I have known her many times speak harshly of him.

Q. How much was he engrossed with actual business at this time ? A. Not very much; I always thought that if Theodore had more business he would have less time for sentiment and romance.

Q. How much time did he spend in actual business as editor ? A. In the early years of his editorial life I think he was a pretty hard worker; he never had his study at home then, and never wrote much at home.

Q. Do you recollect any message which came to you or to the family, from your doctor, in regard to your condition, giving the reason why your illness was of such a lingering character ? A. Yes, sir; I remember that Dr. Putnam said, "There is care and trouble on that woman's mind, and I cannot help it with medicine." He said that there was something he could not reach by the ordinary method, and that it was trouble.

Q. What was the trouble in point of fact ? A. Well, any one of you gentlemen, I think, would have cared for my family as much as Theodore did; I was left entirely with my servants, and they were very poor servants; I could not have my mother with me, because it was impossible for her to live with us on account of the disagreement of Mr. Tilton and herself.

THEODORE'S BAD MOODS.

Q. You intimated that you thought it would be better if your husband had been more fully occupied; will you explain further what you meant by that remark ? A. He spent a great deal of his time at home in moods of dissatisfaction with the surroundings, yearning, and wanting other ministrations; there was nothing in our home that satisfied him.

Q. Why was that ? A. It was on account of my domestic duties; I think it was because I could not minister to him in the way he wanted me to—that is, in reading; his life was largely literary, and I could not meet him there; I had three little children, all of about the same age, at that time.

Q. Were his friends persons who were congenial to you at that early time ? A. Yes, sir; I was happy in the friends that he brought to my house, and felt as if they were an addition to my life.

Q. Tell me who your guests were at the time ? A. I do not think when we boarded with mother that there were many except the church folks; when we left mother's and went into Oxford street literary people came to the house, and that has been so ever since; they would sometimes call in his absence, and when he came home I would laughingly tell him that So-and-so had been there during the day, and he would ask, "What did you have to say?" I would reply, "Well, I am a first-rate listener if they are good talkers; if not, I am a good chatterer myself."

Q. Did you understand that he said that as an expression of doubt as to your ability to entertain people ? A. Yes, sir; there is not the shadow of a doubt of it; I have lived under that always; he was very critical about my language; when under Theodore's influence, I do not think I ever said anything freely or naturally.

HOST AND HOSTESS.

Q. Please state what you did or tried to do in receiving these friends of his ? A. I tried to receive them kindly and pleasantly, always, and I think there is not one of them that will not bear witness to it; they were welcome; I always had a great desire to make my house hospitable to every one that came into it; we had a little picture of a sunshine house; the first year Theodore brought it home, and I said, "Our house will always be like that."

Q. I want to ask you in regard to his attentions to domestic wants—to the needs of the family ? A. He did not know anything about them at all; I took charge of them myself altogether; often he was critical about it, and I would say, "Well, alone I can do no better, but with you I think I could do much better;" and he would say, "I do not call upon you to go to the office to do my work; this is yours; the other is mine."

Q. What was the character of his criticisms ? A. They were very unreasonable, indeed; he would speak to me harshly and severely about any little extravagance, as he considered it; he was very fastidious, and must have the best of everything; but he didn't realize the cost.

Q. Do you mean that he found fault with your domestic management? A. Yes, sir; with my management of my servants, and with my management of the household matters generally.

Q. You speak of his referring to it harshly and severely; how did he treat you in matters of that description ? A. I fail generally when I attempt to be severe, and therefore I do not think I can imitate or describe him; but it was very hard and cruel; he would frequently make some very impulsive remark; I remember his taking me to task and scolding me severely before the butcher in regard to my dealings there; but directly after making a severe remark to me he would always apologize and say that he was sorry, but the apology was in private; it is a sorry story indeed.

Q. Were his demands extravagant ? A. Very much so; he was very particular with regard to his diet, and the table linen, and his own apparel; and the glass and china must be very nice; but these things cost money, so that the expenses which we were subjected to were largely increased, while I would have liked very well to have had it different.

MUTUAL JEALOUSY.

Q. Now, state to the committee what it was that first really disturbed your peace of mind in your family? A. I think that first I was jealous of his attention to the ladies.

Q. When were you first sensible of that? A. I think not until the winter of 1866.

Q. Do you recall any criticism of Mr. Tilton upon your conduct in any respect prior to 1869? A. Oh, yes; my manner to everyone was a trouble to Theodore; I think that was the beginning of my trouble; I saw something that was interesting in everyone; persons that he would find it a perfect bore to talk with I would be interested in, and would entertain; that was a great annoyance to Mr. Tilton, and he said "I gathered about me the most distressing sort of people," and he frequently had to go away; many persons that were pleasant to me were repulsive to him, but all who came—it mattered very little to me who they were—I took an interest in, not that I wanted such and such a person, but the house was open, and I really feel that you should give me credit for that one gift of mind (if it is a gift), of seeing something in almost everyone to be interested in—the poor and rich and the miserable—even those women who have troubled me so much latterly.

Q. When did he begin to talk to you, if at all, in regard to your association with and friendship for Mr. Beecher? A. I think I had no personal visits from Mr. Beecher before 1866; that is the first that I remember seeing him very much.

THEODORE AND BEECHER'S VISITS.

Q. What was the criticism in regard to Mr. Beecher and yourself which Mr. Tilton made? A. I would like to go back a little here, for I think it will show you my manner with Mr. Beecher; when I lived in Oxford street that was the first of this taint with which Mr. —— filled my husband's mind as early as 1865; Theodore then used to begin to talk to me about Mr. Beecher's wrongdoings with ladies which he (Mr. Tilton) had heard from Mr. ——, and night after night, day after day, he talked about Mr. Beecher; he seemed to be worried on that subject, so that when Mr. Beecher came to see me Mr. Tilton immediately began to have suspicions; but in order that I might be perfectly transparent to my husband with respect to my interviews with Mr. Beecher, whenever I was alone with him I used to make a memorandum and charge my mind with all the details of the conversation that passed between us, that I might repeat them to Mr. Tilton; it was so in regard to every gentleman who came to see me and with whom I sat alone; I was very closely watched and questioned, but especially in regard to Mr. Beecher; I attributed those criticisms from Theodore to Mr. ——'s criticisms; I never had a visit from Mr. Beecher that I was not questioned; Theodore would question me till I thought I had told him all that we talked about, and perhaps a day or two afterwards I would throw out a remark which Mr. Beecher had made, and Theodore would say, "You didn't tell me that yesterday;" I would say, "I forgot it;" "You lie," he would say, "you didn't mean to tell me;" "Oh, yes, I did mean to tell you, but I forgot it;" for two or three years I tried faithfully to repeat to my husband everything that I said and did, till I found it made him more suspicious than ever. He believed that I left out many things purposely, while I was conscious of never meaningly omitting anything; I wanted Theodore to know everything that passed between us; I often said that if he would only come home and be there, he would know all.

TILTON'S SUSPICIONS.

Q. You say that he would say, "You lie;" be kind enough to explain to the committee what his manner was in doing that? A. It was passionate and angry; he had no confidence in me; in those days I suffered a great deal; the last two or three years I have not felt so badly.

Q. You say that these suspicions and criticisms continued for about three years? A. They have lasted up to the present day, I think.

Q. When did his complaints against you change from the form of criticism to that of accusation, or something more than mere criticism? A. In the latter part of the winter and in the early spring of 1869-70 he began to talk to me, assuming that I had done wrong.

Q. In what respect? A. With Mr. Beecher.

Q. Criminally? A. Yes; I have been with him days and nights talking this matter over; but I would like to have you know that these conversations lasted for years, and that the change of his thought from the "old to the new," as he called it, was gradual; I used to think that his suspicions of me were caused by his not being at rest in his own mind.

Q. When he assumed that you had been guilty of criminal intimacy with Mr. Beecher, how did you treat the subject? A. For a time I was very angry, and expressed myself to him as strongly as I possibly could; I became angry and said I would not be talked to in that way.

DENYING THE CRIMINAL INTIMACY.

Q. State how you received it at different times, whether you received it silently or denied it? A. I received it in various ways, according to the manner in which he introduced it; sometimes I would think it best to be quiet; I have often taken the plausible mode of dealing with him, and tried to lift his mind from that subject to some other; I have acted according to his moods as far as I could.

Q. State whether or not you invariably denied that you ever had any criminal intimacy with Mr. Beecher? A. I have indeed; I remember that he not only charged me with this in my presence, but often became so audacious as to write to me about it, and that seemed to me unpardonable.

Q. When did he begin that? A. In the summer of 1870, when I was away.

Q. What was the character of that which he wrote to you in this particular? A. He sometimes would write quite lengthily of his own state of mind; his social theories—what we call free-love doctrines —were the one obsorbing theme with him then; I remember replying to him; I have not the letter, but, so far as I can recollect, there was a direct, not question exactly, but affirmation.

Q. What was your reason for adopting these various methods in receiving these accusations? A. Because I felt that he was in a morbid state of mind from troubles of his own; I was not quite willing to treat the matter seriously in regard to myself until he began to publish it abroad.

TILTON'S BREAK-DOWN.

Q. What did you do in endeavoring to soothe and quiet Mr. Tilton, and relieve his mind from the impressions he had in regard to yourself, and in regard to social life? A. I read to him a great deal aloud; I have read to him nearly half the night; he could not sleep; he never has been a good sleeper for years and years.

Q. What did you do particularly in regard to his accusations against you? A. I never could do anything but deny it.

Q. Did you always deny it? A. Oh, yes, sir; always.

Q. Please state what he said on the subject—how he introduced it. A. Well, as I look back upon it now, it seems to me that he would be very glad to bring me into such a state that I would acknowledge some wrong; all his influence in his conversation was exerted in that direction; he would talk of the Bible—he read it and thought of it—and he was becoming persuaded, and was making up his mind in regard to the life he was about to lead; and he would ask me again and again, "What do you think about this?—'Whosoever looketh upon a woman,'" etc.; really, my friends, he was morbid on that subject; I do not think he ever talked about anything else; I sought relief from it day and night, I assure you; he would keep me awake till three or four o'clock in the morning discussing of this particular subject; it came from his giving up his religious faith; altogether it was a breakdown.

TILTON'S MORBID JEALOUSY.

Q. In making those offensive allegations what did he say? A. As often as any way he said, "You will not deny that you have had criminal intercourse," and he tried to frighten me by saying that he had seen certain things.

Q. What things did he say he had seen? A. I remember that once or twice he pretended he saw me sitting on Mr. Beecher's lap at home in the red chair in the parlor; in reply to this I said, "You didn't;" I do not know what you gentlemen will think, but you certainly can see that such a continual talk, year in and year out, would have its influence upon me; I came really to be quite indifferent except in regard to my anxiety about him; it was a sort of morbid jealousy that he had; I was worn out and sick with it.

Q. Was it only in respect to Mr. Beecher that he made these accusations, or in respect to other people also? A. In respect to Mr. Beecher only at that time; about 1870, I believe, he began to think that I had great admiration for several people besides Mr. Beecher.

Q. Did he hesitate to mention names? A. No, sir, he did not.

Q. How many different persons did he mention? A. Two or three gentlemen acquaintances.

Q. Did he ever make to you any charge or accusation even with respect to Mr. Beecher, naming any definite time or place of any criminal act? A. Oh, no, never; he never connected any time with it.

THE BEDROOM SCENE.

Q. Did he ever pretend to you that you had been guilty of any impropriety with Mr. Beecher at his (Mr. Beecher's) house? A. No; he wondered why I went there on two or three occasions; I went on errands; I attended Mr. Burgess a great deal at the time of his death (he was a poor man), and I went to Mr. Beecher two or three times to see him in regard to that man.

Q. Did you ever meet Mr. Beecher at other places by appointment? A. Never at all; not once.

Q. Did Mr. Tilton ever base any accusations against you upon any admission which you had made to him either with respect to an event at Mr. Beecher's or your house, or any other place? A. Yes; he based an accusation against me in his public statement upon an interview which I had with Mr. Beecher in my second-story room, and I deny it in my public statement.

Q. In any conversation with you at any time did he accuse you of any wrong-doing with Mr. Beecher, based upon any admission by you? A. No, sir.

Q. Is it true that in July. 1870, you confessed to your husband any act or acts of impropriety with Mr. Beecher? A. No.

THE CATHERINE GAUNT STORY.

Q. Did you admit to him any wrongs of criminal intimacy with Mr. Beecher at other places? A. No, sir.

Q. Now, please state what conversation occurred in the summer of 1870, along about the month of July, between you and your husband in relation to that subject? A. Well, I said in my statement, not that I had made a confession similar to that which Catherine Gaunt had made at any one time, but that I had said things in many conversations out of which there might have been gathered up such a story as, on reading Catherine Gaunt's up to a certain point, I felt that she had told.

Q. You wrote a letter to your husband from Schoharie; had you at that time read the "Life of Catherine Gaunt" through? A. No, I had not; I had read the "Life of Catherine Gaunt" to a certain point, and, being touched very strongly with it in regard to myself, I sat down and wrote this letter to Theodore.

Mr. Winslow—Had you at that time any reference to adultery, or thought of it? A. No, sir.

Q. What did you refer to? A. I will try to answer that question; the one absorbing feeling of my whole life has been Theodore Tilton; neither Mr. Beecher, I assure you, nor any human being has ever taken away from that one fact my love for him; but I must say that I felt very great helpfulness in my own soul from having had the friendship of Mr. Beecher, and also of other people, as many women as men.

THE SIN.

Mr. Hill—You stated that in the summer of 1870 you made confession in respect to Catherine Gaunt, and that you made it at no one time? A. No, I did not. I think that Theodore gathered up from all our talks that summer that I really found in Mr. Beecher what I did not find in him; he got that, I know; I gave it to him; but I often said, "Theodore, if you had given to me what you give to others, I dare say I should find in you what I find in Mr. Beecher."

Q. In your Schoharie letter you spoke of your "sin;" what did you mean by that? A. Theodore's nature being a proud one, I felt on reading that book that I had done him wrong—that I had harmed him in taking any one else in any way; although, in looking it over, I do not think but that I should do it again, because it has been so much to my soul.

Q. Taking any one else in what respect? A. I do not think if I had known as much as I do now of Tilton that I should ever have encouraged Mr. Beecher's acquaintance; I think I did wrong in doing it, inasmuch as it hurt Theodore; I do not know as I can make myself understood; but do you know what I mean when I say that I was aroused in myself—that I had a self-assertion which I never knew before with Theodore? there was always a damper between me and Theodore, but there never was between me and Mr. Beecher; with Mr. Beecher I had a sort of consciousness of being more; he appreciated me as Theodore did not; I felt myself another woman; I felt that he respected me; I think Theodore never saw in me what Mr. Beecher did.

A WANT OF MARITAL SYMPATHY.

Mr. Sage—Do you mean to say that Theodore put down self-respect in you, while Mr. Beecher lifted it up? A. Yes, I never felt a bit of embarrassment with Mr. Beecher. but to this day I never could sit down with Theodore without being self-conscious and feeling his sense of my inequality with him.

Mr. Winslow—Will you state in a few words what was that sin which you spoke of in that letter? A. I do not think I felt that it was anything more than giving to another what was due to my husband— that which he did not bring out, however.

Q. When you speak of what was due to him, what do you refer to? A. Why the all of my nature; I do not think I feel any great sin about it now.

By Mr. Hill—Do you mean that you thought you let your affections or your regard or your respect go out for Mr. Beecher unduly, and so censured yourself? A. No, sir; I do not think I ever felt that, because I did not think I harmed Theodore in that; I harmed him in his pride by allowing any one else to enter into my life at all; I think that was sin.

Q. When you speak of your sin, you do not mean to be understood as going farther than that? A. No; let me tell you a little more; Theodore, up to that time, in his accusations, would often talk to me by the hour to show me the effect that he said he knew I carried about my personal presence with gentlemen; and I would become nearly crazy in my conscience; he would say that he knew there was no one who carried such an influence as I did; I would say, "Theodore, I do not think that is a fact; if I did, I would never speak to another man in all my life."

Q. Did he define that influence? A. He said I had a sensual influence; I used to become impregnated with this idea of his myself while under his influence, and I wondered if it was so, and would think it over and over; he would often talk to me in that way by the hour, and try to persuade me that it was true; and then when I used to get out from under his influence I was perfectly sure that no man ever felt that way toward me.

Mr. Sage—Was there, in the sin to which you referred, anything that was unjust, or that was giving to Mr. Beecher any affection that belonged to your husband? A. No, sir; I think that the wifely feeling which I gave to my husband was as pure as anything that I could give him; there was nothing more than confidence and respect which I gave to Mr. Beecher; and I teach my daughters that if they give to their husbands what I have given to mine, they will do enough; I would like to have you, gentlemen, realize how very severe that was to me, because it has been day after day and week after week —the hearing that that was the effect of my presence upon persons; it made me sick and caused me to distress myself; it kept me in embarrassment; it was a hard thing to live under.

Mr. Cleveland—Did it make you feel that you were beneath him and not his equal? A. Oh, certainly; I will tell you a little incident to explain this feeling in regard to my personal appearance (my presence was always mean, I knew); I have often been invited to go with him to meet his friends, and very much against my will I have gone; I never could appear as a lady; of course I never could dress as other ladies did; that was not my taste; and when I have been there with them, going at his own desire, he has turned around to me and said, "I would give $500 if you were not by my side," meaning that I was so insignificant that he was ashamed of me; and I remember perfectly, in two or three instances, of going to hotels, where my being short of stature was a dreadful trial to him, and be said, "I wish you would not keep near me;" I would not have gone if I had not been invited by him, and I did not go save to accompany him, dear friends; and I would have cut off my right arm to have been five inches taller; he seemed unwilling that I should be as the Lord made me; I do not know what else it was; one occasion I remember very well; there was a large company of friends at our house; they were all his friends—a gathering of women's rights people—and he particularly requested me not to come near him that night; it was very evident to me that he did not want comparisons made between us; that seems very mean to state, but it hurt me very much to know it.

Mr. Hill—In July, 1870, had you any conversation with Mr. Tilton in regard to his own habits and his own associations? A. Yes, sir, I had.

Q. What was the character of that conversation? A. He had always very freely opened his heart and his thoughts to me in all these conversations, for I think he never had a thought without telling me; no matter how much it hurt, he would tell it, and he made a great many disclosures to me of his life that summer.

A CONFESSION OF ADULTERY.

Q. Did he make any confession to you of criminality with other ladies? A. Yes, sir.

Q. And did you say that was about July, 1870? A. Yes, sir.

Q. You have noticed his statement in which he says you confessed adultery to him about that time, and you say that the confession was the other way—from him to you? A. It was; I do not mean that his confession at that time referred to one; his talk with me referred to several. It was the time when I was making up my mind what to do in regard to living with a person who had reached such a state, and in connection with these ideas which he had grown into; he said he wished me to understand that when he was away from home on a lecturing tour or anywhere visiting with friends, if he desired the gratification of himself he would do it.

Q. State what you refer to in your published statement where you speak of your going to other people to correct impressions with reference to him, and finding that he had anticipated you? A. The world was filled with slanders about him; he did not seem to know it; he thought everything came from me, and he said so; he declared that I was the originator of all this talk about him, and he insisted upon my correcting these impressions.

Q. Do you remember that that was in the summer of 1870? A. Yes; I will give you one instance which occurred with Elizabeth So-and-so; said he, "That woman has been talking against me, and I want you to go around and see her and put an end to it." Well, I immediately did; the next day I put on my things and made a call on her, and said that I was surprised that she should add to the stories that were already in circulation; that I should have thought she would have avoided doing it for my sake; and she said: "Mrs. Tilton, do you know why I didn't? because the night before your husband had told stories of yourself to such-and-such a person that came to me directly, and I was not going to allow an accusation of that character to stand against you." I found, wherever I went, not only the accusation, but the details which he has now published.

Mr. Sage—He was charging you with the same crime that he was committing himself? A. Yes; and it was a very singular thing for him to do; I would go back from these calls utterly speechless; I could say no more to these people; and I said to him, "Theodore, what made you send me there?" he would deny that he had ever said any such things as were attributed to him; there was no talking with him; he was very unreasonable.

THE IMPROPER CARESS AND THE BEDROOM STORY.

Mr. Hill—I want to call your attention to the allegation made by your husband in his published statement with respect to a scene in Mr. Beecher's house, wherein he states that you were looking at engravings, and that there was an improper caress; was there any truth in that? A. No, sir; I said in my statement that it was not true; you must consider my public statement a part of my testimony.

Mr. Winslow—When did you first learn of that? A. In Theodore's statement.

Mr. Hill—Let me call your attention to another charge—that he (Mr. Tilton), discovered yourself and Mr. Beecher in the second story bedroom of your house? A. That I also deny.

Q. Do you deny that it was as he stated it, or do you deny that he found you there? A. He found us often in our common sitting-room, and he has invited Mr. Beecher there; my writing-desk was up there, and we sat there more often than in the parlor, a great deal; Mr. Greeley and almost everybody else went up there; there were folding-doors between the bedroom and the sitting-room, and they were almost always open, and the door which Mr. Tilton said was locked was generally locked, and we entered the room by the other door, leading from the hall into the sitting-room.

Q. Do you recollect an occasion when Mr. Beecher was in either of these rooms, and Mr. Tilton came to the hall entrance of the bedroom? A. Yes, because that has been the one thing that he has always talked about to me.

Q. Explain that occurrence. A. Well, I think Theodore had been with us for quite a little season that morning; he had gone out; Mr. Beecher was sitting in the large chair, and I had drawn up a small one; Mr. Beecher had in his hand a little manuscript that he was going to read; I do not remember what it was; the door from the bedroom to the hall was shut, and I shut the door leading from the sitting-room to the hall, which was usually open; I had no sooner done that (which I did to keep out the noise of the children, that were playing in the hall), and sat down by the side of Mr. Beecher, when Theodore came to the other door; not five minutes had elapsed since he went out.

Q. Was there any hesitation in opening the door? A. Not the slightest.

Q. Were the folding-doors closed? A. No, they were wide open; the door leading from the hall to the bedroom was locked; but that was not uncommon; my closing the other door, which was seldom closed, perhaps did make Theodore suspicious.

Q. Was Mr. Beecher flushed when Theodore came in? A. Not at all.

Q. At what time in the day did that occur? A. About eleven or twelve o'clock.

Q. He was there and left you, and returned in five minutes or less? A. Yes.

Q. Mr. Beecher was there, upstairs; Theodore was there, and you were there; all of you were sitting together, and Theodore went out, and came back in five minutes? A. Yes, it was not more than that.

UNCONSCIOUS WRITING.

Q. Tell us with regard to the paper which Mr. Tilton says you wrote to him the latter part of December, 1870, wherein you stated that Mr. Beecher had been guilty of improper approaches to you? A. Well, the paper which I wrote then was but a couple of lines, so far as I can remember; it was written, as I have told you already, at a time when I was pretty nearly out of my mind; if ever I was worried it was by this constant talking; but what Theodore made me write I cannot tell to this day; I am conscious of doing it on very many occasions; I am conscious of writing for Mr. Tilton many things under his dictation, or copying them off and giving them to him.

Mr. Winslow—Things that were false? A. Oh, yes; that is why I expect before you to appear utterly miserable and weak and forlorn.

Q. What did he say to you to make you write them? A. He had very great embarrassments in every way, especially at that time, when these social scandals were upon him.

Q. What benefit did he tell you would come if you would make these statements? A. He said this statement was to help him in the matter with Mr. Bowen; I did not understand how it was; but instead of going to Mr. Bowen with it, he went to Mr. Moulton, and that quite startled me.

Mr. Hill—You say that the paper was about two lines long? A. Yes, sir.

Q. Can you tell us what was in it? A. No, sir.

Q. If there was anything in it which reflected on Mr. Beecher, was it true or false? A. False.

Q. Did Mr. Beecher make any improper suggestion or request to you? A. Why, no, sir; it was utterly false; I have done many things like signing that paper.

A PSYCHOLOGICAL INFLUENCE.

Q. How happened it that you did these many things—copying off statements which Mr. Tilton had prepared for you, and which you say were false ? What was the influence that operated on your mind ? A. I have always been unable to account for it; I do not know why I did it; there is a certain power that Theodore has over me, especially if I am sick, and he hardly ever came to me when I was in any other condition to do anything of that sort, and I very frequently would say, "Well, it matters very little to me; I shan't be here long any way, and if you want me to do this I will do it."

Mr. Winslow—Had you arrived at a condition of mind on this occasion in which you could not exercise your will ? A. Yes, sir.

Q. Was it his will altogether that influenced you ? A. Yes.

Q. Did you feel that your will was not acting ? A. I did; one or two letters that I sent West will bear witness to that—with regard to the same matter; I wrote a letter to Mrs. —— in one ten minutes, and in the next ten minutes I wrote another letter to her with a statement just contrary to that of the first; the first was written under Mr. Tilton's influence; after having written I said to myself, "Why, I have stabbed Mr. Beecher," and I wrote in the second letter, "For God's sake, don't listen to what I said in the first."

Q. Who suggested the words of that two-line letter in 1870? A. Mr. Tilton; I had hardly any mind or consciousness in those days.

Q. Did he write the words for you to copy, or did he suggest them ? He always wrote the letter and I copied it; I never have written a letter of my own in regard to this matter, except one very small letter, about which I desire to confess: it was with regard to my mother; I do not know whether she had seen it or not; in that letter I gave her a very cruel stab; I wrote that, but the others were entirely of Mr. Tilton's concocting.

Mr. Sage—When Theodore desired you to write those letters, which he dictated or wrote and you copied, were you so much under the influence of his will that you had no power of your own? A. I never exerted my will when he was about.

Q. Had you any power of will, or did his will so dominate you that you were obliged to act under his? A. I have often thought whether I had any power or whether his was a mesmeric condition brought to bear upon me; I certainly was indifferent to any act that I was doing, except to do as he willed me to do.

Mr. Hill—Was that statement prepared during your sickness at the time of your miscarriage in 1870? A. Yes, sir.

Q. Then this peculiar influence of Mr. Tilton over you to which you refer was aggravated by your physical condition ? A. Yes ; I never expected to see the light again.

Mr. Winslow—Was that letter addressed to anybody? A. It was a mere statement.

Q. Did he say what he was going to do with it ? A. He said he was going to use it if he wanted it; he gave me to understand that it referred to his difficulties with Mr. Bowen.

Q. Did you write that letter from your sick-bed? A. Yes, sir; I had pen, ink, and paper brought to me.

Q. Were you lying down or sitting up? A. Lying down.

Q. Was it in the daytime or in the evening ? A. In the night.

Q. How long did Mr. Tilton importune you for this letter? A. About five minutes; it was a matter of indifference to me whether I gave it or not.

THE LETTER TO DR. STORRS.

Mr. Hill—A letter was written, as we understand, by you to Dr. Storrs, or for use before Dr. Storrs. Will you describe the circumstances under which it was written, and tell what was said to you at the time ? A. Theodore had been three or four months writing what he called "a true statement ;" it was written on foolscap, and it made a roll two or three or more inches in diameter ; he came to me one morning after breakfast in the parlor, in the presence of Mr. Carpenter, who had stayed at our house over night, and said that in about fifteen minutes he wanted to meet Dr. Storrs by appointment, and that he had a letter on which would hinge this whole story, and that he wanted to show it, and that he wanted me to copy and sign it; I never would allow him to read that story to me except in little fragments, because I did not believe in it, nor would I allow the children to hear it ; he wanted Florence to hear it often and often, and before he had this letter he asked Annie Tilton and Florrie to go down into the parlor and listen to it ; they said no ; they did not care to read the story ; he said it was my influence that made them refuse ; well, this morning he had the letter written ; it fills one side of a note sheet of my writing, as I copied it ; said he, "I want you to copy that, because it is the hinge of the whole matter," meaning the whole or "true statement ;" I think the first line of it was, "Mr. Beecher desired me to be his wife, with all that that implies ;" I said, "I can't write that ;" said he, "I must have something a great deal better than I can write ;" said I, "I cannot write it ;" "Well, now, come,

Elizabeth," said he, "that is not anything, after all." Said I, "It is not true, and what will Mr. Beecher say?" there stood Frank Carpenter right by my side; there was the writing-desk in the parlor, and he said that I had but fifteen minutes, and I sat down and wrote it.

THE WOODHULL TROUBLE.

Mr. Winslow—What use was he going to make of it? A. He was going to take it to Dr. Storrs.

Q. Why did he want to show it to Dr. Storrs? A. I don't think he gave any reason, except that he had made an appointment with him; he said the whole story was all right, with the exception that he wanted something from me.

Q. Is it true, as Mr. Tilton says, and as he said before this committee, that you wanted to make a a stronger statement than he made? A. It is absolutely false; I thought it was dreadfully wicked, strong as it was; I knew there was trouble, and I thought it would in some way serve Theodore and bring peace to his household; he said that was the best way he could fix it; it was some scheme to get him out of the Woodhull trouble.

Q. Did he say that it would get him out of the Woodhull trouble? A. He said that the writing of the whole statement would; but whether he said so that morning, or not, I don't know.

FRANK CARPENTER'S ACTION.

Q. What part did Mr. Carpenter take in this? A. No part; he stood by the fire and looked on; he did not advise me one way or the other.

Q. Mr. Carpenter says you left the room and readily assented to it; did you leave the room? A. No, sir; there are three parlors; he stood in the back parlor by the fire, and I went to the desk in the middle room.

Q. Was Theodore with you any of the time? A. Part of the time.

Q. You say you told Mr. Tilton you could not write that letter; was that conversation before you went to the desk? A. It was in the middle room, before I took my seat at the desk.

Q. Could Mr. Carpenter hear your conversation or your objection to writing the letter when you made it? A. No; it was a conversation in a low tone of voice.

Q. Have you seen Dr. Storrs within a year? A. I went to see him at his study.

DOCTOR STORRS'S STUDY.

Q. When was that? A. About a week after he called the Council. I had been in considerable trouble about this letter of mine, and, knowing that Dr. Storrs had seen it, I went one morning, without consultation with Theodore, alone, and asked Dr. Storrs to hear me; he could not that morning, but he appointed the next morning at nine o'clock for an interview; that was a little while before the session of the council; I saw him all alone; I told him I went to his church the Sunday before, and that I meant to have seen him there and asked an interview then, and he said that he never saw any one on Sunday after church; then I told him I had been very little in church lately, but that my daughter had attended his church and enjoyed his services, and I thanked him for his kindness to her (he had introduced her into his Sunday-school); I told him that I had called on purpose to say to him that there was a letter in the statement which Mr. Tilton showed him, as I understood, that I had written, and that I wanted him to know that I had not composed that letter, and was not the author of it in any way, that it was false, and that it was added to the statement in order to have some word from me; Dr. Storrs looked up at me and said, "I wish I had known that a week ago, because on that letter alone I believed Mr. Beecher to be a guilty man."

Mr. Winslow—Did he inquire how you came to copy such a letter? A. No.

DR. STORRS IN A HURRY.

Mr. Hill—Did you explain to him? A. No; he wanted to know if I knew of the great sin that I had done: I said I did; he said it was a fearful thing; to which I said yes; I realized it; I had frequently done such things as that.

Q. Did you explain to him the influence of Theodore upon you? A. No, sir, not at length; he was in a hurry.

Q. You went to see him for the single purpose of correcting that impression? A. Yes, sir; he was then going to see Dr. Budington; and he said that if I wanted to talk further he would like me to see his wife.

Q. Have you had any conversation with Dr. Storrs since? A. No, sir.

Q. Do you know Dr. Budington? A. No, sir; never met him.

Q. Did you tell Theodore that you were going to see Dr. Storrs? A. No, sir; but he very soon found it out.

Mr. Hill—I want to call your attention to the letter which was published by your husband in his statement, dated Brooklyn, February 7, 1871, apparently from Mr. Beecher to you; did you ever see it? A. No, sir; I never saw it until it was printed there.

NO CORDIALITY WITH MOULTON.

Q. Did you ever hear about it? A. I was never willing to have anything to do with Mr. Moulton, although Mr. Tilton was; I have never been a cordial visitor at his house; I never had anything to do with him; Mr. Tilton early told me that whatever communication I had on these matters in regard to Mr. Beecher and Mrs. Woodhull must come through Mr. Moulton; but I said, "I shall have nothing to do with any third party—I shall be trusted as I have been hitherto, and if Mr. Beecher or any one else has anything to say to me, it shall not come through Mr. Moulton;" well, there came to me two or three times papers and letters which purported to come from Mr. Beecher, but I did not look at them, because they came through Mr. Moulton; I did not care anything about them; this one, one day when I was sitting in the parlor, Mr. Moulton brought to me and said it was a very important letter; I refused to receive any letter from him in that way, and he said, "Let me read it to you," and he did read something, but it went in one ear and out of the other, so much so that I do not remember what was in it; I know there must have been a letter, but I did not see the handwriting or anything about it; I did not take it in my hands; after reading it he carried it away.

MRS. TILTON'S SICK-BED LETTER.

Q. Can you recall anything in the letter that he read which makes you think that this is the one? A. I remember something about his urging me to have Mr. Moulton as a confidant; the only thing that impressed itself upon my mind was that Mr. Beecher desired me to accept Frank Moulton in some way, as in him we had a common ground; I have a recollection of some such statement, against which I rebelled, in the letter which Mr. Moulton read to me.

Q. Do you recollect a letter beginning, "My Dear Husband—I desire to leave with you, before going to bed, a statement that Mr. Henry Ward Beecher called upon me this evening and asked me if I would defend him against any accusation in a council of ministers," and ending, "Affectionately, Elizabeth?" A. Yes, sir; but that is not my letter.

Q. How was it written? A. In the same way as those which I have already explained; I have no other explanation for any of them; that was written in bed; Mr. Tilton wrote it first, and I sat up in my sick-bed and copied it.

Mr. Cleveland—Is that true of all the letters that have that significance? A. Yes, sir, so far as my authorship of them is concerned.

Mr. Winslow—Was he excited? A. He was always very much excited about his own public difficulties.

Q. Had he been out that evening? A. Yes, he had been to Frank Moulton's.

Mr. Hill—What time did he get home? A. My nurse had gone to bed and he found me in bed; I was very sick, and my nerves were greatly disturbed.

Q. When he first came in what did he say? A. I do not remember.

Mr. Winslow—What led to this act? A. His bringing me pen and ink and paper; he had the letter already written.

Mr. Hill—What did he say about it? A. Really, I positively tell you, I cannot remember; I felt often at that time utterly despairing and miserable, and it mattered to me but little what I did.

Q. Was it when you were sick from a miscarriage? A. Yes.

Q. Do you recollect Mr. Beecher calling that evening? A. Yes.

Q. When? A. But a few hours before I wrote that letter.

Q. Can you remember that interview with Mr. Beecher? A. It was a very similar one to the other; I was half-unconscious, and was very ill-prepared to see either of them; my room was all darkened, and the nurse had gone to hers; she opened the door and said that Mr. Beecher wanted to see me; I certainly do not know what to tell you about that either.

THE RIVALS.

Q. Do you remember writing some paper for Mr. Beecher? A. Yes.

Q. Can you recall the contents of that paper? A. No, I cannot; I think it was to do something for him, because Theodore had done something against him.

Q. Is it true that he said anything to you about a council of ministers? A. I do not remember everything about it; I have tried very hard, dear friends, to get into my mind those scenes, but they are utterly gone out of my brain.

Q. Did you not tell Miss Anthony that you had committed adultery or other wrong with Mr. Beecher, or anything to that effect? A. No, sir.

Q. Did you ever tell any human being that you had been guilty of wrong-doing with Mr. Beecher? A. I never voluntarily did so; once my husband took me in Mrs. * * * 's carriage to the house of a lady, to whom he had been telling stories about me and Mr. Beecher; I went against my will, and when we got there, he said, "I have brought Elizabeth to speak for herself, whether I have slandered her," and I did not deny him; it was the same thing, as when I had copied and signed letters which Theodore had prepared, and I am reminded of this; I do not know whether it was treachery, but many times he has said, "You have gone to Dr. Storrs's, and now he knows that you are guilty;" he found out that I had been to Dr. Storrs's, and he was very angry.

Q. What did he say? A. I do not know, but he was very angry, as you may well suppose he would be; he was violent in manner.

Q. Was he ever profane? A. Very often, and I always left his presence when he began to swear.

Mr. Cleveland—Do you think it possible, in your low state of health, when talking to people about your troubles, that you might have left the impression upon their minds that there was something criminally wrong without intending to do so? A. I do not think I ever did; I understand that Miss Anthony and another lady have both reported that I made confidants of them, and it came in this way: I have, full of anguish of soul, many times talked freely to them, and, on one occasion, Susan Anthony stayed all night with me, and I talked to her.

THE INTERVIEW WITH SUSAN B. ANTHONY.

Mr. Hill—How did that interview with Miss Anthony come about? A. In this way:—she came with Mrs. Stanton one afternoon to our house, and they proposed going to Mrs. Bullard's to dinner; Mrs. Stanton and my husband went first, early in the afternoon, and we understood that Theodore was coming back to bring Susan and myself there; I was not going, however. The evening came and Miss Anthony was very much annoyed to think that Theodore didn't come, and she filled my mind all that evening with stories about Theodore's infidelities; he came home about eleven o'clock; Mrs. Stanton remained at Mrs. Bullard's all night; when Theodore came in Susan began in a very angry way to chide him for not coming after her, and charged him with what she had been telling me about ladies, and he grew very angry at Susan, so much so that she ran upstairs and locked herself up in the front room; I followed, and he said to me, "You have done this thing; you have been talking and putting it into her mind;" "No," I said, "I never was the one to talk against Theodore in that manner;" he was so angry that I feared he would be really crazy; for the first time he threatened to strike me; he went into his own room, and was so much excited that I was alarmed; I thought I would sleep with him and apply water to his head and feet, but Susan would not let me; she said it was not safe, and that I should not stay with him, so I went into her room and went to bed with her, but during the night I went frequently to see how he was; he did not sleep—he was restless; that night I told Susan of my alarm for Theodore; I told her I never saw his brother in such a state when it seemed to me that he was more crazy than Theodore often was, and I went on further to tell her how he was, she having seen this exhibition of his—of his being angry and of his striking; I told her, also, in the conversation "that he had charged me with infidelities with one and another, and with Mr. Beecher particularly, and that when he sat at his table many times he had said that he did not know who his children belonged to;" on a similar occasion I spoke of it to * * *; I was aroused to it by Mrs. Woodhull's being there and by being very much outraged by a visit from Mrs. Claflin and the two sisters of Mrs. Woodhull, whom I called the police to take away; * * * sat with me, and I poured out my soul to her.

POLICE CALLED.

Mr. Winslow—You called the police to take the Claflins away? A. Yes, and they seeing it, went off.

Mr. Hill—You say that you opened out your soul to * * *? A. Nothing more than to tell her what unjust accusations had been put upon me by my husband.

Q. Did you, in each instance with her and with Miss Anthony, take the trouble to say that these accusations are false? A. No; it never occurred to me to do it; I took them to be reasonable persons, and I never thought of their even wondering if it was so.

Q. I want to call your attention to an important statement of your husband that you have written out a confession or an admission of your guilt with Mr. Beecher, and that you intended to send it through your stepfather to the church; is that so? A. Oh, dear, no; I never heard of that before.

MRS. TILTON GOES WEST.

Q. How frequent were Mr. Beecher's calls upon you? A. There was no regularity in them at all; I think never oftener than once in three or four weeks.

Q. Was there ever a time, so far as you know, when Mr. Beecher called upon you so often as twelve times within five or six weeks, as Mr. Tilton alleges in his statement? A. I do not think he called as often as that; I do not think he can have called more than once in two or three weeks.

Q. Explain the circumstances under which you left to go West. A. I went to get rested from

Theodore's constant talkings; I was worn out by them; I went to Mrs. * * * 's, in Ohio, in the fall of 1870, and found · * * * there; she had been there for some time. * * *

Q. Before you went West had you a conversation with your husband in regard to * * * and his treatment of her? A. Yes.

Q. What was the substance of it? A. This came out in his talks with me about persons with whom he had been ; he spoke in this way: "* * * On one or two occasions when I solicited her she utterly refused me, and I had not found it so with other women ;" he made me listen to that; I always had to hear it, and to hear all sorts of things.

A MIDDLE-AGED MAIDEN LADY.

Q. When you went West and saw * * *, did you have any conversation with her about your interview with Mr. Tilton in respect of her? A. Yes ; and she told me it was so ; she said she often thought of telling me before she left home, but that she feared it would add to my burdens; that she tried to think Mr. Tilton was a father to her and did not mean anything wrong, and all that, and that she concluded not to tell me.

Q. You and * * * returned together to New York? A. Yes; Mrs. * * * and I talked the matter over as to whether * * * should stay with her or myself, and I thought she could be a great help to me in my state of health, so she returned with me; I expected to find my house as I left it, but it was altogether different; my husband had sent off my servants; mother said she would remain and oversee matters while I was away; she did for a few days, and then left; she took into the house a middle-aged maiden lady, and she had entire possession.

Q. What was her name? A. * * *.

Q. Did you find that Theodore had been talking over these troubles with her, so that she was completely possessed of his ideas about them? A. Yes, sir; and I have every reason to believe that she ministered to him in every way.

TURNED OUT OF HER HOME.

Mr. Hill—Do you mean in a criminal way? A. Yes, I do ; I was utterly turned out of house and home; when I got there, there seemed to be no place for me; they had not expected my return so soon; they thought I was to remain West all winter; I found her at the head of the table and taking my place entirely, and Mr. Tilton backed her up in all this; I never could have a word to say; she followed me wherever I went; if I went into the china-closet, or anywhere else, she was behind me, looking over my shoulder to see what I was about; this went on until, finally, I was persuaded that she had been told to take possession of the house and occupy it.

Q. Do you recollect an interview at the breakfast table, referred to by Mr. * * *, at which you were grieved by what this person did in your presence? Yes; he sat at the table, she at the head, and I opposite, and Theodore and * * * on one side ; Miss * * *, who was upstairs, had not come down ; I was full of feeling, and could eat nothing; presently I left the table, and * * * (the person at the head) said, "Well, I think Elizabeth is getting crazy;" and Mr. Tilton said, "* * *, don't you think Mrs. Tilton is getting demented ?" "No," said * * * indignantly, "but it is a wonder to me that she has not been in the lunatic asylum," or something like that; Miss * * * criticised that remark of * * *'s; Theodore followed me into the parlor, and said to me that I must discharge that girl immediately ; I was at the piano at the time; I frequently went there and touched a few notes when I was in trouble, as a sort of relief; Mr. Tilton spoke to me defiantly and violently, and * * * heard it, and came in and said to him, "You are not going to scold Mrs. Tilton on my account!" he was very angry with her, and asked her if I had said that he had guiltily approached her, etc., rather boastingly; and she replied to him, "Yes, sir, you did, and you know you did ;" at that he took hold of her and threw her against the wall ; after that scene, Mr. Carpenter came to ask me about it, he having heard of it; Theodore was present, and he said to me, "I wish you to make that straight with Mr. Carpenter," and I immediately denied it.

Q. * * * left the house within a day or two, did she ? A. Yes, she went to my mother's.

Q. How long was she absent from the house ? A. She never came to stay there afterwards ; sometimes she would come and stop with me over night.

STOPPING A GIRL'S TALK.

Q. She states that you had an interview with her in which you said that she might go away to school, and that her expenses would be paid ; do you recollect that? A. Yes, sir.

Q. Please state what interview you had with your husband or any one else about * * * 's going away. A. He came home from a visit with Mr. * * * at Mr. Moulton's house; he learned there that Mr. * * * had this story, and was using it against him, and he said something must be done to stop that girl's talk ; mother had been brought into the matter in some way, and he wanted me to write something and give it to * * * to copy and sign; I said, "If you will write it I will take it to her;" she was then at Mrs. * * *'s, in * * * street, as seamstress; he would not allow her to stay in our house; he said if she would sign such a paper as he wanted he would promise her $500 or $600 a year; I said, "You had better not do that, but if any good can come out of all this trouble, let it be to educate her;" he said, "Yes, I will send her to Mr. * * * in * * *, who has an institution for young ladies;" I thought at last there was an opportunity for her getting an education; I am sure she did not know what she was doing any more than I did; she was very simple-minded; I handed the paper to her and said, "Just copy that and sign your name to it," and she did, right away; I do not think she thought anything about it; her mind was on going to school, and all that (the paper thus signed was a retraction of the stories told about Mr. Tilton's behavior); afterwards, when she was away at school, Theodore threatened me a great many times, and said, "You don't think I sent her away because of my own case; it was because of the story I told her about you;" I said I thought very differently of the matter, and that I would not allow it to stand so; he represented that he sent her away because of some secret that he had given her about me, whereas it was directly the contrary.

Mr. Cleveland—Where did the money come from? A. I think Mr. Moulton furnished it, but I do not know.

MOULTON FURNISHING MONEY.

Mr. Hill—What was the character of your private discussions with Mr. Tilton? A. He would take me into a room and lock the door; this he has done days and days; I think the reason he locked the door was to keep the children from me; he has kept me locked up all day long many a time; this has occurred innumerable times; it was this which wearied my life.

Mr. Sage—While he had you locked up did his mind obtain complete dominion over yours, so that you lost your own will? A. I think it did; I suffered a good deal.

Mr. Hill—How numerous were these interviews? A. They sometimes took place two or three times a week.

Q. Was his manner mild and conciliatory or violent? A. It varied according to his moods. But he always bore down upon me heavily in the way of accusation.

Mr. Cleveland—Did you ever feel in those interviews that his mind might be unsettled? A. I really did.

MRS. BEECHER AS A COUNSELOR.

Mr. Hill—Do you recollect having an interview with Mr. Beecher with regard to your domestic difficulties towards the end of 1870, about the time of Mr. Tilton's valedictory in the *Independent*, one or two days before your sickness? A. Yes, sir.

Q. Please state what occurred at that interview? A. I told him I wanted to talk with him about my difficulties at home; he almost instantly, when he saw the character of my message, said, "Well, I will send Mrs. Beecher to you; she will be a mother to you; tell her all that you would like to say;" he did not seem to have any advice to give particularly; he preferred that Mrs. Beecher should be the adviser, so he brought Mrs. Beecher to me, at mother's house, and introduced me to her, and after a few moments he left us; she asked me to tell her the story of my troubles, and inquired why it was that I thought of a separation.

Q. Did you go over all your troubles to her? A. Yes, in a degree; I told her a good deal of the same sort of thing that I have told you here to-night.

Q. Do you recollect what Mrs. Beecher's advice to you was? A. I think I do, pretty well; she looked at the matter very differently from what I did; I was vacillating in my mind what I should do; she said, did she know that her husband had been faulty in that manner she would not live with him a day; she said she had always known Theodore's tenderness; I felt a little uncomfortable in talking to Mrs. Beecher, because I knew she was very much prejudiced against Theodore; I was not very greatly helped in my mind by that interview with Mrs. Beecher; I only saw her twice; I thought I had better make my mind up for myself; and I finally concluded to live with him, thinking it was a morbid state that he was in, and that he would soon get out of it; my talks with Mrs. Beecher were long and painful, and I cannot recall all that was said.

Q. Do you recollect whether you went back home in consequence of the fact that Mr. Tilton had sent for the children? A. He had sent for the children and he had taken the baby, and then I went back after that.

Q. State what you did in your anxiety and trouble with reference to this Miss * * * and the position which you found her occupying in your house? A. I think she hurt me more than any one in the world; she was more severe and treated me with greater contempt than anybody else ever did, and to such an extent that I could not speak of it to my husband, as he never took any side; nor could I tell mother about it; I did not feel like revealing to her all this trouble and embarrassment and humiliation; I did not feel that there was a place for my head to lie down on in that house, and frequently I went out wandering in the streets ; night after night I walked, with my waterproof cloak on, and would go back and creep into the basement and lie down anywhere, feeling utterly wretched ; once I went away from home, thinking that I would not come back, but I found that I had left my purse at home and had to return ; Mr. Tilton owns a lot in Greenwood, and there I have two babies ; I went there with my waterproof cloak on and with the hood over my head, and lay down on the two graves and felt peace I had been there but a little while before the keeper of the grounds ordered me off; I paid no attention to him ; I did not regard his order until he came again in a few moments and said, "I order you off these grounds; do you hear me?" I rose on my feet and said, "If there is one spot on earth that is mine, it is these two graves ;" and he actually bowed down before me in apology ; though he was a common workman, it was very hearty and it was very grateful to me; he said, "I did not know that these were yours ;" and he left me ; and I stayed there on the little graves the rest of the day.

Q. Were experiences of that character common during your suffering in consequence of Mr. Tilton's introducing other persons into your family, and in consequence of his treatment of you ? A. Yes ; but no one ever knew it, and I cannot endure to tell it now ; at the same time, I trust you will all think the matter over well, and use as little of it as you can.

WANT OF FOOD.

Q. After Mr. Tilton had left the *Independent*, what provision did he make for your family ? A. I suffered very much indeed from want ; I have sometimes had no fire ; many and many a time I have had no food, and Theodore has been utterly indifferent to it; the winter was very severe; I sent away the servants, and had no one but myself in that house; inasmuch as it was a marked house, there came scarcely one human being of all the church people, and I had not a friend to call on me; my brother only called once; I lived by myself; Theodore came there to sleep, but he did not look into the matters to see whether I had this, that, or the other thing; he always took his meals with Mr. Moulton.

Q. Do you think it was on your account or on his account ? A. I think it was on account of the family troubles; I think that the publicity of the Woodhull matters was the cause of my social neglect.

Mr. Storrs—Were the Woodhull women there ? A. Not the Woodhull women; Mrs. Woodhull never came to see me after I returned from the country; but two or three times she had taken her meals there, and on one occasion Mr. Tilton wanted to have her stay over Sunday, and I refused to have any Sunday visitors of that class.

[Several questions followed touching upon Mr. Tilton's bringing of other ladies into his house; Mrs. Tilton said, with regard to some of the ladies she specially named, that she had never thought there was anything criminally wrong in their relations with Mr. Tilton.]

Mr. Cleveland—In looking back on all these years with Theodore, do you feel conscious that you tried to do everything that you could for him as a good wife and as a good mother to your children? A. I do; I have not one pang of conscience on that score; I really yet do not see how I could have done differently.

Q. So that now in this culmination and breaking up of your family you do not feel that you are responsible ? A. I do not; I feel that I have borne and suffered for his sake, and that he alone is responsible for this disruption of my family.

TILTON AND THE PLYMOUTH CHURCH INVESTIGAT-
ING COMMITTEE.

On August 4th the following correspondence was made public. It will be seen that Mr. Tilton has ordered his attorney to bring his case before a court of law for determination. The correspondence is as follows :

MR. SAGE TO MR. TILTON.

BROOKLYN, July 3, 1872.

Theodore Tilton, Esq. :

DEAR SIR—I am instructed by the Committee to state that the letters and documents referred to in your statement presented to us have not been delivered, notwithstanding your several promises to furnish them.

As your statement, in the absence of these documents, is deprived of its greatest force, we think you should desire to place them in our possession ; and I desire to impress on you the importance of delivering them to us at your earliest convenience.

Very truly yours,   H. W. SAGE, Chairman.

MR. TILTON'S REPLY.

174 LIVINGSTON STREET, BROOKLYN, }
August 3, 1874. }

Mr. Henry W. Sage, Chairman of Committee :

MY DEAR SIR—I have just received your note of July 31st—four days after date. Unless you accidentally misdated it, the communication should have come to me several days ago. This leads me to recall a similar dilatoriness of delivery of your original note, first summoning me to your Committee, which I received only four hours before I was to appear, and yet the summons bore date of the day previous. But let these trifles pass.

Your note, just received, surprises me by its contents ; for you seem to have forgotten that, on the last day of my appearance before your Committee, I carried to your meeting not only all the documents which I quoted in my sworn statement (save those in Mr. Moulton's possession), but many more besides, making a double-handful of interesting and important papers vital to *my* case and destructive to *yours*. All these papers I purposed to lay before you, but no sooner had I begun to read them aloud in your presence than one of your attorneys stopped me in the reading, and proposed that I should save the Committee's time by referring these papers to one of your members, the Hon. John Winslow. I acquiesced in this suggestion, and retired from your Committee with the expectation of a speedy conference with Mr. Winslow. Perhaps it was my proper duty to have called on Mr. Winslow, but as the whole Committee had previously set the example of calling in a body on one of the other parties to this controversy, I took it for granted that Mr. Winslow would repeat this precedent by doing me the honor to call at my house—at which he would have been a welcome guest.

But, while waiting for his coming, I was called upon instead by a policeman, who arrested me, and carried me, at thirty minute's notice, before Justice Riley's police court, to answer a charge of libeling the Rev. Henry Ward Beecher, against whom I had spoken not a libel, but the truth.

Up to the time of this arrest, I had employed no lawyer, not needing any. But on finding myself before a police court, and not understanding the motive of my arrest, nor the methods of courts, I requested my friend Judge S. D. Morris, to answer for me in a technical proceeding in which I knew not how to answer properly for myself. Twice already I have been before this unexpected tribunal, and may be called before it a third time on Wednesday next.

Meanwhile, my counsel, to whom I have just shown your note, instructs me to lay no documents, papers, or remaining testimony before your Committee, nor hold any further communication with you in any form, except to send you this present and final letter containing the reasons for this step.

These reasons are the following :

First.—You are a Committee of Mr. Beecher's friends, appointed by himself, expected to act in his behalf, assisted by attorneys employed exclusively for his vindication, holding secret sessions inaccessible to the public, having no power to compel witnesses, giving no opportunity for the opposite side to cross-examine such as voluntarily appear, publishing or suppressing their testimony as you see fit, and so far as my own experience goes, asking me no questions save such as were irrelevant to the case, and omitting to publish in your imperfect and unjust report of my testimony all that was most pertinent to my own side of the controversy.

Second.—The daily papers of Brooklyn and New York have been artfully fed, day by day, with crumbs of fictitious evidence against my own character, as if not Mr. Beecher, but I alone, were the man on trial : and though I have little right, perhaps, to hold your Committee responsible for this daily misrepresentation, which may come through the malice of others, yet the result is the same to me as if you had deliberately designed it ; and that result is this, namely : I expect no justice either from your tribunal, since you cannot compel witnesses to testify, nor from your reporters, since they do not give impartial reports.

Third.—I cannot resist the conviction (though I mean no offense in expressing it) that your Committee has come at last to be as little satisfactory to the public as to myself, and that your verdict (if you render one) could not possibly be based on the full facts, since you have no power to compel witnesses, nor to verify their testimony by oath, nor to sift it by cross-examination.

For these reasons, which ought to have moved me earlier, I have at last instructed my counsel to proceed at once, at his discretion, to carry my case from your jurisdiction

TO A COURT OF LAW.

And in view of this instruction from me, he has in turn instructed me to hold no further communication with your Committee except this present letter of courtesy, in which I have the honor to bid you farewell, in doing which, allow me to add that the respect which I am unable to entertain for your Committee as a tribunal I cannot help expressing for you, each and all, as individuals.

Truly yours,

THEODORE TILTON.

TILTON ON FALLEN WOMEN.

It will be remembered that in 1871 Mr. Tilton published a series of papers called "The Golden Age Tracts." Only four were published, we believe, in pamphlet form No. 1 was "The Rights of Women—a Letter to Horace Greeley ;" No. 2, "The Constitution a Title-deed to Woman's Franchise—a Letter to Charles Sumner;" No. 3, "Victoria C. Woodhull—a Biographical Sketch ;" and No. 4, "The Sin of Sins." Main portions of No. 3 are given in another place. The last of this series has the following title-page :

The Golden Age Tracts, No. 4.
The Sin of Sins, by Theodore Tilton.
"*Shall they fall, and not arise ?*"—Isaiah.
Published at the office of the Golden Age, 9 Spruce St., New York, 1871.

In view of the developments in the Beecher-Tilton matter, this tract may have some significance ; in any case, it is interesting reading, as showing what class of subjects Theodore Tilton's mind was running on at the time that, according to his own story, he was trying to be magnanimous. This tract reads as follows :

THE SIN OF SINS.

"*Shall they fall, and not arise ?*"—Isaiah.

I have been thinking of the uncharitable treatment which society gives to what are called "fallen women." How virtuously we keep them down ! How impossible we make it for them to rise again ! How inexorably we sentence them to a dungeon of shadows, and shut against them every golden gate to a future career ! This morning, in idling along a brook overhung with alders and fringed with ferns, I came upon an unexpected pool which Nature had poured into a crevice between some red-sandstone rocks, and, sitting down beside it, I thought of him who, in his wayside wanderings, stopped at the Well of Sychar, and talked with the Woman of Samaria.

GOOD AND BAD.

It was a good man talking to a bad woman. No, let me retract that last epithet. I am saying the very thing myself which I condemn in the speech of others. Why did I let slip that word "bad"? Did *he* call her so ? Then what right have *I* to stamp her with this stigma ? None.

Let me turn to the narrative.

"Jesus saith unto her,
" 'Go call thy husband and come hither.'
"The woman answered and said,
" 'I have no husband.'
"Jesus said unto her,
" 'Thou hast well said, "I have no husband" ; for thou hast had five husbands, and he whom thou now hast is not thy husband ; in that said'st thou truly.' "

Here was a woman whom the church, had she belonged to it, would have excommunicated. How was she treated by the church's founder ? Here was a woman who would have been ostracized by the world. How was she judged by him "of whom the world was not worthy?" In the long dialogue which he held with her, he uttered no syllable in rebuke of her past life ; he put no insult on her frailty ; he cast no reproach on her wayward love. "Come," quoth she to her neighbors, "Come see a man who told me all things that ever I did." And yet in telling them all he gave her no wounding rebuke—

NO STINGING CONDEMNATION—

No recorded word of criticism—nothing but the same sweet, eloquent persuasion to a higher life which he uttered equally to sinner and saint.

"How is it that thou," she said, "being a Jew, askest drink of me who am a woman of Samaria ? for the Jews have no dealings with the Samaritans ?"

I cannot read such a question by such a questioner without wishing that those other women of Samaria—who walk their fearful pilgrimages up and down Broadway at midnight—for whom there are only bitter wells and who drink only of poisoned waters :—I say, I would to God that these women also could put the same, wondering and delighted question to some Christ of to-day, saying,

"How is it that thou, being pure, wilt come and hold spiritual fellowship with us, being foul ?"

I do not so much puzzle myself about the origin, as I do about the quality of evil. What is sin, and what purity ? What is virtue, and what vice ? What is right, and what wrong ? A man who has never afflicted himself with these queries—who has never held the scourge of this inquest over his own mind—who has never used the smiting rod of this judgment upon his own heart—knows too little of human nature to be either a counselor of others or a monitor to himself. Nor am I ever able to survey the conduct even of the weakest, the faultiest, and the guiltiest of men or women, without being suddenly estopped by that penetrating maxim, "Judge not that ye be not judged, for with what judgment ye judge ye shall be judged." And so I can only pity, and dare not condemn, even the lowest of the fallen, and the worst of the bad.

On the contrary, I appeal to men's two religions—the natural and the revealed. Did not the very brook that bubbled past my feet this morning seem intent to wash the whole world clean ? Is there not likewise a promise that the human heart, though its sins be as scarlet, can become as white as snow ? Then, if Nature and God thus conjoin to purify us, is it not despicable in us to call ill names for the defiling of one another's fame ?

PHARISEES AND SINNERS.

I thought, too, of that other fallen woman—that unwanton wanton, who burst in upon him while he was sitting at a banquet—that aspiring, transfigured, and immortal harlot who "brought an alabaster-box of ointment, and stood at his feet behind him weeping, and began to wash his feet with tears, and did wipe them with the hairs of her head, and kissed his feet and anointed them with the ointment." Where is there a more exquisite tale in literature, or where a more beautiful lesson in charity?

"Now when the Pharisee who had bidden him saw it, he spake within himself saying, 'This man, if he were a prophet, would have known who and what manner of woman this is that toucheth him, for she is a sinner.'" A sinner ? Yes, and therefore an exile from society. A sinner ? Yes, and therefore disentitled to sit at good men's feasts. A sinner ? Yes, and therefore condemned to outer darkness, where there is weeping and gnashing of teeth. "Simon," said the god-like guest to the man-like host, "seest thou this woman ?" No, Simon had never seen her. That is, he saw not the woman, but only the drab—not her womanhood, but only her shame. He was blind. The Master then pricked open his eyes, and sent through them a sudden sunbeam that carried a new light into his cobwebbed soul. "Simon," said he, "I entered into thine house, thou gavest me no kiss ; but this woman, since the time I came in, hath not ceased to kiss my feet. My head with oil thou didst not anoint ; but this woman hath anointed my feet with ointment." The point was pressed home by double antithesis. The Pharisee in his proud propriety was convicted of being outdone in courtesy by a woman of the streets. Her gentle manners, therefore, had not forsaken her. The ministering kindliness of her woman's nature still remained. Kneeling at her Master's feet, the homage which she still knew how to pay to virtue was as fragrant as the perfume in her box.

FORGIVEN.

Then from the Lord's lips came a remark, which, like a bee, carried honey to the woman, but a sting to the man. What must they both have thought of the marvelous audacity of that mild guest, who, in defiance of all the laws of Moses, of all the traditions of the elders, and of all the sanctities of society, suddenly exclaimed to the man, "I say unto thee, her sins, which are many, are forgiven, for she loved much ; " and who, turning at the same time to the woman, repeated the same strange speech, "Thy sins are forgiven—go in peace." I quote and emphasize these words for the sake of asking this question, namely, If forgiven by him, why not, then, forgiven by us all? The birds could not have sung so sweetly as they did this morning, neither could the sky have kept so bright a blue, nor the earth dressed herself in so soft a green, if the human heart, for which the earth and all that it contains were made, must remain forever perverted from its Maker by so strange a fact as that its warmest love should suddenly constitute its chiefest sin.

NEITHER DO I CONDEMN THEE.

Thinking this thought, I then suddenly saw in the gravel-path at my feet the strange handwriting which the man of Nazareth once stooped and wrote upon the ground. I mean, I saw it not in fact, but in fancy. How runs the tale?

"And the Scribes and Pharisees brought unto him a woman taken in adultery, in the very act. 'Now Moses, in the law commanded us that such be stoned ; but what sayest thou?' Jesus stooped down, and with his finger wrote on the ground, as though he heard them not. So when they continued asking him, he lifted up himself, and said unto them, 'He that is without sin among you, let him first cast a stone.' "

Without *what* sin? Not all sins in general, but one sin in particular. The hypocrites, every one of them, had sinned it. And, furthermore, most men since then have been the like sinners, and are to this day. ,

"And again he stooped down, and wrote on the ground, and they which heard it, being convicted by their own conscience, went out one by one, beginning at the eldest, even unto the last; and Jesus was left alone, and the woman standing in the midst. When Jesus had lifted up himself and saw none but the woman, he said unto her, 'Woman, who are those thine accusers? Hath no man condemned thee?' She said, 'No man, Lord.' And Jesus said unto her, 'Neither do I condemn thee; go and sin no more.'"

MEN AND WOMEN AS SINNERS—A COMPARISON.

Did I not say that I knew what he wrote on the ground? Perhaps I err in my imaginings. Nor will I venture to put *his* great thoughts into *my* weak words. But I believe that as the woman's sin was of the earth earthy, he therefore engraved upon the very earth itself the everlasting record of her pardon! So that any woman who should thereafter, in all coming time, fall from her purity even to the street, and be trodden under foot of men, and grovel in the dust, might then and there, in the very soilure and defilement with which she is begrimed, behold the eternal decree, "Thy sins are forgiven —go in peace." It is written of this teacher that "he spake as never man spake." This, I am sure, is true. For, what *man* ever said of a woman taken in adultery, "Neither do I condemn thee." It requires something of the godhead to say that!

During my rambles I reflected on that great impartiality of Nature which sends the sun and the rain alike on the just and the unjust—in contradistinction to the miserable partiality of human judgment as one sees it in this very case. "They say unto him, Master, this woman was taken in adultery, in the very act." If so, then not only the woman was taken, but also the man. But what became of the man? The woman was dragged to the temple to be stoned. The man probably went away among his companions to laugh. Indeed, there is no evidence that he was not her chief accuser, and the ringleader in her punishment. Now let me point the moral which adorns this tale. If the woman's crime merits martyrdom, what does the man's? If *she* was a sinner, what was *he*? And yet how does the world judge between the two culprits? Ah, now as then, and in every such case, the Scribes and Pharisees meet together to forgive the man, and then go away and leave it to Christ alone to forgive the woman!

SLEEPY HOLLOW,

MR. WILKESON'S STATEMENT.

Mr. Samuel Wilkeson was examined by the Plymouth Church Investigating Committee, on Wednesday evening, July 15th. The substance of this important statement was as follows:

In the last week of March, 1872, Theodore Tilton came to my office in New York, and took out of his pocket a worn press proof of a letter which he said he purposed to publish in the next issue of his paper, the *Golden Age*, unless Henry Ward Beecher did him justice, and handed it to me to read. He said that he came to me because I had an interest in its publication through my property in the *Christian Union* newspaper, of which Mr. Beecher was editor, and through my partnership in the house which published his books, and because I was the common friend of himself and Mr. Beecher.

The letter was as follows:

BROOKLYN, Jan. 1, 1871.

Mr. Henry C. Bowen.

SIR: I received last evening your sudden notices, breaking my two contracts, one with the *Independent*, the other with the Brooklyn *Union*. With reference to this act of yours I will make a plain statement of facts. It was during the early part of the rebellion, if I recollect aright, when you first intimated to me that the Rev. Henry Ward Beecher had committed acts of adultery, for which, if you should expose him, he would be driven from the pulpit. From that time onward your references to the subject were frequent, and always accompanied with the exhibition of deep-seated injury to your heart. In a letter which you addressed to me from Woodstock, June 16, 1863, referring to this subject, you said, "I sometimes feel that I must break silence; that I must no longer suffer as a dumb man, and be made to bear a load of grief most unjustly. One word from me would make—a rebellion throughout Christendom, I had almost said, and you know it. You have just a little of the evidence from the great volume in your possession. I am not pursuing a phantom, but solemnly brooding over an awful reality."

Subsequent to this letter, and on frequent intervals from then till now, you have repeated the statement that you could at any moment expel Henry Ward Beecher from Brooklyn. You have reiterated the same thing, not only to me, but to others. Moreover, during the year just closed, your letters on the subject were marked with more feeling than heretofore, and were not unfrequently coupled with your emphatic declaration that Mr. Beecher ought not to be allowed to occupy a public position as a Christian teacher and preacher.

On the 25th of December, 1870, at an interview in your house, at which Mr. Oliver Johnson and I were present, you spoke freely and indignantly against Mr. Beecher as an unsafe visitor in the families of his congregation. You alluded by name to a woman, now a widow, whose husband's death you did not doubt was hastened by his knowledge that Mr. Beecher had maintained with her improper intimacy. As if to leave no doubt on the minds of either Mr. Johnson or myself, you informed us that Mr. Beecher had made to you a confession of guilt, and had with tears implored your forgiveness. After Mr. Johnson retired from this interview, you related to me the case of a woman, of whom you said (as nearly as I can recollect your words) that "Mr. Beecher took her in his arms by force, threw her down upon the sofa, accomplished upon her his deviltry, and left her. * * * * " During your recital of this tale you were filled with anger towards Mr. Beecher. You said, with terrible emphasis, that "he ought not to remain a week longer in his pulpit." You immediately suggested that a demand should be made upon him to quit his sacred office. You volunteered to bear to him such a demand in the form of an open letter, which you would present to him with your own hand, and you pledged yourself to sustain the demand which this letter should make, viz.: "That he should, for reasons which he explicitly knew, immediately cease from his ministry at Plymouth Church, and retire from Brooklyn." The first draft of this letter did not contain the phrase "for reasons that he explicitly knew," and these words, or words to this effect, were incorporated in a second at your motion. You urged, furthermore, very emphatically, that the letter should demand not only Mr. Beecher's abdication of his pulpit, but the cessation of his writing for the *Christian Union*—a point on which you were overruled. This letter you presented to Mr. Beecher at Mr. Freeland's house. Shortly after its presentation you sought an interview with me in the editorial office of the Brooklyn *Union*, during which, with unaccountable emotion in your manner, your face livid with rage, you threatened with loud voice that if I ever should inform Mr. Beecher of the statements which you made concerning his adultery, or should compel you to adduce the evidence on which you agreed to sustain the demand for Mr. Beecher's withdrawal from Brooklyn, you would immediately deprive me of my engagement to write for the *Independent* and to edit the Brooklyn *Union*, and that in case I should ever attempt to enter the offices of those journals you would have me ejected by force. I told you that I should inform Mr. Beecher or anybody else, according to the dictates of my judgment, uninfluenced by any authority of my employers. You then excitedly retired from my presence. Hardly had your violent words ceased ringing in my ears when I received your summary notices breaking my contract with the *Independent* and the Brooklyn *Union*. To the foregoing narrative of fact I have only to add my surprise and regret at the sudden interruption by your own act of what has been on my part a faithful service of fifteen years. Truly yours,

THEODORE TILTON.

I was shocked at the mischievousness of the matter he threatened to publish. I remonstrated with him against its publication. A discussion ensued, on his part passionate and noisy. He complained, first, that Henry C. Bowen had without cause dismissed him from the editorship of the *Independent* and of the Brooklyn *Union*, and ruined him in fame, prospects and estate; that he had crowned this wrong by refusing to pay him a large debt for editorial services, of which he was in pressing need, and compelling him to bring a suit to collect the amount. His next plaint was that Mr. Beecher had not helped him in his troubles. He said that he was lying crushed on the side-walk in Brooklyn under the misfortunes of losing his positions on the two papers, and the incomes derived from them, with the accompanying loss of the public respect and confidence—the loss, in a word, of the entire stored-up capital for his life career, and that Mr. Beecher, who had such power that with his little finger he could have lifted him up and reinstated him, saw him in his agony and ruin, and passed by in silence and indifferent on the other side of the way. Rising into a dramatic rage, and tramping my room from corner to corner, and speaking with intense passion, he declared, "I will have revenge on him. I will pursue him into his grave."

It was clear to me that what Mr. Tilton wanted was money, and that his purpose in coming to me was to raise money. Omitting further details of this interview, he left my office calm and happy, in the prospect of an arrangement I outlined that should immediately give him in hand, without the delays of a contested law-suit, the money Mr. Bowen owed him and that would restore his old relations to Mr. Beecher and Mr. Bowen, and procure for him restorative and flattering mention in the editorial columns of the *Independent*, and cause to be inserted editorially in the *Christian Union* such handsome notice of his newspaper enterprise as should at once gratify and profit him.

What is somewhat well known as the "Tripartite Agreement" came from the negotiation initiated after this interview. Before it was drafted, but after its terms were settled, Mr. Bowen agreed to pay Mr. Tilton forthwith the amount of unpaid salary for which he had brought suit. He likewise promised to publish a card in the *Independent*, over his own signature, that should repair, as fully as it could, the injury done to Mr. Tilton by dismissing him from that paper. On the night of the 2d of April, 1872, when the tripartite agreement was ready for signature, Mr. Tilton was in a happy frame of mind. In conversation he especially overflowed with love and admiration Beecherwards.

This tripartite agreement, which I intended to be an estoppel to two of the parties to it, and a concordat all around, was in the words:

We three men, earnestly desiring to restore each to the other the respect, love, and fraternity in which we once lived happily together in our social life in Brooklyn, and as members of the Plymouth Church, and earnestly desiring to remove all causes of offense existing between us, real or fancied, and to make Christian reparation for injuries done, or supposed to be done, and to efface the disturbed past, and to provide concord, good-will, and love for the future, do declare and covenant each to the other as follows:

I. I, Henry C. Bowen, having given credit, perhaps without due consideration, to tales and innuendoes affecting Henry Ward Beecher, and being influenced by them, as was natural to a man who receives impressions suddenly, to the extent of repeating them (guardedly, however, and within limitations, and not for the purpose of injuring him, but strictly in the confidence of consultation), now feel that therein I did him wrong. Therefore I disavow all the charges and imputations that have been attributed to me as having been by me made against Henry Ward Beecher, and I declare fully and without reserve that I know nothing *derogatory to his reputation as a clergyman or a man. And I expressly disavow the charges, imputations, and innuendoes imputed to have been made by me, and set forth in a letter written to me by Theodore Tilton, on the 1st day of January, 1871 (a copy of which letter is hereto annexed), and I declare that those charges, imputations, and innuendoes are without any foundation in fact, to the best of my knowledge and belief.* And I covenant that, for all future time, I will never, by word or deed, recur to, repeat, or allude to any or either of said charges, imputations, and innuendoes.

II. I, Theodore Tilton, *returning of my free will to a man whom I have revered and loved as a father, thus renew and confirm my faith in Henry Ward Beecher as a grandly good and generous man. I, too, disavow each and all of the imputations and charges in the said annexed letter repeated and contained. And any and all other imputations upon his character and conduct which have been said to come from me I disavow* and covenant never to repeat or renew.

III. I, Henry Ward Beecher, put the past forever out of sight and out of memory. I deeply regret the causes of suspicion, jealousy, and estrangement which have come between us. It is a joy to me to have my old regard for Henry C. Bowen and Theodore Tilton restored, and a happiness to me to resume the old relations of love, respect, and reliance to each and both of them. If I have said anything injurious to the reputation of either of them, or have detracted from their standing and fame as Christian gentlemen and members of my church, I revoke it all, and heartily covenant to repair and reinstate them to the extent of my power.

BROOKLYN, April 2, 1872.

This paper was read at a meeting of four gentlemen, of whom Mr. Tilton was one, at a house in Brooklyn. He was more than satisfied with the paragraph concerning himself. He was charmed with it. He said he could conscientiously and heartily subscribe his name to every word of it. He said he would sign it twelve times over if that would induce Mr. Bowen to sign it once; and, in his eagerness, he took up a pen to sign. But he was restrained by the suggestion of a wise and influential party to the conference, that Mr. Bowen might be less willing to sign the paper if Mr. Tilton should sign first. It was carried away without Mr. Tilton's signature.

In a full and kind conversation between me and Mr. Tilton, after the meeting on the night of April 2 broke up, he replied to a clear-cut question I put to him, that the only wrong Mr. Beecher had ever done him had been to address improper language to his wife, and that for that he held in his hands an ample and satisfactory written apology. I repeated to him mention of a graver injury than that, made to me by a person whose information was alleged to be derived in part directly from himself, in part at second hand, from a confession of his wife. With great spirit he denied the truth of both these statements. He called the informant at second hand a sexually morbid monomaniac, who had imagined every word she uttered. He scornfully said that there was not a shadow of truth in her story. He expressed amazement that the other person should state that he had ever said that there was anything criminal in Mr. Beecher's conduct, and denied in the fullest and most energetic manner that he had ever said so, or said anything that could be so construed by a truthful and healthy mind. And he returned to his previous declaration that Mr. Beecher's sole offense was improper language to his wife, and repeated it anew, and again repeated that the written confession and apology he had in keeping was ample atonement for that wrong.

The next morning, on the 3d of April, Mr. Tilton came to my office, in the Equitable Life Insurance Company's building. He was flushed and sullen. There was a hitch in the money-payment. He said abruptly that he would not sign the agreement; that it would have to be altered before he would sign it. Kindling in anger as he talked, he said that in the negotiation Mr. Bowen had been well taken care of by Mr. Claflin, and Mr. Beecher well taken care of by me, but he had been left out in the cold with the money due from Bowen unpaid. I combated this fancy kindly, and tried to soothe him and hold him to the arrangement he had made, but he flew out wild, and declared with the utmost passion that he would never while he lived sign a paper that should disable him from pursuing Henry Ward Beecher, and he demanded a copy of his paragraph in the tripartite agreement, that he might alter it. I made a copy for him, and he sat down at a table, and began to scratch and interline it; but he rose up, and carried his work away uncompleted. Before he left, I gathered from what he said that Mr. Bowen had refused to pay the full amount of his claim, and that his law-suit would have to go on.

But the full amount was paid within a day or two thereafter, and the tripartite agreement was executed—not the one I had drafted, and which was accepted by all the parties, but a modification of that. I used my last copy of this instrument in my testimony before the committee, and I cannot show the changes of the original by a comparison of the two. I can now only say that all the portions of the agreement (above set forth in full) which are italicized were omitted from the agreement finally executed.

The efficacy of the covenants I aimed at was lost, and the compact was defeated. Tilton, in modifying his paragraph, backed out of his disavowal of his imputations on Mr. Beecher, and his admissions that they were untrue, and carefully secured to himself the largest liberty to pursue the great preacher forever with innuendoes. My testimony before the committee shows the changes in the tripartite agreement as originally drawn, and which all the parties to it had heartily approved, and had promised to sign. It also shows my earnest remonstrances against permitting those changes to be made, and my warnings of the mischievous consequences that would inevitably follow.

BEECHER'S ELDER BROTHER ON THE SCANDAL.

As will be seen by the following interview, Mr. Beecher's elder brother, a resident of Chicago, does not believe the Tilton story. The conversation is as follows:

Of course it is possible, and I must confess that that statement of Tilton's is a tough thing to get around, but I believe that Henry can refute it, and that he will, and will come out all right. I have been in correspondence with my brother Edward, and he is of the opinion that all will be well in the end.

R.—Was not Mrs. Beecher the cause of Tilton's dismissal from the *Independent?*

Mr. B.—She always disliked him and thought him a dangerous man ; in fact, she frequently warned Henry against him when they were the best of friends, believing that injury to him (Beecher) would be the result.

R.—What do you think of Henry Ward's " peculiar ideas upon the marriage relation," of which your brother, Thomas K., speaks in a letter quoted by Tilton ?

Mr. B.—I don't think he has any.

R.—Have you ever talked with him upon the subject ?

Mr. B.—No ; but his training was entirely opposed to any such thing. I am the oldest brother, and Henry is one of the youngest. I have never known any woman except my wife, nor has my brother Edward ever known any woman except his wife, and I believe the same is true of Henry. He was never in the habit of running after women. I believe he looks upon the marriage relation as sacredly as any one. In fact, I know he has suffered great trouble on account of his wife, and has endeavored to be faithful to her, notwithstanding the sore trials she has cost him. It has separated him from his kindred, from his brothers and sisters, who were prevented from coming to the house on her account. Yet he bore with her, and in every way endeavored to arrange matters so that they might visit him. Still I think she loved him, and was faithful to him. On another ground this charge seems weak. Henry never was in the habit of running after women ; but if he had been, would he have been likely to choose an old married woman ? There were plenty of young girls that he could have had if he had been so inclined. There was no difficulty about it. He could have had them if he had wanted to—plenty of them. Then why should he choose an old, faded, married woman ? It is easier for a preacher than any one else, except, perhaps, a doctor, to take advantage of women.

AN ALLEGED LETTER OF MR. BEECHER.

The following note, without date, has been published, and its authenticity vouched for. It was said to have been written when Mrs. Woodhull's story was first published.

" *My Dear Mrs. Tilton :*

" I hoped that you would be shielded from the knowledge of the great wrong that has been done to you, and through you to universal womanhood. I can hardly bear to speak of it, or allude to a matter than which nothing can be imagined more painful to a pure and womanly nature. I pray daily for you, ' that your faith fail not.' You, yourself, know the way and the power of prayer. God has been your refuge in many sorrows before. He will now hide you in his pavilion until the storm be overpast. The rain that beats down the flower to the earth will pass at length, and the stem, bent, but not broken, will rise again and blossom as before.

" Every pure woman on earth will feel that this wanton and unprovoked assault is aimed at you, but reaches to universal womanhood.

" Meantime your dear children will love you with double tenderness, and Theodore, against whom these shafts are hurled, will hide you in his heart of hearts.

" I am glad that this revelation from the pit has given him a sight of the danger that was before hidden by specious appearances and promises of usefulness. May God keep him in courage in the arduous struggle which he wages against adversity, and bring him out, though much tried, like gold seven times fined.

" I have not spoken of myself, No word could express the sharpness and depth of my sorrow in your behalf, my dear and honored friend. God walks in the fire by the side of those he loves, and in heaven neither you, nor Theodore, nor I, shall regret the discipline, how hard soever it may seem now.

" May He restrain and turn those poor creatures who have been given over to do all this sorrowful harm to those who have deserved no such treatment at their hands.

" I commend you to my mother's God, my dear friend ! May his smile bring light in darkness, and his love be a perpetual summer to you ! Very truly yours,

"HENRY WARD BEECHER."

MOULTON—BEECHER—TILTON.

The following important correspondence, made public August 6, explains itself fully. The letters run as follows:

MR. BEECHER TO MR. MOULTON.

JULY 24, 1874.

MY DEAR MR. MOULTON :—

I am making out a statement, and I need the letters and papers in your hands. Will you send me by Tracy all the originals of my papers? Let them be numbered and an inventory taken, and I will return them to you as soon as I can see and compare, get dates, make extracts or copies, as the case may be.

Will you also send me Bowen's "heads of difficulty," and all letters of my sister, if any are with you?

I heard you were sick—are you about again? God grant you to see peaceful times. Yours gratefully.

H. W. BEECHER.

F. D. MOULTON.

MR. MOULTON TO MR. BEECHER.

49 REMSEN STREET,
BROOKLYN, August 4, 1874.

MY DEAR MR. BEECHER :—

I received your note of July 24, informing me that you are making a statement and need the letters and papers in my hands, and asking me to send them to you for the purpose of having extracts or copies made from them, as the case may be, that you may use them in your controversy with Mr. Tilton.

I should be very glad to do anything that I may do, consistent with my sense of what is due to justice and right, to aid you; but if you will reflect that I hold all the important papers intrusted to me at the desire and request and in the confidence of both parties to this unhappy affair, you will see that I cannot in honor give them, or any of them, to either party to aid him as against the other. I have not given or shown to Mr. Tilton any documents or papers relating to your affairs since the renewal of your controversy, which had been once adjusted.

I need need not tell you how deeply I regret your position as foes, each to the other, after my long and, as you, I have no doubt, fully believe, honest and faithful, effort to have you otherwise.

I will sacredly hold all the papers and information I have until both parties shall request me to make them public, or to deliver them into hands of either or both, or to lay them before the Committee, or I am compelled in a court of justice to produce them, if I can be so compelled.

My regret that I am compelled to this course is softened by my belief that you will not be substantially injured by it in this regard, for all the facts are, of course, known to you, and I am bound to believe and assume that in the statement you are preparing you will only set forth the exact facts; and, if so, the documents, when produced, will only confirm, and cannot contradict, what you may state, so that you will suffer no loss.

If, on the contrary—which I cannot presume—you desire the possession of the documents, in order that you may prove your statement in a manner not to be contravened by the facts set forth in them to the disadvantage of Mr. Tilton, I should be then aiding you in doing that which I cannot believe the strictest and firmest friendship for you calls upon me to do. With grateful recollections of your kind confidence and trust in me,

I am very truly yours,

F. D. MOULTON.

REV. HENRY WARD BEECHER, Brooklyn, N. Y.

MR. BEECHER TO MR. MOULTON.

BROOKLYN, July 28, 1874.

MY DEAR FRIEND—The Committee of Investigation are waiting mainly for you before closing their labors. I, too, earnestly wish that you would come and clear your mind and memory of everything that can bear on my case. I pray you also to bring all letters and papers relating to it which will throw any light upon it, and bring to a result this protracted case.

I trust that Mrs. Moulton has been reinvigorated and that her need of your care will not be so great as to detain you. Truly yours,

H. W. BEECHER.

F. D. MOULTON, Esq.

A SECOND APPEAL.

BROOKLYN, August 4, 1874.

F. D. MOULTON, Esq. :—

SIR—Your letter, bearing date August 4, 1874, is this moment received. Allow me to express my regret and astonishment that you refuse me permission even to see certain letters and papers in your possession, relating to the charges made against me by Theodore Tilton, and at the reasons given for the refusal.

On your solemn and repeated assurances of personal friendship, and in the unquestioning confidence with which you inspired me of your honor and fidelity, I placed in your hands for safe-keeping various letters addressed to me from my brother, my sister, and various other parties; also memoranda of affairs not immediately connected with Mr. Tilton's matters. I also from time to time addressed you confidential notes relating to my own self as one friend would write to another. These papers were never placed in your hands to be held for two parties, nor to be used in any way. They were to be held for me. I did not wish them to be subject to risk of loss or scattering, from my careless habits in the manner of preserving documents. They were to be held for me. In so far as these papers were concerned, you were only a friendly trustee, holding papers subject to my wishes.

MR. TILTON HAS MADE A DEADLY ASSAULT

upon me, and has used letters and fragments of letters purporting to be copies of these papers. Are these extracts genuine ? Are they garbled ? What are their dates ? What, if anything, has been left out, and what put in ?

You refuse my demand for these papers on the various pleas that if I speak the truth in my statement, I do not need them; that if I make a successful use of them, it will be an injury to Mr. Tilton, and that you, as a friend of both parties, are bound not to aid either in any act that shall injure the other.

But I do not desire to injure any one, but to repel an injury attempted upon me by the use of papers committed sacredly to your care. These documents have been seen and copied; they have been hawked for sale in New York newspaper offices; what purport to be my confidential notes to you are on the market. But when I demand a sight of the originals of papers of which you are only a trustee, that I may defend myself, you refuse, because you are the friend of both parties!

Mr. Tilton has access to your depository for materials with which to strike me, but I am not permitted to use them in defending myself !

I do not ask you to place before the Committee any papers which Mr. Tilton may have given you. But I do demand that you forthwith place before the Committee every paper which I have written or deposited with you. Yours truly,

H. W. BEECHER.

MR. MOULTON TO MR. BEECHER.

49 REMSEN STREET, BROOKLYN, August 5, 1874.

REV. HENRY WARD BEECHER :—

MY DEAR SIR—In all our acquaintance and friendship I have never received from you a letter of the tone of yours of August 4. It seems unlike yourself, and to have been inspired by the same ill-advisers who had so lamentably carried your private affairs before a committee of your church and thence before the public.

In reply, let me remind you that during the whole of the past four years all the documents, notes, and memoranda which you and Mr. Tilton have intrusted to me have been so intrusted because they had a reference to your mutual differences. I hold no papers, either of yours or his, except such as bear on this case. You speak of "memoranda of affairs not immediately connected with Mr. Tilton's matter." You probably allude here to the memoranda of your difficulties with Mr. Bowen, but these have a direct reference to your present case with Mr. Tilton, and were deposited with me by you because of such reference. You speak also of a letter or two from your brother and sister, and I am sure you have not forgotten the apprehension which we entertained lest Mrs. Hooker should fulfil a design which she foreshadowed to invade your pulpit and read to your congregation a confession of your intimacy with Mrs. Tilton.

You speak of other papers, which I hold "subject to your wishes." I hold none such, nor do I hold any subject to Mr. Tilton's wishes. The papers which I hold, both yours and his, were not given to me to be subject to the wishes of either of the parties. But the very object of my holding them has been, and still is, to prevent the wish of one party from being injuriously exercised against the other.

You are incorrect in saying that Mr. Tilton has had access to my "depository of materials;" on the contrary, I have refused Mr. Tilton such access. During the preparation of his sworn statement he came to me and said his case would be incomplete unless I permitted him the use of all the documents, but I refused; and all he could rely upon were such notes as he had made from time to time from writings of yours which you had written to me to be read to him, and passages of which he caught from my lips, in shorthand. Mr. Tilton has seen only a part of the papers in my possession, and would be more surprised to learn the entire facts of the case than you can possibly be.

What idle rumors may have existed in newspaper offices I know not; but they have not come from me.

In closing your letter you say, "I do not ask you to place before the Committee any papers which Mr. Tilton may have given you; but I do demand that you forthwith place before the Committee every paper which I have written or deposited with you." In reply I can only say that I cannot justly place before the Committee the papers of one of the parties without doing the same with the papers of the other, and I cannot do this honorably except either by legal process compelling me or else by consent in writing, not only of yourself, but of Mr. Tilton, with whom I shall confer on the subject as speedily as possible.

You will, I trust, see a greater spirit of justice in this reply than you have infused into your unusual letter of August 4. Very respectfully,   FRANCIS D. MOULTON.

MR. MOULTON TO MR. TILTON.

BROOKLYN, August 5, 1874.

THEODORE TILTON, Esq.:—

MY DEAR SIR—I have received, under date of July 28, a letter from the Rev. Henry Ward Beecher, in which he expresses the wish that I would go before the Investigating Committee and "clear my mind and memory of everything that can bear on this case"—referring, of course, to the controversy between you and him.

I cannot, in view of my confidential relations with you, make any statement before the Investigating Committee, unless you release me, as Mr. Beecher has done, explicitly from my obligation to maintain your confidence.

If you will express to me clearly a request that I should go before the Investigating Committee and state any and all facts within my knowledge concerning your case with Mr. Beecher, and exhibit to them any or all documents in my possession relating thereto, I shall, in view of Mr. Beecher's letter, consider myself at liberty to accede to the request of the Committee, to state such facts and exhibit such documents. Very respectfully,   FRANCIS D. MOULTON.

MR. TILTON TO MR. MOULTON.

BROOKLYN, August 5, 1874.

FRANCIS D. MOULTON, Esq.:—

MY DEAR SIR—In reponse to your note of this day mentioning Mr. Beecher's request that you should exhibit to the Committee the facts and documents hitherto held in confidence by you touching his difference with me, I hereby give you notice that you have my own consent and request to do the same. Truly yours,   THEODORE TILTON.

MR. MOULTON PROMISES TO PRODUCE THE DOCUMENTS.

At the meeting of the Plymouth Church Investigating Committee held Wednesday evening, August 5th, Mr. Moulton read the following statement:—

GENTLEMEN OF THE COMMITTEE—I have received your invitation to appear before you. I have been ready on any proper occasion to disclose all the facts and documents known to me, or in my possession, relating to the subject-matter of your inquiry, but I have found myself embarrassed because of my peculiar relations to the parties to the controversy. Friendly for years to all of them, and at the time of the outbreak of this miserable business having the kindest feeling toward each, I endeavored to avert the calamity that has now fallen upon all. Most fully and confidentially trusted by all parties, it became necessary that I should know the exact and simple truth of every fact and circumstance of the controversy; so I was made, by mutual consent, in some sort, the arbiter of the affair, and, after the estrangement, the medium of communication between the parties, each saying and writing to me such things as were desired to be said or written to the others, and in such case I gave the information or showed the communication to the person intended to receive or be affected by it. Under these circumstances, I have not felt at liberty to give testimony or facts thus obtained in the sacredness of confidence before a tribunal not authorized by law to require them, however much otherwise I might respect its members and objects, without the consent of the parties from whom I received the disclosures and documents. With the consent or request of Mr. Beecher and Mr. Tilton I have held myself ready, sorrowingly, to give all the facts that I know about the objects of inquiry of the Committee, and produce whatever papers I have to the Committee and leave copies of the same with them if they desired it—with, perhaps, the one stipulation, that if I have to give my evidence orally or to be cross-examined I might bring with me a phonographic reporter, in order that I should have an exact copy of my testimony for my own protection.

I am to-day in receipt from the Rev. Henry Ward Beecher and Mr. Theodore Tilton of their consent and request—thus absolving me thereby from my confidential relations towards them—to appear before you and to give to you the facts and documents with reference to the differences between them.

It appears to me that as Mr. Tilton has given his evidence, and Mrs. Tilton likewise, Mr. Beecher should be requested to add his own, in order that the three principal parties in the case shall have been independently heard on their own responsibility before I am called to adduce the facts in my possession derived from them all. Nevertheless, since I am now fully released from my confidential relations with the parties involved in this sad affair, and since my only proper statement must consist of "the truth, the whole truth, and nothing but the truth," I see no especial reason why it may not be made at one time as well as at another. But as my statement will necessarily include a great multiplicity of facts and papers, I must ask a little delay to arrange and copy them. Accordingly, I suggest Saturday evening, August 8, as an evening convenient for me to lay my statement before the Committee. Yours truly,   FRANCIS D. MOULTON.

BROOKLYN, August 5, 1874.

MR. MOULTON'S STATEMENT.

THE Investigating Committee met August 10, 1874, at 8 P. M. All the members were present. At about five o'clock Mr. Francis D. Moulton, who was expected at the opening of the session, made his appearance, when, with the consent of the Committee, he read the following statement, prefacing it with the remarks:—" I submit to you, first, the invitation signed by your Chairman, July 27, 1874; next the invitation of your Chairman, signed July 28, and next, the invitation of your Chairman, signed August 4 " [laying copies of these invitations on the table before him.]:

GENTLEMEN OF THE COMMITTEE :—When I was last before you I stated that I would, at your request, produce such documents as I had, and make such statement of facts as had come to my knowledge on the subject of your inquiry. I fully intended so to do, and have prepared my statement of facts as sustained by the documents and made an exhibit of all the papers that have come in any way into my possession, bearing on the controversy between the parties. That statement must, of course, bear with more or less force upon one or the other of them. On mature reflection, aided by the advice of my most valued friends, I have reconsidered that determination, and am obliged to say to you that I feel compelled from a sense of duty to the parties, to my relation to their controversy, and to myself, neither to make the statement nor produce the documents. When I first became a party to the unhappy controversy between Beecher and Tilton, I had no personal knowledge, nor any document in my possession, which could affect either. Everything that I know of fact, or have received of papers, has come to me in the most sacred confidence, to be used for the purpose of composing and settling all difficulties between them, and of preventing, so far as possible, any knowledge of their private affairs being brought to the public notice. For this purpose all their matters have been entrusted to me and for none other. If I should now use them, it would be not for the purpose of peace and reconciliation, but to voluntarily take part in a controversy which they have seen fit to renew between themselves.

How faithfully, earnestly and honestly I have labored to do my duty to the parties for peace they both know. The question for me to settle for myself, and no other, is now, ought I to do anything to aid either party in a renewed controversy by use of that which I received and have used only to promote harmony ? On my honor and conscience I think I ought not. And at the risk of whatever of misconstruction and vituperation may come upon me, I must adhere to the dictates of my own judgment, and preserve, at least, my own self-respect.

I call attention again to the fact that yours is a mere voluntary tribunal, and whatever I do here is done by a voluntary and not compelled witness. Whether before any tribunal having the power to compel the production of testimony and statement of fact, I shall ever produce these papers, or give any of these confidential statements, I reserve to myself to judge of the emergency, which I hope, may never come.

Against my wish—as I never have been in sympathy with a renewal of this conflict—a part of these documents have been given to the public. In so far, confidence in regard to them has ceased. It is but just, therefore, and due to the parties, that the whole of those documents, portions of which only have been given, shall be put into your hands, in response to the thrice renewed request of the Committee. I have therefore copies of them which I produce here and place in the hands of the Committee, with the hope and request, that after they have been examined by them, they may be returned to me.

If any controversy shall arise as to the authenticity of the copies or of the documents on that point, I shall hold myself open to speak. With this exception—except in defense of my own honor and the uprightness of my course in all this unfortunate and unhappy business, the purity and candor of which ,I appeal to the consciences of both parties to sustain—I do not propose, and hope I may never be called upon hereafter to speak, either as to the facts or to produce any paper that I have received from either of the parties involved herein.

FRANK MOULTON.

[The letters appear in Mr. Beecher's statement.]

CROSS-EXAMINATION.

After the reading of this statement, Mr. Moulton was subjected to a brief cross-examination, as follows:

Mr. Winslow—Mr. Moulton, the Committee desire me to ask you some questions, notwithstanding the position you take here in your statement. You are well aware, as you show, by the three invitations which the committee have sent you, that we are in good faith pursuing an investigation. You will remember that we were appointed by the Pastor of Plymouth Church, with the sanction and approval of the Examining Committee of that Church, to inquire into all these matters relating to the alleged grievances of Mr. Tilton. The letter of authority that comes to us is not limited. No restrictions are put upon us of any kind. We are invited to examine all the sources of evidence, and we have looked upon you as one of the principal sources of evidence. We have waited some two or three weeks to get your testimony; and I am sure I express the feeling of the Committee when I express a sense of disappointment at the position you take. Of course we know that we are not a Court with compulsory powers. We are, as you state, a mere voluntary tribunal. You can do exactly as you please; we await your pleasure; but what I desire to know is, in behalf of the Committee, whether you have so deliberately formed this purpose as to make it beyond recall, as things now stand.

Mr. Moulton—In reply to what you have said, and with reference to my appearance here, so far as you are concerned in this Committee, I call your attention to the language of your own invitation, namely, this : "We earnestly request that you bring all letters and documents in your possession, which are referred to by Theodore Tilton in his statement before the Committee." I comply with the request of this Committee, and produce copies of the letters referred to by Mr. Tilton, the authenticity of which I am ready within a few moments to establish.

Mr. Winslow—Do you mean to have us understand, Mr. Moulton, that you have personally compared the originals with these copies, so that you know of your own knowledge that they are correct ? A. I mean to state exactly what I have stated.

Mr. Winslow—You have not stated anything on that point. A. Yes, I stated that these are copies of the letters which you requested, referred to in Mr. Theodore Tilton's documents.

Q. Do you state of your own personal knowledge that they are copies, or have you trusted to somebody else to make copies and compose them ? A. I beg pardon, sir ; I am willing to authenticate these copies whenever you wish that they should be authenticated.

Q. Cannot you now be induced, Mr. Moulton, to go on, notwithstanding what has happened, and give us a full statement of all your knowledge in these matters ? A. I stand upon the communication which I have made to you to-day, sir.

Q. And that you do not mean to change ? A. Not without sufficient reason.

Q. Of course I am now referring to the present moment. A. Yes, sir.

Q. There is another point that I would like to ask you about, Mr. Moulton. Considering the great importance of these letters, I submit to you whether it would not be fair and proper that the originals be produced, notwithstanding your readiness to authenticate the copies. You know that in a court copies would not be received where the originals could be produced; and would you not be willing to produce them long enough to have them looked at and examined ? A. In answer to that question I will say, I have not any desire now, nor have I had any desire, to withhold these originals from you ; and I am willing now, or within a few minutes, to produce them. You may send any member of your Committee to see them if you doubt the authenticity.

Q. I do not put it on the ground of doubt, but on the ground of business-like regularity. A. Pardon me ; I call your attention to the language of this statement which I have just made : and if the authenticity, by either party, of these documents is doubted, I hold myself ready to prove their authenticity.

Q. I do not feel called upon to put it on any ground of doubt, because there is no reason of doing it. A. I do not think there is, sir.

Q. It is merely a matter of customary business regularity. A. I have in good faith come here, and have presented to you copies of the original documents. If you doubt ——

Q.—Do not put it in that way, please. A. Pardon me. I referred to my communication ; if there is any doubt I shall remove the doubt.

Q. You were about to say something of your willingness to send for them while you are here, and let us see them. A. Oh, well, you won't doubt then, I think.

Q. If we should conclude that we wanted to see them at some other time, would you send for them ? A. Certainly, sir.

Q. Within the present week ? A. Certainly. I am willing to go with all the members of your present Committee, or any one that you may select, some time during the present week, and show to any accredited member of this Committee the original documents. Is that a fair answer to that question ? Mr. Winslow—That is satisfactory.

Mr. Hall—Perhaps that question could be determined, so far as the Committee are concerned, at the present moment. A. I want the action in reference to these documents determined, according to the expression of the document which I have submitted to you.

Mr. Winslow—Well, if for any reason we want to see the originals, I understand you to say there is no objection. [Mr. Moulton assented.]

Mr. White—I want to inquire whether your objection to giving a fuller statement is based upon the wording of the letters which seem on one construction to limit it to bringing with you the original of the letters or papers referred to in Mr. Tilton's statement before the Committee ; as it seems to me that the letter is susceptible of another explanation, and one which certainly was the understanding of the Committee ? A. Yes, sir ; I will answer your question. I wish to say, and do say, that I have acquiesced just now in the request of your chairman, and that all reasons for the non-production of facts, or the non-exhibition of documents, is given in the communication which I have just read to you.

Mr. White—Well, as I understand it, the first request, antedating all of these, called upon you to come before us and give your testimony in regard to any charges which might affect the character and the Christian standing of Mr. Beecher, in the letter referred to, of Theodore Tilton to Dr. Bacon. A. Your original letter did not say any such thing.

Q. Have you a copy here, that we may see what it did say ? A. I represented to you at the beginning of this interview, the letter from your Chairman, with reference to which I appear ; and as it is a fact that I have fully answered these thrice repeated requests, I submit that this answer is sufficient.

Mr. Sage—Allow me to ask you one question, Mr. Moulton ? A. Certainly.

Q. One letter of mine, which is before me, contains a request to bring with you the originals of all letters and papers referred to in Mr. Tilton's statement to the Committee.

Mr. Winslow—He has covered that by his agreement.

Mr. Moulton—If you doubt or question, or if you require them, you shall have them.

Mr. Sage—When shall we ? A. My dear sir, you can go with me all together to my house if you want to.

Q. The answer is unequivocal that we can have possession ? A. Not that you can have possession, but that you can see them.

Q. Well, do you mean possession long enough to examine them ? A. Yes, sir, in accordance with my statement.

Mr. White—The letters that are referred to, which are produced by you here, three in number, each of them, refer to a request before made, to appear and give your testimony. I desire simply, as one of the Committee, to state that it is my understanding of those requests that they cover the same thing that was embodied in the statement, in the request, of early in July, that you appear and give your testimony in regard to the matter involved in the Tilton letter to Mr. Bacon ; and as they refer to that again, I claim it as my understanding, as one of the Committee, that this request is not limited to the simple production of papers ; but it does include in it the request to give your testimony in regard to all the matters. That is what I have been trying to make appear here. A. I repeat again that I have answered fully, in my interview with you to-day, the request of the Chairman of your Committee.

In answer to a question put by Mr. Tracy, Mr. Moulton replied :

I have stated explicitly, in my communication to this Committee, the grounds upon which I deny to this Committee the statement of facts and the exhibition of documents that have come into my possession in confidence.

General Tracy—Then you do not mean to put that refusal upon the form of the Committee's invitation to you ? A. No, sir.

On motion of Mr. Cleveland, it was voted that Mr. Winslow be authorized to go with Mr. Moulton, and examine and verify the documents.

After some informal conversation in regard to the publication of the proceedings of the present session, Mr. Moulton retired. The Committee remained in consultation until seven o'clock, and then adjourned, to meet again on the evening of Tuesday, the 11th instant, at eight o'clock.

MR. BEECHER'S DEFENSE.

On Thursday, August 13, 1874, the Plymouth Church Investigating Committee met at the residence of Henry Ward Beecher, Columbia Heights, Brooklyn, when the reverend gentleman delivered the following elaborate defense of himself, as against Theodore Tilton's charges and minute history of the relations of the Tilton family:

MR. BEECHER'S STATEMENT.

GENTLEMEN OF THE COMMITTEE: In the statement addressed to the public on the 22d of July last, I gave an explicit, comprehensive, and solemn denial to the charges made by Theodore Tilton against me. That denial I now repeat and reaffirm. I also stated in that communication that I should appear before your Committee with a more detailed statement and explanation of the facts in the case. For this the time has now come. Four years ago Theodore Tilton fell from one of the proudest editorial chairs in America, where he represented the cause of religion, humanity, and patriotism, and in a few months thereafter became the associate and representative of Victoria Woodhull and the priest of her strange cause. By his follies he was bankrupt in reputation, in occupation and in resources. The interior history of which I am now to give a brief outline is the history of his attempts to so employ me as to reinstate him in business, restore his reputation, and place him again upon the eminence from which he had fallen. It is a sad history, to the full meaning of which I have but recently awaked. Entangled in a wilderness of complications, I followed until lately, a false theory and a delusive hope, believing that the friend who assured me of his determination and ability to control the passionate vagaries of Mr. Tilton, to restore his household, to rebuild his fortunes and to vindicate me would be equal to that promise. This self-confessed failure has made clear to me what for a long time I did not suspect—the real motive of Mr. Tilton. My narrative does not represent a single standpoint only as regards my opinion of Theodore Tilton. It begins at my cordial intimacy with him in his earlier career, and shows my lamentation and sorrowful but hopeful affection for him during the period of his initial wanderings from truth and virtue. It describes my repentance over evils befalling him of which I was made to believe myself the cause; my persevering and finally despairing efforts to save him and his family by any sacrifice of myself not absolutely dishonorable, and my growing conviction that his perpetual follies and blunders rendered his recovery impossible. I can now see that he is and has been from the beginning of this difficulty a selfish and reckless schemer, pursuing a plan of mingled greed and hatred, and weaving about me a network of suspicions, misunderstandings, plots and lies, to which my own innocent words and acts, nay, even my thoughts of kindness toward him, have been made to contribute. These successive views of him must be kept in view to explain my course through the last four years.

HIS CONFIDENCE IN MR. MOULTON.

That I was blind so long to the real nature of the intrigue going on around me was due partly to my own overwhelming public engagements, partly to my complete surrender of this affair and all papers and questions connected with it into the hands of Mr. Moulton, who was intensely confident that he could manage it successfully. I suffered much, but I inquired little. Mr. Moulton was chary to me of Mr. Tilton's confidences to him, reporting to me occasionally in a general way Mr. Tilton's moods and outbreaks of passion only as elements of trouble which he was able to control, and as additional proofs of the wisdom of leaving it to him. His comment of the situation seemed to me, at the time complete, immersed as I was in incessant cares and duties, and only too glad to be relieved from considering the details of such wretched complications, the origin and the fact of which remain in spite of all friendly intervention a perpetual burden to my soul. I would not read in the papers about it; I would not talk about it. I made Moulton for a long period my confidant and my only channel of information.

From time to time suspicions were aroused in me by indications that Mr. Tilton was acting the part of an enemy; but these suspicions were repeatedly allayed by his own behavior toward me in other ways and by the assurances of Mr. Moulton, who ascribed the circumstances to misunderstanding or to malice on the part of others. It is plain to me now that it was not until Mr. Tilton had fallen in disgrace and lost his salary that he thought it necessary to assail me with charges which he pretended to have had in mind for six months. The domestic offense which he alleged was very quickly and easily put aside, but yet in such a way as to keep my feelings stirred up, in order that I might, through my friends, be used to extract from Mr. Bowen $7,000, the amount of a claim in dispute between them. The check for that sum in hand, Mr. Tilton signed an agreement of peace and concord—not made by me, but accepted by me as sincere. *The Golden Age* had been started. He had the capital to carry it on for a while. He was sure that he was to lead a great social revolution. With returning prosperity he had apparently no griefs which could not be covered by his signature to the articles of peace. Yet the change in that covenant, made by him before signing it, and represented to me as necessary merely to relieve him from the imputation of having originated and circulated certain old and shameless slanders about me, were really made, as now appears, to leave him free for future operations upon me and against me.

THE LEVER WHICH WAS USED.

So long as he was, or thought he was, on the road to a new success, his conduct toward me was as friendly as he knew how to make it. His assumption of superiority and magnanimity, and his patronizing manner, were trifles at which I could afford to smile, and which I bore with the greater humility since I still retained the profound impression made upon me as explained in the following narrative—that I had been a cause of overwhelming disaster to him, and that his complete restoration to public standing and household happiness was a reparation, justly required of me, and the only one which I could make.

But with a peculiar genius for blunders, he fell almost at every step into new complications and difficulties, and in every such instance it was his policy to bring coercion to bear upon my honor, my conscience, and my affections, for the purpose of procuring his extrication at my expense. Theodore Tilton knew me well. He has said again and again to his friends that if they wished to gain influence over me they must work upon the sympathetic side of my nature. To this he has addressed himself steadily for four years, using as a lever, without scruple, my attachment to my friends, to my family, to his own household, and even my old affection for himself.

Not blind to his faults, but resolved to look on him as favorably and hopefully as possible, and ignorant of his deeper malice, I labored earnestly, even desperately, for his salvation. For four years I have been trying to feed the insatiable egotism, to make the man as great as he conceived himself to be, to restore to popularity and public confidence one who, in the midst of my efforts in his behalf, patronized disreputable people and doctrines, refused when I besought him to separate himself from them, and ascribed to my agency the increasing ruin which he was persistently bringing upon himself, and which I was doing my utmost to avert. It was hard to do anything for such a man. I might as well have tried to fill a sieve with water. In the latter part of the history he actually incited and created difficulties, apparently for no other purpose than to drive me to fresh exertions. I refused to indorse his wild views and associates. The best I could do was to speak well of him, mention those good qualities and abilities which I still believe him to possess in his higher moods, and keeping silent concerning the evil things which, I was assured and believed, had been greatly exaggerated by public report. I could not think him so bad as my friends did. I trusted to the germs of good which I thought still lived in him, to Mr. Moulton's apparent power over him, and to the power of my persistent self sacrifice.

Mr. Moulton came to me at first as the schoolmate and friend of Mr. Tilton, determined to reinstate him, I always suspected, without regard to my interests, but on further acquaintance with me he undertook and promised to serve his friend without doing wrong to me. He said he saw clearly how this was to be done, so as to restore peace and harmony to Mr. Tilton's home, and bring a happy end to all misunderstandings. Many things which he counseled I absolutely refused, but I never doubted his professed friendship for me, after friendship had grown up between us ; and whatever he wished me to do I did, unless it seemed to me wrong.

THE STORM GATHERING.

My confidence in him was the only element that seemed secure in that confusion of tormenting perplexities. To him I wrote freely in that troublous time, when I felt that secret machinations were going on around me, and echoes of the vilest slander concerning me were heard of in unexpected quarters ; when some of my near relatives were set against me, and the tattle of a crowd of malicious women hostile to me on other grounds was borne to my ears ; when I had lost the last remnant of faith in Theodore, or hope for him ; when I heard with unspeakable remorse that everything I had done to stay his destruction had made matters worse and worse ; that my attempt to keep him from a public trial (involving such a flood of scandal as has now been let loose) had been used by him to bring up new troubles ; that his unhappy wife, was under his dictation, signing papers and recantations, and I knew not what ; that, in short, everything was breaking up, and the destruction from which I had sought to save the family was likely to be emptied on other families, the church, the community, with infinite horrors of woe for me ; that my own innocence was buried under heaps and heaps of rubbish, and nobody but my professed friend (if even he) could save us. · To his assurances that he could still do so I gave at least so much faith as to maintain under these terrible trials the silence which he enjoined. Not until Mr. Tilton, having attempted, through Frank Carpenter, to raise money from my friends, openly assailed me in his letter to Dr. Bacon, did I break that silence, save my simple denial of the slanderous rumors against me a year before.

HIS OWN ACTIVE LIFE.

When on the appearance of the first open attack from Mr. Tilton, I immediately, without consulting Mr. Moulton, called for a thorough investigation with a committee of my Church. I am not responsible for the delay, the publicity, or the details of that investigation. All the harm which I have so long dreaded and have so earnestly striven to avoid has come to pass. I could not have futher prevented it without a full surrender of honor and truth. The time has arrived when I can freely speak in vindication of myself. ·I labor under great disadvantages in making a statement. My memory of states of the mind is clear and tenacious, better than my memory of dates and details. During four troubled years, in all of which I have been singularly burdened with public labor,·having established and conducted the *Christian Union*; delivered courses of lectures, preaching before the Theological Seminary of Yale College, written the Life of Christ, delivered each winter Lyceum lectures in all the North and West—all these duties with the care of the great church and its outlying schools and chapels, and the miscellaneous business which falls upon a clergyman more than upon any othe public man. I have kept in regard, and now with the necessity of explaining actions and letters resulting from complex influences apparent at the time, I find myself in a position where I know my innocence without being able to prove it with detailed explanation. I am one upon whom trouble works inwardly, making me outwardly silent but reverberating in the chambers of my soul ; and when at length I do speak, it is a pent up flood and pours without measure or moderation. I inherit a tendency to sadness, the remains in me of positive hypochondria in my father and grandfather, and in certain moods of reaction the world becomes black and I see very despairingly.

If I were in such moods to speak as I feel, I should give false colors and exaggerated proportions of everything. This manifestation is in such contrast to the hopefulness and courage which I experience in ordinary times that none but those intimate with me would suspect one so full of overflowing spirit and eager gladsomeness to have within him a care of gloom and despoudency. Some of my letters to Mr. Moulton reflect this morbid feeling. He understood it, and at times reproved me for indulging it. With this preliminary review, I proceed to my narrative.

FIRST ACQUAINTANCE WITH MR. TILTON.

Mr. Tilton was first known to me as a reporter of my sermons. He was then a youth just from school and working on the *New York Observer*. From this paper he passed to the *Independent*, and became a great favorite with Mr. Bowen. When about 1861 Drs. Bacon, Storrs, and Thompson resigned their places, I became editor of the *Independent*, to which I had been from its start a contributor. One of the inducements held out to me was that Mr. Tilton should be my assistant, and relieve me wholly from routine office work. In this relation I became very much attached to him. We used to stroll the galleries and print-shops and dine often together. His mind was opening freshly and with enthusiasm upon all questions. I used to pour out my ideas of civil affairs, public policy, religion, and philanthropy. Of this he often spoke with grateful appreciation, and mourned at a later day over its cessation.

August was my vacation month, but my family repaired to my farm in June and July, and remained there during September and October. My labors confining me to the city, I took my meals in the families of friends, and from year to year I became so familiar with their children and homes that I went in and out daily almost as in my own house. Mr. Tilton often alluded to this habit, and urged me to do the same by his house. He used to often speak in extravagant terms of his wife's esteem and affection for me. After I began to visit his house he sought to make it attractive. He urged me to bring my papers down there and use his study to do my writing in, as it was not pleasant to write in the office of the *Independent*. When I went to England in 1863, Mr. Tilton took temporary charge of the *Independent*. On my return I paved the way for him to take sole charge of it. my name remaining for a year, and then he becoming the responsible editor. Friendly relations continued until 1866, when the violent assaults made upon me by Mr. Tilton in the *Independent*, on account of my Cleveland letter and the temporary discontinuation of the publication of my sermons in that paper, broke off my connection with it. Although Mr. Tilton and I remained personally on good terms, yet there was a coolness between us in all matters of politics. Our social relations were very kindly, and as late as 1868-9, at his request, I sat to Page some fifty times for a portrait. It was here that I first met and talked with Moulton, whose wife was a member of Plymouth Church, though he was not a member nor even a regular attendant. During this whole period I never received from Mr. Tilton or any member of his family the slightest hint that there was any dissatisfaction with my familiar relations to his household. As late, I think, as the winter of 1869, when going upon an extended lecturing tour, he said: "I wish you would look in after and see that Libby is not lonesome or does not want anything," or words to that effect. Never by sign or word did Mr. Tilton complain of my visits to his family until he began to fear that the *Independent* would be taken from him, nor did he break out into violence until on the eve of dispossession from both the papers—the *Independent* and the *Brooklyn Union*—owned by Mr. Bowen. During these years of intimacy in Mr. Tilton's family I was treated as a father or elder brother; children were born—children died. They learned to love me and to frolic with me as if I was one of themselves. I loved them, and I had for Mrs. Tilton a true and honest regard.

HIS RELATIONS WITH MRS. TILTON.

She seemed to me an affectionate mother and a devoted wife, looking up to her husband as one far above the common race of men, and turning to me with artless familiarity and with entire confidence. Childish in appearance, she was childlike in nature, and I would as soon have misconceived the confidence of her little girls as the unstudied affection which she showed me. Delicate in health, with a self-cheerful air, she was boundless in her sympathy for those in trouble, and labored beyond her strength for the poor. She had the charge at one time of the married woman's class at the Bethel Mission School, and they perfectly worshiped her there. I gave Mrs. Tilton copies of my books when published. I sometimes sent down from the farm flowers to be distributed among a dozen or more families, and she occasionally shared. The only present of value I ever gave her was on my return from Europe in 1863, when I distributed souvenirs of my journey to some fifty or more persons, and to her I gave a simple brooch of little intrinsic value. So far from supposing that my presence and influence were alienating Mrs. Tilton from her family relations, I thought on the contrary that it was giving her strength and encouraging her to hold fast upon a man evidently sliding into dangerous associations, and liable to be ruined by unexampled self-conceit. I regarded Mr. Tilton as in a very critical period of his life, and used to think it fortunate that he had good home influences about him. During the later years of our friendship Mrs. Tilton spoke very mournfully to me about the tendency of her husband to great laxity of doctrine in religion and morals. She gave me to understand that he denied the divinity of Christ, the inspiration of the Scriptures and most articles of orthodox faith, while his views as to the sanctity of the marriage relation were undergoing constant change in the direction of free love.

In the latter part of July, 1870, Mrs. Tilton was sick, and at her request I visited her. She seemed much depressed, but gave me no hint of any trouble having reference to me. I cheered her as best I could and prayed with her just before leaving. This was our last interview before trouble broke out in the family. I describe it because it was the last, and its character has a bearing upon a later part of my story. Concerning all my other visits it is sufficient to say that *at no interview which ever took place between Mrs. Tilton and myself did anything occur which might not have occurred with perfect propriety between a brother and sister, between a father and child, or between a man of honor and the wife of his dearest friend;* nor did anything ever happen which she or I sought to conceal from her husband.

Some years before any open trouble between Mr. Tilton and myself, his doctrines as set forth in the leaders of *The Independent* aroused a storm of indignation among the representative Congregationalists in the West; and as the paper was still very largely supposed to be my organ, I was written to on the subject. In reply, I indignantly disclaimed all responsibility for the views expressed by Mr. Tilton. My brother Edward, then living in Illinois, was prominent in the remonstrance addressed to Mr. Bowen concerning the course of his paper under Mr. Tilton's management. It was understood that Mr. Bowen agreed, in consequence of proceedings arising out of this remonstrance, to remove Mr. Tilton or suppress his peculiar views, but instead of that, Theodore seemed firmer in the saddle than before, and his loose notions of marriage and divorce began to be shadowed editorially. This led to the starting of *The Advance* in Chicago, to supersede *The Independent* in the North-West, and Mr. Bowen was made to feel that Mr. Tilton's management was seriously injuring the business, and Mr. Tilton may have felt that his position was being undermined by opponents of his views with whom he subsequently pretended to believe I was in league. Vague intimations of his "feeling hard" toward me I ascribed to this misconception. I had in reality taken no step to harm him.

HE ADVISES SEPARATION.

After Mr. Tilton's return from the West in December, 1870, a young girl whom Mrs. Tilton had taken into the family, educated, and treated like an own child (her testimony, I understand, is before the Committee), was sent to me with an urgent request that I would visit Mrs. Tilton at her mother's. She said that Mrs. Tilton had left her home and gone to her mother's in consequence of ill-treatment of her husband. She then gave an account of what she had seen of cruelty and abuse on the part of the husband that shocked me; and yet more, when with downcast look she said that Mr. Tilton had visited her chamber in the night and sought her consent to his wishes. I immediately visited Mrs. Tilton at her mother's, and received an account of her home life, and of the despotism of her husband, and of the management of a woman whom he had made housekeeper, which seemed like a nightmare dream. The question was whether she should go back, or separate forever from her husband. I asked permission to bring my wife to see them, whose judgment in all domestic relations I thought better than my own ; and accordingly a second visit was made. The result of the interview was that my wife was extremely indignant toward Mr. Tilton, and declared that no consideration on earth would induce her to remain an hour with a man who had treated her with a hundredth part of such insult and cruelty. I felt as strongly as she did, but hesitated, as I always do, at giving advice in favor of a separation. It was agreed that my wife should give her final advice at another visit. The next day, when ready to go, she wished a final word ; but there was company, and the children were present, and so I wrote on a scrap of paper, "I incline to think that your view is right, and that a separation and a *settlement of support* will be wisest, and that in his present desperate state her presence near him is far more likely to produce hatred than her absence."

Mrs. Tilton did not tell me that my presence had anything to do with this trouble, nor did she let me know that on the July previous he had extorted from her a confession of excessive affection for me.

On the evening of Dec. 27, 1870, Mr. Bowen, on his way home, called at my house and handed me a letter from Mr. Tilton. It was, as nearly as I can remember, in the following terms :

HENRY WARD BEECHER : For reasons which you explicitly know, and which I forbear to state, I demand that you withdraw from the pulpit and quit Brooklyn as a residence.

THEODORE TILTON.

INTERFERENCE IN BUSINESS MATTERS.

I read it over twice, and turned to Bowen and said : "This man is crazy ; this is sheer insanity," and other like words. Mr. Bowen professed to be ignorant of the contents, and I handed him the letter to read. We at once fell into a conversation about Mr. Tilton. He gave me some account of the reasons why he had reduced him from the editorship of *The Independent* to the subordinate position of contributor, namely, that Mr. Tilton's religious and social views were ruining the paper. But he said as soon as it was known that he had so far broken with Mr. Tilton, there came pouring in upon him so many stories of Mr. Tilton's private life and habits that he was overwhelmed, and that he was now considering whether he could consistently retain him on *The Brooklyn Union*, or as chief contributor to *The Independent*. He narrated the story of the affair at Winsted, Conn., some like stories from the North-West, and charges brought against Mr. Tilton in his own office. Without doubt he believed these allegations, and so did I. The other facts previously stated to me seemed a full corroboration. We conversed for some time, Mr. Bowen wishing my opinion. It was frankly given. I did not see how he could maintain his relations with Mr. Tilton. The substance of the conversation was that Tilton's inordinate vanity, his fatal facility for blundering (for which he had a genius), and ostentatious independence in his own opinions and general impracticableness would keep *The Union* at disagreement with the political party for whose service it was published ; and now, added to all this, these revelations of these promiscuous immoralities would make his connection with either paper fatal to its interests. I spoke strongly and emphatically under the great provocation of his threatening to me and the revelation I had just had concerning his domestic affairs.

Mr. Bowen derided the letter of Tilton's which he had brought to me, and said earnestly that if trouble came out of it I might rely upon his friendship. I learned afterward that in the further quarrel, ending in Tilton's peremptory expulsion from Bowen's service, this conversation was repeated to Mr. Tilton. I believe Mr. Bowen had an interview and received some further information about Tilton from my wife, to whom I had referred him ; and although I have no doubt that Mr. Tilton would have lost his place at any rate, I have also no doubt that my influence was decisive, and precipitated his final overthrow. When I came to think it all over I felt very unhappy at the contemplation of Mr. Tilton's impending disaster. I had loved him much, and at one time he had seemed like a son to me. My influence had come just at the time of his first unfolding, and had much to do with this early development. I had aided him externally to bring him before the public. We had been together in the great controversies of the day until after the war, and our social relations had been intimate.

It is true that his nature always exaggerated his own excellencies. When he was but a boy he looked up to me with affectionate admiration. After some years he felt himself my equal, and was very companionable ; and when he had outgrown me, and reached the position of the first man of the age, he still was kind and patronizing. I had always smiled at these weaknesses of vanity, and had believed that a larger experience, with some knocks among strong men, and by sorrows that temper the soul, he would yet fulfill a useful and brilliant career. But now all looked dark ; he was to be cast forth from his eminent position, and his affairs at home did not promise that sympathy and strength which make one's house, as mine has been, in times of adversity, a refuge from the storm and a tower of defense.

Besides a generous suffering I should have had a selfish reason for such, if I had dreamt that I was about to become the instrument by which Mr. Tilton meant to fight his way back to the prosperity which he had forfeited. It now appears that on the 29th of December, 1870, Mr. Tilton having learned that I had replied to his threatening letter by expressing such an opinion of him as to set Mr. Bowen finally against him, and bring him face to face with immediate ruin, extorted from his wife, then suffering under a severe illness, a document incriminating me, and prepared an elaborate attack upon me.

MR. TILTON WITH HIS WIFE'S CERTIFICATE.

On Tuesday evening, December 30, 1870, about seven o'clock, Francis D. Moulton called at my house, and with intense earnestness said, "I wish you to go with me to see Mr. Tilton." I replied that I could not then, as I was just going to my prayer-meeting. With the most positive manner, he said, "You must go ; somebody else will take care of the meeting." I went with him, not knowing what trouble had agitated him, but vaguely thinking that I might now learn the solution of the recent threatening letter. On the way I asked him what was the reason of this visit, to which he replied that Mr. Tilton would inform me, or words to that effect. On entering his house, Mr. Moulton locked the door, saying something about not being interrupted. He requested me to go into the front chamber over the parlor. I was under the impression that Mr. Tilton was going to pour out upon me his anger for colleaguing with Bowen and for the advice of separation given to his wife. I wished Mr. Moulton to be with me as a witness, but he insisted that I should go by myself.

Mr. Tilton received me coldly, but calmly. After a word or two, standing in front of me with a memorandum in his hand, he began an oration. He charged me in substance with acting for a long time in an unfriendly spirit ; that I had sought his downfall ; had spread injurious rumors about him ; was using my place and influence to undermine him ; had advised Mr. Bowen to dismiss him, and much more that I cannot remember. He then declared that I had injured him in his family relations ; had joined with his mother-in-law in producing discord in his house, had advised a separation, had alienated his wife's affections from him, had led her to love me more than any living being, had corrupted her moral nature, and taught her to be insincere, lying, and hypocritical, and ended by charging that I had made wicked proposals to her. Until he had reached this, I had listened with some contempt, under the impression that he was attempting to bully me. But with the last charge he produced a paper purporting to be a certified statement of a previous confession made to him by his wife of her love for me, and that I had made proposals to her of an impure nature. He said that this confession had been made to him in July, six months previous ; that his sense of honor and affection would not permit any such document to remain in existence ; that he had burned the original, and should now destroy the only copy ; and he then tore the paper into small pieces. If I had been shocked at such a statement, I was absolutely thunderstruck when he closed the interview by requesting me to repair at once to his house, where he said Elizabeth was waiting for me, and learn from her lips the truth of his stories in so far as they concerned her. This fell like a thunderbolt on me. Could it be possible that his wife, whom I had regarded as the type of moral goodness, should have made such false and atrocious statements ? And yet if she had not, how would she dare to send me to her for confirmation of his charges ?

I went forth like a sleep-walker, while clouds were flying in the sky. There had been a snow storm, which was breaking away. The winds were out and whistling through the leafless trees, but all this was peace compared to my mood within. I believe that Moulton went with me to the door of Tilton's house. The housekeeper (the same woman of whom Mr. Tilton had complained) seemed to have been instructed by him, for she evidently expected me, and showed me at once up to Mrs. Tilton's room. Mrs. Tilton lay upon her bed, white as marble, with closed eyes, as in a trance, and with her hands upon her bosom, palm to palm, like one in prayer. As I look back upon it, the picture is like some forms carved in marble that I had seen upon monuments in Europe.

THE RETRACTION WRITTEN.

She made no motion, and gave no sign of recognition of my presence. I sat down near her and said, "Elizabeth, Theodore has been making very serious charges against me, and sends me to you for confirmation." She made no reply or sign. Yet it was plain that she was conscious and listening. I repeated some of his statements—that I had brought discord to the family, had alienated her from him, had sought to break up the family, had usurped his influence, and then, as well as I could, I added that he said that I had made improper suggestions to her, *and that she had admitted this fact to him last July.* I said, "Elizabeth, have you made such statements to him ?" She made no answer. I repeated the question. Tears ran down her cheeks, and she very slightly bowed her head in acquiescence. I said, "You cannot mean that you have stated all he has charged." She opened her eyes and began in a slow and feeble way to explain how sick she had been, how wearied out with importunity ; that he had confessed his own alien loves, and said that he could not bear to think that she was better than he; that she might win him to reformation if she would confess that she had loved me more than him, and that they would repent and go on with future concord. I cannot give her language, but only the tenor of her representations. I received them impatiently, I spoke to her in the strongest language of her course. I said to her: "Have I ever made any improper advances to you?" She said: "No." Then I asked: "Why did you say so to your husband?" She seemed deeply distressed. "My friend " (by that designation she almost always called me), " I am sorry, but I could not help it. What can I do?" I told her she could state in writing what she had now told me. She beckoned for her writing materials, which I handed her from her secretary standing near by, and she sat up in bed and wrote a brief counter-statement.

In a sort of postscript, she denied explicitly that I had ever offered any improper solicitations to her, that being the only charge made against me by Mr. Tilton, or sustained by the statement about the confession which he had read to me. I dreamed of no worse charge at that time. That was horrible enough. The mere thought that he could make it and could have extorted any evidence on which to base it, was enough to take away my senses. Neither my consciousness of its utter falsehood, nor Mrs. Tilton's retraction of her part in it could remove the shock from my heart and head. Indeed, her admission to me that she had stated, under any circumstances, to her husband so wicked a falsehood was the crowning blow of all. It seemed to me as if she was going to die, that her mind was overthrown, and that I was in some dreadful way mixed up in it, and might be left by her death with this terrible accusation hanging over me.

I returned, like one in a dream, to Mr. Moulton's house, where I said very little and soon went home. It has been said that I confessed guilt and expressed remorse. This is utterly false. Is it likely that, with Mrs. Tilton's retraction in my pocket, I should have thus stultified myself?

MR. MOULTON ARMED WITH A PISTOL.

On the next day, at evening, Mr. Moulton called at my house and came up into my bedroom. He said that Mrs. Tilton, on her husband's return to her after our interview, had informed him what she had done, and that I had her retraction. Moulton expostulated with me, said that the retraction under the circumstances would not mend matters, but awaken fresh discord between husband and wife and do great injury to Mrs. Tilton without helping me. Mrs. Tilton, he said, had already recanted in writing the retraction made to me, and of course there might be no end to such contradictions. Meanwhile, Tilton had destroyed his wife's first letter, acknowledging the confession, and Mr. Moulton claimed that I had taken a mean advantage, and made dishonorable use of Theodore's request that I should visit her, in obtaining from her a written contradiction to a document not in existence. He said that all difficulties could be settled without any such papers, and that I ought to give it up. He was under great excitement. He made no verbal threats, but he opened his overcoat, and with some emphatic remark showed a pistol, which afterward he took out and laid on the bureau near which he stood. I gave the paper to him, and after a few moments' talk he left.

HIS MOOD WHEN THE APOLOGY WAS WRITTEN.

Within a day or two after this Mr. Moulton made me third visit, and this time we repaired to my study in the third story of my house. Before speaking of this interview, it is right that I should allude to the suffering through which I had gone during the previous days—the cause of which was the strange change in Mrs. Tilton. Nothing had seemed to me more certain, during all my acquaintance with her, than that she was singularly simple, truthful, and honorable. Deceit seemed absolutely foreign to her nature, and yet she had stated to her husband those strange and awful falsehoods. She had not, when daily I called and prayed with her, given me the slightest hint, I will not say of such accusations, but even that there was any serious family difficulty. She had suddenly, in December, called me and my wife to a consultation to a possible separation from her husband, still leaving me ignorant that she had put into his hands such a weapon against me. I was bewildered with a double consciousness of a saintly woman communicating a very needless treachery to her friend and pastor. My distress was boundless. I did not for a moment feel, however, that she was blameworthy, as would ordinarily be thought, but supposed that she had been overborne by sickness and shattered in mind until she scarcely knew what she did, and was no longer responsible for her acts. My soul went out to her in pity. I blamed myself for want of prudence and foresight, for I thought that all this had been the result of her undue affection for me. I had a profound feeling that I would bear any blame and take any punishment if that poor child could only emerge from this cloud and be put back into the happiness from which I had been, as I thought, if not the cause, yet the occasion of withdrawing her. If my own daughter had been in similar case, my grief at her calamity could scarcely have been greater. Moreover, from the anger and fury of Mr. Tilton, I apprehended that this charge was made by him, and, supported by the accusation of his wife, was to be at once publicly pressed against me; and if it was, I had nothing but my simple word of denial to interpose against it. In my then morbid condition of mind, I thought that this charge, although entirely untrue, might result in great disaster, if not in absolute ruin. The great interests which were entirely dependent on me, the church which I had built up, the book which I was writing, my own immediate family, my brother's name, now engaged in the ministry, my sisters, the name which I had hoped might live after me and be in some slight degree a source of strength and encouragement to those who should succeed me, and above all, the cause for which I had devoted my life, seemed imperiled. It seemed to me that my life-work was to end abruptly and in disaster. My earnest desire to avoid a public accusation, and the evils which must necessarily flow from it and which now have resulted from it, has been one of the leading motives that must explain my action during these four years with reference to this matter.

THE APOLOGY.

It was in such a sore and distressing condition that Mr. Moulton found me. His manner was kind and conciliatory; he seemed, however, to be convinced that I had been seeking Tilton's downfall, that I had leagued with Mr. Bowen against him, and that I had by my advice come near destroying his family. I did not need any argument or persuasion to induce me to do and say anything which would remedy the injury of which I then believed I had certainly been the occasion if not the active cause. But Mr. Moulton urged that having wronged so, the wrong meant his means of support taken away, his reputation gone, his family destroyed, and that I had done it. He assured me of his own knowledge that the stories which I had heard of Mr. Tilton's impurities of life, and which I had believed and repeated to Mr. Bowen, were all false, and that Mr. Tilton had always been faithful to his wife. I was persuaded into the belief of what he had said, and felt convicted of slander in its meanest form. He drew the picture of Mr. Tilton wronged in reputation, in position, wronged in purse, shattered in his family where he would otherwise have found a refuge, and at the same time looking upon me out of his deep distress, while I was abounding in friends, most popular, and with ample means; he drew that picture—my prosperity overflowing and abounding, and Tilton's utter degradation—I was most intensely excited. Indeed, I felt that my mind was in danger of giving way: I walked up and down the room pouring forth my heart in the most unrestrained grief and bitterness of self-accusation, telling what my ideas were of the obligation of friendship and of the sacredness of the household; denying, however, an intentional wrong, seeing that if I had been the cause, however remotely, of that which I then beheld, I never could forgive myself, and heaping all the blame on my own head. The case as it then appeared to my eyes, was strongly against me. My old fellow-worker had been dispossessed of his eminent place and influence, and I had counseled it. His family had well nigh been broken up, and I had advised it; his wife had been long sick and broken in health and body, and I, as I fully believed it, had been the cause of all this wreck, by continuing that blind heedlessness and friendship which had beguiled her heart and had roused her husband into a fury of jealousy, although not caused by any intentional act of mine. And should I coldly defend myself? Should I pour indignation upon this lady? Should I hold her up to contempt as having thrust her affections upon me unsought? Should I tread upon the man and his household in their great adversity? I gave vent to my feelings without measure. I disclaimed with the greatest earnestness all intent to harm Theodore in his home or his business, and with inexplicable sorrow I both blamed and defended Mrs. Tilton in one breath.

Mr. Moulton was apparently affected by my soliloquy, for it was that, rather than a conversation. He said that if Mr. Tilton could really be persuaded of the friendliness of my feelings toward him, he was sure that there would be no trouble in procuring a reconciliation. I gave him leave to state to Theodore my feelings. He proposed that I should write a letter. I declined, but said that he could report our interview. He then prepared to make a memorandum of the talk, and sat down at my table, and took down, as I supposed, a condensed report of my talk; for I went on still pouring out my wounded feelings over this great desolation in Mr. Tilton's family. It was not a dictation of sentence after sentence, he a mere amanuensis, and I composing for him. Mr. Moulton was putting into his own shape parts of that which I was saying in my own manner, with profuse explanations. This paper of Mr. Moulton's was a mere memorandum of points to be used by him in setting forth my feelings. That it contains matters and points derived from me is without doubt; but they were put into sentences by him and expressed as he understood them, not as my words, but as hints of my figures and letters, to be used by him in conversing with Mr. Tilton.

NOT MR. BEECHER'S APOLOGY.

He did not read the paper to me nor did I read it, nor have I ever seen it or heard it read that I remember, until the publication of Mr. Tilton's recent documents; and now reading it, I see in it thoughts that point to the matter of my discourse; but it is not my paper, nor are those my sentences, nor is it a correct report of what I said. It is a mere string of hints hastily made by an unpracticed writer as helps to his memory in representing to Mr. Tilton how I felt toward his family. If more than this be claimed—if it be set forth as in any proper sense my letter, I then disown it and denounce it. Some of its sentences and particularly that in which I am made to say that I had obtained Mrs.

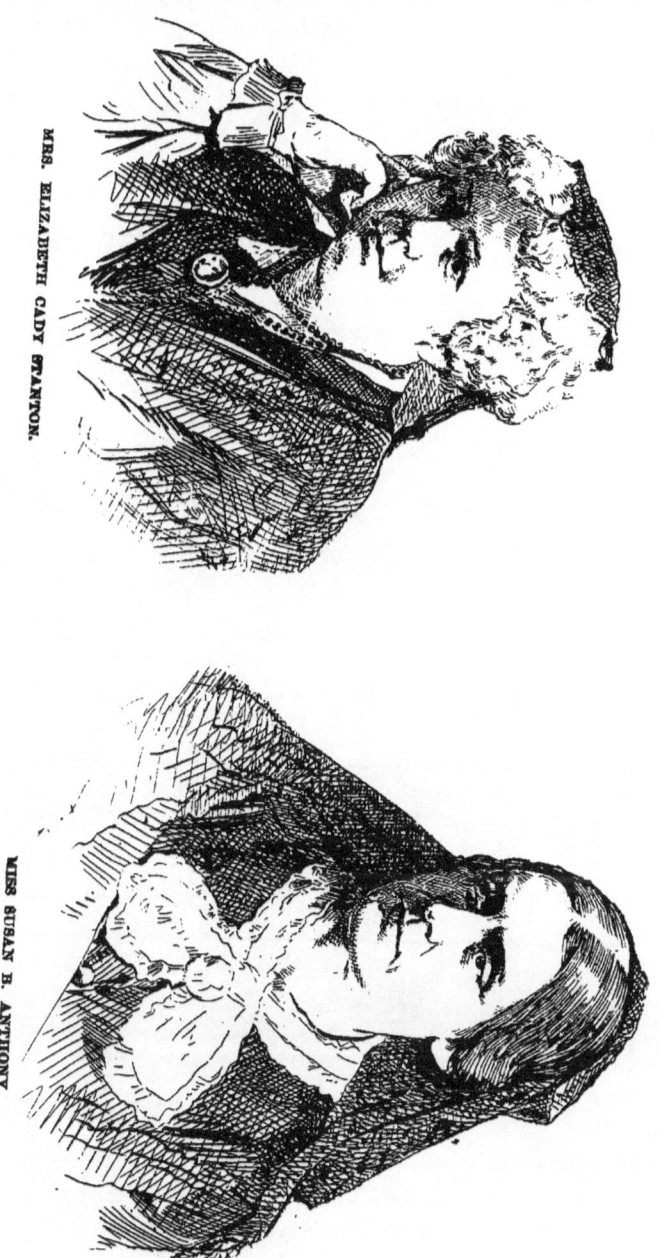

MRS. ELIZABETH CADY STANTON.

MISS SUSAN B. ANTHONY.

Tilton's forgiveness, I never could have said, even in substance. I had not obtained nor asked any forgiveness from her, and nobody pretended that I had done so. Neither could I ever have said that I humbled myself before Tilton as before God—except in the sense that both to God and to the man I thought I had deeply injured, I humbled myself, as I certainly did. But it is useless to analyze a paper prepared as this was. The remainder of my plain statement concerning it will be its best comment. This document was written upon three separate half sheets of large letter paper. After it was finished Mr. Moulton asked me if I would sign it. I said no; it was not my letter. He replied that it would have more weight if I would in some way indicate that he was authorized to explain my sentiments. I took my pen, and at some distance below the writing and upon the lower margin I indicated that I had committed the document in trust to Mr. Moulton, and I signed the line thus written by me.

A few words more as to its further fate. Mr. Moulton, of his own accord, said that after using it he would, in two or three days, bring the memorandum back to me, and he cautioned me about disclosing in any way that there was a difficulty between Mr. Tilton and me, as it would be injurious to Tilton to have it known that I had quarreled with him, as well as to me to have rumors set afloat. I did not trouble myself about it until more than a year afterward, when Tilton began to write up his case (of which hereafter) and was looking up documents. I wondered what was in the old memorandum, and desired to see it for greater certainty; so one day I suddenly asked Moulton for that memorandum, and said, "You promised to return it to me." He seemed confused for a moment, and said "Did I?" "Certainly," I answered. He replied that the paper had been destroyed. On my putting the question again, "That paper was burned up long ago;" and during the next two years, in various conversations, of his own accord he spoke of it as destroyed. I had never asked for, nor authorized, the destruction of this paper. But I was not allowed to know that the document was in existence until a distinguished editor in New York, within a few weeks past, assured me that Mr. Moulton had shown him the original, and that he had examined my signature to be sure of its genuineness. I know that there was a copy of it since this statement was in preparation.

While I rejected this memorandum as my work, or an accurate condensation of my statement, it does undoubtedly correctly represent that I was in profound sorrow, and that I blamed myself with great severity for the disasters of the Tilton family. I had not then the light that I now have. There was much then that weighed heavily upon my heart and conscience, which now weighs only on my heart. I have not the light which analyzes and discriminates things. By one blow there opened before me a revelation full of anguish: an agonized family, whose inmates had been my friends, greatly beloved; the husband ruined in worldly prospects, the household crumbling to pieces, the woman, by long sickness and suffering either corrupted to deceit, as her husband alleged, or so broken in mind as to be irresponsible; and either way it was her enthusiasm for her pastor, as I was made to believe, that was the germ and beginning of the trouble. It was for me to have forestalled and prevented that mischief. My age and experience in the world should have put me more on my guard. I could not at that time tell what was true and what was not true of all the considerations urged upon me by Mr. Tilton and Moulton. There was a gulf before me in which lay those which had been warm friends, and they alleged that I had helped to plunge them therein. That seemed enough to fill my soul with sorrow and anguish. No mother who has lost a child but will understand the wild self-accusation that grief produced, against all reason, blaming herself for what things she did do and for what she neglected to do, and charging upon herself, her neglect or heedlessness, the death of her child, while ordinarily every one knows that she had worn herself out with her assiduities.

CONVERSATIONS WITH MR. TILTON.

Soon after this I met Mr. Tilton at Moulton's house. Either Moulton was sick or was very late in rising, for he was in bed. The subject of my feelings and conduct toward Tilton was introduced. I made a statement of the motives under which I had acted in counseling Bowen, of my feelings in regard to Mr. Tilton's family, disclaiming with horror the thought of wrong, and expressing desire to do whatever lay in human power to remedy any evil I had occasioned, and to reunite his family. Tilton was silent and sullen. He played the part of an injured man, but Moulton said to Mr. Tilton, with intense emphasis, "That is all that a gentleman can say, and you ought to accept it; as our honorable basis of reconciliation." This he repeated two or three times, and Tilton's countenance cheered up under Moulton's strong talk. We shook hands and parted in a friendly way. Not very long afterward Tilton asked me to his house, and said he should be glad to have good old times renewed. I do not remember whether I ever took a meal after this under his roof, but I certainly was invited by him to renew my visits as formerly. I never resumed my intimacy with the family; but once or twice I went there soon after my reconciliation with Mr. Tilton and at his request. I particularly remember a scene which took place at his house, when he talked about his wife and me in a very gracious mood. He began by mourning his sorrows; he was very desolate; the future seemed quite dark. After impressing us with his great patience, he grew generous, praised me to his wife, saying that I had taken upon myself all blame of past troubles, and had honorably exculpated her, and telling me that his wife had likewise behaved very magnanimously, had blamed herself, and declared that I was blameless, and he closed his homily with increasing hope and cheer, saying that deep as was his misery, he did not know but that it would work out in the future a more cheerful home than he had before. I restrained my smiles at the absurdity of the thing, well content to have it evaporate so, and even thinking he was generous in his way. This seemed to me the end of trouble. With a sensitive and honorable man, who had no ulterior designs to accomplish, it would have been the burial of the difficulty. I supposed Mr. Tilton had given up the idea of intentional wrong on my part and forgiven my unintentional wrong. I plainly understand now what I did not then suspect, that my trouble of mind was to be kept alive and nourished, so that I might be used to act on my friend in securing from Mr. Bowen the money which Mr. Tilton claimed to be due as compensation for his expulsion from the two newspapers.

MR. TILTON'S SENSE OF MARITAL PURITY.

Mr. Moulton and Mr. Tilton both strove to obliterate from my mind all belief in the rumors that had been circulated about Mr. Tilton. There was much going on in silencing, explaining, arranging, etc., that I did not understand as well then as now. But of one thing I was convinced, viz. : that Mr. Tilton had the highest sense of marital purity, and that he had never strayed from the path of virtue ; which preservation he owed, as he told me in a narrative of his life, to a very solemn scene with his father, who, on the eve of his leaving home, pointed out to him the nature of amorous temptations and snares, and the evils to be dreaded from unlawful practices. He declared that he had always been kept spotless by the memory of that scene. I was glad to believe it true, and felt how hard it was that he should be made to suffer by evil and slanderous foes. I could not explain some testimony which had been laid before me; but, I said, there is undoubtedly some misunderstanding, and if I knew the whole I should find Theodore, though with obvious faults, at heart sound and good. These views I often expressed to intimate friends in spite of their manifest incredulity, and what in the light of the facts I must now call their well-deserved ridicule. Mr. Moulton lost no occasion of presenting to me the kindest view of Mr. Tilton's character and conduct. On the other hand, he complained that Mrs. Tilton did not trust her husband or him, and did not assist him in his effort to help Theodore. I knew that she distrusted Moulton, and felt bitterly hurt by the treatment of her husband. I was urged to use my influence with her to inspire confidence in Moulton, and to lead her to take a kinder view of Theodore. Accordingly, at the instance of Mr. Moulton, three letters were written on the same day—Feb. 17, 1871 —on one common purpose, to be shown to Mrs. Tilton, and to reconcile her to her husband ; and my letter to her of that date was designed to effect the further or collateral purpose of giving her confidence in Mr. Moulton. This will be obvious from the reading of the letters.

The following is the full text of my letters of that date from a copy verified by one of your Committee, for I have not to this hour been permitted to see the originals, either of them, or of any other papers which I had deposited with Moulton for safe keeping :

BEECHER TO MRS. TILTON.

BROOKLYN, Feb. 7, 1871.

MY DEAR MRS. TILTON : When I saw you last I did not expect ever to see you again, or to be alive many days. God was kinder to me than were my own thoughts. The friend whom God sent to me— Mr. Moulton—has proved above all friends that ever I had, able and willing to help me in this terrible emergency of my life. His hand it was that tied up the storm that was ready to burst upon our heads.

I am not the less disposed to trust him from finding that he has *your* welfare most deeply and tenderly at heart. You have no friend (Theodore excepted) who has it in his power to serve you so vitally, and who will do it with so much delicacy and honor. I beseech of you, if my wishes have yet any influence, let my deliberate judgment in this matter weigh with you. It does my sore heart good to see in Mr. Moulton an unfeigned respect and honor for you. It would kill me if he thought otherwise. He will be as true a friend to your honor and happiness as a brother would be to a sister's.

In him we have a common ground. You and I may meet in him. The past is ended. But is there no future ? No wiser, higher, holier future ? May not this friend stand as a priest in the new sanctuary of reconciliation, and mediate and bless you, Theodore, and my most unhappy self ? Do not let my earnestness fail of its end. You believe in my judgment. I have put myself wholly and gladly in Moulton's hands, and there I must meet you.

This is sent with Theodore's consent, but he has not read it. *Will you return it to me by his hands?* I am very earnest in this wish, for all our sakes, as such a letter ought not to be subject to even a chance of miscarriage. Your unhappy friend,

H. W. BEECHER.

BEECHER TO MOULTON.

Feb. 7, 1871.

MY DEAR MR. MOULTON : I am glad to send you a book which you will relish, or which a man on a sick bed *ought* to relish. I wish I had more like it, and that I could send you one every day, not as a repayment of your great kindness to me, for that can never be repaid, not even by love, which I give you freely. Many, many friends has God raised up to me ; but to no one of them has He ever given the opportunity and the wisdom so to serve me as you have. My trust in you is implicit. You have also proved yourself Theodore's friend and Elizabeth's. Does God look down from heaven on three unhappy creatures that more need a friend than these? Is it no' an intimation o God's intent of mercy to all that each one of these has in you a tried and proved friend? But only in you are we three united. Would to God, who orders all hearts, that by your aid and mediation Theodore, Elizabeth, and I could be made friends again. Theodore will have the hardest task in such a case; but has he not proven himself capable of the noblest things?

I wonder if Elizabeth knows how generously he has carried himself toward me? Of course I can never speak with her again, except with his permission—and I do not know that, even then, it would be best. My earnest longing is, to see her, in the full sympathy of her nature, at rest in him, and to see him once more trusting her and loving her with even a better than the old love. I am always sad in such thoughts. Is there any way out of this night? May not a day star arise?

Truly yours always, and with truest love,

HENRY WARD BEECHER.

MR. BEECHER'S ANTICIPATION OF SUDDEN DEATH.

I have no recollection of seeing or hearing read the letter of Mr. Tilton of the same date. In my letter to Mrs. Tilton I alluded to the fact that I did not expect when I saw her last to be alive many days. That statement stands connected with a series of symptoms which I first experienced in 1856. I went through the Fremont campaign, speaking in the open air three hours at a time three days in the week. On renewing my literary labors I felt I must have given way, I very seriously thought that I was going to have apoplexy or paralysis, or something of the kind. On two or three occasions, while preaching, I should have fallen in the pulpit if I had not held on to the table. Very often I came near falling in the streets. During the last fifteen years I have gone into the pulpit, I suppose 100 times, with a very strong impression that I should never come out of it alive. I have preached more sermons than any human being would believe, when I felt all the while that whatever I had got to say to my people I must say it then or I never would have another chance to say it. If I had consulted a physician, his first advice would have been, " You must stop work." But I was in such a situation that I could not stop work. I read the best medical books on symptoms of nervous prostration, and overwork, and paralysis, and formed my own judgment of my case. The three points I marked were: I must have good digestion, good sleep, and I must go on working. These three things were to be reconciled, and in regard to my diet and stimulants and medicines I made the most thorough and search ing trial; and as the result managed my body so that I could get the most work out of it without essentially impairing it. If I had said a word about this to my family it would have brought such distress and anxiety on the part of my wife as I could not bear. I have for many years so steadily taxed my mind to the utmost, that there have been periods when I could not afford to have people express even sympathy with me. To have my wife or friends anxious about it, and showing it to me, would be just the drop too much.

In 1863 I came again into the same condition just before going to England, and it was one of those reasons why I was wishing to go. The war was at its height. I carried my country in my heart. I had the *Independent* in charge, and was working, preaching, and lecturing continually. I knew I was likely to be prostrated again.

In December, 1870, the sudden shock of these troubles brought on again these symptoms in a more violent form. I was very much depressed in mind, and all the more because it was one of those things that I could not say anything about; I was silent with everybody. During the last four years these symptoms had been repeatedly brought on by my intense work, carried forward on the underlying basis of so much sorrow and trouble.

My friends will bear witness that in the pulpit I have very frequently alluded to my expectation of sudden death. I feel that I have more than once already been near a stroke that would have killed or paralyzed me, and I carry with me now, as I have so often carried in years before this trouble began, the daily thought of death as a door which might open for me at any moment, out of all cures and labors into most welcome rest.

TILTON AND WOODHULL CLIQUE.

During the whole of the year 1871 I was kept in a state of suspense and doubt, not only as to the future of the family, for the reunion and happiness of which I had striven so earnestly, but as to the degree to which I might be personally subject to attack and misconstruction, and the trouble be brought into the church and magnified by publicity. The officers of the church sought to investigate Mr. Tilton's religious views and moral conduct, and on the latter point I had been deceived into the belief that he was not in fault. As to the religious views I still hoped for a change for the better, as it was proposed to drop him from the list of members for non-attendance, and as he asserted to me his withdrawal, this might have been done, but his wife still attended the church and hoped for his restoration. I recollect having with him a conversation, in which he dimly hinted to me that he thought it not unlikely that he might go back into his old position. He seemed to be in a mood to regret the past. And so, when I was urged by the Executive Committee to take some steps, I said I was not without hopes that by patience and kindness Tilton will come back again into his old church works and be one of us again. I therefore delayed a decision upon this point for a long time. Many of our members were anxious and impatient, and there were many tokens of trouble from this quarter. Meanwhile one wing of the Female Suffrage party had got hold of the story in a distorted and exaggerated form, such as had never been intimated to me by Mr. Tilton or his friends. I did not then suspect what I now know, that these atrociously false rumors originated with Mr. Tilton himself. I only saw the evil growing, instead of diminishing, and perceived that while I was pledged to silence, and therefore could not speak in my own defense, some one was forever persevering in falsehood, growing continually in dimensions, and these difficulties were immensely increased by the affiliation of Mr. Tilton with the Woodhull clique.

In May, 1871, Mrs. Woodhull advertised a forthcoming article, shadowing an account of the disturbances in Mr. Tilton's family, but without using names. It was delayed, ostensibly by Mr. Tilton's influence with Mrs. Woodhull, until November, 1872. During this suspension of her publication, she became the heroine of Mr. Moulton and Mr. Tilton. She was made welcome to both houses, with the toleration, but not the cordial consent of their wives. I heard the most extravagant eulogies upon her. She was represented as a genius, born and reared among rude influences, but only needed to be surrounded by refined society to show a noble and communing nature. I did not know much about her; and, though my impressions were unfavorable, her real character was not then really known to the world. I met her three times. At the first interview she was gracious, at the second she was cold and haughty, but at the third she was angry and threatening, for I had peremptorily refused to preside at the lecture she was about to give at Steinway Hall. The most strenuous efforts had been made by both Mr. Tilton and Mr. Moulton to induce me to preside at this lecture and to identify myself publicly with Mrs. Woodhull. It was represented to me that I need not, in so doing, expressly give assent to her doctrines, especially with regard to the marriage relation, upon which point she was beginning to be more explicit in opposition to the views which I, in common with all Christian men, entertained; but it was plausibly urged that I could preside at the lecture and introduce her upon the simple grounds of advocating free speech and liberty of debate. But as I understood that she was about to avow doctrines which I abhor, I would not be induced by this plausible argument to give her public countenance; and after continuing to urge me, up to the very day of the meeting, without any distinct threats, but with the obvious intimation that my personal safety would be better secured by taking this advice, Mr. Tilton himself went over to New York and presided at the meeting where Mrs. Woodhull gave vent, as I understand for the first time in public, to a full exposition of her free-love doctrines.

The very thought I should have been asked under any circumstances, and upon any excuse, to preside or be present at such a meeting, was inexpressibly galling to me. Whatever my astonishment might have been at the motive of Mr. Tilton and Mr. Moulton in asking such a thing (as to which I had not at the time as clear a perception as I now have), the request was nevertheless a humiliating one. At about the same time I found that the circle, of which Mrs. Woodhull formed a part, was the centre of loathsome scandals, organized, classified, and perpetuated with a greedy and unclean appetite for everything that was foul and vile.

The moment that any one, whether man or woman, became noted as a reformer or attained any degree of eminence among the advocates of liberal sentiments, it seemed as if those who claimed a monopoly of reform selected such persons as the special victims of charges and filthy slanders. I was by no means the only clergyman who was made the butt of their private gossip, while it seemed as if no woman of any distinction in the land was left out of their pool of scandal. All the history of their past lives, and even the graves of their friends, were raked over to furnish material and pretexts for their loathsome falsehoods. It was inexpressibly disgusting to me, and I would not associate with these people. Yet Mr. Tilton and Mr. Moulton had some strange theory concerning the management of this particular affair which always made it, in their judgment necessary for them to maintain friendly relations with the group of human hyenas. From this circle, and from Mr. Tilton's intimate associations with it, many rumors and suspicions arose among my own congregation, which led them to press me with questions, and to originate investigations, especially into the affairs of Mr. Tilton, from whom alone, as they generally believed, the rumors against me originated. In this I was constantly and vehemently assured by Mr. Moulton that they were mistaken, and yet their zeal in my defense made them impatient of my silence and anxious to deal in a summary manner with Mr. Tilton. Had I allowed them to do this, it was obvious that Mr. Tilton would have been greatly enraged, that all his former unjust suspicions of me would have been confirmed, and that he would have had every motive which was necessary to induce him to break up the peace between us, and to make some such public attack upon me as he has finally made.

I have no knowledge of Mr. Tilton's friendship for Victoria Woodhull, other than that which the public already has—that he manifested his admiration for her publicly, that he wrote her biography, and that he presided at her Steinway Hall lecture, I mention only because he aroused against himself great indignation and odium.

The winter following (1871-72), Mr. Tilton returned from the lecture field in despair. Engagements had been canceled, invitations withdrawn, and he spoke of the prejudice and repugnance with which he was everywhere met as indescribable. I urged him to make a prompt repudiation of these women and their doctrines. I told him that no man could rise against the public confidence with such a load. Mr. Tilton's vanity seldom allows him to regard himself as in the wrong or his actions faulty. He could never be made to believe that his failure to rise again was caused by his partnership with these women, and by his want of sensible work, which work should make the public feel that he had in him power for good. Instead of this he preferred, or professed, to think that I was using my influence against him; that I was allowing him to be traduced without coming generously to the front to defend him, and that my friends were working against him, to which I replied that unless the laws of mind were changed, not Almighty God Himself could lift him into favor if these women must be lifted with him. Nevertheless I sought in every way to restore peace and concord to the family which I was made to feel had been injured by me and was dependent on my influence for recovery.

LETTERS GARBLED.

But one thing was constant and apparent—when Theodore, by lecturing or otherwise, was prosperous, he was very genial and affectionate to me. Whenever he met rebuffs and was in pecuniary trouble, he scowled threateningly upon me as the author of his troubles, and Moulton himself seemed at times to accuse me of indifference to Tilton's misfortunes. It was in the midst of complications like these, though it may be that a part of these events happened shortly afterward, that in a thoroughly worried and depressed mood, discouraged by the apparent hopelessness of extricating Tilton from his difficulties, or of saving his family from the blight which he has since fastened upon it with even more destructive effect upon its members than I then feared, I wrote a letter to Mr. Moulton, of which Mr. Tilton has given extracts even more wickedly garbled than his other quotations; for he has represented two extracts from this letter as constituting points of two separate letters, and has artfully given the impression that they were written in or after June, 1873, whereas this letter was dated February 5, 1872. He further says that this letter was written for the purpose of being shown to him. I had no idea of such a thing being done, as the letter shows plainly on its face, and did not authorize any such use of that letter, which was supposed by me to be written and received in the most sacred confidence. This letter was as follows, as, I am now informed. An inspection of the original would doubtless refresh my memory concerning the circumstances; but this Mr. Moulton denies to me.

BEECHER TO MOULTON.

MONDAY, Feb. 5, 1872.

My DEAR FRIEND: I leave town to-day, and expect to pass through from Philadelphia to New Haven; shall not be here until Friday.

About three weeks ago I met T. in the cars going to B—. He was kind. We talked much. At the end he told me to go on with my work without the least anxiety, insofar as his feelings and actions were the occasion of apprehension.

On returning home from New-Haven (where I am three days in the week delivering a course of lectures to the Theological students). I found a note from *E.* saying that *T.* felt hard toward me, and was going to see or write me before leaving for the West. She kindly added, "do not be cast down. I bear this almost always, but the God in whom we trust will *deliver us all safely.* * * * * * * I know you do and are willing abundantly to help him, and I also know your embarrassments." There were added words of warning, but also of consolation, for I believe E. is beloved of God, and that her prayers for me are sooner heard than mine for myself or for her. But it seems that a change has come over T. since I saw him in the cars. Indeed even since he felt more intensely the force of feeling in society and the humiliations which environ his enterprise, he has growingly felt that I had a power to help which I did not develop, and I believe that you have participated in this feeling—it is natural you should. T. is dearer to you than I *can* be. He is with you. All his trials lie open to your eye daily. But I see you but seldom, and my personal relations, environments, necessities, limitations, dangers, and plerplexities, you cannot see nor imagine. If I had not gone through this *great year of trouble,* I would not have believed that any one could pass thro' my experience and be *alive* and *sane.*

I have been the centre of three distinct circles, each of which required clear-mindedness and peculiarly inventive, or originating power, viz.:
1. The *Great Church.*
2. The *Newspaper.*
3. The *Book.*

The first I could neither get out of nor slight. The sensitiveness of so many of my people would have made any appearance of trouble or any remission of force an occasion of alarm and notice, and have excited where it was important that rumors should die and everything be quieted.

The newspaper I did roll off—doing but little except give general directions, and in so doing, I was continually spurred and exhorted by those in interest. It could not be helped.

The Life of Christ, long delayed, had locked up the capital of the firm and was likely to sink them—finished it *must* be. Was ever book born of such sorrow as was that? The interior history of it will never be written.

During all this time *you,* literally, were all my *stay and comfort.* I should have fallen on the way but for the courage which you inspired and the hope which you breathed.

My vacation was profitable. I came back, hoping that the bitterness of death was passed. But—T's trouble brought back the cloud, with even severer suffering. For, all this Fall and Winter I have felt that you did not feel satisfied with me; and that I seemed both to you and Tilton as contenting myself with a cautious or sluggish policy—willing to save myself, but not willing to risk anything for

Tilton. I have again and again probed my heart to see whether I was truly liable to such feeling, and the response is unequivocal that I am not.

[No man can see the difficulties that environ me, unless he stands where I do. To *say* that I have a church on my hands is simple enough, but to have the hundreds and thousands of men, pressing me, each one with his keen suspicion, or anxiety, or zeal ; to see tendencies which if not stopped would break out into a ruinous defense of me ; to stop them without seeming to do it ; to prevent anyone questioning me ; to meet and allay prejudices against *T.* which had their beginning years before this ; to keep serene, as if I was not alarmed or disturbed ; to be cheerful at home and among friends, when I was suffering the torments of the damned ; to pass sleepless nights often, and yet, to come up fresh and full for Sunday. All this may be talked about, but the real thing cannot be understood from the outside, nor its wearing and grinding on the nervous system.

God knows that I have put more thought, and judgment, and earnest desire into my efforts to prepare a way for T. and E., than ever I did for myself a hundred fold !

As to the outside public, I have never lost an opportunity to soften prejudices, to refute falsehoods, and to excite a kindly feeling among all whom I met. I am known among clergymen, public men, and, generally, the makers of public opinion, and I have used every rational endeavor to restrain the evils which have been visited upon T., and with increasing success.

But the roots of this prejudice are long. The catastrophe which precipitated him from his place only disclosed feelings that had existed long. Neither he nor you can be aware of the feelings of classes in society on other grounds than late rumors. I mention this to explain why *I know* with *absolute* certainty that no mere statement, letter, testimony, or affirmation will reach the root of affairs and rein-tate them. Time and work will. But chronic evil requires *chronic remedies*.

If my destruction would place him all right, that shall not stand in the way. I am willing to step down and out. No one can offer more than that ; that I do offer. Sacrifice me without hesitation if you can clearly see your way to his happiness and safety thereby.

I do not think that anything would be gained by it. I should be destroyed but he would not be saved. Elizabeth and the children would have their future clouded.

In one point of view I could desire the sacrifice on my part. . Nothing can possibly be so bad as the horror of great darkness in which I spend much of my time. I look upon death as sweeter faced than any friend I have in the world. Life would be pleasant if I could see that rebuilt which is shattered ; but to live on the sharp and rugged edge of anxiety, remorse, fear, despair, and yet to put on all the appearances of serenity and happiness, cannot be endured much longer.

I am well-nigh discouraged. If you, too, cease to trust me, to love me, I am alone. I have not another person to whom I could go.

Well, to God I commit all—whatever it may be here, it shall be well there—with sincere gratitude for your heroic friendship, and with sincere affection, even though you love me not,

I am yours (though unknown to you),   H. W. B.

The letter of Mrs. Tilton, which is here partly quoted, is as follows :

TUESDAY.—I leave for the West Monday next. How glad I was to learn you were your own self Sunday morning ! Theodore's mind has been hard toward you of late, and I think he proposes an interview with you by word or note before leaving home. If so, be not cast down. I bear this almost always, but the God in whom we trust *will deliver* us all safely. I know you do and are willing abundantly to help him, and I also know your embarrassments. I anticipate my Western trip, where I may be alone with him exceedingly.

ORIGIN OF THE. TRIPARTITE AGREEMENT. .

I now come in my narrative to give an account of the origin of the somewhat famous tripartite agreement. Shortly after the foregoing letter was written, Mr. Tilton returned to the city thoroughly discouraged with the result of his lecturing tour. *The Golden Age*, which had then been established for about twelve months, had not succeeded, and was understood to be losing money. His pecuniary obligations were pressing, and although his claim against Bowen for the violation of his two contracts had a year previously been put under the exclusive control of Moulton with a view of settlement, it had not as yet been effected. About this time, Mr. Moulton, who was sick, sent for me and showed me a galley-proof of an article, prepared by Mr. Tilton for *The Golden Age* (and which has since been published in the Brooklyn papers), in which he embodied a copy of a letter written by him to Mr. Bowen, dated January 1, 1871, in which he charged Mr. Bowen with making scandalous accusations against my moral character. This was the first time that I had ever seen these charges, and I had never heard of them except by mere rumor, Mr. Bowen never having, at any time, said a word to me on the subject. I was amazed at the proposed publication. I did not then understand the real object of giving circulation to such slanders. My first impression was that Mr. Tilton designed, under cover of an attack upon me in the name of another, to open the way for the publication of his own pretended personal grievances. I protested against the publication in the strongest terms, but was informed that it was not intended as an hostile act to myself, but to Mr. Bowen. I did not any the less insist upon my protest against this publication. On its being shown to Mr. Bowen, he was thoroughly alarmed, and speedily consented to the appointment of arbitrators to bring about an amicable settlement. The result of this proceeding was that Mr. Bowen paid Mr. Tilton over $7,000, and that a written agreement was entered into by Bowen, Tilton, and myself of amnesty, concord, and future peace. It was agreed that the offensive article, the publication of which had produced such an effect upon Mr. Bowen, and secured a happy settlement, should be destroyed without seeing the light. It was an act of treachery peculiarly base that this article was permitted to get into hands which would insure its publication, and that it was published. I was assured that every vestige of it had been destroyed, nor until a comparatively recent period did I understand how Mr. Tilton secured its publication without seeming to be himself responsible for the deed.

Finally, after vainly attempting to obtain money both from myself and my wife as the price of its suppression, the Woodhull women published their version of the Tilton scandal in the November of 1872. The details given by them were so minute, though so distorted, that suspicion was universally directed toward Mr. Tilton as the real author of this which he so justly calls "a wicked and horrible scandal," though it is not a whit more horrible than that which he has now fathered, and not half so wicked, because those abandoned women did not have personal knowledge of the falsity of their story, as Mr. Tilton has of his.

MR. TILTON'S OUTBREAKS.

To rid himself of this incubus, Mr. Tilton drew up a voluminous paper called "A true statement," but which was familiarly called "Tilton's case." I had some knowledge of its composition, having heard much of it read; but some documents were only referred to as on file, and others had not yet been manufactured. Tilton's furor for compiling statements was one of my familiar annoyances. Moulton used to tell me that the only way to manage Theodore was to let him work off his periodical passion on some such document, and then to pounce on the document and suppress it. This particular "true statement" was a special plea or abatement of the prejudices excited by his Woodhull partnership. It was a muddle of garbled statements, manufactured documents, and downright falsehoods. This paper I knew he read to many, and I am told that he read it to not less than fifty persons, in which he did not pretend to charge immorality upon his wife; on the contrary, he explicitly denied it, and asserted her purity, but charged me with improper overtures to her. It was this paper which he read to Dr. Storrs, and poisoned therewith his mind, thus leading to the attempt to prosecute Tilton in Plymouth Church, the interference of neighboring churches, and the calling of the Congregational Council. After the Woodhull story was published, and while Mr. Tilton seemed really desirous for a short time of protecting his wife, I sent through him the following letter to her:

MY DEAR MRS. TILTON: I hoped that you would be shielded from the knowledge of the great wrong that has been done to you, and through you to universal womanhood. I can hardly bear to speak of it or allude to a matter than which nothing can be imagined more painful to a pure and womanly nature. I pray daily for you "that your faith fail not." You yourself know the way and the power of prayer. God has been your refuge in many sorrows before. He will now hide you in his pavilion until the storm be overpast. The rain that beats down the flower to the earth shall pass at length, and the stem bent but not broken will rise again and blossom as before. Every pure woman on earth will feel that this wanton and unprovoked assault is aimed at you, but reaches to universal womanhood. Meantime your dear children will love you with double tenderness, and Theodore, at whom the shafts are hurled, will hide you in his heart of hearts. I am glad that revelation from the pit has given him a sight of the danger that was before hidden by spurious appearances and promises of usefulness. May God keep him in courage in this arduous struggle which he wages against adversity, and bring him out through much trial, like gold seven times fined. I have not spoken of myself. No words could express the sharpness and depth of my sorrow in your behalf, my dear and honored friend. God walks in the fire by the side of those He loves, and in Heaven neither you nor Theodore nor I shall regret the discipline, how hard soever it may seem now. May he restrain and turn those poor creatures who have been given over to do all this sorrowful harm to those who have deserved no such treatment at their hands! I commend you to my mother's God, my dear friend! May His smile bring light in darkness, and His love be a perpetual Summer to you.
Very truly yours,
HENRY WARD BEECHER.

The whole series of events beginning with the outbreak of the Woodhull story repeatedly brought me a terrible accumulation of anxieties and perils. Everything that had threatened before now started up again with new violence. Tilton's behavior was at once inexplicable and uncontrollable. His card "to a complaining friend" did not produce the effect he pretended to expect from it, of convincing the public of his great magnanimity. Then his infamous article and letter to Mr. Bowen made its appearance in *The Eagle*. It had been suggested that the publication of the "tripartite covenant" would have a good effect in counteracting the slanderous stories about Mrs. Tilton and myself, which Theodore professed to regard, but which his foolish card and the publication of that article had done so much to revive and render mischievous. Mr. Moulton urged me to get from the gentleman who who held the "tripartite covenant" a copy of it for us, when suddenly Mr. Wilkeson came out with it on his responsibility. Its publication in this manner I made strenuous but unavailing efforts to prevent. He had originally kept a copy of it. (Everybody in this business seem to have copies of everything except myself.) On the appearance of that paper Theodore went into a rage. It put him, he said, in a "false position" before the public, and he said he would publish another card giving a statement something like what he afterward wrote to Dr. Bacon, that is, as I recollect the matter, declaring that I had committed an offense and that he had been the magnanimous party in the business. It was necessary to decide what to do with him. Moulton strangely urged a card from me exonerating Theodore (as I could honestly do) from the authorship of the particular scandals detailed in his article to Mr. Bowen and alluded to in the covenant.

AN IMPORTANT LETTER EXPLAINED.

I said I would think it over, and perhaps write something. This was Friday or Saturday. The covenant appeared on Friday morning, and the alarm was sounded on me immediately that Theodore would do something dreadful if not restrained. On Sunday I had made up my mind to write to Mr. Moulton the following letter, garbled extracts of which are given in Mr. Tilton's statement:

BEECHER TO MOULTON.

SUNDAY MORNING, June 1, 1873.

MY DEAR FRANK : The whole earth is tranquil and the heaven is serener, as befits one who has about finished this world-life.

I could do nothing on Saturday. My head was confused.

But a good sleep has made it like crystal. I have determined to make no more resistance. Theodore's temperament is such that the future, even if temporarily earned, would be absolutely worthless, filled with abrupt changes, and rendering me liable at any hour or day to be obliged to stultify all the devices by which we saved ourselves.

It is only fair that he should know that the publication of the card which he proposes would leave him far worse off than before. *The agreement* was made after my letter through you was written. He had had it a year. He had condoned his wife's fault. He had enjoined upon me with the utmost earnestness and solemnity not to betray his wife nor leave his children to a blight. I had honestly and earnestly joined in the purpose.

Then this settlement was made and signed by him. It was not my making. He revised his part so that it should wholly suit him and signed it. It stood unquestioned and unblamed for more than a year. *Then it was published.* Nothing but that. That which he did in private, when made public excited him to fury, and he charges me with *making him appear as one graciously pardoned by me!* It was his own deliberate act, with which he was perfectly content till others saw it, and then he charges a grievous wrong home on me !

My mind is clear, I am not in haste. I shall write for public a statement that will bear the light of the judgment day. God will take care of me and mine. When I look on earth, it is deep night. When I look to the Heavens above I see the morning breaking. But, oh that I could put in golden letters my deep sense of your faithful, earnest, undying fidelity—your disinterested friendship ! Your whole life, too, has been one of God's comforters. It is such as she that renews a waning faith in womanhood.

Now, Frank, I would not have you waste any more energy on a hopeless task. With such a man as T. T. there is no possible salvation for any that depend on him. With a strong nature, he does not know how to govern it. With generous impulses, the undercurrent that rules him is self. With ardent affections, he cannot love long that which does not repay but with admiration and praise. With a strong theatric nature, he is constantly imposed upon with the idea that a position—a great stroke—a *coup d'etat*—is the way to success. Besides these, he has a hundred good things about him, but these named traits make him *absolutely unreliable.* Therefore, there is no use in further trying. I have a strong feeling upon me, and it brings great peace with it, that I am spending my *last Sunday* and preaching my last sermon. Dear good God, I thank Thee. I am indeed beginning to see rest and triumph. The pain of life is but a moment—the glory of the everlasting emancipation is wordless, inconceivable, full of breaking glory. Oh, my beloved Frank, I shall know you then, and forever hold fellowship with you, and look back and smile at the past. Your loving, H. W. B.

There are intimations at the begining and end of this letter that I felt the approach of death. With regard to that I merely refer to my previous statement concerning my bodily symptoms, and add, that on this day I felt symptoms upon me. The main point is that I was worried out with the whole business, and would have been glad to escape by death, of which I long had little dread. I could see no end but death to the accumulation of torture, but I resolved to stop short and waste no more time in making matters worse. I felt that Mr. Moulton had better stop too, and let the whole thing come out. I determined then to make a full and true statement, which I now make, and to leave the result with God. Mr. Tilton had repeatedly urged me, as stated in my letter, not to betray his wife, and I felt bound by every sense of honor, in case I should be pressed by inquiries from my church or family as to the foundations of rumors which might reach them, to keep this promise. By this promise I meant only that I would not betray the excessive affection which his wife, as I had been told, had conceived for me, and had confessed to him. It certainly did not refer to adultery. If there had been such a fact in existence its betrayal would have ruined me as well as her, and a pledge not to destroy myself would have been too absurd to be mentioned in this letter. In reply to this note, which was calm and reserved rather than gloomy, Mr. Tilton wrote that same day a letter of three and half sheets of copy paper. He began as follows :

" MY DEAR FRIEND : You know I have never been in sympathy with the mood out of which you have often spoken as you have written this morning. If the truth must be spoken let it be. I know you can stand if the whole case was published to-morrow, and in my opinion it shows a selfish faith in God."

Having proceeded thus far, Mr. Moulton seems to have perceived that the tone of this letter was rather likely to determine me in my determination to publish the whole case than otherwise ; and as this was opposed to the whole line of his policy, he crossed out with one dash of the pencil the whole of this, and commenced anew, writing the following letter.

SUNDAY, June 1, 1873.

MY DEAR FRIEND : Your letter makes this first Sabbath of summer dark and cold like a vault. You have never inspired me with courage or hope, and if I had listened to you alone my hands would have dropped helpless long ago. You don't begin to be in the danger to-day that has faced you many times before. If you now look at it square in the eyes, it will cower and slink away again. You know that I have never been in sympathy with, but that I absolutely abhor, the unmanly mood out of which your letter of this morning came. This mood is a reservoir of mildew. *You* can stand it if the *whole case* were published to-morrow. In my opinion it shows only a selfish faith in God to go whining into heaven, if you could, with a truth that you are not courageous enough, with God's help and faith in

God, to try to live on earth. You know that I love you, and because I do I shall try and try and try as in the past. You are mistaken when you say that "Theodore charges you with making him appear as one graciously pardoned by you." He said the form in which it was published in some of the papers made it so appear, and it was from this that he asked relief. I do not think it impossible to frame a letter which will cover the case. May God bless you I know He will protect you.

FRANK.

(On the back, crossed out.)

MY DEAR FRIEND : You know I have never been in sympathy with the mood out of which you have often spoken as you have written this morning. I know you can stand if the whole case was published to-morrow, and in my opinion it shows a selfish faith in God to

MR. MOULTON CAUGHT.

In the haste of writing Mr. Moulton apparently failed to perceive what he had written. In the first instance, he wrote on one side of a half sheet of paper, and used the clean side of that half sheet for the purpose of the letter which he sent in the shape he had given. But it will be seen that he deliberately, and twice in succession, reaffirmed his main statement that there was nothing in the whole case on which I could not safely stand. He treats my resolution as born of such morbid despair as he had often reproached me for, and urged me strongly to maintain my faith in him. Tilton yielded to his persuasion, and graciously allowed himself to be soothed by the publication of a card exonerating him from the authorship of the base lies to which the tripartite covenant referred. So once more, and this time against my calmer judgment, I patched up a hollow peace with him.

That I have grievously erred in judgment with this perplexed case, no one is more conscious than I am. I chose the wrong path and accepted a disastrous guidance in the beginning, and have indeed traveled on a "rough and ragged edge" in my prolonged efforts to suppress this scandal, which has at last spread so much desolation through the land. But I cannot admit that I erred in desiring to keep these matters out of sight. In this respect I appeal to you and to all Christian men to judge whether almost any personal sacrifice ought not to have been made rather than to suffer the morals of an entire community, and especially of the young, to be corrupted by the filthy details of scandalous falsehoods, daily iterated and amplified, for the gratification of impure curiosity and the demoralization of every child that is old enough to read.

THEODORE TILTON LEVYING BLACK MAIL.

The full truth of this history requires that one more fact should be told, especially as Mr. Tilton has invited it. Money has been obtained from me in the course of these affairs, in considerable sums, but I did not at first look upon the suggestions that I should contribute to Mr. Tilton's pecuniary wants as savoring of blackmail. This did not occur to me until I had paid perhaps $2,000. Afterward I contributed at one time $5,000. After the money had been paid over, in five $1,000 bills, to raise which I mortgaged the house I live in, I felt very much dissatisfied with myself about it. Finally a square demand and a threat was made to me by my confidential friend, that if $5,000 more were not paid, Tilton's charges would be laid before the public. This I saw at once was blackmail in its boldest form, and I never paid a cent of it, but challenged and requested the fullest exposure.

But after the summer of 1873, I became inwardly satisfied that Tilton was, inherently and inevitably, a ruined man. I no longer trusted either his word or his honor. I came to feel that his kindness was but a snare, and his professions of friendship treacherous. He did not mean well by me nor by his own household ; but I suffered all the more on this account. As he had grown up under my influence and in my church, I could never free myself from a certain degree of responsibility for his misdoings, such as visits a father for a wrong-doing son, and, in times of great mental depression, this feeling sometimes amounted almost to a mania.

Among the last desperate efforts to restrain him from overwhelming himself, his family, myself, the Church, and the whole community with the fetid flood of scandal which he had by this time accumulated, were those connected with the charges of Mr. West, and the subsequent proceedings of the Examining Committee of the Church. The prosecution of Mr. Tilton I felt bound to prevent. In any form I would strive to prevent the belching forth of a scandal ; but in that form it was peculiarly distasteful. It presented no square issues upon which my guilt or innocence could be tried ; it was a roundabout issue, on which Mr. Tilton could have escaped, possibly by showing that he believed the stories he told about me, or that he had not "circulated" them, or by the mere failure on the other side to prove that he had done so, or by the decision that he was a monomaniac and not responsible. Any such halfway decision would leave me in the attitude of overthrow, and yet no party to the case. Moreover, I felt that Mr. Tilton thought I was setting my church against him—and I was bound he should not think that ; for if it had not been for me he would have been dropped two years before for non-attendance, and for his distinct notice to me that he was out of the church. I had got the Examining Committee to postpone the usual action, because he was letting his wife still attend the church, and I thought that would gradually influence him for good. Indeed, he had deluded me with hopes that he would give up his bad women associates and reform his life. I felt. that we had no right to claim him as a member, under the circumstances, for the sole purpose of his public trial. Mr. Moulton insisted, that everything must be done to prevent that trial, as the Examining Committee was likely to be equally divided, whether the facts sustained Mr. Tilton's plea, whether he was out of the Church' or not. I was so determined to carry out my pledges to Moulton, for him, and do all in human power to save him, even from himself, that I was ready to resign, if that would stop the scandal. I wrote a letter of resignation, not referring to charges against me, but declaring that I had striven for years to maintain secrecy concerning a scandal affecting a family in the Church, and that, as I had failed, I herewith resigned. This letter was never sent. A little calmer thought showed me how futile it would be to stop the trouble--a mere useless self-sacrifice—but I showed it to Mr. Moulton, and possibly he copied it. I have found the original of it in my house.

If I could at this moment remember any of the other letters which I have written to Mr. Moulton, I would do so. If he has reserved all my effusions of feeling he must have a large collection. I wished him to bring them all before the Committee. I should have been glad to get such hints as they may contain to refresh my recollection of facts and sequences. I have no fear of their full and fair publication, for 'though they would doubtless make a sad exposure of my weakness, grief, and despondency, they do not contain a line confessing such guilt as has been charged upon me, or a word inconsistent with my innocence, nor any other spirit than that of a generous remorse over a great and more and more irreparable evil. But however intense and numerous may be these expressions of grief, they cannot possibly ever state the anxiety which I constantly felt for the future, the perils of which it is now clear I did not exaggerate ; nor the sorrow and remorse which I felt originally on account of the injury which I supposed I had unwittingly done to a beloved family, and afterward for the greater injury which I became satisfied I had done by my unwise, blind, and useless efforts to remedy that injury, only, as it proved, at the expense of my own name, the happiness of my own family, and the peace of my own church.

HIS LAST WORDS.

GENTLEMEN OF THE COMMITTEE: In the note requesting your appointment I asked that you should make full investigation of all sources of information. You are witnesses that I have in no way influenced or interfered with your proceedings or duties. I have wished the investigation to be so searching that nothing could unsettle its results. I have nothing to gain by any policy of suppression or compromise.

For four years I have borne and suffered enough, and I will not go a step further. I will be free. I will not walk under a rod or yoke. If any man would do me a favor, let him tell all he knows now. It is not mine to lay down the law of honor in regard to the use of other persons' confidential communications ; but, in so far as my own writings are concerned, there is not a letter nor document which I am afraid to have exhibited, and I authorize any and call upon any living person to produce and print forthwith whatever writings they have any source whatsoever.

It is time, for the sake of decency and of public morals, that this matter should be brought to an end. It is an open pool of corruption, exhaling deadly vapors.

For six weeks the nation has risen up and sat down upon scandal. Not a great war nor a revolution could more have filled the newspapers than this question of domestic trouble ; magnified a thousandfold, and, like a sore spot in the human body, drawing to itself every morbid humor in the blood. Whoever is buried with it, it is time that this abomination be buried below all touch or power of resurrection.

MR. BEECHER'S CROSS-EXAMINATION.

ON the same day, namely, August 13, the Committee cross-examined Mr. Beecher, as follows :

By Mr. Storrs—Q. You spoke of Mr. Tilton being a reporter for *The Observer*, was it not for *The Times?* A. *The Observer* never had a reporter in the sense which we use that term, but he was a worker —a man of all work—in the editorial and publishing department of *The Observer ;* I know nothing about his connection with *The Times.*

By Mr. Sage—I would like to inquire how Mr. Moulton first entered this case, and how he came to be your confidant ? A. Mr. Moulton was a schoolmate and friend of Mr. Tilton's, and Mr. Tilton, when his various complicated troubles came upon him, in connection with Mr. Bowen, went to Mr. Moulton and made him his adviser and helper. That is the way he came into the case.

CONVERSATION WITH LOCKED DOORS.

Q. Can you tell us how you came to write that letter of despondency, dated Feb. 5, 1872, to Mr. Moulton ? A. I would come back from a whole week's lecturing and would be perfectly fagged out, and the first thing on getting home there would be some confounded development opening on me. In this state of mind, in which I had not longer any resiliency or rebound in me. So I would work the whole week out. And that is the way it happened time and time and time again. On one of these occasions I went to Mr. Moulton's store. Mr. Moulton had always treated me with the greatest personal kindness. He never had refused by day or by night to see me or to listen to me. I never saw him out of mood toward me after the first few months. He treated me as if he loved me. On this occasion I went down to the store to see him, and his face was cold toward me. I proposed to walk with him, and he walked with me in such a way that it seemed to me as though it was irksome to him to have me with him, and as though he wanted to shake me off. Now, anything like that all but kills me. I don't wish to push myself upon anybody; to feel that I have pushed myself upon any human being who does not want me is enough to kill me; and to be treated so by him at that time made it seem to me as though the end of the world had come. For he was the only man on the globe I could talk with on this subject. I was shut up to every human being. I could not go to my wife, I could not go to my children, I could not go to my brothers and sisters I could not go to my church. He was the only one person to whom I could talk; and when I got that rebuff from him, it seemed as though it would kill me, and the letter was the product of that mood into which I was thrown.

By Mr. Sage—When was this interview with the pistol? A. The first interview was at Mr. Moulton's house, Dec. 30, and the next was at my own on the next day.

Q. Did you consider the interview at Mr. Moulton's house a threatening interview? I have heard from some source that the door was locked. A. That is stated in my statement.

Q. What was your impression from that act of locking the door? A. I did not think anything about it, nor care a snap about it. I only remembered it afterward. His family were away visiting and the family was alone for several days; and, when he came in he not only locked the door, but he took the key out and put it in his pocket. I must have noticed it, or it would not have come to my memory. He said something about not being interrupted in any way. The servant girl was in the house, I think.

Q. Then Mr. Tilton locked the door when you went into the room with him? A. Not that I remember.

Q. Did Mr. Tilton at that time make any charge of adultery? A. No, sir.

Q. What was Mr. Moulton's manner at the time when he demanded the retraction of Mrs. Tilton's—threatening? A. I should describe it as being exceedingly one of intense excitement.

Q. Did it impress you with any sense of personal danger? A. No, sir.

Q. Was it the result of that evening's conversation and full and free expression from you that he came to be your confidant, and that he seemed to sympathize with you? A. No, sir; that was the result probably of some months' intercourse.

By Mr. Claflin—Do you suppose that you or the community would have heard anything of these troubles of Mr. Tilton with his family had he been a successful man? A. I am morally certain that the thing would have been deeper buried than the bottom of the sea if Mr. Tilton had gone right on to a prosperous career, and he had had the food which he had been accustomed to; but Mr. Tilton is a man starves for want of flattery, and no power on God's earth can ever make him happy when he is not receiving some intense—

By Mr. Winslow—I understand by your statement that you first met Mr. Moulton at Mr. Page's studio; is that correct? A. The first meeting with Mr. Moulton that ever led me to know him or think of him as distinct from a thousand other men was that; I had undoubtedly met him before, but not in a way that made any impression upon me; I date my knowledge of the man from that time; he was having his portrait painted at the same time, and we met there occasionally; I remember that on one occasion we walked from Page's studio clear down to his door, or to Fulton Ferry, and talked of public matters all the way, and I recollect being impressed with the feeling that he was an acute fellow, and that he had strong literary tastes, as he has.

Q. Had you ever visited his house in a social way prior to his call at your house on this business? A. Never.

Q. Then you had no intimate personal relations with him? A. None.

Q. So that when he came to you he came rather as Mr. Tilton's friend than otherwise? A. Altogether.

MR. BEECHER'S TRUST IN MR. BOWEN.

Q. When did you come to believe that relation was becoming one of mutual friendship? A. I cannot tell you; but it was some time afterward; the transition was made during the consultations which they held as to how Mr. Bowen should be managed, so as to do, as they said, justice to Mr. Tilton; once or twice he said to me, when I told him something, "There, that is the right thing." I recollect that on one occasion I made a confidential statement to him about some matter that they never could have found out otherwise, and he said (I don't recollect the words, I only have a recollection of the impression that was made upon my mind) that I never should regret putting confidence in him; it sprung from some statement that I had made; he gave token of his pleasure at my trust in him us if to encourage, as it were, a full trust, and he said that I never should regret having put confidence in him—which I shall regret to the day of my death.

Q. In the course of your conversation when the so-called apology was written, did he say anything to you to the effect that there was nothing about the case but what an apology might cover? A. He made the impression on my mind not only that Mr. Tilton had been greatly injured, but that Mr. Tilton was saturated with the conviction that I was using my whole power against him. When any disclosure of my real feelings was made to him, he listened with a kind of incredulity, as if I was acting a part. But when I shed tears, and my voice broke, and I walked up and down the room with unfeigned distress, he seemed to be touched, and finally he said, "Now if that is the way you feel, if Mr. Tilton could be made to see it, this whole thing could be settled."

Q. If you used the words, "He would have been a better man in my circumstances than I have been," what did you mean by them? A. I do not know, I'm sure; the conversation was hypothetically in respect to the betrayal of a friend in an hour of emergency; in respect to undermining Mr. Tilton just at the time when Mr. Bowen and all the world were leaving him; in respect to a want of fidelity; and there is one thing that you are to bear in mind—a thing that I have never mentioned to any of you and that had a very strong influence upon me. I never can forget a kindness done to me. When the war broke out, my son went into a Brooklyn regiment, and after being seven months in a camp at Washington, he played a series of pranks on some of the officers and got himself into great trouble, and Col. Adams recommended him to resign, and he came to me. Well, it broke my heart. I had but one boy that was old enough to go that I could offer to my country, and I told Theodore who was in the office with me. He made the case his own. Mr. Tilton has a great deal in his upper nature. If he could be cut into and his lower nature could be separated from the upper, there is a great deal in his upper nature that is capable of great sweetness and beauty. At any rate he took up my case. He suggested himself that the thing to do would be to get him transferred into the regular army. He said that he knew Sam Wilkeson, a correspondent of the *Tribune,* who was at that time in Washington, and had great influence, and that he would go right on that very night and secure this thing. He did, without a moment's delay, start and go to Washington, and he secured, through Sam Wilkeson, from Simon Cameron, then Secretary of War, the appointment of Henry as a Second Lieutenant in the 4th Artillery service. I have felt ever since that in the doing of that thing he did me most royal service. I have felt it exquisitely; and there has not been a time when I have done anything that hurt Tilton that that thing has not come back to me, and when it seemed as though I had in an hour of his need and trouble stepped aside, and even helped to push him down, I felt it very acutely.

Q. Here are three letters written on Feb. 7, 1871—I am not quite sure whether I understood you correctly in saying that you did not see Theodore's letter of that date? A. I have no remembrance of it; I only know that there was an arrangement made among us to bring an influence to bear upon Elizabeth in consequence of her state of mind; I used to say to him, "Moulton, I am a man walking in the open air and full of work, and Theodore is at loose and doing whatever he pleases, and we can come down and talk to you and have counsel; but what human being has Elizabeth Tilton to talk with her in her trouble? She is shut up at home, sick and unbefriended, and it is not generous for us to let her go without and uncared for. I was always saying that there ought to be somebody who should think of her.

Q. In your letter of the same date to Mr. Moulton this occurs: "Would to God, who orders all hearts, and by His kind mediation, Theodore and Elizabeth and I could be made friends again. Theodore will have the hardest task in such a case!" Precisely what did you mean? A. It is all a muddle to me, as I don't recall the precise working of my mind. I have no vivid recollection of the making up of the letter, or of the precise moods under which I wrote, I cannot give the reason of the sentence, or of that sentence; I only know the general drift which we were on.

Q. I call your attention to it because criticism is made in certain quarters that it referred to Mr. Tilton's marital troubles growing out of your offense? A. Well, but see; isn't it a going back to friendship? Isn't it the restoration of the family?

Q. What you ask for is that you three should be made friends again? A. Yes; that we should all co-operate.

Q. And you say that Theodore will have the hardest task? A. There was a family that by circumstances had been brought to the bitterest antagonisms at a time of the most profound adversity, when Mr. Tilton had got to struggle for his livelihood, for his name, for his position, and for his household. Everything put together, he was in a situation in which he had to exert himself in every way for restoration in every manner; and the point was that she should co-operate with him, as well as with his friends. If she had her sorrow to bear at home, he had his too. That is what I think likely may have suggested these words; but I don't say that it is, because I don't remember. Elizabeth, you know, was at times immensely bitter against Theodore, and felt that she had been the aggrieved one, and I had been led to suppose that she had not been anything like so much aggrieved as I now suppose she has been.

Q. In the same letter of February 7, you say, "Of course I can never speak with her again without his permission, and I don't know that even then it would be best ;" why did you say that ? A. Because either at the time of that letter from Mr. Bowen, or in its immediate vicinity, Mr. Tilton, as I have the impression now, sent word by Mr. Bowen (though I cannot be sure of that) forbidding me ever to enter his house again.

Q. When was that ? A. It was in the vicinity of that whole business; but in what way it came, or what the precise date of it was, I cannot tell. I only know that the message was conveyed to me from him ; but by whom, or how, or when, I have forgotten. It was a distinct thing in my memory, and afterwards he, on one or two occasions, took pains to revoke it after he had become reconciled.

Q. In the same letter occurred the words (which Mr. Tilton in his statement makes appear to come from another letter, but which in fact are from the same letter), "When I saw you last I did not expect ever to' see you again or be alive many days." What was in your mind when you wrote them ? A. Just what I have stated in my statement already.

THE WISH FOR DEATH.

Q. Nothing else ? A. No ; I know I frequently said "I wish I was dead," and Theodore Tilton, he came in and said he wished he was dead, and Mr. Moulton was frequently in a state in which he wished he was dead, and Mrs. Moulton said, "I am living among friends, every one of whom wishes he was dead," or something like that ; I do not know but it was smarter than that; but she put it in a way that was very ludicrous ; every one of us used to be echoing that expression ; we were vexed and plagued together, and I used the familiar phrase, "I wish I was dead."

Q. The outside gossip is that you referred in that line to contemplated suicide ?

Mr. Beecher—How do you propose to cure the gossip ?

Mr. Winslow—I cannot say ; but I want to know if anything of that kind was in your mind. A. It was not. My general purpose in the matter of this whole thing was this [and I kept it as the motto of my life] : By patient continuance in well-doing to put to shame those who falsely accuse me. I meant to put down and preach down this truth. Of course, in my dismal moods, I felt as though the earth had come to an end. Now, in interpreting these special letters, everybody is irresistibly tempted to suppose that everything I said was said narrowly in regard to their text, instead of considering the foregoing state of my mind ; whereas my utterances were largely to be interpreted by the past as well as by the present or the future. I cannot interpret them precisely, as I can a note of hand or a check. A man that is poetical, a man that is oftentimes extravagant, a man that is subject to moods such as make me such as I am, cannot narrowly measure his words. And yet, from this writing of over four years in every conceivable condition, in this large correspondence, proceeding from a mind speaking in hyperbolical moods, and in all manner of states, about everybody and everything—out of this mass they have got only these few equivocal things, "devices," did not refer to me, but to him—his whole style of acting.

Q. Theodore said he was born for war, and Moulton was probably born for diplomacy ? A. Yes.

By Mr. Cleveland—Q. Were the plan and method by which, from time to time, these things were managed by your suggestion or by Mr. Moulton ? A. I made suggestions from time to time, generally without any effect, and the essential course of affairs, so far as it has not been forced upon us from outside influences, has been of his (Moulton's) procuring.

Q. He managed this whole matter with Mr. Tilton ? A. Yes ; he represented himself always as having all the reins in his hands—as having in his hands such power that if worst should come to worst he could compel a settlement ; he intimated to me time and again that he had such materials in his hands respecting Theodore that, as he said once, "If Theodore does not do as I say, I'll grind him to powder."

By Mr. Winslow—"By which we saved ourselves "—this letter says—saved from what ?

By Mr. Winslow—The "earning the future," as I understand, was to procure the silence and burial of the scandal ? A. No, it wasn't either. It refused the plans by which Tilton was to get something to do, and do it, and get some praise for it, and be content.

Q. The "devices;" did that refer to all the plans and arrangements and steps that had been taken ? A. It referred to this. If I had been left to manage this matter simply myself, I should have said "Yes" or "No." That would have been the whole of it ; but instead of that the matter went into Moulton's hands, and Moulton is a man that loves intrigue in such a way that, as Lady Montague said of somebody, "He would not carve a cabbage unless he could steal on it from behind, and do it by a device," and the smallest things and the plainest he liked to do in the sharpest way. He was consulting with parties here and there and elsewhere, and a great deal of whispering was taking place, and finally it would turn out that something was not going to be done that he had said he would do, and he did not tell me why, and I had to guess. There was this wide circuit of various influences through which he was moving all the time.

Q. He had condoned "his wife's fault;" what did you mean by this ? A. Condone has a legal meaning and a general meaning, but the general meaning of condone is to pass over, to make peace, to overlook, and I use the word as a literary man would use it, not as a lawyer. If I used it in a legal phrase the word would have been "offense," not "fault."

Q. In using the word fault do you refer to some particular act of Mrs. Tilton? A. I refer to the complaints he made in general in respect to her; you know perfectly well what was the impression conveyed to me from the beginning to the end, and that was that I had stolen into his house, and that I had taken advantage of the simplicity of his wife to steal her affections to myself and away from him.

Q. And do you mean to say you had that in your mind when you used the word fault? A. I suppose I did.

Q. You say in the same letter that he had "enjoined upon you most earnestly and solemnly not to betray his wife;" in what respect? A. Not to betray this whole difficulty into which his household had been cast; consider how it is; I appeal to every sensitive man and cultured nature in the world if any greater evil can befall than to have a woman, a wife and mother, made the subject of even investigation as it respects her moral character; for no greater harm can befall a woman than to be talked about from house to house with discussions as to the grade of offense, and the probable nature of the offense, and the cause of the offense, and everything about it. Next to stabbing a woman dead is to talk about her virtue; and if the public suppose that in order to interpret these letters I must refer to a vulgar physical gross indiguity, then they are living on a plane where I do not live. You must remember that I was aware that in addition to the trouble involving my name, Mr. Tilton had also, in fits of jealousy, accused his wife of criminal intercourse with several gentlemen of whom I was not one, and had asserted in the presence of witnesses that all her children, except the first, were the children of those gentlemen respectively; in his decent moods he was very anxious to have such accusations unknown to the world; the mere rumor of them would cast an ineffaceable blight upon his children; nothing would have induced me to make this explanation, but that Mr. Tilton has deliberately chosen to cast a blight of precisely the same kind upon those very children by his subsequent course; and all that is left to me is the power to speak of this abominable accusation with the scorn which such a horrible falsehood deserves.

HIS DIFFERENT MOODS.

Q. You can refer to some points which have already been considered, for a moment. A. "I have a strange feeling upon me, that I am spending my last Sunday, and preaching my last sermon."

Q. Do you refer to the same condition of health and mind that you have described? A. I refer to the fact simply that that was my state of mind during this great trouble, although if you were to collect all the language I have used at various times, it might produce an impression that I had wallowed in a sea of unparalleled distress. I have had stormy days, and have suffered more from this than probably all other causes of my life put together. Yet, taking the four years together, I have had more religious peace and more profound insight into the wants and sufferings of men since I have become acquainted with trouble and despair. I have had an experience in the higher regions of Christian life that is worth all the sorrow and suffering that I have had to go through to get to it.

Q. Is it or not true that in the course of these matters Mr. Tilton expressed a strong desire that the secrets of his family should not be known? A. Always; at least that was his mood, except when he fell into a strange mania at times. There were times in which it was very evident that he perfectly longed to be obliged to bring out, or to have somebody bring out, a scandalous story on his family, in order that he might have his credit with the world as to be so magnanimous as still to stay at home, and live with his wife.

Q. You say, "My mind is clear. I am not in haste. I shall write for the public a statement that will bear the light of the judgment-day." A. I have done it.

Q. You didn't do it, however, then. Had you any present purpose of doing it then? A. I thought a good many times that I had better sit down before my memory failed me, and make a memorandum of the course of events and the reasons of my conduct. But I was so busy I could not do it, and every year it became less possible.

Q. Here comes a clause in which you express a profound confidence in Moulton's fidelity; does that correctly represent your own feelings? A. It does, although Mr. Moulton was not the man that I should select as an ideal man; I thought that in that one particular, fidelity to friends, he was the most remarkable man I ever met, by the amount of time he was willing to give, by the amount of anxiety he was willing to encounter, by the doing of work which I suppose is more agreeable to him than to me—that is, of seeing different parties, and of ferreting out stories and of running things back to their source, which I utterly abhor in social relations, and consequently trying to keep me in good heart, and presenting to me the best sides of Tilton's character, which he never failed to do. When I brought to Moulton what seemed to be the bad and treacherous things I learned of Tilton, he said, "Don't believe a word of such things; I will make inquiries," and the next time I would see him he would have a plausible explanation of the whole thing, and I felt as though it was no use to attack Tilton; that he shed every arrow that was aimed against him; I have said this not only in reference to the impressions no produced upon me, but until the time of the Council I was in an abiding faith of Mr. Moulton's truth; until the reply of Mr. Tilton to Bacon's letter I never had a suspicion of his good faith, and of the sincerity with which he was dealing with me, and when that letter was published, and Mr. Moulton on my visiting him in reference to it proposed no counter operation—no documents, no help—I was staggered, and when Tilton subsequently published his statement, after he came to this Committee, when that came out I never heard a word from Moulton ; he never sent for me, nor visited me, nor did a thing. I waited for him to say or do something ; for I had said to Moulton within the last year, "As things are coming, you never are going to manage Tilton ; he is going to manage you." I have said to him once or twice, "Moulton, Tilton is longer-headed than you are, and he has out-witted you ; " and I have said to him, "The time is coming in which I see distinctly you have got to choose between Tilton's statement and mine." He said, "There never will be a time, for I shall stand by you to the death." He said that to me in the last conversation I had with him.

Q. In view of all that has happened, what is your present feeling as to the conduct of Moulton—his sincerity ? A. I have no views to express.

Q. In case of an issue between Tilton and yourself, now, in this published issue which exists between you and Tilton ? A. I have no expectation of help from Moulton.

Q. Has Mr. Moulton any secrets of yours in paper, in document, or in knowledge of any act of yours that you would not have see the light in this house ?. A. Not that I am aware of.

Q. Have you any doubt ? A. I have none.

Q. Do you now call upon him to produce all he has and tell all he knows ? A. I do.

By Mr. Cleveland—Have you reason, in the light of recent disclosures, to doubt his fidelity to you during those four years ? A. The impression made by him during the four years of friendship and fidelity was so strong that my present surprise and indignation do not seem to rub it out. I am in that kind of divided consciousness that I was in respect to Elizabeth Tilton—that she was a saint and chief of sinners—and Mr. Moulton's hold on my confidence was so great that all that has come now affects me as a dream.

A RUINOUS DEFENSE.

By Mr. Winslow—In your letter of Feb. 5, 1872, you speak of the possibility of a ruinous defense of you breaking out ; how could there be any ruinous defense of you ? A. A defense of me conducted by ignorant people, full of church zeal and personal, partisan feeling, knowing nothing of the facts, and compelling this whole avalanche of mud to descend upon the community, might have been ruinous ; I think now as I then felt.

Q. It would be at least injurious ? A. Where you would say injurious, I would say ruinous.

Q. You speak of remorse, fear and despair ? A. I suppose I felt them all ; whether I was justified in so feeling is a question ; when I lived in Indianapolis there was an old lawyer there named Calvin Fletcher, a New England man of large brain, who stood at the head of the bar; he was a Methodist, Christian man ; he took a peculiar fancy to me, and he used to come and see me often when I was a young minister, and I would see him a great deal. He would make many admirable suggestions, one of which was that he never admitted anybody was to blame except the party who uttered the complaint. He says, " I hold myself responsible for having everybody do right by me, and if they do not do right it is because I do not do my duty. And now," said he, " in preaching during your life, do you take blame upon yourself, and don't you be scolding your church and blaming everybody. It is your business to see that your folks are right." Well, it sank down into my heart, and became a spring of influence from that day to this. If my prayer-meetings do not go right it is my fault. If the people do not come to church, I am the one to blame for their not coming. If things go wrong in my family I find the reason in myself. I have foreseen quarrels in the church, and, if I had left them alone they would burst and break out ; but acting under the advice thus given, and doing my own duty, I have had no difficulty in my church.

Q. An anonymous letter to the Committee from a Free Lover, says that you have a reservation in your philosophy which would enable you to say I had no wrong conduct or relations with Mrs. Tilton, having in your own mind a belief that what you are charged with doing was right. What are your ideas on this subject ? A. I am not versed in the philosophy and casuistry of Free Love. I stand on the New England doctrine, in which I was brought up, that it is best for a man to have one wife, and that he stay by her, and that he do not meddle with his neighbors' wives. I abhor every manifestation of the Free Love doctrine that I have seen in theory, and I abhor every advocate of the Free Love doctrine that I have known.

Q. Did you ever know anybody who took hold of it seriously who was not ruined by it ? A. No, sir ; provided they were susceptible of ruin. I have had women write to me that if I did not send them $10 they were ruined, and I wrote in reply that they were ruined before.

Q. You speak about having sent Mrs. Tilton a copy of books. Was that an act of courtesy specially to her ? A. No ; I gave them out to friends. When one book would come out I would give a copy to a friend, and so on. I have not been a great distributor of my own books—only in cases where it would be a real pleasure, and from an intimation that it would be so.

MEETING THE WOODHULLS.

Q. Are you clear in your recollection that you never met the Woodhulls more than three times ? A. I am perfectly clear—that is, to speak to them.

Q. State the times and places. A. On one occasion I was walking with Mr. Moulton in the general direction of Tilton's house, when he said that Mrs. Woodhull was going to be there. I at first hesitated, and he said, "Come in and just see her." I said, "Very well." I went in, and after some conversation down in the parlors, I went up stairs into this famous boudoir room, where she sat waiting, and, like a spider to a fly, she rushed to me on my entrance, and reached out both her hands, with the utmost earnestness, and said how rejoiced she was to see me. I talked with her about five minutes, and then went down stairs. My second interview with her was on one occasion when I had been with some twenty or thirty gentlemen to look at the warehouse establishment of Woodruff & Robinson. We were on the steamer that had been chartered for the occasion. And when I came up Moulton said, "Come with me to town." He never told me there was to be any company. When I came there I learned there was to be something in New York, in the evening, and that there were to be there a number of literary ladies, among whom was Mrs. Woodhull. I was placed at the head of the table, near Mrs. Moulton, I think, on the left. Mrs. Woodhull was next to me, or else she was first and I was next. I do not remember which. At that table she scarcely deigned to speak to me. I addressed a few words to her, for politeness' sake, during the dinner, but there was no sort of enthusiasm between us. My third and last interview was at Moulton's house. She had addressed to me a threatening letter, saying that she would open all the scandal if I did not preside at the Steinway Hall, and in reply to that Mr. Moulton advised that instead of answering her letter, I should see her and say without witnesses what I had to say. She brought with her her great subject. It was in type, and my policy was to let her talk, and say little, which I did, and she went on saying, "You know you believe so and so," and I said nothing, and so on from point to point, until I said, at last, "Mrs. Woodhull, I do not understand your views ; I have never read them thoroughly ; as far as I do understand them, I do not believe in them, and though, I am in favor of free discussion, yet, presiding at meetings is a thing I seldom do for anybody, and I shall not do it for you, because I am not in sympathy with your movement."

Q. Has Mrs. Woodhull any letters of yours in her possession ? A. Two, I suppose, unless she has sold them.

Q. Upon what subject ? A. She inclosed a letter to me with one from my sister, Mrs. Isabella Hooker, inviting me to be present at the Suffrage Convention at Washington. To that letter I replied briefly in the negative, but made a few statements in respect to my ideas of woman's voting. The other letter was just before her scandalous publication. She wrote to me a whining letter saying that her reformatory movements had brought upon her such odium that she could not procure lodgings in New York, and that she had been turned out of the Gilsey House, I think, and asking me in a very significant way to interpose my influence or some other relief for her. To that letter I replied very briefly, saying I regretted when anybody suffered persecution for the advocacy of their sincere views, but that I must decline interference.

By Mr. Claflin—These are two letters, the signatures of which she showed to Mr. Bowen and myself. It was reported that by these letters you were to be sunk forty thousand fathoms deep. I told Bowen before I went there that I knew of the existence of the letters, and that was all they contained. Bowen made the journey clear down from Connecticut on purpose to go up there.

By Mr. Winslow—Q. Did you ever meet her at Tilton's ? A. The first time I ever saw her was at Tilton's.

Q. Did you ever meet her there any other time ? A. Not that I recall. If I saw her I am perfectly sure I would know it. I remember her well on account of the transcendent description I had heard of her and because of Mrs. Hooker's feelings towards her. Mrs. Hooker regarded her as Joan of Arc would a vision of the Virgin Mary, and when I went to see her I went with great expectations, saying to myself, "Here is this woman, who is lauded everywhere, and must be a power to rise to the head."

By Mr. Winslow—Q. Can you tell us what became of Mrs. Woodhull's threatening letter ? A. Mr. Moulton opened it.

Q. Now, as to what occurred in your library and in his bedchamber—I refer to the occasions in which he said you touched his wife's ankle, and were found with a flushed face in the bedchamber of his house ? A. I do emphatically deny that either of these scenes ever occurred.

By Mr. White—Q. In one part of your statement you say that in December, 1870, you heard of many immoralities of Mr. Tilton, and that you believed in their existence. In a later part of your statement you say that you had been subsequently deceived into a belief that Mr. Tilton was not in fault in respect to his moral conduct. How do you reconcile these two statements ? A. Because when the matter came to me from Mr. Bowen, and through the visit of Tilton's family, I was under the full persuasion of the truth of these things. One of the very first things to which Mr. Moulton and Mr.

Tilton had addressed themselves was to disabuse my mind of this belief concerning Mr. Tilton's moral conduct. Tilton alluded to the subject of his own purity with circumstantial and historical statements, and Moulton's conduct specially tends to convince me that all the allegations against Mr. Tilton respecting such matters, were false.

Q. Did you admit at any time to Mr. Moulton or Mr. Tilton or to any other person that you had ever had any relations with Mrs. Elizabeth R. Tilton, or ever commit any act to or with her, or said any word to her, which would be unfit for a Christian man to hold, do, or say with the wife of his friend, or for a father to hold, do, or say with his daughter, or a brother with his sister—did you ever admit this in any form or in any words? A. Never.

By Mr. Tracy—Q. Did you ever, in fact, hold any such relations, do any such act, or utter any such word? A. Never.

By Mr. Cleveland—Q. In your statement you have alluded to one payment of $5,000. Have you furnished any other money to those parties? A. I have furnished at least $2,000 besides the $5,000.

Q. To whom did you pay that money? A. To Mr. Moulton.

Q. In various sums? A. In various sums, partly in cash and partly in checks.

Q. Have you any of those checks? A. I have several. I don't remember how many.

Q. Where are they? A. I have some of them here—one of June 23, 1871, drawn on the Mechanics' Bank, to the order of Frank Moultonn, and indorsed in his handwriting; and one of November 10, 1871, payable to the order of Frank Moulton, and indorsed in his handwriting; and one of May 29, 1872, to the order of F. D. Moulton, and also indorsed in his handwriting. Each of these that are marked "for deposit" across the face have been paid.

Q. As nearly as you can recollect, how much money went into the hands of Mr. Moulton? A. I should say I have paid $7,000.

Q. To what use did you suppose that money was to be appropriated? A. I supposed that it was to be appropriated to extricate Mr. Tilton from his difficulties in some way.

Q. You did not stop to inquire how, or why? A. Moulton sometimes sent me a note saying: "I wish you would send me your check," for so much.

Q. Did you usually respond to the demands of Mr. Moulton for money during those months? A. I always did.

Q. Under what circumstances did you come to pay the $5,000 in one sum? A. Because it was represented to me that the whole difficulty could now be settled by that amount of money, which would put the *Golden Age* on a secure footing, that they would be able to go right on, and that with the going on of them, the safety of Tilton would be assured, and that would be the settlement of the whole thing. It was to save Tilton pecuniarily.

Q. Were there any documents shown to you by Moulton? What did he show you before you made the payments? A. It was the result of intimations and general statements, and I finally said to him: "I am willing to pay $5,000." I came to do it in this way: There was a discussion about that paper. Moulton was constantly advancing money, as he said to me, to help Tilton. The paper was needy. One evening I was at his house. We were alone together in the back parlor, and Moulton took out of his pocket a letter from ——. It was read to me, in which the writer mentioned contributions which the writer had made to Theodore. I understood from him that the writer of this letter had given him some thousands of dollars down in cash, and then taking out two time checks or drafts, which, as I recollected, were on bluish paper—although I am not sure of that. There were two checks, each of them amounting to one or two thousand dollars more, and I should think it amounted in all to about six thousand dollars, although my memory about quantities and figures is to be taken with great allowance, but it produced the impression in me that the writer had given him one or two thousand dollars in cash down, and, as the writer explained in the letter, it was not convenient to give the balance in money at that time, but that the writer had drawn time drafts which would be just as useful to him as money, and Moulton slapped the table and said, "That is what I call friendship," and I was stupid, and said, "Yes, it was." Afterward, when I got home, and thinking about it in the morning—"Why," said I, "what a fool! I never dreamed what he meant." Then I went to him and said to him, "I am willing to make a contribution and put the thing beyond a controversy." Well, he said something like this—"That he thought it would be the best investment that ever I made in my life." I then went to the savings bank and put a mortgage of five thousand on my house. I took a check which was given me by the bank's lawyer, and put it into the bank, and on Moulton's suggestion that it would be better than to have a check drawn to his order, I drew the money in five hundred dollar or one thousand dollar bills, I have forgotten which, but I know that they were large, for I carried the roll in my hand, and these I gave into his hands. From time to time he spoke in the most glowing terms, and said that he was feeding it out to Theodore, and he said that at the time of the first instalment he gave Theodore $300 at once, and that he sent with it a promissory note for Theodore to sign, but that Theodore did not sign it, and sent it back to him, saying that he saw no prospect in the end of paying loans, and that he could not honorably, therefore, expect them, and refused to sign any note, and Moulton laughed significantly, and said that Tilton subsequently took the money without giving any note.

Q. Did you receive any note of security whatever, or evidence of debt from Mr. Moulton, or has there been any offer to return the money to you? A. Nothing of the kind; it was never expected to be returned by either party.

Q. Has Moulton said anything to you about money in a comparatively recent period? A. About the time of the publication of the Bacon letter, I think I had been given to understand that he had offered $5,000 in gold to Tilton if he would not publish that letter, and that at the then stage of affairs, Moulton felt profoundly that Tilton could not come out with a disclosure of all this matter without leaving Moulton in an awkward position, and that he offered $5,000 in gold if Tilton would not publish that letter. It led to some little conversation about a supply of money, and he said that I had better give him my whole fortune than have Tilton go on in his course.

Q. That you had better give your whole fortune to Mr. Tilton? A. Yes, rather than have Tilton go into this fight.

Q. Was that before or after the publication of the Bacon letter? A. I can't be certain about that. It was about that time.

Q. Did Mr. Moulton ever question you in regard to this matter, whether you had ever spoken on that to any one, or expressed any anxiety in your mind about it? A. He did, not many weeks ago, among the last interviews I had with him.

Q. Since the publication of that Bacon letter? A. Yes, I think it was on the Sabbath day after the appointment of this Committee. I preached but once on that day, and on the afternoon of that day he saw me, and said to me in a conversation: "You have never mentioned about that five thousand dollars." I said yes, I had to one or two persons. I mentioned to Oliver Johnson for one, because he was saying something to me one day about what some of Tilton's friends were saying, and I incidentally mentioned that to him, which he never repeated, I suppose, to anybody. Moulton said: "I will never admit that, I shall deny it always."

Q. Have you any objections to state what Tilton's friends were saying to Oliver Johnson and others; what did Oliver Johnson say to you? A. On one occasion he reported to me that among the friends of Tilton he had heard reproaches made against me, that I neither was endeavoring to help Theodore in reputation or in any other way, and that the expression was this, that I had been the instrument of his being thrown off the track in life, and that I would not reinstate him. I replied in substance that so far as reputation was concerned I not only longed and tried to do what I could for Tilton, but that his association with the Woodhull was fatal to him, and I could not make any head against it. With regard to the other, I said to him that I had been willing to help him materially, and that recently I paid $5,000 to him.

Q. Did you see and have a conversation with Tilton soon after the payment of the $5,000? A. On the Sunday morning following the payment of $5,000, as I was going to church in the morning, I met Mr. Tilton standing right opposite the house. He put his arm through mine, and was in his most beatific mood. While walking along down to the church he was talking all the way of grace, mercy and peace to me, and at that time, I recollect thinking, that $5,000 is very mollifying.

By Mr. Claflin—Q. Did you at any time receive the note which the Committee have in evidence, as follows:

"*H. W. B.:*
"Grace, mercy, and peace.   T. T.
"SUNDAY MORNING."

A. Yes. He sent it on Sunday morning by his wife, who had it laid on my pulpit stand.

By Mr. Cleveland—If your mortgage was dated about May 1, 1873, the money, of course, was paid to Mr. Moulton after your mortgage was made? A. Yes, sir; I did not keep the money an hour; I went with it directly from the Mechanics' Bank, where I drew it, and put it into Moulton's hands on the same day, and within a few hours.

Q. At his house? A. I do not know.

Q. Did you have trouble with Mr. Tilton during the latter part of that month; before the 1st of June, 1873? A. I do not know the months in which I have not had trouble with him; but he made a special outburst at the end of the month of May, 1873, on account of the publication of the tripartite agreement which led to my letter to Moulton, June 1, 1873.

Q. Here is a letter dated May 1, 1874, in which Tilton refers to some story of Carpenter about your offering money. Did you receive that letter? A. I did, sir. It was a magnificent humbug. I knew that Mr. Tilton knew that he had been tinkling my gold in his pockets for months and years, and he wrote that letter to be published for a sham and mask.

Q. What did you understand by Carpenter's relations to the money matter? A. My first knowledge of Mr. Carpenter was that he was putting his nose into this business which did not concern him. That was also Mr. Moulton's impression. I asked Moulton one day, "What under the sun is Carpenter doing around here, and meddling with this matter?" He summarily damned him and represented him as a good-natured and well-meaning busybody. I suggested why didn't he tell him distinctly that his presence was not wanted. He said: "Well, he serves us some useful purposes. When we hear of things going on in the clubs or any place in New York, we put Carpenter on the track, and he fetches all the rumors, and so we use him to find out what we could not get otherwise." And I did find that he not only did that, but that Mr. Carpenter was one of those good-natured men whose philanthropy exhibited itself in trying to settle quarrels and difficulties by picking up everything he could hear said, by, for, or against a man, and carrying it to the parties where it would do the most harm possible. He was a kind of genial, good-natured fool; and in all this matter he has been a tool more than a helper. He has never once done anything except in the kindest way, and never once done anything in the whole of this matter from begining to end that was not a stupid blunder. I made up my mind from the beginning that as I was silent to everybody in this matter, I would be especially silent to him, Carpenter. I recollect but one interview with him that had any particular significance. He came to see me once when the Council was in session, and our document was published. There was a phrase introduced into it that Tilton thought pointed to him, and Tilton that night was in a bonfire flame, and walked up and down the street with Moulton. I was in at Freeland's and in comes Carpenter, with his dark and mysterious eyes; he sat down on the sofa and in a kind of sepulchral whisper, told me of some matters. Says I, "That is all nonsense; that it meant ——, and ——, and Carpenter was rejoiced to hear it, and then went out. On another occasion he came to me and, in a great glow of benevolence, said there was to be a newspaper established in New York, and that I was to take the editorship of it, and a half a million was to be raised almost by the tap of a drum. I was greatly amused, but said to him, gravely, "Well, Carpenter, if I should ever leave the pulpit, I think it very likely I should go into journalism. It would be more natural to me than anything else." That was the amount of that conversation. One other conversation I have some recollection of, in April, and that was when Mr. Moulton had a plan on foot to buy the *Golden Age* of Tilton, and send him to Europe, and Carpenter came in and talked with me about it.

I recollect very distinctly that conversation; my eyes were beginning to be enlightened. My education was beginning to tell on me a little, and I said to Mr. Carpenter, distinctly, " Mr. Carpenter, that is a matter which I can have nothing to do with, I don't know but that if Tilton wishes to go to Europe with his family and live there for some time, that his friends would be willing to raise that amount of money ; but that is a matter you must talk with somebody else, and not with me."

Q. Did you say that if Tilton printed his documents you would never ascend that pulpit again ? A. I never said that, and I should never talk about the thing with such a weak man as he.

Q. Who introduced the subject of going to Europe when Carpenter came to see you ? A. He did.

Q. In the statement which you have made and the letters you have published you express great agitation, sorrow and suffering, even to anguish. How do you reconcile that with the tone of your public ministrations, and with the declarations of peace and trust which have fallen from you from time to time in the lecture room ? A. I explain it precisely in the same way as I do the words of Paul, who said that he died deaths daily, that he was the offscouring of the earth—having the care of all the churches—and yet with all this burden on his mind he described himself as living in the most transcendent religious peace and joy that stands on record in human literature. " Godly sorrow worketh joy." The first effect of these troubles to me was most anguishful and depressing, and often-times I lay in them even as a ship heaves on the sea in times of calm, when she can make no progress and yet cannot lie still. But after a little came the reaction, and by the power of the Holy Ghost my mind was lifted above these things, and I said to myself, " It is my business as a man and a minister to live the doctrines I have been preaching." I have always been telling people how to manage sorrow, and telling men how to bear up under their troubles. I determined that I would not flinch, whine or sit down, I would stand up, and I did not care how much the Lord piled on me. I believed He would not put more on me than I could bear, if I rose to it, and I took work wherever it was offered, and I went through the work and grew strong under it, and at intervals had experiences of peace and of resignation and of divine comfort which I had never known before in all my life. And, in the retrospect of all this trouble, I can say truly that I am better capable of interpreting the comfort of the Word of God to the sorrowing heart than ever I should have been if I had not passed through this discipline. I have lost children ; I have lost brothers ; I have had many friends who have died, and some who would not die—and yet under all this I have never been more sustained than I have in this.

Q. Notwithstanding your great suffering during the last four years, do you feel that your health or powers for labor and usefulness are impaired ? A. I work because I like to work. I worked because my whole soul was saying to me : " Go forward and preach." I never measured how long the shadow was of my life. I never put a question to myself once whether I was higher or lower than other Christian ministers. To be called the first preacher in America or the world is only throwing a shadow at me, I have but one feeling about this, and that is just as long as I live every particle of strength, and imagination, and feeling, and reason, and body, and soul, I give to my country and to my kind, and that is all the ambition I have. I never had better health than I have to-day. I do not think the machinery is worn out yet, and I do not propose to be idle, and I shall do again what I did in the beginning of my life. I never asked anybody for permission to work, I shall not ask anybody now. The channels I am working in may flow here or there, but I propose to work fifteen years yet.

TILTONIAN LOVE-LETTERS.

WHATEVER may be the final decision in the Beecher-Tilton case, there can be no doubt that the remarkable series of love-letters which are here given will be read with interest wherever the English language is spoken. These effusions are not the work of a schoolboy and schoolgirl, under the influence of "love's young dream." The authors were more than thirty years of age when the first of them was written, and had then been wedded eleven years. These letters were given to the world to disprove the testimony given by Mrs. Tilton before the Investigating Committee. The following are

MRS. TILTON'S LETTERS TO HER HUSBAND, 1866–1870.

PRAYS TO BE WORTHY OF HER HUSBAND.

APRIL 1, 1866.

MY BELOVED : * * * This evening I have heard Mr. Beecher, in company with A—— and L——. There was no recognition between Mr. B. and myself, he leaving directly after service, nor has he called on me. * * * Whenever I hear any inspiring sentiment of poetry or music my first feeling seeks God, and then you. This my soul knoweth right well. "Make my name familiar as heaven by your prayers," you ask. Ah, I do, my sweet, and shall I make confession to you? When I am naughty, I cannot abide long without a purging of myself, lest you receive the blessing which I, by my willfulness, am unworthy of, and I cry out, "Bless *me too*, O Lord !" And thus are you evermore my helper. My darling, may God make me worthy to be your wife in all the largest and broadest meaning of that word, that His name may be magnified through us. Come to me ere another Sabbath night. The benediction of our Saviour rest upon you.

FEEDS ON HER HUSBAND'S LETTERS.

BROOKLYN, April 6, 1866.

You have been patient and uncomplaining, my sweet, in the matter of my writing you. I know not how I should live without your precious daily letter. They do indeed feed me. I have even thought how I feel your heart in expression toward me as much in your absence as when at home. * * * I am sure you will be unlike most public men—*no* thing can by any possibility wean you from the dear ones at home, while your wife is faithful and pure. I have an ambition to help you, but "this kind cometh not by prayer and fasting."

CONCERNING MR. BEECHER.

FRIDAY NIGHT, DEC. 28, 1866.

MY OWN TRUE MATE: * * * I have been thinking of my love for Mr. B. considerably of late, and those thoughts you shall have. I remember Hannah More says, "My heart in this new sympathy for one abounds towards all." Now, I think, I have lived a richer, happier life, since I have *known* him. And have you not loved me more ardently since you saw that another high nature appreciated me? Certain it is, I never in all my life had such rapture of enthusiasm in my love for you—something akin to the birth of another babe—a new fountain opened enriching all—especially towards *you*, the one being supreme of my soul.

> I love thee with the breath,
> Smiles, tears, of all my life! and, if God choose,
> I shall but love thee better after death.

It is not possible for any human creature to supersede *you* in my heart. Above all, you rise grand —highest, best. I praise God that He is reaching me of His great mercy and love shown by His gift of so great a heart as your own to be *mine*. For many years I did not realize the blessing. What remorse it brings to me! Memories bitter—awful!

But to return to Mr. B. He has been the guide of our youth, and, until the three last dreadful years, when our confidence was shaken in him, we trusted him as no other human being. During these early years, the mention of his name, to meet him, or, better still, a visit from him,—my cheek would flush with pleasure—an experience common to all his parishoners of both sexes. It is not strange then, dar-

.ing, that on a more intimate acquaintance, my delight and pleasure should increase. Of course, I realize what attracts you both to me is a supposed purity of soul you find in me. Therefore, it is, that never before have I had such wrestlings with God that He would reveal Himself to me, and ever in my ears I hear, "The pure in heart shall see God."

Oh, fulfill this promise unto me, my Lord and my God.

Darling husband, I have endeavored to express to you, without cant or any such thing, my true feelings as they appear to me.
Yours,
ELIZABETH.

"WITHOUT YOU, I CAN DO NOTHING."

WEDNESDAY NIGHT, Jan. 2, 1867.

MY OWN: * * * What can I say to you, my darling, to cheer you to-night? I think I never chafed so constantly as during this separation. I am so unwilling to be patient until you return, I do nothing well. I used to believe my daily duties would be more promptly and thoroughly performed if I was not interrupted and absorbed by my husband. I have learned better, sweet. Without you I can do nothing. * * * Bye-bye. Your own darling.

HER HUSBAND'S GENTLENESS OF REBUKE.

AT YOUR DESK,
MONDAY, Jan. 7, 1867.

MY PRECIOUS HUSBAND: I find our language very poor in superlatives when I attempt to describe my soul's love. What a delicious way you have of rebuking and teaching me. * * * Pretending always that you think I am the loveliest and best of little wives. My bump of approbativeness is so thoroughly satisfied when you praise me, though it be true or not, I am content. I go singing and light-hearted about my work. Every difficulty is straightened and life is sweet. * * * What a blessing you are to me in every way.
Yours, entirely,
ELIZABETH.

A LEGACY TO HER CHILDREN.

"THE SHIP'S CABIN,"
AT MY DESK, Jan. 9, 1867.

MY BELOVED : It is quite time you should have a little insight into the manner in which I am using your hard-wrought earnings. . . . . My heart is sick at the figures, while I make confession with shame and sorrow that I can do no better in my situation. . . . ' Once more I would bless you for your delicious letters. They will be a legacy to my children when I no longer live to preserve them.

I will try to take care better of my wretched self, *because the best man in all the world loves me.*

TWINSHIP OF HEARTS.

OUR HOME, Jan. 10, '67.

MY DEAR ONE : I feel how poor and meagre my letters are in comparison with yours. . . . Ah, well, my darling, it is my love that makes you happy. So, all those parts of your letter which give me your soul, though extravagant, thrill me all over with ecstasy. . . . How delightful that we are of one mind. You call me your "heart's twin;" I want to be. . . .

UNION OF SOULS.

FRIDAY EVENING, Jan. 11, 1867.

MY SWEET : . . . You write to-day of the love of two interlocked souls remaining wedded for immortality, and ask whether such love is not more tenderly beautiful than those same souls can possibly feel toward God. Darling, I live in profound wonder and hushed solemnity at this great mystery and soul-loving to which I have wakened the past year. Am I your soul's mate? How few find this pearl of great price in this life! I cannot make myself believe I have capacity to meet your soul's want, though you entirely fill mine. When I look at you, I say: "Yes, my soul is satisfied,—our union is perfect." But, when I turn and look at myself as supplying your need, I bow my head and pray God to add the needed grace. . . . As to my love toward God, I understand it only as I know my love to you: it is one and inseparable. I learned of God, the Father, as I know my children. I learned of Jesus as lover of my soul,—as I know *thee*, my lover, husband, friend. Oh, God, lead us ! "Thou art the way, the Truth, and the Life."

"Forgive us if too close we lean
Our human hearts on Thee."

Good-night.

YOURS.

PASTORAL VISITS.

SUNDAY EVENING, January 13, 1867.

MY DEAREST : * * * Pardon me if so many of my letters are filled with accounts of the pastor's visits. It is because I would have you know all that fills my thoughts that I write so frequently of him.

· Yesterday he made us very happy. It was Saturday. He came in about 11:30 a. m., bringing flowers, as usual. After visiting with me twenty minutes he said, "I am hungry to see your children." "Are you, really," said I ; "then come up directly and see them." I had set apart this day for doll-dressing, as I had not time before Christmas. So he followed me up stairs, where, for one full hour, he chatted and played with them delightfully. * * * After this he invited me to accompany him to Mr. Oving-ton's, which call he had intended to make for some time. He said he had planned going there with his wife, and then to say to her, "Come, mother, Mrs. Tilton lives right up here, let's call on her ; she is all alone this winter." "She might or she mightn't."

Whether he will follow up this plan, I know not.

We had a very pleasant call there, cheering the sick man. We stopped a moment at Moulton's, and then I brought him to A.'s. He had never called on her. There, too, his presence was a blessing. Hav-ing been inspired by our dolls, he then wished me to go with him to the toy stores and advise him in selecting a doll for Hattie S.'s little girl. "It must be as large as my Carroll." But we were not suc-cessful, as such grown-up dollies do not live in Brooklyn. By this time it was my dinner hour, and I jumped into a car and rode home. This is the only time I have *been out* with him since your absence. Thus ended an interview of real pleasure to us both. You, too, would have enjoyed it. I wish you would write him. He has real, high, true status of mind. Oh, if you two dear men were once more reunited in perfect sympathy. * * * As I look at you from this distance, how grand, great, pure, and satisfying you are. * * * Good night.   YOUR DEAR WIFE.

SELF-DEPRECIATION.

MONDAY EVENING, Jan. 14, 1867.

MY BELOVED :   .   .   During the early part of your absence it was well enough to suffer you to believe in my perfection, but as you near home, it is wise to dispel the infatuation little by little, and convince you of the humanity and frailty of your loving

WIFE.

Good-night.

THEODORE INDULGENT IN MONEY MATTERS.

SUNDAY EVENING, Jan. 20, 1867.

MY PRECIOUS HUSBAND ; Oh, cruel fate, that parts us when we yearn for each other! My spirit is not at rest, nor has it been during our separation,—although God has ministered constantly and consciously to me as never before in my life ; yet I long to show you my love renewed and consecrated as I humbly believe it hath been. Theodore, you know I love you. My heart is so full at this moment, and frequently, that I *suffer* to express it. . . Above all, my husband, when you are lonely, can I be indifferent ? I think not ever again. Ah, my sweet, take the love I offer you, believe in it to the cheer-ing of your life.

· Is not my supreme wish to be with you ? Never doubt it. Nothing but the threatened sickness of myself and children deterred me. . .

Your letter expressing great patience toward me in reference to my finances came yesterday also. I thank you with all my heart. You are magnanimous and generous beyond all men. I long to be more entirely what you need. It is the wonder of my life that you are satisfied with me. It is your great goodness, and not in my merit.

GOD MADE A GOOD THING.

JAN. 16, 1867.

MY DELIGHT ? Your letter from Washington, Iowa, received to-day, showed me how great your trial must have been in not meeting me at Chicago. . . ·. The fact is, God made a good thing when he made *you*, my sweet,—not to be irreverent. And better than all he gave you to *me*. I thank him ! I love him, . . . What more can I add but the oft-repeated assurance of my love unalterable ?

Do all love as *we* do? And shall we continue thus, when we meet? This is the nightmare which abides with me. Good-night.

YOUR OWN PET,

HER HUSBAND HER LAST THOUGHT AT NIGHT.

JANUARY 23. 1867. }
SECOND-STORY SITTING-ROOM. }

MY DARLING : It is midnight, but I must breathe out my love to you before sleeping ; for all the evening I have been quietly thinking of you while at my work. . . .

YOUR OWN.

YEARNING TO SEE HIS FACE.

In the Sitting-Room,
Second Story Front,
January 24, 1867.

My Husband: . . . I believe I love you as well as you wish me to; I should be wretched if I loved stronger. I suffer enough as it is. . . . I have an irresistible desire to penetrate somewhere that I may once again look upon your dear face and kiss your sweet lips. Shall I ever again? Good-night. Yours, perfectly.

SHE COMPARES HER HUSBAND WITH MR. BEECHER.

Friday Evening, January 25, 1867.

My Own Dear Husband: . . . I think, in reference to Oliver's opinion of Mr. B., as his remarks were made to Mr. Bowen, and *they* are embittered toward one another, that what Mr. B. said of you may appear very different through the coloring Mr. Bowen may give it. Oh, how my soul yearns over you two dear men! You, my beloved, are higher up than he; this I believe. Will you not. join me in prayer that God would keep *him* as he is keeping *us?* Oh, let us pray for him. You are not willing to leave him to the evil influences which surround him. He is in delusion with regard to himself, and pitifully mistaken in his opinion of you. I can never rest satisfied until you both see eye to eye, and love one another as you once did. This will not come to pass as quickly by estrangement. But, with all the earnestness of my being, I commit you both to God's love. He has signally blessed you both, and He will help His own beloved. Why I so mysteriously was brought in as actor in this friendship, I know not yet. No experience of all my life has made my soul ache so keenly as the apparent lack of Christian manliness in this beloved man. Mattie feels as I do. I saw her to-day. She said she received two letters from you to-day. I do love him very dearly, and I do love you *supremely,* *utterly*—believe it. Perhaps, if I, by God's grace. keep myself white, I may bless you both. I am striving. God bless this trinity! I can nor will no denial take. . . . Hereafter, I guard my temper.

You shall have a true, pure wife by and by.

I am ashamed that I am so often unattractive to the Great Lover of my soul. I am striving to make myself beautiful that He may admire me. You know full well how far short I come, but this is my aim. If He can only say my life is blameless, you and I will then be satisfied. Cheer up, my darling; the work is mighty to which you are called, and you are doing it nobly. I love you as Mrs. Browning loved. Don't you know it? Pray for me always. *I* pray for *you*—tho' I have such assurances of God's love and care for you that you seem high up and safe.

If I could sit in your lap and look into your dear eyes now—I'm afraid it would be more than I could bear. At any rate, I should have a good cry—*that,* I am now going to have without you. It always "baptizes me," to use your word. . . . Angels guard us *all*. Good night. .

Your Own Wife.

CALMS MR. BEECHER.

Monday, Jan. 28, (probably 1867).

My Beloved: . . . Mr. Haskell came over Sunday afternoon. We went to hear Mr. Beecher, who preached an uncommonly fine sermon on the Divinity of man from the text, "Ye are Gods." . . . Mr. B. called Saturday. He came tired and gloomy, but he said I had the most calming and peaceful influence over him, more so than any one he ever knew. I believe he loves you. We talked of you. He brought me two pretty flowers in pots, and said as he went out: "What a pretty house this is—I wish I lived here." . . .

Your Darling.

CANNOT BEAR TO BE PARTED FROM THEODORE.

Second Story Front,
Tuesday, Jan. 29, 1867.

My Very Dear Husband: . . . Greater love hath no woman than this, to leave her children and travel on the rail-cars in the winter with her husband. Perhaps I am selfish, yet to be in your company and rest from the cares of my daily life would be delicious. Surely I am selfish to go to you.

. . . My beloved, if we should meet in this world again, do write me that you have forgiven my cruelties! I will never forget them, and, with God's help, will try to never repeat them. It makes me very happy to have you say you need me, while I wonder that I have any power to comfort; still, no music is sweeter than those dear words. . . . Good night. Your dear little

Wife.

WAITS FOR HIS HOME-COMING.

BROOKLYN, SECOND STORY FRONT, }
Wednesday, Jan. 30, 1867. }

MY DEAR HUSBAND: To borrow your wour words, "I am at peace to-night," have settled down to wait patiently for your home-coming. . . . Do you love me always? Are you not getting used to being wifeless? If you reply by asking me the same question, I say the separation is more and more dreadful to me. . . . Good night. May God bless us both.

YOUR OWN.

BE ACTIVE IN PLYMOUTH CHURCH.

SUNDAY EVENING, February 3, 1867.

MY DEARLY BELOVED : . . . If love be the fulfilling of the law, then are not the conditions for his highest life established ?

I realize with the Vicar of Wakefield how great a wealth we have in our children. They are already high up—beyond us—as Christ looks upon pure living. He has revealed Himself to my babes. Blessed be His name.

The church to-night was filled with medical students, Mr. B. preaching before their Christian Union. He certainly is greatly roused this winter, and works most earnestly. Will you not on your return throw in your inspiration and join me in fulfilling our vows as members of this Christian church ? Your beautiful spirit would help many there as it does everywhere. And, to me, there is no spot so sacred in all this earth as Plymouth Church. Full of delicious memories, if we now, with all its members, bring into it our various rich and growing experiences, its later days would gloriously fulfill the enthusiasms of its beginning. . . . Good night.

YOUR OWN

HER HUSBAND IS HER INSPIRATION.

AT YOUR DESK. }
Tuesday Afternoon, February 5, 1867. }

MY SWEET : . . . The inspiration of my daily life now is the thought of looking upon your dear face again. By-bye. . . .

YOUR DEVOTED WIFE.

GIVE UP THE "INDEPENDENT."

BROOKLYN, Feb. 11, 1867, }
AT YOUR DESK. }

MY DARLING : Here, in your sunny, beautiful library, I sit down at the unusual hour of noon to reply to the letter just received inclosing your woe-begone photograph. Did you have revenge in your heart when you sat for that picture, and did you want to frighten me and make my dreams hideous? It is a false representation of my beloved, nor can I take the responsibility of that haggard old face. . . . Oh, how can I convince you how entirely I love you? God bless you for the confession of your perfect love for me. To be worthy is the aim and endeavor of every moment of my life. Believe this. . . . I am more and more dissatisfied to have for your life's work an editor's. The *Independent's* power is alone, it seems to me, in your editorial and the advertisements. It makes me sorry that what you write is read only once, and nothing saved. You feel it to be your pulpit. The circulation is large, but it is gained by money and premiums, and I cannot bear to see your beautiful genius in the best part of your life idle. Can you not work for your country by lecturing and an occasional editorial somewhere, and rid yourself of the responsibility of the details of a great paper? Then this spring and summer you might devote to reading, writing stories, poetry,—in short, a literary life.

I believe you could make money enough lecturing, and I would manage my affairs to join you most of the time, if such might be the plan of the coming years. Did you think to be like Horace Greeley? Your gifts are too diversified.

I have never had much pride in you as an editor, but I believe as a poet and essayist I might fall to worshiping. I will trouble you no further, but it would gratify me if you would give a passing thought to these suggestions. . . . By-bye,

YOUR OWN DARLING.

HEART-HUNGRY TO SEE HER HUSBAND'S FACE.

THE LIBRARY, 3 P. M., }
TUESDAY, Feb. 12 (probably 1867). }

MY PRECIOUS HUSBAND: My heart at this moment swells and feels out so hungry for you that it makes my head ache. I hope I shall be calm when I first see you, and not have one of my enthusiasms. I'm so safe, and strong, and glad in your love that I am conscious the past year of an entire change toward every one,—an independence like maidens feel when they decide upon one of their choice, which often carries a saucy indifference with it; but my state in this is unlike,—for "my heart, in its new sympathy for one, abounds toward all." . . . Now, in the light of your home-coming, I am waking to a new life. . . . Forgive everything in this wretched scrawl. 'Tis only love the sheet contains,—and that of your

DARLING WIFE.

THROW OFF THE INDEPENDENT.

WEDNESDAY, Feb. 13, 1867.

"What shall I give to my beloved" to-day? He has my heart—my entire life. Is there aught else a woman can give? But it hath little power to cheer or bless, parted by time and space. * * * I shall go to-night to hear Mr. Beecher open the Fraternity course. I am more and more inclined to have you break loose from the *Independent* and lead a more perfect literary life, or else start a new paper which shall be more worthy of you. * * *

"When I sue
God for myself, He hears that name of thine,
And sees within my eyes the tears of two."

My lips hunger to kiss you. Adieu,

YOUR OWN.

MEETS HER PASTOR ON THE STREET.

TUESDAY, Feb. 19, 1867.

MY OWN: * * * I am looking forward to your return most eagerly, because from *you* I draw *my* inspiration. I have been very, very hungry for that part of my life which you hold. * * * I met the pastor on the street yesterday. He is working hard and continuously on his book, of which he has promised Bonner to give the half the 1st of March. * * * Adieu for a little. I love you.

ELIZABETH.

COUPLES HER HUSBAND WITH HER SAVIOUR.

TUESDAY MORNING, Jan. 28, 1868.

MY BELOVED: Don't you know the peculiar phase of Christ's character as a lover is so precious to me because of my consecration and devotion to *you?* I learn to love you from my love to *Him;* I have learned to love *Him* from loving you !

I couple you with Him, nor do I feel it one whit irreverent as a *man bowed down with grief for my sins.* And as every day I adorn myself consciously as a bride to meet her bridegroom, so, in like manner, I lift imploring hands that my *soul's love* may be prepared.

I, with the little girls, after you left us with overflowing eyes and hearts, consecrated ourselves to our work and to *you.*

Do not fear but that God heard, well-pleased, the aspirations of those little children. I will rouse all my energies to make them happy, that they may not suffer with loneliness for you,—while I conantl y inspire them with reverence and love for you. My waking thoughts last night were of you. My rising thoughts this morning were of you. I bless you ; I honor you ; I love you. God sustain us and help us both to keep our vows. Yours entirely,

ELIZABETH, WIFE.

The children each send their pure love.

"YET WILL WE BE STRONG."

FRIDAY, Jan. 31, 1868. }
ONE O'CLOCK, P. M.}

MY DEAR HUSBAND : I have just returned from Mattie's, and I saw your bust, loved it, and could not bear to leave that precious head behind me. * * *

Darling, we must both cultivate our self-respect by *being* what we *seem.* Then will be fulfilled my ideal marriage—to you and you only a wife—but contact of the body with no other ; while, then, a pure friendship with *many* may be enjoyed ennobling us. Let us have not even a shadow of doubt of each other. Tho' all the world are weak, yet will *we* be strong.

God accept and bless us both.

Now are we one.

By-bye. Faithfully yours.

HOW SHE FELT TOWARD BEECHER.

SATURDAY EVENING, Feb. 1, 1868.

MY BELOVED : * * * I *know* that now, mother, children, or friend have no longer possession of my heart. The supreme place is yours for ever. Are you really glad to hear this, my sweet ? When you speak your love for me, it is delicious harmony to my soul. * * * About 11 o'clock to-day Mr.

B. called. Now, beloved, let not even the shadow of a *shadow* fall on your dear heart because of this—now, henceforth, or forever. He cannot by *any possibility* be much to me since I have known *you*. I implore you to believe it, and look at me as in the Day of Judgment I shall be revealed to you. Do not think it audacious in me to say I am to him a good deal—a rest, and (can you understand it?) I appear even cheerful and helpful to him. * * *

After seeing the children, I asked him if he would go with me to Mattie's and see the bust. Without any hesitation he said he would. I immediately got ready, and I took my first walk, to the Court street cars without much difficulty, so that I feel free again, and will walk out every day. * * *

Seeing your dear head, darling, which on second seeing is more than ever to me, Mr. B. expressed great satisfaction with it, feeling that it was far better than he expected to find it, and he believed as correct a likeness as you could have. He is very desirous for Mac to try him. Nothing noteworthy occurred, save that he left me at the door with the remark that "he had had a very pleasant morning." You once told me that you did not believe that I gave you a correct account of his visits, and you always felt depressed much. Sweet, do you still feel this? I strive in my poor word-painting to give you the *spirit* and impression which I give him, and he to me. It would be my supreme wish and delight to have you always with me. This trinity of friendship I pray for always. . . .

YOUR OWN.

"THE BEAUTIFUL IMAGE I HAVE MARRED."

SUNDAY, February 3, 1868.
Nine o'clock a. m.

What may I bring to my beloved this bright morning? A large throbbing heart full of love, single in its aim and purpose to bless and cheer him. Is it acceptable, sweet one? As my body gains daily in strength, my enthusiasm bubbles up perpetually, so that I even felt I saw you reflected in my eyes this morning when my thoughts of you so literally filled me as to gush out of my face. Most truly do I love, and I am resolved never more to repress the expression of it. I have lived under the fatal mistake that I would make you selfish; but, oh, what it has cost me to learn that a large generous love cannot, in its very nature, minister to our best and holiest state.

The picture of your dear face, most constantly with me, is one glowing with love, but *always* bearing the look of one that has suffered. Can I, who am the cause thereof, ever again be indifferent? Nay, the little life which remaineth is consecrated to restore, if possible, the beautiful image I have marred. There is no sacrifice too great that I would not enthusiastically make to this end.

SUNSHINE.

MONDAY, February 4, 1868.

MY DARLING: * * * You say that the four miles walk at Newcastle "was a whole gospel to my soul." I read that over and over, and thanked God with all my soul for giving you that experience.

I see you now walking in the sunshine, heartfull, joyful, praising God. You did not need me then. But I follow on, and would fain catch the hem of your garment as you pass along, that I, too, may have a blessing. I yearn and pray unweariedly to grow worthy of your love.

By-bye. Yours undividedly,

WIFE ELIZABETH.

"STARVING FOR YOU."

WEDNESDAY EVENING, February 5,
IN THE PARLOR.

MY BELOVED: I am starving for you to-night; from some detention in the mails, probably, I have had no letter since Newcastle: that is three days without food. Could I see you now, how my pent-up heart would burst and overflow in your bosom. * * * Good night.

YOURS.

HUMAN LOVE NOT SATISFYING.

WEDNESDAY, FEBRUARY 5 (PROBABLY 1868),
NINE O'CLOCK a.m., AT YOUR DESK.

MY DARLING: My brain has run wild since four o'clock—sleep forsook me. The love of man or to man is not restful, while the love given to God is peaceful beyond expression. Oh! that we might know this blessed experience as a state. * * * By-bye.

YOUR DEAR WIFE.

HER HUSBAND ENJOYS HER LETTERS.

THURSDAY EVENING, February 6, 1868.

MY DEARLY-LOVED HUSBAND: * * * You will hardly be able to understand the relief to my mind that you feel it to be "one of the pleasantest incidents of the day," my letters which await you

I say to myself, If he did not love me they would never be a pleasure, as they are wretched, hurried effusions, breathing only of love. The ardent love from one unattractive, how hard to bear it is. Therefore, I take these words as a signal proof of your love, which wearies not with imperfections, but "suffereth long and is kind."

"Good-night, my sweet."

HOW THE HUSBAND WAS LOVED IN HIS HOME.

FRIDAY EVENING, February 7, 1869.

MY BELOVED : * * * Oh, you are truly and nobly loved in your home. * * *
Good-night. YOUR OWN.

HOW HER HUSBAND LOVED HER.

SATURDAY EVENING, FEB. 8, 1868.

MY PRECIOUS HUSBAND: The closing lines of yours from Delaware City, received to-day, are these words: "I trust you so utterly, I build upon you so entirely, I am satisfied with you so completely, I love you so devotedly, that my whole mind and soul and strength now go out toward you with unutterable yearnings." Theodore, do you *know* what you have written? How a heart so hungry for your love as mine will accept it? That it might be so, I earnestly wish; that it is so, I cannot believe. I linger and pore over every word with joy and trembling. My life will not be a failure when this can be truly said. * * * Good night.

ELIZABETH.

ON HER KNEES IN HER HUSBAND'S STUDY.

SUNDAY, Feb. 9, '68. }
AFTER DINNER. }

MY DEAR HUSBAND: I have been up in the study, where it is cold, clean, and desolate, with my shawl wrapped around me—kneeling at the green lounge where, face to face with God, I sought His blessing for us both. Oh, what strength and power there is in prayer. I feel as though I had my armor on and ready to meet any adversary. Having known this rest and power so blessedly in our experience, why do we toil so frequently with our burdens, when we may lay them down at any moment, before One who is mighty and willing to bear them? * * * Perhaps I do not know myself, yet, I never, in all my life, have carried your memory so perpetually, and with a tenderness equaled only to that I bear towards my babes. * * * Our home, especially on Sunday, suggests your dear love to my mind continually. I caught an inspiration from the Dome* to-day, and wherever I go, my heart pours out its thanksgiving. Have you not a reward for all your hard labor ?

YOUR OWN.

"TENDENCIES THAT WELL-NIGH WRECKED ME."

TUESDAY MORNING, Feb. 11, 1868.

Oh, could I see you now, instead of this undemonstrative way of bidding you "Good morning,— my sweet,"—except for the hope that the discipline of this separation is to work out for me knowledge, patience, and subtler secrets in love,—I would chafe against the fate which parts me from you this winter. But I am so eager to leave behind me *forever*, and to have rooted out from me utterly, the tendencies which in the past hath well-nigh wrecked me, that I live my daily life as they who perform penance. I have, indeed, been thoroughly aroused from the lethargy of indifference which had possessed me so thoroughly. Now I cry out for wisdom, guidance, and a new heart. As you regard your own happiness put your strong arm about me—support and help me. Perhaps you do not think me sincere. Do trust me! * * * Where I write my name, I imprint *a wife's kiss.*

ELIZABETH.

HER THOUGHTS GO WITH HER HUSBAND.

WEDNESDAY, 7 A. M., Feb. 12, 1868.

MY HUSBAND: The moon is still shining clear and bright over my shoulder, as I sit by your desk writing. I have a sense of being near you,—nor could I help thinking as I looked into its broad, bright face, that there was intelligence in it. Your eye could look upon it, and perhaps was gazing through

---

* This allusion is to the glass dome over the stairway, on which are painted the words, "Mine eyes are unto Thee, O God."

the car-window with like thoughts, as you left Quincy for your next appointment. Surely, then, I say to myself, if we both, with natural eye, may look at the same object, are we not side by side? And I almost felt your arm around me. I have not had such a sense of your personal presence since you went away. * * * Farewell.

ELIZABETH, WIFE.

BEECHER'S VISITS ELICIT COMMENT.

FRIDAY EVENING, February 14, 1868.

MY —— : Supply, to gratify your own heart most perfectly, some endearing epithet. I sent you my valentine this morning, and because I have laid out work for the morrow, with the little girls, I come again to you to-night that you may not miss my Saturday letter.

Blessings on you! Blessings on you, beloved! Yours from Crawfordsville (I shall evermore remember that place with gladness) came to-day. To hear that you are happy, cheerful, and love me, is more than even my faith could hope. I wept over it, I laughed over it, I prayed over it, and in the midst of my exultation, Mattie called in ; and, though I was under vows not to read your letters, I did the next best thing, which was to get the bottle of wine you sent me the night you left, and drank your bodily and spiritual health. * * *

Mattie is hungry to hear from you. I think she feels a little care that Mr. B. visits here. See how great a power he and your dear self have over the heart. She said, "Lib., I heard through Mrs. Morrill that Mr. B. called on you Wednesday. I believe he likes you ever so much." Now, my darling, I have often urged him to visit Mattie, believing he would find her more comforting and restful than I can be. *She* would be refreshed and cheered—while, as for me, I who am rich in the fullness of your delicious love, have no need. Save for his sake I am gratified if I may minister, and thank God the while.

Oh, dear Theodore, husband, how much I rejoice in your love—am kept in perfect humiliation that he who knows me so well should love so grandly. This is the theme of all my thoughts. No other sentiment or creature hath power to move me.

The chords of my heart are set to the harmony of love *for you.* Now, how I may be able to express this to you when you return, I know not. That the flame will always burn, I know—but that, by reason of infirmities, it shall glow upon the cheek and through the eye, I know not. In God only is my trust. He knows my heart's desire. I implore you to live "by faith and not by sight," with regard to your dear little wife. Now to Him who is able to keep both soul and body, I commit you this night. Farewell. Yours devotedly,

ELIZABETH.

HER HUSBAND'S SPIRIT.

MONDAY NIGHT, Feb. 17, 1868.

MY OWN: * * * Yes, darling, I have fallen (why not say risen ?) desperately in love with my husband. I have *fallen* quite long enough. I cannot tell why such lines as these in your letters depress me; "I am a cheery, good-hearted, hopeful, and bright man." In my soul I rejoice that you are, but I cannot help thinking that it is because I am not with you ! * * * You invite me to "come and abide with you *forever.*" Ah, how willing and proud am I to accept—if I may bless, but I shrink in terror from the *forever,* if I *curse!* * * * Good night. Yours faithfully,

ELIZABETH.

TRUE MARRIAGE ABOUT TO PERISH.

TUESDAY AFTERNOON, Feb. 18, 1868.

MY DARLING HUSBAND: * * * I have felt so heart-sick that there are so few great men or women. The ideas of a faithful, true marriage will be lost out of the world—certainly out of the literary and refined world—unless *we* revive it. * * * I shall have much to tell you of our dear friend, Mr. B. He has opened his heart as you would love and admire him. To believe in one human being strengthens one's faith in God. Yours always,

ELIZABETH, WIFE.

CHILDREN AND MR. BEECHER.

MY DEAR HUSBAND: * * * Yesterday afternoon I had gone out with Bella to do some errands, when Mr. Beecher called with Hattie Benedict Beecher. He held Flora on his lap and chatted with Alice, to her great delight, and left two cakes of soap that would keep their hands from chapping.

I have often thought that the privilege Mrs. H——'s children had, of the intimacy with Mr. B., had seemed more harmful than good—so it must not be with ours. We both teach them to reverence the good man, and I believe the foundations of our friendship are so high and pure that I mean to *appropriate* our privileges to the best *growth of all.* And you know I have a very high ideal of friendship. By-bye. Yours forever,

WIFE ELIZABETH.

HEART-SICK.

THURSDAY EVENING, February 20, 1868.

MY BELOVED : I am so lonesome and heart-sick for your companionship to-night that I hesitate to write lest my mood might depress you. Good-night. Good angels guard thy sleep,

"HER HUSBAND—HE PRAISETH HER."

FRIDAY AFTERNOON, February 21, 1868.

MY CHOSEN OF MEN : * * * Oh, my sweet, you greatly overrate my attainments to your friends, and create in their minds an ideal which you know by sad experience can never be realized. * * * Think of me tenderly, but tell not of excellencies which have only begun to exist, for I do sincerely feel that I never knew you, and certainly not myself, as the last year has revealed. * * * Farewell.

YOUR DEAR WIFE.

BENEDICTION.

HOME, SITTING-ROOM, February 22, 1868.

MY BELOVED : * * * Nothing more to-night, save my abiding and growing love, with a true wife's benediction.

ELIZABETH.

MR. BEECHER'S "DREAMER."

TUESDAY NIGHT, February 23 (probably 1868).

MY DEAR HUSBAND : * * * I am, as usual, full of thoughts, as to how it will be when again we are united. Mr. B. calls me a dreamer, I hope they may prove realities. * * * Good-night.

YOUR DARLING.

HER HUSBAND AS A FRIEND AND INSPIRER.

MONDAY MORNING, February 24, 1868.

MY DARLING OF DARLINGS : * * * Oh, my beloved, I feel unutterable love and sympathy for you in your anguish and "heart-break"—as you say. It is too true you have given largely, grandly, and beautifully of your best love to friends—aye, even to your wife—while in return you have received most often indifference, and at best, love not deserving the name in comparison with thine own.

Do you wonder that I couple your love, your presence, and relation to me, with the Saviour ? I lift you up sacredly and keep you in that exalted and holy place, where I reverence, respect, and love with the fervency of my whole being. Whatever capacity I have, I offer it to you. The closing lines of your letter are these words : "I shall hardly venture again upon a great friendship. Your love shall be *enough* for the remaining days."

That word "enough," seems to me to be a stoicism in which you have resolved to live your life ; but I pray God He will supply you with friendships pure, and wifely love, which your great heart demands, withholding not Himself as the Chief Love, which consumeth not though it burn, and whose effects are perfect rest and peace.

Again, in one of your letters you close with "Faithfully yours :" that word "faithful" means a great deal ; yes, my darling, I believe it, trust it, and give you the same security with regard to myself, *I am faithful to you, have been always, and shall ever be, world without end.*

Call not this assurance impious. There are some things we *know*—blessed be God !

I sorrow more than you can for your lost friendship,—as my soul stings with remorse that I was the cause,—and yet, for all this, you love me. Henceforth let no one point the finger at your Christianity. The love which is in Christ Jesus abounds in your soul. * * *

MR. BEECHER ROCKS THE CRADLE.

WEDNESDAY, February 26, 1868

MY DEAR HUSBAND : * * * Mr. B. put our baby to sleep, laid him down, and covered him up, the last time he was here ; said whenever we could not quiet him to send for him and he would come. His call amused the children very much. * * * Oh ! how proud I am of you ! I'm sure we will be happier in the future. Had we began our lives where we start !

Farewell.

YOUR OWN.

PRAYERS.

HOME PARLOR, Thursday, February 27, 1868.

MY OWN DEAR HUSBAND : * * * Good-night my darling. I get nearer to you in prayer than any other way, from the assurance that He who sees me at the same time, holds you. "Though sundered far, by faith we meet." What should I do had God taken you to Himself, and I could not even write to you ? I pray in his infinite mercy He call me *first*.

Yours, E.

STRIVINGS TOWARD HAPPINESS.

HOME PARLOR, Feb. 28, 1868.

MY DEAREST : I have just returned from prayer-meeting. The room was crowded and the exercises of unusual interest. I am inclined to appreciate these privileges, for they are passing away. Mr. Beecher cannot many years longer sustain his remarkable freshness of mind, and there can never be another who can fill his place to us. He had just returned from Pennsylvania where he has been all the week, lecturing twice. * * * I have not heard but once from you this week, and that was Monday. There is much lost in the days which bring me no word of love. Yet I know in whom I trust. Your labors, and even your very absence, proves your love. How much I want to do to make you happy when you come home ! I can do no great things ; but all the many little things which love will suggest, these I will do for my beloved.

A EULOGY ON HER HUSBAND.

HOME, SATURDAY EVENING, Feb. 29, 1868.

Ah ! did any man ever love so grandly as my beloved? Other friendships, public affairs, all "fall to naught" when I come to you ! Though you are in Decorah to-night, yet I have felt your love, and and am very grateful for it. I had not received a line since Monday, and was so hungry and lonesome that I took out all your letters and indulged myself as at a feast—but without satiety, and now I long to pour out into your heart 'of my abundance. I am conscious of three jets to the fountain of my soul, to the Great Lover and yourself, to whom as *one* I am eternally wedded ; my children ; and the dear friends who trust and love me. * * * May God's peace abound with you.

YOUR OWN DEAR WIFE.

HE DWELLS IN HER THOUGHTS.

SUNDAY EVENING, March 1, 1868.

MY BELOVED : You have been in my thoughts all day. The morning dawned mild and clear : it was communion Sabbath. * * * Mr. B. was in his best mood, carrying us with him as he talked of the Christian's victory over death, and the revelations which will then be made known to us, when the body, with all its burdens and hindrances, shall fall off. * * *

Tell me continually of your love. I need the encouragement. It won't harm me ; I will be proud and happy. Good night.

YOUR OWN FOREVER.

RECIPROCITY.

WEDNESDAY MORNING, March 4, 1868.

Yes, darling, I know you want me ! if ever I may serve you, it is when overtaxed and weary. I am most grateful that *then* you turn to me. Oh how almost *perfectly* could I minister this winter. My heart glows so perpetually, I am conscious of great inward awakening toward you. If I live I shall teach my children to begin their loves where now I am. I cannot conceive of anything more delicious than a *life* consecrated to a faithful love. * * * Adieu,

YOUR OWN DEAR WIFE.

WANTED—A WORD.

FRIDAY EVENING, March 6, 1868.

MY PRECIOUS HUSBAND : I wish I might coin a new word of endearment that would express the fullness of my soul's love. * * *

YOUR DEARLY BELOVED WIFE.

SHE WILL NEVER SCOLD HIM AGAIN.

NURSERY, SUNDAY EVENING, March 8, 1868.

MY BELOVED : All alone, save Eliza in the kitchen ; children all asleep about me ; while I have been trying to imagine my state when I shall again live with you, and behold your precious form. *This*, I think, I have decided—no more chidings, scoldings ! An inexpressible tenderness has grown up in my soul toward you. I never before saw my path as clear as now—that whatever you may do, say, or be, it becometh me to be the Christian wife and mother ! ! * * *

Mr. Beecher gave us a pleasant episode yesterday—a visit of more than an hour. He said, with great earnestness, you never could know the gratification your letter appreciating "Norwood" gave him. He meant to give you the American edition and me the English ; or *vice versa*, so that we might have one each. * * * Good night.

SHE GOES TO A WEDDING.

HOME PARLOR, March 10, 1868.

MY DEARLY BELOVED : This day I have departed widely from the usual routine, by attending the wedding of Mary W—— and Charley D——. I went to gratify mother and Mrs. W., who were very urgent. Mr. Beecher married them beautifully, yet not equal to *our* ceremony. * * * Good night.

ELIZABETH, WIFE.

LOVE'S PERFECT FRUIT.

WEDNESDAY AFTERNOON, March 11, 1868.

MY BELOVED HUSBAND : * * * We have learned of love as few have been permitted, and I bless God for every pang and tear it cost, if only the perfect fruit appear at last. * * * Farewell.

YOUR OWN ELIZABETH.

INFIDELITY.

YOUR DESK, Friday a. m., March 13, 1868.

MY DEAR HUSBAND : * * * Intimations of the Chief-Justice's infidelity make me feel that *you* alone of all men can *stand !* Well, beloved, so long as I live, we will stand *together* for all truth and purity of action. Say you not amen to this ? * * * I know of no joy equal to your home-coming. Adieu.

YOUR DEAR WIFE.

WATCHING THE ALMANAC.

SUNDAY EVENING, March 15, 1868.

MY DEARLY BELOVED : I find myself running to the calendar as often to discover the day of your return, as before my babes are born I watch the date of their birth. I have settled my mind to receive you two weeks from to-day. Do not disappoint me. But I shall have nothing to say to you save love, for have I not faithfully told you each day's events and experiences ? * * * If the *thought* of seeing you is so delicious, what will be the reality ?

YOUR OWN ELIZABETH.

SHE WANTS HER HUSBAND ALL TO HERSELF.

HOME PARLOR, March 17, 1868.

MY DEARLY BELOVED : * * * But I insist that when you return you shall be prevented from seeing visitors, and for a little while rest with me. I shall be the Griffin, like our friend Mrs. B., to frighten away intruders. * * *

YOUR OWN.

THE END OF THE JOURNEY.

WEDNESDAY MORNING, March 18, 1868.

MY DEARLY-BELOVED : My heart is filled with gladness that your "journey is almost done," and I shall soon have you to soothe, comfort, and cheer. If there be any power in love to do this, be assured I shall test it. * * *

YOUR OWN DEAR WIFE.

SORROWING OVER HIS ABSENCE.

JANUARY 1, 1869.

MY PRECIOUS HUSBAND : * * * I feel I have very much to make me happy, yet I am wilfully unhappy with my beloved full of labors and far away. The weather is fearfully stormy,—snow, hail, rain, and all at once. There will be few calls made I think. Our house looks beautifully. The table is furnished with cold turkey, cold ham, tongue, pickled oysters, jelly, mottoes for the children, cake, lemonade, and coffee. Oh ! I wish you were here. Since I made you *once* happy in receiving your friends, I feel encouraged to think I may always. * * * Adieu. Yours, utterly.

ELIZABETH, WIFE.

HER HUSBAND'S SATISFACTION WITH HER LETTERS.

FRIDAY MORNING, January 22, 1869.

MY DEARLY BELOVED : * * * If my poor, dull, heavy "letters do you good as a medicine." I have cause for gratitude, I am sure. * * * Forgive me that I want so much love. Yes, my soul cries ; Give, give. I believe I am big enough to supply even your big heart with love if you'll only let me. Farewell.

WIFE, BELOVED.

HATEFUL LITTLE SPRITES.

THURSDAY, NOON, January 26, 1869.

DEARLY BELOVED : It is with delight and for refreshment that I hasten, as opportunity offers, to sit down without interruption to write and think of you. Is it, not true that I write of you as well as to you ? Oh ! my own dear husband, could I but enjoy your companionship now a little while—I cannot understand why the demons weariness, faultfinding, ungenerous selfishness, and many hateful little sprites, perpetually hang about me when you are with me, to modify and lessen our possible enjoyment. * * *

Good-bye, and good night. Your own dear wife, who is proud and fond of her husband.

E——.

'SHE THANKS HIM FOR HIS KIND WORDS.

WEDNESDAY NOON, January 27, 1869.

MY BELOVED : How can I make you know my grateful love for your tender words written at Ann Arbor, and just this moment received ? They are as healing balm to my aching heart. Mama has replied to my note which I sent you this morning in the same cruel manner, and I have felt quite broken by it. But, I, too must "let her drop." I could more easily forget, were I out of the neighborhood. But I return to your letter, so delicious and restful. I thank God with my whole being for this gift of love's assurance this morning. * * * Be very happy, for you have *made me glad.* Yours utterly,

ELIZABETH, WIFE.

OLIVER AND ELIZABETH.

BROOKLYN, THURSDAY MORNING, Feb. 4, 1869.

MY DEARLY-BELOVED HUSBAND: * * * My darling, I must believe that this beautiful home which you have made for us must have given you a greater amount of satisfaction than we generally secure from earthly labors. * * * I was glad to hear from you in the *Independent* this week. Oliver told me of Mr. Bowen's desire to publish *his* reply last week to the Methodist assailant. This led to the object of his visit to me, which was to inquire of me the origin of the story told him by a lady from Brooklyn, whose letter you saw before going West. I then told him at length—how that he knew himself how I felt years ago regarding him, for I had sought an interview alone with him at the *Standard* office, and all that had passed there, I had told Mattie B——, but at present my feelings toward him had changed entirely, because my husband was no longer young, and that very few, indeed, I could not name *one* whom I thought possible to influence him for harm. Besides, I had learned to trust in the friendship of my husband. I realized how sincere his attachment was for you, and I believed in it. But I had felt a growing indifference for some time past between him, Oliver, and myself, and therefore I had been always more glad to welcome Mary Ann than himself to my house. We had a very frank, conscientious talk, ending by my telling him that I desired with all my soul to feel no ill thought or suspicion toward any human being, and I only wished to live to attain to this. I felt very much better in spirit after it, and think that *here* now we are again in sympathy.

The reception to Lucretia Mott has fallen through, because of that dear old lady's unwillingness to be lionized. * * * Mr. B. does not come as often as in the fall. His labors are heavy, and he too *feels* just like work, more than for several years past. * * * Farewell. Your darling,

ELIZABETH, WIFE.

HER HEART IS FULL OF TENDERNESS.

FRIDAY NIGHT, Feb. 5, 1869.

MY BELOVED: I come to thee, for my heart overflows in tenderness and desire for you. * * * I took Flory with me to prayer-meeting to-night as an escort. We had a very rare time; something that would have pleased you thoroughly. * * * I love you with all my soul, and always do in my highest moods. * * * If we could only run to each other in our best moments, and flee away when they do, would it not be delicious? * * * Good night,

YOUR DEAR WIFE.

A WHITE NIGHT.

SATURDAY NIGHT, Feb. 6, 1869.

MY VERY DEAR HUSBAND: * * * Your words "my return trip" I have read over and over again. How long it seems since we took the ride in the carriage through New York to the cars! That was a *white* night—as you say—memorable for true feeling in both of our hearts. I hope my heart will always leap at your coming. * * * Do not be discouraged, my sweet. If you live and labor your best, God knows, and does not require you to bear *my* infirmities. *Alone* we live and alone we do and must appear. It is my *greatest misery* if I make you to fall by loss of temper, deception, or any such thing. That my presence should ever affect you for evil makes me cry as did Cain: "My punishment is greater than I can bear!" I do not think he suffered any more keenly than do I. Good night.

YOUR FOND BUT IMPATIENT WIFE.

SHE CONSECRATES HERSELF TO HER HUSBAND.

SUNDAY, Feb. 7, 1869.

MY BELOVED: I have just finished reading to Emma, Lowell's "Extreme Unction," and a chapter in "Norwood" of Parson Buell's grief at the death of his wife. It is very touching, and I realized for a moment what that agony must be, the parting at the river between a husband and wife who have truly loved—how inevitable it is! God only can sustain the one who remains, while He enables the one who departed to say, "I shall be satisfied!"

Allow me to say, without cant, that God has given me a blessing to-day,—He has enabled me to do something for Him, and that conscious privilege overflows my heart utterly. At home He helped me to be patient, willing, yea glad, to spend myself for others; and in the Bethel—my little, little room was crowded. The interest increases in my class. They all love me, I *feel* it—because I, too, love every one. I do indeed feel grateful for the encouragement they give me, in these new labors. I tell you rather more at length than usual of my work here, because I earnestly wish your sympathy, and to feel free to talk *with you* of everything in which I'm interested, as in "auld lang syne." However imperfect we may appear to each other, yet the dear Lord does not hesitate to use us. Now, to-night, I give myself to you—my *best, my worst*—"just as I am." Take me once again into your confidence, bear with my follies as in early days. I consecrate myself to you so long as I shall live, before God this night, as a fitting close of this Sabbath day. Forgive all my infirmities, and help me to overcome to final victory. Wilt thou? So will I you, if you permit. The freedom with which you write of Paul * gives me great pleasure. Then the fountain is unsealed and we flow together. I talk not so much of him. Yet this new mysterious feeling *I know*, which I never before have uttered—a kind of awe, or waiting, listening to learn what he will do for me, and an agony of fear at times, lest I should fall by reason of sin—what he could bring. Already, in many things, I am a *changed woman*, through his precious ministrations. Yet, fearing such a statement may be too positive, let me modify it by a *woman changing.* * * *

YOUR OWN.

THE "LIFE OF CHRIST."

WEDNESDAY NIGHT, February 10, 1869.

MY DEARLY LOVED HUSBAND: I will take up my home-story from where I left off yesterday morning; mailing the financial letter to Des Moines. About an hour later Mr. B. came in, bringing the manuscript sheets of his first chapter in the "Life of Christ" to read to me. He had read them to no one else, and wanted to know how his opening chapter would sound. I liked it, and you will, I think. It is fresh and interesting. After he had finished reading, I ran up-stairs and brought a little sketch of one of my Bethel lessons on "Mary, the Mother of Jesus," as an example of woman's faith, which I read to him. His visit was refreshing and comforting to me. * * * But I am too tired to think or write more. How blessed to know that these bodies are not always to clog and hinder us. Accept and welcome my spirit of love, which is as fresh and ardent as ever, faithful and ever devoted to you. Blessings on you, my dearly beloved.

ELIZABETH, WIFE.

SHE IS THOROUGHLY SATISFIED IN HER HUSBAND.

THURSDAY, February 11, 1869.

MY DARLING: * * * You will find a worn and weary woman thoroughly satisfied when once again she may rest in your bosom. I cannot sleep until I return thanks for the letter of good cheer reaching me to-day, written on the cars to Chicago. I had been waiting all the week for a word, and had fallen in spirits, but, as the hymn says, "What a change a word can make," I took my letter in the room and, by the spot where the Heaven opened once for little Paul to enter, I knelt down and gave thanks for your life, for your love, and again (as in many, many times) *there* the heavens have opened and brought peace to my soul. If tears could atone for sin, my soul would be clean therefrom, for alone and often I cry unto God to "create in me a clean heart." * * * Joseph is with mother, having that long-expected settlement. Father is firmly set upon a separation. I would be happier were she to seek an asylum for a season before that step be taken. Oh, my beloved, may you never suffer as I have

---

* Paul was the dead son of Mr. and Mrs. Tilton.

over a mother turned to an enemy. . . . I rejoice in the spirit of your editorial; it has the good old ring in it. Now may not home influences dull the strain! Elizabeth, behold what you do, or undo! So I keep in mind. Good night, my sweet. Yours always,

WIFE ELIZABETH.

THE CHILDREN GET VALENTINES.

, MONDAY, February 15, 1869.

MY BELOVED: . . . My spirit sank to find another list of engagements added to defer your home-coming! . . . The children were well pleased with your valentines. Mine is the sweetest of all. . . . I appreciate and am satisfied in your love. God unite us utterly and bless us.

YOUR OWN DEAR WIFE.

" DO HURRY HOME."

SECOND STORY FRONT, FRIDAY MORNING,
February 19, 1869.

DEARLY BELOVED: . . . Yesterday was an exciting, busy day, and I would not write you, though I yearned, almost cried, for you many times. Our separation this winter has been cruel; as an inevitable I bear it, but with cheerfulness not. . . . Do hurry home, love. I am yours utterly. My heart is fixed to bless you. Our children are all well and happy. Carroll says at the breakfast-table spontaneously, "Oh! I do wish my papa was home." Do believe that we all love you and long for you. Send for the letters I have written you, for I want you to know all I've said and felt. By-bye.

YOUR OWN DARLING.

"Am I not your own sweet little wife?"

A REMARKABLE TRIBUTE TO HER HUSBAND'S LOVE.

TUESDAY EVENING, February 28, 1869.

MY BELOVED: "This is the last day of winter." Little Carroll said as he got into bed to-night: "Papa will soon be here." " Yes," I replied, " spring will certainly come, and I hope in three Sundays more papa will come as surely." . . . I will go back a little, and tell you yesterday's story, a day so full as to crowd out entirely my writing you. First of all, then, my heart overflowed toward you, because of your generous, kind letter concerning mother. She was quite touched by it, and desired me to give you her thanks for your sympathy. . . . My head and heart have been so full of divorce cases since you left—this difficulty of mother's following on the heels of Mrs. M—k, has been a kind of experience of which I have had quite enough. Were I a lawyer I would certainly change my profession, or beg, rather than investigate such miseries. . . . Now, my sweet, after so long a tale, let me for our mutual refreshment turn to our own sweet love. I bless God that it abideth. Among the terrible changes of many hearths God has kept us steadfast with a glowing love, admiration, and respect for each other. O, let us praise His name forever. All the differences and misunderstandings we have had are, as Whittier says,

Like mountain ranges overpast.

" If God be for us, who can be against us?"

Give me your patience while I spread out before you the fruitage of your beautiful love, like the rare-cut flowers of a bouquet. They are the closing words of your letters—select and precious, reminding me of the soul-stirring benedictions of the Apostles' epistles. Fruit No. 1:

"But among all my losses, I have lost no jot or tittle of ever-increasing love for the sweetest of wives and the fairest of children."

"My heart longs for you to-day."

"Grace, mercy, and peace ever thine."

"You and the chicks, and the house, and all, are in my thoughts every day and hour."

"Good-bye and all hail."

" With overflowing love, I am now, and ever, yours devotedly."

"I send you now as ever the fervid love of yours devotedly."

"I think you and I are yet to walk in Paradise together."

"I would rather have my wife and children at this moment than all the honors under the sun."

"Every day of my life I love you more and more, and shall unto the end."

"With my whole soul I am yours faithfully."

"If now I had a little personal comforting and petting from the little lady at No. 136, I would be perfectly satisfied."

"But Paul and I keep our companionship. To you, his mother, be God's peace."

"I love you fervently and entirely."

"Blessings on you always."

Then fearing that these extreme delights "would make a woman mad outright," you have six epistles ending:

"Yours in dust and ashes."

"Yours Doggedly."

"God help your sorrowful and groaning husband!"

"Yours, achingly," etc.

How like you the receiving a letter from yourself ?

I keep a list of these delicious tit-bits most tenderly, believe it. Thou knowest I love theee. Good-night.

WIFE ELIZABETH.

THE SAME OLD STORY.

FRIDAY NIGHT, March 5, 1869.

MY OWN DEAR HUSBAND: The sheet on which I write is one of a box of paper and envelopes presented by one of my "mothers," who called to take me to church to-night, and desired me to use it in writing to you. . . . I am sure I need you very much. My prayer is night and day that I may not harm your free spirit, nor be selfish in loving you any more. . . .

. I am very tired, sweet; too tired to write, but not to love. Love never exhausts. Good-night. Your own forever.

ELIZABETH.

SHE SYMPATHIZES WITH HER HUSBAND'S TOIL.

SATURDAY MORNING, March 6, 1869.

MY DARLING: I have looked with great annoyance and pain on the map to learn your whereabouts, and realized the immense labors you were going through before your letter, just received, desired me to do so. Don't make a Western tour again; with your salary, and the engagements near home, we will try to pay off our debt and educate our children. . . . Farewell.

YOUR DEAR WIFE.

SHE WANTS TO JOIN HER HUSBAND.

TUESDAY NIGHT, March 9, 1869.

. MY DARLING : My mind has been in conflict all day between my desire to meet you with Frank Moulton in Michigan, and my ability to do so. But my caution has finally prevailed. The *thought* of spending two or more weeks with you alone has done me good,—a delicious romance it was, and I am content ; though, like reading a poem, there is disappointment at the unreality. . . . Good-night. I am very tired. "But thou knowest that I love thee."

ELIZABETH, WIFE.

SHE BECAME AN ACTIVE SUFFRAGIST.

SATURDAY MORNING, March 13, 1869.

MY BELOVED : Friday I took Annie to call with me on some of my Bethel women, and after to a meeting of the Executive Committee of the Equal Rights Association, meeting at the *Revolution* office. You will be amused to know that Susan made me Chair*woman*, and said afterwards that "I did as well as Theodore himself." I always want to represent you well.

LOOKING FOR HER BELOVED.

THURSDAY MORNING, March 18, 1869.

MY DARLING HUSBAND : Do not blame your dear little wife for apparent neglect this last fortnight, because only once in two or three days has she been able to write to her beloved. *You know* that inability, and not a lack of desire, has made me silent. . . . I have been extremely busy ; though I insist that my hands are never as full as my heart. You will enjoy home-life with us, won't you ? I am impatient to prove my love in ways more substantial than pen-talk. . . . The days before you return, though full of labors, are tedious to endure. May God hasten and bless your safe coming to my arms and my heart. . All send love and welcome. Be happy, for more of soul-deep treasure is yours than is often given.

YOUR OWN.

EAGERNESS OF EXPLAINING.

SATURDAY, March 20, 1869.

MY BELOVED: I have endeavored to meet you at every appointment with one or two letters. Why they have not reached you is a mystery. I am nearly beside myself thinking that in *one week* I am yours and you are mine again. I kept waking up all last night, and my first thought was a desire and a prayer for you. I am overflowing with grateful love for your tender, precious words from Springfield. I have written this week eighteen letters.* The house will be empty, swept, and garnished, I trust, when you return. Take care of yourself, that, with body and soul, we may realize God's fullest blessing in our reunion. Yours, earnestly and entirely,

ELIZABETH, WIFE.

FROM THE SUMMER HOME.

MONTICELLO, July 29, 1869.

MY BELOVED: * * * My darling, I am very tired, but desire these few lines will welcome you as a wife's fond kiss on your return home. Rest assured that my heart is with you always. More anon. Your pet. E.

Love to the girls.

ANXIOUS FOR ORTHODOXY.

AUGUST 3, 1869.

MY DEAR HUSBAND: * * * Oh, dear Theodore, may I not persuade you to love the Lord Jesus Christ? Do not let this entreaty estrange us more, for my pillow *oft* is wet with tears and prayers that we may come into sympathy in our religious natures. Do have patience with me, for, as the time remains to us, I feel as though my heart would break if I did not speak to you—not that I am right in any sense, and you are wrong; God forbid! but we are not one in feeling, and it is *impossible* for me to be indifferent, especially while God blesses me with dear children * * * I am extremely glad that Mr. Greeley is to be with you. I hope you will have unalloyed comfort with him. Give him my love, as you know I have it for him. Make him as comfortable as you can. Your letters coming daily are my sustenance really, although they give me only your outer life. * * * Good night. Your dear wife,

ELIZABETH.

HER HUSBAND'S FRIENDS.

MONTICELLO, August 6, 1869.

MY DEAR HUSBAND: * * * I rejoice in the cheery tone in which you write, and that so many good people are brightening your solitary and lonely home. Father Tilton, Alice Carey, Mrs. Ames, Susan, Mr. and Mrs. Manning! Surely you have had rare entertainments. Good night. I am

YOUR DEAR WIFE.

REMEMBRANCES.

MONTICELLO, SUNDAY, August 15, 1869.

MY DEAR HUSBAND: These days are full of the memories of the sickness and suffering of little Paul a year ago! * * * Mr. Beecher wrote me a very summary, characteristic letter, which I would inclose save for the fear you would lose it. Remember me to our girls.

YOURS ALWAYS.

EXPRESSING LOVE.

MONTICELLO, TUESDAY.

MY DARLING: I was not going to write you to-night, but your Sunday's letter was such a beautiful picture of yourself and children that I wished to express my love once more and send a kiss to my sweet darlings. Come soon. YOUR BLESSED PET.

SHE HANGS UP A SENTENCE.

MONTICELLO, August 18.

MY BELOVED HUSBAND: I fear my letter distressed you, as I found occasion to express my fears to you, and perhaps hid the love that was throbbing in my heart for you all the while. I shall soon have been absent from you as long as you were from me on your Western visit, which I then hoped and prayed would never occur again. Oh, when I do see you you shall have a taste for a few minutes of a woman's pure love, *if I know how to express it.* I have just mailed a note of appreciation to Mr. Cuyler for his beautiful tribute to you. * * * I have taken your sentence in large letters "with love unbounded" and hung it over my mantlepiece.

YOURS ALWAYS.

---

* These letters were addressed by Mrs. Tilton to various persons interested in the Woman's Suffrage Movement, whom she wished to bring together in Brooklyn at the anniversary meeting.

HER HUSBAND'S "BEAUTIFUL VISIT."

MONTICELLO, August 31, 1869.

MY OWN DEAR HUSBAND : Thanks for your prompt letter. I do indeed feel lonely without you, but try to be brave. * * * Your most beautiful visit is a constant delight to think upon. I am very grateful for it. *. * * I long for you these moonlight nights. * * * You made many friends here. We are rich in this regard, ever to find friends. Love to all my loved ones, and my heart's unrest for yourself.

SUNDAY NOT SUNDAY WITHOUT HER HUSBAND.

MONTICELLO, MONDAY EVENING, Sept. 4.

MY DEAR HUSBAND: * * * You speak of coming up next Sunday. If so, do prepare to spend the remaining two weeks with me, that we may return together. You can write your editorials here, and the rest you need after the last week's excitement. * * * We had a ride this afternoon, and yesterday we strolled in the fields, but I could not say, as the Sabbath before I did, I was perfectly happy, or as happy as any one could be in this world, for you were absent. * * *

YOURS ALWAYS.

HER PRIDE IN HER HUSBAND'S FAME.

GARRISON'S, WEST POINT, }
MONDAY NIGHT, Jan. 3, 1870. }

MY DEAR HUSBAND: Before you had fairly seated yourself in the cars, I learned from the conversation of a gentleman in the depot that the 10:45 express was then ready and that an effort would be made to reach New York before night. I therefore determined to share my fortunes with my fellow-travelers and spend the day in the cars rather than in Albany. We reached Poughkeepsie past 3, and here—West Point—half-past 6. I intended to push on home, but could hardly expect to do so before midnight, and as Alice desired a change, I yielded, and am in a neat little hotel at the head of the ferry-house here, very comfortable, where the hostess always reads the *Independent* and wishes more to see its editor than any other living man. Such a sentiment from this simple-hearted woman was like wine to my tired body and soul. * * *

LOVE PERPETUALLY.

MY DEAR HUSBAND : I do not at all realize that my winter's correspondence has begun. We have fallen from the habit of daily writing because of the frequent home-comings, but it will be very sweet for me to give my daily story, and sweeter still to listen to yours, the first strain of which I caught to-day, and I sorrowed for your hard fate, but rejoiced in the victory. . . . Believe that I will cherish your love and memory perpetually, talk of you often to our darlings, and reward your arduous labors by learning to be a financier. The taste of saving I never really knew before, and, unlike other tastes, it lingers in delight. I sent extracts from Lucille for last week's *Revolution.* Do not forget me in your prayers.

CRAVING SENTIMENT.

THURSDAY EVENING, January 13, 1870.

MY DEAR HUSBAND : You once said, and have often acted, that I was always craving sentiment. It is verily true. I am what I am, therefore, to such a nature as mine. Jesus Christ, as He discovers Himself to me, is unutterably precious. Let my tongue cleave to the roof of my mouth, if I fail to bear testimony to His *unchangeable love.* Your letter reached me yesterday. How it lightened my day like a glory ! You are well beloved by *one human,* and, therefore, it is love struggling and unperfected. I do not, however, comfort myself in my humanity—rather, whenever I am victor over it. Oh ! how slow is the warfare ! . . . To-day has been a quiet day. Mr. Beecher called ; he is in fine spirits, making calls. He devotes Wednesdays and Thursdays to this work, "till further notice ;" has three hundred to make ; made twenty to-day ; enjoys it immensely. He called on the Wheelocks to-day, and kissed them all around—Lizzie Wood included, he said. I told him that Alice had named her doll Rose Wentworth. Thus ends another of my matter-of-fact epistles, but so endeth not the love of your darling wife and four precious children.

SHE RENEWS HER LOVE AND HOPE.

SATURDAY MORNING, January 15, 1870.

MY DEARLY-BELOVED : I feel the old-time delight to hear from your lips that you are lonesome and homesick. I am grateful—yea, happy. *I renew my love and hope.* Last night I went to prayer-meeting. One great argument against public life and city life is that the children are deprived of their right to their parents. They each one send much love to their dear papa. I read your letters to them. By-bye, my own darling. I am, yours,

ELIZABETH.

"STEPPING HEAVENWARD."

TUESDAY NIGHT, February 1, 1870.

MY BELOVED : We are having a cold spell of weather. The wind whistles wildly down the chimney of our sitting-room where I write. I am reading "Stepping Heavenward" to aunty. The tears are trickling down her face all the while. I have said at other absences I should be happy when you got home, and you have seen how I failed to prove to you the fact. Still it does seem to me we shall be happy of a truth this return. Good-night, darling. I am,

YOUR OWN WIFE.

SOME NOTES.

WEDNESDAY AFTERNOON, February 2, 1870.

MY DEAR HUSBAND : I find you in haste, as ever, surrounded with people. So is my life. I do not believe it right in either of us. Concentration of one's affections upon one's duties is impossible. I ask your love and confidence. Good night.   YOUR DARLING.

THURSDAY, February 3—night. (Probably 1870.)

MY DARLING : I have joined the Woman's Club in Brooklyn, and paid my fee of $3. You are proposed as an honorary member, and will be accepted, no doubt. Good night, beloved. I am,

YOUR OWN DEAR WIFE.

THE following are

TILTON'S LETTERS TO HIS WIFE—1865–1870:

"NONE WHOM I WOULD EXCHANGE FOR MY OWN."

ST. LOUIS, Dec. 31, 1864.

MY DEARLY BELOVED WIFE: It is midnight,—the last hour and moment of the year! I am sitting alone in my room at the hotel, thinking of home, and full of home-sickness. Under my window a ser-enading band is playing "Home, Sweet Home," in honor of a military officer here. I feel as if they are playing it in mockery of *me*.

The city here is full of bonfires, a custom here on Christmas and New Year's eves. The fire-bells have been ringing a salute to speed the parting and welcome the coming year. Already my date of 1864 is wrong; I ought now to say 1865.

I think of our year of family-history—full of small yet important events; the growth of the chil-dren ; the ripening of own minds ; the growing affection between us all, ripening with time; the goodness of God in sparing our lives; the daily discipline of cares, trials, sorrows, joys,—all the changes of life, fashioning us, as under the molding of Providence, into constantly new creatures, and, I trust, into higher and better lives. . . .

I have seen, in my daily visits to the new cities and families of my tour, many sweet and pleasant ladies and children, but none, anywhere, whom I would exchange for my own! I suspect that, at this late hour, you are all abed and asleep. I would like to catch a glimpse of all your faces, and to steal a kiss from all your cheeks. This would be more comfort than all the pleasant attentions which I am securing from the half-friendship and skin-deep kindness, which the world calls hospitality.

And now, Happy New Year! May God bless, protect, abide with you all,—wife and children, and all the household, to whom, now as ever, I send my love.

Yours, brimful of affection,

THEODORE.

"NEVER KNEW BEFORE THE PAIN OF ABSENCE."

ASHLEY HOUSE, BLOOMINGTON, Ill., }
Thursday, Jan. 5, 1865.   }

MY DEARLY BELOVED WIFE: Not having touched a pen for four days, I just this moment find leisure to resume the story of my travels. . . .

On New Year's afternoon (that is Monday afternoon) I took the train for Alton, Ill. . . .

The next morning I visited the grave of Elijah Lovejoy, who was killed, twenty-seven years ago, in that place, because he spoke against Slavery His grave is in a cemetery on a high hill, from which I could see the confluence of the Missouri and Mississippi Rivers—a broad and liberal landscape, picturesque and beautiful. Alton is the roughest and hilliest city I ever saw—being all like Brooklyn at the slope of Columbia street. . . .

On Wednesday morning I left Alton, and at noon reached Springfield. . . . Lieut.-Gov. Bross gave me welcome, . . . and in the afternoon took me to the home of Abraham Lincoln—a plain two-story, wooden building, painted brown, looking like the residence of a man neither poor nor rich—a house like many a one in Salem or Danvers, except that its color was not the New England white. To my surprise, its present occupants are a family named Tilton, who received me with great cordiality, and with whom I spent the entire afternoon till dark. . . . They gave me a cordial invitation to come again, bringing you, and making a family-visit. Inclosed is a little card of flowers which Miss Tilton plucked from the garden while flowers were yet in bloom. . . .

After breakfast this morning, I walked out upon the prairie, which here is not flat, but rolling. I found just outside the city a beautiful grove, where I paced up and down, musing of home. The weather a fall of golden glory—not cold for the season—all Nature smiling like. a weedding-day. But there is always something in such a rare beauty of sky and sunshine to make me sad and lonesome. I walked up and down like a pilgrim—struggling to keep tears out of my eyes. I chide myself, and I am punished for not having brought with me some picture of you and the children. Even a *picture* of you would comfort me now. My love is kindled like a coal under a breath, whenever I think of you. I never knew before the pain of absence. You are the dearest, sweetest, kindest, and best of women, and the children, the dear children are like yourself! Kiss them all for,

PAPA.

"MY ONE AND ONLY LOVE AMONG WOMEN."

CINCINNATI, BURNET HOUSE, }
Sunday Evening, January 9, 1865. }

MY DEAR WIFE AND FRIEND : At last I have your two letters, which I have been chasing for three days. I overtook them in Cincinnati this morning, and have already read them half a dozen times over. I can appreciate the greed of soldiers to get letters from home. They are "good news from a far country." I have now, in all, four letters from your dear pen. The previous two I have handled so much—reading them so often in the cars—that their edges look worn and roughened. They four make a little manuscript volume, which I keep in a spare corner of my pocket. What I read most often are the rare and flavorsome sentences in which you offer me your love, like a ripe fruit. Heaven bless you, my true wife ! . . .

Your last letter was without date, though I judged it to have been written before New Year's day. Did I tell you of my disappointment on that day ? *I* was in St. Louis, and *you* in Brooklyn ; but there was a telegraph-wire between ; and so I wrote the following dispatch :

To Mrs. Theodore Tilton, 48 *Livingston street, Brooklyn :*
Happy New Year from the banks of the Mississippi !

THEODORE TILTON.

But I was told by the operators that it could not be put through on that day. I was going to send a similar one to Mr. Beecher. It seemed to me on that day as if I were half-way round the world,—I was at such a distance from your dear, sweet self.

You mention that you do not receive my letters daily. I write one each day, but sometimes they are mailed on the railroad, and sometimes in a hotel. I never can tell when my letter will start after I have mailed it. This accounts for the irregularity. . . .

Your account of your holiday presents to the children, near and far of kin, has suddenly awakened in my mind the suspicion that I never before fully appreciated your interest and anxiety in this matter. I am glad you did as your heart prompted. I am sorry that heretofore I have not better understood the full extent of your wishes as to making gifts. I think you never before took pains to make me so full a statement of your inward promptings on this subject. Birthdays and holidays have not been so much to me as to you. I will think more of them hereafter for your sake.

I will send no messages to the children this time ; for I mean to write them a special letter after I have finished this, if I get time. In case I get *no* time, I here send kisses for all three, and *you* shall be the express to deliver the burden. Sweet little cheeks ! I wish I could kiss them myself at this very moment. . . .

I find myself so broadened in mind by travel, and particularly in that part of travel which consists in making new friendships, that I shall hereafter insist on *your* going with me, for the sake of similar advantages to yourself, as well as for the sake of companionship for me. I am beginning to think less and less of books, and more and more of men and human life, as means of education. *You* are too closely shut up at home. You must go more into society,—not to evening-parties, but on journeys with *me*. . I regret keenly that you have not been with me this long trip. My journey has been as much to *me* as Mr. Beecher's English journey was to *him.*.

Oh ! if you and I could only have plucked these roses *together !* May God bless you, and carry me safely to your side and into your arms once again. Above all else in the world,—books, name, or fame,—I love *you*, my one and only love among women,—first last, and perennial.

As now I write, my feelings rise within me with such a thrill as sometimes shoots through me at the touch of your hand within mine, or of your lips to mine.

Passing daily through multitudes of strangers, who glide among one another without mutual recognition, or mutual interest in each other's welfare, I have lately been much more than ever impressed with the wonderful simplicity of God's plan for binding together human society, namely: by creating in each breast some strong and dominating love for *one* human being.

I look at the multitudinous faces of my audience, and say to myself, "After all, what are all these to me, in comparison with one dear quiet face far away?" Were it not for the love of mother to child, or husband to wife, our society, civilization, the peace and order of the world,—all would fall asunder in a day!

Therefore it is that the sacredness of human affections is beyond the sacredness of all other anointed things. Whatever rends apart two lives which have been bound into one is a cruelty to all mankind,—a blow at the unity of civil society.

This is the reason why Slavery, that tears families to pieces, has torn the States also to pieces. As one does not appreciate how exquisitely the human frame is nerved and corded until the whole be jarred by some pain unendurable, so no one can tell what the human heart is fibred with till it be made to ache. Then it proves itself a wondrous thing.

Yet how great is the multitude of hearts that daily ache! What rending of ties between lovers! What breakages in human friendships! What ingratitude of children to parents! What unkindness of man to man!

My sweet love, I begin to see, as never before, that the centre of the world, to an honorable man, is his own family—his wife's sitting-room—his children's play-places—his HOME. I hope hereafter, if God should spare my life, to be more careful how my face is made to cast a shadow upon my home. I have been too often negligent of your requests that I should give more time to your dear self and the children. As my heart now feels, I am ready to promise never to seek my old selfish seclusions again, but to spend my home-life in your sweetest of all company.

Our children live so much in the moods of their parents that I hope our dear little chicks will see that you and I love one another unto perpetual happiness and unbroken peace. LOVE is the heavenly magic. It is the gilding that would brighten many a dull house. Love is ours, I know, in rich measure already—only let us make it finer and finer gold!

I hardly know why I should have fallen into this strain to-night, and especially *here;* for I am sitting at a public table, in a great hotel, with people walking up and down on all sides of me, and my ears full of busy bustlings; but I am strong in the conviction that the great favor of God, shown to me in the gift of so many new-found friends and well-wishers, is working out in my heart, for its chief and crowning effect, a purer, deeper, stronger, holier love for that sweet woman, that friend of friends, on whose finger I myself, and not another, put a wedding-ring! Yours for life and death, THEODORE.

"MY WHOLE HEART TURNS TOWARD YOU."

BURNETT HOUSE, CINCINNATI, }
Tuesday, midnight, January 10, 1865. }

DEAR PET: I have accomplished my lecture, and, before going to bed, I take my pen to say Goodnight to my dear, yearning, prayerful wife, who, perhaps at this very hour, is lying awake thinking of her runaway husband.

My day's story is this: I spent my forenoon in the room of General R——, at his invitation. We had a "long talk." What it was about cannot be exactly defined, for it touched many topics, mostly moral, ethical, and spiritual. He is a Roman Catholic—though neither of us made any allusion to that fact. . He is a fine-looking, frank-faced man, built like our friend Mr. G——, though of a different temperament. We unbosomed to each other our interior aspirations toward the higher life—spoke of the unsatisfactoriness of this world's applause, of the great selfishness of the fame-seekers, and of various kindred themes of human desire.

Good night, my dear girl! Sweet dreams of your husband fill your thoughts! My whole heart turns toward you with great yearnings and with love unutterable. Peace be with you! Amen! THEODORE.

"I HAVE CLUNG TO YOU AS WITH AN ANCHOR."

WEDDELL HOUSE, CLEVELAND, Jan. 13, 1865.

MY DARLING WIFE: . . . Yesterday morning . . . I was invited . . . to visit the father and mother of Lieutenant-General Grant. . . .

Your letters are like wine to my thirst. On opening the envelope I am always disappointed if the letter is not a long one. I am glad Mr. Beecher called on you. I will write to thank him for it. I have not had a line from him, but I have had two brief notes from Mr. Greeley.

You say, "I am glad you write you are homesick." I reply, I am glad *you* write the same. If God spares me to return, I am sure our loves will be nobler than ever. I feel myself spiritually profited by my experiences of travel. I have clung to you as with an anchor every day of my absence. The thought of your constant love fills me with tenderness and yearning. And the dear children grow dearer and dearer. Kiss them all for their father's sake. Remember me always in your prayers. Dear, sweet pet, good-night!

THEODORE.

SPEND ALL THE MONEY YOU NEED.

THE INDEPENDENT EDITORIAL ROOMS, No. 5 BEEKMAN STREET, NEW YORK, July 31, 1865.

MY DEAR PET: Your letter this morning came with a thousand welcomes. It has kept my blood gay all day long. Bless you, dear pet, for loving such a troublesome, taxing, wayward, fault-finding husband! . . .

Spend all the money you need to make yourself comfortable. Don't fail to ride out plentifully,—never mind the cost.

Forgive all my faults, and look into my heart, and see how I love you. Ever yours,

THEODORE.

FLORENCE'S EIGHTH BIRTHDAY.

THE INDEPENDENT EDITORIAL ROOMS, No. 5 BEEKMAN STREET, NEW YORK, Aug. 4, 1865.

MY DEAR PET: This is Florence's eighth birthday! How many times to-day you have thought of it,—absent among the mountains! The dear child and her sister have had their heads full of it all day, for I am now writing in the late afternoon.

First of all, I gave to Florence a Bible, gilt-edged and brass-clasped; also, a pretty knife, pearl-handled; also, some of Mr. Park's flowers to make a crown for her head; also, some spending money, with liberty to use it at her pleasure. Oliver Johnson sent her a neat leather reticule,—something like Libby's. At 4 o'clock to-day, the children were to go with the Judge down to Coney Island,—the party being too large to make room for myself in the carriage. So I think the birthday will be memorable with her. She has appeared very happy and talked very wisely.

It is good for the children that you should be occasionally absent from them, it develops their resources. . . .

I have not been able, in any of my thoughts to-day, to realize how rapidly the girls are creeping away from their childhood. Mattie * is my only baby,—*she* remains in my mind, perpetually the same young thing whom we laid under the ground. *Her* birthday into Heaven! So life, and death, and immortality, have each added a thought to this day's reflections. Yours, with unspeakable love,

THEODORE.

"I TAKE FOR GRANTED YOUR CONTINUAL LOVE."

NEW YORK, Aug. 5, 1865.

DEAR PET: No letter from you this morning! Never mind,—don't trouble yourself to write every day. I take for granted your continual love. But your letters are my chief delight during these days of absence. . . .

Mr. Beecher has been in this morning, inquiring for you and the chicks, and leaving his love for all. He is not well,—dyspeptic and bilious. . . .

With ever-growing love for you and dear Carroll, and with regards to Libby and Emma, I am, now and ever,

THEODORE.

"I AM LONGING FOR YOU."

NEW YORK, Aug. 10, 1865.

MY DEAR PET: I seize a moment before steamboat-time to write a line to your dear self. Your letter this morning was thrice welcome. I am longing for you beyond all former hunger. . . .
Ever yours,

THEODORE.

"I THANK GOD FOR MY SWEET WIFE."

SUNDAY EVENING, Aug. 20, 1865.

MY DARLING: I am sitting at my writing-table in Keyport, having just put both the children to bed in the green-room.

---

* Mattie was a child who died in infancy.

My Sabbath has been very delightful. I went to church this morning, and spent the afternoon with Florence and Alice, reading the history of David and Goliath. The children have been delightful companions.

As evening drew on, they became more and more confidential, talking a good deal of you and Cad. I helped them undress, and put them to bed—allowing no one else to disturb the charm. Alice had at first some hesitation in saying her prayers aloud, but overcame the scruple bravely.

I tremble at the thought of *losing* either of the pets. Life is *awful*, looked at through love. "We have these treasures in earthen vessels." I have been several days thinking how I could contrive to make the world endurable without your companionship. Nor is it possible for true lovers ever to measure the depth of their own true love until a separation searches both hearts, or death slays one.

What we possess we may not always undervalue, though possession quiets and allays the irresistible longings which arise during separation.

It seems to me that, if you were taken away from me altogether, this world would seem no longer worth tarrying in. I thank God for my sweet wife, and the beautiful-minded children He has given us. May you and I become more and more like unto little children, and so be the more and more fit for the Kingdom of Heaven. Ever yours,   THEODORE.

"I WISH YOU WERE HERE."

MONDAY EVENING, KEYPORT, August 20, 1865.

MY SWEET WIFE : I have put the children to bed, showing myself a perfect mother to them, and I now sit and lament awhile over my lonesome separation from yourself. I have a fat envelope, which I carry in my breast-pocket, stuffed full of your letters from Monticello ; and, when I am specially alone, and lonely, I take them out, and pick here and there some choice sentiment of your love, and smell it as I would a honeysuckle.

For instance, to-day's letter brought me *this* sweetness, "Oh, when I *do* see your face again. you shall have a taste for a few minutes of a woman's pure love, if I know how to express it." My darling, I wish you were here at this moment ! I fancy what I would do if you were to ring the door-bell *just now*. . . .

Well, you are *not* here, and lamentation begins again. But the children and I are all in the green-room, and we have superb times together. I am their motherly father, and your divorced husband,
                                                                                    THEODORE.

SWEET RECOLLECTIONS.

NEW YORK, Wed., Oct. 25, 1865.

BEST OF PETS: . . . Mr. Beecher preached a sermon on Sunday evening, aimed at the *Independent.* I have a reply in this week's paper. Mr. Bowen heartily sustains me in my course. I have not seen Mr. Beecher, and I suppose his difference is a difference only of opinion, and not of good will. But I am right, and won't be shaken from the rock under my feet.

I have had such sweet recollections of our Sunday, and of my last visit home, that I have been ever since the happiest of men. Nothing is more deeply rooted in my conviction than that I owe more to your pure love and wifely example than to all the world beside. Heaven bless you ! You are the best of good women ! Kiss the children for their father's sake, and let them kiss you in the same behalf. Yours forever, .

                                                                                    THEODORE.

"MY HEART RESTS UPON YOU."

SUNDAY NOON, WASHINGTON, March 28, 1866.

O MY ESPOUSED SAINT: How could you so cruelly disappoint my expectation of meeting you here to-morrow ? . . . I am half of opinion that you are coming after all, and mean to take me by a joyful surprise. Whenever you come, I will cry welcome ! To-day is the first day of leisure which I have had since my arrival in this city. But this leisure brings homesickness, and unutterable desire to see your sweet self and the little folks.

I chide myself because I have written you so few letters, and these such scrawny fruit. But every day, from early morning to midnight, my time has been occupied with busy cares, creating a kind of bewilderment of mind which makes writing impossible. My letters to the *Independent* have been actually forced out of me—toilsome tasks, done against my will, and unsalted with any zeal of composition. And, if I were to write you a love-letter which should prove as barren as a husk, you would rather none had been written.

But, when your last note reminded me that I have not written to you from Washington as copiously or as warmly as I wrote from the West, I felt that you wronged me by not reflecting on the difference between my situation here and my situation there. Here, every moment of my day is busy ; there, I did nothing all day but sit either in a car or a hotel, and wait for the evening. Even to-day, which I have called a day of leisure, my leisure will end in an hour from now, for I am going somewhere (I don't know where) to make an address to a congregation of negroes.

I went to church this morning out of pure hunger to hear some Christian hymn-singing. I don't care greatly for sermons, but I am a believer in hymns. I felt as lonely in the midst of the congregation as a monk who says prayers in a solitary cell. The text was, "And they went and told Jesus." The discourse was very good, but not as good as the text.

I thought, during all the exercises, of how many different lives I lead,—sometimes all absorbed with public affairs, sometimes in an entirely different world and only at verse-making, sometimes a still totally different person and moulding my thoughts for public speech and the popular assembly. Different inclinations, leading to entirely different pursuits, so overmaster me each in turn, that sometimes I have one personality and sometimes another. I am sure it is not everyone who either experiences such a life or can even comprehend it.

But, whichever wind blows, I find in a little while that you, my dearest, are my sheet-anchor. I need your presence and influence, not only for the comfort of my life, but for the stability of my mind. I feel to-day as if I could humbly kiss your lips. O my wife! I more and more realize the exceeding great influence which your nature has, unconsciously to both of us, exerted upon mine. I know that I am a better man because God gave you to me. But I tremble to think that I may perhaps have meanly reciprocated this bounty by selfishly living too much to myself and too little for you.

Sitting here to-day, and thinking of you afar off, I am proud of your character, of your affection for me, of the little children of our love, and of all the sweet pictures of the home-faces that I now see with my mind's eye.

When I think that you have spent your life for my sake, my heart overflows with gratitude for the gift of your pure and disinterested love. Never any other woman so filled my ideal of womanly nobility. My heart rests upon you, and is satisfied. Would to God I could see you here to-day! I know I am too uneven and tumultuous to show you always a courteous and knightly front. But my heart bears no false witness when it testifies that its supreme and undefiled affection on earth is now and evermore for you, and for no other.

Grace, mercy and peace be with you on this Sabbath day! Make heaven familiar with your husband's name by your prayers for his daily strengthening in a Christian life. And now, with blessings and benedictions on the sweetest mother of the best of children, I send kisses and tears to each and all. Forever thine,

THEODORE.

"THE CHILD-LIKE MOTHER."

NEW YORK, June 3, 1866.

MY DEAR PET: . . . The enclosed letter I forgot to mail yesterday. I am sorry I was absent when Henry Ward called with it at my office.

With love to the children and their child-like mother, I am yours forevermore,

THEODORE.

"JOYS THAT ARE NEVER TO BE FORGOTTEN."

AT THE OFFICE,
Tuesday Morning, Aug. 21, 1866.

MY WELL BELOVED WIFE: I enjoyed your recent visit as much as I ever enjoyed a similar occasion in all my life,—in some respects, more than all preceding similar visits. The memory of it lingers in my mind as the fragrance of the garden clings to one's garments long after walking through it.

It is only now and then, I suppose, in the lives of the best of good people, that they appear to each other at the very highest point of moral development and spiritual ripeness. But it is certain you showed yourself very lovely to me on that beautiful Sunday evening. I register that scene in my memory,—classing it with the other choicest remembrances of my life,—ranking it among the joys that are never to be forgotten. I would to God I were not so easily overcome by my own worldly-mindedness as to be brought so quickly and fatally down from my heavenly moods to the earth. But this belongs to the infirmity of human nature. I have walked like a king ever since that evening. No labor has been too arduous, no sacrifice too great for me. It is such fruition that our mutual love ought always, or oftener, to bear. May God make us wise, rich, and pure! For ever yours,

THEODORE.

"NO WOMAN HERE IS LIKE MY WIFE."

NEWPORT, R. I.,
Monday Afternoon, August 23, 1866.

MY BEST BELOVED: A great company is gathering here at this moment. Carriages are rolling up at the door; ladies and gentlemen are getting out; congratulations are going on; but I don't care for the fashionable display, and have excused myself from mingling in the parade. I never before had a realizing thought of so much fashion brought into contact with so much nature. Here one sees at the same glance the ocean and its waves, and silk dresses and scented handkerchiefs. I don't relish the comparison.

. Nevertheless, if people are to lead fashionable lives at all, let them lead them in the compensating presence of Nature. I am getting somewhat homesick, notwithstanding the great kindness of my host, and the great ingenuity he has displayed in providing manly pleasures for my own special circle of his guests.

. . . I half repent me of my long stay—particularly since I am quite aware that you have been lonesome meanwhile. Your brief note, which I received yesterday, mentioning the sickness of Alice, and your own disappointment at not seeing your husband, chid me into compunction for *my* dallying in this place while *you* were repining in another.

No woman here is like my wife ; no children like our children,—none so fair-looking,—none so well-behaved. Rich men's houses often lack poor men's treasures. I am here in the midst of great luxury, but am more than ever content with my own moderate resources.

I have been reflecting that God has been exceedingly kind to you and to me. Our love and marriage, our children, our friends, our good repute among people whose good opinion is golden, our daily comforts,—all make me thankful for my lot as it is, rather than restless after what it is not.

I have penned these lines just to fill a few moments of leisure with that pleasantest of all occupations,—thinking of my wife and children. This makes the second letter which I have written to you to-day. So, you see, I do not forget you.

THEODORE.

BASS-FISHING.

CUTTYHUNK ISLAND. {
Martha's Vineyard Sound, August 24, 1866. }

MY DEAR PET : I am at this moment the only one not in bed on this island. It is late at night, and everybody has gone to his bunk, except one man, who prefers first to write to his wife.

This day has been one of the most romantic days of my whole life. First of all, let me tell you that this place is one of the Elizabeth Isles, that lie off Newport almost thirty miles. This is about a a mile long and a mile broad ; high rocks all around the edge; the soil grassed for sheep, but growing almost nothing else; and the population, including men, women, and children, being only a few fishermen's families, numbering not more than one hundred souls.

Some New York and Philadelphia gentlemen, finding that the place was solitary and the bass-fishing fine, put up a club-house here a year or two ago. These gentlemen all departed to-day, about half an hour after we arrived. They made us promise, however, that we would occupy their bunks, use their flannel jackets and oil-skin trowsers, and fish with their rods. Their hospitality was magnificent, and we accepted it.

Accordingly, Mr. J——, Mr. McM——, and myself, are here, lodged like three princes, having three negroes to cook for us.

The yacht lies in the harbor. To-day I have been fishing for bass, but caught none, owing to a severe wind blowing directly toward the shore, making it almost impossible to throw out a bait far enough.

Tell father that the fishermen here sit on a rock, using a short rod and reel, a line about six hundred feet in length, and that one of the gentlemen caught, some days ago, a bass weighing fifty-seven pounds. The average weight of bass here taken is twenty-five pounds. The only bass caught to-day weighed only five pounds and a half. But while trolling for blue-fish with the boat this morning, I took a fine fellow that weighed seven and a half.

In fishing for bass, two men always stand together, one with the fishing-rod and the other with a gaff, or great pole with an iron grappling, to pierce the fish and lift him up the steep rocks. One gentleman caught a few days ago, ten bass that weighed 312 pounds, and the comment on this feat was, "Rather small fish!" Our Jersey fishermen know nothing of such huge fish as are here taken.

To-night the wind howls, the moon silvers the sea, the lighthouse shines, and universal grandeur and loveliness pervade Nature, I am sitting by a hot fire, as if the night air were wintry. I feel like Alexander Selkirk, "Monarch of all I survey." I almost imagine that I am not in my own country,—in fact, that I am hardly in this old and familiar world,—but translated to some strange and unaccountable place. If you could look out with me on this night's picture of the ocean, seen from these cliffs, which are older than mankind, you would never forget the sight.

But, as I am to wake before the dawn to-morrow, I must go to bed before midnight. So good-night.

. Ever yours,

THEODORE TILTON.

"TEACH THEM TO ADORE THEIR MOTHER."

NEWPORT, Monday, Aug. 27, 1866.

MY DARLING: . . . I have not wished that you were here, except for the pleasure of your company, for I do not think you would find much enjoyment in the society of the ladies now at this house. The young are frivolous, and the old are stupid. I have no more to say to either class than just to be civil. · . . .

The weather is glorious,—perfect, and without blemish. I believe I ordinarily see too little of Nature for my soul's good; for communion with these great waves and grand clouds makes a man humble and devout. In all my more solemn thoughts, I find myself constantly thinking of your own dear self—my soul's true associate for time and eternity.

Kiss the dear children, and teach them to love their father, but adore their mother.

"OUR DEAR CHILD WHO ROSE INTO HEAVEN."

TROY HOUSE, TROY, Nov. 12, 1866.

MY DARLING : I have arrived in Troy, taken my supper, and now drop you a line of remembrance before going to bed. I feel that to-day I have begun my winter's work in earnest. On leaving home this morning, I cast a lingering look behind, and exclaimed inwardly (as Eve, in the Garden, ex claimed outwardly):

"Must I leave thee, Paradise ?"

I will confess to a feeling, on coming away from home to-day, of unusual disquiet of mind,— something akin to bitterness of spirit. This was occasioned exclusively by my dread of such long ab sences from home as I am now threatened with. My loneliness, however, passed away during the day. . . .

Twilight and nightfall came upon our train as it was passing Newburg. I never see that city in the night, with its bank of light, but I think of our dear child who rose from it at midday into Heaven. I thought anew of all our moonlight sail down the river that night, carrying that precious corpse in the bow of the steamboat, while the moonbeams silvered the box in which our jewel was locked. But no sorrow entered into my thoughts at the recollection. It is thus that "Time," as the proverb says, "is the great consoler." At this distance from that grave no suggestion of Mattie's death comes to my mind with pain : on the contrary, every backward look upon her birth, her sickness, her death, her perpetual weekly tribute of fresh flowers from our hands,—all these thoughts are full of a strange and sweet delight to my mind. . . .

Good night, my darling ! Kiss the children for their father's sake,

THEODORE.

"I WISH YOU WERE HERE."

BURLINGTON, Nov. 13, 1866—10 p. m.

MY DARLING : . . . The weather is golden—perfect—indescribable. The Green Mountains and Lake Champlain are among God's best works. The moon, that pursued me up the Hudson, tar ries with me in my chamber to-night. But I wish you were here, instead of Diana and her chilliness.

THEODORE.

IDEAL OF A WIFE.

ALTOONA, PA., Monday night, November 26, 1866.

MY DARLING : After riding all day—reading, thinking, napping, and catching cold—I have brought up in this well-remembered place about bed-time. Here, two years ago, I was cast away by the floods. . . . I am glad you came with me to the cars. It made me more cheerful than if I had left you in the tearful mood in which you and Florence stood in the parlor this morning. *Your* tears compelled me to be somewhat reserved, lest *I* should have tears to match.

Your parting question, whether or not your love totally and thoroughly satisfied me, would have been answered by a very demonstrative hug round the neck, were it not that spectators were looking into the carriage, and the *Herald* might have contained, the next day, a report of the scene.

I do not think it possible for a human being to love another more heartily and more sublimely than *you* love *me*. And I believe that my love, in return, is as much as it is possible for a man to bear toward a woman.

Whether a wife loves more than a husband, or a husband more than a wife, I am unable to say. I know *one* thing, however, and that is : I would not exchange my wife for any other in the world. If I were to-day on unmoored ship, I would anchor in the self-same harbor of peace which your own true love has made for me.

You still chide yourself for a fancied failure in filling your husband's ideal of a wife. No—you have *created* my ideal of a wife, and (like God's mercy) are ," better than I could ask or think." · .

You know that, though I am given to enthusiasm, and therefore to the intense expression of warm affection, nevertheless I never speak flatteries, and not often praise. But, now that I am face to face with a three months' absence from home, your own love, example, character, and rebuke of my imper fectness by your true moral nobility, are the chief inspiration of my life and labor. So good-night.

Ever yours,   THEODORE.

A HISTORY OF THE GREAT SCANDAL.

A MOMENTARY ILLUSION.

PITTSBURG, PA., Tuesday, Nov. 27, 1866.

MY ABSENT DARLING: I have safely reached the city of my first Western appointment. At this moment, of all the moments of the day, I wish you were here. It is the twilight hour; the room is cosy and cheerful; the soft coal fire is bright ; the rocking-chair is empty; and everything invites you to step into this snug and pretty chamber. I am driven nowadays to live much in the imagination. I actually succeed sometimes, particularly while half-dozing in the cars, in putting myself back into my own house and home. But the momentary illusion quickly breaks into the reality of my loneliness and separation. Last evening, some envious and churlish breath of cold air caught hold of my throat, and to-day I have had a homœopathic physician. . . . I am now waiting for my Committee, who will be here in a few moments. Wherefore, my beloved, good-by. Ever thine.

THEODORE.

"A MOST VILLAINOUS DINNER."

YOUNGSTOWN, O., Wednesday afternoon, Nov. 28.

MY DEAR PET : I have just repeated one of the delights of my boyhood : I have taken a sail in a canal boat. Eight miles of the distance between Pittsburg and this place must be performed in the old-fashioned way of mules and a rope. It seemed like the middle ages renewed, as I crossed my legs on the Captain's binnacle this morning, surveyed the country, forgot progress, and remembered the past. Safely brought to Youngstown, I am quartered in the most wretched of hotels, and have just eaten a most villainous dinner. Congratulate yourself that you are not here to-day. If you couldn't eat anything at the Continental, what would you do here ? My meeting is to be held in the Methodist Church, and, as the skies are now raining cats and dogs, I presume my audience will be overwhelming. But, last night, at Pittsburg, the Academy of Music was a complete jam. Notwithstanding my cold (which is better to-day), I did my work completely. Love to all.

THEODORE.

"IN THE MIDST OF GREAT LABORS."

AKRON, O., Saturday, Midnight, December 1, 1866.

MY DEAR WIFE : I am in the midst of great labors. I feel that I am summoned, this winter, to a greater task than I have ever before attempted. My audiences are very large,—larger than I had dared to hope. My reception by the people is very kind,—far beyond my desert. Every day my work appears more and more serious. I feel a solemn sense that I am pursuing my true vocation. I am conscious of speaking with a genuine earnestness, night after night. My bodily health stands well thus far, though my voice is not at its best.

But I feel the lack of a wife's companionship to such a degree that I write this letter on purpose to speak of it. If you could have read to me this afternoon, I could have got asleep. A half-hour's sleep would have had a golden value. I don't sleep at night as well I ought. I speak of it this early because I may yet find it necessary to ask you to meet me in the West. I cannot abandon my winter's work, unless I actually break down under it. Neither ought I to go forward with it, except with all the helps which can be offered. Of these you are the chief.

Now, I am not saying that you must come, or that I yet absolutely *need* you to come ; I am only saying that it may be necessary for you to come by-and-by. I can tell better after another week or a fortnight.

Meanwhile, this note is a fulfilment of the promise which I made when I told you that I would write daily of my secret thoughts. And the predominant thought of all these is, whether or not I shall prove adequate to the great task, and the great opportunity, and the great reward of this winter's promised plans. The moment I am through with my lectures, I crave that kind of quiet, which comes better from your companionship than from any other source in the world. On the other hand, the personal fatigues of travel are greater than I would willingly see you subject to for my sake,—particularly since I must travel daily, and sometimes by night. There is a serious question whether you could stand this trial of your bodily strength.

I feel the great importance of making no failure this winter. And the only probable failure will be a failure of health. If this disaster should arise, it will arise chiefly through the unsoothed and uncomforted reaction which follows speaking, and which sometimes follow it so as to prevent sleep.

I have made one strong determination, and that is : that I will not force Nature by any stimulants nor sedatives—neither wine to excite, nor ale to allay, my blood. I am taking conscientious care of my body and soul. And since I have been on this tour, I have had some of the sweetest moments of my life. But they need a sharer. Let us both think of it first, and decide afterwards. Good night.

THEODORE.

A HISTORY OF THE GREAT SCANDAL.

I TAKE NO PATTERN AFTER GREAT MEN.

SUNDAY NIGHT, AKRON, O., Dec. 2.

MY DARLING: I have just been moved to write a long letter to Mrs. B——w about May. It is chiefly about having a purpose in life, and how to carry it out. Of late I have been thinking much of my own life.

You know that I don't attach as much importance as many do to certain churchly ideas of the Christian life. It seems to me that the truest method, and the surest, of developing a Christian character. is never to swerve from one's own inward idea of right, whether or not this ideal be in conformity with the prevailing conventional notions of good men, or of the best of men.

I have been looking back upon my ten years of public life, and judging of its motives. Looking back thus, I can see that I have always been earnest and straightforward, but always too much in the interest of myself, and too little willing to be counted as nothing in comparison with the work to which I have been set as an instrument.

Lately I have been endeavoring to ascertain what are my earthly ambitions; to struggle with them and conquer them. I have no ambition to be rich—I never had; none to be in political office; none for social or fashionable preëminence; none, that I can detect, for oratorical distinction; and not a great deal for a literary reputation. My public notoriety occasionally flushes me with pleasure. But, on the whole, I believe I can truthfully say that I have, in great measure, put aside the idols which I used to worship.

I once believed, judging by my personal experience, that public life, particularly such a life as that of a young man prematurely famous—is bad for the character and crippling to the soul. I used to feel this at times in keen self-reproaches.

But, when one has at first tasted the sweets of reputation, and at last of their insipidity, I think he gets a more sober, philosophic, and just view of what is valuable, and what is valueless, in life, than in almost any other way.

As a consequence, many of the men of great fame whom I intimately know make no such ruling impression on my mind as many of my private friends do.

But, if I had no reputation myself, I should still be dazzled by theirs, as I was once dazzled years ago. For instance, I like Mr. Beecher in many respects as well as I ever did. But he has ceased to be my soul's prop—ceased to inspire me to my best life. I believe he is not as morally great as he once was. I do not now refer at all to his political views. His political views have made no change in my feelings toward him as a friend. But there was an older virtue which has since gone out of him—an influence which used to brighten my life when I came under its ray; an influence, however, which became gradually quenched like a vanishing sunbeam.

Henceforth I take no patterns after public men—great men—famous men. They are not so good as my wife and children. Half an hour's talk with Mrs. —— makes me a better man than a half dozen sermons could do. I have had a sweet Sabbath day—one that has baptized my soul.

I spoke to 1,000 children this afternoon, and I have been in a glow ever since. This will account for the fact that I have written two such sermons in letters. But now I end. Good night. Forever yours,

THEODORE.

"ANY MAN IS A FOOL TO BE JEALOUS."

LAPORTE, IND., December 6, 1866.

MY DARLING: I have ridden all day long, and am just arrived, at dark, about an hour before my lecture. I am so excited in mind by a sense of my being imprisoned away from home, and barred out by impassable walls, hindered from seeing you by cruel obstacles, that I can do nothing at this moment but make an outburst of my feelings.

I ought now to be composing myself for my task, but I feel more like taking flight eastward in the next train.

All day long I have been reading Griffith Gaunt. Go to the bookstore, buy a copy, and read it,—that is, if you would like to be doing the same thing with myself. I am not yet far enough in the story to know the moral meaning, but it has excited me considerably. It turns on jealousy? I am not jealous, nor do I know the feeling. I think any man is a fool to be jealous. If he is jealous *without* cause, he is foolish; if *with* cause, more foolish.

But I am somewhat disturbed, and have been for a long while past, at the diminishing faith which I entertain for human nature. Human characters do not seem so lovely to me as they once did. Perhaps this view is temporary,—the result of a passing shadow. Or rather, perhaps, it is because I do not entertain so good an opinion of my own character—its moral strength and unbending rectitude—as I once supposed I could justly entertain.

During my travels I have had profound reflections on my life. I am a weak man, supposed to be strong; a selfish man, supposed to be the world's lover and helper; an earthly-minded man, supposed to be more Christian than my fellows. I cannot endure the mockery,—it breeds agony in me.

At this moment I am completely wretched, yet expecting in ten minutes to step forth to a public welcome! The outside life is one thing; the inside, another. I dare not show the inside to the world. And yet I must show it perpetually to God.

I am endeavoring to live a manly life,—not what the over-generous world shall so esteem, but what, in my inmost conscience, I shall know to be such. I have had many wrestlings of my soul with Heaven of late. I feel myself scarred, spotted, miserable and unworthy. From this feeling during the day, I have taken refuge in my lecture at night,—sometimes turning it almost into a sermon. I have come to feel exactly as the Prodigal felt. An inward revelation of a man's self to himself is an awful thing. It lifts one's face to the Eternal Word. Henceforth my prayer is, that God may keep me nearer to Himself. My life is so unprofitable that I sometimes dare not turn round and look upon it.

You cannot guess for what one thing I most yearn to see you. It is to kneel by your side at our familiar evening prayer. My prayers of late have seemed all spiritless without you. I am never so true a man as in my prayers,—when I have prayed with my arm around your neck. It seems to me now that I cannot live this winter without at least seeing you once or twice,—if for no other moments than those first those greatest of all moments.

I see, with agony in the retrospect, how my life has been marred by social influences coming from your mother,—how they disastrously have affected us both. If you should ever appear to me anything less than the ideal woman, the Christian saint, that I know you to be, I shall not care to live a day longer.

I cannot write further. I must stop and go to my audience. It is dreadful to be so full of feeling as I am at this moment. God bless you!

THEODORE.

"YOU ARE MY WHOLE WORLD."

LAPORTE, Ind., Dec. 7, 1866.

MY DARLING: . . . At every place where I stop, I get seven or eight letters,—for instance, last evening I found six awaiting my arrival. But, during all my absence, I have seen only one, solitary, precious, and prized piece of your handwriting.

Give my love to the chicks, kissing them each in the order, and pulling their ears gently for their papa's sake. You are my whole world. Ever and forever thine.

THEODORE.

"HOW CLEARLY YOU HAVE OUTSTRIPPED ME."

AURORA, ILL., Dec. 7, 1866.

MY DELICIOUS DARLING: It is a comfort to get out of the cars, and to sit down to pen and ink, and send you my love.

. . . A good landlord and a contented hostler make a good inn.

. . . The chief burden of my reflections has been, How shall I henceforth keep myself nobler in spirit, more patient under crosses, more heroic to attain true manhood, more consonant with God's will? My life seems to have been thus far a folly. I am ashamed of it. I have been winning what the world prizes,—honor, reputation, influence,—but all these, to the possessor, are like the golden apple of the fable; they fall to ashes in his grasp.

Seated by the car-window, gazing on the prairies, thinking of God's blessing in allowing my selfish heart to beat against your unselfish one,—a wife of whom I am unworthy,—I see how clearly you have outstripped me in what, after all, constitutes true Christian character, true nobility, and the true object of human life.

A thousand miles are at this moment between us, but you seem to be near me and around me, like a guardian angel. O my sweet wife! if sometimes I am undemonstrative, and carry my love unexpressed, yet at other times it glows and burns within me like a holy fire!

I see in myself so many points of weakness wherever you stand against me as my prop, that I am convinced, in my reflective moods, that I owe my good name and fame in the world more to your influence on my character than to my inherent character itself.

You charged me, when I came away, to write my secretest thoughts, and not to chronicle external events. I love the people among whom I am here thrown. These Westerners are a noble race. They grip my hand with a splendid welcome. But, after all, in all their thrift, their activity, their prosperity, there is something in nearly every man whom I meet that savors too much of this world. I see in you, and in a few women, more greatness, such as Christ would have called great, than in all the motley, rushing company of brave and hardy men whom I encounter day by day.

And I, too, am no better than they. But you, and Mrs. ——, and the Saints, are far ahead of us all in the pilgrimage toward Zion.

I have thoroughly tested the vanity of all that part of this life which most people think best worth the living. Henceforth I wish to join you, and the company of the good, the pure, the prayerful, the self-denying, the Christ-loving.

Indeed, my sweet pet, the other world seems not far off even when this world seems near. Let us be wedded anew,—with love inseparable and everlasting.

THEODORE.

"GRIFFITH GAUNT" AND "FELIX HOLT."

ON THE CARS, NORTHERN INDIANA, Dec. 7, 1866.

MY DARLING : This rattling train shakes my pencil, but I must endeavor to write to say that I have just finished "Griffith Gaunt."

It is a powerful and interesting story,—well constructed, though not remarkably well written. I don't care particularly whether you read it or not. It has not baptized and anointed me like our mutual reading of "Felix Holt." Do you not often recall that sweet evening in Twelfth street, when, late at night, we finished that heroic story ?

I can see you at this moment lying propped on the sofa, your red shawl around your shoulders, and your water-proof cloak over your feet. That night, and the day that followed it, filled me as full of human happiness as my heart could hold.

"Griffith Gaunt" ends in a far sweeter and more agreeable manner than one expects when he is in the midst of its pages. But I have never met a character in any romance equal to one which, if I were a romancist, I could draw from a certain woman I know.

The novels turn too much on love as a passion, as a jealousy, as a madness, as an intense adoration for the time being ; and it is only here and there that one sees in a novel the true and perfect love of a true and perfect woman,—the love that dwells in the soul rather than in the heart.

Men and women who have the mere natural *instinct* for loving, love with the heart ; but they who have a true *genius* for loving, love with their soul.

The noblest part of love is honor, fidelity, constancy, self-abnegation,—not the clasp of the hand, nor the kiss of the lips, nor the estasy of fondness. Sometimes that which more delights the heart most cheats the soul. It is for this reason that lovers ought sometimes to be separated.

Now to bear each other in memory, in daily and hourly pictures of the fancy, in constant mutual communings of soul without contact of the flesh, in perpetual nearness notwithstanding miles of distance, in an abiding reverence, unfeigned, lofty, and ennobling,—this is the great prerogative of true love.

No man loves a woman as a woman loves a man, until he has attained to such an experience as this of the union of two souls by their noblest possible interchange. But, in some lives this comes not at all ; and, in the best lives, it comes only at the crowning moments. O that we were heroic enough to seek always to live our best possible life ! I am trying more than ever.

God help us both. Thine immortally.

THEODORE.

"THE SWEETEST FAMILY."

PRINCETON, Ill., Dec. 8, 1866.

MY SWEET PET : . . At this distance from home, I realize how much of my happiness consists in the daily sight of your dear black eyes. If ever a man had love, reverence and pride for his wife, I am he. You now seem the one bright spot on the Atlantic coast. I picture you at this moment as sitting in the sunshine of our library,—perhaps at the writing desk, perhaps at the Bombay table.

I hope that the sun is as golden over Brooklyn to-day as here.

The children of course are with you. Florence is reading a book ; Alice is cutting a paper doll , and Cad is stealing the scissors from his mamma's work-basket.

Oh, if I could enter upon your little group unaware at this moment ! God bless you all ! I have the sweetest family that ever Heaven gave to an unworthy man.

I know not what agonies of separation are in store for us through the stroke of death. I know, however, that if I were now to unseal the fountain of my feelings, I could make *my* heart ache in a moment at the thousand miles that part us to-day. Oh, little flock, unto one and all be grace, mercy, and peace ! Thine forever,

THEODORE.

"THE FULL-BLOWN ROSE OF WOMANKIND."

ILLINOIS, December 11, 1866.

MY SWEET WIFE : I am in Galesburg, where I have had a long and quiet afternoon, all to myself. I spent it in walking about town, dodging the committee, evading callers, looking at the public buildings, and enjoying one of the most perfect of winter days. I then returned to my room, took a nap, dreamed that I was at home, and have just now lighted my lamp to write my daily letter to the full-blown rose of womankind.

"THESE BEECHERS."

GALESBURG, Ill., Wednesday Morning, December 12, 1866.

MY DARLING : . . . I was up till midnight after my lecture last evening, talking with Edward Beecher, mainly about his backsliding Brooklyn brother. Dr. Beecher impresses me as a man thoroughly true, sincere, simple-hearted, and morally noble. He said that the brothers and sisters never wrote to one another, or seldom, and that he did not know whether any one or all of them agreed with Henry or with himself. I trust that my own children, if they live to grow up, will be more necessary to each other's happiness than these Beechers appear to be. . . .

I occasionally take out your two letters (which are all that I have thus far received), and read them over two or three times. During the remainder of my tour you must oblige me with a line at every station,—something to meet me there,—even if only a single page, with your name and love signed thereto.

I am as dependent upon your love and sympathy as the children are. This you will not believe, but it is true. More and more you grow into the picture of the perfect wife. "There is none upon earth that I desire beside thee." To think of you as tripping up and down stairs, putting the chicks to bed, sitting at the tea-tray, or anywhere and everywhere gliding about the house—this is one of my meditative employments and spiritual delights. . . . Ever yours,

THEODORE.

"HOW I LONG TO SEE YOU."

QUINCY, Illinois, December 12, 1866.

MY DARLING OF DARLINGS : I have just written two letters to the little girls, and have only a minute left for adding a kiss for their mother. Oh, how I long to see you ! I yearn, and long, and pine to be at home. I never knew the strength of my home-attachments till this winter. I never comprehended how thoroughly we are a part of each other, till this separation. I bleed like a grape-vine broken off. But I cannot say that I am not cheerful. My work seems important. and my winter (if I am spared through it) will be the most useful one of all my life. I am lecturing in dead earnest. I have a message to deliver. I could not endure to speak night after night on any merely literary or entertaining theme. I believe I love my country purely and passionately, and seek her honor and integrity. I must work while yet the strength and life last. I have always had a sense that neither would last for many years.

Ever yours,

THEODORE.

A FEELING OF ENVY.

ST. JOSEPH, Mo., December 14, 1866.

MY DARLING : . . . I have just arrived here, in company with Major-General C——. He commands at Fort Riley, a post about one hundred and fifty miles farther west. I look upon him with envy, because he is hastening home to a lovely wife, while I am daily speeding away from one still lovelier.

Yours faithfully,

THEODORE.

"DEAR, HISTORIC, NOBLE KANSAS."

ELDRIDGE HOUSE, LAWRENCE, Kan., }
SUNDAY AFTERNOON, Dec. 16, 1866. }

MY DARLING: I am in dear, historic, noble Kansas—the State that was consecrated to Liberty amid sacrifices, sufferings, tears, and blood—the State which, to-day, is the Massachusetts of the West.

Leaving St. Joseph, Mo., on Saturday morning, about two hours after midnight, I came in sight of the bluffs of Fort Leavenworth in the early gray of the dawn. While the steamer was plowing her toilsome way through the ice of the Missouri, I paced the deck alone, musing on the strange and illustrious early history of the young State, whose soil was the battle-ground of the first struggles in the war for American Liberty. There was something bewitching in the early hour; the day was dim; a storm of hail and snow was falling; the scene was solemn, still, and grave; my heart was touched at the thought that I was passing through a tempest into Kansas as Kansas had passed through a tempest into Freedom. I have never felt in all my life a more passionate, delightful, and consecrating love for my country, than swelled within me in that stormy dawn. But I felt that other men had been heroic, and I tame; that other men had suffered for their country, I never; that other men had *fought* for Liberty, and I had only *spoken* for it. I felt that I had henceforth no right to squander my years in selfish pursuits, and resolved to live for my country's sake in the future. It is so easy to slip down from a high, pure, unselfish life into the commonplace greed of ordinary daily experience, that I find myself in need of special scenes and associations to renew to me my oft-failing purpose of living for the good, not for myself, but for my fellow man. . . .

After the meeting I walked with the Presbyterian minister to a high hill, on which the University stands, and looked upon a prospect equal in extent and beauty to the scene that one beholds from Eagle Rock, at Orange.

From the walk I returned to write this letter to the one dear woman who is now never a moment out of my thoughts; O my darling! I believe I am in some respects become a different and better man by reason of my Western experience. I have had many communings with God; many yearnings for a purer life; many desires for others, and fewer for myself; many resolutions that I would be true to Liberty, Justice, and my country; many dear and tender memories of my wife and little ones. I have been greatly praised by good and noble men out here; but I seek to consider every flattering word unsaid and undeserved. I do not wish to be caught in the net of vanity and self-conceit. I wish henceforth to chasten my thoughts, ennoble my purposes, sacrifice my selfish ambitions, and live as "under the great Task-master's eye." I have several times suddenly felt, during my absence from home, that I have been earnestly and devoutly prayed for by your dear self. I know your love; I trust it; I live in it; yet I do not deserve it; but I cannot be happy without it. You have my whole heart. I see you as the noblest of women. May heaven bless you daily, since you are a blessing from heaven to your faithful lover and husband,

THEODORE TILTON.

"SQUANDERING ONE'S SELF IN FORTUNE-SEEKING."

DEC. 17, 1866.

MY SWEET PET: . . . My letters have just arrived from the office. To my great joy, they contain two from yourself—the one which you directed to Laporte, and the one which you directed to Quincy. Nothwithstanding they are nearly three weeks old, the are welcome and precious. The letters which you directed to Akron will be forwarded to me at Springfield, Ill. Until to-day's mail I had received from you, in all, only two letters, though I must have written to you during that time not less than fifteen.

I perceive that your letters are mostly written at midnight. Please do not feel burdened to write at unseemly and wearisome hours. No duty is laid upon you to write every day—certainly not to write every night. Of course you know how greedily I devour your letters, reading them over and over again; but I remember that, when I returned from the West two years ago, I found you so thin and reduced that at first I was frightened. Don't sit up late at night. Keep yourself fresh and young.

. . . The difference between Kansas and Missouri—even to one day's observation—is almost incredible. Freedom, justice, New England habits,—Sunday-schools, good women,—these I saw in Lawrence as signally as one sees them in Massachusetts. But this Missouri City, through which I took a carriage-ride to-day, seems to be given up to money-getting. I don't believe in squandering one's life in fortune-seeking. I am glad that I have not dedicated my life to merchandise, or numbered myself with those who "buy, sell, and get gain." I am a poor man to-day, and am glad of it. If I had spent the time, and had chosen the means, to get rich, I would have been a still more worthless fellow than the scapegrace who now signs himself your affectionate husband,

THEODORE TILTON.

A VISION OF HOME.

NORTHWEST MISSOURI, }
IN THE CARS, Dec. 18, 1866. }

MY BELOVED PET: I have now four letters of yours in my pocket. They make me rich. I often take them out and read little choice sentences of love over and over again.

I have been thinking of the difference between separation by distance and separation by death. It seems now as if I could not endure to pass a day without writing to you; it would be a violence to my feelings. Even now, when this old, shaking, and jolting rail-car almost makes it impossible for me to write, I nevertheless cannot help writing. I believe that, if you were not on the earth, but in Heaven, I could not help writing you a letter every day. My feelings overflow, and if I do not express them, I suffer pain.

Mrs. ——'s letter, received yesterday, gave me a little glimpse of your perfect love for your husband. She said that you showed her one of my letters while sitting with her in church, and that she never knew any woman to lavish so much love upon a man as you upon me. That was the sweetest word in all her letter. I thank you for your profession of affection. Perhaps I ought not to speak of changes in myself, as not being the best judge in my own case; and I sincerely believe that your devotion, fidelity, and lavishment of love, are making me a better man. In one of my letters I mentioned that sometimes I felt as if you were praying for me at that moment. I have had the same impression many times since. Against such a guardian influence I dare not do or think wrong. You are a wall about me day and night. I have never lived so victorious a life, in my soul, as during these lonely winter-days. If selfish thoughts come up, I chide them down. If the spirit of this world seizes my blood, I remember that the only greatness is in moral strength, in self-denial, in the patient performance of duty, in a steadfast forelooking to the Eternal Life.

The more I think of the whole subject of religion, of theology, of the church, of doctrines, of creeds, I am inclined to undervalue, or rather see the little value, of everything but the Christian character.

All my life long I have had a daily familiarity with religious creeds, exercises, and worship; and still, after all, I am yet to lay a first foundation of a true Christian character. I see so much in my travels that goes to show how men content themselves with low lives instead of high, and vulgar thoughts instead of pure, with selfish greed instead of generous self-sacrifice, that hereafter I mean to take pattern, not after men, but after the Great Teacher. The words that keep ringing in my ears are, "Be ye therefore perfect, as your Father in heaven is perfect." Our lives are to be not merely good, but the best; our thoughts not merely high, but the highest; our purposes not only noble, but the noblest.

Now, my darling, I have found out a way of visiting home without your knowing it. I have bought a little Scotch cap, which I carry in my pocket except while I ride in the cars. Once on my head, it feels like a gentle hand laid against my forehead. As soon as I get weary in my ride, I draw the cap over my eyes, shut out the day-light, step across the Mississippi, the prairies, the Alleghanies, and the East River, back to Brooklyn. I glide my night-key, without noise, into my own door, and step into the hall on tip-toe. First of all I sit a moment in the great arm-chair, and look around at the pictures, the statuette, and the dome. Then I creep softly into the parlor, and sit on the red lounge. Nobody is at the piano or organ. Where can the folks be? I see a light in the library. It is midnight. You are sitting at your desk writing a letter to me, not dreaming that I am at that very moment looking over your shoulder. But, like one in a dream, if I put out my hand to touch you, I cannot do it. There you sit. I can only see you, love you, and bless you. I cannot make known my presence. I suppose this is the experience of the disembodied dead who has revisit the living. Meanwhile, the living, unaware of the dead, cry:

Oh for the touch of a vanished hand,
And the sound of a voice that is still.

I leave you at your desk, and glide up-stairs. The two little girls are fast asleep in one bed. I peep into my own chamber, and see a bed and pillow uncrushed by any sleeper. The pictures on the walls give me solace and welcome. I open the door of the dark room, and remember its delights of naps, and nestlings, and prayers. I take a glimpse of Cad and Libbie. I go into the third story, to see if you have any company in the guest chamber. No, nobody but the pictured soldier who has returned to find his wife dead. Better he had fallen in the wars. I say to myself, "Am I a ghost or not? Am I alive or dead?" I come down-stairs again, take another look at the dear writer at her desk, and then suddenly rush out of the house, hastening back, over hill and valley, river and lake, to get to my appointment two thousand miles from home, where I wait wistfully until the letter which I saw you writing shall be delivered to my hand.

I told you that I have now four of your letters. I saw you write them all! O my sweet sister, wife, and angel—all in one—love me for evermore. Yours devoutly,

THEODORE.

JOIN ME IN CHICAGO.

JEFFERSON CITY, Mo., December 18, 1866.

MY DARLING: While riding in the rickety cars this morning, I wrote you a letter in lead-pencil, but had no opportunity to mail it till arriving here, so I shall inclose it in the same envelope with this.

Jefferson City is the capital of Missouri—a town beautifully situated. The state-house stands on a bluff overlooking the Missouri River, commanding a spectacle as grand as one sees in looking from Newburg down the Hudson toward the gate of the Highlands. It is when I see such sights as I have seen this afternoon, and such as I now see out of my window this moonlight evening, that I feel like a "miser" truly "miserable," to be enjoying them all alone. The hills are thickly clad with snow; the broad river is half covered with ice; the sky is the perfection of clearness; and the moon is approaching her full.

"How is it possible," I say to myself, "that I did not bring her with me on this journey?" Certainly the journey has its fatigues, but certainly also it has its delights. . . .

I am more and more of the opinion that I shall ask you to join me in Chicago in January, and perform the easier part of my tour in company with your otherwise lonesome but affectionate husband,

THEODORE.

"DELIGHTFUL WORDS FROM HOME."

THE ILLINOIS PRAIRIE, December 20, 1866.

MY SWEET WIFE: I told you yesterday, that so many delightful words from home as were spoken to me by my handful of letters would throw me into my best vein last evening. Accordingly I enjoyed my lecture last evening as well as I ever enjoyed making a public speech in my life. The hall was as elegant and nearly as large, as Music Hall, Boston, or old Tripler Hall, New York. Its chandeliers, its red-cushioned chairs, its grand platform, and its noble audience (notwithstanding the storm) made the scene brilliant and inspiring. The assemblage was composed of both Radicals and Rebels,

But I have no difficulty with the Rebels,—They all like frank, square-cutt, sharp-edged speech. I find that they respect me more for being a Radical than they would if I were a conservative. . . .

Going afterwards to my room, I was so full of life and spirits that I sat down immediately and wrote a little story for Florence. . . . Oh, if I could have a letter from you at every place waiting on my arrival ! . . .

I have taken no pains to see the newspapers,—what they say of me ; and half that I see, I don't stop to read. But I think you will be amused at the inclosed reference to yourself. No, I've lost the paper after all. But it had an article from the Cincinnati *Gazette* describing me as an unmarried man, and a reply by the Cincinnati *Commercial*, mentioning the "olive plants around Mr. Tilton's table."

To you, the mother-stalk of these plants, and to the tender plants themselves, I send my love. As ever.

THEODORE.

AT LINCOLN'S GRAVE.

SPRINGFIELD, Ill., Dec. 20, 1866.

MY SWEET VIOLET:—I visited this afternoon the grave of Abraham Lincoln. Two oak trees stand over it, dropping their crisp and dead leaves on the grass. I send you one of the leaves in the letter, and I shall send one to May. As I walk around the grave, or the vault,—for it is not a hillock, but a structure of masonry,—I brought up the picture of the good man kissing our dear Florence. If she should be spared to old age, she will have that incident as a story to tell to her grandchildren. I never thought that Abraham Lincoln was one of the great men of the world, but I had always a tender feeling towards him, akin to personal affection. The great fault of our American statesmen and public leaders is a lack of the moral courage which, of all endowments, makes men most truly great. More and more I believe in absolute fidelity to Liberty, Justice and Equality. Every public man who compromises these great principles retards the progress of his country. Mr. Lincoln's fame rests on his Proclamation,—a measure to which he was driven somewhat against his will. He was willing to save Slavery if he could thereby save the Union. This willingness to compromise with wrong shows a mind not great in the highest sense. But he was a noble, grand, and illustrious man, after all. His faults were somewhat like George Washington's, and were such as

Leaned to Virtue's side.

I was tenderly affected by my visit to his resting-place, and wished that you were with me to share my thoughts and feelings. How true it is, as Burke says, that death canonizes a great character ! The world magnifies its favorite names into colossal fame. Abraham Lincoln's name and fame will probably overtop the records of all other men of the nineteenth century. The Romans gave a crown of oak-leaves to a true hero. The two oak trees under which I stood to-day, seem to know, by their gifts, that a true hero lies in their shade at rest beneath. Ever yours,

THEODORE.

A HOPE OF "MARRYING AGAIN."

ALTON, Ill., Dec. 21, 1866.

MY DARLING : I am growing very familiar with the Mississippi River. It has become a companion and friend. Out of the window of my hotel I look upon it to-day,—broad, ice-covered, ridged with low banks, and gleaming in the sun. This has been a spring-like day. One of my neighbors, an old lady in the opposite house, has opened her window to give a breath of the sunshiny air to her household plants. The ice is melting, and running like a brook in the streets. A pleasure-boat like mine (when I had one) is sailing in the open channel of the river between the cakes of ice. But O the mud in the thoroughfares ! You never saw such mud in your life, at home. Small dogs get drowned in it. I believe that the flatboats sometimes float in it. This city has visibly grown and intensified since I spoke here two years ago. All the large Western cities are wonderfully wide-awake, active, busy, and hurried. New York is leisurely compared with Chicago. And Brooklyn ? Such a city does not exist in the West.

I have walked round the town a good deal, bought two little picture-cards for the children, sat for my photograph, grumbled a little at receiving no letter from home, but finally have shoved my table near enough to the window to look out upon the glorious river, in the hope that my peace shall be like unto it, according to the promise. The warm half-summer air has created in me a kind of lassitude, and I feel in a languishing mood, rather homesick, and a little melancholy. And yet a gentleman was in my room a few moments ago, who asked me if I do not enjoy hugely my lecturing engagements and the consequent sight-seeing. Truly "Every heart knoweth its own bitterness, and a stranger intermeddleth not with its joy."

Feeling unusually weary to-day, I brought up your accidental mention that you had lately fainted. My darling, I have always noticed that, when I have been absent from home for a considerable period, I return to find you degenerated in health. Be less disturbed in your mind. It is your spirit that wearies your flesh. You have a great soul in a small frame. Sitting up late is not to be pardoned by your too-indulgent husband. But when you *are* weak and weary, I hope that, as unto St. Bernard in his exhaustion, many more of the ministering angels will guide you daily round about.

This afternoon I crossed the presence of an angel—my own sweet angel of flesh and blood, with black eyes and pretty curls. I was lying on the sofa, trying to make-believe I was in my own house, and that you were coming up-stairs in a few minutes to read to me from the "Pilgrim's Progress." But no, you staid away. Are you not coming to Chicago? Don't say no. Get Ellen Davis to keep house for you, and come and join me. To judge from your letters, you will not be any more wearied by the travel than you are with the house and its loneliness. I do not abandon the hope of marrying you again next January. Ever your own, THEODORE TILTON.

"THE STAR OF THE EAST."

ALTON HOTEL, Illinois, December 21, 1866.

MY DOVE: . . . You see how often I am driven to the comfort of writing you letters, since I am denied the luxury of seeing you face to face. The moment my heart begins to ache, that moment I seize my pen. My love-letters have all been the pouring of oil on my own wounds. Some people have a beautiful liberty of expression through music—sitting at the keys of a piano, and translating their thoughts into "concord of sweet sounds." *My* gates of utterance are only two—speech and pen. My speech goes now to the public, my pen to you. I give thanks daily for Uncle Sam's kindness in carrying a mail-bag between myself and my lady-love. Suppose we lived in the stage-coach days, and were, as now, a thousand miles apart! It would take a letter a month to trip across the prairies from the Mississippi to Brooklyn.

To-morrow I shall dedicate myself to writing for the *Independent.* I have an army, a legion, of readers in the West. Almost every man who speaks to me says, "Well, sir, I read what you write every week." This has lately been said so often that I tremble at the responsibility of writing for so many devouring readers. I shall spend my holiday at hard work. In fact, writing has become a necessary diversion of my mind from speaking. Reading does not answer the purpose. Books are rather flat to me in my present temper of mind.

Still, I think I would be content to-morrow if the Little Lady were here to read aloud to her husband. If indeed you were here, what fine times we would have! Are you not coming? Some morning, when the sky is unusually bright, I shall know that the Star of the East is coming to the West. "Hail, holy light!" Yours ever,

THEODORE TILTON.

A DISQUISITION ON LYING.

ALTON, Ill., Dec. 22, 1866.

MY DEAR PET: . . . I sat down with the idea of writing for the *Independent.* But, apparently finding nothing in my brain worth saying to my public readers, I have switched off from the main track, and am here scribbling another of my daily nothings to the one dear creature who thinks that my chaff is always wheat. What is it that you find in my letters to excite your praises?

I am sure that, after I have written, and turn around to read them, they appear to be poor and meagre enough. Now and then I come upon some womanly, Christian, profound sentence or expression in your letters, that proves (what I knew before) that the art of writing beautiful letters does not belong to literary men and women more than to other men and women. As in a mirror one shows his face to himself, so in a letter one shows his heart to his friend. The writing may be poor, and yet the letter good. But, in a perfect sentence, which is made to fit like a glove around the modeled shape of some worthy thought, there is something in the mere expression, independent of the thought, that sometimes has a charm indescribable.

Some of the finest literature in the world is contained in wise and rich letters,—many of them never destined to be read by more than one reader. The most interesting books are biographies, mainly on account of their personality. But letters are still more personal. A letter is mutually enkindling—it puts both writer and reader in a glow of love and good-will toward the other. Letters, like prayers, ought never to admit an untrue word,—never a conventional for a direct expression,—never any of the little lies of polite usage.

For instance, I don't like a letter to end with, "I am your obedient servant." No form of expression, however customary, ought to be used which is not strictly honest. Accordingly, to a man whom I did not like, I would never say, "My Dear Sir," but simply, "Sir." The more I see of the little fibs current in society, the more I despise them. Let us teach our children to speak the truth; and, to this end, let us speak it ourselves. I have long thought that the habit of communicating to each other, as husbands and wives, as friends and friends, our secretest and deepest-hidden thoughts, without disguise and without misrepresentation, would finally breed a greater reverence for honesty and truthfulness than now prevails.

If a man willfully misstates an outward fact, it is a lie, and he sins against society. But, if he willfully deceives by representing his thoughts to be better than they are, which is usually the case with men who indulge in religious cant, and are the prayer-mongers at Friday-night meetings, then such a man equally is guilty of lying, although his sin of falsehood is not so much against society as against himself. I believe that, of all the virtues, the greatest is to speak the truth. With which moral, as Robert Browning says, "I drop my theorbo."

This is enough sermonizing for Saturday night. O, my little, black-eyed pet. I love you better than my life itself.

THEODORE.

DISSATISFIED WITH THE CHURCHES.

ALTON, Ill., December 23, 1866.

MY DARLING : I have been reading a biography of Mrs. Pomeroy, the dead wife of the Kansas Senator. She was a noble Christian woman, of an unusually rich Christian experience. The biography was prepared by her sister, Mrs. Bascom, with whom I sojourned awhile in Princeton, in this State. I was struck with a little passage as follows :

"It was," said she (lying on her death-bed, after waking from sleep), "a prophetic state. I have looked into the future. I know of things that are to be hereafter." . . .

Such experiences are not uncommon with good men and women near death. I never can read of such an experience except with a thrill. The future is not so far from us. The Kingdom of God is around us. The veil is thin which divides our eyes from the vision of Jordan. Sometimes in sleep, sometimes in wakefulness, there comes to us a glimpse " of the glory that is to be revealed." In Kirke White there is a passage about the lark soaring till the unrisen sun smites her breast. So our souls take sometimes a sudden ascent above the flesh, until the undawned light of Heaven gilds them with a fore-gleam of glory. Our customary notions of the other life are distorted, misshapen, and deformed. Our prevailing theologies have covered our eyes with stained windows.

Oh, for a direct gaze into the pure blue ! " For now we see through a glass darkly, but then face to face."

I have lately said to myself, "Let me forget all that I have been taught of sectarianism, of hide-bound theologies, of stereotyped creeds ; and let me, instead, go direct to God, and ask for His light to shine on my face as on Moses' of old.". I am dissatisfied with the churches and their teachings. They stand between our minds and the light. They mean well, but they know not what they do. I believe in God's daily revelations to the human soul. As He makes daily gift of the sun to the earth, so He makes daily disclosure of His glory to our souls. But, if we shut our eyes, either of our bodies or our souls, we cannot expect to see. I am striving to tear off, little by little,—since I cannot do it at a stroke,—some of the bandages that have hitherto bound me blind. "Mine eyes unto Thee, O God." Your best lover,

THEODORE.

"MY DEAR LOVE, PET, WIFE, AND GUARDIAN."

ROCKPORT, Ill., Dec. 26, 1866.

MY DARLING : All I have to add is my LOVE. This was quickened by two of your letters (including one from Alice) which arrived this evening,—forwarded from Alton. Alice speaks of a letter by Floy, but none such has reached me. Give your letters seven days' time ; then, perhaps, I shall not get ahead of them. Moreover, address their envelopes in very large and distinct handwriting. Please see that Mrs. —— writes. I ought to have a letter from *you* at every place I stop at, and from *her* as often as she is willing to write,—the oftener the better. Letters are my meat and drink. I re-read *all* your letters every day. My dear love, pet, wife, and guardian, you are more than half my life.

Ever yours, THEODORE.

"THE OTHER MAN."

DUBUQUE, Ia., Dec. 27, 1866.

MY DARLING : I came hither this morning, and found your letter awaiting me. Hereafter, I trust I shall receive all your letters. This makes the third time I have crossed the Mississippi, not counting the recrossings. The beautiful river this morning was nowhere to be seen. It flows silently under a bridge of solid ice. I crossed in a sleigh. The ride was more than a mile from bank to bank. The far-Western atmosphere—by which I mean Iowa, Minnesota, and Kansas—is very pure, dry, and health-ful. To-day is a perfect specimen of such atmospheric healthfulness. After breakfast I toiled up the steep bluffs, clad in my furs to keep off Jack Frost. My panting and struggling rewarded me with rosy cheeks, but I had no wife near by to kiss them. My health is excellent, but I think I am looking older than usual. Last night the villainous time-table robbed me of my rest. But I am having a long day of leisure to make up for the theft. I have been busy about three hours in getting off answers to lec-ture committees.

If I had six tongues instead of one, I could employ them all, and every night. I had a touch of homesickness this morning. It came from the sunshine that poured into my room from the lustrous southeast. The wall, the carpet, the chairs, all glowed and glittered under the touch of the goldsmith.

I wanted then a certain shining face to sit in my rocking-chair, in whose eyes I might look, and on whose lips I might hang.

I allow these, and such like moods, to fill me awhile with a delicious sadness; and then I fight them down, and go to work. I don't expect, however, to be lonesome much longer; for I am to meet you in Chicago. Now that the *other* man has gone off lecturing (as your letter mentions), you can afford to come to *me*. You ought to be enjoying what I am enjoying on this magnificent trip,—for instance, this afternoon,—a dinner party. Leave home, children, kith and kin, and cleave unto him to whom you originally promised to cleave. You promised the *other* man to cleave to *me*, and yet you leave *me all alone* and cleave to *him*.

O, frailty! thy name is woman.

If you can get anybody to pour tea for you, and to take sauce from the servants, and to receive pastoral visits, I shall expect to meet you under the roof of Robert Hatfield.

Yours eternally, THEODORE.

"MY LOVE, MY DELIGHT, MY MINISTERING SPIRIT."

MARION, GA., Dec. 28, 1866.

MY DARLING: . . . After my lecture, two letters were put into my hand. I said to myself, "If one of these is from my wife, I will read both; but, if neither is from *her*, I will not read either." The first one I looked at was your own dear handwriting, the letter giving the account of the visit by Oliver and Mary, and dated Dec. 19. I feel I am pretty sure of finding a letter from you in each place at which I stop. What do you suppose was the second letter of the two by to-night's mail? It was an invitation for me to go into a neighboring town and preach two sermons next Sunday!

I am more and more setting my heart on meeting you in Chicago. Nevertheless, you know that I will listen to reason; and, if you find insuperable obstacles, say so, and I shall be satisfied, and respect your decision. I believe that to-night is the first real instance of physical weariness which has yet befallen me in all my pilgrimage. I am going straight to bed. So adieu, my love, my delight, my ministering spirit!

THEODORE.

PRIVATE WORTH vs. PUBLIC REPUTATION.

VINTON, IA., Dec. 29, 1866.

MY DARLING: . . After lighting my lamp this evening, I arranged all the letters which I have received from my dear pet, each according to its date, and I shall read them all over again to-morrow, from beginning to end. They make a little pocket-volume which I carry with me wherever I go, and which I read whenever I grow homesick.

To-morrow afternoon I am to have another meeting of the town-children. Every Sunday, without exception, since the beginning of my pilgrimage, I have made a speech to an audience of children, and the audiences have always been crowded to overflowing. I have observed that every Western family includes children and a dog. The family with whom I dined to-day included five children and a dog. The mother of the six seemed equally proud of them all. She was rather a striking character—a woman worthy of much respect. I cannot help feeling more than an ordinary admiration for a woman who, living in narrow and mean circumstances in a new and rude country, crowding a large family (dog and all) within two small rooms, and working like a drudge day by day, nevertheless in spite of all discouragements and heart-sinkings, succeeds in bringing up her children well, and glows with a matronly pride as she looks at her brood and tells a stranger their names.

The older I grow, the less do I regard public reputation, and the more do I revere private worth. A man, like myself, who, for a little dexterity in speaking or writing, gets a reputation that outmeasures real desert, is not to be compared, in point of moral heroism, with hundreds and thousands of the brave men and women who live in log cabins and under thatched roofs. Let us henceforth be noble, unselfish, courageous, and humble. Ever yours,

THEODORE.

"THE WORST SERMON I EVER HEARD."

VINTON, IA., December 30, 1866.

MY DARLING: I have had a day filled with thoughts of my loved ones at home. The weather has been bleak and cold, with spasms of wind and touches of snow. After breakfast I muffled myself in my furs, and walked awhile along the edge of Cedar river—a winding, picturesque stream, covered with ice and fringed with trees. A company of white pigeons were dipping their beaks in the only air-hole which I could anywhere discover in the frozen river. Poor things, they were afraid of me, and flew away, perhaps to thirst all day long—for the weather is so cold that a drop of water cannot live out of doors.

I picked up a dead blue-bird this morning—a beautiful creature, which I suppose was either wounded by some hunter, or else had frozen to death. I plucked two feathers from his wings, which I inclose for the little girls. Returning from my morning walk, I warmed myself, and then went to church. What a sermon ! It was from the text, "The end of all things is at hand ; " but I thought the end of the sermon would never be at hand. I believe, on the whole, it was the worst sermon I ever heard in all my life.

In the afternoon, as usual, I had my meeting of children ; all the Sunday-schools in town participated. From this meeting I have just returned to my lonely room. After speaking I most feel my loneliness. Roused and tired, I come back to house myself within companionless walls. It is then that I crave your sweet companionship. You are as needful to me in my public as in my private life. What a delightful Sunday evening we might spend together if you were now here ! I shall stay at home, lie on my lounge, read, meditate, and love. I live a strange life ; but it has its discipline, and its benediction. Ever yours,

THEODORE.

REVIEWING HIS LIFE.

VINTON, INDIANA, December 31, 1866.

MY DARLING: This is the last night, and the last hour, of the Old Year. I have returned from my lecture and its crowd to my chamber and its solitariness. It is quite probable that you are sitting up at this late hour, meditating, and perhaps sorrowing. I have been all day working for the *Independent*, all the evening in making a long speech, all the later hours before midnight in seeing friends, and now I am alone with yourself, So I have had no time for thoughts appropriate to the season, unless I indulge them now.

I feel no disposition to make resolves, seeing how easily the best intents to live well are thwarted by one's own weakness against daily temptations. In reviewing my life, and comparing my present views, aims, and temper with former years, I believe the chief changes are these: I have now less care for reputation and applause, and more admiration for a sterling character. But I believe that I have less self-respect than in former days. I once thought myself a good, true, and upright man. But now, when I judge myself by Christ's rule of the thought as well as of the deeds—what I think as well as what I feel— I find myself a constant sinner.

Lately I have many times bowed my head like a bulrush. I have once or twice done right under strong provocation to do wrong, and I have several times done wrong under a mere gossamer of temptation. The carriage of my mind in perfect justice toward my fellow-men is a hard thing to accomplish every day. It is a white day when I even partly succeed. O New Year ! bring me the gift of a higher ideal of life, and a stouter heart to achieve it. Your passionate lover,

THEODORE.

A RESOLVE TO PERFORM A DAILY, ACT OF KINDNESS.

WATERLOO, IOWA, New Year's Night, 1867.

MY DARLING: I wish you a Happy New Year. I wonder how *you* have spent the day. *I* spent it mainly in a wagon ride of thirty miles over the prairies from Vinton to Waterloo—starting at nine in the morning and arriving at three in the afternoon. Bitter cold the day has been, and yet I enjoyed my ride as almost a luxury. There is something wonderfully invigorating in this Iowa atmosphere. Wrapped securely against the cold, one makes his journey with perpetual refreshment of soul. During all my ride I was thinking of what good resolution would be most profitable for me to make, with the least fatality of breaking it as soon as made. At last I determined that to resolve that I would be a better man would simply be vague and untangible; to resolve that I would be more unselfish, or more self-denying, or more prayerful, would be simply to repeat old good-intents which I had grown into a habit, long ago, of non-fulfilling; and accordingly I resolved that, instead of attempting to attain some improved inward state, I would chain my mind to the daily performance of some outward act which would react upon my mind and heart within. Finally I fixed my resolution at this: "Resolved, That I will henceforth make it my bounden duty to perform each day some act of kindness, however small, to some fellow-creature." I shall try *this* plan of improving my character; and I think it will work out a better result than much of my religious, and perhaps somewhat morbid, meditations, reveries, and longings. Will you join me in the resolution? Let us carry it out hand in hand.

. . . Oh, how my heart bounds at the sight of your handwriting! I never have loved you half as well as during your winter's separation. Day by day, and hour after hour, I think of you, live in you, cast my honors at your feet, invoke Heaven's blessing on your life, and place you before me as my pattern of saintship in this world. You are a darling! Your sweet letters make my blood dance with joy. I pour out my soul upon you to-night. May the New Year bring you a horn of plenty, full of benedictions, and empty them all into your lap ! You are the best, the truest, the purest, and the wifeliest of women. I kiss you good-night.

THEODORE.

LOVE RIPENS LATE.

CEDAR FALLS, Ia., Jan. 3, 1867.

MY SUPREME PET : . ، . Your letters are a well of living water, from which I drink daily, quenching my soul's thirst. I have preserved every scrap of your handwriting, together with the children's ; and the package is a little book of sacred writings. They are a Newer Testament than the New, I think, on the whole, you do me as much good as St. Paul, who hadn't a very great opinion of women! But, if he were alive now, and were acquainted with you and your loving ways, what an Epistle he could write! . . .

At this moment, in the parlor of this hotel, a bride and groom are receiving calls. The pair are youngsters,—as you and I were once. I looked at them with a smile, and said to myself, "Poor creatures! you think you are happy; you imagine that you know what love is ; but you have not yet tasted your happiness, and have not yet known your love. *Wait ten years.*" Love ripens late.

I thank God that my heart is at peace; that my wife is the best of human characters; that I crave nothing more for my wedded life henceforth than that I may grow to be more worthy of God's sweet gift of the dearest of pets to one of the least deserving of men. . . . Your own

THEODORE.

"LIFE'S MAIN PURPOSE OUGHT TO BE TO LOVE."

MT. VERNON, Ia., Jan. 3, 1867.

MY LITTLE MISTRESS : . . . Last evening, at the close of my lecture, I had a protracted interview with my boyhood friend, ——, whom I had lost sight of since that early day. He is a handsome young man, served with distinction in the army as a Lieutenant-Colonel, and is now engaged at.—— in mercantile business. But he has had an unhappy—in fact, a blighted—life, through a marriage which has ended in divorce, and in a little daughter of 9 years to remind him equally of his happiness and his misery. He told me all the particulars in a manly, straightforward way, never casting any reproach upon the divorced woman, and always alluding to her in terms which impressed me as very gentlemanly and magnanimous. Of course I allowed myself to form no final opinion of the case, since I had heard but one side. But poor —— and his history touched my heart. I sat with him till long after midnight, since which time I have been thinking of the goodness of God in preserving you and me from any such shipwreck of our hearts. After all, it is more and more apparent to my mind that the one great object of our mortal lives is to love. If we do not love, we might better never have been born. It is a very great saying, "Love is the fulfilling of the Law." Business, public labors, riches, reputation—all these are merely *incidents* in the life whose *main purpose* ought to be to love. Let us, therefore, more than ever before, love one another with kindness, forbearance, earnestness, and wisdom. Then, if we should have achieved nothing besides a perfect union of two loving hearts, we shall have wrought out for ourselves a heaven on earth, and perhaps afterwards the heaven above the earth. Yours forever,

THEODORE TILTON.

MEDITATIONS IN A GRAVEYARD.

ON THE CARS FROM INDEPENDENCE TO }
CEDAR RAPIDS, Ia., Jan. 4, 1867. }

MY DARLING : An old man is sitting in the next seat, half-dozing, talking to himself, and smiling as if he were in great merriment. He has found an invisible circle of pleasure within his own mind, and he sits in the centre of it, crowned with joy. Occasionally he lurches his head, lifts his forefinger, and gesticulates like a grandfather entertaining his pets. I would give a good deal to look in upon the inward spectacle—the imaginary picture—that is creating so much fun in his brain.

This old man has set me to thinking of the fountains of happiness. They are many, if we only knew where to find them. They are like springs in meadows; we walk near them and among them every day, but we never think of looking under the grass to discover them. I remember in Carlyle some such remark as this: that "Happiness is cheap if we only applied to the right merchant for it." The chief happiness of our lives is in little things. And, if we do not learn the art of being made happy by trifles, we shall never learn it at all.

For instance, what happiness could I find in my weary journeyings if I did not glean it here and there from little, meagre incidents—enjoyed awhile, and then forgotten? I had a very happy hour this morning. Wrapped in my furs, I wandered along the picturesque banks of a frozen stream, and found myself first in a grove of oaks, and then in a graveyard. I am fond of idling among tombs; and I shall finally be a complete idler among them forever. Sweet, sad, and solemn thoughts came into my mind. I was fed by the scene, as I am sometimes fed by plaintive music. Every grave had its history of a human life, begun and ended. *My* life, long ago begun, might perhaps be already nearly ended. I confess that the thought was not without a certain delightful, and yet, perhaps, delusive satisfaction. My hour's pilgrimage through the white marbles—too white and new in this fresh and new country to show yet a trace of moss or lichen—made death itself look fresh, new, and agreeable. The sheep ran loose and nibbled about those unfenced graves. The flocks seemed familiar and welcome companions of the dead. At some of the mounds, perhaps, they represented more innocence than the guilty clay sleeping beneath. But, after all, innocence or guilt, in most of us, depends more on the measure of our temptation than on the measure of our virtue. Many a strong man is conquered and falls, while many a weak man escapes because unattacked. The more I look into my own heart, trembling at what I there see, the more charitable I grow towards the common infirmities of human nature. How morally sublime was Christ's word to the woman: "Neither do I condemn thee."

The graveyard contributed to my soul's contentment to-day. It set me at peace with all the world. Some little children walked past, and I loved them at first sight. I saw a party of skaters cutting circles in the distance, and I rejoiced at their sport. Sombre, snow-bearing clouds came toiling up from the horizon, and I saluted them with welcome. Even the dry grass under my feet had something lovable in it. On the whole, I do not often achieve a happier morning; and yet my happiness came altogether from little things,—indeed, things so little that, except for my having here idly penciled them down to please your own heart by keeping it in communion with mine, I should hardly have held them fast in remembrance for half a day.

I still adhere to my resolution to do some act of kindness, daily, to some fellow-creature. And I find that, thus far, all such acts have been of the category of these self-same little things. But they have given me happiness in the doing. And happiness is not a little, but a great, thing. Now, the best part of happiness is love. Therefore let us continue to love one another unto the end. Thine immortally,

THEODORE.

"SEPARATION A GREAT MISTAKE."

LAFAYETTE, Ind., Jan. 15, 1867.

MY DEAR PET: . . . I am thinking, while writing these lines on my knee, toasting my feet at the grate, what a happy man I ought to be! Indeed, I think my state of mind for the last two or three days has been somewhat unmanly. Last evening and this morning I was even fretful and peevish. I have no such feeling now. God is good. He does not suffer us to be tempted beyond what we are able to bear. That is, I suppose, if we *try* to bear it. Our efforts to accomplish results in external things are always more full of endeavor than our efforts to rule our inward state. At the same time, I see that I have made a great mistake in permitting myself to be separated from you three months. This absence from home, and particularly from yourself, is telling on me visibly. It is breeding a kind of demoralization in my faculties. True, I have my secret and contemplative hours—my happy and profitable moods. But, during the greater part of all these long and toilsome days and nights, my soul is at ebb-tide. There is something in your personal influence over my habits of thought which I sadly lack during the separation. I have an inward, dull pain of unintermitting longing for home,—something, I suppose, like that which the soldiers felt in camp,—an incurable disease. I feel it in my heart this moment. Good-bye.

THEODORE.

"ECONOMY MUST NOT PINCH YOUR DAILY PURSE."

LAFAYETTE, Ind., Jan. 16, 1867.

MY DARLING: . . . Of course I wish you to economize as much as possible till I get rid of the burden of carrying a house on my back. But I do not wish your economy either to pinch your daily purse or to worry your daily peace. We have been, in many and various respects, so abundantly prospered in this life, that we ought to be willing to bear our pecuniary difficulties with cheerfulness and patience. By and by I hope to work myself clear of all incumbrances. But, meanwhile, it is better to be contented than to be rich, and nobler to endure than to complain. Until I had roofed your head and carpeted your feet, I felt discontented with my lot and fortunes. But having performed a gentleman's duty of putting my wife in a pretty house, I shall endeavor to perform a Christian's duty of "Owing no man anything," and particularly that other part which consists in, "Loving one another." Ever yours,

THEODORE.

MEETING ONE OF MRS. TILTON'S OLD FRIENDS.

VINCENNES, IND., January 18, 1867.

MY DARLING: . . . At my lecture this evening I came on one of your old friends—no other personage than —— ——. She looks much more womanly and sensible than when I used to know her in the days of her youth. Her husband, who seems a pleasant gentleman, is the Rector of an Episcopalian Church here, and is in a very good position. I think that she has, on the whole, made a good use of herself in the way of developing her character during these past fifteen years. I could see in her countenance Whittier's lines of

Care, and sorrow, and child-birth pain.

I felt greatly drawn toward her for your sake, as one of your companions in the merry days when you, too, were an unfledged bird without a gray feather in your wing.

Time is crow-footing our cheeks; I am a grayer man than when I started from home. Every lecture adds one hair more to "the crown of glory." Sometimes I am in haste to see Florence's children and Alice's wooer. Meantime, if I could see the mother of those two girls, I would begin my own wooing over again. Grace, mercy, and peace, to all under your roof. Ever yours,

THEODORE TILTON.

"MY SHOCK AT CHICAGO."

OTTAWA, ILL., January 21, 1867.

MY DARLING : I am well aware, as you intimate, that the chief charm of letters from friendship and love is not in the recital of facts and events, but in the revelation of feelings and thoughts. Nevertheless, it is a rather dangerous practice for persons to scrutinize, question, catalogue, and describe, one's feelings and thoughts. To give evidence of a warm feeling, or a tender thought, is better than to give a description of either or both.

Not a day passes over my head but I have some rare, and high, and beautiful transfiguration of yourself before my soul; by this I see an image that fills me with love, reverence, and humility. If, at that moment, I should happen to have a pen in my hand, and happen to be writing you a letter, of course any letter would glow and burn with intense feeling of the moment. But if, after the feeling has passed away, I should turn back to conjure up its faded figure, and should write of the emotion which *was* rather than of that which *is*, my letter would neither be true, valuable, nor worthy of your kiss upon its page.

I have often told you how much I prize truthfulness,—that is, the scrupulously-exact truth, without concealment and without distortion,—in all intercourse between intimate friends, and particularly between husband and wife. This truthfulness applied to such daily letter-writing as yours and mine, requires that I should be true to the state of my mind at the time when I write, and that I should not attempt to write while in one mood as if I were in another.

For instance, I mentioned in my hasty lines of this morning, that my letter was prosaic and unsentimental, adding that my fountain of poetry and sentiment had not flowed freely for a week past. This statement is unhappily too true. My mind has been barren ever since my shock at Chicago. That was a touch from a lion's paw; the wound does not easily heal. It is now ten or twelve days since that Saturday evening of the greatest disappointment of my whole life ; and, from that hour to this, I have not clothed a solitary thought of my mind in gay colors, but have the rather plucked

Every flower that sad embroidery wears.

I understand well enough that I was overcome on that occasion by physical, quite as much as by mental influences ; that my mind was wrought to an unusual exaltation at an unfortunate moment, when my body was feeble under an unusual fatigue ; and that, consequently, my brain drank my blood dry. But, as a natural consequence, I have been, ever since, more of the earth earthy, and less of the heavens, heavenly.

For the last few days, therefore, I have had less craving either for the love of woman, the love of man, or the love of God, than at any former period of my pilgrimage. Of course, I expect my feeling to return, and to return like a flood, baptizing me afresh. But, until it shall return, and run its sweet riot through my veins as heretofore, making the closing weeks of my journey as memorable in my heart's experience as were the opening, you must be content with a somewhat sombre rigmarole from a somewhat sedate correspondent.

Nevertheless, I could now write as cheerily as ever in my life, if I choose to strain a point of conscience. But I do not mean to degrade myself in my own eyes by cheating any one else, particularly my own wife, into a belief that I am filled with a feeling which I do not possess.

I am trying to ennoble my character ; I cannot, therefore, permit it at any moment to appear more noble than it is. I have had a special, hard, and long struggle with myself this very afternoon, and have not yet achieved the victory. I find it easy to be a gentleman toward the outer world, but hard to be a Christian in my inner self.

"This," as a culprit says in signing his testimony, " this is my true confession."

Yours ever,   THEODORE TILTON.

LOST LETTERS.

BATTLE CREEK, Mich., Jan. 30, 1867.

MY OTHER SELF : . . . There is something in the exchange of letters that ranks next to the greeting of palm to palm. When I receive one of your letters the sheet seems to contain more than you were writing; it is something which has been touched by your hand, which has caught a pulse of your feeling, and which represents more than the words can possibly say. I have always felt a little guilty after throwing away even an envelope on which you had written my name. Think, therefore, what a bankruptcy I suffered when I lost the packet of all your daily letters for six weeks! I lost them from my too great care; for I carried them in my pocket, which I could always reach, and would not trust them to my valise, which was not always under my eye. I had filed them carefully, put each in its order of date, interleaved them with the few letters which the children wrote, and kept the roll as sacred archives. I meant, on my return home, to put them in an iron safe, and bequeathe them to the children, to show to Florence's sons and daughters how much their grandfather and grandmother loved one another in the olden time. But those delightful manuscripts belong now to the lost literature of the world. Ever yours, THEODORE.

A "SUPREME MOMENT."

ANN ARBOR, Mich., Feb. 1, 1867.

O LOVING AND BELOVED: I have been pacing up and down the hall of a stone mansion during the twilight, indulging in high, solemn, and devout thoughts. The dimness of the closing day was made doubly dark by the gloomy carpet, the black-walnut stairways, and the dusky-papered halls. Strains of sad music came floating back to my remembrance. Old scenes repainted themselves to my mind's eye. I looked backward and looked forward.

John Foster, wandering up and down the aisles of his chapel at Chichester, by moonlight, was not more of a dreamer than I allowed myself to be during this one, delicious, lonely, and heart-aching hour. It was a sad and sweet season. Almost every day brings me at least one "supreme moment." To-day, twilight was to-day's "supreme moment."

Sometimes I think of life at its true value. Selfishness falls away ; ambition retires ; love reigns ; and peace fills my soul like a fountain. God knows whether or not my winter of meditation and of attempted improvement of my character, has wrought out any other than an imaginary result. Sometimes I think I have advanced to a higher plane than before ; then I am filled with doubt, and sometimes I am in the very dust. But at least one thing is certain : I hold myself to a higher ideal, and judge myself by a severer criticism than in the olden days. And yet I am conscious of departing more and more from the peculiar religious and theological views which you regard as sacred. Perhaps this statement may give you trouble but certainly this fact has given me peace. Ever yours,

THEODORE TILTON.

"ONCE A PRINCESS, NOW A QUEEN."

ANN ARBOR, Mich., February 3, 1867.

MY DARLING OF DARLINGS : . . . It is a sweet delight to have a wife who interweaves herself into all her husband's highest and purest thoughts. I keep turning my soul towards yours day by day, and sometimes hour by hour ; and I am sure that, if I could not write to you often and think of you oftener, I would grow cramped and barren in the highest realm of my thought. I sometimes call your name aloud, for the simple sake of hearing its sound. My love has grown young and boyish during this winter. I find in myself a conscious return to the ancient moods of our early courtship. I would like to have you for a companion this evening on a starlit walk, such as young lovers take. I keep bringing you before my mind, not as the mother and matron, but as the maiden and bride. And yet, on soberer reflection, you are sweeter, dearest, noblest to me as the ripe, rich-hearted woman, the mother of beautiful children, and the wife of a gray-haired man ! You were once a Princess ; you are now a Queen. O Elizabeth ! the crown is on your head, and you don't know it. But the halo is plain enough to be seen by your loving worshiper,

THEODORE TILTON.

I LOVE YOU AS FERVENTLY AS MAN EVER LOVED.

FLINT, Mich., Feb. 5, 1867.

MY QUEEN AND MISTRESS : . . . But I was speaking of your letter. It is so full of your love that you have this day set yourself unconsciously before me in such noble proportions as to hide all the rest of the universe ; and nothing, either in Heaven above or earth beneath, seems at this moment so great, so pure, or so beautiful, as your own true love for your unworthy husband.

In fact, this morning I was suffering from undue fatigue, owing to an entirely sleepless night, and my mind was in an unclean and groveling frame—haunted with low thoughts. I am a hard subject for self-conquering, as you know. And this morning I could not get any honorable or manly mastery over myself, although I tried hard for the victory.

But when your dear letter came, my soul took wings like a lark. "A word in season, how good it is." A little piece of white paper, with a loving woman's handwriting on it, changed the whole face of Nature, and the whole temper of my spirit, in a single moment. How powerful and how beneficent is the influence of love ! And I now see, by the light of my winter's experience, that you have been profoundly right in demanding, not only a constant mutual love, but a constant mutual expression of it. Hereafter, I shall judge the needs of *your* heart by the needs of mine, and be more prodigal in my daily outpouring of what has hitherto been too often unexpressed. Sometimes we allow our loves simply to be taken for granted, whereas we should both enjoy *each other's* love the more by coining *our own* into a repeated confession of words. "Confession is good for the soul," says the proverb. And I hereby confess that I love you as fervently as any man ever loved any woman on the earth, or perhaps in the heavens. . . .

Dearly beloved, God bless you for evermore! Yours,

THEODORE.

"I DON'T BELIEVE IN ORTHODOXY."

ON THE CARS, CHICAGO TO MILWAUKEE, }
Tuesday, Feb. 12, 1867, }

MY DARLING: . . . I am satisfied that whoso makes no intimate or confidential friends, both among men and among women—friends with whom he girdles himself round about as with a halo—friends who are props to keep him lifted perpetually toward his highest life—friends whose friendship is a kind of sacred wedding that knows no sex, such a man neglects one of the greatest opportunities for intellectual, moral, and spiritual growth.

The old religious teachings, the Orthodox view, the dread of punishment, the Atonement, have less and less power over my mind. Of course you will mourn over this. But I must be an honest man. I don't believe in Orthodoxy, and therefore I will not pretend to do so. From you, as from God, I have no secrets; so I tell you day by day my thoughts. And these are my thoughts this morning. But the car is now growing crowded; a man has taken a seat at my elbow, and I must stop writing. Blessings on your saintly head. Ever yours,

THEODORE.

HOW WOULD JESUS HAVE APPEARED AS A MARRIED MAN?

OSHKOSH, WIS., Feb. 14, 1867.

MY DEAR, ORTHODOX WIFE: I have been speculating considerably lately on the character and career of Jesus; and I wonder whether you will be shocked when I mention one of my meditations. It is this: How would He have appeared in the character of a married man? Certainly, even to your reverential and adoring view of Him as "God manifested in the flesh," there ought to be nothing profane in the supposition. If He consented to be born of a woman, why might He not have consented to be married to a woman? And, if He was the son of an earthly parent, why might He not have been the Father of a mortal child? He loved some of His disciples better than others,—as, for instance, John. He undoubtedly loved some few women devotedly, perhaps passionately. Now, why might He not have loved one, chief and chosen among those women, on whom He might have poured the whole fullness of His heart, and on whose finger He might have set a marriage-ring, making her, indeed, like the Church, the "Pride of Christ?" I confess that, if a new historic investigation should reveal the proof that Jesus was a married man, instead of an unmated lover of all the world, I would see an additional glory in the most wonderful of all historic characters. Nor do I know of any evidence to show that He was ever married.

If either Mary or Martha, or any other saintly woman, had been His wife, the fact would probably have been mentioned; and yet what would we have known of His friend Peter's wife except for the fact that her mother was once sick of a fever? Men's wives are not necessarily known to history. Of course, the probability is, that Jesus was never married; yet this is by no means a certainty.

And, as there remains a possibility that He was, it is a pleasing reflection for me that, while He was living in Capernaum, in the house of Peter (one of His disciples), He might there have enjoyed also the still-sweeter companionship of a wife of His own. I know that even Renan says "Jesus never married." Even admitting the fact, however, this does not deny the *propriety* of His marrying, if He had chosen to marry.

But, if Jesus had taken a wife and fathered a family, I believe that this fact would have so completely humanized Him in the eyes of all the world that He never would have been regarded as God, or the Only-Begotten Son of God. And yet, if, as the son of Mary, He had become the husband of a Galilean girl, and these twain had dwelt in a cottage by the Lake of Genezaret, and unto them had been born children like those of whom he said, "Suffer them to come unto me," let me inquire whether or not you would love the character of Jesus any less than you love it now? Answer. Your Heterodox husband,

THEODORE TILTON.

PEACE OF MIND.

MIDNIGHT, OSHKOSH, Wis., Feb. 14, 1867.

MY ABSENT PET : I am more and more astonished at the spiritual joy which one may reap in the barren places of his life, if only he be determined to find peace instead of being satisfied with indifference. I have many hours wherein I am alone, and yet not lonely,—many experiences of longings, ending in delightful contentment,—many half-agonies, which suddenly change to inward glory and strange delight. My winter has been full of marvels to my soul. I shall have no excuse, hereafter, if I do not better govern my unruly moods. Life has taken a new aspect as I have lately looked upon it. Forgetting myself, I now discover a thousand other and sweeter things to remember.

Laying aside ambition, the great object of living seems to be the Christian development of my inmost character. I never wish to lose sight of the ideals which I have borne before my mind this winter,—never wish to fall behind the degree of attainment which I think I have made in their realization at times.

I make this bold statement of progress because, with all my fatigues of body, unusual duties, homesickness, and nightly wakefulness, I have, nevertheless, had greater peace of mind this winter—greater joy in my spiritual life—than ever before in all my experience. I think that over many temptations, particularly over my somewhat characteristic downfalls into morbidness of mind, I have had signal victories. Certain it is that I meet no man, day by day in my travels, who appears to be more at peace than myself.

I have almost ceased to fret at anything, to be displeased at anybody, to speak an ungentle word, or to carry any daily trouble. Perhaps this sounds like a singular tale of self-satisfaction. I would not make such a statement to anybody but yourself. Nor do I count on any long continuance of this even and resigned temper. But at least I may enjoy it while it lasts, and may confess it to my wife's ear, that she too may enjoy it with her husband. Our minds might be made beautiful ministers of our daily happiness, if only we had the skill and patience to handle our faculties well. The difference between high spiritual contentment and deep spiritual gloom is often a mere difference in the activity of the will. Resolving to be happy is itself half the victory over the unhappiness. I could be miserably restless and discontented at this moment if I were to take away the curb with which I seek to bribe my spirit. I foresaw, some weeks ago, that I must either conquer myself, or else be conquered, and, ever since, I have been fighting a battle of the giants. To-night I am in the enjoyment of a little victory. So I report it to headquarters. Good night. Yours ever,

THEODORE.

THE LITTLE CHILDREN.

RIPON, Wis., Feb. 15, 1867.

MY WIFE AND CHIEF FRIEND: . . . Your letter received this evening asks me this question: "Theodore, do you realize the depth and sacredness of my love for you?" Yes, my darling, I realize it fully; I realize it as never before in all my life. I realize it each day afresh, and with renewed gratitude to God for the gift of such a wife, of whom I am unworthy. I realize that it is not possible for any woman to love any man more than *you* love *me*. And I am humbled and rebuked by your strong and wonderful love. It daily chides me to a better life.

And now I ask, in return, Do you realize how supremely you are loved, and how sacredly you are reverenced, by your husband? I have often thought that it could not be in the character of any other human being on the face of the earth to excite mingled love and reverence so much as these feelings are excited by my dear wife. I count your love for me as the chief reward and pleasure of my life: and I repay it into your own bosom by an outpouring of all the wealth of my own heart's love for my own heart's mate.

This winter, to me, has been a season of many sweet and tender experiences. For instance, I have never before been so lovingly drawn to all the children I have meet. But now, the sight of a child anywhere, thrills me with delight. This evening, for half an hour before my lecture, I held a sweet, sick, loving child in my arms. who looked up into my face with pure and perfect love.

Yesterday a little lame girl in the street almost made me weep. Mr. H——'s little daughter has several times come down before daylight in the morning, clad in her night-gown, to kiss me before my departure by the early train. I have had a good many children in my arms since I left Brooklyn. Alice asked, in one of her pretty notes, if I found any little children to comfort me in my absence : tell her I find many,—some of them very lovely,—but none of them quite so dear as the three little chicks who live in Livingston street, and whose names I could name. The only little children to whom I have sent valentines are these same three little children of Livingston street. . . . Sitting by this study-fire, at this midnight hour, the whole house asleep, and with only a ticking clock to keep me company, I feel myself drawn toward you with unutterable yearnings of love. The lamp-light brightens my wedding-ring, and makes it doubly golden against my finger. I hereby kiss the token, in sign of wedding you anew, now and forever. Amen ! Yours lovingly,

THEODORE.

MR. BEECHER'S "KIND ATTENTIONS."

LA CROSSE, Wis. Feb. 21, 1867.

MY DARLING : . . . I am sorry to hear that Mr. Beecher had a poor house in Brooklyn. In view of his kind attentions to you this winter, all my old love for him has revived, and my heart would once more greet him as of old. I sometimes quarrel with my friends on the surface, but never at the bottom. With yourself, O friend above all friends ! I am in perpetual love. Yours,

THEODORE.

TILTON AND THE "INDEPENDENT."

ON THE TRAIN, WINONA TO NORTHFIELD, }
Minn., February 23, 1867. }

MY SWEET WIFE : Last evening I undertook to write you a letter from Winona, but was fairly conquered by the too interesting family that sat around my writing-table, and so I fear I sent you a very barren line. This morning, elbowed by a close neighbor in this crowded car, I have still a very poor opportunity to write ; but I have something particular to say, and desire to say it without delay. Except for the expression of your love in your letters,—which is always their sweetest part,—the most welcome thing, next in order, in all your winter's correspondence, was your suggestion that I should change or modify my relations with the *Independent.*

The letter which first broached the subject gave me such a frantic delight that I waved the sheet over my head, and gave you silently three cheers. You expressed in words what had long been in my unexpressed thoughts. Your few sentences seemed suddenly to open a golden door to my emancipation, and my blood tingled at the prospect. Of course I have formed no purpose of leaving the paper. Perhaps my duty will compel me to stay with it. Such a step as you propose requires much precaution. Nevertheless, it is a joy unspeakable to know how closely your mind keeps track of mine, and how instinctively you sympathize with even the undetected movement of my own thought.

I have never seriously looked upon my connection with the *Independent* as properly the work of my life. But I have looked upon the great progressive movements which I have advocated in the *Independent* as offering the most useful career which I could choose. In fact, I did not choose my career —it was chosen for me by events. I hold it to be my daily and bounden duty to advance, by all means in my power, the great idea of political equality. Providentially put in charge of the *Independent,* I have used that journal as the potent instrument for advancing this idea.

In editing the *Independent,* I have been allowed by its proprietor the most unlimited freedom of speech. Mr. Bowen has never once sought to restrain me in the utterance of any opinion which I have entertained. I know of no publisher who has treated his editor with more thorough respect— no publisher who has left, systematically and unvaryingly, the absolute independence of his editor so untouched, or even unshadowed, by counter-influence from the publication office.

At the same time, the business-management of the *Independent* often grates upon my feelings and tastes. I dislike the excessive grasping after subscribers ; the undignified offers of premiums ; the constant, noisy blowing of one's own trumpet of self-advertisement.

The whole subject of my relations with the paper has occupied my mind greatly during the winter. I have not heretofore mentioned the subject to yourself, partly because I never once suspected that you were entertaining similar thoughts, and partly because I have not yet been able to discern any "conclusion of the whole matter." I do not know in what frame of mind I shall find Mr. Bowen on my return.

Before I left he promised me an interest in the paper as soon as we could agree as to terms ; that is, after my lectures were over, and we could sit down and talk out the matter to the full. The more I think of the future, the less I am inclined to enter into a business partnership with him. He is a man of fine qualities. I shall speak well of him against all his detractors. He has enough inherent nobleness to excuse many and grievous faults. But, if I were in a business partnership with him, I should then become responsible for his very peculiar and distasteful methods of advertising business. My sensibilities would be constantly pained. At least, so I fear. Perhaps, however, all prospect of such a partnership will be destroyed on my return by his own disinclination. In that case, the question is already settled for me.

If, however, he shall again propose to make me a partner, the subject will not require a hasty decision, and you and I can make up our minds, after mutual consultation and good advice. At present, it seems to me that, if Mr. Bowen should be willing that I should edit the *Independent* without cumbering myself with the details of the office—editing it as during the past winter—leaving me free to come and go as I choose, and holding me responsible only for my own editorial columns ; if he should cordially accede to such an engagement (for the time being at least) I should consider the question of my duty settled.

I have had abundant evidence this winter—never such evidence before—that the *Independent* has as much influence on public opinion as can be claimed for any other American journal. I have been thanked and blessed by thousands of good men and women this winter, who, as they have taken my hand, have expressed their joy at the radical course of the *Independent.* But I shall not remain its editor for the sake of an editor's conspicuous position before the public.

For the future, out of the most solemn experiences of my life—experiences of what I have kept you informed day by day for the past three months—I have resolved to harbor no worldly ambition, to seek no place for the honor which it may confer, to grasp at nothing lower than Heaven itself, and to live my life solely as "under the Great Taskmaster's eye." Meanwhile, O my darling! you are the best of counselors and the sweetest of friends. God bless you evermore. Yours devoutly,

THEODORE.

NO INTENTION OF PAINING MRS. TILTON.

ON THE TRAIN, LEAVING MINNESOTA, {
February 28, 1867. }

MY DARLING : ' . . . This cloudy, murky morning finds me too tired, too sleepy, to say anything not altogether matter-of-fact. I must mention, however, that I had no intention of paining you by anything that I said about my religious speculations. I am not conscious of holding any different religious views from those which I brought away with me last November, and which you already know full well. Nor can I remember anything which I have said that might be calculated to make you uneasy. But you know I have always written in a hurry. Yours absolutely,

THEODORE.

PLANS FOR THE FUTURE.

ON THE TRAIN, CHICAGO TO PRINCETON, {
Friday, March 1, 1867. }

MY DARLING : . . . Only three more lectures, and then home ! The prospect is joyous. My love for you is unbounded. My plans for the future (if God shall enable me to execute them) shall be mainly for our own sake rather than for mine. Henceforth I do not mean to live much to myself. My past life fills me with regret at my overmuch self-seeking.

This winter I have daily given myself away to somebody, and I have found therein the sweetest pleasure of my whole life. "It is more blessed to give than to receive." *You* learned the secret years ago ; but *I* have learned it only lately. Henceforth I trust that we shall be able to practice it together.

Oh, my darling ! No yearning of yours, expressed in your letters, can possibly be greater than mine, that we may love one another fervently, unselfishly, and divinely ; that the remaining years of our life—if, indeed, *years* remain for us—shall be spent as in God's sight, and that, day by day, " that mind may be in us which was in Jesus Christ our Lord."

Heaven bless you, my darling ! This is the daily prayer of your one true lover,

THEODORE.

SWEETEST, LOVELIEST, NOBLEST WOMAN !

ALLYN HOUSE, HARTFORD, {
Wednesday, March 13, 1867. }

MY DARLING : . . . I think that I have never had four happier days in all my life than the four which I have just set aside in my memory,—the four days of delight at home, after my last four months of absence and heart-ache.

How much felicity there is in human life, if only we take the right method to find it !

You are the sweetest, loveliest, and noblest woman now living on the earth.

Which I say because it is the truth. Ever yours,

THEODORE.

DAYS IN DARKNESS.

TUESDAY, March 18, 1867, OSWEGO, N. Y.

MY DEAR WIFE : . . . But I cannot thus afford to be led away captive of gloominess and bad blood. I must endeavor more completely to conquer myself in future. "Greater is he who ruleth his own spirit than he who taketh a city." Despondency is my lurking enemy. It lies in wait for me in my most familiar haunts. And it most often entraps me under my own roof.

But I think my two or three recent days in darkness have been, on the whole, a moral benefit, in that they have revealed to my mind its most easily temptable points. It was good for the Pilgrim to go into the Valley of the Shadow of Death. "No chastening for the present is joyous, but grievous; nevertheless, afterwards it worketh out the peaceable fruit of righteousness."

So, after my overthrow, I rise again well out of the dust, and re-begin the battle of self-conquests,— to be again, I doubt not, defeated a thousand times. Well, during all the winter I was as one clothed in King's apparel; and it is now high time, therefore, that I should, for a little while, wear beggars' rags. The soul's life must have its needful changes from joy to sorrow. I came home from the West respecting myself too highly. My crown then was suddenly taken off and cast to the earth. I am now dispossessed of my portion, and wander like an exile banished from my former complacent self. But, O happy misfortune! that carries a man first into miserable wretchedness in order that it may then carry him, like the Prodigal, back to his Father's House.

As Luther thanked God for his sins, so I too can thank God for my sorrowful glooms.

Be assured that, whatever happens, whether clouds or clear skies, I love you boundlessly and forever.

THEODORE.

RETROSPECTION.

ROCHESTER, N. Y., March 21, 1867.

MY DEAR PET: I am, at this midnight hour, in the same hotel, and in the same room, wherein you and I were quartered eleven and a half years ago, on our wedding tour! What a history these years unfold to our backward gaze! Gray hairs have stolen upon us since them. Time and care have jointly wrinkled our brows. Joys and sorrows have checkered our path. Four children have been given to us on earth, and one of these has been taken back to Heaven. You have had sickness, and I have had toil. Both of us may now look back to that wedding-pilgrimage, and smile at how little we then knew of human life! Thank God, the years grow richer as we grow older! Not yet conquerors of ourselves, we are nevertheless, nearer the victory now than then. I would not exchange the present for the past! With what self-complacency I looked upon my life in those "green and salad days!" How strong I thought myself for the battle! The revelations of later years subdue a man's pride by teaching him his weakness. At this retrospective moment, in this charmed chamber, I am humble, sad, and calm. Life is sober, as I now look upon it. Death is near, as I now think of it. Heaven is sweet, as I now wait for it. I have not made the best, or even a good, use of my last ten years. I have less faith in my moral integrity now than at any former period of my life. It is hard to live well. Nevertheless, my dear pet, we will try again to realize more perfectly our ideals. May God bless us both, now and ever. Amen! Yours,

THEODORE.

"I FELT QUITE LIKE A CHILD."

ON THE CARS, BET. CLEVELAND AND COLUMBUS, O.,
WEDNESDAY, Jan. 6, 1868.

MY DEAR WIFE: . . . I have had more happiness this morning than at any time since my departure from home. At last my spirit is at peace, and I am reconciled to my winter's work. Many pleasant thoughts have stolen, like sunbeams, into my musings this afternoon—thoughts of my home, of my wife and children, of Paul, and of all the great hereafter. I have been murmuring hymns in a low voice, and making little prayers to God. I feel quite like a child—prattling to myself and to my Father in Heaven. I have taken a good deal of comfort in reading the New Testament in French. Then, too, the blessed sunshine is itself a Gospel of peace and tranquility. . . .

The sun, the sky, the spring-like air, all conspire to keep me humming to myself:

> Sweet fields beyond the swelling flood,
> Stand dressed in living green.

Winter or summer, the earth is never so beautiful as when it suggests Heaven.

I think you and I are yet to walk in Paradise together. Thine here and there,

THEODORE.

"THE SWEETEST FAMILY GOD EVER GAVE TO A MAN."

HUDSON RIVER R. R., THIRTY-FIRST ST. DEPOT,
Jan. 26, 1868.

MY DARLING: I am housed in the sleeping-car for the beginning of my Westward journey. . . . You have never seemed so noble to me as during last evening and this day. You are not only all, but more than all, that any man can need, or even can deserve. . . Since I have been in the car, I have been wondering if any of my fellow-passengers have left such beautiful families as mine behind them. I think sometimes that I have the sweetest family that God ever gave to a man. God grant that I may return to you all.

With unutterable love, I am yours, "Now, henceforth, and forever,"

THEODORE.

THE EVANESCENCE OF LIFE.

DETROIT, MICH, Jan. 29, 1868.

MY DARLING: . . . All this interferes with my letter writing. But I feel a great disposition to write you very long and very loving letters. Oh, how fleeting is time, and how vanishing is life! The days seem to have wings. Life seems to be gliding away like a swift stream. I am like an arrow shot every day from a new bow. You must be content with a very little of me till I can get home and give you my whole self. I love you fervently and entirely. Blessings on you always.

THEODORE.

A "MEMORABLE INTERVIEW."

MONONGAHELA HOUSE, PITTSBURGH, PA., }
Jan. 30, 1868. }

MY DARLING: . . . Our memorable interview, on the evening before I left home, lingers with me like a sunset in the sky. It makes all my thoughts rosy, and all my feelings pure. I seem, all of a sudden, to have grown ten years younger in hope, and ten years older in strength. The knowledge of your love, your confidence, your respect, your satisfaction in *me*,—this is more than all the rest of the world can give, and far more than I can ever deserve. . . . Affectionately thine,

THEODORE.

"QUITE MERRY-HEARTED."

KENNARD HOUSE, Cleveland, O., Feb. 4, 1868.

MY DEARLY-BELOVED WIFE: . . . . I am quite merry-hearted. Low spirits have not come near me for a week. The fact that I am doing something for the enrichment of my family is a great joy to me. I bound up and down like an India-rubber ball !

Good afternoon ! Lovingly yours,

THEODORE.

"THE CHIEF RULING INFLUENCE OF MY LIFE."

CRAWFORDSVILLE, Ind., }
Sunday Morning, Feb. 9, 1868. }

MY DEAR ANGEL: I dreamed of you all last night, and awoke thinking of you this morning. How much I want to see you ! How I yearn after you ! How my soul blesses you day by day ! I can never describe how precious your love of your husband has appeared to him during these few weeks past. Your singleness, your fervor, your purity, your devotion,—they fill my mind and heart with reverence, adoration, and humility.

I regard my last evening spent with you at home as the most memorable point in my whole life. You opened for me that night the gate of Heaven, which had so long seemed shut.

Ever since, I have had nothing but glory, thanksgiving, and praise. If ever a man was made a new creature, that man was I,—no more despondency,—no more repining,—no more vain regrets,— no more loss of self-respect,—no more grovelling in the dust. On the contrary, I am once again a man among men, and a Christian among Christians. Now, this transformation I owe to yourself, to your irrepressible love and devotion, to your ceaseless prayers, and to your victorious faith.

You always have in your power either to crown or dethrone me. You have the chief ruling influence of my life. Your words, your wishes, your looks, your thoughts, act on me like magic. When I am doing you any injury, or slight, or hardness, I am made so miserable that I do not wish to live. When I am making you happy, I walk like a Prince newly come into his Kingdom.

Your letters, since I have been from home this last time, have been the dearest you ever penned. They are royal in their love. Each one fills me with renewed pride and joy in my wife. O my darling, in comparison with such love as you express, how poor is the friendship of all other friends ! I have never seen any one who loves as you do. You have the richest of all human hearts. I am pledged to you forever. My vows I shall keep, and not break. With God's help, and with yours, I shall be the faithfulest man in the world. Blessings on your soul, this Sabbath-day. Ever yours,

THEODORE.

YEARNINGS.

ON THE TRAIN, CRAWFORDSVILLE, IND., }
February 10, 1868. }

MY GOOD AND COMFORTING WIFE: . . . I send kisses for the dear children, and yearnings for their dear mother. My heart is eager, greedy, and miserly in its desire to possess you all once more. Ever thine,

THEODORE.

"A MUTUAL-ADMIRATION SOCIETY."

JACKSONVILLE, ILL., February 12, 1868.

MY DARLING : Though the hour is midnight, I will not allow myself to go to bed till I have left a few lines to be mailed to you in the morning. Two of your letters came to me to-day, making me happy and rich. Every line of your handwriting seems like fine gold for preciousness. I have numbered your letters, as David numbered Israel, and yet without David's sin in doing it.

This morning, on the train, I had them all out, and looked them all over once more. They are a little volume of dear, sweet, sacred writings. I fear that my responses are not worthy of them. You seem to be in a mood of overflowing affection, confidence, pride, and rejoicing, on account of your husband. Well, so am I on account of my wife. We certainly are a Mutual-Admiration Society. My prevailing feeling toward you of late has been, you are the chief prop and pillar of my life. You never were so needful to me, and never so helpful to me, as now. I not only think of you, but rely upon you, and live for you constantly. I have great peace.

Indeed, I have had no cloud on my mind since we brushed away all clouds on that storm-dispelling night. I trust they have gone forever. Certainly, I have ever since been a cheery, good-hearted, hopeful, and bright man. Sometimes you show yourself to me so large, generous, strong, and devout a character, that I am uplifted for a month by the very contagion of it. If I had come away from home in a low, instead of a high, state of mind, this night would not have found me so surrounded as I am with something brighter than the day itself. I am lonesome, but not sad; I yearn for you, and yet am cheerful ; I think of you longingly, and yet am content to be writing to you, out of sight and far away.

· It is a man's spirit that either saves or destroys. The broken-spiritedness which for months past I suffered would soon have left on me an ineffaceable work. My very face, however, has so changed that the Dayton *Journal* says : "Mr. Tilton is an unusually handsome man." That editor did not know who it was that gave me my new look. It was the mother of Paul. You did not pack my trunk half so full of clothes as you packed my heart full of good hope and cheer. In fact, for the " spirit of heaviness " you gave me " the garment of praise." So, from my beautiful chamber, from my wood-fire, from my book-laden table, from my fair-papered walls, my heart sends you salutation to-night.

"Come and abide with me forever." Yours faithfully.

THEODORE.

A HOME-SCENE.

LINCOLN, Ill., February 13, 1868.

MY SWEET WIFE : . . . Peace be with you all ! The little trifling facts mentioned in the children's notes were enough to bring all the home-scenes—dolls, baby-rags, and all—visibly to my mind. I could see Cad sitting with his Grandma, in ignorance of the Noah's Ark awaiting him at home : Alice playing pranks with little Miss B——, dressed as a man; Florence with her sedate head, meditating on her new knife; and Paul with his toes held out to be named at the fire. . . . With kisses all around, I am affectionately yours, · THEODORE TILTON.

ONE, SWEET, LIFE-LONG LOVE.

SHERMAN HOUSE, CHICAGO, Feb. 16, 1868.

· MY BELOVED WIFE :— . . . I see now more than ever—I saw last night—how that nobody on earth could ever take your place in my mind and heart. Perhaps I may say, without undue self-complacency, that I was never in my life so true to any one, sweet, life-long love, as I am now. O, if I could kiss your dear head this morning, I would be content with this life and all its cares. Ever yours,

THEODORE.

" A TONIC TO MY WHOLE SYSTEM."

CLINTON, Ia., Feb. 20, 1868.

PET : Heigho ! Five of your letters have just come to me, all in a bunch ! " Here's richness !" They have put me into such a merry humor that my blood has been laughing up and down my veins. They made an actual handful,—nay, more than that : a heartfull.

. . . How I would like to be at home to-day ! Or else, how I would like to see you here ! The weather is warm enough for grass to grow, birds to build, and hearts to love. You ask me if I like to read the reiteration of your love. Yes, my darling ! Every bird loves to hear his mate sing. Your love for me, as expressed in your letters, is my chief joy and rejoicing in this world. It makes life seem a braver thing to me. It makes my journeys nothing but trifles, and my hardships a bagatelle. It puts vigor into my step, and joy into my work. I look round at my fellow-travelers in the cars, and my co-workers everywhere, and ask myself, "I wonder if these people have as much spring and motive for work as I now have ?" The thought of giving you a home free and clear of debt is a tonic to my whole system. I am somewhat wearied, thin, and pale, but never was so cheering in all my life, never so free from fretfulness, never so thankful for my prosperity, and never so happy in my love for wife, and children. This makes a man of me day by day. . . .

Give the chicks my dearest love, and a kiss all round. Faithfully yours, THEODORE.

BENEFITING HER AND THE CHILDREN.

DECORAH, Ia., March 1, 1868.

MY DEAR WIFE ; . . . I have been looking at my little collection of home-photographs and wishing that I could to-night see the real faces. How precious you all seem ! My heart grows big when I think of one and another of my family. What a wife and what children God has given me! Truly I am blessed as few men are. To-night I am grateful that my labors, travel, and absence all go to benefit you and the dear children. This thought, whenever it fully takes possession of my mind, turns my daily burden into a gossamer. My whole heart is filled with love imperishable, and so I laugh at my trials and welcome my cares. Ever since Mrs. G——'s misfortunes were made known to me, I have been seriously anxious to place you out of the reach of any similar arrow of bitterness. How that woman's heart must daily suffer a new death! I cannot but think that her necessitous situation (for which there seems hardly to be a sufficient excuse) must irresistibly cast a shadow over her remembrances of her husband. Mr. G—— once told me that he was worth a million of dollars! Now his wife is a beggar! What a world this is for doing and undoing,—for crowning and discrowning! "Let him that thinketh he standeth, take heed lest he fall."

. . Lovingly and longingly, THEODORE.

WORK AN ENEMY TO GLOOM.

BERLIN, Wisconsin, March 5, 1868.

MY DEAR PET: It is a late bed-time, but I drop a line to say good-night!

This afternoon I wrote you a long, dreary, and dismal letter, which, when I had ended it, I tore to pieces. I did not wish to afflict you with my despondent moods. But I feel now, late at night, as merry as a lark at early morning. I have been laughing all to myself in this solitary chamber, over the ludicrous escape of the Giantess from Mr. Barnum's fire! But all this day had been so dreary with falling rain, and so lonely in this hotel of strangers, that I had a shadowing time until the evening brought with it my lecture. Work is an enemy to gloom.

Your two letters, both received to-day, were like two sprigs of geranium sent from the pots in our parlor window. . . .

I wish I could lift the latch and catch a glimpse of Paul, and Floy, and Alice, and Cad, and their mother just now. But no. I am alone. Good-night, my many darlings! Lovingly yours,

THEODORE.

A LOVE-LETTER WRITTEN IN A CABOOSE CAR.

NORTHWESTERN RAILWAY, }
HOWARD TO CHICAGO, March 6, 1868.

MY DARLING : If you wish to see an interesting sight, look at me at this moment. I am in the caboose of a freight car, writing on the baggageman's desk, while the train is on its slow way to Chicago. Half a dozen men are smoking about me, and wondering what I am about. Perhaps they think I am some adventurous young merchant sending to New York a sudden order for goods ; or a belated clergyman caught in the act of finishing his sermon ; or some newspaper correspondent inditing his dispatches. Nobody guesses that I am writing a love-letter to the sweetest of women and the truest of wives.

I did not lecture this evening ; for, although I had an appointment at Harvard, yet, in consequence of the storm, I offered to release the Committee from their engagement—an offer which they willingly accepted. So I have taken an 8 o'clock train for Chicago, where I expect to arrive before morning—say at 3 a. m. I shall go to the Tremont House for the remainder of the night, try to sleep very late in the morning, and then dine at Colonel E——'s in the afternoon.

Your letter, which reached me at Harvard, and which I have read three times over, informed me of Miss R——'s departure for Marietta; and of Miss J——'s uniting with Plymouth Church. You say that God has given you unusual exaltation, peace, and happiness. You deserve it all, because you strive so devotedly and unselfishly to do right. You "seek not your own." You live for others. So God rewards you abundantly.

Mrs. G——, whom you mention as being at church, has been much in my thoughts of late. I am full of pity for her widowhood and poverty. Widowhood is itself a poverty, and needs no addition of beggary to make it miserable. If I were out of debt, and had money in my pocket, I would privately send her a check for $1,000. No woman's misfortunes ever more completely took hold of my heart.

"I more than ever," you say, "feel the meanness of the other life." So do I. During my late sojournings, I have had this feeling frequently and keenly.

Cold winds are rattling against the train at this moment, making me shiver at the thought of wandering alone on these bleak moors. In earlier years, I sometimes thought of going down unto death as of a traveller venturing alone through a barren waste on a wild night. But, in late years, all my thoughts of death have taken a more summer-like and rosy hue. And I can truly say that those bonds which chiefly unite me to this world are the same which, I trust, will bind me equally in the other; I mean my heart's affections. You and the children are what I live for on earth. Shall I not live for you, still more for you in Heaven? So both the worlds keep drawing us closer and closer to a converging point,—the heart's peace. We have it here already, in part; but, by and by, we shall have it in perpetual fullness.

In this caboose, surrounded by a noisy, riotous, song-singing company of rude men, I am, nevertheless, at this very hour, full of a sweet peace, which mocks the riot of my fellow-travelers within, and mocks the howling of the storm without. The flesh is often, and generally, master of the soul; but the soul has her hours of victory over all that is fleshly, earthly, and mortal. *You* had such an hour last Sunday morning; I am having such an hour on this Saturday night.

You write, "Tell me continually of your love; I need the encouragement." Am I ever tired of telling it? Do I not think of it all the day long? Do I not keep humming it to myself, like a sweet song? If I do not sufficiently in words express it, it is because it is not sufficiently expressible by any words. But I can write it over and over again, if you are not tired of the tale, though, when I have written all that I can write, "The half has not been told."

At this hour, I suppose, the chicks have gone to bed, fresh and clean from their Saturday night's bath.

God bless you, one and all. Affectionately yours,

· THEODORE TILTON.

"PRECIOUS BEYOND ALL FORMER DEARNESS."

TREMONT HOUSE, CHICAGO, March 7, 1868.

MY DARLING : . . . Day by day, I seem to find some reason for loving you better than ever before. You are precious to me beyond all former dearness. The years may bring sorrows, but they also heighten love. Whatever you write of your own fond love for your husband, I reciprocate eagerly and joyfully toward yourself. So, lovingly, Good-night !

THEODORE.

" PEACE AND JOY, AS FROM THE HOLY GHOST."

MICHIGAN SOUTHERN RAILROAD, March 13, 1868.

MY DARLING : . . . This golden sky, shining above these prairies and gilding their brown grasses is like the spiritual light which we all need to illumine our dead thoughts. I have peace and joy to-day, as from the Holy Ghost. Your own dear self shall hereafter find me more full of peacefulness and joyfulness than heretofore. Your letters have been unconscious testimony to the high and noble state of mind in which you have been since the first of February. Never before have you put so much of your spirit into pen and ink. Every letter which you have sent has been like a buoy under me, helping me to swim in a sea of troubles. Nothing has so much influenced me this winter as your letters. Like the imposition of hands, they have imparted a strength—a benediction. I have fed upon your loving words and grown stronger in love. A true woman is indeed a helpmeet to a man.

I have no news to chronicle. I keep looking forward to the time of my going home. The thought of being once again with you is as sweet as the sudden singing of that spring-bird which I heard to-day. May God bring us once more together in renewed love and with indissoluble bonds. Ever yours,

THEODORE.

" NOT TO BE MINISTERED UNTO, BUT TO MINISTER."

TOLEDO, OHIO, March 15, 1868.

MY DEARY! . . . I have been full of worship all day long. A fragment of the Scriptures has been running through my head, as if trying to work itself down into my life : The words, "Not to be ministered unto, but to minister." How they rebuke a life of self-seeking, and inspire to a life of self-sacrifice ! Sometimes I get such an overpowering view of what it is to live the true Christian life that I feel like forsaking all else and following Christ,—following Him, I mean, not merely in a sentimental, reflective, and emotional way, but in denying myself the things which I am mostly engaged in seeking, and in enduring hardness as a good follower of Jesus Christ. The truth is, we must take counsel with each other as to the best means of avoiding the sinfulness of being too much to ourselves. Of course this remark applies a thousand times more to me than you. But I trust I am growing less and less selfish. At least, something in my inmost heart seems to tell me so. Aid me to advance my soul. This is the true use of woman to man, and of man to woman,—to inspire each other to mutual and co-equal progress in the Christian life. For *I* wish to walk in the way in which *you* are going. Good-night.

THEODORE.

A PILGRIMAGE FOR THE RAISING OF $20,000.

ASHTABULA, O., March 24, 1868.

MY DARLING! . . . Stretched out on a bed, in a sunshiny room, this afternoon, watching the lights and shadows on the wall, I have been reviewing my lecture-season and its incidents. I have lectured seventy-five times, and have received $8,368. Two more appointments remain before reaching home, and one after that. How much I ought to deduct for my expenses (of which I have kept an account) I can hardly say; perhaps about $1,000, or more. I calculate that one more season like this and the last (if God should provide it for me) will clear my house. I am always carrying my house on my mind; sometimes lightly, sometimes burdensomely; sometimes as a half-hatched chicken carries its shell round its head, and sometimes as Atlas carried the earth on his shoulders.

At the beginning, I did not understand the magnitude of the task which I had undertaken. To start out on a pilgrimage for the raising of $20,000 looked like an easier thing than it proves to be.

It is a three years' labor, and each year a heavy and exhaustive tax on one's strength. Heretofore, when I heard a man speak of a "thousand dollars" or "five thousand dollars," the phrase had a light and airy sound. But, whenever I now hear of so much money, I instantly think of the toils endured in raising it. Never before, in all my life, have I been so impressed with the reasonableness of economy as during the last winter's journeyings.

I have increasing respect for those worldly-wise people who use their common sense in practical money-saving and thrifty investments. Every cent of the money with which I am paying for my house has cost me a throb of my pulse, and heart, and brain. In fact, I playfully said to a lady, a few even-ngs ago, "Every lecture which I deliver gives me a gray hair."

Then, too, my love for you has never been so high, strong, and pure, as now. Your winter's letters —which have expressed your love for me as you never expressed it before—have won me to you as with a new marriage. I feel more sacredly knit to you than at any former time. It seems to me that I have looked deeper into your soul this winter than you ever showed it to me before. My heart is full of blessings for you. I shall greet you, on my return, as a pilgrim greets the shrine of his worship. I have faithfully kept my vows, and shall faithfully keep them. May God's blessing sweeten our reunited lives.

Yours, forever,

THEODORE.

HIS TROUBLES AND THEIR CAUSE.

AT THE OFFICE, NOV. 3, 1868.

MY DEARY: Your kind and loving note falls so pleasantly on my spirits that I would immediately go home this afternoon were it not that I have engaged to go out this evening.

There is so much sunshine pouring into my little office at this moment that I think I never knew a brighter day in my life ; and I hope that some of the light and warmth will steal into and remain within my cold and cruel heart.

It is the greatest regret of my life that I do not seem constituted so as to make you as happy as you deserve to be ; but I have the best of intentions—and the worst of success.

The cause of so much of my trouble at home is my general anxiety about everything. Latterly I worry more or less concerning every matter which I touch. I have hardly ten minutes a day of uninterrupted freedom from care. This may seem an exaggerated statement; but it is the painful truth. I feel as if I were growing old before my time. Lights that used to burn within me have been quenched. Hopes are faded; ambition is killed; life seems a failure.

As I cannot bear to see any expression of pain, or sorrow, or regret, on your face, I cannot bring myself to speak to you familiarly on any subject connected with any of our sorrows—not even Paul, our chief. I am literally *tormented* at having no grave for his crumbling clay. Every allusion to the subject has been a pang through my heart.

Then, too, all my religious doubts and difficulties have been, and are, and I fear must be, shut within myself, because I cannot open my mouth to you concerning them without giving you a wound. You are the finest-fibred soul that ever was put into a body; you jar at my touch, and I am apt to touch too rudely.

As for my own character, I saw, at the time of Paul's death, what it was to be a man, and how far short of it I am myself ; and I have ever since been utterly overwhelmed with my own worthlessness, selfishness, degradation, and wickedness. At some time I expect to recover from this slough of despond ; but not now. I must remain longer in suffering before I can emerge into peace. I have been overthrown, and, before I rise, I must be made to feel, like Antæus, that strength comes from touching the ground.

But the chief of all my miseries is this: that I impart them to others. Let me say, with the utmost fervor of protestation, that neither you, nor the children, nor the house, nor the servant, nor anything that is within our gates—not one alone—nor all combined—no, none of these persons or things, *has the slightest originating share in my troubles.* Those troubles (such as they are) are of my own making. Would to God they were also of my own enduring! But they have to be inflicted upon others— upon yourself and the children. It is this fact that doubles my affliction.

But your kind and tender words, penciled in the studio this morning, were very precious to me— sweeter than honey in the honeycomb. I write this letter on purpose to thank you for them. God bless you evermore. Lovingly yours,

THEODORE.

HER "SWEET COMPANIONSHIP."

COLUMBUS, O., Jan. 11, 1869.

MY DEAR PET: . . . O would you were here at this lonely midnight-hour.

I hunger and thirst for your sweet companionship. Home seems never so pleasant to me as when I am shut out of it. What we possess is not so passionately loved as what we yearn for. You, and the chicks, and the house, and all, are in my thoughts every day and hour. Good night.

THEODORE.

"WORRIED AT NOT HEARING FROM HOME."

STEUBENVILLE, O. Jan. 12, 1869.

MY DEAR WIFE: I am hungering and thirsting to hear from home. It is now nine days since I have been absent, during which the only line I have received from you was the lead-pencil note. . . .

To-day, all day long, I have felt the pinch and pang of expectation. . . .

I will not say that I am worried at not hearing from home, for I suppose the reason has been some failure of mail-trains. But I feel the deprivation greatly. Perhaps you have not allowed your letters sufficient time to reach me. Let me hear from you as often as possible. Also, ask the children to send me frequently some scraps of their handwriting.

. . . I have been treated here with great kindness. But oh ! to be home again. Ever yours.

THEODORE.

PRAYING.

GRANVILLE, O., Jan. 12, 1869.

MY DEAR PET : . . . I continue to take great comfort in my French Testament. I read it daily, and I pray much. . . . If you and I were together, we would pray a great deal. "More things are wrought by prayer," says King Arthur, "than this world dreams of." Then, you remember, he adds, "Wherefore let thy voice rise like a fountain for me night and day." I need not ask you to pray for your husband. I know you do; and may God answer all your many prayers, and reward all your many tears offered and shed in my behalf. . . . Lovingly yours,

THEODORE.

HIS AND HER EXTRAVAGANCE.

AKRON, O., Jan. 15, 1869.

MY DEAR WIFE : Ever since last October I have been lecturing every week,—sometimes every night, and the proceeds have all been swallowed up in my extravagant debts. If this spendthrift tendency of mine is ever to be curbed, it must be by your helpful criticism of it,—not by a parallel liberality of outlay by yourself. I am putting myself daily to as much fatigue as human nature can endure, in order, if possible, to clear off my obligations to my creditors, and to keep afterwards abreast with the world. Your letter, a few days ago, stating that you could not live on your salary, made me sick at heart; and temporarily I felt like giving up my journey and going home. To-day you send me a bill of $58 for Cad's clothes.—an amount which I regard as so great for a family of our resources as to be almost as wicked as my own outlays for pictures. In all the three weeks of my last absence, I have not made, above expenses, $400. Not one penny of all my lecture-earnings for years has ever yet gone into a bank. I look upon our money-spending tendencies as cruelly wrong. At this moment I am well-nigh broken down in voice, and know not how I shall get through with to-night's lecture. Am I wrong when I say that I cannot look with equanimity on squandering so much money in fine dresses for the children ? My heart suffers a pang in saying this; but I cannot help saying it. We must either sell our establishment in Brooklyn, or else manage it on a less expensive scale. I have made a vow to buy not another picture, and not another unnecessary article, during the present year. It is with something like a shudder that I look forward to the prolonged slavery of public lecturing every winter; and, if the proceeds are to be freely thrown away by both of us, I may as well stop it now. I have suffered for ten days past an agony of remorse at the fruitless exertions I have made by three years of speaking,—fruitless because their harvest has been unprofitably spent. Judging by all the families I visit, *I know that we are literally throwing away our inheritance.* At last I am aroused; and I appeal to you to put a peremptory check upon any and every unnecessary expenditure which *you see me make.* Dress the children in calico for a year, and let me get out of my misery. Yours in dust and ashes,

THEODORE TILTON.

"IN A HEARTBREAK."

EMPIRE HOUSE, AKRON, O., Jan. 15, 1869.

MY DEAR WIFE : I am in a heart-break,—yes. I have been on my knees in this chamber, crying more bitterly than any child. Two years ago, in this same spot, I had a terrible wrestling with my soul. The moment I entered the room to-day, the old experience was revived. Since that occasion,—

which I can never lose out of my memory,—I seem to have suffered much and profited little. My life looks very much like a waste,—a blank,—a blight. Of all the past, I thought to-day that I had saved nothing but Paul,—and him, too, I have lost. The little key in my pocket seems not to bring him nearer, but to keep him farther away. All the afternoon I have been weeping, trembling, and agonizing. I am well-nigh sick with very grief. My eyes are red and full of pain. I have been saying, "Little Paul, come and help your father." My life seems utterly wretched and unworthy. I cannot bear to look in upon myself. I wrote to you about our failure to live within our means ; but this shortcoming is nothing to what I feel in myself of moral truthlessness. It seems to me as if I were a spiritual castaway. I ought not to trouble you with these disclosures; but, if I do not utter them to you, they must go unuttered. Your own confessions seem to indicate that you are in a perpetual trouble. Ah ! the morning of life is rosy, but the noon is sometimes leaden and gray.

I make a great many re-beginnings, but do not get along far before I lose the little that I have gained. You ask for "glimpses in my heart." It is a dark place to look into. God help your sorrowful and groaning husband! Yours affectionately, THEODORE.

"LIFTED TO A HIGHER LEVEL."

FRIDAY, MIDNIGHT, AKRON, O., Jan. 15, 1869.

MY DEAR WIFE : I will add a few words more before going to bed,—I mean, add them to the letter which I have written to you to-day.

My whole frame seemed weak this evening on the platform. My eyes were very sore, and kept stinging round the edges. But I was in a very calm mood. My spirit was at rest. The great agony of this afternoon has lifted me to a higher level. For a few minutes I never suffered more in all my life than when my heart this afternoon went to pieces once again over Paul's key, and death, and presence in my room. I now feel perfectly tranquil. You are probably fast asleep at this hour. I can almost peep into your bed-room,—I see the picture so vividly before me. I give you my blessing. Now, I wonder if it be worth anything? Not much. It is the prayer of the righteous, and not of the wicked, that avails with God.

Tell the children that I have been thinking of them very tenderly to-night. Yours fondly, THEODORE.

"THE BEST AND TRUEST WOMAN."

MATTOON, Ill., March 4, 1869.

MY DARLING : . . . Your last night's letter was full of love, and I drank your tender words like a mine of comfort. My chief title to self-respect is, that I have won, and kept, the unblemished love of the best and truest woman whom I have ever known. Why you should love me so heartily, so earnestly, and so devotedly, I see nothing in myself to deserve. My first thought on waking this morning was, how few men ever know what it is to be loved so purely, so deeply, so passionately, and so sacredly, as I am loved by my ever-loving wife.

I hope that my remaining life on the earth (whether short or long) will exhibit to you a daily proof that this beautiful affection is reverently returned. . . . Ever yours. THEODORE.

"A DAY'S MARCH NEARER HOME."

SPRINGFIELD, O., March 15, 1869.

MY DEAR PET : . . . Every morning I say to myself, "A day's march nearer home." I never before have so longed for home as now. I am impatient for a sight of my own house and its familiar faces. Now that the time draws near, I feel less able to bear my separation than when I was in the midst of my tour. . . .

I am determined that, on getting home, I shall spend a great deal of time in taking care of you, reading to you, talking with you, and petting you.

I hunger and thirst for you and the children, every day and hour. Give my love to them all. Ever yours, THEODORE.

MISSING THE CHILDREN.

BROOKLYN, August 7, 1869.

MY DEAR PET : . . . Give my love to the children. How dear they all seem ! Although this house never looked prettier than it does now,—specially on this clear, crisp, cool morning,—yet the absent voices and faces are dreadfully missed by its wifeless and childless master. . . . Lovingly yours. THEODORE.

"ETHEREAL HAPPINESS."

AT THE OFFICE, August 24, 1869.

MY DARLING : . . . How I long to see you once again ! For two or three days past, I have been in a high and tranquil frame of mind, uplifted above wrong and untempted to evil. Whenever I am in such a state, I yearn to be with you more than with any other person in the world. No one else satisfies my soul. But alack ! I am so seldom, and for so short a time, in this ethereal happiness, that I have to speak of it as a novelty.

Commend me to the dear children. Kiss them one and all. Yours lovingly,

THEODORE.

"THE MOST WRETCHED SUMMER OF MY LIFE."

SATURDAY NIGHT, BROOKLYN, August 28, 1869.

MY DEAR WIFE : . . . I will confess frankly that I have passed the most wretched summer of my life, and no one knows it but myself ; indeed, no one who has been with me has seen me other than outwardly gay-and cheerful. All the exhibitions which I have made of myself to my friends have been of unusual hilarity. This has been the utmost shallowness of superficiality. *One* thing I *have* enjoyed; that is, my work. It has been unusually heavy, and therefore unusually beneficent. But, leaving my work aside, all my other pleasures have been pains. For two or three weeks I resolutely repressed all allusions to my feelings, when writing to you, not wishing to mar your vacation. But, as the time of your home-coming cannot be very far off, I open the flood-gates to-night. I will, therefore, say that I have missed you for the past month with something of the same awfulness and heart-break as if I had lost you forever by death. . . .

But I have discovered, by searching my soul, that I love you more than any human ought to love another. I have seen some noble women this summer, whom I admire, and whom, in a certain way, I love. All my life I have known something of the nature and experience of true friendship.

From my early years I have loved, and loved *you*. But all the past experiences of my heart's affections have been as nothing compared with the unusual and solemn sense which I have had, during all the hilarities of this Newport week, that the only human being who touches my highest nature is yourself. This being the case, I am filled with distress to think that I must keep you uninformed, for the sake of your own tranquillity, of many of my thoughts.

I would to God I were a man worthy of your goodness, your self-denial, and your singleness of heart. Occasionally, in some supreme hour, I am your fit mate ; but, at all other hours, you are high above me. But, if you know the inward reverence which I have borne toward you for many days past, even while appearing to be absorbed in the companionship of other ladies, and particularly at Newport, I am sure you would almost dread to be so much loved by any human (and therefore infirm and wayward) creature like myself.

I have several times tried to keep myself from writing you any such letter as this, because it is unlike most of my past correspondence. It is my request that no other eye shall ever see it except your own. Indeed, after this letter is in the mail, I shall probably grieve to think I wrote it. But, on the other hand, I shall never feel content until I have, in some measure, confessed to you that, all summer long, I have trembled at the thought that you are almost as much to me as God Himself, and yet that I am constantly treating *you* as ungratefully as I treat *Him*. Yours, in frankness,

THEODORE.

IN THE OIL REGIONS.

PITTSBURGH, PA., Jan. 10, 1870.

MY DARLING WIFE: I owe the short remainder of this evening to *you*, and shall fulfill my debt. . . .

You have never seen the oil-regions. I have been in them four days. During the time have seen hardly less than a thousand oil-wells, some of them a thousand feet deep; some of them yielding a hundred barrels a day, and making their owners as rich as Princes; and some of them dry, useless, and profitless—a means of ruining many speculators. I must have passed the very spot to-day where Washington crossed the Allegheny on a raft. If that thrifty gentleman had suspected the existence of petroleum, he might have spent his life in sinking wells, building derricks, and tanking oil, and have never become the Father of his Country.

. . . Give my love to the children, and say that I shall take an early opportunity to write them a letter. But, as a general rule, my only chance to get a pen in my hand is between my lecture and my bed-time; and oftentimes the Committee steal away even this little bit of coveted leisure. . . .

My remembrances to Sophia, and to the other members of "my house and heart."

Lovingly yours,

THEODORE.

"PITIFUL INK."

SPRINGFIELD, Jan. 16, 1870.

MY DEAR WIFE: A fierce rain is falling, and the window-panes are pelted with it. My sojourn is in a stately house, situated on a high ridge of land, and overlooking the Lagonda Valley. The exposed and commanding situation gives me all the voices of the storm. Heaven's great organ blows to-night.

I repeat my cry of "No letters." *One* letter, indeed, I *did* receive last evening, but it was the one you had sent to Tidioute a week before. I have received *none* direct from home. It was because I worried myself with thinking that something was wrong that I sent you the telegram from Columbus. The answer to that telegram came promptly; I received it on the same day that I sent the dispatch.

I am writing these lines from the most vexatious of inkstands,—a little aged glass bottle, with an ebb-tide of muddy ink at the bottom of it. I wanted to write you a long and gossipy lingo. But here, in a rich man's house, I have hardly ink enough to sign my name. Mem. : when strangers (particularly if they be literary men) make a visit to *our* house, provide them with good ink if even you have to give them a bad breakfast. . . .

A happy pair, a ten weeks' bride and groom, are in the house,—both young, handsome, and jubilant, —the light of the honeymoon shining in their faces,—"youth at the prow and pleasure at the helm." O the merry, merry days when *we* were young ! . . .

I cannot pen with this pitiful ink the love which my heart prompts me to send ; for there is only ne more drop in the bottle, and *that* I must save for directing the envelope. Affectionately yours,

THEODORE.

"THERE IS BUT ONE HOME."

DES MOINES, Iowa, January 30, 1870.

MY DEAR PET : In this far-away town, the extreme western limit of my journey, I feel my home-oickness more than ever before. To-morrow morning I begin my slow march eastward ; but I shall feel like a sailor tossed on the sea until I get to my final haven of rest in my own house. There is but one home. . . . Affectionately yours,

THEODORE.

"OVERFLOWING LOVE."

DETROIT, December 16.

MY DEAR PET : I am well,—splendid appetite,—good sleep o' nights,—cheerful and merry-hearted, —never more full of animal spirits in all my life. If you were here, I would kiss you on both cheeks, and we would dance up and down the long parlor, and would celebrate outwardly the festival which I feel within me.

With overflowing love to yourself and the dear children, I am, now as ever, yours wholly,

THEODORE.

"O GOLDEN EARLY DAYS !"

FOND DU LAC, Wis., February 10.

MY DARLING : . . . At this moment, in the midst of these recollections, the sound of a piano in the next room makes me half believe that you, the young maiden Elizabeth of fifteen years ago, are the player.

O golden early days ! Yours ever,

THEODORE TILTON.

EXPLANATION OF AN ABSENCE.

NEW YORK, February 19, 1870.

MY DARLING : Don't think I have deserted you altogether.

Last night, after the meeting, I found myself engaged so late at the St. Denis that, rather than walk home, I staid all night. Wendell Phillips, Mary Greer, Julia Ward Howe, James Redpath, Frederick Douglas, and others, were there, and I wanted to be among them.

The telegraph-office was shut, or I would have sent you a message to be delivered early this morning.

It may be that I shall be home to-night, but probably not.

If I am not there at twelve, consider that I shall remain in New York.

At five this afternoon we (that is, the aforesaid persons) were all to be at Mrs. Botta's.

I fear I have troubled you by staying away. If so, forgive me, and be assured that I would rather be home than here. With a hundred kisses, yours,

THEODORE.

EDITING MORE AGREEABLE THAN POLITICS.

HOUSE OF REPRESENTATIVES, April 3, 1870.

MY SPOUSE : This day is as golden as a wedding-ring. The sun shines, the birds sing, the crocuses bloom in the Capitol grounds, and I am sick at heart with being here without a sight of your face for nigh a month. Neither sun, nor birds, nor flowers, can make any reparation for my loss.

. . . I have become almost a bachelor. My stay from home appears longer than my stay in the West. The reason of this is, that my days and evenings are crowded more full of busy incidents. I have learned whole volumes of human nature since I have been staying here. Moreover, I have been fortunate in watching how the great engine of the Government is worked, like a man who has access to the machine-room of a steamship. I am thoroughly convinced that my present editorial profession is far more agreeable than if I were a Congressman or any kind of politician: So you must quench your ambition to be the Hon. Mrs. Tilton. Yours, with love to chicks,

THEODORE.

"UNDIVIDED AND EVER-GROWING LOVE."

APRIL 6, 1870.

DARLING OF MY HEART: This is Sunday—day of thoughts of home. I am alone in my room, wishing you were here to bear me company. I shall go this afternoon to speak to Henry Highland Garnet's school. I meant to go to church this morning, but have been writing to the *Independent*. I have met a good woman here, who shows me in her face exactly how you will look when you grow old. She is the wife of Senator G——. . . .

I shall probably remain ten or twelve days more. Can you not make me a little visit during that time? Think twice before you finally say No. Meanwhile, accept my undivided and ever growing love, and kiss the children for their father's sake.

THEODORE.

Mr. Tilton's letters, which end here, were followed, three months afterward, by his wife's confession to him of her intimacy with Mr. Beecher. This confession was made (according to Mr. Tilton's sworn statement) on the 2d of July, 1870. The letters above given, it will be noticed, cover the exact period which is mentioned in Mrs. Tilton's testimony as having been a period marked by ill-treatment by her husband, namely, from 1866 onward. They negative that testimony in every important point.

MOULTON'S STATEMENT.

On Friday, August 21st, the following remarkable letter and statement was published. It treats fully of the relations of our "Mutual friend," Mr. Francis D. Moulton, with the famous Beecher-Tilton romance:

To the Public:

I became a party almost accidentally in the unhappy controversy between Mr. Beecher and Mr. Tilton. I had been a friend of Mr. Tilton since my boyhood, and for Mr. Beecher I had always entertained the warmest admiration.

In 1870 I learned for the first time that Mr. Beecher had given Mr. Tilton so grave a cause of offense that, if the truth should be made public, a great national calamity would ensue. I believed that the scandal would tend to undermine the very foundations of social order, to lay low a beneficent power for good in our country, and blast the prospects and blight the family of one of the most brilliant and promising of the rising men of the generation. This disaster—as I deemed it and still regard it—I determined to try and avert.

For nearly four years I have labored most assiduously to save both of these men from the consequences of their acts, whether of unwisdom or passion—acts which have already seriously involved them in needless and disastrous quarrel, which is made the pretext of pouring on the community a flood of impurity and scandal deeply affecting their own families, and threatening like a whirlpool, if not stilled, to draw into its vortex the peace of mind and good repute of a host of others. More than all, I saw that, because of the "transgression of another," innocent children would be burdened with a load of obloquy which would weigh most heavily and cruelly on their young lives.

All these considerations determined me to take an active part in the transactions which have since become so notorious.

This decision involved me in great anxiety and labor, for which the hope of saving these interests could be my only compensation. Even that reward has now failed me, and instead of it an attempt is made to throw on me a part of the shame and disgrace which belongs to the actors alone.

One of them, whom I have zealously endeavored to serve, has seen fit, with all the power of his vast influence and matchless art as a writer, to visit on me the penalties of his own wrong-doing,—at the same time publicly appealing to me to make known the truth, as if it would justify his attack on me!

I feel that the failure of my exertions has not been owing to any fault of mine. I worked faithfully and sincerely, under the almost daily advice and direction of Mr. Beecher, with his fullest approbation, confidence, and beaming gratitude, until, as I think, in an evil hour for him, he took other advisers. I have failed; and now, strangely enough, he seems to desire to punish me for the sad consequences of the folly, insincerity, and wickedness of his present counselors.

Mr. Beecher, in his statement, testifies that he brought on this investigation without my knowledge or advice.

Even while mourning what seemed to me the utter unwisdom of this proceeding, I have done all I could honorably do to avert the catastrophe. I have kept silent, although I saw with sorrow that this silence was deeply injuring the friend of my boyhood.

Prompted by a sense of duty—not to one only, but to all the parties involved—I denied the united and public appeals made to me by Mr. Beecher and Mr. Tilton to produce the evidence in my possession; partly because I felt that the injury thereby done to Mr. Tilton was far less calamitous than the destruction which must come on all the interests I had for years tried to conserve, and especially on Mr. Beecher himself, if I should comply with this request.

But I stated clearly that in one emergency I *should* speak—namely, in defense of my own integrity of action if it should be wantonly assailed.

I left Mr. Beecher untrammeled by the facts in my hands to defend himself, without the necessity of attacking me.

But the published accusations of Mr. Beecher affecting my character, my own self-respect, the advice of friends, and public justice make it imperative that "the truth, the whole truth, and nothing but the truth" should now be fully declared.

I give to the public, therefore, the statement I had prepared to bring before the committee, without the alteration or addition of a sentence and scarcely a word—certainly without the change of a single syllable—since I read Mr. Beecher's statement and evidence, or because of it.

This paper I withheld from the committee when before it in a last despairing effort for peace, at the earnest solicitation of some of Mr. Beecher's friends, and with the approval also of some of the most valued of my own.

I do not now give it to the committee, but to the public, because its production concerns myself rather than the principals in the strife. It is made for my own protection against public accusations, and not to aid either party to the controversy.

For the needless and cruel necessity that now so imperatively compels its production I have the most profound grief—for which there is but a single alleviation: namely, that the disclosure of the facts at this time can scarcely work more harm to him whom I at first tried to befriend by withholding them from the public, than they would have caused him in January, 1871, when, but for my interference, the public most assuredly would have been put in possession of the whole truth.

This publication, to which Mr. Beecher forces me, renders fruitless four years of constant and sincere efforts to save him. It leaves him and Mrs. Tilton in almost the same position in which I found them, excepting in so far as their own late disingenuous untruthfulness in their solemn statements may lower them in the estimation of the world.

I reserve to myself the right hereafter to review the statements of Mr. Beecher in contrast with the facts as shown by the documents herewith subjoined, and others which I have at my hand,—the production of which did not seem to be necessary until some portion of the published evidence of Mr. Beecher demanded contradiction.

(Signed), . FRANCIS D. MOULTON.

STATEMENT OF FRANCIS D. MOULTON.

GENTLEMEN OF THE COMMITTEE : I need not repeat to you my great, very great sorrow to feel obliged to answer your invitation, and, with the permission of the parties, to put before you the exact facts which have been committed to me, or come to my knowledge in the unhappy affair under investigation. In so doing I shall use no words of characterization of any of them, or of inculpation of the parties, nor shall I attempt to ascribe motives, save when necessary to exactly state the fact, leaving the occurrences, their acts of omission and commission, to be interpreted by themselves. In giving conversations or narrative, I, of course, can in most cases give only the substance of the first, and will attempt to give words only when they so impressed themselves upon my mind as to remain in my memory, and of the latter only so much as seems to me material.

I have known Mr. Theodore Tilton since 1850 intimately, in the kindest relations of social and personal friendship. I have known Rev. Henry Ward Beecher since 1869, and then casually as an acquaintance and an attendant upon his ministrations up to the beginning of the occurrences of which I shall speak.

Seeing Mr. Tilton's valedictory, as editor of the *Independent*, on the 22d of December, 1870, I inferred that there had been some differences between himself and Mr. Henry C. Bowen, the proprietor, but learning that Tilton had been retained as contributor to that journal and editor of the Brooklyn *Union*, of which Bowen was also proprietor, I supposed that the differences were not personal or unkind. Up to that time, although I had been a frequent visitor at Tilton's house, and had seen himself and Mrs. Tilton under all the phases of social intercourse, I had never heard or known of the slightest disagreement or unkindness existing between them, but had believed their marital relations were almost exceptionally pleasant. On the 26th day of December, 1870, being at Mr. Tilton's house, he came home from an interview with Mr. Bowen, and told me with some excitement of manner that he had just had a conference with Bowen, and that in that interview Bowen had made certain accusations against Beecher, and had challenged him (Tilton), as a matter of duty to the public to write an open letter, which Bowen was to take to Beecher, of which he showed me the original draft which is as follows:

[FIRST DRAFT—MARKED "A."]

December 26, 1870—BROOKLYN.

Henry Ward Beecher:

SIR: I demand that, for the reasons which you explicitly understand, you immediately cease from the ministry of Plymouth Church, and that you quit the City of Brooklyn as a residence.

(Signed) THEODORE TILTON.

Tilton explained that the words "for the reasons which you explicitly understand," were interlined at the request of Bowen, and he further stated that he told Bowen that he was prepared to believe his charges because Beecher had made improper advances to Mrs. Tilton. Surprised at this, I asked him, "What?" when he replied, "Don't ask me; I can't tell you." I then said, "Is it possible you could have been so foolish as to sign that letter on the strength of Bowen's assertion, and not have Bowen sign it too, although, as you say, he was to carry it to Beecher?" He answered "Mr. Bowen gave me his word that he would sustain the charges, and adduce the evidence to prove them whenever called upon, I said, "I fear you will find yourself mistaken. Has the letter gone?" He answered, "Bowen said he would take it immediately." I afterwards learned from Beecher that Bowen had done so, because on the first of January following Beecher gave me the copy he received, as I find by a memorandum made at the time on the envelope, and I find by a later memorandum on the envelope that the original draft was given to me by Mr. Tilton on the 5th of the same month. I insert here the following memorandum of the facts above stated, made at the time, giving the hour when it was made:

BROOKLYN, December 26, 1870.

Theodore Tilton informed me to-day that he had sent a note to Mr. Beecher, of which Mr. H. C. Bowen was the bearer, demanding that he, Beecher, should retire from his pulpit and quit the city of Brooklyn. The letter was an open one. H. C. Bowen knew the contents of it, and said that he, Bowen, would sustain Tilton in this demand.

3:45 P. M.

In a day or two after that Mr. Tilton called on me at my house and said that he had sent word to Bowen that he was going to call on Beecher within half an hour, or shortly; that Bowen came up into the office with great anger, and told him if he should say to Beecher what he, Bowen, had told him concerning his (Beecher's) adulteries, he would dismiss him from the *Independent* and the *Union*. Tilton told him that he had never been influenced by threats, and he would not be in the present case, and he subsequently received Bowen's letter of dismissal.

What those charges were, and the account of the interview, will appear in the following letter, addressed to Bowen by Tilton, bearing date the 1st of January, 1871, which also gives in substance and in more detail what Tilton had said to me in the two conversations which I have mentioned:

TILTON TO BOWEN.

BROOKLYN, January 1, 1871.

Mr. HENRY C. BOWEN,

S R: I received last evening your sudden notices breaking my two contracts—one with the *Independent*, the other with the Brooklyn *Union*.

With reference to this act of yours I will make a plain statement of facts.

It was during the early part of the rebellion (if I recollect aright) when you first intimated to me that the Rev. Henry Ward Beecher had committed acts of adultery for which, if you should expose him, he would be driven from his pulpit. From that time onward your references to this subject were frequent, and always accompanied with the exhibition of a deep-seated injury to your heart.

In a letter which you addressed to me from Woodstock, June 16, 1863, referring to this subject, you said: "I sometimes feel that I *must break silence,* that I *must* no longer suffer as a *dumb man,* and be made to bear a load of grief *most unjustly.* One word from me would make a *revolution* throughout Christendom, I had almost said—and *you know it.* . . . You have just a little of the evidence from the great volume in my possession. . . . I am not pursuing a phantom, but solemnly brooding over an awful reality."

The underscorings in this extract are your own. Subsequently to the date of this letter, and at frequent intervals from then till now, you have repeated the statement that you could at any moment expel Henry Ward Beecher from Brooklyn. You have reiterated the same thing not only to me but to others.

Moreover, during the year just closed, your allusions to the subject were uttered with more feeling than heretofore, and were not unfrequently coupled with your emphatic declaration that Mr. Beecher ought not to be allowed to occupy a public position as a Christian preacher and teacher.

On the 26th of December, 1870, at an interview in your house, at which Mr. Oliver Johnson and I were present, you spoke freely and indignantly against Mr. Beecher as an unsafe visitor among the families of his congregation. You alluded by name to a woman, now a widow, whose husband's death you had no doubt was hastened by his knowledge that Mr. Beecher had maintained with her an improper intimacy. You avowed your knowledge of several other cases of Mr. Beecher's adulteries. Moreover, as if to leave no doubt on the mind of either Mr. Johnson or myself, you informed us that Mr. Beecher had made to you a confession of his guilt, and had with tears implored your forgiveness. After Mr. Johnson retired from this interview, you related to me the case of a woman whom you said (as nearly as I can recall your words) that . . .

During your recital of the tale you were full of anger towards Mr. Beecher. You said, with terrible emphasis, that he ought not to remain a week longer in his pulpit. You immediately suggested that a demand should be made upon him to quit his sacred office. You volunteered to bear to him such a demand in the form of an open letter, which you would present to him with your own hand; and you pledged yourself to sustain the demand which this letter should make—namely, that he should, for reasons which he explicitly knew, immediately cease from his ministry of Plymouth Church and retire from Brooklyn.

The first draft of the letter did not contain the phrase "for reasons which he explicitly knew," and these words (or words to this effect) were incorporated in a second, at your motion. You urged furthermore (and very emphatically) that the letter should demand not only Mr. Beecher's abdication of his pulpit but cessation of his writing for the *Christian Union,* a point on which you were overruled. This letter you presented to Mr. Beecher at Mr. Freeland's house. Shortly after its presentation you sought an interview with me in the editorial office of the Brooklyn *Union,* during which, with unaccountable emotion in your manner, your face livid with rage, you threatened with a loud voice that if I ever should inform Mr. Beecher of the statements which you had made concerning his adultery, or should compel you to adduce the evidence on which you agreed to sustain the demand for Mr. Beecher's withdrawal from Brooklyn, you would immediately deprive me of my engagement to write for the *Independent* and to edit the Brooklyn *Union,* and that in case I should ever attempt to enter the offices of those journals you would have me ejected by force. I told you that I should inform Mr. Beecher or anybody else, according to the dictates of my judgment, uninfluenced by any threat from my employer. You then excitedly retired from my presence. Hardly had your violent words ceased ringing in my ears, when I received your summary notices breaking my contracts with the *Independent* and the Brooklyn *Union.* To the foregoing narrative of facts I have only to add my surprise and regret at the sudden interruption, by your own act, of what has been, on my part towards you, a faithful friendship of fifteen years,

Truly yours,

(Signed)

THEODORE TILTON.

In this letter I have omitted the sentence quoted as the words of Mr. Bowen, after the words, "as nearly as I can recall your words, that"—simply desiring to say that it contained a charge of a rape, or something very nearly like ravishment, of a woman other than Mrs. Tilton, told in words that are unfit to be spread upon the record, but, if desired, the original is for the inspection of the Committee.

On Friday evening, the 30th of December, being the night of the Plymouth Church prayer-meeting, Tilton came to me and said, in substance, that by his wife's request he had determined to see Beecher, in order to show to Beecher a confession of his wife of the intercourse between them, which he (Tilton) had never up to that time mentioned to him (Beecher), and the fact of the confession, of which his wife had told him that she had never told Beecher, although her confession had been made in July previous in writing, which writing he (Tilton) had afterwards destroyed; but that his wife, fearing that, if the Bowen accusations against Beecher were made public, the whole matter would be known, and her own

FRANCIS D. MOULTON.

FRANK B CARPENTER.

conduct with Beecher become exposed, had renewed her confession in her own handwriting, which he handed to me to read, which was the first knowledge I had of its existence.

Tilton did not tell me how his wife came to make the confession in July, nor did I at that time or ever after ask. Indeed, I may state here, once for all, that I refrained from asking confessions of the acts of all the parties further than they chose to make them to me voluntarily for the purpose for which I was acting.

Tilton wanted me to go down and ask Beecher to come up and see him at my house, which I did. I said to Mr. Beecher, "Mr. Tilton wants you to come and see him at my house immediately." He asked, "What for?" I replied, "He wants to make some statement to you in reference to your relations with his family." He then called to some one in the back room to go down and say that he should not be at the prayer-meeting, and we went out together.

It was storming at the time, when he remarked, "There is an appropriateness in this storm," and asked me, "What can I do? What can I do?" I said, "Mr. Beecher, I am not a Christian, but if you wish I will show you how well a heathen can serve you." We then went to my house, and I showed him into the chamber over the parlor, where Mr. Tilton was, and left them together. In about an hour Mr. Beecher came down and asked me if I had seen the confession of Elizabeth. I said I had. Said he, "This will kill me," and asked me to walk out with him. I did so, and we walked to Mr. Tilton's house together, and he went in. On the way he said, "This is a terrible catastrophe; it comes upon me as if struck by lightning."

He went into Tilton's house and I returned home. Within an hour he returned to my house, and we left my house again together, and I walked with him to his house. Tilton remained at my house while Beecher was absent at Tilton's house, and when he returned there was no conversation between them. When we arrived at Beecher's house he wanted me to stand by him in this emergency, and procure a reconciliation if possible. I told him I would, because the interests of women, children, and families were involved, if for no other reason. That ended the interview that night. During this evening nothing was said by Beecher as to the truth or falsity of Mrs. Tilton's confession, nor did he inform me that he had obtained from her any recantation of the confession, which I afterwards learned he had done.

I returned to my house and had some conversation with Tilton, in which he told me that he had recited to Beecher the details of the confession of his wife's adulteries, and the remark which Beecher made was, "This is all a dream, Theodore," and that that was all the answer that Beecher made to him. I then advised Tilton that, for the sake of his wife and family, and for the sake of Beecher's family, the matter should be kept quiet and hushed up. The next morning as I was leaving home for business Tilton came to my house and with great anger said that Beecher had done a mean act; that he had gone from that interview of last night to his house and procured from Elizabeth a recantation and retraction of her confession. He said for that act he would smite him; that there could be no peace. He said: "You see that what I have told you of the meanness of that man is now evident." Tilton said that Beecher at the interview of last night had asked his permission to go and see Elizabeth, and he told him he might go, which statement was confirmed by Beecher himself, and Beecher left him for that purpose. I said to Tilton: "Now don't get angry; let us see if even this cannot be arranged. I will go down and get that retraction from him."

I was then going to my business, so that I was unable to go that morning, but went that evening, saw Beecher, and told him that I thought he had been doing a very mean and treacherous act—treacherous first, towards me, from whom he wanted help, in that he did not tell me on our way to his house last night what he had procured from Mrs. Tilton, and that he could not expect my friendship in this matter, unless he acted truthfully and honorably towards me. I further said: "Mr. Beecher, you have had criminal intercourse with Mrs. Tilton; you have done great injury to Tilton otherwise. Now when you are confronted with it you ask permission of the man to again visit his house, and you get from that woman who has confessed you have ruined her, a recantation and retraction of the truth for your mere personal safety. That won't save you."

At that interview he admitted with grief and sorrow the fact of his sexual relations with Mrs. Tilton, expressed some indignation that she had not told him that she had told her husband, and that in consequence of being in ignorance of that fact he had been walking upon a volcano—referring to what he had done in connection with Bowen and with reference to Tilton's family. He said that he had sympathized with Bowen, and had taken sides with him as against Tilton, in consequence of stories which were in circulation in regard to him, and especially of one specific case where he had been informed that Tilton had had improper relations with a woman whom he named, and to whom a letter from his wife will make a part of this statement, and had so stated to Bowen. And he told me that he would write to Bowen and withdraw those charges, and gave me the rough draft of a letter which he wrote and sent to Bowen, which letter is here produced marked "C":

BEECHER TO BOWEN.

BROOKLYN, January 2, 1871.

MY DEAR MR. BOWEN: Since I saw you last Tuesday I have reason to think that the only cases of which I spoke to you in regard to Mr. Tilton were exaggerated in being reported to me, and I should be unwilling to have anything I said, though it was but little, weigh on your mind in a matter so important to his welfare. I am informed by one on whose judgment and integrity I greatly rely, and who has the means of forming an opinion better than any of us, that he knows the whole matter about Mrs.——, and that the stories are not true, and that the same is the case with other stories. I do not wish any reply to this. I thought it only due to justice that I should say so much. Truly yours,

(Signed)   H. W. BEECHER.

Mr. Beecher told me that Mrs. Beecher and himself, without knowing of the confession of Mrs. Tilton to her husband, had been expressing great sympathy towards Mrs. Tilton, and taking an active interest with her against her husband. I said, "Mr. Beecher, I want that recantation ; I have come for it." "Well," said he, "what shall I do without it ?" I replied, "I don't know ; I can tell you what will happen with it." He asked, "What will you do if I give it to you ?" I answered, "I will keep it as I keep the confession. If you act honorably I will protect it with my life, as I would protect the other with my life. Mr. Tilton asked for that confession this morning, and I said, "I will never give it to you ; you shall not have it from my hands until I have exhausted every effort for peace." Mr. Beecher gave me back the paper, the original of which I now produce in Mrs. Tilton's handwriting, marked "D," as follows :

MRS. TILTON'S RECANTATION.

DECEMBER 30, 1870.

Wearied with importunity and weakened by sickness, I gave a letter inculpating my friend Henry Ward Beecher, under assurances that that would remove all difficulties between me and my husband. That letter I now revoke. I was persuaded to it, almost forced, when I was in a weakened state of mind. I regret it and recall all its statements.

(Signed)   E. R. TILTON.

I desire to say explicitly Mr. Beecher has never offered any improper solicitations, but has always treated me in a manner becoming a Christian and a gentleman.

(Signed)   ELIZABETH R. TILTON.

Afterwards Mr. Tilton left with me another letter, dated the same night of the recantation, December 30, bearing on the same topic, to be kept with the papers, which was in his wife's handwriting. It is here produced and marked "E," as follows :

MRS. TILTON'S RETRACTION OF HER RECANTATION.

DECEMBER 30, 1870—Midnight.

MY DEAR HUSBAND : I desire to leave with you before going to sleep a statement that Mr. Henry Ward Beecher called upon me this evening, asked me if I would defend him against any accusation in a *council of ministers*, and I replied solemnly that I would in case the accuser was any other person than my husband. He (H. W. B.) dictated a letter which I copied as my own, to be used by him as against any other accuser except my husband. This letter was designed to vindicate Mr. Beecher against all other persons save only yourself. I was ready to give him this letter because he said with pain that my letter in your hands addressed to him, dated December 29, "had struck him dead and ended his usefulness."

You and I both are pledged to do our best to avoid publicity. God grant a speedy end to all further anxieties. Affectionately,

(Signed)   ELIZABETH.

When I went home with the recantation I found Tilton there and showed it to him. He expressed his surprise and gratification that I should have been able to get it, and I then showed to him how very foolish it would have been in the morning to have proceeded angrily against Beecher. I made another appeal for peace, saying that, notwithstanding great difficulties appeared in the way, if they were properly dealt with they could be beaten out of the way. He expressed his willingness and desire for peace.

When I saw Beecher I made an agreement, at his request, to go and see him on Sunday, January 1. I went to his house in accordance with the engagement. He took me into his study, and then told me again of his great surprise that Elizabeth should have made the confession of his criminal commerce with her to her husband without letting him (B.) know anything about it, making his destruction at any moment possible, and without warning to him. He expressed his great grief at this wrong which he had done as a minister, and friend to Theodore, and at his request I took pen and paper, and he dictated to me the following paper, all of which is in my handwriting except the words, "I have trusted this to Moulton in confidence," and the signature, which latter are in Mr. Beecher's. It is here produced and marked "F."

LETTER OF CONTRITION.

BROOKLYN, January 1, 1871.

In trust with F. D. Moulton.

MY DEAR FRIEND MOULTON: I ask through you Theodore Tilton's forgiveness, and I humble myself before him as I do before my God. He would have been a better man in my circumstances than I have been. I can ask nothing except that he will remember all the other hearts that would ache. I will not plead for myself. I even wish that I were dead; but others must live and suffer.

I will die before any one but myself shall be implicated. All my thoughts are running towards my friends, towards the poor child lying there and praying with her folded hands. She is guiltless—sinned against; bearing the transgression of another. Her forgiveness I have. I humbly pray to God that he may put it into the heart of her husband to forgive me.

I have trusted this to *Moulton* in confidence.

(Signed)   H. W. BEECHER.

This was intrusted to me in confidence, to be shown only to Tilton, which I did. It had reference to no other fact or act than the confession of sexual intercourse between Beecher and Mrs. Tilton, which he at that interview confessed, and denied not, but confessed. He also at other interviews subsequently held between us in relation to this unfortunate affair unqualifiedly confessed that he had been guilty of adultery with Mrs. Tilton, and always in a spirit of grief and sorrow at the enormity of the crime he had committed against Mr. Tilton's family. At such times he would speak with much feeling of the relation he had sustained towards them as pastor, spiritual adviser, and trusted friend. His self-condemnation at the ruin he had wrought under such circumstances was full and complete, and at times he was so bowed down with grief in consequence of the wrong he had done that he threatened to put an end to his life. He also gave to me the letter the first draft of which, marked "A," is above given, in reference to which he said that Bowen had given it to him; that he had told Bowen that Tilton must be crazy to write such a letter as that; that he did not understand it, and that Bowen said to him, "I will be your friend in this matter." He then made a statement which Tilton had made to me at my house of the charge that Bowen had made to him (Tilton); said that Bowen had been very treacherous towards Tilton, as well as towards himself, because he (Beecher) had had a reconciliation with Bowen, of which he told me the terms, and that Bowen had never in his (Beecher's) presence spoken of or referred to any allegation of crime or wrong-doing on his part with any woman whatever. He gave me, in general terms, the reconciliation, and afterwards gave me two memoranda, which I here produce, which show the terms of the reconciliation. The first is in the handwriting of Bowen, containing five items, which Beecher assured me were the terms which Bowen claimed should be the basis of reconciliation. It is as follows, and is marked "G":

BOWEN'S TERMS.

First—Report and publish sermons and lecture-room talks.
Second—New edition Plymouth Collection and Freeland's interest.
Third—Explanations to church.
Fourth—Write me a letter.
Fifth—Retract in every quarter what has been said to my injury.

The second paper is a pencil memorandum of the reconciliation with Bowen in Beecher's handwriting, giving an account of the affair. It is marked "H," as follows:

RECONCILIATION WITH BOWEN.

About February, 1870, at a long interview at Mr. Freeland's house, for the purpose of having a full and final reconciliation between Bowen and Beecher, Mr. Bowen stated his grievances, which were *all* either of a business nature or of my treatment of *him personally* (as per memorandum in his writing).

After hours of conference everything was adjusted. We shook hands. We pledged each other to work henceforth without a jar or break. I said to him : "Mr. Bowen if you hear anything of me not in accordance with this agreement of harmony, do not let it rest. Come straight to me at once, and I will do the same by you."

He agreed. In the lecture-room I stated that all our differences were over, and that we were friends again. This public recognition he was present and heard, and expressed himself as greatly pleased with. It was after all this that I asked Mr. Howard to help me carry out this reconciliation, and to call on Mr. Bowen, and to remove the little differences between *them*.

Mr. Howard called, expressed his gratification.

Then it was that without any provocation he, Mr. Bowen, told Mr. Howard that this reconciliation did not include one matter, that he (Bowen) "knew *that* about Mr. Beecher which if he should speak it would drive Mr. Beecher out of Brooklyn." Mr. Howard protested with horror against such a statement, saying: "Mr. Bowen, this is terrible. No man should make such a statement unless he has the most absolute evidence." To this Mr. Bowen replied that he had this evidence, and said, pointedly, that he (Howard) might go to Mr. Beecher, and *that Mr. Beecher would never* give his consent that he (Bowen) should tell Mr. Howard this secret.

Mr. Bowen *at no time* had ever made known to Mr. B. what this secret was, and the hints which Mr. Beecher had had of it led him to think that it was *another matter,* and not the slander which he now finds it to be.

In that interview Beecher was very earnest in his expression of regret at what had been done against Tilton in relation to his business connection with Bowen, and besought me to do everything I could to save him from the destruction which would come upon him if the story of his (Beecher's) intercourse with Mrs. Tilton should be divulged. In compliance with the directions of Beecher, January 1, 1871, I took the paper marked " F," which he had dictated to me, to Tilton, detailed to him Beecher's expressions of regret and sorrow, spoke to him of his agony of mind, and again appealed to him to have the whole matter kept quiet, if for no other reason, for the sake of the children. To this Tilton assented. I found him writing the letter to Bowen of that date which I have before produced, marked " B." He told me also of the contracts he had with Bowen with a penalty, when he left the *Independent,* to be editor of the Brooklyn *Union* and special contributor to the *Independent* at a salary of one hundred dollars per week, with another salary of equal amount for his editorship of the Brooklyn *Union* and a portion of the profits. Copies of these contracts I cannot produce, because both papers were delivered to Bowen after the arbitration of the controversy of which I am about to speak. These contracts provided that they could be terminated by mutual consent, or upon six months' notice, or upon the death of either party, or at once by the party who wished to break or annul them paying to the other the sum of twenty-five hundred dollars. Tilton insisted that that sum, with his arrears of salary, was justly due him, and that he should bring suit against Bowen unless he settled, and he gave me an authorization to settle his affairs with Bowen, which paper I gave to Mr. Bowen when I went down to treat with him, retaining this copy, marked " I ":

MOULTON'S AUTHORIZATION.

BROOKLYN, January 2, 1871.

Mr. H C. Bowen.

SIR: I hereby authorize Mr. Francis D. Moulton to act in my behalf in full settlement with you of all my accounts growing out of my contracts for services to the *Independent* and the Brooklyn *Daily Union.* (Signed)

THEO. TILTON.

Acting in the interest of Beecher. I told Tilton that this controversy with Bowen, if possible, should be peacefully settled lest it might reöpen the other matters relating to Beecher's conduct in Tilton's family and the charges made by Bowen against Beecher. To this Tilton assented, giving me the authorization above quoted.

At my earliest convenience I called upon Bowen at his office upon this business, telling him that I wanted him to settle with me, as I was authorized by Tilton by this letter (handing him the letter) to settle for the breaking of his contract with Tilton as contributor to the *Independent* and as editor of the Brooklyn *Union.* I also handed him an article written by Tilton for the *Independent,* which he (Tilton) claimed was in part performance of his contract, which article was subsequently returned to Tilton by Bowen through me. Bowen said that he did not consider that he owed Tilton any money at all for breaking the contracts—that he had terminated them, having, in his opinion, sufficient reasons for so doing. "Well," I said, "Mr. Bowen, your contracts are specific." He said he "knew they were, but they provided for arbitration in case of any differences between the parties." I replied, in substance, that the arbitration only referred to differences between the parties as to the articles to be published as editor and contributor by Tilton, and as to Bowen's conduct as publisher, and that there was a fixed sum as penalty for breach of the contracts. The interview terminated with his refusal to settle the claim I demanded, which refusal I reported to Tilton, advising him still not to sue Bowen.

The following correspondence is with reference to my meeting Mr. Bowen on this business. The letter marked " J 1 " is my note to Mr. Bowen, and his reply, marked " J 2 ":

MOULTON TO BOWEN.

BROOKLYN, January 9, 1871.

Mr. Henry C. Bowen.

DEAR SIR: Referring to a recent interview with you, I would state that in consequence of illness I have been detained at home, and as I deem it of great importance to the interests of all concerned in the affairs about which we talked that you and I should meet at an early moment, if you will call at my house, No. 143 Clinton street, I shall be glad to see you at any hour convenient to yourself to-morrow. Truly yours, (Signed)

F. D. MOULTON.

BOWEN TO MOULTON.

90 WILLOW STREET,
BROOKLYN, January 10, 1871.

SIR: I am not very well myself, but will try to call at your house Thursday evening at eight o'clock. I am engaged to-morrow evening. I can go this evening if you will inform me that it will be convenient for you to see me. Unless I learn from you to the contrary, I will see you on Thursday evening. Very respectfully, (Signed)

HENRY C. BOWEN.

Mr. F. D. Moulton.

In pursuance of this correspondence we met at my house and entered into negotiations about the settlement of the contract with Tilton. At that time, during the interview, I showed Bowen the letter of January 1 of Tilton (which he—Tilton—had placed in my hands to use in accordance with my own discretion), heretofore given, marked "B." Bowen during the reading of the letter seemed to be much excited, and at only one point of the letter questioned the accuracy of its statements, which states as follows: "that alluding by name to a woman, now a widow, whose husband's death no doubt was hastened by his knowledge that Mr. Beecher had maintained with her an improper intimacy." To that he said, "I didn't make that allusion; Mr. Tilton made it." I went on to the close of the letter and finished it, when Bowen said to me, "Has Tilton told Beecher the contents of this letter?" I replied, "Yes, he has." Said he, "What shall I do? What I said at that interview was said in confidence. We struck hands there, and pledged ourselves to God that no one there present would reveal anything there spoken." I said to him, "It would be an easy matter to confirm what you say, or prove that what you say is false. Mr. Oliver Johnson was there, and I have submitted this letter to Mr. Johnson, in Mr. Tilton's presence, and he tells me that there was no obligatory confidence imposed on any of the parties concerning anything said at this interview, save a special pledge, mutually given, that nothing should be said concerning Mr. Beecher's demonstrations towards Mrs. Tilton. Mr. Johnson also says—and this confirms what you say in regard to one point, namely, that the allusion to the widow was made by Theodore Tilton, and that you said that you had no doubt that her husband's death was caused by his knowledge of her improper intimacy with Mr. Beecher. Quoting your language, he says that you said, 'I have no doubt about it whatever.' Mr. Johnson also says that your statements in regard to Beecher were not intimations of his adulteries, but plain and straightforward charges of the same. He says that you said that you knew of four or five cases of Mr. Beecher's adulterous intercourse with women. Mr. Johnson says also that you at that interview plainly declared that Mr. Beecher had confessed his guilt to you." I also said to him: "Mr. Tilton states that you said, 'I can't stand it any longer. You and I owe a duty to society in this matter. That man ought not to stay another week in his pulpit. It isn't safe for our families to have him in this city.'" I also said to him, "Mr. Johnson also states that at the interview of December 26, at your house, Willow street, you voluntarily pledged your word to Mr. Johnson that you would take no further measures in regard to Mr. Tilton without consultation with him (Mr. Johnson), and that you had said substantially the same thing to him previously, during private conversations between you and him."

I then said to Bowen that I thought he was a very treacherous man, and for this reason, that I knew he had had a reconciliation with Beecher—or rather I was informed of it—which was perfected in the house of God, and that within forty-eight hours from that time he had avowed to Mr. Howard that he could, if he chose, drive Mr. Beecher out of town. I told him further that I was also informed that, prior to that reconciliation, he had made no charge against Beecher's character to Beecher, but only behind his back; and I said: "Mr. Bowen, I have the points of settlement between you and Beecher, in your own handwriting, and there is no reference to any charge of crime of any kind against Beecher." Mr. Bowen made no denial of these assertions of mine, but seemed, on the contrary, abashed and dejected, and in reply to my question, "What do you say to these charges which you have made against Beecher?" he declined to say anything about them, but repeated the question, "What can I do?" I answered, "I am not your adviser; I cannot dictate to you what course you should pursue; but you have done great injustice to Mr. Tilton and to Mr. Beecher, and you ought to take the earliest means of repairing the injury. I should think it would be but just for you to restore Tilton to the *Independent*, but I don't believe he would go back if you should offer it to him." His reply was, "How can I do that now?" I told him I didn't know; he must find a way to settle his own difficulties. He again expressed his willingness to arbitrate the question of money, between himself and Tilton, growing out of the contract. I told him that I would not arbitrate; that a plain provision of the contract provided that he should pay what I demanded, and he must fulfill it. Mr. Bowen rose to leave, and said, before leaving, whenever I wanted to see him he would be happy to come to my house and confer on this subject; and he did, on several subsequent occasions, visit me at my house whenever I sent for him to consult on this matter. The means I have of giving so accurately the conversation between myself and Bowen as to conversations had with Tilton and Oliver Johnson are, that prior to my meeting with Bowen, as I told him, I had an interview with Oliver Johnson in the presence of Tilton, where the whole matter was discussed, and a memorandum of Oliver Johnson's statement, in which he gave his recollection of the interview of December 26, when Tilton and Johnson were present, was taken down by Tilton in short-hand, in my presence, and copied out at the time in Johnson's presence, which memorandum has been in my possession ever since, and from which I read each statement, one after the other, to Mr. Bowen. I here produce it, marked "K":

OLIVER JOHNSON'S STATEMENT.

· At the interview of December 26 (Willow street, No. 90). Mr. Bowen voluntarily pledged his word to Mr. Johnson that he (H. C. B.) would take no further measures in regard to Mr. Tilton without consultation with Mr. Johnson. Mr. Bowen likewise had said substantially the same thing to Mr. Johnson previously, during private conversations between those two persons.

There was no obligatory confidence imposed on any of the parties concerning anything said at this interview save a special pledge mutually given that nothing should be said concerning Mr. Beecher's demonstrations towards Mrs. Tilton.

Mr. O. J. says that Mr. Bowen's statements in regard to H. W. B, were not intimations of H. W. B.'s adulteries, but plain and straightforward charges of the same. H. C. B. stated that he knew four or five cases of Mr. B,'s adulterous intercourse with women.

O. J. says that H. C. B. at this interview plainly declared that H. W. B. had confessed his guilt to H. C. B.

H. C. B.—I cannot stand it any longer. You and I owe a duty to society in this matter. That man ought not to stay another week in his pulpit. It is not safe for our families to have him in this city.

The allusion to the widow was made by T. T., and H. C. B. said he had no doubt that her husband's death was caused by his knowledge of her improper intimacy with H. W. B. "I have no doubt about it whatever."

To make an end of the statement as to the controversy between Tilton and Bowen, I further state that various negotiations were had between Bowen and myself, which resulted finally in an arbitration in which H. B. Claflin, Charles Storrs, and James Freeland were referees ; that there was very considerable delay arising from my own absence South in the early spring on account of sickness, Mr. Bowen's absence during the summer, and Tilton's absence during the fall and winter on his lecturing tour ; so that the arbitration did not terminate until the 2d of April, 1872. This arbitration was determined upon by me, and my determination given to Mr. Claflin in the following note, which I sent, marked "K 2":

MOULTON TO CLAFLIN.

BROOKLYN, April 1, 1872.

MY DEAR MR. CLAFLIN: After full consideration of all interests other than Theodore's, I have advised him to arbitrate, on grounds which he will explain to you, and which I hope will accord with your judgment and kind wishes towards all concerned. Cordially yours,

(Signed)   FRANCIS D. MOULTON.

Tilton and Bowen and myself appeared before the arbitrators, and all made statements. In Tilton's statement was included the letter marked "B," before given, which he had put into type, which fact influenced me to consent to the arbitration in order to do away with the necessity for its publication.

After full hearing—nothing having been submitted to the arbitrators except the business differences of Tilton and Bowen—the arbitrators made an award that Mr. Bowen should pay Tilton the sum of seven thousand dollars, for which he (Mr. Bowen) drew his check upon the spot and the contracts were given up to him.

After the above settlement a paper, which has been called the "tripartite agreement," was signed by Bowen and Tilton, Beecher signing it subsequently. The inducing cause to this arbitration was the fact that Tilton had commenced a suit against Bowen and prepared an article for the *Golden Age*, in which he embodied his letter (marked "B") to Mr. Bowen and a statement of the circumstances. He submitted that article to me, and I begged him to withhold it from publication. I also brought Beecher and Tilton together, and Beecher added his entreaties to mine. To prevent its publication and close the suit which might work injury to Mr. Beecher and others, I agreed to submit Mr. Tilton's claim to arbitration, to which I had been invited before by Mr. Bowen, but which I had refused as before stated. In this interview between Beecher, Tilton, and myself I said, "Perhaps we can settle the whole matter if I can see Mr. Claflin, for Claflin knows Bowen will, and understands the importance of all those interests." Beecher said he would send Claflin to me, and I might confer with him upon the matter. In consequence of this Mr. Claflin called on me and we conferred upon the matter, and subsequently the arbitration was agreed upon. At the conclusion of the arbitration the parties signed the "tripartite covenant," which was drawn up (as I understand) by Mr. Samuel Wilkeson. It was first signed by Bowen. In the form in which it was first drawn it bound the parties to say nothing of any wrong done or offense committed by Beecher, and fully exonerated him therefrom. After Bowen had signed it it was handed to Tilton to sign, and he refused. He was willing to sign an agreement never to repeat again the charges of Bowen, saying that if for no other reason, if the matter should thereafter come to light it would appear that there had been something between Beecher and Mrs. Tilton, and it might be used as evidence to the injury of himself and family as well as of Beecher, and therefore it was not for the interest of either Tilton or Beecher to sign it in the form first proposed. No copy of the " tripartite covenant " was confided to me. Appended to this covenant and made a part of it was a copy of the proof-sheet article for the *Golden Age*, so that it might be known exactly to what scandal it referred. How that " tripartite covenant " came to be published I know not. As a part of that settlement it was arranged that Tilton should write a letter to Bowen to be published in the *Independent*, with certain comments to be made by Bowen. The original draft of these, in full recantation and withdrawal of all charges and matters of difference between Tilton and Bowen, is herewith produced and marked " L " :

RECONCILIATION OF TILTON AND BOWEN.

Theodore Tilton.

We have received the following note from an old friend:

"OFFICE OF THE ' GOLDEN AGE,'
(Original date blotted,)
"NEW YORK, April 3, 1872.

" *Henry C. Bowen, Esq.*

"MY DEAR SIR: In view of misapprehensions which I lately found existing among our mutual friends at the West, touching the severance of our relations in the *Independent* and the Brooklyn *Union*, I think it would be well, both for your sake and mine, if we should publicly say that, while our political and theological differences still exist, and will probably widen, yet that all other disagreements (so far as we ever had any) have been blotted out in reciprocal friendliness and good will.

"Truly yours,

(Signed)   "THEODORE TILTON."

It is so long since Mr. Tilton's pen has contributed to the *Independent* that we give to his brief note his old and familiar place at the head of these columns. While we never agreed with some of his radical opinions (and quite likely, as he intimates, we never shall), yet we owe to his request as above printed the hearty response which his honest purposes, his manly character, and his unstained integrity elicit from all who know him well. The abuse and slanders heaped upon him by some unfriendly journals have never been countenanced by the *Independent*. Regretting his opposition to the present Administration, we nevertheless wish abundant prosperity to the *Golden Age* and its editor.

H. C. B.

The above proposed card was subsequently and voluntarily changed by Mr. Bowen into a still stronger and more friendly notice of Mr. Tilton.

After the tripartite covenant was signed it came to the knowledge of Beecher, as he informed me, that Bowen was still spreading scandals about him, at which he was angered and proposed to write Bowen a letter stating the points that had been settled in their reconciliation and agreement, and the reason why Mr. Bowen's mouth should be closed in regard to such slanders. I find among my papers a pencil and ink memorandum of the statements intended to be embodied in that letter, which was submitted to my judgment by Beecher. It is in his handwriting and is produced, marked " M." It reads as follows :

BEECHER'S STATEMENT OF BOWEN'S SETTLEMENT.

I. That he allowed himself to listen to unfounded rumors.

II. That he never brought them either (1) to me (2) nor in any proper manner to the church; (3) that he only whispered them, and even that only when he had some business end in view.

III. That he did not himself believe that anything had occurred which unfitted me for the utmost trust shown,

(1) By continuing for twelve or fifteen years a conspicuous attendant at Plymouth Church.

(2) By contracts with me as editor of the *Independent*.

(3) By continued publications of my sermons, etc., making the privilege of doing so—even as late as the interview at Freeland's—one of these points of settlement.

(4) By a settlement of *all difficulties* at Freeland's (and a reconciliation which was to lead to work together), in which *not a single hint* of any *personal* immorality, but every *item was business*.

IV. As a result of such agreement—

(1) I was to resume my old familiarity at his house.

(2) To write him a letter that could give his family to show that I had restored confidence.

(3) To endeavor to remove from him the coldness and frowns of the parish, as one who had *injured me*.

(4) *A card* to be published, and which was published, giving him the right to put in the *Independent* sermons and lecture-room talk, etc.

(5) I was invited to go to Woodstock and be his guest, as I was at Grant's reception.

V. Of the settlement by a committee whose record is with Claflin, I have nothing to say. I did not see Mr. B. during the whole process, nor do I remember to have spoken with him since.

VI. Now the *force of the statement that he did not himself believe* that I had done *anything immoral* which should affect my standing as a *man*, a *citizen*, and a *minister*, illustrated by the foregoing facts, is demonstrated by his conduct when he *did* believe that Theodore Tilton committed immoralities, his dispossession of the *Independent*, his ignominious expulsion from the *B. U.*, his refusal to pay him the salary and forfeit of contract.

As a part of this transaction, Beecher sent me the following note, marked "N":

BEECHER TO MOULTON.

MONDAY.

MY DEAR FRIEND : I called last evening as agreed, but you had stepped out. On the way to church last evening I met Claflin. He says that B. *denies* any such treacherous whisperings, and is in a right state.

I mentioned my proposed letter. He liked the idea. I read him the draft of it (in lecture-room). He drew back, and said better not send it. I asked him if B. had ever made him statement of the very *bottom* facts: if there were any charges I did not know. He evaded and intimated that if he had he hardly would be right in telling me. I think he would be right in telling *you*—ought to. I have not sent any note, and have destroyed that prepared.

The real point to avoid is, to an appeal to church and then a council.

It would be a conflagration, and give every possible chance for *parties*, for hidings and evasions, and increase an hundred-fold this scandal, without healing anything.

I shall see you as soon as I return.

Meantime I confide everything to your wisdom, as I always have, and with such success hitherto that I have full trust for future.

Don't fail to see C. and have a full and confidential talk. Yours ever.

From the time of the tripartite covenant nothing occurred to disturb the relations between Beecher Tilton, and Bowen, or either of them, so far as I know, until the publication in *Woodhull and Claflin's Weekly* of an elaborate story concerning the social relations between Beecher, Tilton, and Mrs. Tilton. After that publication appeared it again came to the knowledge of Beecher that Bowen was making declarations derogatory to his character. This was followed by the publication of the "tripartite covenant," which Beecher informed me was done by Mr. Samuel Wilkeson, and also that Beecher was not a party to its publication, nor knew anything about it, There afterwards appeared an account of an interview between Bowen, H. B. Claflin, and Mrs. Woodhull, published in the Brooklyn *Eagle*, in which an attempt was made to obtain from her any letters which she might have showing that Beecher was guilty of criminal conduct, which attempt failed. Whereupon Beecher addressed me the following note, which I here produce, marked "N 2":

BEECHER TO MOULTON.

I need to see you this evening any time till half-past ten. Can you make appointment ? Will you call at 124, or shall I ? At what hour ? I send Claflin's letter. Keep it. Answer by telegraph.

H. W. B.

I shall take tea at Howard's, 74 Hicks, and should you call, let it be there. Or I will go round to your rooms. I want to show you a proposed card.

I also produce a letter of Claflin to Beecher of June 28, 1873, which was enclosed with the above, marked "N 3":

CLAFLIN TO BEECHER.

NEW YORK, June 28, 1872.

MY DEAR MR. BEECHER : I have yours. It was distinctly understood that the call on Woodhull was entirely private, and not to be reported. I told Bowen Woodhull had no letters from you of the least consequence to him or anybody else, and I was entirely satisfied after the interview that I was entirely right. I went there at Bowen's earnest solicitation, knowing it could not harm you and might satisfy him, as I think it did. It was in bad faith to publish the meeting. All present must have been disgusted at the utter lack of what Woodhull professed to have, but could not produce. Truly your friend,

H. B. CLAFLIN.

P. S.—Wish you would call and see me if you pass the store. I am always in at about eleven A. M.

H. B. C.

Beecher, when we met in pursuance of his note, produced to me a memorandum of a card which he proposed to publish in the *Eagle*, and which he submitted to my judgment, and gave me leave to alter the same as I thought fit. That paper is herewith produced, marked "N 4":

BEECHER'S PROPOSED CARD.

BROOKLYN, June, 1873.

I have seen in the morning papers that application has been made to Mrs. Victoria Woodhull for certain letters of mine supposed to contain information respecting certain infamous stories against me. She has two business letters, one declining an invitation to a suffrage meeting and the other declining to give her assistance solicited.

These, and all letters of mine in the hands of any other persons, they have my cordial consent to publish. I will only add in this connection that the stories and rumors which have for a time been circulated about me are grossly untrue, and I stamp them them in general and in particular as utterly false.

I saw the editor of the Brooklyn *Eagle* at his office, and after consultation with him the card was published as follows:

To the Editor of the Brooklyn Eagle.

SIR: In a long and active life in Brooklyn it has rarely happened that the *Eagle* and myself have been in accord on questions of common concern to our fellow-citizens. I am for this reason compelled to acknowledge the unsolicited confidence and regard of which the columns of the *Eagle* of late bear testimony. I have just returned to the city to learn that application has been made to [Mrs.] Victoria Woodhull for letters of mine supposed to contain information respecting certain infamous stories against me. [I have no objection to have the *Eagle* state, in any way it deems fit, that Mrs. Woodhull] or any other person or persons who may have letters of mine in their possession, have my cordial consent to publish them. In this connection [and at this time] I will only add that the stories and rumors which have, for some time past, been circulated about me are untrue, and I stamp them in general and in particular as utterly [untrue].

Respectfully, (Signed)

HENRY WARD BEECHER.

In order that the emendations made by myself and Mr. Kinsella may be observed at a glance, I have enclosed in brackets the words which are not in the original. It will be thus seen how much of this card was the composition of Mr. Beecher, and how much he relied upon the judgment of others in its preparation.

I would have submitted this card to Beecher before publication, but he was absent. For obvious reasons I held myself excepted from this call for publication, *as was well* understood by Beecher. I know nothing further of the relations of Bowen and Beecher in this connection which is of importance to this inquiry. I have traced them thus far because that controversy at each stage of it continually threatened the peaceful settlement of the trouble of Tilton and Beecher, an account of which I now resume.

Another curious complication of the relations of the parties arose from the publication by Mrs. Woodhull of the story in her journal. It is a matter of public notoriety that Mrs. Isabella Beecher Hooker, the sister of Beecher, had espoused the cause of Mrs. Woodhull on the question of woman suffrage, and had been accused still further of adopting her social tenets.

Beecher's relations to Mrs. Tilton had been comunicated to her. This had been made a subject of communication from Mrs. Hooker to her brother, and, after the publication by Mrs. Woodhull, Mrs. Hooker addressed the following note to her brother, which contains so full and clear an exposition of all the facts and circumstances that I need not add a word of explanation. I produce Mrs. Hooker's letter to Beecher under date of November, 1, 1872, marked "N 5":

MRS. HOOKER TO BEECHER.

HARTFORD, November, 1, 1872.

DEAR BROTHER: In reply to your words "if you still believe in that woman," &c., let me say that from her personally I have never heard a word on this subject, and when, nearly a year ago, I heard that when here in this city she said she had expected you to introduce her at Steinway, I wrote her a most indignant and rebuking letter, to which she replied in a manner that astonished me by its calm assertion that she considered you as true a friend to her as I myself.

I enclosed this letter to Mr. Tilton, asking him to show it to you if he thought best, and to write me what it all meant. He never replied nor returned the letter to me as I requested; but I have a copy of it at your service. In the month of February, after that, on returning from Washington, I went to Mrs. Stanton's to spend Sunday. At Jersey City I met Mrs. W., who had come on in the same train with me, it seemed, and who urged me in a hasty way to bring Mrs. Stanton over on Monday for a suffrage consultation as to spring convention. Remembering her assertion of the friendship between you, and of her meeting you occasionally at Mr. Moulton's house (I think this is the name), I thought I would put this to test, and replied that if I could be sure of seeing you at the same time I would come. She promised to secure you if possible, and I fully meant to keep my appointment, but on Sunday I remembered an appointment at New Haven which I should miss if I stopped in New York, and so I passed by, dropping her a letter by the way. Curiously enough, sister Catherine, who was staying at your house at this time, said to me here, casually, the latter of that same week: "Belle, Henry went over to New York to see you last Monday, but couldn't find you." Of course my inference was that Mrs. W. either had power over you, or you were secretly friends. During that Sunday Mrs. Stanton told me precisely what Mr. Tilton had said to her, when in the rage of discovery he fled to the house of Mrs. ——, and before them both narrated the story of his own infidelities as confessed to his wife and of hers as confessed to him. She added, that not long after she went to Mr. Moulton's and met you coming down the front steps, and on entering met Tilton and Moulton, who said: "We have just had Plymouth Church at our feet and here is his confession "—showing a manuscript. She added that Mrs. Tilton had made similar statements to Miss Anthony, and I have since received from Miss A. a corroboration of this, although she refused to give me particulars, being bound in confidence, she thinks. From that day to this I have carried a heavy load, you may be sure. I could not share it with my husband, because he was already overburdened and alarmingly affected brain-wise, but I resolved that if he went abroad, as he probably must, I would not go with him, leaving you alone as it were, to bear whatever might come of revelation. I withstood the entreaties of my husband to the last, and sent Mary in my stead, and at the last moment I confided to her all that I knew and felt and feared, that she might be prepared to sustain her father should trial overtake them. By reading the accompanying letters from them you will perceive that from outside evidence alone he had come to the conclusions which I reached only through the most reliable testimony that could well be furnished in any case and against every predisposition of my own soul. Fearing that they would hasten home to me and thus lose all the benefit of the journey (for, owing to this and other anxieties of business, John had grown worse rather than better up to that very time, though the air of the high Alps was beginning to promote sleep and restoration), I telegraphed by cable, "No trouble here—go to Italy," and by recent letters I am rejoiced to hear of them in Milan in comfortable health and spirits. From the day those letters came the matter has not been out of my thoughts an hour, it seems to me, and an unceasing prayer has ascended that I might be guided with wisdom and *truth*. But what is the truth I am farther from understanding this morning than ever. The tale as published is *essentially* the same as told to me—in fact, it is impossible but that Mr. Tilton is the authority for it, since I recognize a verisimilitude, and, as I understand it, Mrs. T. was the sole revelator. The only reply I made to Mrs. Stanton was that if true you had a philosophy of the relation of the sexes so far ahead of the times that you dared not announce it, though you consented to live by it. That this was in my judgment wrong, and God would bring all secret things to light in His own time and fashion, and I could only wait. I added that I had come to see that human laws were an impertinence, but could get no further, though I could see glimpses of a possible new science of life that at present was revolting to my feelings and my judgment; that I should keep myself open to conviction, however, and should converse with men, and especially women, on the whole subject, and as fast as I *knew* the truth I should stand by it, with no attempt at concealment. I think that Dr. Channing probably agrees with you in theory, but he had the courage to announce his convictions before acting upon them. He refused intercourse with an uncongenial wife for a long time, and then left her and married a woman whom he still loves, leaving a darling daughter with her mother, and to-day he pays photographers to keep him supplied with her pictures as often as they can be procured. I send you the article he wrote when, abandoned by all their friends, he and his wife went to the West and stayed for years. Crushed by calumny and abuse, to-day they are esteemed more highly than ever, and he is in positions of public trust in Providence.

You will perceive my situation, and, by all that I have suffered and am willing to suffer for your sake, I beg you to confide to me the whole truth. Then I can help you as no one else in the world can. The moment that I can know this matter as God knows it He will help you and me to bring everlasting good out of this seeming evil. If I could say truthfully that I believe this story to be a fabrication of Mr. and Mrs. Tilton's imposed upon a credulous woman—mere medium, whose susceptibility to impressions from spirits in the flesh and out of it is to be taken into account always—the whole thing dies. But if it is essentially true there is but one honorable way to meet it, in my judgment, and the precise method occurred to me in bed this morning, and I was about writing you to suggest it when your letter came.

I will write you a sisterly letter, expressing my deep conviction that this whole subject needs the most earnest and chaste discussion—that my own mind has long been occupied with it, but is still in doubt on many points—that I have observed for years that your reading and thinking has been profound on this and kindred subjects ; and now the time has come for you to give the world, through your own paper, the conclusions you have reached and the reasons therefor. If you choose I will then reply to each letter, giving the woman's view (for there is surely a man's and a woman's side to this beyond everywhere else), and by this means attention will be diverted from personalities and conc;n-trated on social philosophy—the one subject that now ought to occupy all thinking minds.

It seems to me that God has been preparing me for this work, and you also, for years and years. I send you a reply I wrote to Dr. Todd long ago, and which I could never get published without my name (which for the sake of my daughters I wished to withhold), although Godkin of the *Nation*, Holbrook of the *Herald of Health*, Ward of the *Independent*, and every mother to whom I have read it all told me it was the best thing ever written on the subject, and the men said they would publish it if they dared, while Mrs. —— urged me to give my name and publish, and said she would rather have written it than anything else of its length in the world, and if it were hers she would print it without hesitation. I send also a copy of a letter I wrote John Stuart Mill on his sending me an early copy of his "Subjection of Women," and his reply. I am sure that nearly all the thinking men and women are somewhere near you, and will rally to your support if you are bold, frank, and absolutely truthful in stating your convictions. Mrs. Burleigh told Dr. Channing she was ready to avow her belief in social freedom when the time came ; she was weary now and glad of a reprieve, but should stand true to her convictions when she must. My own conviction is that the one radical mistake you have made is in supposing that you are so much ahead of your time, and in daring to attempt to lead when you have anything to conceal. Do not, I pray you, deceive yourself with the hope that the love of your church or any other love human or divine, can compensate the loss of absolute truthfulness to your own mental convictions. I have not told you the half I have suffered since February ; but you can imagine, knowing what my husband is to me, that it was no common love I have for you and for the truth, and for all mankind, women as well as men, when I decided to nearly break his heart, already lacerated by the course I had been compelled to pursue, by sending him away to die, perhaps, without me at his side.

I wish you would come here in the evening some time (to the Burton cottage), or I will meet you anywhere in New York you appoint, and at any time. Ever yours, BELLE.

Read the letters from John and Mary in the order I have placed them. I will send those now and the other documents I have mentioned another day, waiting till I know whether you will meet me.

On the 3d of the same month, Mrs. Hooker addressed a letter to her brother, the Rev. Thomas K. Beecher, which I produce, marked "N 6" :

MRS. HOOKER TO REV. THOMAS K. BEECHER.

[Please return this letter to me when you have done with it.]

HARTFORD, Sunday, November 3, 1872.

DEAR BROTHER TOM : The blow has fallen, and I hope you are better prepared for it than you might have been but for our interview. I wrote H. a single line last week thus, "Can I help you ?" and here is his reply : "If you still believe in that woman, you cannot help me. If you think of her as I do you can, perhaps, though I do not need much help. I tread the falsehoods into the dirt from whence they spring, and go on my way rejoicing. My people are thus far heroic, and would give their lives for me. Their love and confidence would make me willing to bear far more than I have. Meanwhile the Lord has a pavilion in which he hides me until the storm be overpast. I abide in peace, committing myself to Him who gave Himself for me. I trust you give neither countenance nor credence to the abominable coinage that has been put afloat. The specks of truth are mere spangles upon a garment of falsehood. The truth itself is made to lie. Thank you for love and truth and silence, but think of the barbarity of dragging a poor, dear child of a woman into this slough. Yours truly."

Now, Tom, so far as I can see it is he who has dragged the dear child into the slough and left her there, and who is now sending another woman to prison who is innocent of all crime but a fanaticism for the truth as revealed to her, and I, by my silence, am consenting unto her death.

Read the little note she sent me long ago, when, in a burst of enthusiasm over a public letter of hers which seemed wonderful to me, I told her how it affected me, and mark its prophetic words :

"NEW YORK, August 8, 1871.

"MY DEAR, DEAR FRIEND : I was never more happy in my life than I am this morning, and made so by you whom I have learned to love so much. From you, from whom I had expected censure, I receive the first deep, pure words of approval and love. I know my course has often been contrary to your wishes, and it has been my greatest grief to know that it was so, since you have so nobly been my defender. But all the time I knew it was not I for whom you spoke, but all womanhood, and I was the more proud of you that your love was general and not personal. I am often compelled to do things from which my sensitive soul shrinks, and for which I endure the censure of most of my friends. But I obey a Power which knows better than they or I can know, and which has never left me stranded and without hope. I should be a faithless servant indeed were I to falter now when required to do what I cannot fully understand, yet in the issue of which I have full faith. None of the scenes in which I have enacted a part were what I would have selfishly chosen for my own happiness. I love my home, my children, my husband, and could live a sanctified life with them, and never desire contact with the wide world. But such is not to be my mission. I know what is to come, though I cannot yet divulge it. My daily prayer is that Heaven may vouchsafe me strength to meet everything which I know must be encountered and overcome. My heart is, however, too full to write you all I wish. I see the near approach of the grandest revelation the world has yet known, and for the part you shall play in it thousands will rise up and call you blessed. It was not for nothing that you and I met so singularly. Let us watch and pray, that we faint not by the wayside before we reach the consummation. We shall then look back with exceeding great joy to all we have been called upon to suffer for the sake of a cause more holy than has yet come upon earth. Again I bless you for your letter. Affectionately and faithfully yours,   VICTORIA C. WOODHULL."

Oh, my dear brother, I fear the awful struggle to live according to law has wrought an absolute demoralization as to truthfulness, and so he can talk about "spangles on a garment of falsehood," when the garment is truth and the specks are the falsehood.

His first letter to me was so different from this. I read it to you, but will copy it lest you have forgotten its character:

"APRIL 25, 1872.

"MY DEAR BELLE: I was sorry when I met you at Bridgeport not to have had longer talk with you about the meeting in May. I do not intend to make any speeches on any topic during anniversary week. Indeed, I shall be out of town. I do not want you to *take any ground this year except upon suffrage.* You know my sympathy with you. Probably you and I are nearer together than any of our family. I cannot give reason now. I am clear; still, you will follow your own judgment. I thank you for your letter. Of some things *I neither talk, nor will I be talked with.* For love and sympathy I am deeply thankful. The only help that can be grateful to me or useful is *silence* and a silencing influence on all others. A day may come for converse. It is not now. Living or dead, my dear sister Belle, *love me,* and do not talk about me or suffer others to in your presence. God love and keep you. God keep us all. Your loving brother,   H. W. B."

The underscoring is his own, and when I read in that horrible story that he begged a few hours' notice, that he might kill himself, my mind flew back to this sentence, which suggested suicide to me the moment I read it: "Living or dead, my dear sister Belle, *love me,*" and I believed even that.

Now, Tom, can't you go to brother Edward at once and give him these letters of mine, and tell him what I told you; and when you have counseled together, as brothers should, counsel me also, and come to me if you can. It looks as if he hoped to buy my silence with my love. At present, of course, I shall keep silence, but truth is dearer than all things else, and if he will not speak it in some way I cannot always stand as consenting to a lie. "God help us all."

Yours in love,   BELLE.

If you can't come to me, send Edward. I am utterly alone, and my heart aches for that woman even as for my own flesh and blood. I do not understand her, but I know her to be pure and unselfish and absolutely driven by some power foreign to herself to these strange utterances, which are always in behalf of freedom, purity—truth, as she understands it—always to befriend the poor and outcast, and bring low only the proud, the hypocrites in high places. The word about meeting at Mrs. Phelps' house I have added to the copy. If you see Henry tell him of this.

The reply to this letter by the Rev. Thomas K. Beecher to his sister is as follows, and needs but a single remark—the thought of a good man as to the value of testimony in this case. I refer to the last sentence of the postscript. This is produced, marked "N 7":

REV. THOS. K. BEECHER TO HIS SISTER.

ELMIRA, November 5, 1872.

DEAR BELLE: To allow the Devil himself to be crushed for speaking the truth is unspeakably cowardly and contemptible. I respect, *as at present advised,* Mrs. Woodhull, while I abhor her philosophy. She only carries out Henry's philosophy, against which I recorded my protest twenty years ago, and parted (lovingly and achingly) from him saying, "We cannot work together." He has drifted, and I have hardened like a crystal till I am sharp-cornered and exacting. I cannot help him except by prayer. I cannot help him through Edward. In my judgment Henry is following his slippery doctrines of expediency, and, in the cry of progress and the nobleness of human nature, has sacrificed clear, exact, ideal integrity. Hands off, until he is down, and then my pulpit, my home, my church, and my purse and heart are at his service. Of the two, Woodhull is my hero, and Henry my coward, *as at present advised.* But I protest against the whole batch and all its belongings. I was not anti-slavery; I am not anti-family. But, as I wrote years ago, whenever I assault slavery because of its abominations, I shall assail the church, the state, the family, and all other institutions of selfish usage.

I return the papers. *You* cannot help Henry. You must be true to Woodhull. I am out of the circle as yet, and am glad of it. When the storm-line includes me I shall suffer as a Christian, saying: "Cease ye from man."

Don't write to me. Follow the truth, and when you need me cry out. Yours, lovingly,

(Signed)   TOM.

P. S.—I am so overworked and hurried that I see upon review that my letter *sounds* hard—because of its sententiousness. But believe me, dear Belle, that I see and suffer with you. You are in a tight place. But having chosen your principles I can only counsel you to be true, and take the consequences. For years, you know, I have been apart from all of you except in love. I think you all in the wrong as to anthropology and social science. *But* I honor and love them who suffer for conviction's sake. My turn to suffer will come in due time. In this world all Christians shall suffer tribulation. So eat, sleep, pray, take good aim and shoot, and when the ache comes say even hereunto were we called. But I repeat —You can't help Henry at present.

P. S.—I unseal my letter to enclose print and add : You have no *proof* as yet of any offense on Henry's part. Your testimony would be allowed in no court. Tilton, wife, Moulton and Co. are witnesses. Even Mrs. Stanton can only declare *hearsay.* So if you move, remember that you are standing on uncertain information, and we shall not probably ever get the facts, and I'm glad of it. If Mr. and Mrs. Tilton are brought into court nothing will be revealed. Perjury for good reasons is with advanced thinkers no sin.

It will be observed in the letter of Mrs. Hooker, that she speaks of having refused to go to Europe with her husband, and that she remained at home in order to protect her brother in this emergency of his life.

A letter came into my hands with the others from Mr. Hooker to his wife, under date of Florence, Italy, November 3, 1871, which tends to show that all this matter had been discussed between Mr. Hooker and his wife long before the publication by Mrs. Woodhull. I extract so much from the letter as refers to this subject. The remainder is a kindly communication of an absent husband to a loved wife, about wholly independent matters which have nothing to do with this controversy. It is produced, marked "N 8":

MR. HOOKER TO HIS WIFE.

FLORENCE, Sunday, November 3, 1872.

MY PRECIOUS WIFE : I hope you were not pained by what I wrote on Friday about the H. W. B. matter. I am getting much more at peace about the matter, but I cannot look upon it in any other light, and it is a relief to me to speak my mind right out about it, and then let it rest. I could not have been easy till I had sworn a little. The only mitigation of the concealment of the thing that I can think of is this—and it seems to me that some excuse, or at least explanation, may be found here—viz. : that a consideration of the happiness of both Mr. T. and his wife required it, or seemed to, and the very possible further fact that he preferred to disclose it, but took the advice of a few of his leading friends in the church, and was overruled by them, they agreeing to take the responsibility of the concealment. This would take off somewhat from the hypocrisy of the thing, but leaves the original crime as open to condemnation as ever. But enough of this. Only let me request you to keep me informed of all that occurs, and do not rely upon my getting the news from the papers. I see by an extract from the Boston *Advertiser* that Mrs. W. has employed two Boston lawyers (it gives their names) to bring suit against the *Republican* and *Woman's Journal*, so that it looks as if the exposure is near at hand. I want to say one word more, however. Can you not let the report get out after the H. matter becomes public, without being exactly responsible for it, that you have kept up friendship with Mrs. W. in the hope of influencing her not to publish the story, you having learned its truth—and that is substantially the fact as I have understood it—and that you gave up going to Europe with me, so as to be at home and comfort H. when the truth came out, as you expected it to do in the course of the summer ? This will give the appearance of self-sacrifice to your affiliation with her, and will explain your not coming abroad with me—a fact which has a very unwifelike look. I know that you will otherwise be regarded as holding Mrs. W.'s views, and that we shall be regarded as living in some discord, and probably (by many people) as practicing her principles. It would be a great relief to me to have your relations to Mrs. W. explained in this way, so creditable to your heart. There is not half the untruth in it that there has been all along in my pretended approval of Mrs. Woodhull's course, and yet people think me an honest man. I have lied enough about that to ruin the character of an average man, and have probably damaged myself by it. . . .

After Beecher had seen these letters of his sister, Mrs. Hooker, he came to me, in trouble and alarm, and handed me all the letters, together with one under the date of November 27, which I herewith produce, with the enclosure, cut from the Hartford *Times*, to which it alludes. It is marked "N 9":

MRS. HOOKER TO BEECHER.

HARTFORD, Wednesday 27, 1872.

DEAR BROTHER : Read the enclosed, clipped from the *Times* of this city last evening. [See enclosure below.] I can endure no longer. I must see you and persuade you to write a paper which I will read, going alone to your pulpit and taking sole charge of the services. I shall leave here on eight A. M. train, Friday morning, and unless you meet me at Forty-second street station, I shall go to Mrs. ——'s house, opposite Young Men's Christian Association, No. — Twenty-third street, where I shall hope to see you during the day. Mrs. —— kindly said to me, when last in New York, "My daughter and I are now widows, living quietly in our pleasant home, and I want you to come there, without warning, whenever you are in New York, unless you have other friends whom you prefer to visit."

So I shall go as if on a shopping trip, and stay as long as it seems best.

I would prefer going to Mrs. Tilton's to anywhere else, but I hesitate to ask her to receive me.

I feel sure, however, that words from her should go into that paper, and with her consent I could write as one commissioned from on high.

Do not fail me, I pray you; meet me at noon on Friday as you hope to meet your own mother in heaven. In her name I beseech you, and will take no denial. Ever yours in love unspeakable,

(Signed)   BELLE.

[Enclosure mentioned in above letter.]

BEECHER AND MRS. TILTON.

"Eli Perkins," of the New York *Commercial*, a prominent Republican paper, has this to say :

"Nast's very boldness—his terrible aggressiveness—is what challenges admiration and makes *Harper's Weekly* a success.

"When I asked him if he didn't think it a great undertaking to attack Mr. Greeley, he said :

"'Yes ; but I knew he was an old humbug. I knew I was right, and I knew right would win in the end. I was almost alone, too. The people were fooled with Greeley, as they are fooled with Beecher, and he will tumble further than Greeley yet.'

"We had a talk about Beecher and Tilton, and putting this with other conversations with personal friends of Mr. Tilton, and with newspaper men in New York, I am satisfied that a terrible downfall surely awaits the one who has erred and *conceals* it."

Beecher then informed me of his apprehension that his sister, in her anxiety that he should do his duty in presenting this truth as she understood it, and in protecting Mrs. Woodhull from the consequences of having published the truth, from which she was then suffering, would go into his pulpit and insist upon declaring that the Woodhull publication was substantially true ; and he desired me to do what in me lay to prevent such a disaster. I suggested to him that he should see Mrs. Hooker, speak to her kindly, and exhort her not to take this course, and that Tilton should see her, and so far shake her confidence in the truth of the story as to induce her to doubt whether she would be safe in making the statement public. In this course Beecher agreed, and such arguments and inducements were brought to bear upon Mrs. Hooker as were in the power of all three of us, to prevent her from doing that which would have certainly brought on an exposure of the whole business. During the consultation between Beecher and myself as to the means of meeting Mrs. Hooker's intentions, no suggestion was ever made on the part of Beecher that his sister was then or had been at any other time insane.

All these letters I received from Beecher, and they are those to which he alludes, in his communication of the 4th instant, as the letters of his sister and brother delivered to me, and which I did not believe that I could honorably give him up, because I thought—and I submit to the Committee, I was right in thinking—that they form a part of this controversy, and were not, as he therein alleged, simply given to my keeping as part of his other papers, which he could not keep safely on account of his own carelessness in preserving documents.

Beecher was exceedingly anxious that Tilton should repudiate the statement published by Woodhull, and denounce her for its publication, and he drew up, upon my memorandum book, the form of a card to be published by Tilton, over his signature; and asked me to submit it to him for that purpose, which I here produce, marked "N 10":

BEECHER'S PROPOSED CARD FOR TILTON.

In an unguarded enthusiasm I hoped well and much of one who has proved utterly unprincipled. I shall never again notice her stories, and now utterly repudiate her statements made concerning me and mine.

Beecher told me to say to Tilton, substantially: "Theodore may for his own purpose, if he choose, say that all his misfortune has come upon him on account of his dismissal from the *Union* and the *Independent*, and on account of the offense which I committed against him; he may take the position against me and Bowen that he does ; yet the fact is that his advocacy of Mrs. Woodhull and her theories has done him the injury which prevents his rising. Now, in order to get support from me and from Plymouth Church, and in order to obtain the sympathy of the whole community, he must publish this card; and unless he does it he cannot rise." He also said the same thing to Tilton in my presence. To this Tilton answered in substance to Beecher: "You know why I sought Mrs. Woodhull's acquaintance. It was to save my family and yours from the consequences of your acts, the facts about which had become known to her. They have now been published, and I will not denounce that woman to save you from the consequences of what you yourself have done."

To resume: After I had carried to Mr. Tilton the paper of apology which had reference to Beecher's adultery, and had received assurances that all between Tilton and Beecher should be kept quiet, I immediately conveyed that information to Beecher. He was profuse in his professions of thankfulness and gratitude to me for what he said were my exertions in his behalf. Soon after that I was taken sick, and while on my sick bed, on the 7th of February, I received the following letter from Beecher, marked "O":

BEECHER TO MOULTON.

February 7, 1871.

MY DEAR MR. MOULTON: I am glad to send you a book which you will relish, or which a man on a sick bed *ought* to relish. I wish I had more like it, and that I could send you one every day, not as a repayment of your great kindness to me—for that can never be repaid, not even by love, which I give you freely.

Many, many friends has God raised up to me; but to no one of them has he ever given the opportunity and the wisdom so to serve me as you have. My trust in you is implicit. You have also proved yourself Theodore's friend and Elizabeth's. Does God look down from Heaven on three unhappy creatures that more need a friend than these?

Is it not an intimation of God's intent of mercy to all, that each one of these has in you a tried and proved friend? But only in you are we three united. Would to God, who orders all hearts, that by your kind mediation, Theodore, Elizabeth, and I could be made friends again. Theodore will have the hardest task in such a case; but has he not proved himself capable of the noblest things?

I wonder if Elizabeth knows how generously he has carried himself towards me? Of course, I can never speak with her again, except with his permission, and I do not know that even then it would be best. My earnest longing is to see her in the full sympathy of her nature at rest in him, and to see him once more trusting her, and loving her with even a better than the old love. I am always sad in such thoughts. Is there any way out of this night? May not a day-star arise?

Truly yours always, with trust and love.

(Signed)   HENRY WARD BEECHER.

On the same day there was conveyed to me from Beecher a request to Tilton that Beecher might write to Mrs. Tilton, because all parties had then come to the conclusion that there should be no communication between Beecher and Mrs. Tilton or Beecher and Tilton, except with my knowledge and consent, and I had exacted a promise from Beecher that he would not communicate with Mrs. Tilton, or allow her to communicate with him, unless I saw the communication, which promise, I believe, was, on his part, faithfully kept, but, as I soon found, was not on the part of Mrs. Tilton.

Permission was given to Beecher to write to Mrs. Tilton, and the following is his letter, here produced, marked "P":

BEECHER TO MRS. TILTON.

BROOKLYN, February 7, 1871.

MY DEAR MRS. TILTON: When I saw you last I did not expect ever to see you again or to be alive many days. God was kinder to me than were my own thoughts. The friend whom God sent to me (Mr. Moulton) has proved, above all friends that ever I had, able and willing to help me in this terrible emergency of my life. His hand it was that tied up the storm that was ready to burst upon our head. I am not the less disposed to trust him from finding that he has your welfare most deeply and tenderly at heart. You have no friend (Theodore excepted) who has it in his power to serve you so vitally, and who will do it with so much delicacy and honor. I beseech of you, if my wishes have yet any influence, let my deliberate judgment in this matter weigh with you. It does my sore heart good to see in Mr. Moulton an unfeigned respect and honor for you. It would kill me if he thought otherwise. He will be as true a friend to your honor and happiness as a brother could be to a sister's. In him we have a common ground. You and I may meet in him. The past is ended. But is there no future?—no wiser, higher, holier future? May not this friend stand as a priest in the new sanctuary of reconciliation, and mediate and bless you, Theodore, and my most unhappy self? Do not let my earnestness fail of its end; you believe in my judgment. I have put myself wholly and gladly in Moulton's hands, and there I must meet you. This is sent with Theodore's consent, but he has not read it. *Will you return it to me by his hands?* I am very earnest in this wish for all our sakes, as such a letter ought not to be subject to even a chance of miscarriage. Your unhappy friend,

(Signed)   H. W. BEECHER.

This was a letter of commendation, so that Mrs. Tilton might trust me, as between her and her husband, as fully as Beecher did. In the meanwhile Mr. Beecher's friends were continually annoying him and writing him about Tilton and the rumors that were afloat with regard to both, and on the 13th of February Beecher received the following letter from his nephew, F. B. Perkins, which he (Beecher) handed me, with a draft of a reply, on the 23d of the same February, which he sent without showing me again, and upon that draft I made the following note. I herewith produce these documents, marked "Q," "R," and "S" respectively:

PERKINS TO BEECHER.

Box 44, Station D, }
New York, February 13, 1871. }

My Dear Uncle : After some consideration, I decide to inform you of a matter concerning you. Tilton has been justifying or excusing his recent intrigues with women by alleging that you have been detected in the like adulteries, the same having been hushed up out of consideration for the parties. This I *know*.

You may, of course, do what you like with this letter. I suppose such talk dies quickest unanswered. I have thought it best to let you know what is being said about you, and by whom, however ; for, whether you act in the matter or not, it has been displeasing to me to suppose such things done without your knowledge. I have thought other people base, but Theodore Tilton has in this action dived into the very sub-cellar of the very backhouse of infamy. In case you should choose to let him know of this, I am responsible, and don't seek any concealment.

Very truly yours,

(Signed) ·   F. B. Perkins.

To Rev. Henry Ward Beecher.

P. S.—I can't say Tilton said "adulteries." He was referring to his late intrigues with Mrs. —— and others, however he may have described them. What I am informed of is the excuse by implicating you in "similar" affairs.

(Signed)   F. B. P.

BEECHER TO PERKINS.

February 23, 1871.

My Dear Fred : Whatever Mr. Tilton formerly said against me—and I know the substance of it—*he has withdrawn*, and frankly confessed that he had been misled by the statements of one who, when confronted, backed down from his charges.

In some sense I am in part to blame for his indignation. For I lent a credulous ear to reports about *him*, which I have reason to believe were exaggerated or wholly false. After a full conference and explanation there remains between us no misunderstanding, but mutual good-will and reconciliation have taken the place of exasperation. Of course, I shall not chase after rumors that will soon run themselves out of breath if left alone. If my friends will put their foot silently on any coal or hot embers, and crush them out, *without talking*, the miserable lies will be as dead in New York in a little time as they are in Brooklyn. But I do not any the less thank you for your affectionate solicitude, and for your loyalty to my good name. I should have replied earlier, but your letter came when I was out of town. I had to go out again immediately. If the papers do not meddle, this slander will fall still-born—dead as Julius Cæsar. If a *sensation* should be got up, of course there are enough bitter enemies to fan the matter and create annoyance, though no final damage.

I am your affectionate uncle,

(Signed)   H. W. B.

NOTE BY MOULTON IN RELATION TO THE ABOVE.

"H. W. Beecher agreed to hold this letter over for consideration, but sent it before seeing me again. I at first approved of the letter, but finally concluded to consult with T. T., who offered a substitute, the substance of which will be found in pencil on copy of H. W. B.'s reply to P."

The following is a copy of the substitute referred to :

An enemy of mine, as I now learn, poisoned the mind of Theodore Tilton by telling him stories concerning me. T. T. being angered against me because I had quoted similar stories against him, which I had heard from the same party, retaliated. Theodore and I, through a mutual frend, were brought together, and found upon mutual explanations that both were the victims of the same slanderer.

No further correspondence was received from Perkins in this connection to my knowledge, except the following note to Tilton, herewith produced and marked "T" :

PERKINS TO TILTON.

May 20, 1871.

Mr. Tilton : If there had not been others by I would have said to you at meeting you this noon what I say now : our acquaintance is at an end ; and if we meet again you will please not recognize me.

(Signed)   ⫶   F. B. Perkins.

Meanwhile Mrs. Morse, the mother-in-law of Mrs. Tilton, who was from time to time an inmate of his family in Livingston street, had, as I was informed both by Mr. and Mrs. Tilton, learned from her daughter the criminal relationship heretofore existing between Beecher and herself, and who could not understand why that matter had been settled, and who had not been told how it had been adjusted, and who had had a most bitter quarrel with Tilton, accusing him of not having so carried his affairs as to keep what fortune he had, and who had called upon Beecher about the relations between Tilton and Mrs. Tilton, and who had, as Beecher had informed me, filled the minds of Mrs. Beecher and himself with stories of Tilton's infidelity and improper conduct to his wife, wrote the following letter to Beecher, under date of January 27, 1871, which she delivered to me the next day, as appears by my memorandum thereon, together with the draft of an answer which he said he proposed to send to Mrs. Morse. Her letter is herewith produced, marked "U," and Mr. Beecher's draft of reply, marked "V," and are as follows:

MRS. MORSE TO MR. BEECHER.

[Received January 27, 1871 ; received from H. W. B. January 28, 1871.]

MR. BEECHER: As you have not seen fit to pay any attention to the request I left at your house now over two weeks since, I will take this method to inform you of the state of things in Livingston street. The remark you made to me at your own door was an enigma at the time, and every day adds to the mystery, "Mrs. Beecher has adopted the child." "What child?" I asked. You replied, "Elizabeth."

Now, I ask what earthly sense was there in that remark? Neither Mrs. B., yourself, nor I can have done anything to ameliorate her condition. She has been for the last three weeks with one very indifferent girl. T. has sent ***** with the others away, leaving my sick and distracted child to care for all four children night and day, without fire in the furnace or anything like comfort or nourisment [sic] in the house. She has not seen any one. He says, "She is mourning for *her sin.*" If this be so, one twenty-four hours under his shot, I think, is enough to atone for a lifelong sin, however henious [sic]. I know that any change in his affairs would bring more trouble upon her and more suffering. I did not think for a moment when I asked Mrs. B. as to your call there, supposing she knew it, of course, as she said you would not go there without her.

I was inocent [sic] of making any misunderstanding if there was any ; you say, keep quiet. I have all through her married life done so, and we now see our eror [sic]. It has brought him to destruction, made me utterly miserable, turned me from a comfortable home, and brought his own family to beggary. I don't believe if his honest debts were paid he would have enough to buy their breackfast [sic]. This she could endure and thrive under, but the publicity he has given to this recent and most *crushing of all trouble* is what's taken the life out of her. I know of twelve persons whom he has told, and they in turn have told others. I had thought we had as much as we could live under from his neglect and ungovernable temper. But this is the death-blow to us both, and I doubt not Florence has hers. Do you know when I hear of you cracking your jokes from Sunday to Sunday, and think of the misery you have brought upon us, I think with the Psalmist : "There is no God." Admitting all he says to be the invention of his half-drunken brain, still the effect upon us is the same, for all he's told believe it. Now he's nothing to do, he makes a Target of her night and day. I am driven to this extremity : to pray for her release from all suffering by God's taking her himself, for if there's a heaven I know she'll go there.

The last time she was in this house she said: "Here I feel I have no home, but on the other side I know I shall be more than welcome." Oh, my precious child ! how my heart bleeds over you in thinking of your sufferings. Can you do anything in the matter?

Must she live in this suffering condition of mind and body with no aleviation [sic] ?

You or any one else who advises her to live with him when he is doing all he can to kill her by slow torture is anything but a friend.

I don't know if you can understand a sentence I've written, but I'm relieved somewhat by writing. The children are kept from me, and I have not seen my dieing [sic] child but once since her return from this house.

I thought the least you could do was to put your name to a paper to help reinstate my brother (in the Custom House). Elizabeth was as disappointed as myself. He is still without employment, with a sick wife and five children to feed, behind with rent, and everything else behindhand.

If your wife has adopted Lib [sic] or you sympathize with her, I pray you do something for her relief before it is too late. He swears so soon as her breath leaves her body he will make this whole thing public, and this prospect, I think, is one thing which keeps her living. I know of no other. She's without nourishment [sic] for one in her state, and in *want*—actual want. They would both deny it no doubt, *but it's true.*

BEECHER TO MRS. MORSE.

Mrs. Judge Morse.

MY DEAR MADAM : I should be very sorry to have you think I had no interest in your troubles. My course toward you hitherto should satisfy you that I have sympathized with your distress. But

Mrs. Beecher and I, after full consideration, are of one mind—that, under present circumstances, the greatest kindness to you and to all will be, in so far as we are concerned, to leave to time the rectification of all the wrongs, whether they prove real or imaginary.

It will be observed that in the letter of Mrs. Morse she says Tilton has sent ***** with the others away. I purposely omit the name of this young girl. There was a reason why it was desirable she should be away from Brooklyn. That reason, as given me by Mr. and Mrs. Tilton was this: She had overheard conversations by them concerning Mrs. Tilton's criminal intimacy with Beecher, and she reported these conversations to several friends of the family. Being young, and not knowing the consequences of her prattling, it seemed proper, for the safety of two families, that she should be sent to a distance to school, which was accordingly done. She was put at a boarding-school at the West, and the expenses of her stay there were privately paid through me by Beecher, to whom I had stated the difficulty of having the girl remain in Brooklyn; and he agreed with us that it was best that she should be removed, and offered to be at the cost of her schooling. The bills were sent to me from time to time as they became due, a part of them through Mrs. Tilton. Previous to her going away she wrote the following letters to Mrs. Tilton—marked "W" and "X"—and they were sent to me by Mrs. T. as part of these transactions :

* * * TO MRS. TILTON.

BROOKLYN, January 10, 1871.

MY DEAR MRS. TILTON : I want to tell you something. Your mother, Mrs. Morse, has repeatedly attempted to hire me, by offering me dresses and presents, to go to certain persons and tell them *stories* injurious to the character of your husband. I have been persuaded that the kind attentions shown me by Mr. Tilton for years were dishonorable demonstrations. I never at the time thought that Mr. Tilton's caresses were for such a purpose. I do not want to be made use of by Mrs. Morse or any one else to bring trouble on my two best friends, you and your husband. Bye-bye,   * * *

These notes are in Mrs. Tilton's handwriting and on the same paper used by her in correspondence with me.

FROM THE SAME TO THE SAME.

JANUARY 12.

MY DEAR MRS. TILTON : The story that Mr. Tilton once lifted me from my bed and *carried* me screaming to his own, and attempted to violate my person, is a wicked lie.

Yours truly,   * * *

While this young lady was at school she did inform a friend of Mrs. Tilton, Mrs. P., of the stories of the family relations. These stories were written to Brooklyn, and came to the knowledge of my friends, creating an impression upon their minds unfavorable to Mr. Tilton, and might possibly lead to the reopening of the scandal. I, therefore, took pains to trace them back, and found that they came from Mrs. P., to whom the school-girl had told them. I, therefore, called upon Tilton and asked if these stories could not be stopped. Soon afterwards he produced to me a letter dated the 8th of November, 1872, written by Mrs. Tilton, with a note to me on the back thereof, to disabuse Mrs. P.'s mind as to this girl's disclosures. The letter is here produced, marked "Y" :

MRS. TILTON TO MRS. P.

BROOKLYN, November 8, 1872.

MY DEAR MRS. P. : I come to you in this fearful extremity, burdened by my misfortunes, to claim your promised sympathy and love. . . . I have mistakingly felt obliged to deceive * * * these two years, that my husband had made false accusations against me *which he never has to her or any one.*

In order that he may not appear on his defense, thus adding the terrible exposure of a lawsuit, will you implore silence on her part against any indignation which she may feel against him ? for the one only ray of light and hope in this midnight gloom is his entire sympathy and co-operation in my behalf.

A word from you to Mr. D*** will change any unfriendly spirit which dear mother may have given him against my husband.

You know that I have no mother's heart that will look charitably upon all, save you. Affectionately, your child,   (Signed)   ELIZABETH.

Of course you will destroy this letter.

Also, I produce—out of the order of time—a letter of Mrs. Tilton, marked "Y 2," sent to me a year afterwards for money for the purpose of paying this young person's school expenses, and also a statement of accounts and letter of transmission, and note acknowledging receipt for quarter ending June, 1871, from the principal of that school, marked "Z 1" and "Z 2." All these sums were paid by Beecher, and I forwarded the money to settle them through Mrs. Tilton, or sent the money directly to the principal of the school at her request :

MRS. TILTON TO MOULTON.

TUESDAY, January 18, 1872.

DEAR FRANCIS : Be kind enough to send me $50 for * * * I want to enclose it in to-morrow's mail. Yours gratefully,   (Signed)   ELIZABETH.

Statement of Account.

—— FEMALE SEMINARY.

Miss * * *
         To * * *   Dr.

For boarding	.. $76.50
For tuition, primary class	10.80
For washing	7.23
For fire (2 months)	4.00
For music (double lessons), $36; use piano, $4.50	40.50
For advanced items	
Books and stationery	$4.14
Music	5.10
Physician and medicine	6.00
Seat in church	1.00—16.24

Amount | $155.27

June, 1871.

—— June 8, 1871.

MRS. TILTON : I send you with this a statement of Miss * * * 's bill for the past half school year.

* * * is doing very well in her studies, and is quite a favorite with us. Sometimes she is not very well, but I think, on the whole, her health is improving.

Could you not come and make us a visit, and bring Mr. Tilton with you? A little rest would do you both good. Very respectfully yours,

—————

* * * is making very good progress in music, and in some of her common branches, as arithmetic, geography, and spelling.

—— SEMINARY, December 18, 1874.

F. D. Moulton, Esq.

DEAR SIR: Yours containing check for $200 in full for Miss. * * * 's school-bill is received. This pays all her indebtedness to this date. Very truly yours,

—————

Beecher was very anxious to ascertain through me the exact condition of Tilton's feelings towards him, and how far the reconciliation was real, and to get a statement in writing that would seem to free him (Beecher) from imputation thereafter. I more than once applied to Tilton to get a statement of his feelings towards Beecher, and received from him on the 7th of February, 1871, the following letter, which I produce, marked " AA ":

TILTON TO MOULTON.

· BROOKLYN, February 7, 1871.

MY VERY DEAR FRIEND: In several conversations with me you have asked about my feelings towards Mr. Beecher, and yesterday you said the time had come when you would like to receive from me an expression of them in writing. I say, therefore, very cheerfully, that, notwithstanding the great suffering which he has caused to Elizabeth and myself, I bear him no malice, shall do him no wrong, shall discountenance every project (by whomsoever proposed) for any exposure of his secret to the public, and (if I know myself at all) shall endeavor to act towards Mr. Beecher as I would have him in similar circumstances act towards me.

I ought to add that your own good offices in this case have led me to a higher moral feeling than I might otherwise have reached. Ever yours affectionately,   (Signed)

THEODORE TILTON.

To Frank Moulton.

From that time everything was quiet. Nothing occurred to mar the harmony existing between Tilton and Beecher, or the kindly relations between Tilton and Mrs. Tilton, during the summer of 1871, except idle gossip which floated about the City of Brooklyn, and sometimes was hinted at in the newspapers, but which received no support in any facts known to the gossiper or the writer, or through any communication of Mr. or Mrs. Tilton or Mr. Beecher. And I received no letters from Beecher alluding to this subject upon any topic until his return, on the 30th September, from his vacation, showing that in fact the settlement was enabling him to regain his health and spirits. I produce this note, marked "BB":

BEECHER TO MOULTON.

SATURDAY, September 30, 1871.

MY DEAR FRIEND: I feel bad not to meet you. My heart warms to you, and you might have known that I should be here, if you loved me as much as I do you. Well, it's an inconstant world! Soberly, I should be glad to have you see how hearty I am, ready for work, and hoping for a bright year.

I have literally done *nothing* for three months, but have "gone to grass." Things seem almost strange to come back among men and see business going on in earnest.

I will be here on Monday at ten A. M. I am, my dear Frank, truly and gratefully yours,

(Signed) HENRY WARD BEECHER.

Taking advantage of this lull in the controversy it may be as convenient here as anywhere to state the relations of Mrs. Tilton to the matter and her acts towards the several parties. I shall be pardoned if I do it with care, because my statement, unhappily for us both, must be diametrically opposite to one published as hers. I had been on terms very familiar, visiting at Mr. Tilton's house. I had seen and known Mrs. Tilton well and kindly on my part, and I believed wholly so on hers, and, as I have before stated, I had never known or suspected or seen any exhibition of inharmony between her and her husband during those many familiar visits, and of course I had no suspicion of infidelity upon the part of either towards the other. The first intimation of it which came to me was in the exhibition of her original confession, of which I have before spoken. The first time I saw that confession was on the 30th of December, 1870. The first communication I had from Mrs. Tilton after I had read her confession on the Friday evening, as before stated, was on the next morning, the 31st of December, 1870, the date being fixed by the fact cited in her letter showing that she gave her retraction to Beecher on the evening previous. The letter from her is as follows, marked "CC":

MRS. TILTON TO MOULTON.

SATURDAY MORNING.

MY DEAR FRIEND FRANK: I want you to do me the greatest possible favor. My letter which you have, and the one I gave Mr. Beecher at his dictation last evening, ought both to be destroyed.

Please bring both to me and I will burn them. Show this note to Theodore and Mr. Beecher. They will see the propriety of this request. Yours truly,

(Signed) E. R. TILTON.

I could not of course accede to this request of Mrs. Tilton, because I had pledged myself to Beecher that her retraction on the one side, and her confession to Tilton on the other—which are the papers she refers to as " my letters which you have, and the one I gave Mr. Beecher"—should not be given up, but should be held for the protection of either as against the other.

I learned in my interview with Beecher on the 1st day of January, 1871, that he had been told by his wife and others that Mrs. Tilton desired a separation from her husband on account of his supposed infidelities to her, and that Mrs. Tilton had applied to Mrs. Beecher for advice upon that subject. This being the first I had heard of any asserted infidelity of Tilton to his marriage vows, either the next day or second day after I asked Mrs. Tilton if it were so, and if she had ever desired a separation from her husband on that or any other account, wishing to assure myself of the facts upon which I was to act as mediator and arbitrator between the parties. She stated to me that she had not desired a separation from her husband, but that application had been made to Mr. and Mrs. Beecher through her mother, upon her own responsibility, to bring it about, and on the 4th day of January she sent me the following letter, which, although dated January 4, 1870, was actually written January 4, 1871, and dated 1870, as is a common enough mistake by most persons at the beginning of a new year. But it bears internal evidence of the time of its date, and also I know that I received it at that time, it being impossible that it should have been a year previous. I produce it, marked "DD":

MRS. TILTON TO MOULTON.

174 LIVINGSTON STREET, }
BROOKLYN, January 14, 1870 (?). }

Mr. Francis D. Moulton :

MY DEAR FRIEND : In regard to your question whether I have ever sought a separation from my husband, I indignantly deny that *such was ever the fact*, as I have denied it a hundred times before. The story that I wanted a separation was a deliberate falsehood, coined by my poor mother, who said she would bear the responsibility of this and other statements she might make and communicated to my husband's enemy, Mrs. H. W. Beecher, and by her communicated to Mr. Bowen. *I feel outraged* by the whole proceeding, and am now suffering in consequence more than I am able to bear. I am yours, very truly,   (Signed)   ELIZ. R. TILTON.

As bearing upon this topic of her husband's infidelity and her desire for separation, I produce another letter, dated January 13, 1871, written by Mrs. Tilton, and addressed to the person whose name I have heretofore and still suppress, as the one with whom Bowen had alleged an improper connection with Tilton, and because of which improper connection Beecher had been informed Mrs. Tilton was unhappy, and desired the separation. It is marked "EE" :

MRS. TILTON TO ——.

174 LIVINGSTON STREET, {
BROOKLYN, January 13, 1871. }

MY DEAR FRIEND AND SISTER : I was made very glad by your letter, for your love to me is most grateful, and for which I actually hunger. You, like me, have loved and been loved, and can say with Mrs. Browning :

> " Well enough I think we've fared,
> My heart and I."

But I find in you an element to which I respond ; when or how, I am not philosopher enough of the human mind to understand. I cannot reason—only feel.

I wrote to you a reply on the morning of my sickness, and tinged with fears of approaching disaster, so that when mail day arrived I was safely over my sufferings, with a fair prospect of returning health. I destroyed it lest its morbid tone might shadow your spirit. I am now around my house again, doing very poorly what I want to do well. All these ambitions and failures you know, darling, and when, in your last letter to Theodore—those good, true letters—you tell indirectly of your life with your parents, I caught and felt the self-sacrifice, admired and sincerely appreciated your rare qualities of heart and mind. I am a more demonstrative and enthusiastic lover of *God* manifested in his children than you will believe, and my memories of you fill me with admiration and delight. I have caught up your card-picture, which we have, in such moments, and kissed it again and again, praying with tears for God's blessing to follow you, and to perfect in us three the beautiful promise of our nature. But, my sweet and dear ——, I realize in these months of our acquaintance how almost impossible it is to *bring out* these blossoms of our heart's growth—God's gifts to us—to human eyes. Our pearls and flowers are caught up literally by vulgar and base minds that surround us on every side, and so destroyed or abused that we know them no longer as our own, and thus God is made our only hope.

My dear, dear sister, do not let us disappoint each other. I expect much from you—you do of me. Not in the sense of draining or weariness to body or spirit—but trust and faith in human hearts. Does it not exist between us ? I believe it ! My husband has suffered much with me in a cruel conspiracy made by my poor, suffering mother, with an energy worthy of a better cause—to divorce us by saying that *I* was seeking it because of Theodore's infidelity, making *her* feeling *mine*.

These slanders have been sown broadcast. I am quoted everywhere as the author of them. Coming in this form and way to Mr. Bowen, they caused his immediate dismission from both the *Independent* and *Union*. Suffering thus both of us so unjustly—(I knew nothing of these plans)—anxiety night and day brought on my miscarriage ; a disappointment I have never before known—a *love babe* it promised, you know. I have had sorrow almost beyond human capacity, my dear ——. It is my mother ! That will explain volumes to your filial heart. Theodore has many secret enemies, I find, besides my mother, but with a faithfulness renewed and strengthened by experience *we* will, by silence, time, and patience, be victorious over them all. My faith and hope are very bright, now that I am off the sick-bed, and dear Frank Moulton is a friend indeed. (He is managing the case with Mr. Bowen.) We have weathered the storm, and, I believe, without harm to our *Best*. "Let not your heart be troubled," dear sweet—I love you. Be assured of it. I wish I could come to you. I would help you in the care of your loved ones, for *that* I can do. "My heart bounds towards all." Then your spirit would be free to write and think.

But hereunto I am not called. My spirit is willing. My dear children are all well. Floy, on her return at the holiday vacation, found me sick, and we concluded to keep her with us, and she has entered the Packer. Our household has indeed been sadly tossed about, and the children suffer with the parents ; but *the end has come*, and I write that you may have joy and not grief, for that is past ! I am glad you love Alice. I have kissed her for you many times. I will teach all my darlings to love you and welcome your home-coming. Ralph is a fine, beautiful boy, and to be our only baby—very precious therefore. Carroll is visiting Theodore's case with Mr. Bowen.) We have wars at Keyport. I hope your mother is now better and that you have reached the sunshine. Our spirits cannot thrive in Nature's gloom. Give much love to your parents. I am yours, faithfully and fondly,   (Signed)

SISTER ELIZABETH.

This letter requires a word of explanation. It will be observed that in the course of the correspondence between Bowen and Beecher, there had been claimed infidelities on the part of Tilton with a certain lady whose name is not disclosed, although well known to all the parties, and much of the accusations against Tilton connected him with that lady, and it was averred that they came from his wife. The above letter was written to that lady long after the accusations had been made against Tilton, and after they had been communicated to his wife, and I bring it in here as bearing on the question whether Mrs. Tilton desired a separation from her husband, as had been alleged, on account of his infidelities with this lady.

I have already stated that I had, as a necessary precaution to the peace of the family and the parties interested, interdicted all the parties from having communication with each other—except the husband and wife—unless that communication was known to me, and the letters sent through me or shown to me. Mr. Tilton and Mr. Beecher, as I have before stated, both faithfully complied with their promise in that regard, so far as I know. I was away sick in the spring of 1871, as before stated, and went to Florida. Soon after my return Beecher placed in my hands an unsigned letter from Mrs. Tilton, in her handwriting, undated, but marked in his handwriting, "Received March 8, 1871." I here produce it, marked "FF":

MRS. TILTON TO BEECHER.

WEDNESDAY.

MY DEAR FRIEND: Does your heart bound *towards all* as it used? So does mine! I am myself again. I did not dare to tell you till I was sure; but the bird has sung in my heart these *four* weeks, and he has covenanted with me never again to leave. "Spring has come." * Because I thought it would gladden you to know this, and not to trouble or embarrass you in *any way*, I now write. Of course I should like to share with you my joy; but can wait for the Beyond!

When dear Frank says I may once again go to old Plymouth, I will thank the dear Father.

Such a communication from Mrs. Tilton to her pastor, under the circumstances and her promise, seemed to me to be a breach of good faith. But desirous to have the peace kept, and hoping if unanswered it might not be repeated, I did not show it to Tilton, or inform him of its existence.

On Friday, April 21, 1871, Mr. Beecher received another letter, of that date, unsigned, from Mrs. Tilton, which he gave to me. It is here produced, marked "GG," as follows:

MRS. TILTON TO BEECHER.

FRIDAY, April 21, 1871.

MR. BEECHER: As Mr. Moulton has returned, will you use your influence to have the papers in his possession destroyed? My heart bleeds night and day at the injustice of their existence.

As I could not comply with this request, for reasons before stated, I did not show this letter to Tilton, nor did I call Mrs. Tilton's attention to it.

On the 3d of May Mr. Beecher handed me still another letter, unsigned, but in Mrs. Tilton's handwriting, of that date, which is here produced, marked "HH":

MRS. TILTON TO BEECHER.

BROOKLYN, May 3, 1871.

MR. BEECHER: My future either for life or death would be happier could I but feel that you *forgave* while you forget me. In all the sad complications of the past year my endeavor was to entirely keep from *you* all suffering; to bear myself alone, leaving you forever ignorant of it. My weapons were love, a large untiring generosity, and *nest-hiding!* That I failed utterly we both know. But now I ask forgiveness.

The contents of this letter were so remarkable that I queried within my own mind whether I ought not to show it to Tilton; but as I was assured by Beecher, and verily believed, and now believe, that they were unanswered by him, I thought it best to retain it in my own possession, as I have done until now. But from the hour of its reception what remained of faith in Mrs. Tilton's character for truth or propriety of conduct was wholly lost, and from that time forth I had no thought or care for her reputation only so far as it affected that of her children.

After this I do not know that anything occurred between myself and Mrs. Tilton of pertinence to this inquiry, or more than the ordinary courtesies or civilities when I called at her house, and I received no other communication from her until shortly before the question of the arbitration of the business between Bowen and Tilton was determined upon. I had learned that Mrs. Tilton had been making declarations which were sullying the reputation of her husband, and giving it to be understood that her home was not a happy one, because of the want of religious sympathy between herself and husband, and because he did not accompany her to church as regularly and as often as she thought he ought to do, and she thought it would be well for the children to do, and sometimes speaking of her unhappiness, without defining specially the cause, thus leaving for the busybodies and intermeddlers to infer causes of unhappiness which she did not state. I thought it my duty to the parties to caution her in that regard, and I said to her that I thought she ought not, in the presence of others, to upbraid her husband with their differences in religious feeling or opinions, and that it was not well for her to make any statement which should show her home unhappy, or that she was unhappy in it, because it might lead to such inquiries as might break it up, as well as the settlement, which she was so desirous to maintain for the sake of both families—Mrs. Beecher's and her own.

This conversation drew from her the following letter, marked "II":

MRS. TILTON TO MOULTON.

SUNDAY MORNING, February 11, 1872.

MY DEAR FRIEND FRANCIS: All the week I have sought opportunity to write you, but as I cannot work in the cars as Theodore does, and the time at our stopping places must be necessarily given to rest eating, and sight-seeing, say nothing of lecture-going, I have failed to come to you before.

It was given to you to reveal to me last Sabbath evening two things (for which God bless you abundantly with his peace): First, the truth that until then I had never seen nor felt, namely, *whenever* I remember *myself* in conversation with others to the shadowing of Theodore I become his *enemy!* And the second truth was that *I* hindered the *reconstruction more than any one else.*

Whenever I become convinced I know I am immovable. Henceforth silence has locked my lips and the key is cast into the depths! Theo. need fear me no longer, for I would be the enemy of no one.

I have not been equal to the great work of the past year. All I have done is to cause the *utter misery* of those I love best—my mother, husband, Mr. B, and my dear children!

But how greatly I prize your counsel and criticisms you will never know. You do not at all terrify me; only convince, and I bless you.

Pardon this hasty line, which I am sure you'll do, since you forgive so much else. Good night. Affectionately,

(Signed)   ELIZABETH.

After the signing of the "tripartite covenant," April 2, 1872, Theodore desired that I should return him the paper containing his wife's confession, in order, as he said to relieve her anxiety as to its possibly falling into wrong hands, and she was very desirous that this paper should be destroyed. As I held it solely for her protection, and under pledge to him, I gave it to him, and he told me afterwards that he gave it into her hands, and that she destroyed it. She also confirmed this statement.

Some time after that—it is impossible for me to fix the date precisely—I learned from Beecher that Mrs. Tilton had told him that when she made her confession to her husband of her infidelity with him (Beecher) her husband had made a like confession to her of his own infidelities with several other women. This being an entirely new statement of facts to me, and never having heard Mrs. Tilton, in all my conversations with her, although she admitted freely her own sexual intercourse with Beecher, make any claims that her husband had confessed his infidelity, or that he had been unfaithful to her, I was considerably surprised at this intimation made at so late a period, and I brought it to the attention of Tilton, in the form of a very strong criticism of his course towards me, that he had kept back so important a fact, which might have made a great difference as to the course that ought to be taken. Tilton promptly and with much feeling denied that he had ever made such a confession, or that his wife even claimed that he had, and desired me to see Mrs. Tilton, and satisfy myself upon that point; and he went immediately with me to his house, that I might see Mrs. Tilton before he should have the opportunity to see her, after he had learned the alleged fact. We went to the house together and found her in the back parlor. On our way to the house, Tilton said to me: "Frank, what is the use of my trying to keep the family together when this sort of thing is being all the time said against me? You are all the time telling me that I must keep the peace, and forget and forgive, while these stories are being circulated to my prejudice." On arriving at the house I asked Mrs. Tilton to step into the front parlor, where we two were alone. I then put the question to her: "Elizabeth, did you tell Mr. Beecher that when you made your confession to your husband of your infidelity with Beecher, your husband at the same time made a confession to you of his own infidelity with other women?" I said, "I want to know if this is true for my own satisfaction." She answered: "Yes." I then stepped with her into the back parlor, where her husband was waiting, and I said to him: "Your wife says that she did tell Beecher that you confessed your infidelity with other women, at the time she made her confession to you." Elizabeth immediately said: "Why, no, I didn't tell you so. I could not have understood your question, because it isn't true that Theodore ever made any such confession, and I didn't state it to Mr. Beecher, because it is not true."

I was very much shocked and surprised at the denial, but of course could say nothing more, and did say nothing more upon that subject, and left and went home. The next morning I received the following letter from Mrs. Tilton, without date, so that I am unable to give the exact date of this transaction; but I know it was after the tripartite covenant. The letter is here produced and marked "JJ":

MRS. TILTON TO MOULTON.

DEAR FRANCIS: I did tell you *two* falsehoods at your last visit. At first I entirely misunderstood your question, thinking you had reference to the interview at your house, the day before. But when I intelligently replied to you, I *replied falsely.* I will now put myself on record truthfully.

I told Mr. B. that at the time of my confession T. *had* made similar confessions to me of himself, *but no developments as to persons.* When you then asked, for your own satisfaction, "Was it so?" I told my second lie. After you had left I said to T., "You know I was obliged to lie to Frank, and I now say, rather than make others suffer as *I now do*, I must lie; for it is a physical impossibility for me to tell the truth."

Yet I do think, Francis, had not T.'s angry, troubled face been before me, I would have told you the truth.

I am a perfect coward in his presence, not from any fault of his perhaps, but from long years of timidity.

I implore you, as this is a side issue, to be careful not to lead me into further temptation.

You may show this to T. or Mr. B., or any one. An effort made for truth.

Wretchedly,

(Signed)   ELIZABETH.

This letter was wholly unsatisfactory to me, because nothing had occurred the day previous to which she could possibly have referred. After the publication, on the 2d of November, 1872, in *Woodhull and Claflin's Weekly*, of the story of Tilton and Beecher's conduct in relation to Mrs. Tilton, and as my name was mentioned in the article as one possessing peculiar knowledge upon the whole subject, I was continually asked by my acquaintances, and even by strangers, upon their ascertaining who I was, whether that publication was true; and I found great difficulty in making an answer. A refusal on my part to answer would have been taken to be a confession of the truth of the charges. Therefore, when people inquired who had no right to my confidence, I answered them in such prase as, without making a direct statement, would lead them to infer that the charges could not be sustained.

In some cases I doubt not that the inquirers supposed that I, in fact, denied their truth; but upon that point I was very studious not directly to commit myself. Finding that my very silence was working injury to the cause of the supression of the scandal, I told Tilton that I wished to be authorized by his wife to deny it.

I thought it certainly could not possibly be true to the extent, and in the circumstances with the breadth, in which it was stated in that newspaper. Soon after I received the following paper, without date, from Mrs. Tilton, which is produced and marked "KK":

MRS. TILTON TO MOULTON.

Mr. Moulton.

MY DEAR FRIEND : For my husband's sake and my children's, I hereby testify, with all my woman's soul, that I am innocent of the crime of impure conduct alleged against me. I have been to my husband a true wife; in his love I wish to live and die. My early affection for him still burns with its maiden flame ; *all the more* for what he has borne for my sake, both private and public wrongs. My plan to keep back scandals long ago threatened against me I never approved, and the result shows it unavailing; but few would have risked so much as he has sacrificed for others ever since the conspiracy began against him, two years ago.

Having had power to strike others, he has forborne to use it, and allowed himself to be injured instead. No wound is so great to me as the imputation that he is among my accusers. I bless him every day for his faith in me, which swerves not, and for standing my champion against all my accusers.

(Signed)   ELIZABETH R. TILTON.

Upon the strength of that I thereafterwards said that Mrs. Tilton denied the story. About the 16th December, 1872, Mr. Carpenter and Dr. Storrs undertook to look up the reports, with the intention, as I understood, of advising some public statement, or as being concerned in some investigation of the matter, and Mrs. Tilton wrote for them the following paper bearing that date, which I produce, marked "LL"

MRS. TILTON'S STATEMENT.

DECEMBER 16, 1872.

In July, 1870, prompted by my duty, I informed my husband that H. W. Beecher, my friend and pastor, had solicited me to be a wife to him, together with all that this implied. Six months afterwards my husband felt impelled by the circumstances of a conspiracy against him, in which Mrs. Beecher had taken part, to have an interview with Mr. Beecher.

In order that Mr. B. might know exactly what I had said to my husband, I wrote a brief statement (I have forgotten in what form), which my husband showed to Mr. Beecher. Late the same evening Mr. B. came to me (lying very sick at the time), and filled me with distress, saying I had ruined him—and wanting to know if I meant to appear against him. This I certainly did not mean to do, and the thought was agonizing to me. I then signed a paper which he wrote, to clear him in case of a trial. In this instance, as in most others, when absorbed by one great interest or feeling, the harmony of my mind is entirely disturbed, and I found on reflection that this paper was so drawn as to place me most unjustly against my husband, and on the side of Mr. Beecher. So in order to repair so cruel a blow to my long-suffering husband, I wrote an explanation of the first paper and my signature. Mr. Moulton procured from Mr. B. the statement which I gave to him in my agitation and excitement, and now holds it.

This ends my connection with the case.

(Signed) ELIZABETH R. TILTON.

P. S.—This statement is made at the request of Mr. Carpenter, that it may be shown confidentially to Dr. Storrs and other friends, with whom my husband and I are consulting.

This paper was delivered to me, and the theory of the confession then was that Mr. and Mrs. Tilton should admit no more than the solicitation; but that endeavor to make an explanation of the business fell through, and after it was shown to those interested, as I was told, the paper remained with me.

I received no further communication from Mrs. Tilton until the 25th of June of this year (1874), and that communication came to me in this wise. When Tilton showed me his Dr. Bacon letter, I most strongly and earnestly advised against its publication, and said to him in substance, that while I admitted the wrong and injustice of Dr. Bacon's charges that he (Mr. T.) had lived by the magnanimity of Beecher and that he was a dog and a knave, when I believed he had acted a proper and manly part in endeavoring to shield his family, yet that its publication would so stir the public mind that an investigation would be forced upon him and Beecher in some manner which I could not then foresee, and that the truth would in all probability have to come out, or so much of it that Mrs. Tilton and Beecher would be dishonored and destroyed, and he himself be subjected to the severest criticism. Notwithstanding my advice, he was so wrought up with the continued assaults upon him by the friends of Beecher that he determined on the publication of the letter.

He said to me, in substance, that as the course I had advised in the matter in regard to the church investigation had been so completely set aside by Beecher's friends, and they had so far ignored all propositions coming from me as to the best mode of disposing of the matter, they evidently did not any longer intend to be guided by my counsel or wishes; and if Beecher and his friends set me aside in the matter, he (Mr. T.) could see no reason why he should any longer yield to my entreaties or follow my lead. The only modification that I was able to get of the Bacon letter was this: It originally read that Beecher had committed against him and his family "a revolting crime."

I insisted that that should be changed into "an offense committed against me," which was done, and the letter was published in that form.

The reasons which actuated me to require this change by Tilton in his letter were in the hope that reconciliation and peace might still be possible. As the letter as amended would state an offense only, and also that an apology sufficient in the mind of Tilton had been made for that offense, if Beecher, in reply to the Bacon letter, should come out and state that it was true that he had committed an offense against Tilton for which he had made the most ample apology, which had been accepted by Tilton as satisfactory, and as the matter was nobody's business but that of the parties interested, he would never become a party to any investigation of the subject, and that Tilton had acted not unjustly or unfairly towards him in what he had done; that in such case the affair might possibly have been quieted and peace maintained. But if the words "revolting crime" remained in the letter all hope of reconciliation or escaping the fullest investigation would be impossible. After the publication of that letter I so advised Mr. Beecher, his friends and counsel, but that advice was unheeded; and I also gave Mr. Beecher the same advice at a consultation with him for which he asked in a letter, which will hereafter in its proper place be produced. Some days subsequent to this advice of mine to Tilton, I received the following letter, of date June 25, 1874, from Mrs. Tilton, which is the last communication I have had with or from her on the subject. It is herewith produced, and marked "M M":

MRS. TILTON TO MOULTON.

JUNE 25, 1874.

MR. MOULTON: It is fitting I should make quick endeavor to undo my injustice towards you.

I learned from Theodore last night that you greatly opposed the publication of his statement to Dr. Bacon. I had coupled you with Mr. Carpenter as advising it.

Forgive me, and accept my gratitude.

(Signed) ELIZ. R. TILTON.

Having now placed before the committee my statement of the facts concerning Mrs. Tilton, and the documentary evidence that I have to support them, and as they are diametrically opposed to nearly all that Mrs. Tilton appears to declare in her published statement, I deem it my duty to myself, and my position in this terrible business, to say that during this affair, Mrs. Tilton has more than once admitted to me and to another person to my knowledge—whom I do not care to bring into this controversy—the fact of her sexual relations with Beecher, and she never has once denied them, other than in the written papers prepared for a purpose which I have already exhibited; but on the contrary, the fact of such criminal intercourse being well understood by Beecher, Tilton, and Mrs. Tilton to have taken place, my whole action in the matter was based upon the existence of that fact, and was an endeavor, faithfully carried out by me in every way possible, to protect the families of both parties from the consequences of a public disclosure of Mrs. Tilton's admitted infidelities to her husband.

I now return to the documentary evidence, and the necessary explanations thereof, which I have of the condition of the affair as regards Beecher himself, after the fall of 1871, as disconnected with the affairs of Bowen which I have already explained. About this time I received the following letter, marked "MM 2":

MRS. WOODHULL TO BEECHER.

15 EAST THIRTY-EIGHTH STREET, 19th, 11th, 1871.

Rev. H. W. Beecher:

DEAR SIR: For reasons in which *you* are deeply interested as well as myself, and the cause of truth, I desire to have an interview with you, without fail, at some hour to-morrow. Two of your sisters have gone out of their way to assail my character and purposes, both by the means of the public press and by numerous private letters written to various persons with whom they seek to injure me and thus to defeat the political ends at which I aim.

You doubtless know that it is in my power to strike back, and in ways more disastrous than anything that can come to me; but I do not desire to do this. I simply desire justice from those from whom I have a right to expect it; and a reasonable course on your part will assist me to it. I speak guardedly, but I think you will understand me. I repeat that I must have an interview to-morrow, since I am to speak to-morrow evening at Steinway Hall, and what I shall or shall not say will depend largely upon the result of the interview. Yours very truly,

(Signed)   VICTORIA C. WOODHULL.

P. S. Please return answer by bearer.

The foregoing letter occasioned Mr. Tilton much anxiety lest Mrs. Woodhull, in proceeding against Mr. Beecher and his sisters, would thereby involve Mrs. Tilton.

Accordingly, knowing that Mr. Beecher and Mrs. Woodhull were to have an interview at my house on the next day, he came to it, uninvited, and urged Mr. Beecher to preside on that evening at Steinway Hall. After Mrs. W. left, Tilton repeated this urgency to Beecher.

On that evening I went to Steinway Hall with Tilton; and finding no one there to preside, Tilton volunteered to preside himself, which, I believe, had the effect of preventing Mrs. Woodhull's proposed attack on the Beecher family at that time. On the 30th of December, 1871, Mrs. Woodhull also sent a letter to Beecher, desiring that he would speak at a woman's suffrage convention at Washington, to be held on the 10th, 11th, and 12th of January following. That letter Beecher forwarded to me with the following note of the date of 2d of January, 1872, herewith produced, and marked "NN":

BEECHER TO MOULTON.

BROOKLYN, TUESDAY EVENING, 2d January, 1872.

MY DEAR MOULTON; 1. I send you V. W.'s letter to me, and a reply which I submit to your judgment. Tell me what you think. Is it too long? Will she use it for publishing? I do not wish to have it so used. I do not mean to speak on the platform of *either* of the two suffrage societies. What influence I exert I prefer to do on my own hook; and I do not mean to *train* with either party, and it will not be fair to press me in where I do not wish to go. But I leave it for *you*. Judge for me. I have leaned on you hitherto, and never been sorry for it.

2. I was mistaken about the *Ch. Union* coming out so early that I could not get a notice of *G. Age* in it. It was *just the other way*, to be delayed, and I send you a rough proof of the first page, and the *Star* article.

In the paper to-morrow a line or so will be inserted to soften a little the touch about the *Lib. Christian*.

3. Do you think I ought to keep a *copy* of any letters to V. W.? Do you think it would be better to write it again, and not say so much? Will you keep the letter to me, and send the other if you judge it wise?

4. Will you send a line to my house *in the morning* saying what you conclude?

I am full of company.

Yours truly and affectionately,

(Signed),   H. W. B.

There is a paragraph in this note which needs a word of explanation. I had advised Beecher, in order that he might show that there was no unkindly feeling between him and Tilton, to publish in the *Christian Union* a reference to the *Golden Age*. He agreed to do so, but instead of that he had a notice which I thought was worse than if he had said nothing, and the allusion in the second paragraph of this letter is to a letter which I had written to Beecher upon the two topics—this and Mrs. Woodhull.

A retained copy of my letter I herewith submit, marked "OO";

MOULTON TO BEECHER.

My Dear Sir: First with reference to Mrs. Woodhull's letter and your answer: I think that you would have done better to accept the invitation to speak in Washington, but if lecture interferes your letter in reply is good enough, and will bear publication.

With relation to your notice of the *Golden Age* I tell you frankly, as your friend, that I am ashamed of it, and would rather you would have written nothing. Your early associations with, and your present knowledge of the man who edits that paper, are grounds upon which you might have so written that no reader would have doubted that in your opinion Theodore Tilton's public and private integrity was unquestionable. If the article had been written to compliment the *Independent* it would receive my unqualified approval.

On the 5th of February, 1872, I received from Mr. Beecher the letter which I here produce, of that date, and marked " PP ":

BEECHER TO MOULTON.

MONDAY, February 5, 1872.

My Dear Friend : I leave town to-day, and expect to pass through from Philadelphia to New Haven. Shall not be here till Friday.

About three weeks ago I met T. in the cars going to B. He was kind. We talked much. At the end he told me to go on with my work without the least anxiety, in so far as his feelings and actions were the occasion of apprehension.

On returning home from New Haven (where I am three days in the week, delivering a course of lectures to the theological students), I found a note from *E.* saying that *T.* felt hard towards me, and was going to see or write me before leaving for the West.

She kindly added, "Do not be cast down. I bear this almost always, but the God in whom we trust will *deliver us all safely*. I know you do and are willing abundantly to help him, and I also know your embarrassments." These were words of warning, but also of consolation, for I believe E. is beloved of God, and that her prayers for me are sooner heard than mine for myself or for her. But it seems that a change has come to T. since I saw him in the cars. Indeed, ever since he has felt more intensely the force of feeling in society, and the humiliations which environ his enterprise, he has growingly felt that I had a power to help which I did not develop, and I believe that you have participated in this feeling. It is natural you should. T. is dearer to you than *I* can be. He is with you. All his trials lie open to your eye daily. But I see you but seldom, and my personal relations, environments, necessities, limitations, dangers, and perplexities you cannot see or imagine. If I had not gone through this great *year of sorrow*, I would not have believed that any one could pass through my experience and be *alive* or *sane*. I have been the centre of three distinct circles, each one of which required clear-mindedness and peculiarly inventive or originating power, viz.:

1. The *great* church.
2. The *newspaper*.
3. The *book*.

The first I could neither get out of nor slight. The *sensitiveness* of so many of my people would have made any appearance of trouble or any remission of force an occasion of alarm and notice and have excited, when it was important that rumors should die and everything be quieted.

The newspaper I did roll off, doing but little except give general directions, and in so doing I was continually spurred and exhorted by those in interest. It could not be helped.

The "Life of Christ," long delayed, had locked up the capital of the firm, and was likely to sink them—finished it *must* be. Was ever book born of such sorrow as that was ? The interior history of it will never be written.

During all this time *you*, literally, were all my *stay and comfort*. I should have fallen on the way but for the courage which you inspired and the hope which you breathed.

My vacation was profitable. I came back hoping that the bitterness of death was passed. But T.'s troubles brought back the cloud, with even severer suffering. For all this fall and winter I have felt that you did not feel satisfied with me, and that I seemed, both to you and T., as contenting myself with a cautious or sluggish policy, willing to save myself but not to risk anything for T. I have again and again probed my heart to see whether I was truly liable to such feeling, and the response is unequivocal that I am not. No man can see the difficulties that environ me, unless he stands where I do.

To *say* that I have a church on my hands is simple enough—but to have the hundreds and thousands of men pressing me, each one with his keen suspicion, or anxiety, or zeal ; to see tendencies which, if not stopped, would break out into ruinous defense of me ; to stop them without seeming to do it ; to prevent any one questioning me ; to meet and allay prejudices against T. which had their beginning years before this ; to keep serene, as if I was not alarmed or disturbed ; to be cheerful at home and among friends when I was suffering the torments of the damned ; to pass sleepless nights often, and yet to come up fresh and full for Sunday ;—all this may be talked about, but the real thing cannot be understood from the outside, nor its wearing and grinding on the nervous system.

God knows that I have put more thought and judgment and earnest desire into my efforts to prepare a way for T. and E. than ever I did for myself a hundred-fold. As to the outside public, I have never lost an opportunity to soften prejudices, to refute falsehoods, and to excite kindly feeling among all whom I met. I am thrown among clergymen, public men, and generally the makers of public opinion, and I have used every rational endeavor to repair the evils which have been visited upon T., and with increasing success.

But the roots of this prejudice are long. The catastrophe which precipitated him from his place only disclosed feelings that had existed long. Neither he nor you can be aware of the feelings of classes in society, on other grounds than late rumors. I mention this to explain why *I know* with *absolute* certainty that no mere statement, letter, testimony, or affirmation will reach the root of affairs and reinstate them. TIME and WORK WILL.

But chronic evil requires *chronic remedies*. If my destruction would place him all right, that shall not stand in the way. I am willing to step down and out. No one can offer more than that. That I do offer. Sacrifice me without hesitation, if you can clearly see your way to his safety and happiness thereby. I do not think that anything would be gained by it. I should be destroyed, but he would not be saved. E. and the children would have their future clouded. In one point of view I could desire the sacrifice on my part. Nothing can possibly be so bad as the horror of great darkness in which I spend much of my time. I look upon death as sweeter-faced than any friend I have in the world. Life would be pleasant if I could see that rebuilt which is shattered. But to live on the sharp and ragged edge of anxiety, remorse, fear, despair, and yet to put on all the appearance of serenity and happiness, cannot be endured much longer.

I am well-nigh discouraged. If you, too, cease to trust me—to love me—I am alone; I have not another person in the world to whom I could go.

Well, to God I commit all. Whatever it may be here, it shall be well there. With sincere gratitude for your heroic friendship, and with sincere affection, even though you love me not, I am yours (though unknown to you),

(Signed)   H. W. B.

This letter was to let me know that Elizabeth had written him, contrary to her promise, without my permission, and also to inform me of his fears as to the change in Tilton's mind, and its clear statement of the case as it then stood cannot be further elucidated by me. On the 25th of March I received a portrait of Titian as a present from Mr. Beecher, with the following note, as a token of his confidence and respect. It is produced, and marked "QQ":

BEECHER TO MOULTON.

MY DEAR FRIEND: I sent on Friday or Saturday a portrait of Titian to the store for you. I hope it may suit you.

I have been doing ten men's work this winter—partly to make up lost time, partly because I live under a cloud, feeling every month that I may be doing my last work, and anxious to make the most of it. When Esau sold his birthright he found "no place for repentance, though he sought it carefully with tears." But I have one abiding comfort. I have known you, and found in you one who has given a new meaning to friendship. As soon as warm days come I want you to go to Peekskill with me.

I am off in an hour for Massachusetts, to be gone all the week.

I am urging forward my second volume of "Life of Christ," for "the night cometh when no man can work."

With much affection and admiration, yours truly,

H. W. B.

March 25, 1872. Monday morning.

After Tilton had written a campaign document against Grant's Administration, and in favor of Mr. Greeley's election, Beecher discussed with me the position taken by Tilton. Beecher also gave me a copy of his (Beecher's) speech opening the Grant campaign in Brooklyn. After the speech was delivered he sent me the following note of May 17, 1872, which I here produce, marked "RR":

BEECHER TO MOULTON.

MAY 17, 1872.

MY DEAR FRANK: I send you the only copy I have of my speech at the Academy of Music on Grant, and have marked the passage that we spoke about last night, and you will see just what I said, and that I argued then just as I do now.

Pray send it back, or I shall be left without a speech!

I read Theodore's on Grant. I do not think it just. It is ably written; it is a case of *grape-shot*.

Yet, I think it will overact; it is too strong—will be likely to produce a feeling among those no already intense, that it is excessive. Yours sincerely and ever,

H. W. B.

Don't forget to send back my *speech!*

About the time of this occurrence Beecher and Tilton met at my house on friendly terms. In fact I cannot exhibit better the tone of Tilton's mind in the winter and spring of 1871-72 than to produce here a letter, written to me at that time without date, but I can fix the date as early as that. It is here produced, and marked "SS";

TILTON TO MOULTON.

HUDSON RIVER RAILROAD, Monday Morning.

MY DEAR FRANK: I am writing while the train is in motion—which accounts for the apparent drunkenness of this shaken chirography. Mrs. Beecher sits in the next seat. We are almost elbow to elbow in the palace car. She is white-haired and looks a dozen years older than when I last had a near view of her. My heart has been full of pity for her, notwithstanding the cruel way in which she has treated my good name. Her face is written over with many volumes of human suffering. I do not think she has been aware of my presence, for she has been absorbed in thought—her eyes rooted to one spot.

A suggestion has occurred to me, which I hasten to communicate. She is going to Florida, and may never return alive. If I am ever to be vindicated from the slanders which she has circulated, or which Mr. Bowen pretends to have derived from her and Mrs. Morse, why would it not be well to get from her and Mrs. Morse a statement under oath (by such a process as last evening's documents make easy and harmless) of the exact narrations which they made to him and to others.

It would be well to have *them* say what they said before *he* gets a chance to say what they said to *him*. Speak to Mr. Ward about it. Of course I leave the matter wholly to you and him.

I am unusually heavy-hearted this morning. My sullen neighbor keeps the dark and lurid past vividly before my mind. If she actually knew the conduct which her priestly husband has been guilty of, I believe she would shed his blood—or perhaps, saving *him*, she would wreak her wrath on his *victims*. There is a look of desperation in her eyes to-day as if she were competent to anything bitter or revengeful. But perhaps I misjudge her mind. I hope I do.

I shall not be home till Thursday afternoon instead of morning, as I said—leaving for Washington at nine P. M. that evening. Ever yours,

THEODORE.

On the 3d of June, 1872, Beecher received from Mrs. Woodhull the following letter of that date, which I here produce, marked "TT":

MRS. WOODHULL TO BEECHER.

48 BROAD STREET, June 3, 1972.

Rev. Henry Ward Beecher.

MY DEAR SIR: The social fight against me being now waged in this city is becoming rather hotter than I can well endure longer, standing unsupported and alone as I have until now. Within the past two weeks I have been shut out of hotel after hotel, and am now, after having obtained a place in one, hunted down by a set of males and females, who are determined that I shall not be permitted to live even, if they can prevent it.

Now, I want your assistance. I want to be sustained in my position in the Gilsey House, from which I am ordered out and from which I do not wish to go—and all this simply because I am Victoria C. Woodhull, the advocate of social freedom. I have submitted to this persecution just so long as I can endure to; my business, my projects, in fact everything for which I live suffers from it, and it must cease. Will you lend me your aid in this? Yours very truly,

VICTORIA C. WOODHULL.

The above letter was sent to me enclosed in note from Beecher of the same date, which is here produced and marked "UU":

BEECHER TO MOULTON.

MONDAY EVENING, June 3, 1872.

MY DEAR MR. MOULTON: Will you answer this? Or will you see that she is to understand that I can do nothing? I certainly shall not, at any and all hazards, take a single step in that direction, and if it brings trouble—it must come.

Please drop me a line to say that all is right—if in your judgment all *is* right. Truly yours,

H. W. B.

This letter of Mrs. Woodhull, together with those before produced asking Beecher to speak at a suffrage convention, are all the letters I have from her to Beecher. To this letter no reply was made.

After the publication of the tripartite covenant by Mr. Wilkeson, which I believe was on the 29th of May, 1873, the story of the troubles between Beecher and Tilton was revived, with many rumors, and those claiming to be friends of Beecher were endeavoring, as Tilton thought, to explain the terms of that covenant in a manner prejudicial to him. Some enemies of Beecher were endeavoring to get some clue to the proofs of the facts lying at the bottom of these scandals.

After the publication of this "tripartite covenant" was made, Tilton deemed, from the comments of the press, that the statement reflected upon him, and he desired that in some way Beecher should relieve him from the imputation of having circulated slanderous stories about him without justification, for which he had apologized, and by advice of friends he prepared a card for me to submit to Beecher to have him sign and publish in his vindication. The original card I herewith produce, marked "UU 1":

A CARD FROM HENRY WARD BEECHER.

A letter written by Theodore Tilton to Henry C. Bowen, dated Brooklyn, January 1, 1871, narrating charges made by Mr. Bowen against my character, has been made public in a community in which I am a citizen and clergyman, and thrusts upon me, by no agency of my own, what I could not with propriety invite for myself, namely, an opportunity to make the following statements:

I. By the courtesy of Mr. Tilton, that letter was shown to me at the time it was written, and before it was conveyed to Mr. Bowen, two and a half years ago. By legal and other advisers, Mr. Tilton was urged to publish it then, without delay, or a similar statement, explaining his sudden collision with Mr. Bowen, and his unexpected retirement as editor of the *Union*, and contributor to the *Independent*. But although Mr. Tilton's public standing needed such an explanation to be made, and although he had my free consent to make it, yet he magnanimously refrained from doing so, through an unwillingness to disclose to the public Mr. Bowen's aspersions concerning myself. Mr. Tilton's consideration for my feelings and reputation, thus evinced at the beginning, has continued to the end, and I have never ceased to be grateful to him for an uncommon manliness in accepting wounds to his own reputation for the sake of preventing aspersions on mine.

II. The surreptitious and unauthorized publication last Sunday of Mr. Tilton's letter—a publication made without the knowledge either of Mr. Tilton or myself—gives me the right to say that Mr. Bowen long ago retracted his mistaken charges in the following words, under his own hand and seal, dated —— ——, namely:

III. In addition to Mr. Bowen's voluntary statement, above given, I solemnly pronounce the charges to be false, one and all, and to be without any color of reason or foundation in fact.

IV. All my differences with Mr. Bowen, and all temporary misunderstandings between Mr. Tilton and myself growing out of these, were long ago settled justly, amicably, and in the spirit of mutual good will. (Signed) HENRY WARD BEECHER.

Beecher felt much aggrieved at this claim upon him by Tilton, feeling that the matter had been all settled and adjusted, and he answered Tilton's application in this regard by the letter herewith produced under date June 1, 1873, marked "UU 2":

BEECHER TO MOULTON.

SUNDAY MORNING, June 1, 1873.

MY DEAR FRANK: The whole earth is tranquil and the heaven is serene, as befits one who has about finished his world-life. I could do nothing on Saturday—my head was confused. But a good sleep has made it like crystal. I have determined to make no more resistance. Theodore's temperament is such that the future, even if temporarily earned, would be absolutely worthless, filled with abrupt charges, and rendering me liable at any hour or day to be obliged to stultify all the devices by which we have saved ourselves. It is only fair that he should know that the publication of the card which he proposes would leave him far worse off than before.

The *agreement* was made after my letter through you was written. He had had it a year. He had condoned his wife's fault. He had enjoined upon me with the utmost earnestness and solemnity not to betray his wife nor leave his children to a blight. I had honestly and earnestly joined in the purpose. Then this settlement was made and signed by him. It was not my making. He revised his part so that it should wholly suit him, and signed it. It stood unquestioned and unblamed for more than a year. *Then it was published.* Nothing but that. That which he did in private when made public excited him to fury, and he charges me with *making him appear* as one *graciously pardoned by me!* It was his own deliberate act, with which he was perfectly content till others saw it, and then he charges a grievous wrong home on me!

My mind is clear. I am not in haste. I shall write for the public a statement that will bear the light of the judgment day. God will take care of me and mine. When I look on earth it is a deep night. When I look to the Heavens above I see the morning breaking. But, oh! that I could put in golden letters my deep sense of your faithful, earnest, undying fidelity, your disinterested friendship!

Your noble wife, too, has been to me one of God's comforters. It is such as she that renews a waning faith in womanhood. Now, Frank, I would not have you waste any more energy on a hopeless task. With such a man as T. T. there is no possible salvation for any that depend upon him. With a strong nature, he does not know how to govern it. With generous impulses, the undercurrent that rules him is self. With ardent affections, he cannot love long that which does not repay him with admiration and praise. With a strong, theatric nature, he is constantly imposed upon with the idea that a position, a great stroke, a *coup d'état*, is the way to success.

Besides these he has a hundred good things about him, but these named traits make him absolutely unreliable.

Therefore there is no use in further trying. I have a strong feeling upon me, and it brings great peace with it, that I am spending my *last Sunday* and preaching my last sermon.

Dear, good God, I thank thee I am indeed beginning to see rest and triumph. The pain of life is but a moment; the glory of everlasting emancipation is wordless, inconceivable, full of beckoning glory. Oh, my beloved Frank, I shall know you there, and forever hold fellowship with you, and look back and smile at the past. Your loving,

H. W. B.

Meanwhile, charges were preferred against Tilton for the purpose of having him dismissed from Plymouth Church. This action, which seemed to threaten the discovery of the facts in regard to the troubles between Beecher and Tilton, annoyed both very much, and I myself feared that serious difficulty would arise therefrom. Upon consultation with Beecher and Tilton I suggested a plan by which that investigation would be rendered unnecessary, which was, in substance, that a resolution should be passed by the church amending its roll, alleging that Tilton, having voluntarily withdrawn from the church some four years before, therefore the roll should be amended by striking off his name. This course had been suggested to me by Mr. Tilton about a year and a half before, in answer to a letter by Beecher, dated December 3, 1871, marked "UU 3":

BEECHER TO MOULTON.

My Dear Friend : There are two or three who feel anxious to press action on the case. It will only serve to raise profitless excitement, when we need to have quieting.

There are already perplexities enough.

We do not want to run the risk of the complications which, in such a body, no man can foresee and no one control. Once free from a sense of responsibility for *him*, and there would a strong tendency for a kindly feeling to set in, which is now checked by the membership, without attendance, sympathy, or doctrinal agreement.

Since the connection is really formal, and not vital or sympathetic, why should it continue, with all the risk of provoking irritating measures ? Every day's reflection satisfies me that this is the course of wisdom, and that T. will be the stronger and B. the weaker for it.

You said that you meant to effect it. Can't it be done promptly ? If a letter is written it had better be very short, simply announcing withdrawal, and, perhaps, with an expression of kind wishes, &c.

You will know. I shall be in town Monday and part of Tuesday. Shall I hear from you ?
December 3, 1871.

But when the meeting of the church was held for that purpose it was charged there that Tilton had slandered the pastor. Tilton, therefore, took the stand, and said in substance that if he had uttered any slanders against Beecher he was ready to answer them, as God was his witness. Beecher thereupon stated that he had no charges to make, and the matter dropped. But when the resolution was passed, instead of being put so as to exonerate Tilton, it was declared in substance that, whereas certain charges had been made against him, and as he pleaded to those charges non-membership, his name be dropped from the roll.

This action of the church very much exasperated Tilton, who thought that Beecher should have prevented such a result, and that he might have done so, if he had stood by him fully and fairly as agreed. In that, however, I believe Tilton was mistaken, because Mr. William F. West, who preferred the charges against Tilton, did it against the wish of Beecher, and without any consultation with him, as appears by the following letter of June 25, 1875, produced here, and marked "VV":

MR. WEST TO BEECHER.

New York, June 25, 1873.

Rev. H. W. Beecher :

Dear Sir : Moved by a sense of duty as a member of Plymouth Church, I have decided to prefer charges against Henry C. Bowen and Theodore Tilton, and have requested Brother Halliday to call a meeting of the Examining Committee in order that I may make the charges before them.

Thinking that you would perhaps like to be made acquainted with these facts, I called last evening at Mr. Beach's house, where I was informed that you had returned to Peekskill.

I therefore write you by early mail to-day. Yours very truly,

WM. F. WEST.

Meanwhile, through the intervention of Dr. Storrs and others, as I understood, an ecclesiastical council had been called. The acts of this council in attempting to disfellowship Plymouth Church were very displeasing to Beecher, and caused him much trouble, especially the action of Dr. Storrs, which he expressed to me in the following letter, dated March 25, 1874, which is here produced and marked "WW":

BEECHER TO MOULTON.

[Confidential.]

MY DEAR FRANK : I am indignant beyond expression. Storrs's course has been an unspeakable outrage. After his pretended sympathy and friendship for Theodore he has turned against him in the most venomous manner—and it is not sincere. His professions of faith and affection for me are hollow and faithless. They are merely *tactical*. His object is plain. He is determined to *force* a conflict, and to use one of us to destroy the other if possible. That is his game. By stinging Theodore he believes that he will be driven into a course which he hopes will ruin me. If ever a man betrayed another he has. I am in hopes that Theodore, who has borne so much, will be unwilling to be a flail in Storrs's hand to strike at a friend. There are one or two reasons, emphatic, for *waiting* until the end of the council before taking any action :

1. That the attack on Plymouth Church and the threats against Congregationalism were so violent that the public mind is likely to be absorbed in the ecclesiastical elements and not in the personal.

2. If Plymouth Church is *disfellowshiped* it will constitute a blow at me and the church, far severer that at him.

3. That if council does *not disfellowship* Plymouth Church, then, undoubtedly, Storrs will go off into Presbyterianism, as he almost, without disguise, *threatened* in his speech, and, in that case, the emphasis will be *there.*

4. At any rate, while the fury rages in council, it is not wise to make any move that would be *one* among so many, as to lose effect in a degree, and after the battle is over one can more exactly see what ought to be done. Meantime I am *patient* as I know how to be, but pretty nearly used up with inward excitement, and must run away for a day or two and hide and sleep, or there will be a funeral.

Cordially and trustingly yours,   H. W. B.

March 25, 1874.

No one can tell under first impressions what the effect of such a speech will be. *It ought to damn Storrs.*

While these proceedings were pending, Rev. Mr. Halliday, the assistant of Beecher, called upon him and upon me to endeavor to learn the facts about the difficulties between Beecher and Tilton. I stated to Halliday that I did not think that either he or the church were well employed in endeavoring to reopen a trouble which had been adjusted and settled by the parties to it, and that it was better, in my judgment, for everybody that the whole matter should be allowed to repose in quiet. The result of the interview between Halliday and Beecher was communicated to me in the following letter, undated and unsigned, so that I cannot fix the date, but it is in Beecher's handwriting, and is here produced and marked "XX":

BEECHER TO MOULTON.

SUNDAY—A. M.

MY DEAR FRIEND : Halliday called last night. T.'s interview with him did not satisfy but disturbed. It was the same with Bell, who was present. It tended directly to unsettling.

Your interview last night was *very beneficial,* and gave confidence. This must be looked after.

It is vain to build if the foundation sinks under every effort.

I shall see you at 10:30 to-morrow—if you return by way of 49 Remsen.

The anxiety which Beecher felt about these stories, and the steps he took to quiet them, together with the trust he reposed in me and my endeavors to aid him in that behalf, may perhaps be as well seen from a letter headed "25, '73," which I believe to be June 25, 1873, and directed, "My Dear Von Moltke," meaning myself, and kindly complimenting me with the name of a general having command of a battle. It is here produced and marked "YY":

BEECHER TO MOULTON.

25, '73.

MY DEAR VON MOLTKE : I have seen Howard again. He says that it was not from Theodore that Gilkison got the statement, but from Carpenter.

Is he reporting that view ? I have told Claflin that you would 'come with Carpenter if he could be found, and at any rate by 9 to-night (to see Storrs), but I did not say anything about Storrs.

I sent Cleveland with my horse and buggy over to hunt Carpenter.

Will you put Carpenter on his guard about making such statements ?

From him these bear the force of coming from headquarters. Yours truly and ever,

H. W. BEECHER.

Meanwhile Halliday had had an interview with Tilton, the result of which, as unsettling the matter between Tilton and Beecher, was very anxiously awaited by Beecher, who communicated to me, and who was also quite as anxious that Tilton should take no steps by which the matter between them should get into the newspapers or be made in any manner a matter of controversy. With this view he stated the situation on the same night of the interview of Halliday and Tilton in the following letter, which is without date and was written in pencil in great haste, and is here produced, marked " ZZ ":

BEECHER TO MOULTON.

SUNDAY NIGHT.

MY DEAR FRIEND :

1. The *Eagle* ought to have nothing to-night. It is *that* meddling which stirs up our folks. Neither *you* nor Theodore ought to be troubled by the side which you served so faithfully in public.

2. The deacons' meeting I think is adjourned. I saw Bell. It was a friendly movement.

3. The only near next danger is the women—Morrill, Bradshaw, and the poor dear child.

If papers will hold off a month we can ride out the gale and make safe anchorage, and then when once we are in deep, tranquil waters, we will all join hands in a profound and genuine *Laus Deo*, for through such a wilderness only a Divine Providence could have led us undevoured by the open-mouthed beasts that lay in wait for our lives.

I go on 12 train after sleepless night. I am anxious about Theodore's interview with Halliday. Will you send me a *line* Monday night or Tuesday morning, care of H. P. Kennard, Boston, Mass.

I shall get mails there till Friday.

I have now produced to the committee all the letters and documents bearing upon the subject-matter of this inquiry which I have in my possession, either from Beecher, Tilton, or Mrs. Tilton, previous to the Bacon letter, and there is but one collateral matter of which I desire to speak.

I saw questions put in the cross-examination of Tilton, as published in the Brooklyn *Eagle*, and also published in the newspapers—with how much of truth I know not—that Mr. Samuel Wilkeson had charged that Tilton's case in controversy with Bowen was for the purpose of blackmailing him and and Beecher, and that he (Wilkeson) knew that there had been no crime committed against Tilton or his household by Beecher. Beecher never intimated to me that he thought there was any desire on Tilton's part to blackmail him ; and as I had the sole management of the money controversy between Tilton and Bowen, which I have already fully explained, I know there was no attempt on Tilton's part to blackmail, or get anything more than what I believe his just due from Bowen. So that I am certain that Mr. Wilkeson is wholly mistaken in that regard.

The question whether Wilkeson knew or believed that any offense had been committed will depend upon the fact whether he knew of anything that had been done by Beecher or Tilton's wife which called for apology at the time he wrote the tripartite covenant. It will be remembered that the tripartite covenant was made solely in reference to the disclosures which Bowen had made to Tilton and Tilton had made to Bowen, and Tilton's letters set forth that the only disclosure he made to Bowen of Beecher's acts towards himself were of improper advances made to his wife and that he so limited his charge in order to save the honor of his wife. These questions will be answered by the production of the letter of April 2, 1872, written by Samuel Wilkeson, which are marked " AAA ":

WILKESON TO MOULTON.

NORTHERN PACIFIC RAILROAD COMPANY,
SECRETARY'S OFFICE, 120 BROADWAY,
NEW YORK, April 2, 1872.

MY DEAR MOULTON : Now for the closing act of justice and duty.

Let Theodore pass into your hand the written apology which he holds for the improper advances, and do you pass it into the flames of the friendly fire in your room of reconciliation. Then let Theodore talk to Oliver Johnson.

I hear that he and Carpenter, the artist, have made this whole affair the subject of conversation in the clubs. Sincerely yours,

SAMUEL WILKESON.

This letter, it will be observed, contains no protest against blackmailing, either on Tilton's part or my own, upon Beecher or Bowen, and is of the date of the tripartite covenant. Wilkeson also, hearing of Tilton's troubles, kindly offered to procure him a very lucrative employment in a large enterprise with which he was connected, as appears from a letter dated January 11, 1871, which I herewith produce marked "BBB 1":

WILKESON TO TILTON.

NORTHERN PACIFIC RAILROAD COMPANY, }
JANUARY 11, 1871. }

DEAR TILTON : You are in trouble. I come to you with a letter just mailed to Jay Cooke, advising him to secure your services as a platform speaker to turn New England, Old England, or the great West upside down about our Northern Pacific.

Pluck up heart ! You shan't be trampled down. Keep quiet. Don't talk. DON'T PUBLISH. Abide your time, and it will be a very good time. Take my word for it.

SAMUEL WILKESON.

It will be observed that this letter was dated after the letter of apology, and after the letter of Tilton to Bowen, and Wilkeson could hardly have desired to employ in so grave an enterprise one whom he then knew or believed to be attempting to blackmail his employer. And besides, his kindly expressions and advice to Tilton seem to me wholly inconsistent with such an allegation.

I think it just, in this connection, to state a fact which bears, in my mind, upon this subject. On the 3d of May, 1873, I knew that Tilton was in want of money, and I took leave, without consulting him, to send him my check for a thousand dollars, and a due-bill for that amount to be signed by him, enclosed in a letter which I here produce, marked " BBB 2," all of which he returned to me with an endorsement thereon. The following is the document :

MOULTON TO TILTON.

NEW YORK, May 3, 1873.

DEAR THEODORE : 'I enclose to you a check for one thousand dollars, for which please sign the enclosed.

Yours,

F. D. MOULTON.

[Endorsement on above by Tilton.]

DEAR FRANK : I can't borrow any money—for I see no way of returning it. Hastily,

T. T.

After the above paper was returned to me, on the same day, I sent him the thousand dollars, leaving it to be a matter as between ourselves, and not a money transaction.

I know, to the contrary of this so far as Beecher is concerned, that Tilton never made any demand on him for money or pecuniary aid in any way or form. He asked only that Beecher should interpose his influence and power to protect him from the slanders of those who claimed to be Beecher's friends; while Beecher himself, with generosity and kindness towards Tilton which had always characterized his acts during the whole of this unhappy controversy, of his own motion insisted, through me, in aiding Tilton in establishing his enterprise of the *Golden Age*, for which purpose he gave me the sum of five thousand dollars, which I was to expend in such manner as I deemed judicious to keep the enterprise along, and if Tilton was at any time in need personally, to aid him. It was understood between myself and Beecher that this money should go to Tilton as if it came from my own voluntary contributions for his benefit, and that he should not know—and he does not know until he reads this statement, for I do not believe he has derived it from any other source—that this money came from Beecher, or thinks that he is in any way indebted to him for it. I annex an account of the receipt and expenditure of that sum, so far as it has been expended, in a paper marked " CCC " :

STATEMENT OF ACCOUNT.

1873.

May, 2, received..	$5,000
May 3, paid..	$1,000
July 11, paid..	650
August 15, paid...	250
September 12, paid..	500
September 30, paid..	500
December 16, paid...	200
1874.	
February 24, paid...	500
March 30, paid..	400
May 2, paid...	250
May 26, paid..	300
Total	$4,550

I also annex two letters of March 30, 1874, from the publisher of the *Golden Age*, which will tend to vouch the expenditure of a part of the above amount. They are marked "DDD" and "EEE" respectively:

RULAND TO MOULTON.

THE GOLDEN AGE, New York, March 30, 1874.

[Private.]

DEAR MR. MOULTON: We are in a tight spot. Mr. —— is away, and we have no money and no paper. Can't get the latter without the former. We owe about $400 for paper, and the firm we have been ordering from refuse to let us have any more without money. Haven't any paper for this week's issue. Truly yours,

O. W. RULAND

If you can do anything for us. I trust you will, to help us tide over the chasm.

FROM SAME TO SAME.

THE GOLDEN AGE, New York, March 30, 1874.

DEAR MR. MOULTON: I am more grateful than I can tell you for the noble and generous way you came to the rescue of the *Golden Age* this afternoon. Truly your friend,

O. W. RULAND.

I think proper to add further that Tilton more than once said to me that he could and would receive nothing from Beecher in the way of pecuniary assistance. I remember one special instance in which the subject was discussed between us. Beecher had told me that he was willing to furnish money to pay the expenses of Tilton and his family in traveling abroad, in order that Tilton might be saved from the constant state of irritation which arose from the rumors he was daily hearing. I rather hinted at that informed Tilton of this fact, and he repelled even the intimation of such a thing with the utmost indignation and anger. Therefore, I only undertook the disbursement of this sum at the most earnest and voluntary request of Beecher.

As I have brought before the Committee the somewhat collateral matter of the letters of Mrs. Woodhull to Beecher to influence him into the support of her doctrines and herself socially, which I thought but just to him, it seems but equally just that I should make as a part of my statement a letter, that came into my possession at the time it was written, from Tilton to a friend in the West—and not for the purpose of publication—explaining his position in regard to Mrs. Woodhull and the injurious publication made against him and his family and Mr. Beecher. The letter I here produce, marked "FFF1":

TILTON TO A FRIEND IN THE WEST.

174 LIVINGSTON STREET, BROOKLYN,
December 31, 1872.

MY DEAR FRIEND: I owe you a long letter. I am unwell and a prisoner in the house, leaning back in leather-cushioned idleness, and writing on my chair-board before the fire. Perhaps you wonder that I have a fire, or anything but a hearthstone broken and crumbled, since the world has been told that my household is in ruins. And yet it is more like your last letter—brimful of love and wit, and sparkling like a fountain in midwinter.

Nevertheless you are right. I am in trouble: and I hardly see a path out of it.

It is just two years ago to-day—this very day—the last of the year—that Mr. Bowen lifted his hammer, and with an unjust blow smote asunder my two contracts, one with the *Independent* and the other with the Brooklyn *Union*. The public little suspects that this act of his turned on his fear to meet the consequences of horrible charges which he made against Henry Ward Beecher. I have kept quiet on the subject for two years through an unwillingness to harm others even for the sake of righting myself before the public. But having trusted to time for my vindication, I find that time has only thickened my difficulties until these now buffet me like a storm.

You know that Bowen long ago paid to me the assessed pecuniary damages which grew out of his breaking of the contracts, and gave me a written vindication of *my* course, and something like an apology for *his*. This settlement, so far as I am concerned, is final.

But Bowen's assassinating dagger drawn against Beecher has proved as unable as Macbeth's to "trammel up the consequence." And the consequence is that the air of Brooklyn is rife with stories against its chief clergyman, not growing out of the Woodhull scandal merely, but exhaled with ever-fresh foulness, like mephitic vapors, from Bowen's own charge against Beecher.

Verily, the tongue is a wild beast that no man can tame, and like a wolf it is now seeking to devour the chief shepherd of the flock, together also with my own pretty lambs.

For the last four or five weeks, or ever since I saw the Woodhull libel, I have hardly had a restful day; and I frequently dream the whole thing over at night, waking the next morning unfit for work.

Have you any conception of what it is to suffer the keenest possible injustice? If not, come and learn of me.

To say nothing of the wrong and insult to my wife, in whose sorrow I have greater sorrow, I have to bear the additional indignity of being misconstrued by half the public and by many friends.

For instance, it is supposed that I had a conspirator's hand in this unholy business, whereas I am as innocent of it as of the Nathan murder.

It is hinted that the libelous article was actually written by me ; whereas (being in the north of New Hampshire) I did not know of its existence till a week after it had convulsed my own city and family. My wife never named it in her letters to me lest it should spoil my mood for public speaking. (You know I was then toiling day and night for Mr. Greeley's sake.)

Then, too, it is the sneer of the clubs that I have degenerated into an apostle of free-love ; whereas the whole body of my writings stands like a monument against this execrable theory.

Moreover, it is charged that I am in financial and other relations with Mrs. Woodhull ; whereas I have not spoken to, nor met, nor seen her for nearly a year.

The history of my acquaintance with her is this : In the spring of 1871, a few months after Bowen charged Beecher with the most hideous crime known to human nature, and had slammed the door of the *Independent* in my face, and when I was toiling like Hercules to keep the scandal from the public, then it was that Mrs. Woodhull, hitherto a total stranger to me, suddenly sent for me and poured into my ears, not the Bowen scandal, but a new one of her own, namely, almost the same identical tale which she printed a few weeks ago. Think of it ! When I was doing my best to suppress *one* earthquake, Mrs. Woodhull suddenly stood before me portentous with another. What was I to do? I resolved at all hazards to keep back the new avalanche until I could securely tie up the original storm. My fear was that she would *publish* what she told to me, and, to prevent this catastrophe, I resolved (and, as the result proves, like a fool, and yet with a fool's innocent and pure motive) to make her such a friend of mine that she would never think of doing me such a harm. So I rendered her some important services (including especially some labors of pen and ink), all with a view to put and hold her under an obligation to me and mine.

In so acting towards her, I found to my glad surprise and astonishment that she rose almost as high in my estimation as she had done with Lucretia Mott, Elizabeth Cady Stanton, Isabella Beecher Hooker, and other excellent women. Nobody who has not met Mrs. Woodhull can have an adequate idea of the admirable impression which she is capable of producing on serious persons. Moreover, I felt that the current denunciations against her were outrageously unjust, and that, like myself, she had been put in a false position before the public, and I sympathized keenly with the aggravation of spirit which this produces. This fact lent a zeal to all I said in her defense.

Nor was it until after I had known her for a number of months, and when I discovered her purpose to libel a dozen representative women of the suffrage movement, that I suddenly opened my eyes to her real tendencies to mischief ; and then it was that I indignantly repudiated her acquaintance, and have never seen her since.

Hence her late tirade.

Well, it is over, and *I* am left to be the chief sufferer in the public estimation.

What to do in the emergency (which is not clearing but clouding itself daily) I have not yet decided.

What I *could* do would be to take from my writing-desk, and publish to-morrow morning, the prepared narrative and vindication, which, with facts and documents, my legal advisers pronounce complete.

This would explain and clarify everything, both great and small (including the Woodhull episode, which is but a minor part of the whole case), but if I publish it, I must not only violate a kind of honorable obligation to be silent, which I had voluntarily imposed upon myself, but I must put my old friend Bowen to a serious risk of being smitten dead by Beecher's hand.

How far Bowen would deserve his fate I cannot say ; but I know that all Plymouth Church would hunt him as a rat.

Well, perhaps the future will unravel my skein for me without my own hand ; but whatever happens to my weather-beaten self, I wish to you, O prosperous comrade, a happy New Year. Fraternally yours,

THEODORE TILTON.

P. S.—Before sending this long letter (which pays my debt to you), I have read it to my wife, who desires to supplement it by sending her love and good will to the little white cottage and its little red cheeks.

The first intimation of the insanity of Tilton arose in this wise : Prior to Sunday, March 29, 1874, a publication was made of a statement by a reporter of the Brooklyn *Union* purporting to be the result of an interview with Mr. Thomas G. Shearman, clerk of Plymouth Church, to the effect—I quote from memory—that Tilton was insane, and that he stated that Mrs. Tilton had mediumistic fits—whatever disease that may be—in which she had stated matters affecting the character of Beecher, and to the statement of neither of them, for that reason, was any credit to be given. This publication, as

It tended not only to excite Tilton to a defense of his sanity, but also as coming from the clerk of Plymouth Church, might be supposed to be an authoritative expression of its pastor, annoyed Beecher very much, and he wrote the following letter, marked "FFF 2," which I herewith produce :

BEECHER TO MOULTON.

SUNDAY NIGHT, March 29, 1874.

MY DEAR FRANK : Is there to be no end of trouble ? Is wave to follow wave in endless succession? I was cut to the heart when C. showed me that shameful paragraph from the *Union*. Its cruelty is beyond description. I felt like lying down and saying, "I am tired—tired—tired of living, or of trying to resist the devil of mischief." I would rather have had a javelin launched against me a hundred times than against those that have suffered so much. The shameful indelicacy of bringing the most sacred relations into such publicity fills me with horror.

But there are some slight alleviations. The paragraph came when the public mind was engaged with the council and with Theodore's letters. I hope it will pass without further notice. If it is *not taken up* by other papers it will sink out of sight and be forgotten ; whereas, if it be assailed, it may give it a conspicuity that it never would have had. But I shall write Shearman a letter, and give him my full feeling about it. I must again [be], as I have heretofore been, indebted to you for a judicious counsel on this new and flagrant element. My innermost soul longs for peace ; and if that cannot be, for death, that *will* bring peace. My fervent hope is that this drop of gall may sink through out of sight, and not prove a mortal poison. Yours ever,

H. W. BEECHER.

I have written strongly to Shearman, and hope that he will send a letter to T. unsolicited. I am sick, head, heart, and body, but must move on! I feel this morning like letting things go by the run!

The letter of retraction, as proposed by Tilton, not being forthcoming, I felt it my duty, in his interest, to take such measures as should result in an apology from Shearman to Tilton. I accordingly carried to him a copy of the paper having the article, and laid it upon his desk in his office, and said to him that if the statements in this article were not actually made by him he ought to retract them. Although it lay on his desk he said to me that he had not seen the article and did not mean to see it. I told him that he must see it, and if it was not true that he must say so. He said he didn't want to read it and wouldn't read it. I then left him. Afterwards I saw Tilton and told him what I had done, and he said, " We will go up together," which we did, and met Mr. Shearman. Mr. Tilton called his attention to the statement in the Brooklyn *Union* as having come from him (Shearman), concerning himself and his wife, that one was crazy and the other subject to mediumistic fits. Said he, "Mr. Shearman, this is untrue, and if you are not correctly reported your simple duty is to say so ; and if you have made such a statement I demand that you retract and apologize. If you do not, I shall hold you responsible in any way I can for such injurious statement." Shearman then read the paragraph in the *Union*, and made an explanation in this wise: that he might probably have repeated to somebody a story which Tilton had told him of the mediumistic states of Mrs. Woodhull, and perhaps have made the mistake of using Mrs. Tilton's name instead of Mrs. Woodhull's. Tilton said to him, " Mr. Shearman, you know that you are deliberately uttering falsehood, and I won't allow you to think even that you can deceive me by such a statement as you are making now. You must make such an explanation of this statement in the *Union* as shall be satisfactory to me, or, as I said before, I shall hold you responsible." During the first part of this conversation Mr. Shearman called in a witness from his outer office, but when the conversation became earnest and Tilton began charging him with an untruth, Shearman bid the witness retire, which he did. Tilton and I then left the office.

Within a few days of this interview Tilton procured the affidavit of the reporter of the *Union* that the statement that Shearman had been reported as making he did in fact make. On March 30, Shearman sent to me for delivery to Tilton a note, of which I produce a copy under that date, marked "GGG." The original was delivered up to Shearman afterwards.

SHEARMAN TO TILTON.

BROOKLYN, March 30, 1874.

DEAR SIR: My attention has been called to a newspaper paragraph which I have not seen, but which I am told is to the effect that I stated to a reporter that you had described Mrs. Tilton as having, in a mediumistic or clairvoyant state, made some extraordinary statements of a painful nature.

I have for some years past made it a rule never to send corrections to newspapers of anything relating to myself, no matter how erroneous such statements may be.

But I have no objection to saying to you personally that this story, if correctly quoted here, appears to be an erroneous version of the one and only statement which I had from you over a year ago, viz.: that Mrs. Woodhull did exactly the thing here attributed to Mrs. Tilton.

I do not know that I ever repeated that story in the presence of any reporter for the paper in question, but I have done so in the presence of others, and I may of course, by an unconscious mistake, have used your wife's name in the place of another and wholly different person. If so, I beg that you will assure Mrs. Tilton of my great regret for such an error. Yours obediently,

T. G. SHEARMAN.

When I took this note to Tilton he refused to receive it, saying: "I will not receive any such note from Shearman. He knows it contains a falsehood and I cannot take it from him. You may carry it back to him." I did so, and stated to him Tilton's answer. Afterwards he substituted for that note another, under date of April 2, 1874, which is here produced, marked "HHH":

SHEARMAN TO TILTON.

BROOKLYN, April 2, 1874.

DEAR SIR : Having seen a paragraph in the Brooklyn *Union* of Saturday last, containing a report of a statement alleged to have been made by me concerning your family and yourself, I desire to assure you that this report is seriously incorrect, and that I have never authorized such a statement.

It is unnecessary to repeat here what I have actually said upon these subjects, because I am now satisfied that what *I did* say was erroneous, and that the rumors to which I gave some credit were without foundation. I deeply regret having been misled into an act of unintentional injustice, and am glad to take the earliest occasion to rectify it.

I beg, therefore, to withdraw all that I said upon the occasion referred to as incorrect (although then believed by me), and to repudiate entirely the statement imputed to me as untrue and unjust to all parties concerned. Yours, obediently,

Theodore Tilton, Esq.   T. G. SHEARMAN.

In no part of that negotiation did Mr. Shearman suggest to me that there were any doubts as to Tilton's sanity, and denied both to me and to him that he had ever said anything to the contrary, or that Mrs. Tilton was in any way incapacitated from telling the truth by reason of mediumistic fits o' other physical disability. Shearman's action was communicated to Beecher, but meanwhile it had come to be spread about that Beecher had made a similar accusation as to the sanity of Mr. and Mrs. Tilton to that of Shearman.

A member of your committee, Mr. Cleveland, communicated the fact to Beecher, to which Beecher made an indignant denial, as appears by his note to Mr. Cleveland, who communicated a copy of it to me in a note under date of April 2, which I here produce, marked "III" :

BEECHER TO CLEVELAND.

(Copy.)

MY DEAR CLEVELAND : You say that I am supposed to have reported to some members of the council substantially the same story that is attributed to Shearman.

How can any human being that knows me believe any such impossibility ? I never opened my lips to any human being on the subject. I will defy any man to face me and say that by word, look, or intimation I ever alluded to it. I have been as dumb as the dead. They that dare to say I have spoken of it are liars, if they mean to themselves, and the bearers of lies if they received it from others.

I have a feeling too profoundly sacred to make such sacrilege possible.

April 2, 1874.   H. W. BEECHER.

CLEVELAND TO MOULTON.

Frank Moulton, Esq.

DEAR SIR : Herewith you have copy of a note received from Mr. Beecher respecting the matter of which it speaks.

Not seeing you when I called this A. M., and leaving the city, I send by Mr. Halliday. Mr. Beecher wants to see you *before* or *after* the meeting this evening. Truly yours,

H. M. CLEVELAND.

Having retained the friendship of the principal parties to this controversy down to to-day, I have not thought it proper to produce herewith any letters that I have received from either of them excepting the single one exonerating me from blame and showing errs. Tilton's confidence in me, which I thought was due to myself to do because of the peculiar statement attributed to her ; nor have I produced any papers or proposals for a settlement of this controversy since it has broken out afresh, and since the publication of Tilton's letter to Dr. Bacon and the call of Beecher for a Committee ; nor have I since then furnished to either party, although called upon by both, any documents in my possession that one might use the same against the other. I have endeavored to hold myself strictly as a mediator between them, and my endeavor has been, even down to the very latest hour, to have all the scandals arising out of the publication of the facts of their controversies and wrongs buried out of sight, deeming it best that it should be so done, not only for the good of the parties concerned and their families, but that of the community at large.

If any evidence were needed that, in the interest of the parties, and especially of Beecher, I was endeavoring to the latest hour to prevent the publication of all these documents and this testimony, and that I retained the confidence of at least one of the parties in that endeavor, I produce a letter of July 13, 1874, being a note arranging a meeting between myself and Beecher in regard to this controversy. It is marked "JJJ":

BEECHER TO MOULTON.

July 13, 1874.

My DEAR FRANK : I will be with you at seven or a little before. I am ashamed to put a straw more upon you, and have but a single consolation—that the matter cannot distress you *long*, as it must soon end ; that is, there will be no more anxiety about the *future*, whatever regrets there may be for the past.

Truly yours and ever,

H. W. BEECHER.

If there is any paper or fact supposed by either of the parties, or by the Committee, to be in my possession, which will throw any further light upon the subject of your inquiry, I shall be most willing to produce it if I have it, although I do not believe that there is any such ; and I am ready to answer any proper question which shall be put to me in the way of cross-examination by any of the parties concerned or their counsel, as fully as my memory or any data I have will serve, so that all the facts may be known. For if any part of them be known, I deem it but just to truth and right that all should be known. As, however, controversy has already arisen as to the correctness of the reports of evidence taken before the committee, I must ask leave, if any cross-examination is to be had orally, to be accompanied by my own stenographer, who shall take down the evidence I may give, as a necessary measure for my own protection.

Leaving to your Committee, without comment, the facts and documents herewith presented,

I have the honor to remain, yours truly,

FRANCIS D. MOULTON.

BESSIE TURNER'S STORY.

It will be remembered that Mr. Moulton's complete statement was published on Friday, August 21st, 1874. In it occurs the following paragraph:

It will be observed that in the letter of Mrs. Morse she says. Tilton had sent * * * with the others away. I purposely omit the name of this young girl. There was a reason why it was desirable that she should be away from Brooklyn. That reason, as given by Mr. and Mrs. Tilton, was this:—She had overheard conversations by them concerning Mrs. Tilton's criminal intimacy with Beecher, and she had reported these conversations to several friends of the family. Being young, and not knowing the consequences of her prattling, it seemed proper, for the safety of the two families, that she should be sent to a distance to school, which was accordingly done. She was put at a boarding school at the West, and the expenses of her stay there were privately paid through me by Beecher, to whom I had stated the difficulty of having the girl remain in Brooklyn; and he agreed with us that it was best that she should be removed and offered to be at the cost of her schooling. The bills were sent to me from time to time as they became due, a part of them through Mrs. Tilton. Previous to her going away she wrote the following letters to Mrs. Tilton—marked " W " and " X "—and they were sent to me by Mrs. T. as part of these transactions:

* * * TO MRS. TILTON.

BROOKLYN, January 10, 1871.

My Dear Mrs. Tilton: I want to tell you something. Your mother, Mrs. Morse, has repeatedly attempted to hire me, by offering me dresses and presents, to go to certain persons and tell them *stories* injurious to the character of your husband. I have been persuaded that the kind attentions shown me by Mr. Tilton for years were dishonorable demonstrations. I never at the time thought that Mr. Tilton's caresses were for such a purpose. I do not want to be made use of by Mrs. Morse or anyone else to bring trouble on my two best friends, you and your husband. Bye-bye.

* * *

On the following day (Saturday, August 22,) the Plymouth Church Investigating Committee published the following as the Testimony of Bessie Turner, the young person whose name Mr. Moulton had suppressed:

THE SCHOOL GIRL'S EXAMINATION

By Mr. Tracy:

Q. Were you formerly intimate in Mr. Theodore Tilton's family in Brooklyn ? A. Yes, sir.

Q. How long ? A. For eight years.

Q. When did you leave there for the last time ? A. In February, 1871.

Q. And you had been there eight years, then ? A. Yes, sir, as near as I can remember. It may have been longer.

Q. Where were they living when you went to live with them ? A. They were boarding with Mrs. Morse, Mrs. Tilton's mother, at No. 48 Livingston street.

Q. Where did they go to housekeeping? A. At No. 174 Livingston street.

Q. Their present place of residence ? A. Yes, sir.

Q. And did they reside there continuously until you left them ? A. Yes, sir.

Q. Were you an adopted child ? A. Yes, sir; I was just the same as one of their own family. Mrs. Tilton has been a mother to me always; she took me in when I was a child.

Q. Will you tell us whether Mr. and Mrs. Tilton lived happily or otherwise when you first went with them ? A. When I first went with them, as I remember it, their married life was apparently happy, and I did not see anything for some time to the contrary.

Mr. Winslow—That was in 1863 ? A. Yes, sir.

By Mr. Tracy—How long had you been with them when you first noticed infelicities in their life?
A. I think about a year after they lived in Livingston street; about 1865.

Q. What did you observe? A. Well, I observed that Mr. Tilton was a very selfish man, very hard, very fastidious, very difficult to please, very dogmatical in his manner, very irritable and unsociable in his disposition ; one day he would be apparently very happy some part of the day, and then in about an hour, it may be, he would be so cross and ugly that nothing and nobody could please him.

Q. How was Mrs. Tilton? A. Mrs. Tilton was always the same—of a lovely and amiable disposition ; I never saw any change in her ; she was the most devoted wife and mother that I ever saw in my life, in every sense of the word ; the moment he came home she always knew his footstep and his ring (if he had not a night-key with him), and she dropped her work, no matter what she was doing, and was always ready to minister to his comfort and bring his slippers and dressing-gown ; all the time she was looking out for his comfort and his pleasure.

Q. Were her habits domestic, or otherwise? A. Remarkably domestic, considering—especially considering that she was the wife of a public man ; if Mrs. Tilton had been a gay, worldly sort of a woman, fond of going into society and of going out at night and all that sort of thing, there might be some cause for remark ; but she is the very last person in the world that ought to be accused of anything like that which is now charged ; I never heard of anything so perfectly outrageous, and it seems particularly so with Mrs. Tilton, because she is such a lovely Christian woman, and such a devoted wife and mother ; she lives up to what she believes always, and has done so ; I think I can say that there could not be a flaw picked with Mrs. Tilton in any respect.

Q. Well, state whether or not the difficulty continued to increase from the time you first observed it? A. Yes, sir, I think it did, with Mr. Tilton ; I noticed Mrs. Tilton crying and sobbing whenever she was with him, and he had for several years (for three years anyway) a way of locking her up in a room and talking very loud to her; he would go in and lock the door, and I would hear him scolding and swearing at her, and then she would cry, and I have heard her say several times, "Why, Theodore, I do the best I can ; you know that I make every dollar go just as far as I possibly can;" she would be remonstrating with him in that way and crying; or if she was not crying she was praying; of course, I never said a word to a soul about it, but I knew that he was treating her badly; I have known it for several years.

Q. Was this abuse, then, largely about money and expenditures of the household? A. No, sir, I don't know that it was particularly; after any gentlemen had been there I always noticed that he would lock the door and have a long talk with her; Mr. X. used to go there Sabbath evenings occasionally, and he (Mr. Tilton) always had her shut up in the room after Mr. X. went away; he was very jealous of her both with gentlemen and ladies.

Q. How was he jealous of her with ladies? A. I don't think he wanted any one to like her, particularly any one that did not show a very great liking for him.

Q. Can you instance a time when you remember seeing her shut in a room after Mr. X. had left? A. Yes, sir ; I can't give the date ; but some little time before I left there, one Sabbath evening, after Mr. X. had gone away.

Q. What did he say when he shut her up? Did he scold her? A. I cannot say that ; the doors were shut, and I simply knew that something was going on, that she was crying and sobbing, and that I heard him talking very loud ; I saw him in one instance with his fist in her face ; I don't know what it was about, but I know she was cowering down very timidly under his fist, and that he was talking very loud.

Q. How long was that before you left? A. About two years, I guess.

Q. Is there anything further that you remember about their domestic affairs? A. I don't know that there is anything that I can recall just now which I have not stated.

Q. Did you use to see Mr. Beecher there occasionally? A. Occasionally—yes, sir ; I think he came perhaps two or three times a month ; I let him in on one or two occasions.

Q. Did you ever see anything in the conduct of Mr. Beecher and Mrs. Tilton to indicate any marked affection between them, or anything of that kind? A. No, sir ; I never saw anything.

Q. Not anything? A. No, sir.

BY MR. WINSLOW.

Q. Where was he generally received? A. In the back parlor.

Q. Did you use to see ladies there—friends of Mrs. Stanton? A. Yes, sir; Mrs. Stanton was a very frequent visitor there, and Miss Susan B. Anthony and Miss Anna Dickinson and Mrs. —— was there on one occasion ; then there were the Misses W.

Q. When was it that the oldest Miss W. was there? A. I think it was about two or three years before I left.

Q. How long did she stay there? A. Some months, I think.

Q. Did Mr. Tilton seem to be very fond of her? A. Yes, sir ; he seemed to be very fond of her ; ,

17

he was with her a great deal ; he used to caress her and kiss her ; he was very much taken with her in every way ; Mrs. Tilton made it very pleasant for her ; she had flowers on the table and flowers in her room, because she was very fond of flowers ; Mr. Tilton used to take her riding a great deal ; he often took her to the theatre, and his attentions to her were so marked that it seemed to me Mrs. Tilton was very much neglected : he did not seem to think of Mrs. Tilton though, while Miss W. was around—unless somebody else was there.

Q. When strangers were there, how was his conduct ? A. I noticed particularly during the last year or so that I was there that whenever anybody was around that I could seem to see that he made a special effort to be very attentive to Mrs. Tilton—very plausible and very nice—I know I used to have my eyes opened pretty wide sometimes ; I never said a word to anybody until I made statements to Mrs. Morse, Mrs. Richards and Mrs. Beecher, but I used to think some day this would all come out ; I don't refer to this scandal, but to his treatment of Mrs. Tilton.

Q. Was he attentive to other ladies that visited there besides this Miss W.? A. Well, his attention was never as marked, I think, with any other ladies that were there, unless it was with Mrs. Stanton and Miss Anthony.

Q. How was it with them ? A. He seemed to think a great deal of Mrs. Stanton and Miss Anthony; I saw her sitting on his lap on one occasion when I was coming into the parlor, and she jumped up pretty quick.

Q. Miss Anthony? A. Susan B. Anthony.

Q. What was his conduct with Mrs. Stanton? A. Well, I never saw him caressing her, but he used to be alone with her a great deal in his study; they used to play chess until two or three o'clock in the morning; frequently they were up until after the family had gone to bed—quite late.

Q. How are you able to say that they sat up until two or three o'clock in the morning? A. Because I was quite awake and heard the clock strike.

Q. Before they retired? A. Yes, sir. I can testify on one occasion the clock struck two, and on another three.

Q. And they retired after that? A. Yes, sir.

Q. Was your room near Mrs. Tilton's? A. It was right next to Mr. and Mrs. Tilton's.

By Mr. Hill—Which Miss W. was he so attentive to? A. Miss A. W.

Q. What about the other Miss W.? A. She was there afterward, Miss B. W.; she was sick there, very sick, indeed.

Q. I understand you to say that you never saw anything between Mr. Beecher and Mrs. Tilton that attracted your attention at all? A. No.

Q. Did Mr. Tilton, in any manner, attempt your ruin? A. Yes, sir.

Q. Will you state the circumstances? A. He did on two occasions while Mrs. Tilton was away ; I don't remember where she went ; Horace Greeley was in the house at the time; I think Mrs. Tilton was in Scoharie; Mr. Tilton and I were there all alone, except Mr. Greeley and the servant; Mr. Greeley was there making a visit to Mr. Tilton; the first time I had been sleeping, and woke up and found myself in his arms.

By Mr. Winslow—At night or in the daytime? A. At night; I hardly realized where I was; he must have lifted me out of my bed, and put me in his : when I woke up and found where I was I asked what he was doing that for; he said that he was lonesome, and wanted me to come and be with him ; I said that wasn't right, and I went back to my own room ; there was nothing said about it at the time ; I was quite young and used to be with him a great deal, just like one of the children, and I used to comb his hair, and he used to kiss me as he did other children frequently ; I never had any impure thought in regard to the man ; when he came to me a second time, and tried to get into bed with me, I got very indignant, and as he would not leave the room, I went into another, and locked the door after me ; I had never thought of locking the door before ; I left the house the next day, and did not come back until Mrs. Tilton returned ; afterward Mrs. Tilton told me that Mr. Tilton had made a confession of this to her, and she wanted to know if this was so ; I said yes, it was so ; I thought of telling her several times, but I knew she had a great deal of trouble, and I thought, perhaps, this would trouble her a great deal more.

By General Tracy—Were both events near together ? A. Yes, sir ; I think pretty near together.

Mr. Hill—Was it during the same absence of Mrs. Tilton ? A. Yes ; Mrs. Tilton was absent this time, too.

Q. Had she come back from Scoharie ? A. No, sir.

Q. In the winter of 1869–70 did you not go to Mrs. Putnam's in the West? A. Yes, sir.

Q. And you stayed how long? A. I left there in the fall, I think, and stayed nine months ; I think I returned late in the fall of 1870.

Q. Did you return with Mrs. Tilton? A. Mrs. Tilton went out to Mrs. Putnam's, and I came back with her ; Mr. Tilton met us at Jersey City.

Q. What occurred after you came back in the fall of '70 from Mrs. Putnam's? A. Mr. Tilton met us in Jersey City ; as we came along he was very attentive and devoted to Mrs. Tilton, but I could see that she was very much troubled and depressed in spirits from the time she went into the house—from the time she saw him ; there was a Miss —— keeping house for him ; she occupied Mrs. Tilton's seat at the table and put on a great air of authority, and was really rude to Mrs. Tilton ; she seemed to want to give an impression of the position that she occupied and of what she could do and would do ; everything went on very well, but I could see that Mr. Tilton had Miss —— just where he wanted her ; that she was altogether on his side ; she showed that at breakfast, and Mrs. Tilton was crying all the time at the table ; he was very sweet and very polite to her and said, " My dear, won't you have some of the broiled steak ? " " My dear, won't you have something of this, or something of that ? "— never letting on to see her tears, though she was crying so that she could not eat ; I could see through him all the time ; I was watching him ; something told me that there was a villain behind all those actions ; they were just for effect ; I could see that ; finally Mrs. Tilton excused herself and left the table ; as soon as she had gone Mr. Tilton looked at me very sweetly and said, " Bessie, my dear, don't you think Elizabeth is demented ? Don't you think she acts like a crazy woman ? " I looked him square in the eyes ; I was so indignant that I didn't know what to say, but I said, " No, but it is a wonder to me that she has not been in the lunatic aslyum years ago." He changed countenance, and probably saw that he was treading on dangerous ground when he talked to me about Mrs. Tilton ; then Miss —— looked at me, as much as to say, " If I dared I would box your ears well for you," but I did not care for Miss —— at all ; Mr. Tilton got up at once, before I finished my breakfast, and went into the front parlor, on the same floor ; he locked one door, and tried to fasten the glass folding-doors ; I could see him through the crack, and could hear him talk very loud to Mrs. Tilton ; I was on the alert and was going to watch him ; I went to the door and listened, and I saw him with his fist in her face, and he said to her, " Damn it, this girl shall leave the house ; " then I went in and said, " You shan't damn Mrs. Tilton on my account. It is not the first time you have had your fist in her face ; you shan't do it on my account ; " said he, " Leave the room ; " I said, " I won't ; " said he, " Damn you, leave the room ; " I said, " I won't ; " then he struck me a heavy blow with such force that it threw me clear across the room, and knocked my head against the doorpost ; I got up and recovered my senses, and went back to Mrs. Tilton and tried to shield her ; I was afraid he would knock her over.

By Mr. Winslow—Did it hurt you ? A. Yes, sir, it hurt me fearfully ; I suffered from it for days ; what seems to be the most ridiculous thing about this was that in a few minutes he said to me, " Bessie, my dear, you hurt yourself, didn't you ? how did you come to trip so ? " What a ridiculous thing that was, as though I had tripped and banged my own head, or knocked my own senses out ! I said, " You must be a fool, or I am one ; " the audacity of the man after doing that thing, trying to make me think I had banged my own head ; it seemed so perfectly ridiculous ; that man has the most assurance of anybody I ever knew ; at the same time he sat down and wanted to take me on his lap, but I jerked myself away, and he said, " Bessie, my dear, I have been a martyr for years ; " then he tried to make me believe he was crying, but I knew he wasn't, and he said he wanted to talk with me about Mrs. Tilton, and he spoke of her criminality with Mr. Beecher, and Mr. X——, and Mr. Y——, and Mr. Z—— (naming three highly respectable gentlemen, one of whom is an intimate sympathizer with Mr. Tilton), and he said, " No wonder my hairs are going down in sorrow to the grave." I said I didn't believe one word of it— it was all wicked lies—and he talked, and talked, and talked, and talked, and talked, and talked, but he did not make me believe anything about Mrs. Tilton ; and that morning he had the audacity to stand up in the presence of his wife and say, " Bessie, did I ever, in word, look, or deed, offer to insult you ? " " Yes, you did," I said, " you know you did ; " he said, " You're a liar ; " he was very defiant, evidently thinking I would be afraid of him ; I think he has the idea that he is some Apollo, some god, that everybody ought to look up to and worship ; poor Mrs. Tilton, she has had a hard life with that man.

Q. Have you heard him say anything about the paternity of the children ? A. Yes ; he said that none of them belonged to him except Florence.

Q. When did you say that was ? A. It was on the very day that I returned from Mrs. Putnam's.

Q. It was the day when you " tripped " on the floor ? A. No, sir, not when I " tripped," but when he knocked me over ; this was in the fall of 1870—late in the fall of that year.

Q. After that did he continue to abuse Mrs. Tilton ? A. Oh, yes ; he locked her up and scolded all night long ; and she was crying and crying ; and when she was not crying she was praying.

Q. Did she leave him and go away and take the children ? A. I think she was afraid of him, and I think two or three nights afterward she took the children—Alice and Carroll—and went to Mrs. Morse's ; I went with her, and that same night or the night after he came around and got on his knees and vowed how much he loved her, and asked her if she would come back to his bosom again, and all that sort of nonsense ; and poor Mrs. Tilton, who was always ready to trust and believe him, believed him then and went back, and he told her she had better go to bed ; she was tired and sat down a moment, and then she went to bed ; as soon as she had gone to bed he went over all this talk and all this rigmarole with me again, which he had gone over before about Mr. Beecher, Mr. ——, and Mr. ——, and Mr. ——. But I did not believe it ; it was a wicked lie, and I told him I never would believe him ; he mentioned that he had seen Mr. Beecher taking improper liberties with Mrs. Tilton before his own eyes, in the library.

Q. In what library? A. In Mr. Tilton's library.

Q. Did he say what he had seen in regard to the other men? A. No, sir; I think not.

Q. How long did she live with him after she went back with him from her mother's, before she left him again? A. I think she staid some little time. She went away the second time and was gone eight or ten days, and was staying at her mother's. I went with her.

Q. At that time was he having difficulty with Mr. Bowen? A. Yes, sir; very great difficulties.

Q. Do you know what means Mr. Tilton resorted to to get her to go back? A. He resorted to every means possible.

Q. Did he send for the children? A. Yes, sir; in the first place he sent Miss Annie Tilton, his only sister, around to say that he wanted his children; he sent her several times, and, I think, he came around himself several times.

Q. Do you know whether he got his children during Mrs. Tilton's absence? A. I think Florence went with him.

Q. Did Mrs. Tilton go back home? A. Yes, sir, and I went with her.

Q. Was she taken sick soon after? A. Yes, sir, soon after.

Q. Very sick? A. Very sick, indeed. It was thought that she would not live.

Q. What doctor attended her, do you know? A. Dr. Skiles.

Q. After her return did you communicate to any one how he had abused her, and how he attempted abuse you? A. Yes, sir; to Mr. Richards, to Judge Morse, to Miss Isabella Oakley, to Mr. Beecher, and to Mrs. Bradshaw.

Q. What did you tell Mr. Beecher about it? A. I told him how Mr. Tilton had abused her, and that I had known of his abusing her for years; I told him how ugly he was, how unkind he was to her, and that what I thought everybody thought, and that he was representing that he was the abused one, and that Mrs. Tilton was all in the wrong, and that I thought my evidence ought to be pretty good, considering that I had been there for eight years: I told him all about it, and then I said that he offered to insult me, and stated the circumstances to him.

Q. You stated it also to Mr. Tilton's brother? A. Yes, sir.

Q. When did you leave there for the last time? A. On the 17th of February, 1871.

Q. How came you to leave? A. Mrs. Tilton had tried to cover all this matter over about his knocking me down; she said her husband was in a passion and did not know what he was saying, and asked me if I would forgive him all this; I wanted to do anything I could to help Mrs. Tilton, and I said, "Yes, that would be all right;" she seemed to be reconciled to him, and I never thought anything about it for the time being; on one Sunday I was up in his study, I think, and he told me that Mrs. Tilton was going to do something nice for me; previous to this time she had said to me, "Bessie, how would you like to go to a boarding school?" I said I would like it very much, but that the news seemed too good to be true; she said I might go anywhere I wanted to; I thought that was very nice; at the same time I wondered that night how they got money so quick, because Mr. Tilton had been turned out of the *Independent*, and he had no money, he said; I did not inquire into that, but I thought of this to myself; after Mrs. Tilton had talked to me in this way, Mr. Tilton, on Sunday, up in the study, said that Elizabeth was going to do something nice for me; that she had always intended to send me to school, and that the time had come when she would do it; a few days after that it was decided where I should go; Dr. ——, who was president of the seminary where I attended three years, was a warm friend of Mr. Tilton, and he selected that academy for me to go to.

Q. Who selected it—Mr. Tilton? A. Yes, sir.

Q. You went on the 7th of February, 1871? A. Yes, sir.

Q. How long were you at the academy? A. Two years and a half.

Q. Did Mrs. Tilton make any request of you, before you left, about signing a paper? A. She did.

Q. What did she say to get you to do it? A. She said that public opinion was very much against Mr. Tilton; that he was her husband; that she could not bear all these things that were being said of him; that Mr. Bowen was against him, and turned him out of the *Independent*, and she wished me to retract the statement I had made by signing this paper, which was :—"I hereby certify that all these stories about Mr. Tilton and myself are wicked lies;" I signed my name to it, and I afterwards learned that this was all a plot of Mr. Tilton to get me out of the way.

Q. You did not understand it at that time? A. No, sir; I would not have gone under those conditions.

Q. But Mrs. Tilton had not said this to you? A. No, sir; I signed that statement to please Mrs. Tilton, although I must say that at the time I felt very wrong about it.

Q. How many days was this interview between you and Mr. Tilton in the study on Sunday before you left? A. I think not more than two days.

Mr. Sage—How long did Mr. Tilton furnish you with money for your expenses? A. Mr. Tilton did not furnish it; it was Mr. Francis Moulton that furnished the money; it was furnished up to a year ago last Christmas—to January, 1873.

General Tracy—Did Mr. Tilton, in any of these conversations, tell you what he had himself seen between Mr. Beecher and Mrs. Tilton ? A. He said that on several occasions when Mr. Beecher was in his (Tilton's) library talking with Mrs. Tilton he took improper liberties with her; he said that there were several instances in his own library which he saw himself.

Q. Did he state any reason for supposing she had been criminally intimate with the other men that he named ? A. No.

Q. Did he at any time on this day say that she had made any confession to him in regard to Mr. Beecher ? A. He said she had confessed to him that she had been criminally intimate with Mr. Beecher; she was present when he said that, and she said, "Oh, Theodore ! how can you tell that child such base lies ?" and then she burst out crying.

Q. When was that ? A. This all occurred on that one day that we went back, in the fall of 1870.

Q. Did you ever see any acts of intimacy between Mr. Tilton and this Miss —— ? A. He was locked up with her on several occasions, and twice I met him coming out of her room as I was going up-stairs.

Q. In the daytime or at night? A. Once or twice at night, and several times during the day; in the daytime I have known that he was in her room.

Q. How did you know that he was there? A. I saw him go in and I saw him come out.

Q. How did you know that the door was locked? A. I heard them lock it on one or two occasions; I was in Mr. Tilton's library; I also heard Miss —— say so; Miss Anthony was there, and they had great trouble; many words passed; there was a great deal of talk, and I heard Mrs. Tilton say something to Miss —— about being with her husband, and she (Miss ——) said that he had been often in her bedroom, that he should go there twenty times a day if he wanted to, and that it was none of her (Mrs. Tilton's) business whatever; I was not in the room, but I heard Miss —— make those remarks.

Q. Where—in Miss ——'s room? A. No, sir; but in Mrs. Tilton's sitting-room.

REPORT

OF THE

INVESTIGATING COMMITTEE.

On Friday evening, Aug. 28, 1874, the Plymouth Church Investigating Committee made the report given below on the charges preferred by Theodore Tilton against Henry Ward Beecher.

All Brooklyn got ready to go to meeting in the middle of the afternoon, while the Examining Committee was finishing up unfinished business in the Trustees' room at the Church. The Friday evening meetings of Plymouth Church begin at 8 o'clock, but the committeemen came at 6 o'clock from the conference, which they hope will be the last at which Mr. Tilton need be considered, only to find the women and men of the congregation, and a great many not of the congregation, already out in the street waiting for the sun to set and the church doors to open. They had to wait awhile, but it was a beautiful, still evening, and they were mostly good-looking and well dressed, and made an interesting crowd. Some of them through their familiarity with the various passages by which entry into the church can be obtained had already gone in and picked out seats—for pew-holders had no rights on that night that anybody was bound to respect—when at 6:30, Mr. Wells, the white-haired sexton, threw open the gates and the doors, and invited "members of the congregation to the floor," all others to the galleries. It takes 3,000 people to fill Plymouth Church, and in an hour it was filled, cockloft and all. Rev. Mr. Halliday was busy in the lobbies passing around camp-chairs and pleasant smiles, but before 8 o'clock, or anything like it had come, he had to give it up, for the lobbies were full and the passages outside overrun, and at every window that was open a dozen heads were looking curiously in. Rev. E. Beecher was heartily cheered as he came out of nowhere and sat on the edge of the platform, blushing and benevolently smiling, while the organ began a voluntary. Brother Shearman, clerk of the church, appeared and was violently applauded, and in a minute or two church was organized for a business meeting, Moderator Freeland, also a benevolent and smiling old gentleman, in the chair. After the hymn and prayer the gentlemen of the Investigating Committee came out of the north lobby and filed upon the platform. Mr. Sage, the Chairman, sat at the extreme left as he faced the people, looking smiling and tired. Mr. Cleveland, smiling and nervously playing with his cane, sat next him; then Mr. Winslow, with gold spectacles and his mouth set for a perpetual smile. Mr. Storrs sat rather solemnly at the Moderator's left hand, and Mr. White was on the Moderator's right, with Mr. Shearman between. If Mr. Claflin was present he did not sit on the platform. The crowded floor and galleries began a round of applause as the committee of twenty-eight regular and nobody knows how many irregular sessions was thus set boldly before them, and it took a good while to settle down to the hearing of the report. The document printed below is not without points, and Professor Ray·

mond, who read it, being a professor of elocution, brought out all the points, and the three thousand people applauded every point, whether made for Mr. Beecher or against Mr. Tilton or against Mr. Moulton with tremendous vigor. When the report was something more than half read it began to be noticed that the three thousand people had suddenly become three thousand and one, and that the one man extra was also paying close attention to Professor Raymond's points. Moulton had come in. He had left word with a friend in the audience that he was to be sent for in case he should be attacked in the report. He was first seen standing in a dense crowd at the north side of the platform close to Brother Blair, and with first half a dozen, then twenty, then fifty people turning round to look at him. People all over the house stood up to look at him, and leaned over the galleries at the imminent risk of their necks, and buzzed and whispered about him. Moulton came out from the crowd and sat down at a table, taking notes of the passages in the report which touched on his actions. He looked warm and excited. By and by he sent a note up to the platform saying that he wished to speak, and said that he should occupy the floor about ten minutes if allowed. But it was a church meeting, and he had no claim to the floor. Whether he was so informed or not he said nothing, but kept on taking notes. The report was adopted after a long interval of cheers and applause, and Brother Blair said something which took him a great while, although 3,000 people called "question" on the acceptation and adoption of the report. Then Brother Raymond began to talk, standing about six feet from where Moulton's head rested against the edge of the platform. He warmed to his work, and spoke of Moulton's "infernal lies." Moulton was on his feet in a moment, and half the church got up to see him. He threw out his left hand at Brother Raymond and called him a liar, and in a moment a whirlwind of confusion beset the place. A policeman's cap was seen struggling up from the doorway, and Police Captain Byrne, in plain clothes, also came up, and during the rest of the evening stood behind Moulton's chair. The 3,000 were at fever-heat, and every touch of Brother Raymond's brought storms of applause from them. There was no quieting them. They listened, but they fidgeted. Such as could pressed up to the chancel and clambered up on the platform steps, and more and more of the police caps began to be seen working in from the crowd in the lobby. When Brother Raymond had done the question came upon the motion to accept the committee's report and adopt the resolutions thereto appended.

"All those in favor," said the Moderator, "will signify it by saying aye," and 3,000 "ayes" from the floor where the voters were, from the gallery where they were not, and from the windows and lobbies where the crowds could just hear what was going on shook the big square room.

"All those opposed," began the Moderator, smiling, "but no, we must have a rising vote. All those in favor of this motion will signify it by rising."

"Count 'em," said somebody in jest, and then there was a laugh, and the number was lumped at 3,000. Moulton did not get up.

"All those opposed," said the Moderator, smiling again, and Moulton did get up. Nobody saw him at first. He is not a tall man, and he stood under the edge of the platform with his eyes flashing. When they did see him there was a storm of hisses, and everybody got to his feet. Shouts and cries of all sorts filled the air in an instant. "Put him out" was the loudest of the cries. "He's not a church member, and has no right to vote!" shouted Mr. Ovington and a friend, from the north aisle, and everybody said or shouted what seemed to him fit, the Moderator's cries of "Order!" being least heeded of any. It seemed as if the crowd would never be stilled again. The committeemen got up and tried to get Mr. Camp, the organist, to play something and drown the noise. But the noise was so great that Mr. Camp couldn't hear. Mr. Moulton had sat down long ago, and by and by the stentorian voice of a lawyer who had a resolution to offer, rose over the tumult, and people began to listen from force of habit, and so got still. Then nothing happened till Mr. Moulton had made up his mind to go home. This was just as the organ had played through the Doxology in long métre, and the people were beginning to sing, "Praise God, from whom all blessings flow." Moulton got up. Either the Doxology had warned people that nothing more was coming, or else a desire to see Moulton suddenly arose, or else a desire to "rush" him. At any rate, when he got up a hundred people seized their hats. The 200 people in the lobby, through which he had to pass, put on their hats, and as Moulton and the policeman forced their way through the cry "Rush him!" repeated again and again, mingled with the second verse of the Doxology. And a very threatening and noisy crowd followed, not to say accompanied, Mr. Moulton in a hurry through the long and narrow passage-way that leads from the back door of the church around to Orange street. Here there was already a crowd, and a crowd shoved aside by the police surrounded his carriage as Moulton got into it and rapidly drove away. And then Plymouth Church emptied itself, and the lights were put out, and the streets were full of people going home, and talking over the unexpected events of the evening.

THE REPORT

was read by Professor Raymond, and was as follows:

The Examining Committee of Plymouth Church beg leave to report that in consequence of the publication of certain statements of Theodore Tilton the committee was requested by the pastor of the church to authorize an investigation by a subcommittee into the imputations made against his character. On July 6, 1874, this committee accordingly appointed Brothers H. W. Sage and H. M. Cleveland such committee, requesting them to associate with themselves Messrs. Claflin, Winslow, Storrs, and White, who are not members of the Examining Committee. The charges having been brought to the church or to the Examining Committee against our pastor it was the duty of the sub-committee simply to ascertain whether there was any foundation in fact for the charges, and a trial before the body of the church. The sub-committee has, in our judgment, faithfully and impartially discharged its duties, and has presented to us a report which is here annexed:

To the Examining Committee of Plymouth Church:

DEAR BRETHREN: The pastor of Plymouth Church, the Rev. Henry Ward Beecher, addressed to us a letter June 27, 1874, of which the following is a copy:

BROOKLYN, June 27, 1874.

GENTLEMEN: In the present state of the public feeling, I owe it to my friends and to the church and the society over which I am pastor to have some proper investigation made of the rumors, insinuations, or charges made respecting my conduct, as compromised by the late publications made by Mr. Tilton. I have thought that both the church and the society should be represented, and I take the liberty of asking the following gentlemen to serve in this inquiry, and to do that which truth and justice may require. I beg that each of the gentlemen named will consider this as if it had been separately and personally sent to him, namely:

From the Church—Henry W. Sage, Augustus Storrs, Henry M. Cleveland.
From the Society—Horace B. Claflin, John Winslow, S V. White.

I desire you, when you have satisfied yourselves by an impartial and thorough examination of all sources of evidence, to communicate to the Examining Committee, or to the church, such action as then may seem to you right and wise.

HENRY WARD BEECHER.

The committee named having signified their willingness to serve in the grave matters so referred to them, Mr. Beecher sent the following letter to the Examining Committee of Plymouth Church:

JULY 6, 1874.

DEAR BRETHREN: I inclose to you a letter in which I have requested three brethren from the church, and three from the Society of Plymouth Church (gentlemen of unimpeachable repute, and who have not been involved in any of the trials through which we have passed during the year), to make a thorough and impartial examination of all charges or insinuations against my good name, and I to report the same to you; and I now respectfully request that you will give to this committee the authority to act in your behalf also. It seemed wise to me that the request should proceed from me, and without your foregoing knowledge, and that you should give to it authority to act in your behalf in so far as thorough investigation of the facts should be concerned.

HENRY WARD BEECHER.

Thereupon the Examining Committee duly authorized the committee named in the letter of June 27 to act in their behalf also.

Second--Your committee cannot here refrain from referring to the inexpressible regret which they in common with all good men feel, that uncontrollable circumstances have made it necessary to discuss in the most public manner the unhappy scandal which is the subject of the present inquiry. But, accepting the situation as we found it when we entered upon the high and solemn trust thus imposed, we have been profoundly impressed from the beginning with the grave importance of the work before us. For a considerable time vague and indefinite rumors were in circulation touching in a vital manner the Christian integrity of our beloved pastor. But nothing had appeared from a known responsible source in a tangible form until the letter of Mr. Theodore Tilton to the Rev. Dr. Bacon, which was published the twenty-fifth day of June, 1874. It was the appearance of this letter that moved Mr. Beecher two days afterwards to request immediate investigation. It will be seen by the terms of such request that some proper investigation is asked for by him of the rumors, insinuations, or charges made respecting his conduct as compromised by the late publications made by Mr. Tilton. We were invited to make an impartial and thorough investigation "of all sources of evidence," and to advise such action as may seem right and wise.

' *Third*—In conducting this investigation we have faithfully endeavored to make it thorough and impartial, and to obtain such facts as are relevant to the inquiry from all attainable sources of evidence. For this purpose we have summoned or requested the attendance of the following persons to testify before the committee : Mrs. Elizabeth R. Tilton, Mrs. H. W. Beecher, Samuel Wilkeson, John R. Howard, Theodore Tilton, Samuel E. Belcher, Mrs. N. B. Morse, Oliver Johnson, Rev. R. S. Storrs, D. D. ; Dwight Johnson, Isaac H. Bailey, Mrs. Putnam, John W. Mason, Rev. W. W. Patton, Mary C. Ames, Richard P. Buck, Francis B. Carpenter, Albert F. Norton, Thomas M. Vaill, E. M. Holmes, Hon. N. B. Morse, Mrs. Mary B. Bradshaw, Joseph Richards, Miss Elizabeth A. Turner, Francis W. Skiles, M. D.; Charles Corez, M. D.; Dr. Minton, Miss Oakley, Mrs. Elizabeth A. Ovington, Mrs. Wallace, Rev. S. B. Halliday, Thomas G. Shearman, Benjamin F. Tracy, Francis D. Moulton, Franklin Woodruff, John W. Harmon, Rev. Henry Ward Beecher. Most of the persons named have attended as requested before the committee. One notable exception is Francis B. Carpenter. Mr. Francis D. Moulton promised to testify fully, but has failed to do so. He has submitted three short statements in writing to the committee, consisting chiefly of reasons why he declined to testify, and of promises to testify at the call of the committee. The committee have called him three times, with the result stated. In addition to the evidence of the persons named we have examined a considerable number of letters and documentary evidence which in some way were supposed to relate to the subject matter of inquiry. We have held in the prosecution of our investigation twenty-eight sessions.

Fourth.—Mr. Tilton, in his letter to Dr. Bacon, published on the twenty-fifth day of June, 1874, states that knowledge came to him in 1870 that Mr. Beecher had committed an offense against him, which he forbore to name or characterize, and in the same letter introduced what he alleged to be extracts from a letter signed by Mr. Beecher, and dated January 1, 1871. This alleged letter, the whole of which appears in Mr. Tilton's subsequent statement before the Committee, has come to be known as the letter of apology. When this Committee commenced its labors there was, therefore, no allegation before them except such vague allusion to an offense of some sort said to have been committed by Mr. Beecher against Mr. Tilton, and for which, according to the same authority, he had apologized. It will thus be seen that the question before the Committee then was what, if any, offense had Mr. Beecher committed against Mr. Tilton.

Fifth.—At an early-period of the investigation Mr. Tilton was called before the Committee and made an extended written statement, and in a sense specific charges, which showed that the offense referred to in the Bacon letter, so called, was, as Mr. Tilton now alleges, adultery with his wife, Elizabeth R. Tilton. By this statement so made by Mr. Tilton, the field of inquiry was somewhat enlarged by the alleged facts, letters, and circumstances therein set forth. It is proper in this connection to state the offense as alleged by Mr. Tilton during some four years, and until recently, to numerous persons, in writing and otherwise, was an improper suggestion or solicitation by Mr. Beecher to Mrs. Tilton. But as time passed and purposes matured, this charge passed and matured into another form and substance. The offense committed by Mr. Beecher, as now alleged by Mr. Tilton, is stated substantially in the third and fourth subdivisions of his statement before the Committee. The charge in effect is, that Mr. Beecher at his residence, on the evening of October 10, 1868, or thereabouts, committed adultery with Elizabeth R. Tilton, wife of Theodore Tilton ; that this "act was followed by a similar act of criminality between the same parties at Mr. Tilton's residence on the subsequent Saturday evening, followed ' ulso by other similar acts on various occasions, from the autumn of 1868 to the spring of 1870, the places being the two residences aforesaid, and occasionally other places, to which her pastor would invite and accompany her, or at which he would meet her by previous appointment." The remainder of Mr. Tilton's extended statement is made up of citations of alleged facts and circumstances which he seems to consider relevant and important, as evidence sustaining his charges above stated.

The committee have given the evidence their most careful consideration, and find therefrom that in 1861, Mr. Beecher became editor and Mr. Tilton assistant editor of the *Independent*, and that during this relation they became warm and intimate friends. On or about 1863, Mr. Tilton began to urge Mr. Beecher to visit his (Tilton's) house, and he became more intimately acquainted with Mr. Tilton's family. He urged him to do much of his editorial writing in his study, as it was more convenient to write there than at the office of the *Independent*. Mr. Beecher visited his house, and a friendly relation sprang up between the wife and family of Mr. Tilton and Mr. Beecher, which continued down to December in 1870. That the friendly relations existing between Mr. Beecher and Mrs. Tilton were always well known and understood, and met with Mr. Tilton's cordial approval. Some years before any open trouble appeared between Mr. Beecher and Mr. Tilton, his (Mr. Tilton's) doctrines as set forth in the *Independent*, of which he had become editor, aroused a storm of indignation and opposition in the West, where this paper was widely circulated. After much discussion, this led to the starting of the *Advance* newspaper in Chicago to supersede the *Independent*. Mr. Tilton, while editor of the *Independent*, a leading religious newspaper, had come to deny the inspiration of the Scriptures and the divinity of Christ. His social views about this time also underwent a radical change in the direction of free love. This marked change in the religious and social views of Mr. Tilton was a source of great grief and sorrow to Mrs. Tilton. Mrs. Tilton seemed to be a very religous woman, amounting almost to enthusiasm, and when this change occurred in her husband she naturally sought her pastor for counsel and sympathy. She set forth in strong terms the suffering her husband's course was causing her. It now appears that during these years Mrs. Tilton became strongly attached to Mr. Beecher, and in July, 1870, confessed to her husband an overshadowing affection for her pastor.

On or about the 10th of December, 1870, Mrs. Tilton separated from her husband, going with her children to her mother's house. She sent for Mr. Beecher, and on his visiting her she made to him a statement of her sufferings and the abuse which she had received at the hands of her husband, which greatly shocked Mr. Beecher. He asked and received permission to send to Mrs. Tilton his wife, whose judgment in such matters he considered better than his own. Subsequently he agreed in advising with his wife that it was desirable that Mrs. Tilton should separate from her husband. Mr. Tilton, however, subsequently forced his wife to return to his house by sending for and obtaining possession of the youngest child, who was sick with the croup, during Mrs. Tilton's temporary absence from her mother's house. She suffered a miscarriage the next day after her return, on the 24th, which resulted in a serious illness, continuing until after the 1st of January, her physician being in daily attendance on her from the 24th to the 30th of December, inclusive. Early in December this year, owing to the marked change in Mr. Tilton's religious and social views, Mr. Bowen felt constrained to give him notice that his services as editor of the *Independent* would terminate at a day named in the notice. Subsequently to this notice, and on or about the 20th of December, Mr. Bowen had entered into a contract with Mr. Tilton, by which he was to be the editor of the Brooklyn *Daily Union*, and chief contributor of the *Independent*, for five years ; but within a few days after making this contract Mr. Bowen received such information of Tilton's immorality as alarmed him, and led to an interview between himself, Tilton, and Oliver Johnson, at the house of Bowen, on the 26th day of December, 1870. At this interview Mr. Tilton sought to retain his place in Bowen's confidence by offering to join Bowen in an attack on Mr. Beecher. This interview resulted in the insolent letter which Mr. Tilton wrote and signed on the 27th of December, demanding that Mr. Beecher leave Plymouth pulpit and Brooklyn. That evening Mr. Bowen, on his way home, delivered this letter to Mr. Beecher. Mr. Beecher, on reading it, expressed his astonishment at the receipt of such a letter, and denounced its author. Mr. Bowen then derided the letter, and gave him some account of the reasons why he had reduced Tilton from the editorship of the *Independent* to the subordinate position of contributor, saying that Mr. Tilton's religious and social views were ruining the paper, and that he was now considering whether he could consistently retain him as editor of the Brooklyn *Union* or chief contributor of the *Independent*. They conversed for some time, Mr. Bowen wishing Mr. Beecher's opinion, which was freely given. Mr. Beecher said he did not see how Mr. Bowen could retain his relations with Mr. Tilton. Mr. Beecher spoke strongly of the threatening letter and the revelation he had just had concerning Tilton's domestic affairs. Mr. Bowen read Tilton's threatening letter, and said that if trouble came he would stand by Mr. Beecher. It seems that Mr. Bowen communicated to Mr. Tilton on the following day the conversation had with Mr. Beecher, and his intention to stand by him. Mr. Beecher, though he had no doubt that Tilton would have lost his place saw that his influence was decisive, and anticipated Tilton's overthrow. It now appears that on the 29th of December, 1870, Mr. Tilton having learned the advice Mr. Beecher gave Mr. Bowen, and which was likely to bring him face to face with loss of place and position, extorted from his wife, then lying ill of miscarriage, a document implicating Mr. Beecher—a document evincing her love for her pastor, and accusing him of having made an improper solicitation. On the following day he sent Moulton to Beecher, requesting an interview with Mr. Beecher at Moulton's house that evening. Mr. Beecher accordingly met Tilton at Moulton's house. Tilton received him with a memorandum in his hand, and proceeded to charge Mr. Beecher with being unfriendly to him, with seeking his downfall, spreading injurious rumors about him, undermining him, and advising Bowen to dismiss him, injuring him in his family relations, joining his (Tilton's) mother-in-law in producing discord in the house, advising a separation, alienating his wife's affection from him, with gaining her love more than any living being, with corrupting her moral virtue, with teaching her to be insincere, lying, and hypocritical, and ending by charging that he made wicked proposals to her. Tilton then produced a written paper, purporting to be a memorandum of a confession made in July previous to him by his wife of her love for Mr. Beecher, and that he had made proposals to her of an impure nature.

Mr. Tilton, in the twenty-second subdivision of his statement before the Committee, referring in time to December, 1870, states his grievance and cause of complaint of Mr. Beecher, touching Tilton's business relations with Mr. Bowen, in these words: "That he (Mr. Beecher) then participated in a conspiracy to degrade Theodore Tilton before the public *by loss of place, business, and repute.*" It is clear that on the twenty-ninth day of December, when the so-called memorandum of confession was procured from Mrs. Tilton, the chief inciting cause of that step on Tilton's part was his belief that Mr. Beecher had caused him "*loss of place, business, and repute.*"

Mr. Beecher says this charge of impure proposals fell upon him like a thunderbolt. Could it be possible that Mrs. Tilton, whom he had regarded as the type of so much moral goodness, should have made such false and atrocious statements? Tilton requested Mr. Beecher to repair to his house, where Elizabeth was waiting for him, and learn from her lips the truth of the stories in so far as they concerned her. The interview was bad, and resulted in a written retraction of the charges of Mrs. Tilton, who seemed in great distress. In a sort of postscript to the retraction she denied explicitly that Mr. Beecher had ever offered any improper solicitations to her, that being the only charge made by Tilton, or referred to in the statement about the confession in July. On the next evening Moulton called at Mr. Beecher's house, and went up into his bedroom. He said that he and Tilton had learned that Mrs. Tilton had given the retraction. He expostulated and said the act was unfriendly, and would not mend matters, and that Mrs. Tilton had already recanted the retraction. That Tilton had already destroyed his wife's first paper of confession. Moulton claimed that Mr. Beecher had acted unfairly; that all difficulties could be settled without such papers, and that Mr. Beecher ought to give it up. Moulton was under great apparent excitement. He made no verbal threats, but displayed a pistol and laid it on the bureau near which he stood. The paper was given to him, and after a few moments' talk he left. It is an amazing pity that at this juncture Moulton was not handed over to the police. It would have saved much that followed, which is deeply deplored. Mr. Beecher's distress at the situation was boundless. He saw the peril of being even falsely accused. He blamed himself for much that had occurred. He could not tell how much of the impending trouble could be attributed to Mrs. Tilton's undue affection for him, which it was his duty to have repressed. "My earnest desire," he says, "to avoid a public accusation, and the evils which must necessarily flow from it, and which have now resulted from it, has been one of the leading motives that must explain my action during these four years in this matter." While in a morbid condition of mind, produced by those distressing difficulties, Moulton again called on him. His manner was kind and conciliatory. He professed, however, to believe that Mr. Beecher had been seeking Tilton's downfall; had leagued with Mr. Bowen against him, and by his advice had come near destroying Tilton's family. Mr. Beecher expressed many and strong regrets at the misfortunes of that family. Moulton caught up some of these expressions and wrote them down, saying that if Tilton could see them there would be no trouble in procuring a reconciliation. This paper, which is dated January 1, 1871, was entrusted by Mr. Beecher to Moulton's keeping without reading it, nor was it read to him. This paper, sometimes called the apology, and sometimes the confession, is in no proper sense Mr. Beecher's production or a correct report of what he said. No man will believe, for instance, that Mr. Beecher said: "I humble myself before him (Tilton) as I do before my God." Another sentence: "Her forgiveness I have." Mr. Beecher states it was not said, nor the semblance of it. Pausing here, a very important question arises in this connection. To what does the apology refer? It declares Mrs. Tilton "guiltless," and yet Tilton says it refers to adultery, which Mr. Beecher denies. Without now considering the weight of credit to which the respective parties are entitled where there is a conflict between them, we believe, and propose to show from the evidence, that the original charge was improper advances, and that as time passed, and the conspiracy deepened, it was enlarged into adultery.

The importance of this is apparent. Because if the charge has been so changed, then both Tilton and Moulton are conspirators and convicted of a vile fraud, which necessarily ends their influence in this controversy. What is the proof that the charge in the first instance was adultery ? It is said that it was, and 'that the memorandum in the hands of Tilton, in his wife's handwriting, was to such effect. But this is denied by both Mr. Beecher and Mrs. Tilton, and the written paper is not produced. It is said further that Mr. Beecher confessed the fact of adultery. But this, again, is denied by him, and such alleged confession is inconsistent with the retraction he received that evening from Mrs. Tilton. If he had confessed, what service could the retraction render ? Why procure one at all if, as alleged, Mr. Beecher had that evening confessed adultery to Tilton and Moulton, or to either ? What then was the charge preferred on the evening of December 30 ? We answer it was improper advances, which, of course, Mr. Beecher denied. What occurred in the matter of retraction that evening, and all the subsequent conversations, acts, and letters of the various persons directly concerned in dealing with the scandal, are consistent with this view, and with no other. The retraction procured referred to improper advances and to nothing else. Is it likely that if the main offense had been charged Mr. Beecher would have been satisfied with anything short of a retraction of that ?

There is a sort of postscript to the retraction, in which the charge of improper advances is explicitly denied—thus showing, we submit, that this was the charge that was in the mind of both Mrs. Tilton and Mr. Beecher, and no other offense. But look further : Mr. Tilton in the last four years has many times said verbally, and in writing, that the charge was the lesser offense. This is important under the rule that where a complainant has made different and inconsistent statements of the offense he alleges, his credibility is damaged, and in most cases destroyed. In the written statement of the offense shown to Dr. Storrs by Tilton and Carpenter, which was made in Mrs. Tilton's handwriting, under the demand of her husband, who says he dictated the precise words characterizing the offense, the charge was an impure proposal. This statement Mrs. Tilton retracted, and says she protested against it as false when signed, and afterwards saw Dr. Storrs and told him so. Dr. Storrs, in a letter to the committee, confirms the retraction. In the manuscript prepared by Tilton, which he called "the true story," the offense was stated to be improper advances. This "true story" Tilton was in the habit of reading to newspaper men, personal friends, and to others, without, it would seem, much discrimination, considering how anxious he professed to be not to make known his secret. Mr. Belcher testifies that he met Tilton on the ferry-boat about two weeks after the publication of the Woodhull scandal, and they talked the matter over. He says that Tilton was at first mysterious and non-committal, but on their way home in Brooklyn, Tilton invited him into his house, where the "true story" was exhibited to Mr. Belcher, and a prolonged conversation was had, which lasted until midnight, and during all this not one word was said or hinted by Tilton that he believed Beecher had committed adultery. On the contrary, he asserted his unshaken confidence in his wife's purity, and complained only of the improper solicitation. Ex-Supervisor Harmon, who, like Mr. Belcher, is one of our well-known and reputable citizens, testifies to substantially the same experience with Tilton as to the nature of the charge. Mr. Harmon goes further, and testifies not only that Tilton read to him the "true story," in which there was no allegation of adultery, but that Tilton described to him his first interview with Mr. Beecher on the evening of December 30, and then informed Mr. Harmon that he at that time charged Mr. Beecher with the offense of improper advances. Mr. Harmon explicitly states that in all his conversations, which were numerous, with Tilton for more than two years, he at no time alleged adultery as the offense of which he complained. The testimony before the committee shows similar statements by Tilton to various other persons up to within a recent period. The further fact that Tilton treated the matter during four years as an offense which could be properly apologized for and forgiven is wholly inconsistent with the charge in its present form. Tilton, in his written statement, complains that Mr. Beecher "abused his (Tilton's) forgiveness." It is believed no case of adultery on record can be produced where an injured husband upon learning of his wife's infidelity kept the fact to himself for six months, and then, after private complaint to the offending party, receives and accepts an apology for the offense, and declares it forgiven ; and this followed by a restoration of the courtesies of friendship. All these and other considerations to be hereafter referred to show that in no event could the offense have been the crime of adultery. It might have been the charge of the lesser offense ; but it is not conceivable that Tilton, in view of his conduct, believed even that. Still further, that the so-called apology was not for the main offense Tilton himself in his cross-examination clearly proves. Mark his words ! He says that the day after it was procured he was in Moulton's room, and there met Mr. Beecher, when the following scene occurred : "He (Beecher) burst out in an expression of great sorrow to me, and said he hoped the communication which he had sent me by Mr. Moulton was satisfactory to me. He then and there 'told Mr. Moulton' he had done wrong ; *not so much as some others had* (*referring to his wife, who had made statements to Mr. Bowen that ought to be unmade*) ; *and he there volunteered to write a letter to Mr. Bowen concerning the facts which he had misstated.*" Here is clear light as to what the apology does *not* refer to. It disposes of the apology forever as a paper referring to adultery. It refers to nothing of the kind. If the wrong done to which Mr. Beecher refers was adultery, how could these words be used in reference to it, "He had done wrong ; not so much as some others " ? The absurdity of such a claim is clear.

Those words and the apology are susceptible of but one construction. They refer, as Mr. Beecher says, to his deep regret for statements which he and his wife had, under certain information a few days before, made to Mr. Bowen, which led him to execute a purpose already entertained of removing Tilton from the Brooklyn *Union* and the *Independent*. It appears also that the next day Mr. Beecher did write the letter to Mr. Bowen which Tilton says he volunteered to write, and which referred to Tilton's business troubles with Bowen.

Next consider Moulton's course with a view of still further testing what was in his mind as well as in Tilton's as to the character of the offense. If Moulton understood the charge to be adultery, then he is entitled to the credit of the invention or discovery that this crime could be the subject of an apology, and a ready forgiveness and reconciliation on the part of the offender and the injured husband. That Moulton did not believe or understand that the offense was adultery is shown by the same class of evidence that has been cited in reference to Tilton. He repeatedly declared to many persons there was no adultery. Fortunately we have a statement in writing setting forth Moulton's estimate of the nature of the offense.

Mr. Beecher wrote a letter dated June 1, 1873, to Moulton, in which, among other things, he complains of Tilton's threatening and inconsistent conduct, and declares his purpose to waste no more energy in trying to satisfy Tilton, who at this time was complaining of the publication of the tripartite agreement, so called. In this letter Mr. Beecher says : "My mind is clear, I am not in haste, I shall write for the public a statement that will bear the light of the judgment day. God will take care of me and mine." These are not the words of a guilty mind. Moulton replies on the same day. Publicity was no part of his profound policy, and he hastens to object. At first he writes these words, "If the truth must be spoken, let it be. I know you can stand if the whole case were published to-morrow." Apparently fearing this might rather tend to determine Mr. Beecher to publish the whole case than otherwise, he crossed out these and other lines with a pencil and commenced anew. In this new effort on the same paper these words occur, "You can stand if the whole case were published to-morrow." Moulton was right. The pity is that Mr. Beecher did not publish forthwith, and so become once more free and end the machinations of Tilton and the mutual friend. These two, whatever else they wanted or designed, did not believe their purposes would be then subserved by publicity. Tilton soon became gracious and kindly. But what shall be said of Moulton, who now asserts for the first time that adultery was the offense ? Is it possible this man is so low in his moral perceptions as to believe that a minister of the Gospel, and that too of Plymouth Church, could stand up before his church and the world against the crime of adultery? No. Tilton says his wife was possessed of the idea that adultery with her pastor was all right, and no sin. That she did not discover her mistake from reading Saint Paul, but "Griffith Gaunt." But we have no evidence that this hallucination had reached and tainted the diplomatic mind of Moulton. It is right that we should say here that we do not believe the sinless character of adultery was a dogma believed in or even known to Mrs. Tilton, except perhaps as a notion of the Woodhull school, of which her husband had become a disciple and shining light, and with which she had no sympathy.

There is but one fair conclusion to be drawn from Moulton's letter of June 1 to Mr. Beecher. He knew that Mr. Beecher had been falsely accused of impure advances, and that he desired in his inmost soul to suppress the scandal. Yet if the simple truth were published he could stand. Knowing this he said so. Whatever Moulton may say now, since his malice has been excited by certain exposures, is of little consequence. He now openly stands with Tilton where he has secretly been from the beginning. We conclude, therefore, in view of these facts and circumstances, that the original charge of impure advances, false though it was, has been dropped by these accusers, and adultery at this late day has been substituted as an after-thought. We brand this performance as a fraud that ought to end all controversy as to the innocence of Mr. Beecher. Pursuing the narrative a little further we find Moulton, who first appeared as Tilton's friend after procuring the so-called apology, quietly becoming the friend of both the parties, the mutual friend. Mr. Moulton, as he discloses his character in these proceedings, appears to be a very plausible man, with more vigor of will than conscience. One thing is unfortunately clear, that from this time on he contrived to obtain and hold the confidence of Mr. Beecher, both in his ability and purpose to keep the peace in good faith. Mr. Beecher knew he had been falsely accused of an impure offense, and that a reputable woman by some means had been induced to make the accusation. It is true the charge had been withdrawn, and its force was in a sense broken. Still the fact remained, he had been accused.

Mr. Beecher naturally felt that the situation was critical. For him, a clergyman of world-wide fame, to be even falsely accused was a calamity. He felt—and in the light of results may we not say he was right ?—that a public charge of such an offense would, as he expressed it in his letter to Moulton of February 5, "make a conflagration." For reasons of malice and revenge it became apparent that Tilton was preparing to make a deadly assault upon him. This, Mr. Beecher believed, it was his supreme duty to prevent by all possible honorable means. Moulton professed to deprecate Tilton's purpose, and declared if Mr. Beecher would trust to him he could and would prevent it. And so now began a series of letters and steps under the direction and advice of the diplomatic mutual friend, having for their object, as Mr. Beecher believed, the suppression of the scandal and the restoration, in some measure, if practicable, of Tilton to position and employment.

In passing judgment upon the means employed to secure these results it is fair to remember that all through these four years Mr. Beecher was performing great labors, and had more and greater responsibilities upon him than at any other period of his life. Moulton said : "Leave these disagreeable matters to me. I will see that Tilton acts right. I will keep him in control. It is true that in certain moods he is threatening and unjust. But he soon recovers, and is kind and reasonable." As time passed along it was evident that Tilton was most troublesome when he was unprosperous in business affairs. The reference in his statement to "loss of place and business " is significant. At times Mr. Beecher became discouraged, as indicated in his letters to Moulton.

Much has been said, and not without some justice, of the extraordinary words and tenor of Mr. Beecher's letters. But in interpreting these letters it must be remembered—first, that Mr. Beecher, under the excitement of deep feeling, uses strong words and emotional expressions. This is and always has been a marked quality of his mind; second, in this,sore trouble he was dealing with Tilton, who had shown himself at times fickle, malicious, revengeful, and mercenary. In the light of these facts there is not a letter from Mr. Beecher, nor an act of his, however ill-judged, through these four years of anxiety and grief, that cannot be accounted for upon the plain theory that he was fighting to suppress an outrageous scandal which consisted of a false accusation against him made by a reputable woman; and further, that he was endeavoring to help a man whom he felt he had unduly injured in his business matters upon representations which he was afterwards made to believe, chiefly by Moulton, were not well-founded.

The statement of this branch of the case would not be complete without reference to the fact that Mr. Beecher had a warm friendship for Mrs. Tilton, which began in her early womanhood, and that Mrs. Tilton, reciprocating this friendship, began, as her domestic troubles came on, to look more than ever to Mr. Beecher for sympathy and advice. That this feeling on Mrs. Tilton's part became, under the circumstances, so strong as to diminish the proper influence that belongs to every good husband is not unlikely.

In the course of events, and especially in December, 1870, Mr. Beecher received the impression from Tilton and Moulton that he had estranged Mrs. Tilton's affections from her husband. The possibility that such a fact as this might be added to the responsibilities then resting upon Mr. Beecher constituted, as he expressed it in his letter of February 5, in part, one of "the environments that surrounded him." This was, to him, the occasion of deep grief and anguish. Mr. Beecher conceived that possibly he had been derelict in duty—he, the strong man and pastor—in not repressing at once any undue affection for him on the part of this distressed Christian woman who was yearning for sympathy that she found not in her household. And we cannot but express our regret at two errors into which it is apparent Mr. Beecher fell. While we recognize the appalling disaster which seemed imminent when he was confronted by a professedly injured husband, with a charge on the part of his wife of an impure proposal from him to her—a disaster which threatened to brand with infamy a name which, through years of public service as philanthropist and minister of God, had maintained the most honored place in the world's esteem—yet we feel that in an hour of such demoralization as this calamity might justly work, the pastor should have sought counsel from Christian men of his own brotherhood, rather than rely upon the counsel of a man of whom he knew so little and whose character as the sequel proved, he so sadly misjudged. And it is also apparent from Mr. Beecher's own statement, in view of the profound sorrow into which he was plunged and the expression which he gave to his feelings, that he had erred in not guarding so closely his relations with the family of Mr. Tilton that there could be no possibility for fear in his own mind even of an undue affection by Mrs. Tilton for him, through any heedless friendship or agency of his.

Mr. Tilton, in his statement before the committee, speaks of his home as one of unusual harmony —"an ideal home." But, upon his cross-examination it clearly appeared it was anything but a happy or harmonious home. The truth as to this is material both as affecting Tilton's credibility and as showing the character of Mrs. Tilton's domestic troubles, and the influences that reached her daily life.

Her painful testimony reveals a jealous husband accusing her of infidelities with different men and of exerting a sensual influence over all. She declares that her husband had frequently compelled her when sick to copy, or from his dictation write, confessions which she herself did not understand, and in her despairing condition of mind cared little about it. At times he threatened her, locked her up, and declared himself ashamed of her presence when among friends whose society was more attractive to him. Her account reveals him full of selfish exactions; indifferent to her wants; neglectful in her illness; forcing disreputable women into her society, till sometimes she fled for peace to the graves of her children. Mrs. Tilton declares he did not hesitate to avow his right to commit adultery on his lecturing tours whenever he chose. And yet, in season and out, we find this man dribbling out his charges of dishonor against his wife. This is a dismal revelation from the "ideal home," but one cannot read it and believe it possible that she has invented this recital of her husband's character and life. This account of the domestic misery of the Tilton family is corroborated by the testimony of several witnesses, and very fully by Miss Elizabeth A. Turner. who is now twenty-three years of age, and was an inmate of the family eight years. This young woman is a teacher of music in a ladies' seminary in Pennsylvania. She is a person of unusual intelligence, and her appearance and manner before the Committee impressed all who heard her testify that she was sincere and reliable and well understood the facts of which she was speaking.

The condition of this family, in connection with the distressing circumstances referred to, and that appear in the history of this difficulty, conspired to make the occasion one full of peril, not only to Mr. Beecher, but to others whom he felt bound to respect to the last moment, to say nothing of the great interests of his beloved Plymouth Church, and other interests of high concern, all of which must be involved, if publicity should be given to the false and scandalous matter that was seeking expression from the heated and malicious mind of Theodore Tilton. Will innocent men pay blackmail? Will innocent men, and especially clergymen, fight as for their lives to suppress an injurious scandal, even though it be born of extortion, falsehood, and revenge? These are questions which unhappily history has too often answered in the affirmative. It is easy, now that we see what manner of men Tilton and Moulton are to wonder that Mr. Beecher should intrust any interest of his to their keeping When we look back upon the record made by this sad story we feel like visiting. even upon the suffering head and heart of our pastor, the severest censure. And this not the less because we revere and love him, and know that no man in all our land is more beloved. It is, we might say, because he is so beloved—because that in him centre so many and so great interests of church and humanity—because he stands to-day foremost among men of master minds, of eloquence and power, that we would chide him in no uncertain words for imperiling so much and so often the precious interests confided to him by the God who made him, and who we have unshaken faith to believe will deliver him from all dangers.

The charge made by the accuser is one easily preferred, and not easily disproved. It is not enough for the accuser to say : "I make this charge, now let it be disproved or be taken as confessed." All tribunals, both ecclesiastical and legal, in their wisdom have required, in determining charges of this kind, such proof of facts and circumstances as point unmistakably to the guilt of the accused, and as are not consistent with any theory of innocence. Lord Stowell, as cited by Greenleaf, one of the best writers known to our jurisprudence, and especially on rules of evidence, says:

In every case almost, the fact is inferred from circumstances that lead to it by fair inference as a necessary conclusion ; and unless this were the case, and unless this were so held, no protection whatever could be given to marital rights. What are the circumstances which lead to such a conclusion, cannot be laid down universally, though many of them, of a more obvious nature, and of more frequent occurrence, are to be found in the ancient books ; at the same time it is impossible to indicate them universally, because they may be infinitely diversified by the situation and character of the parties, by the state of general manners, and by many other incidental circumstances, apparently slight and delicate in themselves, but which may have most important bearings in decisions upon the particular case. The only general rule that can be laid down upon the subject is, that the circumstances must be such as would lead the guarded discretion of a reasonable and just man to the conclusion ; for it is not to lead a rash and intemperate judgment moving upon appearances that are equally capable of two interpretations.

Greenleaf further illustrates the kind of evidence required to prove adultery as follows :

Adultery of the *wife* may be proved by the birth of a child and non-access of the husband, he being out of the realm. Adultery of the *husband* may be proved by habits of adulterous intercourse, and by the birth, maintenance. and acknowledgment of a child. A married man going into a known *brothel* raises a suspicion of adultery, to be rebutted only by the very best evidence. His going there and remaining alone for some time in a room with a common prostitute is sufficient proof of the crime. The circumstance of a woman going to such a place with a man furnishes similar proof of adultery.

The citations are pointed but useful.

Under the guidance of these precedents and principles it is essential to observe that there is nothing whatever disclosed by the evidence that proves that the accused parties have ever been found together under any suspicious circumstances, such as in some unusual house or place, or consulting together in some secret way to avoid observation and exposure. There is no proof of clandestine correspondence, nor attempts in that direction. Mr. Beecher's letters were, as a rule, opened, arranged, and read by his wife. She testifies that she has read and answered as many as 1,000 in three months. Such as reached the *Christian Union* office were opened by others, and those that went to the church were opened, by the direction of Mr. Beecher, by the clerk, before being placed on the desk. No sort of restrictions were imposed as to his letters. The usual facts and circumstances suggestive of wrong-doing are utterly wanting in this case. What then does the case, as put by the accuser, rest upon? We answer—upon mere words and assertions, supported by no circumstances whatever that are the usual indications of adultery.

Tilton says he knew the fact from his wife's confession, July 3, 1870, and from her subsequent confessions to Moulton and to her mother, Mrs. Morse. This is thus answered : First, that Mrs. Tilton says in effect that this confession, whatever it was, was extorted from her by an imperious, malicious husband, and by means that, in a moral sense, were fraudulent. Pretenses were made that she must say something to extricate Theodore out of his business perplexities. She was made to believe there was a conspiracy against her husband. The fact that Mrs. Tilton withdrew the charge when Mr. Beecher first confronted her after he had heard of it, on the evening of December 30, is in order in this connection, together with the further fact that she has ever since denied the truth of the charge when free from the dominating influence of her husband. She explicitly denies that the charge was adultery. We now see her coming before the committee with expressions of joy that at last she can come and speak the truth ; and in the most solemn manner she denies absolutely the charge, and proceeds to set forth facts and circumstances which demonstrate that this unhappy woman has for years been the plastic victim of extorted falsehoods. Tilton's allegation that she confessed to her mother, Mrs. Morse, is pronounced false by the mother, who testified before the committee. The source of the scandal, then, is alleged words of Mrs. Tilton, which she explains in such a manner as to deprive the allegation of all force and credit. Then comes Mr. Beecher, who solemnly declares that whatever words, by whatever means, have been drawn from Mrs. Tilton by her husband, he is innocent of any and all impropriety, towards her, without relating to improper advances or to adultery.

It is not for the committee to defend the course of Mrs. Tilton. Her conduct, upon any theory of human responsibility, is indefensible. Our hope is that it may be made clear, as the testimony affords much reason to believe it may be, that this distressed woman was so beset by her designing husband, when in states of mind differing little, if at all, from mental aberration, brought on by illness and domestic sorrow and gloom, as to induce her, at least passively, to make a charge of improper advances by Mr. Beecher. But when her attention was pointedly called to the great wrong she had done, she quickly took it back in sorrow and penitence as follows :

DECEMBER 30, 1870.

Wearied with importunity and weakened by sickness, I gave a letter implicating my friend Henry Ward Beecher, under assurances that that would remove all difficulties between me and my husband. That letter I now revoke. I was persuaded to it—almost forced—when I was in a weakened state of mind. I regret it and recall its statements.

E. R. TILTON.

I desire to say explicitly Mr. Beecher has never offered any improper solicitation, but has always treated me in a manner becoming a Christian and a gentleman.

ELIZABETH R. TILTON.

There is medical testimony before the committee, given by two eminent physicians, Doctors Minton and Corey, to the effect that such cases of mental power and domination by a husband of strong will over a wife weakened by disease and domestic trouble are not infrequent. Dr. Corey, who is eminent and has large experience in mental diseases and phenomena, says such conduct on the part of Mrs. Tilton, when subjected to the influences referred to, is even consistent with an honest mind. We observe that Moulton parades a letter purporting to have been written by Mrs. Tilton to him (JJ), in which she says she is "a perfect coward in his (Tilton's) presence," and "it is a physical impossibility for me to tell the truth." In another letter, same to same, "KK," she says, "With all my woman's soul I am innocent of the crime of impure conduct alleged against me." In her statement, procured under the direction of Tilton and Carpenter, of December 16, 1872, and which was taken by them to Dr. Storrs, Mrs. Tilton shows that she was made to believe that a conspiracy was formed against her husband. Her words are : "Six months afterwards (that is, July 3, 1870) my husband felt impelled by the circumstances of a conspiracy against him, in which Mrs. Beecher had a part, to have an interview with Mr. Beecher." This refers to the interview of Tilton with Mr. Beecher, procured by Moulton on the evening of December 30, 1870, when Tilton produced a written charge, in two lines, in the handwriting of Mrs. Tilton. It will be seen it was under the influence of startling statements of conspiracy against her husband that Mrs. Tilton was moved to appear to act on this occasion. We find her subsequently in a letter asking Mr. Beecher's "forgiveness for the sufferings she had caused him."

We hear much from Tilton of confessions made by his wife to him. We are obliged to receive his statements on this point, if at all, without corroboration. But on one occasion, when Tilton was assailing his wife, we learn from the testimony of Miss Elizabeth A. Turner in what manner Tilton's accusations were met by his wife. Question : "Did he (Tilton) at any time on this day say that she had made any confession to him in regard to Mr. Beecher ?" Answer : "He said she had confessed to him that she had been criminally intimate with Mr. Beecher ; she (Mrs. Tilton) was present when he said that, and she said, 'Oh Theodore, how can you tell that child such base lies ?' and then she burst out crying." Question : "When was that ?" Answer : "This all occurred on the day that we went back in the fall of 1870." This was the day when this witness testified that a scene of violence occurred. The witness believing that Tilton was about to strike his wife, interfered to save her, and was knocked down by Tilton. This witness is the same person who it is said by Tilton and Moulton was sent to boarding-school to get rid of her, because she had heard Tilton make charges against Beecher. It is further said that Mr. Beecher was so anxious to have her leave town and keep away that he paid some

$2,000 for her school expenses. There is no doubt the $2,000 were paid, but for quite another purpose. Miss Turner and Mrs. Tilton both agree in saying that it was Tilton's plan to have her go away because she had stated to her friends that Tilton had twice attempted intimate relations with her while in bed and during the absence of Mrs. Tilton in the country. Tilton was fast losing place and position because of his social views and practices, and feared the publicity of this girl's statement, who at that time was twenty years of age. The absurdity of supposing that Mr. Beecher would invest $2,000 apiece to get persons to leave town to whom Tilton had been peddling his scandal against him is transparent. Persons to whom Tilton had talked in some form of the scandal, sometimes in one shape and then in another, were too numerous to justify an investment of $2,000 on each of them by anybody whose wealth could not be counted by millions.

It should be noted that just as Miss Turner was leaving for the boarding-school, Tilton procured from her, with the aid of his wife, a letter denying the reports of his improper liberties. Here again we find Tilton a manufacturer of evidence.

It is not for us to pass judgment on Mrs. Tilton uncharitably. She has suffered unparalleled trials. Moulton quotes her as saying in a letter to him, as we have seen, that it was physically impossible for her to tell the truth in her husband's presence. It will be noted that the pretended confession was obtained in that presence; and, further, that it was when she was away from home and from home at Schoharie that she stated her sin to be like that of Catherine Gaunt, an undue affection for her pastor. In this letter to her husband she says: "I felt unfalteringly that the love I felt and received harmed no one, not even you, until the heavenly vision dawned upon me." And again: "Oh, my dear Theodore, though your opinions are not restful or congenial to my soul, yet my integrity and purity are a sacred and holy thing to me. Bless God with me for Catherine Gaunt and for all the pure leadings of an all-wise and loving Providence." This letter was written June 29, 1871, about a year after the pretended confession. In no sense can its words be construed as referring to adultery. Tilton, when before the committee, when reference was first made to this Schoharie letter, seemed to think that the offense in the story of "Griffith Gaunt" was adultery, and accordingly relied upon this letter as incontrovertible evidence of his charge. In this he was mistaken. It is a principle of the common law that a married woman cannot commit or be held to commit a crime perpetrated in the presence of her husband, and this upon the idea that the husband's presence and influence amount to duress, and that she is therefore not responsible.

Whether it is necessary to invoke this rule of law to excuse Mrs. Tilton or not, we may see in what Tilton was able to extort from her without her volition or real assent something of the reasons which moved the early expounders of the English common law to assert the doctrine referred to.

We have now reviewed, as briefly as we could, the evidence before us. There are many facts and details we have not discussed. We have cited the more important of these and discussed the salient points. We have carefully examined the evidence relied on by the accuser to sustain the charges we are asked to believe.

Finally, who is this accuser, that he makes so bold a face? We may learn by the testimony, as well as by common report, without descending to unpleasant particulars or personalities, that Theodore Tilton has in recent years become a very different man from what he was formerly reputed to be. He will hardly deny that. Both before and after his espousal of the new marital philosophy signs of degeneracy were setting in which have made him a discredited man in this community. In the new role his culmination and downfall are well stated in recent words by an able writer, who, in sketching his career, says that, "In process of time he comes before the world as the indorser of Victoria C. Woodhull, and lends his name to a biography of her which would have sunk any man's reputation anywhere for common sense. Such a book is a tomb from which no author rises again." Such is the accuser. Who is the accused? It is Henry Ward Beecher. The pastor of Plymouth Church has been a clergyman with harness on forty years. Twenty-seven of these years he has been here in this church, which as all the world knows has so often been stirred to good deeds and to a better life by his eloquent ministration.

This man has been living in the clear light of noonday, before his people and before all men, a life of great Christian usefulness and incessant work. None have known him but to admire and love him. They who have been most intimate with him at home and abroad report nothing of his life or conversation but what comes of purity of soul. We are asked by Theodore Tilton and his coadjutor, Moulton, to believe that this man, with his long and useful life and high character to sustain him, is unworthy of our confidence, regard, or respect. Christian character and great services, which are usually considered a tower of strength and defense when one is assailed, are to go for naught, according to Mr. Tilton. We are invited to give up this beloved and eminent man and send him and his good name and fame into the vortex of moral destruction. We are to do this, upon what? Upon some wild, absurd and contradictory assertions of Mr. Tilton, who in all this work does not succeed in disguising his malicious and revengeful designs.

No tribunal administering justice ever held a charge of adultery proved by mere alleged words, written or spoken, that are denied and not connected with circumstances and appearances pointing unmistakably to the guilt of the accused. Upon a review of all the evidence, made with an earnest desire to find the truth, and to advise what truth and justice shall require, we feel bound to state that, in our judgment, the evidence relied on by the accuser utterly fails to sustain the charges made.

We herewith submit a complete stenographic copy of all the evidence before the committee, with some unimportant or irrelevant exceptions.

STATEMENT OF CONCLUSIONS.

First—We find from the evidence that the Rev. Henry Ward Beecher did not commit adultery with Mrs. Elizabeth R. Tilton, either at the time or times, place or places, set forth in the third and fourth subdivisions of Mr. Tilton's statement, or at any other time or place whatever.

Second—We find from the evidence that Mr. Beecher has never committed any unchaste or improper act with Mrs. Tilton, nor made any unchaste or improper remark, proffer, or solicitation to her of any kind or description whatever.

Third—If this were a question of errors of judgment on the part of Mr. Beecher, it would be easy to criticise, especially in the light of recent events. In such criticism, even to the extent of regrets and censure, we are sure no man would join more sincerely than Mr. Beecher himself.

Fourth—We find nothing whatever in the evidence that should impair the perfect confidence of Plymouth Church or the world in the Christian character and integrity of Henry Ward Beecher.

And now let the peace of God that passeth all understanding rest and abide with Plymouth Church and her beloved and eminent pastor, so much and so long afflicted.

> HENRY W. SAGE,
> AUGUSTUS STORRS,
> HENRY M. CLEVELAND,
> HORACE B. CLAFLIN,
> JOHN WINSLOW,
> S. V. WHITE,
> *Committee of Investigation.*

Dated BROOKLYN, August 27, 1874.

The evidence taken has also been transmitted to us. Most of it has been already made public. The publication of the remainder will be considered by us at a further meeting; one point, however, being settled, that nothing shall be withheld from publication which can afford a pretext for censuring the pastor of this church. The expediency of publishing evidence injurious to other parties is a question which cannot be hastily determined. While we should have unhesitatingly done our duty in case a different conclusion had been reached, we rejoice to say that, without one dissenting voice, this committee find nothing in the evidence to justify the least suspicion of our pastor's integrity and purity, and everything to justify and command on the part of Plymouth Church and society a degree of confidence and affection towards its pastor greater, if possible, than it has ever yet felt to him. It is not the office of this committee to review his errors of judgment in managing a complex trouble or struggling against the most infamous conspiracy known to the present age. It is for us simply to consider what moral culpability, if any, is developed upon his part, and of this we find no proof, although, under a delusion, artfully brought about by his enemies, our pastor was for a long time made to believe himself in fault.

In conclusion, we recommend to the church the adoption of the following resolutions:

Resolved, That the evidence laid before the Examining Committee not only does not afford any foundation for putting the pastor of this church, Rev. Henry Ward Beecher, on trial, but on the contrary, establishes to the perfect satisfaction of this church his entire innocence and absolute personal purity with respect to all the charges now or heretofore made against him by Theodore Tilton.

Resolved, That our confidence in and love for our pastor, so far from being diminished, are heightened and deepened by the unmerited sufferings which he has so long borne, and that we welcome him with a sympathy more tender and a trust more unbounded than we ever felt before to his public labors among us, to our church, our families, our homes, and our hearts.

> D. W. TALLMADGE,
> Clerk Examining Committee.

DR. PATTON'S RECOLLECTIONS.

Th3 Rev. W. W. Patton, D.D., of Chicago, in answer to a letter from the Chairman of the Plymouth Church Investigating Committee asking him to appear before the Committee and give any information in his possession touching the charges against the Rev. H. W. Beecher, or, if he could not appear in person, to send a written statement of the same, forwarded the following paper to the Chairman of the Committee :

Mr. H. W. Sage, Chairman:

In accordance with the promise in my brief note this day sent to you, I now prepare a statement of what I know about the charges brought against the Rev. Henry Ward Beecher. Perhaps a historical order and form may be the best.

In November, 1871, I was in Ohio, and met Mrs. Putnam, of Marietta, or that vicinity. She requested an interview, that she might give me a better understanding of Mr. Theodore Tilton, with whose utterances on certain theological and social topics I had expressed editorial dissatisfaction in the *Advance*. At the interview, at which her husband was also present, she informed me that she had been intimately acquainted with both Mr. and Mrs. Tilton from their early childhood, and had esteemed them highly. About a year previous, Mrs. Tilton came to her house to take refuge, as she said, as with a mother, from the sore abuses of her husband, whose actions were as bad as his principles. Thus Mrs. T. affirmed to Mrs. P. that her husband filled the house with female visitors whose sentiments on love and marriage were offensive ; that he would have them there for days at a time ; that he would treat her with entire neglect, and lavish attention on them ; that he would sometimes say, in their presence, to her : "I love such a person (naming one) more than I do you ; " that he would speak insultingly of her appearance, and say that it was a shame for such a fine-proportioned man as he to be compelled to walk on the street with such a dried-up little woman as she ; that he would often accuse her of being the mistress of Henry Ward Beecher, and would sometimes propose a separation, saying that he would go with his set, and she might go with Mr. Beecher ; and that he had also tried to induce her to take the children and live abroad in Europe. But she was unwilling to leave him, hoping that eventually he would retrace his steps and be his old self again, as regarded morals and religion. Finally his treatment became such that she could not endure it longer, and so had come a broken-hearted woman to her early friend, Mrs. Putnam. 'Mrs. P. further stated that a young woman had also been to her (whom I suppose to have been Bessie Turner, though Mrs. P. mentioned no name) who had lived for years as an inmate of Mr. Tilton's family, assisting Mrs. T., and that this young woman represented that these complaints of Mrs. T.'s were true ; that she had seen and heard many such things in the house; that Mr. T. had insulted her modesty, also, in such ways as caused her to leave, after long patience, owing to her love for Mrs. T.; that, on one occasion, she heard him abusing his wife outrageously in the next room ; and was so enraged thereby that she stepped in and said : "Theodore Tilton, if you dare to treat your wife so again I will expose your character ;" that he replied : "You have exposed me already to Mrs. Putnam ;" that she answered : "If you repeat your conduct to Mrs. Tilton, I will expose you to the public ;" and that he instantly raised his hand and knocked her down. Mrs. Putnam further said that, when Mr. Tilton's business troubles came upon him, Mrs. T. pitied him so much, and was so afraid that he would go to destruction, that she went back to him, and so did the young woman ; but that afterwards the latter was spirited away to some unknown place by Mr. Tilton, so that Mrs. Putnam had been unable to ascertain where she was. Such had long been the unfavorable reports current respecting Mr. Tilton's habits, and such was my perfect confidence in Mr. Beecher, that this statement of his accusation against Mr. B. and his own wife did not even raise a suspicion in my mind against Mr. Beecher. It only operated to produce an impression of the fearful corruption of Mr. Tilton, and to explain, apparently, his editorial course on social reform.

When the public scandal was started, in *Woodhull and Claflin's Weekly*, a copy of which a friend in New York sent to me, I was astounded ; because it was so contrary to my faith in Mr. B.; because it was plainly based on *something*, which Mrs. Woodhull believed would be with reluctance investigated, or she would not have ventured to make such large and specific accusations ; and because she referred by name to so many responsible persons as possessing knowledge of the facts. I then recalled the fact that Mrs. Tilton had told Mrs. Putnam that her husband had thrown these very accusations in her face, and I placed that by the side of Mr. Tilton's intimacy with Mrs. Woodhull and his suicidal act in writing her life. Could it be, that Mrs. Woodhull had knowledge of his family affairs, which placed him in her power ? Yet nothing more than a passing suspicion was aroused; though I saw that unless the persons named by Mrs. W. explicitly and publicly contradicted her story, Mr. Beecher, or Mr. Tilton, or both, would be compelled to admit or deny the alleged facts, or to explain what degree of truth attached to the charge. But I saw no reason for alluding to the matter editorially in the *Advance.* While in this state of mind, I was shocked to receive, on the first day of January, 1873, a letter from my brother, resident in the City of New York, stating that he had learned that Beecher was guilty; that he being known, with his wife, to be a warm friend and ardent admirer of Mr. Beecher, had, on that ground, been applied to by Mr. Frank B. Carpenter, the artist, to take stock in a new daily paper, which was to be started in New York, under the editorship of Mr. B.; that Mr. C. told him that Beecher was guilty; that the fact was known to some of his intimate friends; that it was necessary to do something to break his fall before the public; that on consultation with Mr. Beecher as to a method by which he could withdraw from the ministry without exciting suspicion unduly, it had been agreed to see whether a new daily political paper could not be started for him, on the ground that Greeley was dead, and Bennett and Raymond, and thus no conspicuous editor remained, and that, as Mr. Beecher was now 60 years of age, and had now celebrated his pastoral silver-wedding, the time was auspicious for him to withdraw from his pastorate with yet unweakened faculties, and to give his remaining years to an honorable and useful work, at the head of a great political paper. My brother said further, that, on his mentioning to Mr. Carpenter that I was likely to leave the *Advance,* and that possibly it would be well to engage me on the proposed paper, Mr. Carpenter warmly assented, and suggested that I should be sent for. So my brother begged me to come on immediately, whether I felt inclined to the project or not, as my advice might be of value in so important an affair. This letter stunned me. I slept but little that night. The statements were so plain that I knew not how to doubt, and as little could I reconcile myself to believe. The next day I wrote to my brother that if the facts were as he represented, on Mr. C.'s authority, I could have absolutely nothing to do with the proposed paper; that the scheme would be a failure in all respects, was based on a wrong principle, and could not receive my co-operation; but that I would comply with his urgent request, and proceed to New York in a few days. This I did, informing no one but my wife of the occasion of my going or of the news which I had received, but carrying around a heavy heart. The letter from my brother I burned, lest by any possibility it should fall into other hands and spread the report.

I reached New York, January 8, I think, saw my brother, who confirmed more at length what he had written, and tried that same day to see Mr. Carpenter, as also the next morning, but in vain. He did not come home from Brooklyn that night; he devoting at that time his whole energies to Mr. Tilton and Mr. Beecher, to the entire neglect of his own business. But the second evening he came to my brother's, and we spent two or three hours talking over the matter. He said that the newspaper had been laid aside for the present, for the reason that, on mature consideration, Mr. Beecher thought it would excite suspicion rather than allay it, and because it was hoped that an investigation might be evaded, and Mr. Beecher be able to stand on his past reputation. And yet he said that no one could tell what a day might bring forth; that Mr. Tilton was almost beside himself with excitement over the exposure; that his daughter Florence had learned of it from Mrs. Morse (Mrs. Tilton's mother), who said to her one day up stairs : " Florence, in this very room, Henry Ward Beecher committed adultery with your mother ;" that Florence had threatened to rise up in Plymouth Church lecture-room and demand an investigation, and had declared that there was but one name she hated worse than Tilton, and that was Beecher ; and that she was a girl of spirit, and might carry out her threats. Finding that I had learned from Mrs. Putnam all about the estrangement of Mr. and Mrs. Tilton (though I declined to mention Mrs. P.'s name), Mr. Carpenter admitted that there had been misunderstandings at one time, but said that both had been to blame, and that they were now reconciled, and that I heard an exaggerated account of their troubles, as Mrs. Tilton would assure me in person. He then detailed the facts of the dismissal of Mr. Tilton from the editorship of the *Independent,* the subsequent amicable arrangement of his salary and work, in connection both with that paper and the Brooklyn *Union,* and the occasion of the sudden and almost immediate breaking of the contract by Mr. Bowen. He said that Bowen wanted Tilton to make much of Beecher and Plymouth Church in the *Union,* and inquired why Mr. T. had not been at church for six months past ; that this drew out from Mr. T. a reference to Mr. Bowen's accusations against Mr. Beecher in his letter from Woodstock, and a statement of Mr. Tilton's own charge against him ; that Mr. Bowen proposed the note demanding Mr. Beecher's withdrawal from Plymouth Church and from Brooklyn, and offered to carry it and back it up ; that the note was taken by Mr. Bowen ; that he returned the next day in an opposite frame of mind, demanding the Woodstock letter, and insisting on silence about it; that Mr. Carpenter could not explain the change, but had heard that, when Mr. Bowen handed the letter to Mr. Beecher, he said : "See what a viper you have nursed in your bosom ;" that Mr. Beecher may have told Mr. Bowen something to Mr. T.'s disadvantage, or may have threatened to attack Mr. Bowen in some exposed part ; that, at all events, he dismissed Mr. T. on the spot for refusing compliance with his demands.

Furthermore, when the arbitration was held to recover damages for this breach of contract, it was decided (1.) That Mr. Bowen should pay Mr. Tilton $7,000. (2.) That Mr. T. should surrender the Woodstock letter. (3.) That Mr. Bowen should insert conspicuously in the *Independent* an editorial eulogistic of Mr. Tilton, and (4.) That Mr. Beecher should copy this into the *Christian Union*, and should add further eulogy of his own; all of which was duly carried out. Mr. Carpenter also said that Oliver Johnson had knowledge of these charges of Mr. Bowen against Mr. Beecher, and of similar matters, but after the publication of Mrs. Woodhull he had been put in as managing editor of Mr. Beecher's paper, the *Christian Union*, though he could not affirm that there was any connection in the two facts. I remarked that this appointment, in view of Mr. Johnson's known sentiments on religion, which were understood to have ousted him from the *Independent*, excited much comment. He spoke as to Mr. Beecher and Mrs. Tilton (though without affirming or denying the broadest form of the charges, except to say that a denial could be made of the *precise form* of statement made by Mrs. Woodhull), almost exactly as given in the published statements of Mr. Tilton and Mr. Moulton; including the written confession or charge of Mrs. Tilton; the date and fact of the interviews of Beecher and Tilton, at Moulton's house; the visit to Mrs. Tilton's sick-room by Beecher and the securing the retraction; the written reversal of that again, the same night, by Mrs. Tilton; the way and time in which Mr. Moulton obtained from Mr. Beecher Mrs. Tilton's paper; the fact that Moulton had all the important documents, and was trying to keep the peace and protect all parties, etc., etc. In the whole course of the conversation not a word was said by Mr. Carpenter implying that Mr. Beecher claimed to be innocent of the charge of having at least made base proposals to Mrs. Tilton; on the contrary, he spoke freely of Mr. Beecher's admissions of guilt with respect to her in this way, and of the fact that several persons in his congregation knew of his impurity, and quoted Mr. Beecher's words to him, to this effect: "Men talk of the courage required to face the cannon's mouth; but that is nothing compared with what I have had to exercise, these years back, in looking in the face and preaching to persons who knew that I had been guilty of such things." He assured me that Mr. Beecher had been very desirous, at first, to have the newspaper project succeed, and to withdraw from the ministry, saying to Mr. C. that "his work was about done in that line, that it had principally been a destructive work, pulling to pieces the old theology, and that some one else must now arise with constructive ability to make a new scheme." He said he had just come from a conference with Dr. Storrs on the subject, to see what could be done to save the public fall of Mr. Beecher; and he pulled from his vest-pocket a small piece of paper on which were minuted down three or four points which could be made before the public in denial of Mrs. Woodhull's statement without touching anything else.

I replied that such a policy could never succeed, and that I did not believe that Dr. Storrs, on reflection, would counsel any deception of the public by sending forth a denial of one statement, as though that covered the whole of the real case, when he knew that actual guilt nevertheless existed. Mr. Carpenter made his statements to me in the presence of my brother (who is now in Europe), said that he was in daily intercourse with Beecher and Tilton on the subject, and explained that the part of the plan about the newspaper was, that Tilton should go abroad for two or three years, correspond with the paper, get a new set of associations with his name in the public mind, and then come home, and go, perhaps, on the editorial staff. Finally, he offered to take me to Mr. Beecher, that I might hear the same things from his lips. My reply was: "I could not endure the pain of such an interview. These many years I have honored Mr. Beecher as a man and a minister, while differing from some of his theological and reformatory views, the effect of which I fear, and our occasional personal intercourse has been friendly ; and I could not bear to look him in the face, in the hour of his humiliation, unless positive duty required it. But here are his lifelong ministerial associates, Drs. Storrs, Budington, and others ; it is for them to deal personally with him, under such painful admissions." Then he urged me to go and talk with Mr. and Mrs. Tilton. This I also refused to do, as I did not wish to be implicated in any manner with Mr. Tilton, and wanted to be able to say that I had never exchanged a word with him on this subject, my faith in him not being particularly strong. Nor did I alter my purpose, when a few days later Mrs. Carpenter communicated to me a request from Mrs. Tilton to call on her. Perhaps I erred in these decisions; but my heart was sad, and I had heard too much already. Had I even imagined that Mr. Beecher denied these charges to these confidential friends, I should have gone to see him ; but I would not unnecessarily humiliate him, on their invitation, to hear him confess. [I should have added here, in the copy of this statement sent to the Committee, that, at that time, Mr. Beecher had made no denial of the charges before the public, and these statements of Mr. Carpenter seemed to harmonize with that fact. W. W. P.]

While returning to Chicago I seemed gradually to discern duty. I had learned from Mr. Carpenter that the actual facts were known to quite a circle of persons, including two or three editors and several prominent clergymen. So I advised with the Rev. Dr. Bacon, of New Haven, and we agreed that nothing could be said or done at present but to await developments ; as possibly Mr. Carpenter might be mistaken in some of his assertions ; but that at some time an investigation must take place, as Plymouth Church could not afford to have such charges remain without denial or disproof. So, on reaching home, I published in the *Advance* an editorial entitled "Mistaken Silence," which made no use of the information I had privately received, but based a call for a denial by Mr. Beecher upon what had already come before the public, including Mr. Tilton's letter to a "Complaining Friend."

Having done this, I felt that my duty was discharged for the time being. But I at once communicated my private information to Henry Ward Beecher's brother William, that he might take such steps as he thought wise to ascertain the whole truth.

I will only add, that, as I made written memoranda just after my interviews with Carpenter, while everything was fresh and deeply impressed on my mind, I feel certain of the substantial correctness of this statement. But I subsequently, at different times, inquired of my brother as to the accuracy of my memory in the leading facts, and his recollection accorded exactly with mine. When I saw Mr. Carpenter, he was very cordial to Mr. Beecher, and anxious to help him through his troubles ; but, soon after, my brother wrote me that Mr. Carpenter had changed his mood, and "was denouncing Mr. Beecher as a coward and a liar ! "

This is all that now occurs to me as worthy of mention in connection with my knowledge of this sorrowful matter. If, through your Committee, God can dissipate the darkness, millions besides myself will rejoice. Yours truly,

WILLIAM W. PATTON.

CHICAGO, August 27, 1874.

THOMAS K. BEECHER ON THE BEECHER-TILTON MATTER.

The following characteristic letter, signed by Rev. Thomas K. Beecher, of Elmira, whose letter to Mrs. Hooker, published in Mr. Moulton's statement, caused so much discussion, has appeared. It runs as follows :

Rev. Thomas K. Beecher, whose letters have proved so injurious to his brother's reputation.—The "Daily Graphic," September 1.

Returning to the world from a month of quietness in the woods, I find that a confidential letter of mine, written as a sequel to a confidential and startling conversation with a much loved, but, as I think, deluded sister, has been by successive breaches of trust allowed to transpire and become public property.

The intent of this letter appears sufficiently upon the face of it. It aimed to caution and if possible dissuade my sister from a costly act of fanaticism. It was written without other knowledge of facts than what had been stated to me by her ; and by her were sincerely believed. In writing to her, therefore, to avoid controversy, the truth of her allegations was assumed, or at least not questioned. Assuming them to be true, the letter exhorted her to be faithful to her own convictions, true to her friend, but at the same time to be extremely cautious as to her conduct, based, as it seemed likely to be, upon the most untrustworthy evidence.

Since the year 1854 I have not been permitted as much as two hours in all of earnest conversation with my honored brother Henry Ward. We have been both of us too busy to find time for the visits which I at least hungered for. Nor can I recall any occasion whatever on which we discussed or even alluded to the subjects—marriage, divorce, the family, the relation of the sexes, female suffrage—or any phase whatever of these questions, delicate or dirty, which are now pushing up through the scum of general discontent and demanding attention.

Clearly, therefore, I am not now, and never have been, a witness competent to testify as to my brother's views and tendencies upon these latter-day questions.

The divergencies of view between my brother and myself, to which the letter alludes, and which have prevented a hearty co-operation between us, were of a kind which when known rebound to his credit in popular esteem, and to my disgrace—demonstrating him a wise man and me a fool. He, an enthusiastic lover of freedom ; a believer in the nobility of human nature ; a prophet of progress, purity, and happiness ; an instant and urgent anti-slavery man ; a promoter of free thought and free speech in all directions ; an ingrained and thorough-paced, hopeful, cheerful, American citizen, accepting the Declaration of Independence and a manifest destiny of glory. I, in contrast, penetrated by a mournful conviction that human nature is essentially corrupt and moribund ; and except as guided, taught, governed, and enlivened, tends to evil and disaster continually ; that of all woes freedom is the most comprehensive ; that the slave is better off than the master ; that the oppressed are better off than their oppressors ; that the cry of progress is a delusion ; that men need government, rebuke, humility; and until men are broken in spirit through prolonged despair they are not in position to receive the kingdom of Heaven as very little children, and thrive by what they receive and by what is done for them of God. He, in short, looks upon every great popular movement as a tide obeying a divine guidance, and he makes haste to go with it ; I look upon the same movement as a strong delusion of the Adversary—the Prince of this world—which shall deceive, were it possible, the very elect ; and accordingly I shrink back from it and caution all with whom I have influence against being carried away by it.

Once and only once have we, in practical affairs, worked together, and that was for the preservation of the Union, and the maintenance of constitutional government.

These divergencies of view are fundamental. They are to his credit as a popular leader, and to my costly discredit.

Of his personal truth, purity, honor, and piety, I have never had for a moment a doubt *that was based upon any trustworthy information.* Many things have been told me with such an air of truth that they have staggered me and filled me with fear and forebodings, which I suppose I have shared with thousands of the best of my fellow-men ; and with them still I acknowledge a profound relief when the man in question stands forth and denies all fault of whatever kind, save that which impeaches his sagacity and discretion only.

I learn by the *Nation* [New York], (for I have read incredibly little) that the late "trial by newspaper " of my brother results in an issue of veracity between him and Mrs. Tilton on the one side, and Mr. Tilton and Mr. Moulton on the other. This being so, I hasten to put on record most gratefully that I know of nothing whatever, past or present, that hinders me from giving to my brother the most implicit, contented, and loving credence; and to say, finally, that any use of my letter to his disadvantage is a renewal of the indiscreet, if not dishonorable acts, by which alone it became public property at the first. Respectfully yours,

THOS. K. BEECHER.

ELMIRA, September 2, 1874.

BEECHER'S SWORN DENIAL OF THE TRUTH OF TILTON'S CHARGES.

ON Monday, Sept. 7, Mr. Beecher's attorneys, Messrs. Shearman & Sterling, served upon Mr. Tilton's attorneys, Messrs. Morris & Pearsall, the following formal answer to the suit brought by Tilton. This answer contains the solemn oath of Henry Ward Beecher that Tilton's charges are untrue in every respect. Monday, Oct. 5, is the day set down for the trial. The document, which is accompanied by the needed certification from the Clerk of the Circuit Court for Grafton county, N. H., where Mr. Beecher's affidavit was made, runs as follows:

THE CITY COURT OF BROOKLYN.—Theodore Tilton, plaintiff, against Henry Ward Beecher, defendant.—Answer.

The defendant answers to the complaint:

I. That each and every allegation in the said complaint contained, (except that the plaintiff and Miss Elizabeth M. Richards were married on Oct. 2, 1855, and lived together as husband and wife up to 1874,) is utterly false.

II. That this defendant never had, at any time or at any place, any unchaste or improper relations with the wife of the plaintiff, and never attempted or sought to have any such relations.

(Signed,) SHEARMAN & STERLING,
Attorneys for Defendant.

State of New Hampshire, County of Grafton, ss.
Henry Ward Beecher being duly sworn, says:

I. That he is the defendant herein, and resides in the city of Brooklyn, Kings County, N. Y., but is temporarily residing in the Twin Mountain House, Coos County, N. H.

II. That he is sixty-one years of age, and his occupation is that of a clergyman.

III. That the foregoing answer is true of his own knowledge.

HENRY WARD BEECHER.

Sworn and subscribed before me this 20th day of August, 1874.

HARRY BINGHAM,
Justice of the Peace,

MOULTON'S VINDICATION.

DETAILED ANSWERS TO THE CHARGES OF BLACKMAIL AND BAD FAITH MADE BY MR. BEECHER.

On Friday, September 11th, the following statement was published:

To the Public:

I have waited patiently, perhaps too long, after giving to the public the exact facts and documents as they were given to me, in the statement prepared for the Committee of Investigation, of which they made no use: nor did they call upon me for any explanation, or try to test the coherence of the facts by cross-examination, which, of course, I held myself ready to undergo, after I felt myself compelled to make an *exposé* of the facts in full.

I had hoped that Mr. Beecher himself would, ere this, have made a denial of any intimation, insinuation, or averment in his statement, that I had acted in any way dishonorably towards him, or had endeavored, in the interests of Mr. Tilton, to extort or obtain by cajolery or promise, any money from him; and as such a withdrawal, in accordance with truth as Mr. Beecher knows it, would have rendered it unnecessary for me to take any further part in the controversy between the principals in this terrible affair, I trusted that I never would have felt myself called upon to make further statements which, if made, must be in the nature of accusations against him.

Failing in this hope, it seems to my friends and to myself, that as a question of veracity is so sharply raised between Mr. Beecher and me, and as there are a large number of well-meaning and confiding men and women who desire, if possible, to believe him, and, although if the case between us were to be determined only by the thinking, scrutinizing people of the country, it would not be necessary to add another word; yet, to prevent these good, religious persons from being led astray in their convictions, not only as regards Mr. Beecher, but that I may maintain the station in their minds which I feel I ought to hold as a man of honor and purity of motive and action in this disgraceful business, I propose, by the aid of documents which I hold, and the necessary narrative to make them intelligible, and by a comparison of Mr. Beecher's statements with the documents heretofore published, to show that it is impossible for his statement to the committee to be true in many very important particulars, and that the issue of truthfulness is not between his personal averments and mine, but between him and the facts themselves.

From his insinuations and inferences, if not the direct statements, feeling that my character as a man as well as my truthfulness as a witness have been impugned, I will endeavor, in the first place, to reinstate myself so far as I may by showing at how late a day he held other and entirely different opinions of me.

It will be observed that in my statement prepared for the committee I said that I refrained from producing any documents or "any papers or proposals for the settlement of this controversy since it has broken out afresh, and since the publication of Tilton's letter to Dr. Bacon and the call of Beecher for a committee," and the reason was that in making the statement before the committee, I thought it unjust to the parties to parade before the committee the mutual concessions and arrangements made by the parties whom I hoped, even at that late hour, might be saved from themselves by an adjustment of the strife.

I extract the following from Mr. Beecher's statement to the committee:

"Until the reply of Mr. Tilton to Bacon's letters, I never had a suspicion of his (Moulton's) good faith and of the sincerity with which he was dealing with me; and when that letter was published, and Mr. Moulton, on my visiting him in reference to it, proposed no counter-operation—no documents, no help—I was staggered."

If this averment were true, he was rightly "staggered," and he rightly lost faith in me; for if I failed, in his then hour of peril, to do everything that in me lay to his satisfaction to rescue him, I was not the friend that I had professed to be, or that he acknowledged me to be, and was unworthy of his confidence or the confidence of any other.

It will be observed that the letter of appointment of the Investigating Committee, of which Mr. Sage is chairman, bears date Brooklyn, June 27, 1874, which was drawn out by the publication of the letter from Tilton to the *Golden Age* on the 21st (?) of the same month.

Mr. Beecher's statement was made before the Committee on the 13th of August, wherein the accusation that I had deserted him at first appears. Now, I aver that from the time of the preparation of the Bacon letter, before the 21st of June, down to the 24th day of July, I was in almost daily consultation with Beecher and his counsel, at their request, as to the best method of meeting that publication and averting the storm that was imminent; and until the 4th of August I enjoyed his entire confidence and regard as much as I ever had so far as any expression came from him; and, instead of manifestations of distrust, he gave me, both verbally and in writing, the highest praise for my friendly intervention. I repeat one instance of his oral commendation because I can substantiate it by a witness who was present. After we had been in consultation at my house, on the 5th of July, upon this subject, I walked with him, still continuing the conference, up past Montague Terrace, where we found Mr. Jeremiah P. Robinson, my business partner, standing at his door. We stopped and spoke to him on some indifferent subject, when Beecher, putting his arm around my neck and his hand upon my shoulder, said to Mr. Robinson : "God never raised up a truer friend to a man than Frank has been to me." Mr. Robinson replied : "That is true," and we passed on.

On the 24th of July I received a letter from Mr. Beecher, asking me to return to him certain letters and papers in order to aid him in making his statement to the Committee. As previous to the 10th, when Tilton made his sworn statement, I had refused the same request from him, I did not think it right to grant that of Beecher, because it seemed to me to be taking sides in the controversy as between them, which I ought not to do; and especially, as he was about to make a statement of facts which were within his own knowledge, I did not see why he should need documents to aid him if the statement was to be a truthful one. I gave a verbal refusal to his counsel, who brought me the letter, and desired him to take the letter back to Beecher, which he declined to do. On that day I left town on imperative business and was gone until the 4th day of August, when I wrote Beecher a letter giving an answer to his request in form, stating substantially these reasons, which letter he has published, together with a reply, which was the first manifestation of unkindness of feeling I received from him.

It must be borne in mind that the point of veracity which is thus raised between us is not whether my efforts for the adjustment of this controversy were wise or well directed, but whether it is true that I made *any* efforts to aid him, or deserted him, as he asserts. Upon that point let the facts answer, which are, fortunately for me, so substantiated by documentary evidence that as to them there can be no doubt. This is exactly what I did do.

When I was first informed by Tilton that he was preparing a reply to Dr. Bacon for publication, I said to him that I hoped he would do no such thing, as it would lead to an exposure of all the facts. He said, in substance, that Dr. Bacon being a leading Congregationalist of New England, his statement would seriously damage him there, if not refuted, in his character as a public man, and that he must reply or be deemed the "dog and knave" that the Doctor had characterized him, and be forever held to be simply a "creature of Beecher's magnanimity ;" that he had given to Beecher, as I knew myself from being present at the time, an opportunity to repair the mischief which Bacon had done him, asking Beecher merely to write a letter to Bacon making it clear that he (Tilton) was not the creature of Beecher's magnanimity. I said to him : "Do you remember that Beecher pleaded the embarrassments of his situation, which hindered him from doing such a thing as that without in reality making a confession ?" Tilton replied : "Beecher has acted in this matter simply with reference to saving himself, and thus leaves nothing for me but my own vindication by myself."

While the Bacon letter was being prepared I did not see it, but after it was written I thought it was but just to all the interests for which I was caring that I should see its contents, and therefore accepted an invitation from Tilton to hear it read. I again objected with great vehemence and warmth to its publication in the presence of witnesses—one of whom was Mr. Frank Carpenter, who, as his friend, had been brought by Tilton into the case without my intervention. After considerable discussion, finding it impossible to control its publication, I then sought to alter the phraseology of the inculpating portion of it in such a manner as would still leave opportunity for such a reply from Beecher as might satisfy Tilton and would prevent the disclosure of Mr. Beecher's acts. To all my arguments and urgings, Tilton replied that he would not hold me responsible at all for the consequences ; that he accepted them all for himself alone, and that he could not take my advice upon this subject, since Beecher and his friends had chosen to disregard my counsel by continuing their attacks upon him. After much persuasion I induced him to strike out the words in the letter as originally written—"Mr. Beecher has committed against me and my family a revolting crime"—and instead thereof to insert the words: "has committed against *me* an offence which I forbear to name or characterize ;" thus omitting the word "family," and substituting a softer word, "offence," susceptible of various interpretations, instead of "revolting crime" against the family, which might have been regarded as capable of only one. When thus modified even, I told Tilton that I would rather give him, from my own pocket, five thousand dollars in gold than to have him publish it.

During the time of the composition of the paper, while my importunities with Tilton were going on, I had frequent consultations with Beecher in regard to the letter, in which I told him that I should do everything in my power to prevent its publication, which I most assuredly did, as more than one person can testify. He understood as fully from me as I had from Tilton that he (Tilton) might be goaded in self-defense to expose Beecher for misbehavior toward his family. The evening that I caused the change in the phraseology above stated was the first time I had heard it read, and was a day or two before its publication; and afterwards, on the day it went to press, and before I knew that it had gone, at the office of the *Golden Age,* I again urged Tilton, with every power of persuasion that I had, not to publish it, and suggested certain other changes which would render Beecher's course in regard to it less difficult.

Immediately after the publication I sent for General Tracy, Mr. Beecher's counsel, to come to my house in the evening, where I read him the letter, and he was much incensed at its contents. I called his attention to the change in the phraseology that I had procured from Tilton, and tried to show him that this letter, bad as it was, would, if properly met, be the means of arriving at a final settlement and peace between the parties and safety for the families, for which purpose I had made a written analysis of the letter, in order to show how I thought the parties might be reconciled. I showed him that it did not charge a crime, but an offence, for which it quoted an apology, and that Tilton in the letter itself stated that a settlement had once been brought about between him and Beecher upon the basis of that apology. which he deemed an honorable one, and which would have been observed but for the attacks upon him of Beecher and his friends, and the speech of Bacon to the students of Yale, and the articles in the *Independent,* which speech and articles Tilton had already given Beecher an opportunity to qualify so far as they related to him (Tilton).

At first Mr. Tracy did not accept this view of the case, but came to me a short time afterwards and said that, after thinking over my remarks and plans, he "had become converted to my view of the case." The question then was as to the best course for Beecher to take in relation to the letter; and upon this matter I consulted with Tracy, and he agreed with me that we should undertake to settle the controversy upon the basis of an "offence."

A few days after the publication of the letter, I met Tilton in company with three of his friends, when I again strongly represented the mistake which in my judgment he had made, especially towards himself, by the publication; and told him that he owed it to himself, his family, and his friends, and to me in an especial degree, as well as all other interests involved, to help me to find a way still to suppress all further publication, and to bring peace and reconciliation between himself and Beecher. He said, in the presence of a witness, that he would say nothing more, and be satisfied if Beecher made no reply to the letter, and that he would not, publicly or privately, insist upon a reply; and after discussing the policy of silence or a reply by Mr. Beecher, I dictated to the party then present the following, which I said I would advise that Beecher should say in substance in his lecture-room to his church as a reply to the letter, or, if not, that he should be silent, with either of which courses Tilton had already expressed himself satisfied. The paper is marked "A."

MOULTON'S PROPOSED STATEMENT FOR BEECHER.

"This church and community are unquestionably and justly interested through the recent publication by Theodore Tilton in answer to Dr. Leonard Bacon, of New Haven.

"It is true that I have committed an offence against Theodore Tilton, and, giving to that offence the force of his construction, I made an apology and reparation, such as both he and I at the time declared full and necessary. I am convinced that Mr. Tilton has been goaded to his defence by misrepresentations, or misunderstanding of my position towards him. I shall never be a party to the reopening of this question, which has been honorably settled as between Theodore Tilton and myself. I have committed no crime; and if this society believes that it is due to it that I should reopen this already too painful subject, or resign, I will resign. I know, as God gives me the power to judge of myself, that I am better fitted to-day, through trials and chastening, to do good, than I have ever been."

This paper I now have, in the handwriting of the gentleman who took it down at the time, and who can testify to the accuracy of this statement. Upon hearing it read Tilton pledged himself to peace and final settlement, if Beecher would either speak or write the substance of the words above quoted or keep silent.

Within a day or two—I think, the next day—I saw Beecher at my own house, and in the presence of a witness had a consultation in reference to the Bacon letter, and discussed the best way of meeting that letter. We first considered the policy of entire silence; next, what was best to say in case anything was said; and, at his request, I gave him a copy of the paper above set forth. He said he would like to submit it to a few of his friends, saying at the same time: "I will copy it in my own handwriting, and not give it as yours." It was fully agreed there that he would make no reply or take any steps in relation to the Bacon letter without consulting me, and that he would either keep silence or make a statement substantially like that which I had given him, as Tilton had told me in the presence of witnesses that he was committed to peace if Beecher should take either of those courses.

I saw Tracy, and asked him if Beecher had submitted to him any paper with reference to the Bacon letter. He said that Beecher had shown him a memorandum which looked like my handiwork. I asked him what he thought of it. He answered that he approved of it in the main, but made objection to the words "I have committed no crime," saying that as adultery was no crime at common law there would be an opportunity for criticism upon that word as not being a sufficient denial. He suggested another doubt as to the propriety of the proposed action, because he did not know whether Tilton would keep faith or not. I replied that I thought he had already made a mistake in assuming everything against Tilton, and that if he should treat him with trust and confidence he would get trust and confidence in return. "But," I said, "Mr. Tracy, the trouble with you and the parties you represent is that you expect everything from Tilton, and are willing to do nothing yourselves that requires courage and confidence." He said he had had a talk a short time previous with Tilton, who had spoken, in his opinion, like an insane man, because he replied to his remark that the world would never forgive him for having condoned his wife's offense by saying : "I take a higher view than you or the world do upon this question, and I don't believe that I am to blame for having condoned my wife's offence, or that it will help the man who has committed the crime against my family to plead that I have." I said to Tracy that I thought he was acting more foolishly than Tilton in assuming, from such a remark as that, Tilton's insanity. I said : "You will get yourself and the people you represent into trouble by just such statements, which only tend to incense ; they do not tend to peace." Tracy said that he did not believe that Tilton ever intended peace. I replied : "There you make a mistake again, for I never yet have failed in any emergency, so far as I know, to get Tilton to acquiesce in what was fair to save all parties, except in the matter of the Bacon letter, and if you now go upon the assumption that he is a reasonable being, and as magnanimous as any of the other parties involved, you can have peace, and if you do not the responsibility must be upon yourselves." He spoke in this conversation of Tilton's great ability, and remarked that Tilton impressed him more and more strongly as a man actuated by high purposes. "But," said he, "he lacks balance." We parted, agreeing to confer further upon this topic.

On Sunday afternoon, July 5, after church services, I met Mr. Beecher walking with his wife in the street. He left her at Mr. Howard's, and went with me to my house. I expected, if he said anything, that he would have taken the opportunity of Sunday to make the statement to his people of his course which I had prepared with reference to the Bacon letter, but had learned that he had not so done. After we reached my house, I said to him, "Well, Mr. Beecher, you did not speak from your pulpit the words we talked over. I wish you had, because the great sympathy manifested for you in this community would have made such words acceptable." "Well," said he, "you know we agreed upon silence, and you are responsible if I have made any mistake in not speaking." "Very well," said I. "I adhere still to the policy of silence as best ; but if you say anything through the pressure that is brought to bear upon you, in my judgment what I wrote out is best, as Tilton has committed himself to a settlement if that is said ; and if it is said, and he demands anything further, so far as I am concerned, I shall destroy every paper and everything I have bearing upon the subject; and if he wants to open the fight he will have to open it without any aid or confirmation from me." Mrs. Moulton was present, and Mr. Beecher asked her opinion of what I had written for him to say, and she told him that it was the only hope she had ever seen for a settlement, aside from a frank and manly confession on his part of his sin, and asking man's forgiveness for it as he expected God's. He said to her that he would consider it, but that I was responsible for his having kept silence.

We then went together towards Mr. Howard's house, he going to find Mrs. Beecher, whom he had left there to continue his walk, and while going there we met Mr. Robinson, when the conversation took place that I have before related. Perhaps I should have added that the reason why he made the remark he did to Mr. Robinson was because I had almost at the beginning of the affair told Mr. Robinson of all the facts concerning Beecher as I knew them and have now made them public, and had received from him valuable advice as to my conduct in regard to them, all of which I had communicated before that time to Mr. Beecher.

As we walked on together, in the course of further conversation, Beecher for the first time told me that he had acquiesced in the appointment of a Committee of Investigation, at which I expressed considerable surprise, and told him I thought it was a mistake, but we would try to get along even with that. He said he had had the naming of the committee himself, and gave me the names of most of them. I said : "I hope Shearman will have nothing to do with this committee." He replied : "We have purposely left him out because we do not want any element in it that will cause trouble." I said : "If this matter is to go before a Committee of Investigation I think I shall employ General Butler as my counsel to advise me in this matter. As you know, he was my counsel in another case, and I think well of his efforts in my behalf. Beecher appeared pleased at my suggestion. I may as well remark here, once for all, that I did not send for General Butler as counsel until after Tilton's sworn statement was prepared, and he arrived on the day it was delivered to the committee by Tilton, as will appear hereafter. As General Butler's name has been connected more or less with the progress of this case, I may as well state that from the time he came into the case he has labored unceasingly to prevent any disclosure or publication of the facts. He has done everything he possibly could, both in advising me and acting with the other parties to the controversy, to avert the consequences of the exposure which has been made. In every phase the affair has taken, his counsel to me has always been that I should try and have the difficulty reconciled, and that I should hold myself entirely impartial between the parties, acting as a friend to each ; which advice I have endeavored to follow, and have only been driven from that position by circumstances which are too well known. I will further say that I never sent for him or counselled with him, except at the solicitation of the counsel for Mr. Beecher, until after Mr. Beecher's letter of August 4, when he demanded of me his papers and letters.

It seemed to me necessary to have counsel, as many of the documents and papers were of a nature to implicate others, and it became important to know how far I might be liable for the use of their contents.

Mrs. Tilton made her first statement before the Committee on the evening of July 8, without the knowledge of her husband, as both he and she say, and because of which she says, " He asked who the gentlemen were; said no more, rose, dressed himself, and bade her good-bye forever." The next day, July 9, I saw General Tracy, and we consulted as to how Tilton should act, and as to what he ought to say with reference to the denial of his wife before the Committee of adultery on Beecher's part. I made an appointment with Tracy and Tilton to meet at my house that evening on this subject. Mr. Tracy told me that Mrs. Tilton had made a very fine impression upon the Committee. I told him that he must convey, with great impressiveness, to Tilton this fact, and of the kindness with which she had spoken of her husband. I warned Tracy that Tilton might be quite severe in his characterization of his conduct, because he had allowed Mrs. Tilton's statement to be taken by the Committee without his (Tilton's) knowledge, and called to his mind something that had happened in November, 1872, in regard to revelations that Tilton had made to him in confidence as to the Woodhull story, when Mr. Woodruff and myself were present, Tilton prefacing them with the statement : " You are to receive certain confidences; but if you do, will you feel yourself at liberty to act as the counsel of Beecher if we ever come into collision ?" to which you replied, " Certainly not." I said; " Mr. Tracy, Tilton thinks now your being counsel for Beecher is a violation of the promise, and will undoubtedly use severe language in regard to it. But since the interests you have at heart and we are now in charge of are so grave, you had better endeavor to conciliate him and not return his denunciations if he indulges in them. Appeal as strongly as you can to the great love I know he still retains for his wife, and try to rouse the pride which he has in her and his family."

Mr. Tracy came to the interview, as I had arranged, and met as I had expected the denunciations of Mr. Tilton, but received them with great forbearance, and then, with strength and pathos of language, with tears flowing down his cheeks, he made so eloquent and manly an appeal to Tilton, picturing with great force his wife's tenderness and gentleness and apparent truthfulness before the committee, and her high eulogy of her husband, that Tilton was greatly moved and pacified therewith, and seemed desirous for reconciliation and renewed peace for his wife's sake. Tracy said to him also that as the committee, to his knowledge, felt that there was an offence committed by Beecher against him, they would undoubtedly make any report that he (Tilton) could suggest upon the basis of almost any offence this side of adultery—indeed, that he could quite guarantee they would.

In consequence of the assurances in this conversation, Tilton, who, as he informed us, had left his home never intending to go back to it, did go back, as he afterwards told me, and there had a reconcilation with his wife, which is thus described in the statement of Mrs. Tilton to the committee:

" The midnight following I was awakened by my husband standing by my bed. In a very tender, kind voice he said he wished to see me. I arose instantly, followed him to his room, and sitting on the bed-side he drew me into his lap, said he was proud of me, loved me ; that nothing ever gave him such real peace and satisfaction as to hear me well spoken of; that, meeting a member of the committee, he had learned that he had been mistaken as to my motive in seeing the committee, and had hastened to assure me that he had been thoroughly wretched since his rash treatment of me the night before. &c.

" Then and there we covenanted sacredly our hearts and lives—I most utterly, renewing my trust in the one human heart I loved. The next day how happy we were ! "

When Tilton left my house that night he said that he would go home, and with Elizabeth, agree upon a report to be made by the Committee which would be satisfactory to them. This fact is confirmed by Mrs. Tilton in her statement as follows:

" Theodore wrote a statement to present to the Committee when they should call upon him, to all of which I heartily acceded."

Mrs. Tilton evidently did not understand that the report was one to be made by the Committee, but to the Committee by Tilton. He returned the next day with such a report which he had copied out as follows, and which is marked B :

" The undersigned, constituting the Committee of Plymouth Church, to whom were referred certain recent publications of Dr. Leonard Bacon and Mr. Theodore Tilton, hereby present their unanimous report.
" The Committee sought and obtained a personal interview with each of the three following-named persons, to wit: Mr. Tilton, Mrs. Tilton, and the pastor, all of whom responded to the searching questions of the committee with freedom and candor. Documents, letters, and papers pertaining to the case were carefully considered. A multiplicity of details, needing to be duly weighed, occasioned a somewhat protracted investigation. The committee hope that the apparent tardiness of their report

will be compensated to the parties by rectifying an erroneous public sentiment under which they have all suffered misrepresentation.

"I. The Committee's first interview was with Mrs. Elizabeth R. Tilton, whose testimony was given with a modesty and touching sincerity that deeply moved those who listened to it. Her straightforward narrative was an unconscious vindication of her innocence and purity of character, and confirmed by evidences in the documents. She repelled with warm feeling the idea that her husband was the author of calumnious statements against her, or had ever treated her with other than chivalrous consideration and protection. She paid a high tribute to his character, and also to the fortitude with which he had borne prolonged injustice.

"II. The Committee further find that Mr. Tilton, in his relations with the pastor, had a just cause of offence, and had received a voluntary apology. Mr. Tilton declined to characterize the offence for the following reasons: First, because the necessary evidence which should accompany any statement would include the names of persons who had happily escaped thus far the tongue of public gossip; next, that the apology was designed to cover a complicated transaction, its details difficult of exact or just statement; and last, that no possible good could arise from satisfying the public curiosity on this point. Mr. Tilton, after concluding his testimony, respectfully called the attention of the Committee to the fact that the clerk of the church had spoken calumniously of Mrs. Tilton during the late council, and had since unqualifiedly contradicted and retracted his statements as untrue and unjust, and he (Mr. T.) requested the Committee to ratify and confirm that apology, making honorable record of the same in their report, which is hereby cheerfully done.

"III. The Committee further find that the Rev. Henry Ward Beecher's evidence corroborated the statements of Mr. and Mrs. Tilton. He also said the church action of which Mr. Tilton had complained had not been inspired by the pastor, but had been taken independently by the church; that the popular impression that Mr. Tilton had been in the habit of speaking against him was unjust to Mr. T., and was owing mainly to the unwelcome introduction into the church of charges against Mr. T. by a mere handful of persons, who, in so doing, had received no countenance from the great mass of the congregation or from the pastor. He said that the apology had been invested by the public press with an undue mystery; that after having been led by his own precipitancy and folly into wrong he saw no singularity of behavior in a Christian man (particularly a clergyman) acknowledging his offence. He had always preached this doctrine to others, and would not shrink from applying it to himself.

"The Committee after hearing the three witnesses already referred to, felt unanimously that any regrets previously entertained concerning the publication of Mr. Tilton's letter to Dr. Bacon should give way to grateful acknowledgments of the providential opportunity which this publication has unexpectedly afforded, to draw forth the testimony which the committee have thus reported in brief, but in sufficient fullness, as they believe, to explain and put at rest forever a vexatious scandal. The committee are likewise of opinion, based on the testimony submitted to them, that no unprejudiced court of inquiry could have reviewed this case as thus presented in person by its principal figures without being strikingly impressed with the moral integrity and elevation of character of the parties; and accordingly the committee cannot forbear to state that the Rev. Henry Ward Beecher, Mr. Theodore Tilton, and Mrs. Tilton (and in an especial manner the latter), must and should receive the increased sympathy and respect of Plymouth Church and congregation.

(Signed)"

Meantime Beecher had been engaged in preparing his own statement for the Committee, and had the night before come down from Peekskill for that purpose and also to attend the Friday evening prayer-meeting the next day, and I suppose had not learned what had been done. Very early Friday morning I received the following note, which I here insert marked "C:"

BEECHER TO MOULTON.

"FRIDAY MORNING, July 10, '74.

"MY DEAR FRANK: Can you be seen this morning? and, if so, when and where? Any time after ten would suit me best, but any *other* hour I will make do. I came into town last night.

"Yours ever, H. W. BEECHER."

I replied to him in substance—for I have not a copy—having been up very late the night before—indeed, I believe I was still in bed when I received it—that I was quite tired, and would have to be busy, expecting to meet Tracy and Tilton again that day before Tilton should go before the committee in the evening. In response to my reply I received from Beecher the following reply marked "D:"

BEECHER TO MOULTON.

"MY DEAR FRANK; My papers are all here, and it would be far more convenient to have you here if you are not too tired. Yours, H. W. BEECHER."

In reply to this I informed Mr. Beecher that I was to meet Tilton at my house, that I would be in consultation with him, and advised him to come there and meet him also, as I hoped matters were in process of adjustment, and received from him on the same day the following note, marked "E:"

BEECHER TO MOULTON.

"MY DEAR FRANK.—I do not know as it is necessary to trouble you. I only wanted to read you the heads and outline of a statement. When I do speak I intend to be believed. Of course, I shall not publish until I have seen you. But time is short. The crisis is at hand. I will not go forward long as heretofore. When I say will not, I mean cannot. Events are masters, just now.

"There is no earthly reason for conference with Mr. T. It makes nothing better; everything worse. The matter is in a nutshell. No light is needed, only choice. Yours gratefully.

"July 10, '74. "H. W. BEECHER."

I frankly confess that I felt hurt at this note, because I believed that I had been acting for the best in his behalf, and that matters were in process of adjustment. It seemed to me to be another cry of despair on his part, whereas I believed instead that he should have conferred with Tilton as his counsel had done.

During the day of the 10th, Tilton's report, drafted for the Committee above quoted, was submitted to Mr. Tracy, who said that with a few alterations that were not material, he thought he could have it adopted by the Committee.

On the evening of the same day—the 10th of July—in response to the invitation of the Committee, and in pursuance of the policy that had been marked out in our conferences with General Tracy, Tilton appeared before the Committee and made a brief statement. Neither Tilton nor myself knew at that time what were the terms of the commission of the Committee, or what were to be the extent and purpose of their inquiry, but both supposed that its purpose was to endeavor to settle the trouble between Beecher and Tilton, and not for the purpose of a full investigation of all the facts. This idea I had got from Mr. Beecher in the conversation which I have before related; and I had therefore supposed, as I stated to him, that I thought we could get along with the Committee.

The first statement of Tilton before the Committee not having been made public, I cannot know its terms, but he reported to me the substance of it as I find it made by him in his preface to his sworn statement of July 20, to the same committee; and as he was addressing the same individuals as to the facts which had taken place before them, I assume it to be a true statement. It is as follows:

"I call you to witness that on my first brief examination before your Committee I begged and implored you not to inquire into the facts of this case, but rather seek to bury them beyond all possible revelation."

On the morning of the next day, the 11th, a new and double complication arose. It consisted first of the sudden and unexpected announcement by Mrs. Tilton to her husband at six o'clock A. M., that she meant to desert her home and family, and in a few moments afterwards she carried this intention into effect by going to make her abode with Mr. and Mrs. Ovington; next, by the simultaneous publication, in that morning's newspapers, of the letter of appointment of the Committee by Beecher, dated the 27th of June previous, but which letter had been kept back and not sent to the church until Tuesday, July 7. That letter called to have "some proper investigation made of the rumors, insinuations, or charges made respecting my conduct as compromised by the late publication made by Mr. Tilton. * * * * * I desire that when you have satisfied yourselves by an impartial and thorough examination of all sources of evidence, to communicate to the Examining Committee or to the church such action as may seem to you right and wise."

On the same day Tilton came to see me, and announcing to me his wife's desertion and calling my attention to the above publication, was excited by these simultaneous events, which seemed to him to be part of a prearranged plan of action, and also excited him to great indignation. He said that Beecher was again playing him a trick, as he had done before when he attempted to settle the matter, by now appointing a committee to make examination of the facts, then getting his wife surreptitiously to go before the committee and exonerate him fully from the charges of adultery, then tempting her openly to desert her husband, so as to show that he, Tilton, had always been in the wrong, and was simply the creature of his magnanimity; and that now Beecher should have a full statement of all the facts and documents if it destroyed him, his wife, or his family; that justice should be done at length and the truth be known; that if Plymouth Church chose to accept an adulterer for its pastor they should have the opportunity to do it; and that he was going home to prepare his full statement, and wanted me to give him the documents and evidence with which to do it. Upon my refusing to do so, he said that I was a traitor to him, because I had gone into this controversy in the beginning as his friend. I tried to pacify him; said everything I could to quiet him, assuring him that although we had been mistaken as to the purpose of the Committee, yet, as Beecher had named them all, he had done so in his own interest and would be surely able to control them. He said that Beecher, by the terms of his letter of appointment, had challenged him before the world, and he accepted the challenge. I told him that I saw nothing in the letter which prevented him from standing upon the terms of the Bacon letter that an offence only had been committed. But he said that this was simply folly on my part—indeed, called me a fool for so believing, and said: "If you choose to desert me in this emergency of my life, I will stand by myself and fight it alone." I appealed again to him for his children's sake, saying: "I cannot be in sympathy with any course of yours that will simply blast them and ruin your household and yourself." But he was obdurate, and left me, reiterating his determination to make a full statement of the facts. Indeed, I had never seen a man so much changed as he had been in a few hours. In reference to this change in Tilton I quote the following from Mrs. Tilton's statement:

"I rose quietly, and having dressed, roused him only to say, 'Theodore, I will never take another step by your side. The end has indeed come!' He followed me to Mr. Ovington's to breakfast, saying I was unduly excited, and that he had been misrepresented, perhaps, but leaving me determined as before. How to account for the change which twenty-four hours had been capable of working in his mind than many years past, I leave for the eternities with their mysteries to reveal."

The causes of the change had, indeed, been revealed to me in a much shorter time.

I did not call upon Mr. Beecher upon this matter because I believed he was in sufficient trouble already, and I was devoting all my energies to keep Tilton within the bounds of reason as to his own course.

On the same day—the 11th—I received an invitation from the Committee to appear before them on the 13th, which is as follows, marked " F : "

SAGE TO MOULTON.

"BROOKLYN, July 11, 1874.

" *Francis D. Moulton, Esq.:—*

"DEAR SIR:—The Examining Committee of Plymouth Church (at the request of Mr. Beecher) have appointed the following gentlemen—viz: From the church—Henry W. Sage, Augustus Storrs, Henry M. Cleveland ; from the society—Horace B. Claflin, John Winslow, S. V. White—a committee to investigate, in the interest of truth and justice, certain charges made by Theodore Tilton in his recent letter to Rev. Leonard Bacon, which compromise the character of Rev. Henry Ward Beecher. The committee are informed that you have some knowledge of matters involved in the case, and instruct me respectfully to invite you to appear before them on Monday evening next, July 13, at eight o'clock, at the residence of Augustus Storrs, Esq., 34 Monroe place, and furnish them with such facts as are within your own knowledge in the matters under investigation. Very truly yours,

"H. W. SAGE, Chairman."

It will be observed that the Committee only desired that I should "furnish them such facts as were within my own knowledge in the matter under investigation." The curious phraseology of this requirement would be quite patent to any one, as the Committee could hardly suppose that I had been called in to be a personal witness of any intimacies, guilty or innocent, between Beecher and Mrs. Tilton, and my statement, if so confined, would have been necessarily very short; and I might well suppose that the invitation was so worded in order that I might make no disclosure.

On my return to my house on Monday afternoon, at ten minutes to six o'clock, I received the following note from Mr. Beecher, marked " G: "

BEECHER TO MOULTON.

"MONDAY, 5 P.M.

"MY DEAR MOULTON: Will it be convenient for you to call around here any time this evening after half-past six ? I shall be in, and can be secure from interruption. I need to see you. Truly yours, and ever,

"H. W. BEECHER."

To which I immediately replied in a note as follows, marked " H: "

MOULTON TO BEECHER.

"MONDAY, 5:50 P.M.

"MY DEAR SIR : I shall be at home until 7:15 P.M. I am almost tired, or would go to you. There will be no interruption here. Truly yours,

"FRANCIS D. MOULTON.

"Your last note grieved me. I have an invitation to appear before your Committee this evening."

In reply to which I received the note heretofore published in my former statement, marked " JJJ," which is as follows :

"JULY 13, 1874.

"MY DEAR FRANK : I will be with you at seven or a little before. I am ashamed to put a straw more upon you, and have but a single consolation—that the matter cannot *distress* you long, as it must soon end: that is, there will be no more anxiety about the future, whatever regrets there may be about the past. Truly yours, and ever,

"H. W. BEECHER."

In pursuance of this note Mr. Beecher called on me and I read him the statement which I was to make to the Committee that same evening, and he approved of its tone and character, and declared it, as I therein stated, honorable to both parties so far as I was concerned. I had also read the same to Tilton, and he agreed in the same opinion as to the propriety of its tone. What I did say has already been published, and contains, in the closing part, the advice to the Committee which I had before given to Beecher, which was as follows :

"I hold now, as I have held hitherto, the opinion that Mr. Beecher should frankly state that he had committed an offence against Mr. Tilton, for which it was necessary to apologize, and for which he did apologize, in the language of the letter a part of which has been quoted ; that he should have stated frankly that he deemed it necessary for Mr. Tilton to have made the defence against Dr. Leonard Bacon which he did make, and that he (Beecher) should refuse to be a party to the reopening of this painful subject. If he had made this statement he would have stated no more than the truth, and it would have saved him and you the responsibility of a further inquiry. It is better now that the Committee should not report, and in the place of a report Mr. Beecher himself should make the statement which I have suggested ; or that, if the Committee does report, the report should be a recommendation to Mr. Beecher to make such a statement."

The interview was somewhat hurried, as I left him to go to the Committee.

Seeing in some newspaper a supposed interview of a committeeman, who claimed to speak for Beecher, in which was reported Beecher's opinion of what I had said before the Committee, I called upon him (Beecher) in reference to that and other business, and after the usual kindly salutations I told him that I thought his committeemen were acting very foolishly in attempting to throw slurs or imputations upon me, and recited the facts, as I felt certain that he did not authorize or countenance the report. He told me that he had not seen the paper at all, and knew nothing about it. We then commenced a discussion of the situation, and I spoke of the fact that Tilton was preparing a statement, at which he expressed regret and sorrow. I told him Tilton had deemed the publication of the correspondence as to the appointment of the Committee a challenge to him to come forward and make a full statement of all the facts; and that he regarded the act of his wife leaving his house a hostile one, prompted by the Committee under the inspiration of Beecher. He said—as had already been published by an interviewer—that he had not authorized the publication of the letter of appointment at all; that he had intended to keep things quiet in accordance with my suggestion; but that now he thought he was compelled to make a statement, which statement he read to me, and which, while it took very much blame upon himself as to his course towards Tilton and his family, of course denied all guilt, but which thoroughly exonerated Tilton from any dishonorable act towards him. I expressed myself to Beecher, as I was, very much pleased with this statement, and said that if it was made to the Committee before Tilton should make his, as Beecher informed me he intended to do, I had no doubt that I could prevail upon Tilton to agree to the statement proposed and to allow the whole matter to drop; and as evidence of his disposition to do so, I showed Beecher a report which Tilton had once consented might be made by the Committee, provided Beecher's statement exonerated him (Tilton) from any dishonorable act. This report was in Tilton's handwriting, a copy of which I showed Beecher, and is marked "I:"

PROPOSED REPORT OF COMMITTEE BY TILTON.

"The Committee appointed to inquire into the offense and apology by Mr. Beecher, alluded to in Mr. Tilton's letter to Dr. Bacon, respectfully report that upon examination they find that an offence of grave character was committed by Mr. Beecher against Mr. and Mrs. Theodore Tilton, for which he made a suitable apology to both parties, receiving in return their forgiveness and good-will. The Committee further report that this seems to them a most eminently Christian way for the settlement of differences, and reflects honor on all the parties concerned."

Said Beecher: "Will Tilton agree to that?" I answered: "He would have agreed to that, and I hope he will continue in that mind; for although he is writing his statement, yet I am dealing with him as I have dealt heretofore, allowing him to exhaust himself in writing out the statement and then using my influence to suppress the publication, and I have no doubt I can do it again."

The conversation then turned as to what reply Tilton ought to make to Beecher's statement, which he had first read to me, if it were accepted by the Committee. Thereupon, Beecher stepped to his desk, and wrote out the following for me to take to Tilton as the substance of what he should say in reply to Beecher's statement, and I was to use my very best exertions and all the influence I could over Tilton to have him agree to it. That paper, every word of which was written by Mr. Beecher, so that there is no opportunity for mistaking its language, I have in my possession. It is marked "J."

BEECHER'S PROPOSED STATEMENT FOR TILTON TO MAKE.

"The statement of Mr. Beecher being read, and if striking favorably, then a word sent, substantially, thus, to Committee:

"I have been three years acting under conviction that I had been wronged, but was under the imputation of being the injurer. I learn from a friend that Mr. B. in his statement to you has reversed this and has done me justice. I am willing, should he consent, to appear before you with him, and dropping the further statements, which I felt it to be my duty to make for my own clearance, to settle this painful domestic difficulty—which never ought to have been made public—finally and amicably."

I left Mr. Beecher with this proposed statement for Tilton in my hand, went to Tilton, tried to persuade him not to publish, not to make his statement to the Committee on the evening of the 20th, at which time they had summoned him, but found him exceedingly obdurate, and busy in preparing his statement. He again asked me for documents and papers, which I refused, and I then left him.

Several publications were made about this time as to what was to be the nature of Tilton's statement, which caused great anxiety to Mr. Tracy and myself, who had consultations on this matter. Accordingly, on Sunday, the 19th, I received the following note from Mr. Tracy to meet me, evidently written in consultation with Beecher, because the note-paper bears precisely the same water-mark and is of the same texture as that of the notes which I had just previously received from Mr. Beecher from his house. It is here inserted, marked "K."

TRACY TO MOULTON.

"BROOKLYN, July 19, 1874.

" *F. D. Moulton.*
"MY DEAR SIR: Will you name a time and place to-day where I can see you. I think it important.
"Yours truly,
B. F. TRACY."

We met, and it was there determined between us, upon my suggestion, that I should make one more attempt to prevent Tilton making his statement to the Committee. Previous to the reception of this note, at Tracy's suggestion, I had summoned my counsel by telegraph to meet me in New York on Monday, the 20th. At the meeting on Sunday I found Tracy impressed with the idea that the documents relating to this affair had been destroyed, and that Tilton could not verify by the originals any statements from them. I answered him that that was not the case; that all the documents were in my hands, with the single exception of Mrs. Tilton's confession, which had been returned to Tilton and destroyed, as Beecher knew; and that I should feel myself obliged to produce them before any tribunal which would compel testimony.

On the morning of the 20th, by arrangement with Tracy, I went with my counsel to Tilton's house, and there we both strenuously and urgently argued with him against the making of his statement to the Committee that evening. We represented to him that such a statement would be ruin to himself, his family, and to Beecher, and that it was not for the interest of either, or of the community, that so great a calamity should happen as the exposure of all these facts. Tilton reiterated that he had been challenged by Beecher; that he had given his word to the Committee that he would appear, and that if they were there he would do so, and that if he should refuse to appear Beecher's advisers would insist that he had no facts and was afraid to appear. It was then suggested to him that if the Committee did not meet that evening and he held himself in readiness to appear before them, that would be a sufficient answer to any such charge, and he was again persistently urged to take that course if a meeting of the Committee could be prevented. Tilton exhibited great reluctance even to that, whereupon I felt obliged to tell him that I should consider this course in thus presenting the matter against Beecher a personal affront to myself, and that in such case I should take all the means in my power to prevent his statement being effectual. To this appeal, put to him in the strongest language I could command, Tilton finally consented, first, that if the Committee were not present, so that he might be excused from appearing before them that evening, he would not publish his statement, or let its contents be known until a future meeting of the Committee, when I suggested to him the course that had been agreed upon by Beecher, and the statement which had been prepared by Beecher might be submitted to the Committee, and an amicable report made.

After getting Tilton's consent I drove around to Mr. Tracy's house, took him into the carriage, and we drove to my house together, with my counsel. When we arrived there we narrated to Mr. Tracy what had taken place at Tilton's, and he (Tracy), agreeing that this course was best, undertook to get an adjournment of the Committee till Wednesday evening, and suggested that it might be difficult to find them before the meeting, in which case it was understood that he himself would not be present on that evening. I undertook to see Tilton and have him agree that if Tracy should not be present he would refuse to go on until a subsequent meeting, on the ground that he desired Tracy to be there to cross-examine him after he had made his statement.

Mr. Tracy left my house for that purpose, and soon after returned and reported that he had called upon the Chairman and left him a formal note, saying that he could not be present at the meeting of the Committee and requesting the adjournment; that he had been to see another member of the Committee, Mr. Cleveland, but failed to find him. He then left, saying that even if the Committee held a meeting he would not be present.

I then saw Tilton, stated the difficulties about getting an adjournment of the Committee, and asked his acquiescence in the arrangement not to deliver his statement to the Committee if Tracy was not there. I made efforts to detain him at dinner until after eight o'clock, in order that the Committee might adjourn before he came. He left my house after eight o'clock, and, not soon returning, in about an hour after I sent a messenger to the Committee to learn what was being done, who returned with the word, to the unspeakable grief and surprise of myself and my counsel—who had co-operated with me in the interest of Mr. Beecher, as I had requested him—that Tilton was reading his statement to the Committee! Almost in despair, but with a last lingering hope of preventing the public exposure of this unspeakably pernicious scandal, and to make one last effort, I went down to the house of the Committee and waited the coming out of Tilton, and conjured him not to give any copy of his statement for publication, hoping that the Committee would see, as I did, that the necessities of the welfare of the whole community required that it should not be made public; and I got him to consent so to do; and on the next day I was present when he refused the request of a personal friend to allow it to be published in the *Herald*. The manner of its publication has been explained in the card of Mr. Maverick, a publication made without Mr. Tilton's consent or knowledge, and to the indescribable grief of both of us.

After the publication I saw nothing but strife and wretchedness, and nothing was left for me to do but to hold myself sternly aloof and allow the parties to fight it out without the aid of any documents or knowledge in my possession.

On the 24th of July I received a note from Beecher by the hand of Tracy, written on the same cross-lined, water-marked paper as the note of Mr. Beecher of the 19th of July, requesting that I would send him the papers and documents in my possession, which note is inserted, marked "L:"

BEECHER TO MOULTON.

" July 24, 1874.

— "MY DEAR MR. MOULTON: I am making out a statement, and need the letters and papers in your hands. Will you send by Tracy all the originals of my papers. Let them be numbered and an inventory taken, and I will return them to you as soon as I can see and compare, get dates, make extracts or copies, as the case may be.

"Will you also send me *Bowen's heads* of difficulty and all letters of *my sister*, if any are with you. "I heard you were sick. Are you about again? God grant you to see peaceful times.

"Yours faithfully,
"H. W. BEECHER.

"F. D. Moulton."

I said to Mr. Tracy that he had better take back that note, as I could not, in honor and conscience, give up the documents to either party to aid them in the preparation of statements against each other. Mr. Tracy suggested that perhaps I might send copies, to which I answered that that would seem to me the same breach of honorable obligation as to send the originals, and that it was impossible for me to have them copied, as I was about to leave town.

On the day of my arrival home, August 4, I received an invitation from the Committee to come before it the next day, asking me only to bring the documents referred to in Tilton's statement. Having seen in the public prints that it was said that Beecher had received no answer from me to his request of July 24, I sent him the letter which has been published, of the date of August 4, explaining in form what I had said in substance through Mr. Tracy.

At ten minutes to eleven of that evening a letter was brought to me purporting to be signed by H. W. Beecher, but not in his handwriting, asking for the production of all the documents before the Committee, but which afterwards, Mr. Sage, Chairman of the Committee, certified to be a correct copy of the original, which is here inserted, marked "M:"

BEECHER TO MOULTON.

"BROOKLYN, July 28, 1874.

"MY DEAR FRIEND: The Committee of Investigation are waiting mainly for you before closing their labors. I, too, earnestly wish that you would come and clear your mind and memory of everything that can bear on my case. I pray you also to bring all letters and papers relating to it which will throw any light upon it, and bring to a result this protracted case.

"I trust that Mrs. M. has been reinvigorated, and that her need of your care will not be so great as to detain you.

Truly yours,
"H. W. BEECHER.

"F. D. Moulton.

"H. W. SAGE, Chairman."

(Correct copy of original.)

The letter of Beecher's of August 4, heretofore published, was the first indication that I had ever had from Henry Ward Beecher of unfriendliness, and I have the very best reason for knowing that the harsh portions of it were the suggestions of others and not of his own mind.

After receiving these notes of Beecher's, I came to the conclusion that if Tilton also consented I would make the full statement before the Committee which I have since published. When I began the preparation of my statement I did not design to include the letters of Mrs. Hooker and her brother, or Mr. Hooker, because, as they had only a collateral bearing upon the controversy, I was very unwilling to drag the name of Mrs. Hooker, for whom I entertain the highest respect, into this matter. But having seen in the newspapers an attack upon Mrs. Hooker's sanity, inspired by the friends of Mr. Beecher; and Beecher, through the advice of his counsel as I believe, having asserted that I retained letters of his brother and sister that were not given into my keeping as part of the documents in this controversy, I felt it at once due to the lady's position and myself that they should appear, and hence they were inserted.

After Tracy had learned by my published letter that I would go before the Committee and make a full statement, he desired most earnestly that I should do no such thing, bringing to bear every argument that occurred to him to dissuade me therefrom, and among others that if I made the statement it would have to come out in the cross-examination that I had received money from Beecher for the use of Tilton, and that Beecher's friends would thereupon make a charge of blackmail against me. I told him in the presence of my counsel—for whom I had again sent at his (Tracy's) request—that that would not come out on cross-examination, for the facts in regard to the money were already fully disclosed in my statement, and that in that transaction there was nothing dishonorable on Beecher's part or my own, that I should fear seeing the light of day. Tracy strongly assured me that I ought not, under any circumstances, to disclose the letters and documents in my possession; that I was bound, by every principle of honor and sacred obligation, to keep them private; and that it would be better, both for Tilton and Beecher, that I should do so.

At his suggestion I called a meeting on Monday morning of some of Mr. Beecher's friends, and some of my most valued friends who could be got together, to lay before them this proposition. At that meeting my counsel advised that there were two honorable courses before me. One was to seal my lips as to personal statements, and produce no documents but those of which extracts had been made and already been put before the Committee, as it would be but just to both parties that, a part of a paper being seen, the whole should be known; or to make a full and complete statement of all the facts and documents, both parties having consented. These alternatives were discussed in the meeting of my friends, and by a majority of them it was determined that less harm would come to the community, to the families of the parties, and to the parties themselves if I took the former course. Yielding to the advice of those I so much respected, I concluded to go before the Committee and make the simple statement of an intention not to take part in the controversy, and producing only the letters which had in part been before them in Tilton's statement, reserving the right to protect my own honor and purity of action in this matter if attacked, as I have since done.

In order that the exact credit due to Mr. Beecher's statement may be seen and its value as testimony may be fully appreciated, as compared with the facts and documents that I shall hereafter bring forward in my own vindication, I am compelled to notice some other patent misstatements in this special plea of counsel made in behalf of Mr. Beecher, if not by himself; and one of the first in order which claims attention is the averment in his statement that "the only copy of Mrs. Tilton's confession was torn in pieces in his own presence" on the night of the 30th of December, 1870, an act about which he could hardly be mistaken. On the contrary, I have stated that that paper of "confession" was delivered into my hands the night of the meeting of Beecher and Tilton at my house, when Beecher was first charged with his adulteries with Mrs. Tilton; and afterwards, when I demanded the retraction of him, he asked me: "What will you do with it if I give it up?" I answered: "I will keep it as I keep the confession. If you act honorably I will protect it with my life, as I would protect the other with my life." I may be allowed to say here that at this remark I made reference to the pistol in my overcoat pocket, which I always carried in the night, as emphasizing the extremity of my defense of the papers. Yet Mr. Beecher says, "He made no verbal threats, but opened his overcoat and with some emphatic remark he showed a pistol." Why misrepresent? Is it possible that he gave his confidence at once to a man who extorted a paper from him with a pistol? Yet Beecher's Committee make a point of this prevarication in their argument for the accused!

After the tripartite covenant I handed back that same paper to Tilton at the request of his wife, in order that she might be satisfied, and herself destroy it.

Now, which of these statements is true? Let contemporaneous facts and acts answer.

It will be remembered that that meeting was on Friday night, the 30th of December, 1870. Mrs. Tilton sent me a note, heretofore published, dated the next Saturday morning, in the following words:

"SATURDAY MORNING.

"MY DEAR FRIEND FRANK: I want you to do me the greatest possible favor. My letter which you have, and the one which I gave Mr. Beecher at his dictation last evening, ought both to be destroyed. Please bring both to me and I will burn them. Show this note to Theodore and Mr. Beecher. They will see the propriety of this request.   Yours truly,

"E. R. TILTON."

The "letter" referred to, of course, it will be seen, is the "confession," the only letter I then had of hers referring to this matter.

And again, to show that I cannot be either mistaken or untrue, I refer to Mrs. Tilton's note to Beecher of April 21, following, heretofore published:

"FRIDAY, April 21, 1871.

"MR. BEECHER: As Mr. Moulton has returned, will you use your influence to have the papers in his possession destroyed? My heart bleeds night and day at the injustice of their existence."

Would not Tilton have caused such a paper to be preserved after he had founded an accusation upon it? This falsehood was put in by Beecher's lawyers lest Tilton might produce a copy, as my statement had not then been published with its documentary evidence.

Still another variation from the truth occurs in Beecher's statement in regard to the destruction of the "letter of contrition." In his explanation of it he speaks as follows:

"I did not trouble myself about it till more [sic] than a year afterward, when Tilton began to write up his case [of which hereafter] and was looking up documents. I wondered what was in this old memorandum, and desired to see it for greater certainty, so one day I suddenly asked Moulton for that memorandum and said, 'You promised to return it to me.' He seemed confused for a moment, and said, 'Did I?' 'Certainly,' I answered. He replied that the paper had been destroyed. On my putting the question again, he said, 'That paper was burned up long ago;' and during the next two years, in various conversations, of his own accord, he spoke of it as destroyed. I had never asked for nor authorized the destruction of this paper."

Upon this point I have said in my statement that I retained that "letter of contrition" as one of the papers necessary to keep peace between the parties, and I now add that this was well known to Beecher, and I shall prove it at last from his own mouth. It will be remembered, so far from Beecher believing, within more than a year afterwards, that it had been destroyed and burned up, that in April, 1872, Mr. Samuel Wilkeson, Beecher's friend and partner in the publication of his book—and who thinks that Beecher's destruction will knock their enterprise of the publication of the "Life of Christ" "higher than a kite," and who acted in the capacity of counsel in his behalf in drawing up the tripartite covenant—wrote me the following letter, heretofore published in my statement, dated the same day with that remarkable covenant:

"NORTHERN PACIFIC RAILROAD COMPANY }
SECRETARY'S OFFICE, 120 BROADWAY, }
NEW YORK, April 2, 1872. }

"MY DEAR MOULTON:—Now for the closing act of justice and duty. Let Theodore pass into your hand the written apology which he holds for the improper advances, and do you pass it into the flames of the friendly fire in your room of reconciliation. Then let Theodore talk to Oliver Johnson. I hear that he and Carpenter, the artist, have made this whole affair the subject of conversation in the clubs. Sincerely yours, SAMUEL WILKESON."

Did Beecher or his friend want me to burn a "letter of contrition" in April, 1872, which Beecher avers I had told him and he believed had been burned long previous? But again, in Beecher's letter of June 1, 1873, he says: "The *agreement* [tripartite covenant] *was made after my letter through you was written.* He [Tilton] had had it a year." Yes, from January 1, 1871, to April 2, 1872. Does Beecher really believe himself when he says that I told him that letter was long before burned up? He had not seen his letter of June 1, when this falsehood was told for him. In view of such false statements, is the anxiety of his counsel to get his letters and papers out of my hands, so they could square their statements by them, at all wonderful?

As bearing upon the want of veracity in the matter that we have just considered as to the destruction of the "letter of contrition," I take leave to call attention to a like misstatement as to the original preparation of this same "letter."

I have stated that it was written out according to the dictation of Mr. Beecher. As an honorable man, looking only to a settlement between the parties, and at that moment certainly without any other possible motive which could be imputed to me, I could have only desired to reproduce exactly the words of Beecher, which I did do with exactness; and the most cursory examination of the phrases will show them to have been *his* words and not *mine*. I am not in the habit of using such language; indeed, I hardly believe myself capable of composing it. I should not myself have used the phrase, "Humble myself before him as I do before my God." I was not used to that kind of expression, nor the phrase, "Toward the poor child lying there praying with folded hands." I never called a woman of nearly forty years old a "poor child" in my life. I did not know that she "was lying" anywhere with folded hands. Beecher did, because he says in his statement to the Committee that she "lay there white as marble," like a statue of the old world, palm to palm, like one praying, thus reproducing four years afterwards almost the identical phrase and picture which he conveyed to me, and which I put in the "letter of contrition." I could not have used the phrase, "I have her forgiveness," because I did not know whether he had it or not except as he told me, and if I had acted upon my belief in the matter I should suppose that he had not. This letter, after being prepared by me, was read by him before he put his signature to it.

The explanation put by Beecher in his statement—that "this paper was a mere memorandum of points to be used by him [me] in setting forth my [his] feelings. * * * But they were put into sentences by him [me] expressed as he [I] understood them, not as my [his] words, but as hints of my [his] figures and letters, to be used by him in conversing with Tilton. * * * It is a mere string of hints, hastily made by an unpractised writer, as helps to his memory in representing to Mr. Tilton how I felt towards his family"—all this explanation is a mere afterthought, made up for the purpose of explanation merely. Beecher always treated this letter as his own in all the after conversations we had upon the subject.

Mr. Samuel Wilkeson, Mr. Beecher's friend and acting counsel, could have known nothing of that paper except from Beecher, as I had never told him or anybody else save Tilton anything of its contents, and both Beecher and Wilkeson supposed it was delivered by me to Tilton, as it was intended to be. And in his letter heretofore published, speaking in the interest of Beecher, Wilkeson calls it "the written apology *which he holds* for the improper advances." In Beecher's letter of June 1, 1873, just before quoted, he speaks of it as "my letter that he [Tilton] had over a year;" not "a memorandum for the purposes of conversation," written by an unpractised writer, which did not represent his thought.

I have said this was an afterthought. The reason for so believing, outside the intrinsic evidence from the documents, is that when this controversy was about being renewed because of the publication and speeches of Dr. Leonard Bacon, which brought it on again, I was in consultation with Beecher upon what might be the effect of them, and predicting that if Bacon went on he would surely reopen the whole matter. In that conversation Beecher said to me—and I remember his words exactly, because it was quite a startling proposition—"Can't we hit upon some plan to break the force of my letter to Tilton? Can't we hit upon some form of note from you to me in which you shall state that that letter was not in fact a letter at all, but simply a memorandum of points of my conversation made by you for the purpose of expressing more accurately my thought and feeling towards Tilton and his family?" I said, "I will think of that, but we must wait, I think, until the necessity arises before determining what I ought to do in that regard." He said, "I will prepare such a note, and you read it over carefully and see whether or not it is possible for you to sign it." I said, "Very well, prepare the note and I will consider it, but as you put the proposition now, of course it wouldn't be true." He never showed me such a note if he prepared it.

Another instance to show how this lawyer's statement of Beecher cannot be trusted, I find stated in these words : "I never resumed my intimacy with the family ; but once or twice I went there soon after my reconciliation with Mr. Tilton, and at *his* request."

Is this averment true? I confess that I believed it substantially true at the time I prepared my published statement, supposing that Beecher was acting according to his distinct instruction to Mrs. Tilton in his letter of February 7, 1871, and in accordance with his promise to me to have no further communication with Mrs. Tilton except through myself. I extract as follows, the whole letter having been published :

"In him [Moulton] we have a common ground. You and I may meet in him. The past is ended. But is there no future—no wiser, higher, holier future? May not this friend stand as a priest in the new sanctuary of reconciliation and mediate and bless you, Theodore, and my most unhappy self? Do not let my earnestness fail of its end. You believe in my judgment. I have put myself wholly and gladly in Moulton's hands, *and there I must meet you.*

"This is sent with Theodore's consent, but he has not read it. Will you return it to me by his hands. I am very earnest in this wish for all our sakes, as such a letter ought not to be subjected to even a chance of miscarriage. Your unhappy friend,

"H. W. BEECHER."

Could Beecher have written that sentence of me if, as his Committee reports, forty days before I had extorted a paper from him with threats by a pistol, for which they say I ought to have been handed over to the police?

And, therefore, I put forth in my statement what, when I prepared it, I believed to be true. I said :

"On the same day there was conveyed to me from Beecher a request to Tilton that Beecher might write to Mrs. Tilton, because all the parties had then come to the conclusion that there should be no communication between Beecher and Mrs. Tilton or Beecher and Tilton except with my knowledge and consent, and I had exacted a promise from Beecher that he would not communicate with Mrs. Tilton or allow her to communicate with him unless I saw the communication, which promise, I believe, was, on his part, faithfully kept, but, as I soon found, was not on the part of Mrs. Tilton. Permission was given to Beecher to write to Mrs. Tilton, and the following is his letter : "

—which is the letter of February 7, 1871, from which the above extract is made. I had no intimation that he received any correspondence from Mrs. Tilton that did not go through my hands, and certainly that he made none to her, or visited her. But since the preparation of that statement there have come into my hands certain letters from him to Mrs. Tilton, that now show me that he was unfaithful to his promise to me, and that he kept up his intercourse clandestinely with her, in violation of his solemn promises, his plighted faith to the wronged husband, to his own imminent and deadly peril, without the knowledge of his [Beecher's] wife—for doing all which things there could have been but one incentive. It becomes necessary, therefore, on the question of veracity of his statement as to the renewal of his intimacy with Mrs. Tilton, that some of these letters should be compared.

In her letter dated January 13, 1871, written to a female friend—which certainly will not be claimed to have been dictated by Tilton—Mrs. Tilton says :

"My faith and hope are very bright, now that I am off the sick bed, and dear Frank Moulton is a friend indeed. (He is managing the case with Mr. Bowen.) We have weathered the storm, and I believe without harm to ou: *best* * * * * These slanders have been sown broadcast. I am quoted everywhere as the author of them. Coming in this way and form to Mr. Bowen, they caused his [Tilton's] immediate dismission from both the *Independent* and the *Union*. Suffering thus, both of us, so unjustly—(I knew nothing of these plans)—anxiety night and day brought on my miscarriage; a disappointment I have never before known—a *love-babe* it promised, you know. I have had sorrow almost beyond human capacity, dear—— *It is my mother!* "

I do not quote the whole letter, as it has been already published, and may be referred to. The peculiarity of the language of this extract should be noted. We find Mrs. Tilton on the 30th of December, sick in bed with what she states to have been a miscarriage a few days before of what promised to be a "*love-babe*, you know "—a very curious expression from a woman nearly forty years old, and the mother of six children, to describe a child begotten in lawful wedlock; specially when, as Mrs. Tilton now asserts, she and her husband had been fiercely quarrelling for many months, and, Bessie Turner testifies, even to blows. Within six weeks of her getting off her sick bed, arising from that confinement, where Beecher says she lay white as marble, with eyes closed as in a trance, with her hands on her bosom, palm to palm, like one in prayer, she writes the following invitation to Beecher, which I received from his hand :

"WEDNESDAY.

"MY DEAR FRIEND : Does your heart bound *towards all* as it used? So does mine. *I am myself again* [sic.] I did not dare to tell you till I was sure, but the bird has sung in my heart these *four* weeks, and he has covenanted with me never again to leave. 'Spring has come.' Because I thought it would gladden you to know this, and not to trouble or embarrass you in *any way*, I now write. Of course I should like to share with you my joy, but can wait for the beyond ! When dear Frank says I may once again go to old Plymouth I will thank the dear Father. "

There can be but one meaning in these phrases under such circumstances. "I am *myself again*. I did not dare to tell you *till I was sure*, but the bird has sung in my heart these *four weeks*, and he has covenanted with me never again to leave. 'Spring has come,'" &c. "*Of course, I should like to share with you my joy.*"

I assume it will not be claimed that Tilton extorted from his wife this letter. Was this so significant hint to come " when she was all right " answered ? The reply to that question will be found in two notes to Elizabeth from Beecher, the shorter one enclosed within the other. The first is as follows, marked " N " :

BEECHER TO MRS. TILTON.

"The blessing of God rest upon you! Every spark of light and warmth in your own house will be a star and a sun in my dwelling. Your note broke like spring [sic] upon winter, and gave me an inward rebound toward life. No one can ever know—none but God—through what a dreary wilderness I have wandered! There was Mt. Sinai, there was the barren sand, there was the alternation of hope and despair that marked the pilgrimage of old. If only it might lead to the Promised Land!—or, like Moses, shall I die on the border. Your hope and courage are like medicine. Should God inspire you to restore and rebuild at home, and while doing it to cheer and sustain outside of it another who sorely needs help in heart and spirit, it will prove a life so noble as few are able to live! and, in another world, the emancipated soul may utter thanks!

"If it would be of comfort to *you*, now and then, to send me a letter of true *inwardness* [sic]—the outcome of your inner life—it *would* be safe, for I am now at home here with my sister ; and it is *permitted to you* [sic] and will be an exceeding refreshment to me, for your heart experiences are often like bread from heaven to the hungry. God has enriched your moral nature. May not others partake ?"

This is in Beecher's handwriting, but without direction or signature, but the note enclosed in pencil tells us the direction of it, as the words, "Your note broke like spring upon winter, " tells also to what note it was in reply to, because that quotes the words of Mrs. Tilton's, "Spring has come, " asking him to "share her joy," she being "all right" now. The enclosure is on a slip of paper, marked " O " (but which I do not produce here, reserving it for presentation before another tribunal).

Was there ever a plainer case of renewal of intimacy, to say the least, than this ? Mark, also, amid the prayers to God contained in the longer note, Beecher's suggestion that Elizabeth can write him now " *with safety*," because *he is living alone with his sister—i. e., his wife is away!*

If this stood alone it would be all-sufficient to prove that he speaks falsely who says that Beecher never visited Mrs. Tilton except at her husband's request after the *settlement*, and fill my purpose; but I do not choose to leave it in its solitude as a single act, and therefore I reproduce from my statement the letter from Mrs. Tilton to Beecher, which bears date May 3, 1871 :

" MR. BEECHER: My future, either for life or death, would be happier could I but feel that you *forgave* me while you forget me. In all the sad complications of the past year my endeavor was to entirely keep from *you* all suffering ; to bear myself alone, leaving you forever ignorant of it. My weapons were love, a large untiring generosity, and *nest-hiding!* That I failed utterly we both know. But now I ask forgiveness."

Perhaps Tilton extorted this letter, too, from his wife.

The italics are those of the writer. Will Beecher, in his first sermon after his vacation, please explain what sort of a " spiritual weapon " " *nest-hiding* " is, with which " a poor dear child of a woman " " keeps all suffering from her pastor " so as to leave him " for ever ignorant of it," unless, indeed, " nest-hiding " is a carnal weapon, for in that case no explanation is needed. There are indications in this note that perhaps Beecher did not keep his appointment, and that may have been the reason for its writing.

Whether this note was answered I do not now produce documentary evidence to show, nor is it necessary upon the question whether Beecher renewed his intimacy with her after the settlement, because I produce another note of January 20, 1872, undirected, but enclosed in an envelope, addressed " Mrs. Elizabeth Tilton, Livingston Street, Brooklyn," bearing the postmark of the same date. It is marked " P " :

BEECHER TO MRS. TILTON.

" 20 JANUARY, 1872.

" Now may the God of Peace that brought again from the dead our Lord Jesus, that great shepherd of the sheep, through the blood of the everlasting covenant, make you perfect in every good work to do his will, working in you that which is well-pleasing in his sight through Jesus Christ.

" This is my prayer day and night. This world ceases to hold me as it did. I live in the thought and hope of the coming immortality, and seem to myself, most of the time, to be standing on the edge of the other life, wondering whether I may not at any hour hear the call ' Come up hither.'

" I shall be in New Haven next week to begin my course of lectures to the theological classes, on preaching. My wife takes boat for Havana and Florida on Thursday.

" I called on Monday, but you were out.

" I hope you are growing stronger and happier. May the dear Lord and Saviour abide with you.

"Very truly yours, "H. W. BEECHER."

I again call attention to the mixture of prayer and business in this note by the following words : "My wife takes boat for *Havanna* and Florida on Thursday. I called on Monday, but found you were out."

But this is not the only note which establishes renewed intimacy. I produce another note, undirected and unsigned, but enclosed in an envelope postmarked the same day, directed, "Elizabeth Tilton, care of Theodore Tilton, Esq., Brooklyn." This is the only one addressed to his care, and its contents are such that a husband might read as coming from a pastor to his parishioner, except that the husband was using the intimacy of the pastor with his wife for the purpose of blackmailing him. But why leave it unsigned? It is here inserted, marked "Q:"

BEECHER TO MRS. TILTON

"MAY 6, '72.

"MY DEAR FRIEND: I was glad to see you at church yesterday. It is always a great comfort to me when you are, and a token of God's favor.

"I go to-night to Norwich, N. Y., where my grand-daughter, six years old, is dying, and her mother, my Hattie, awaiting her own confinement. I seem to live amidst funerals. The air is heavy much of the time with the odor of the grave.

"I am again at work on the 'Life,' making haste while the day lasts—'the night cometh when no man can work.'

"I pray for you, that God would dwell in you by that spirit of Divine love by which we are cleansed from anger, impatience, and all self-assertion, and kept in the sweetness of that peace which passes all understanding. That it may please God to lift you up out of all trouble, and to keep you under the shadow of His wings, is my prayer for you. By His spirit animosity may be utterly slain, and your better self may be clothed with the invincible spirit of a love which, springing from God and abiding in him, will carry with it *His victory*."

And these letters, written too by a Christian minister to a woman whom he now characterizes in his statement thus: "I am in that kind of divided consciousness that I was in respect to Elizabeth, that she was a saint and chief of sinners." He knew all of her then he does now, unless indeed he does know *more* now, and yet he wants "refreshment" from her "true inwardness."

I need not prolong this statement by the production of documents to show that the intimacy between Beecher and Mrs. Tilton did not cease after January 1, 1871, when he had solemnly settled the past injury with the husband, and promised me that it should cease, and when he now states it did cease, for all these letters are subsequent to his settlement with Tilton, and some of them more than a year after.

I call attention to the fact that I have drawn no inferences as to the effect of these letters. I have only compared them, shown the relations of their several parts to their surroundings, except that I do insist that they show a renewal of intimacy with his family not under the supervision of either Tilton or myself, which is the point at issue between Beecher and me in this regard. I have avoided stating in terms the effect upon my mind, because, in my former statement, having given only the results of conversations, I have been criticised; and disbelief of the facts I stated has been attempted because I did not state the precise words and manner of the admissions of the fact of sexual intercourse with Mrs. Tilton by Beecher. It has been said that, being a "man of the world," I drew inferences from his pure and unguarded expressions which they did not authorize, and therefore as to these letters I have left the inferences to be drawn by those who read them in the light which dates and facts now throw upon them.

But to answer this criticism in another direction, and to show the impossibility that I could be mistaken, not seeking to shelter myself under any supposed misunderstanding, but taking all the burden of veracity between Beecher, Tilton, and myself, I now proceed to give such portions as are necessary of some few of the conversations in which Beecher made confession of adultery:

I have before stated that the first confession was made on the night I went for the "retraction" of Mrs. Tilton: that I there told him: "Mr. Beecher, you have had criminal intercourse with Mrs. Tilton, and you have done great injury to Tilton otherwise;" and I say further in my published statement: "that he confessed and denied not, but confessed." As he did not deny this charge, so explicitly made by me, whatever inferences I may have made from his words at other times, he certainly could not have mistaken mine at this time. When speaking of the relations of a man and a woman, "criminal intercourse" has but one "legal or literary meaning," even to a clergyman.

It, however, seems necessary that I should go still further, which I do, and I say that on that evening he confessed to me his relations with Mrs. Tilton in language so vivid that I could not possibly forget or mistake it. He said, "My acts of intercourse with that woman were as natural and sincere an expression of my love for her as the words of endearment which I addressed to her. There seemed to be nothing in what we did together that I could not justify to myself on the ground of our love for each other, and I think God will not blame me for my acts with her. I know that at present it would be utterly impossible for me to justify myself before man." This is impressed upon my mind because it was the first enunciation of a justification of the doctrines of free-love that I had ever heard.

Not only on the occasion of handing back Mrs. Tilton's "retraction" and when giving me the letter of contrition of January 1, 1871, did he particularize with regard to the feelings that influenced him to do as he did with Mrs. Tilton, but in many of the conversations I held with him he strongly adverted to the absorbing love which he felt for the woman, and to the joys of his intercourse with her, which he always justified because of that love. Indeed, on one occasion when speaking of it, he said so pure did the intercourse seem to him that the little red lounge on which they had been together seemed to him "almost a sacred thing."

If my testimony is to avail anything in this matter, I here commit it now fully to the statement heretofore made by me, which I then softened by omitting details, the language of which I thought it best for public morality should be suppressed. And I call attention to the fact made in my previous statement that, in the presence of myself and another witness, whom I still feel reluctant to bring forward—of course not Mr. Tilton—both Mrs. Tilton and Mr. Beecher admitted in language not to be mistaken, that a continued sexual intimacy had existed between them, and asked advice as to the course to be taken because of it.

I trust I shall be pardoned for giving an instance or two out of the many that I might cite of the inconsistency of Mr. Beecher with himself. The theory of his statement is that Mrs. Tilton had confessed to her husband in the first place only his [Beecher's] "excessive love for her," and he maintains stoutly that in that confession there was nothing more confessed than that *he* had made "improper advances" to *her*. But again, he says the document was one "incriminating" him. Lastly, he gives an account of his interview with Mrs. Tilton when he got the retraction. This he describes in the following words :

"I added that he (Tilton) said that I had made improper suggestions to her, and that she admitted this fact to him last July. I said : 'Elizabeth, have you made such statements to him ?' She made no answer. I repeated the question. Tears ran down her cheeks, and she very slightly bowed her head in acquiescence. I said : 'You cannot mean that you have stated all that he has charged?' She opened her eyes, and began in a slow and feeble way to explain how sick she had been, how wearied out with importunity ; that he had confessed his own alien loves, and said that he could not bear to think that she was better than he ; that she might win him to reformation if she would confess that she had loved me more than him, and that they would repent and go on with future concord."

The point between us is this: I averred in my statement that the document which Beecher saw as well as myself, was her confession that he had committed adultery with the wife. Which was it ? A confession only of excessive love and improper advances on his part, or, as he describes it, an "incriminating" confession ? Without stopping to advert to the fact that Mrs. Tilton, in her confession, which went to Dr. Storrs, says that he asked her to be a wife to him, with all that that implies, and the singular fact appears that she does not therein say she said no to him, need I advert upon the likelihood of her making a negative with her great love for him if he took the initiative ? Let us now judge Mr. Beecher by his own statement. He went to Mrs. Tilton and asked her if she had confessed all that her husband had charged, which he said were "improper advances." She bowed her head in acquiescence. He said, "How could you do that ?" She now gives the reason and says Tilton had confessed his own *alien loves*, and said that he could not bear to think that she was better than he, and that "she might win him if she confessed she loved me more than him, and that they would repent and go on in future concord."

Assuming this report of the conversation to be true, and the reason given by Mrs. Tilton for her confession, I am led to ask how would it tend to show that the husband, who had confessed his adultery to his wife, had a wife as bad as he was because she confessed to him that she had been tempted by her pastor and friend, and had refused his solicitations, under circumstances of the greatest possible temptation ? It can only be reconciled upon the theory that Tilton's confession of "alien loves" also included a declaration that he had not sinned in act with them. This supposition, however, both Beecher and Elizabeth reject with scorn. Both declare the same equivocal words as hers as to Tilton mean adultery only. May not, then, her "love" with Beecher, so "excessive," mean the same thing ? If that theory as to themselves is true, would not such a confession to Tilton by his wife, instead of convincing him that she was as bad as he was an adulterer, tend to show to him that she was the best of all women, and withstood temptation better than her grandmother Eve ? Why confess her own entire worthiness in order to convince her husband of her unworthiness ? On the contrary, does not this language plainly show that her confession was precisely what I have declared it was in the written confession, and what it was in fact.

Let me give a single other instance. When called upon in his cross-examination to explain his phrases in the letter of June 3, 1872 :—"I have determined to make no more resistance. Theodore's temperament is such that the future, even if temporarily earned, would be absolutely worthless, filled with abrupt changes and rendering me liable at any hour or day to be obliged to stultify all the devices by which we saved ourselves"—he says :

"Devices did not refer to me, but to him [Moulton]—his whole style of acting.
"Q. Theodore said he was born for war, and Moulton probably born for diplomacy ? A. Yes.
"By Mr. Cleaveland—Were the plan and method by which from time to time these things were managed by your suggestions or by Mr. Moulton ? A. I made suggestions from time to time, generally without any effect, and the essential course of affairs, so far as it has not been forced upon us from outside influences, has been of his [Moulton's] procuring."

Again he answers to another question as follows :

"Q. The 'devices'—did that refer to all the places and arrangements and steps that had been taken ? A. It referred to this : If I had been left to manage this matter simply myself I should have said 'yes' or 'no.' That would have been the whole of it, but instead of that the matter went into Moulton's hands, and Moulton is a man that loves intrigue in such a way that, as Lady Montague said of somebody, 'he would not carve a cabbage unless he could steal on it from behind and do it by a device.'"

Let us see if this is true. I certainly did not manage the "device" of getting the retraction from Mrs. Tilton of December 30, 1870. I did not manage the "device" of the reconciliation with Bowen in 1870. I did not manage the "device" of the tripartite covenant. I did not suggest his proposed letter to Claflin, and of his sending me to him to ascertain whether he had learned the "very bottom facts." I did not suggest the "device" of putting the card in the Brooklyn *Eagle* denying the facts—I only made it more intelligible. I did not suggest the "device" of attempting to stop the mouth of Mrs. Hooker, for I could know nothing about it until Beecher came to me with it.

I did not suggest the "device" of his proposed card to Tilton, by which he should repudiate the Woodhull statement. I did not manage or suggest the "devices" of the two letters of February 7th, 1871, that I should be made a priest at the altar of reconciliation, because it appears from the letters themselves I was then on a sick-bed. I did not suggest the "device" as to his letters to Mrs. Woodhull, for he wrote them and then sent them to me for my approval. I did not suggest the "devices" of silence, or of writing to Shearman to send letters of explanation to Mr. Tilton, nor the letter to Mr. Cleveland, of which he sent me a copy ; nor of sending Cleveland with his horse and buggy to hunt Carpenter, in order to shut up his mouth, lest his statement should appear "to have come from head-quarters," as Beecher wrote me he had done it. Neither did I manage the "device," since the publication of the Bacon letter, of the proposed statement for Tilton to make to the Committee, in reply to the one which he [Beecher] was to make.

These all, as appears from the letters and documents themselves, are the emanations of Mr. Beecher's own diplomacy, to cover up the fact that he had given bad advice to the wife of his friend upon a misstatement of the truth as to a domestic difference. Is Mr. Beecher to be believed when he states all these were my "devices ; " or rather, was not his state of mind better described by himself in his cross-examination where he is asked to explain—what indeed is unexplainable on any other theory than the truth of his guilt—his letter of February 7, 1871 ? I quote :

"Q. In your letter of the same date to Mr. Moulton this occurs: 'Would to God, who orders all hearts, and by his kind mediation, Theodore, Elizabeth, and I could be made friends again. Theodore will have the hardest task in such a case.' Precisely what did you mean ? Why that last sentence ? A. It is all a muddle to me, as I don't recall the precise working of my mind."

It is indeed true that his mind is all "a muddle " in undertaking to carry through the explanation made by his lawyers. Yet even this poor excuse, that "he cannot recall the workings of his mind," he does not leave to himself, because in his written statement he says : "I labor under great disadvantages in making a statement. *My memory of states of mind is clear and tenacious,* better than memory of dates and details ; " and yet, in his cross-examination he utterly breaks down upon "the state of his mind," and declares it "all a muddle."

But it is not my purpose, nor will it be profitable, to push the analysis of this statement of Mr. Beecher's lawyers further. From these specimens of its inconsistencies, and from these contradictions of the facts, I shall leave the truth of our respective statements to be judged of by all good men who take an interest in them.

I have here at first given what I am sorry to say is a prolix but faithful narrative of every event and act in which I took part, with the documents and papers, occurring since the inception of the Bacon letter. And I ask the judgment of every candid mind upon the question of veracity first herein stated, whether the statement of Henry Ward Beecher before the Committee—that "when that [Bacon] letter was published, and Mr. Moulton, on my visiting him in reference to it, proposed no counter-operation—no documents, no help—I was staggered, and when Tilton subsequently published his statement, after he came to this Committee, when that came out I never heard a word from Moulton ; he *never sent for me,. nor visited me, nor did a thing* ; I waited for him to say or do something "—can be true in general or in either particular ?

His averment covers the whole period from before the 21st of June to the hour he made his statement. Does he not know that he himself placed in my hands his proposition in his own handwriting as to what Tilton should say in reply to his statement before the Committee, written more than three weeks after the publication of the Bacon letter ? Does he not know he visited my house in reference to my own statement, to be made before his Committee, when he came according to his letter of appointment of July 13 ? Does he not know that I wrote out for him my view of the words by which he could shield himself from the consequences of that Bacon letter, to be used in his pulpit, which he copied out to show to his friends ? Does he not remember when he put his arms around my neck, during that consultation of the 5th of July, fourteen days after the Bacon letter, and in the presence of my business partner spoke of me as the "best friend that God ever raised up to a man ? " In view of these facts thus vouched, how can he stand before the community otherwise than as a convicted falsifier and slanderer of "his only and best friend," who was loyally doing all he could to save him day by day ?

From this bitter issue there is in my own mind for Beecher but one escape, to which I gladly turn—that these statements are put into his mouth by his lawyers and advisers, and are not his own ; and while that may well protect him from the charge of ungrateful, wicked lying, at the same moment it disposes of his statement to the Committee as evidence in this controversy, not being the truth told by himself or another, but the special plea of his counsel.

Whatever may have been my own mistakes in acting for him, whatever may have been the faults and foolishness of my advice in his behalf, to save him in the years of his deadly peril, thank God they brought him into no such terrible dilemma as this, by which his character as a man of truth and Christian piety is forever gone, or his pretended statement ceases to be evidence in his own behalf.

I have gone through all these facts with another purpose also, and that is that I may in some degree reinstate myself with the public from the charge of treachery and broken faith to Mr. Beecher, which, if true, ought to render any word I might say in my own behalf as to any other charge useless.

If I have not thereby succeeded in substantiating my truthfulness as a witness, my purity of motive, and the loyalty of my conduct towards Beecher--always acknowledging everything of unwisdom or want of judgment in my actions that may justly be alleged against me—all that I may say further in regard to the charges of blackmail so liberally visited upon me by Mr. Beecher may as well remain unsaid.

As to the charge of blackmailing upon Rev. Mr. Beecher, I premise by saying that whatever money transactions were had with him in this regard were had through myself alone ; and therefore if blackmail was levied upon Mr. Beecher, as he avers, it was done by my procurement and consent, and for which I am alone blamable, as I confirm his own statement that Tilton never spoke to him on the subject of money. Beecher's account of the blackmailing is substantially as follows, being abbreviated from various parts of his statement and cross-examination :

"Money has been obtained from me in the course of these affairs in considerable sums, but I,did not at first look upon the suggestions that I should contribute to Mr. Tilton's pecuniary wants as savoring of blackmail. This did not occur to me until I had paid perhaps $2,000. Afterward I contributed at one time $5,000. After the money had been paid over in five $1,000 bills—to raise which I mortgaged the house I live in—I felt very much dissatisfied with myself about it."

Again he gives this account of the $7,000 in his cross-examination—all the money that he says he ever paid :

"Q. By Mr. Cleveland—In your statement you have alluded to one payment of $5,000. Have you furnished any other money to those parties ? A. I have furnished at least $2,000 besides the $5,000.
"Q. To whom did you pay that money ? A. To Mr. Moulton.
"Q. In various sums ? A. In various sums, partly in cash and partly in checks.
"Q. Have you any of those checks ? A. I have several : I don't remember how many.
"Q. Where are they ? A. I have some of them here : one of June 23, 1871, drawn on the Mechanics' Bank to the order of Frank Moulton, and indorsed in his handwriting ; and one of November 10, 1871, payable to the order of Frank Moulton and indorsed in his handwriting ; and of May 29, 1872, to the order of Frank D. Moulton, and also indorsed in his handwriting. Each of these that are marked for deposit across the face have been paid.
"Q. As nearly as you can recollect, how much money went into the hands of Mr. Moulton ? A. I should say I have paid $7,000.
"Q. To what use did you suppose that money was to be appropriated ? A. I supposed that it was to be appropriated to extricate Mr. Tilton from his difficulties in some way.
"Q. You did not stop to inquire how or why ? A. Moulton sometimes sent me a note saying, 'I wish you would send me your check for so much.'
"Q. Did you usually respond to the demands of Mr. Moulton for money during those months ? A. I always did.
"Q. Under what circumstances did you come to pay the $5,000 in one sum ? A. Because it was represented to me that the whole difficulty could be now settled by that amount of money, which would put the affairs of the *Golden Age* on a secure footing ; that they would be able to go right on, and that with the going on of them the safety of Tilton would be assured, and that would be the settlement of the whole thing. It was to save Tilton pecuniarily."

It will be observed that in this account of the $7,000—all that he claims he ever paid—Mr. Beecher does not allege that the thought of blackmailing was in his mind until after he had paid the $2,000, or that Tilton had ever asked him for any money. It will also be observed that he produces certain checks to the Committee in his cross-examination, but does not give the several amounts of those checks, but does the dates. But being in the position of being required to tell the whole truth, he entirely conceals the fact that a large portion of the $2,000 was paid for the education and support of the girl Bessie Turner, now his swift witness before the Committee, contradicting two written statements which have been published, made by her relative to the same facts, wherein she designates what she tells before the Committee as a "wicked lie." See her letter :

BESSIE TURNER TO ELIZABETH TILTON.

"JANUARY 12.
"The story that Mr. Tilton once lifted me from my bed and *carried* [sic] me screaming to his own, and attempted to violate my person is a wicked lie. Yours truly,
"BESSIE."

She now says that she was carried "sleeping," not "screaming." For a young woman of twenty *she slept reasonably soundly*, as she did not wake up till after she was in his bed !

Her character for truth and virtue has been by Beecher's advisers thus forever ruined to save him, because, as the story was first told, no young girl was ever "lifted from her bed and carried screaming to his own " by a ruthless ravisher and remained pure, especially as the witness nowhere suggests that he was interfered with.

The checks which he produced before the Committee, which are not published, will be seen, I have no doubt, to have been payments on her account, as their dates show them to be six months apart, as her half-yearly bills became due, with perhaps a single exception. Let me say to Mr. Beecher that if he will apply to the principal of the Steubenville (O.) school he can find out just how much he has paid there, and Mrs. Tilton can tell him what became of the rest of the supposed two thousand dollars. All this matter of the support of this girl was arranged by Mrs. Tilton and Beecher, Tilton doing nothing about it, and a portion of the money was paid to Mrs. Tilton herself, as appears by the following letter, extracted from my published statement:

"TUESDAY, January 18, 1873.

" DEAR FRANCIS: Be kind enough to send me $50 for Bessie, I want to inclose it in to-morrow's mail. Yours gratefully,

" ELIZABETH."

Would not ingenuous truth have required Mr. Beecher to state that this large sum was paid for this young girl's support in order to relieve him from his difficulty and prevent the exposure of the recital of his own acts, which she had heard in the family, in the neighborhood where they were most likely to be taken up ? Did he not know the facts ? Will anybody believe him when he intimates in his examination that he did not know? Is it possible that he never asked his dear friend Moulton where this money was going to, especially as he is careful to instruct Moulton to "feed out " the $5,000 to Til-ton. Instead he puts forward the phrases: "Money has been obtained from me in the course of these affairs in considerable sums; but I did not at first look upon the suggestions that I should contribute to Mr. Tilton's pecuniary wants as savoring of blackmail "—thus putting the amount of the $2,000 and the $5,000 in his statement as if they went together to Tilton for the same purpose.

In order to give color to this allegation of blackmail, trumped up after the charges against Tilton of forging letters and insanity had failed them, Beecher's lawyers make the following report of the conversation of July 5 in answer to a question prepared for that purpose:

" Q. Did Moulton ever question you in regard to this matter whether you had ever spoken on that to any one, or expressed any anxiety in your mind about it ? A. He did, not many weeks ago, among the last interviews I had with him.

" Q. Since the publication of that Bacon letter ? A. Yes; I think it was on the Sabbath day after the appointment of this committee. I preached but once on that day, and on the afternoon of that day he saw me and said to me in a conversation: ' You have never mentioned about that $5,000.' I said, ' Yes, I had, to one or two persons. I mentioned to Oliver Johnson for one, because he was saying something to me one day about what some of Tilton's friends were saying, and I incidentally mentioned that to him, which he never repeated, I suppose, to anybody.' Moulton said: ' I will never admit that; I shall deny it always.' "

In regard to this statement Beecher is wholly mistaken, if he does not intend to falsify. I remember that part of the conversation very well and what I said on that occasion to him, which was: " General Tracy, your counsel, says that you must never say anything about the payment of any money on account of Tilton, because that will go very much against you. Have you ever said anything ?" Beecher replied: " Only to Oliver Johnson, who will keep it to himself, and I never will say anything about it to anybody else." That was all that was said upon the matter of keeping silence about that money.

Now when the fact is seen that I especially and exactly set forth, as well the money paid Mrs. Tilton and for Bessie's support as the $5,000, in my statement prepared for the Committee, without being called upon to do so by anybody, and while I supposed it rested wholly between Beecher and myself, and Beecher himself says it did wholly rest between him and Johnson, why should I have, at the very hour that I was looking forward to the probability of making my statement before the Committee that I have made, stated to Beecher that I never would admit it to anybody ? I frankly confess that I never had told it to anybody, and never meant to tell it to anybody, not on Beecher's account, because I thought the advance of $5,000 to the *Golden Age* was an act of nobleness and generosity on his part, and so said in my statement, and my only desire to keep it secret was lest it should get to Tilton that he was under obligations to Beecher. It never occurred to my thought, under any circumstances whatever or in any form, that it could enter into the imagination of man that this was an extortion of money from Beecher. On the contrary, he knew that I myself had advanced sums in aid of Tilton's enterprise, who had never accused me of any improper intimacy with or advances towards his wife. My partners had subscribed and advanced money for the purpose of supporting the *Golden Age*. Many other prominent citizens of Brooklyn had done the same thing, and I had no thought that Beecher was doing anything other and different from what the rest of us were doing—except that he had perhaps an additional personal motive—to sustain an enterprise which we all favored, and the results of which were looked upon as an honor to journalism.

It will also be observed, upon a careful examination of Beecher's own statement, although attempted to be concealed by ambiguous phrases, that the suggested payment of $5,000 first came to me from him, and was not made by me to him ; and that part of his statement which relates to what I told him in regard to the kind friend who had made an advance to Theodore Tilton in cash and notes would have been quite nearly correct if he had added the rest of the truth which I then told him—that Tilton had refused to receive that advance from the party offering to make it; and that I also told him at the same time that Tilton, I was sure, would not take any money from him, and therefore it was arranged between us that it should be given to Tilton in small sums as coming from me, as I had already made him like advances. Nor did the amount of $5,000 which Beecher subscribed seem to me at all extravagant for him to give. Having been for many years in the possession of a reputed income, from his salary and literary labor, of from forty to fifty thousand a year, and having apparently reasonably economical habits of living, I supposed him to be a man of very considerable, if not large, fortune, from his almost necessary accumulations, and I leave him to explain why it was, with such ample income, from which he ought to have accumulated a large fortune with habits of prudence and no *known* extraordinary expenses, to explain how he had impoverished himself and impaired his credit to so great an extent as not to be able to raise the paltry sum of $5,000 from among his rich parishioners without mortgaging his house, unless, indeed, he felt called upon to support others as he did Bessie.

I will venture to mention the name of another gentleman who has shown himself in this controversy to be a staunch and fast friend of Beecher, and who, before ever he proposed it to me, had advised Beecher that he ought to subscribe in aid of Tilton, and to whom Beecher, as he reported, made the reply that he had offered to give money in order to aid Tilton, but he would not receive it. I now refer to Mr. Thomas Kinsella, of the Brooklyn *Eagle*, who has so loyally supported Beecher in this his final struggle for his pulpit and good name.

It will also be observed that Beecher in his statement says that I was to "feed out" this money to Tilton, which exactly comports with what I said in my statement, that I was to give it to him from time to time as I found he needed it, and that I had not yet paid all of that sum to him, as the account in my published statement shows. Why, then, with that knowledge and that statement by Beecher that this money was to be "fed out," does Beecher speak of the "mollifying effect" of $5,000 to Tilton, which he now confesses he knew Tilton had not received, and why say that Tilton had had "his gold jingling in his pockets" for years? Or are these insinuations and flings on so solemn an occasion only the "jokes" which Mrs. Morse, Mrs. Tilton's mother, says "he cracked from Sunday to Sunday, while he leaves his victim suffering in cold and hunger at home, mourning for her sin?" I quote from Mrs. Morse's letter of January 27, 1871, published in my former statement.

"But this is a death-blow to us both, and I doubt not Florence [Tilton's daughter] has hers. Do you know, when I hear of your cracking your jokes from Sunday to Sunday, and think of the misery you have brought upon us, I think with the Psalmist: 'There is no God.'"

Mrs. Morse is now one of his witnesses before Beecher's Committee and his adopted mother, from a spiritual marriage with her daughter, as will be shown by the following letter, which I here insert, marked "R":

MRS. MORSE TO BEECHER.

"OCTOBER 24.

"MY DEAR 'SON': You must pardon me for the request I now make. Can you help me in any way by the first of November? I am still alone, with no prospect of any one, with a rent of $1,500 and an income of $1,000. The consequence is, with other expenses, I shall be by the first of the month terribly behindhand, as I agreed to pay in monthly installments.

"I know full well I have no claim upon you in any way [sic], excepting your sympathy for my lonely and isolated condition. If I could be released from the house I should gladly do so, for I'm convinced it's too far out. All who have been to see my rooms say so. My darling spent most of yesterday with me. She said all she had in the way of money was forty dollars per week, which was for food and all other household expenses aside from rent, and this was given her by hand of Annie Tilton every Saturday. If you know anything of the amount it takes to find food for eight people you must know there's little left for clothing. She told me he [T.] did not take any meals home from the fact she could not get such food as he liked to *nourish his brain*, and so he took his meals at Moulton's. Just think of that!

"I am almost crazy with the thought. Do come and see me. I will promise that the 'secret of her life,' as she calls it, shall not be mentioned. I know it's hard to bring it up, as you must have suffered intensely, and we all will, I fear, till released by death. Do you pray for me? If not, *pray do*. I never felt more rebellious than now, more need of God's and human help. Do you know I think it strange you should ask me to call you 'son'. When I have told darling, I felt if you could, in safety to yourself and all concerned, you would be to me all this endearing name. Am I mistaken?
"MOTHER."

This letter bears date October 24. I fix the date to be in 1871, because it was at that time that Mrs. Morse had the house for which she was paying $1,500 rent, and is the time when Tilton was allowing his wife $40 per week for household expenses. This letter was given me by Beecher as written by Mrs. Morse, Elizabeth's mother, and is a call on him for money, which may explain the necessity for mortgaging his house otherwise than by paying $5,000 to me. It is the outside family that is always the most onerous to a man.

It will be remembered that Elizabeth confessed that Beecher asked her to be his wife, with all that the name implies. Mrs. Morse tells him—and she would not dare tell him so if it was not so—"Do you know I think it strange you should ask me to call you 'son'. When I have told darling, I felt if you could, in safety to yourself and all concerned, you would be to me all this endearing name. Am I mistaken?"

The delicacy of this adopted mother, who says : "Do come and see me. I will promise the 'secret of her life,' as she calls it, shall not be mentioned," will be appreciated, especially because she knows it is cruel to bring it up, "as you must have suffered intensely, and we all will, I fear, till released by death."

Who believes that this note to Mr. Beecher—a married man—accompanied by a demand for money, with the reminder of the "secret" of a daughter's life, means only that Beecher once gave some bad advice about a separation between man and wife, which, so far as I know, never took place ?

The trouble is, Beecher mistakes the persons who blackmailed him. It was Mrs. Morse and Bessie, and nobody else, and they are now repaying him by testifying in his behalf. If such conduct as this goes unpunished and unrebuked, unchristian men will be prone to agree with the Psalmist and Mrs. Morse, that "there is no God ".

Upon the whole, there were very curious relationships among these parties by adoption, of which I think it would trouble a heraldry office to make a family tree, and which seem to have been a mystery even to Mrs. Morse, for she says in her first letter which I have quoted above: "The remark you made to me at your door was an enigma to me, and every day adds to the mystery ; 'Mrs. Beecher has adopted the child.' 'What child ?' I asked. You said, 'Elizabeth.' Now I ask what earthly sense was there in that remark !" Mrs. Beecher had adopted Elizabeth ; Beecher had adopted her mother, and wanted Elizabeth to be all that a wife could be to him ; and Mrs. Morse says she believes he would be all the endearing name of son can be to her, and wants to know if she is mistaken. Query : Under this arrangement, what relation is Mrs. Beecher to Beecher if she had adopted the child of his mother, and her husband had married the daughter of her mother ? Who wonders that Mrs. Morse thought it a mystery ?

I am not specially acquainted with the habits of men or women who obtain money by blackmail, but I had supposed if they so obtained money they did what they pleased with it, and not have it doled out by a third person in little sums as he deemed there was need, without the knowledge of the blackmailer where it came from, who obtained the money by threats and extortion.

Again, Beecher says that "my confidential friend" told him that Tilton would publish his statement unless another $5,000 was paid, which he refused to do. Does Beecher mean that I was that friend ? If he meant so, why did he not say so ? He knows that I never suggested that he should pay a dollar, or ever believed that the matter could be compromised by the payment of money, as it might have been by other proper action, if he had acted like a noble and courageous man, as I at one time hoped he might do and might be. This statement is insinuated to prejudice me in advance after he learned, on the 4th of August last, he could not use the best friend that "God ever raised up to a man " to act dishonestly and falsely to serve his selfish purposes. The charge is as false as another answer made on cross-examination to injure me by showing that I opened his letters, as follows :

"Q. By Mr. Winslow—Can you tell us what became of Mrs. Woodhull's threatening letter ? A. Mr. Moulton opened it."

The falsehood of this answer can be shown in a moment. That threatening letter—as indeed both letters from Woodhull to Beecher—were sent to me—was dated June 3, 1872, and was sent enclosed in a note from Beecher to me of the same date, with a request to answer it, as follows :

"MY DEAR MOULTON : Will you answer this ? Or will you see that she is to understand that I can do nothing ? I certainly shall not, at any and all hazards, take a single step in that direction, and if it brings trouble—it must come. Please drop me a line to say that all is right—if, in your judgment, all is right. Truly yours,   H. W. B."

Why does this minister of the Gospel make such reckless statements? Again, let me ask, does any man wonder, when they fall into such contradictions with his own letters, that Beecher and his lawyers should have desired so much to get possession of my documents, in order that they might square their statements and escape these contradictions ?

And in the whole course of all the negotiations had with his friends or his counsel as to the settlement of this controversy after the publication of the Bacon letter, I challenge any one to say that the word money was ever used by me, or by Tilton in my presence, as a method of settling this matter. True, before that publication I said to Tilton—what I say here openly and freely—that from my own fortune I would give $5,000 in gold to save its publication. And I also stated the fact that I so said to Beecher; and I also said to him that he had better give his whole fortune if that would stop it (and I believed it much larger then than I do now), in order to convince him how necessary it was, in my judgment, that this controversy should not be reopened.

No letter will be produced, I venture to say, from Tilton, and, I know, none from me or from mine, asking Beecher to take any course except to keep silence and cover his own sins as well as he might in this unhappy affair; and the only thing that seems to me like blackmailing him because of his connection with Mrs. Tilton is the plain demand for her mother (and, as now appears, his adopted mother), Mrs. Morse, that he should use his influence as a Christian minister to reappoint her brother in the Custom-House at New York. "And Elizabeth was disappointed that he did not, too."

I now produce certain letters of Mr. Beecher, which seem to contain an answer to his charge that when he paid the $5,000 he thought it was blackmailing, and was very much "dissatisfied with himeelf" for doing it. If he was so dissatisfied he certainly did not make it known to me, who had, as he says, extorted the money from him. It will be remembered that the $5,000 was paid on the 2d of May, 1873. The 7th of the following July brought me a very cordial invitation to visit him at his house in the country, contained in the following letter of that date, marked "S":

BEECHER TO MOULTON.

" PEEKSKILL, July 7, 1873—Monday, 7 P. M.

"MY DEAR FRANK :—I have just arrived. I called Saturday evening, to learn that you would not return till Monday. Can you come up Tuesday, or Wednesday, or Thursday? Let me know by letter or telegram. The trains are A. M., 8, 9:10, 10:45; P. M., 2, 4, 4:15, 5:30, 6:20, and 7. The four P. M. is express and good train ; if you come in the afternoon you should allow forty-five minutes from City Hall to reach Forty-second street station, and about one hour from your store.

"I have not seen you since the card. I will take good care of you, and even if others don't think so much of you as I do, I will try and make up. My vacation is begun, and am I not glad? Next week we expect company.

"The drouth is severe—no real soaking since the last of May, and things are suffering ; but yet the country is beautiful. The birds are as good to me as David's harp. I only need some one to talk to, and that one is *you*.

"Come when you can, and, coming or going, believe me faithfully and affectionately yours,
" H. W. B."

It will be seen that to complete his happiness he only wanted "some one to talk to, and that one is you,"—the man who had just extorted money from him as blackmail so that he felt " dissatisfied with himself," and to whom he says, " coming or going, believe me faithfully and affectionately yours, H. W. B."

On the 9th came another invitation in a letter of that date, which I insert, marked "T" ·

BEECHER TO MOULTON.

" THURSDAY EVENING, 9 July, 1873.

"MY DEAR FRANK:—Why not come on Saturday and spend Sunday ? You must get your comfort out of Nature and me, and not notice any withholding of countenance elsewhere.

"I preach in the village in the morning, but you can lie on the hill-side—in peace.

"The afternoon and evening will be open for all gracious influences which forests hide or heavens distill. The birds are not yet silent, though their pipes are somewhat feebler. Flowers are burnt, grass withered, grain reapt, grapes not ripe, strawberries gone, blackberries not come, raspberries in good condition and abundant, also watermelons, and, besides, a demijohn of—water!

"I want to see you and show you a letter, etc. Do you hear what Bowen is doing? Will he publish ? Find out if anything is on hand. Truly yours, H. W. B.

"Send me a line Friday if you shall come, so that I may *meet the train ;* otherwise pay your own hack hire."

This, it will be seen, promises me every inducement and entertainment if I would come. Besides, he wants to see his blackmailer and to "show him a letter, &c." For what purpose ?—to be blackmailed again ? . He also wants to know what Bowen is doing, and whether he will publish any statement. Was ever blackmailer treated by his victim as before ? The only punishment he threatens to put upon his blackmailer is that if he will not so arrange his business that his victim can have the chance of meeting him and driving him home in his carriage, he shall have to pay his own hack hire.

I also produce another letter of July 14, 1873, which, if it is not a full refutation of the charge that, up to that time, I had blackmailed Beecher or aided in blackmailing him, or that he believed I had done anything except in his interest, a charge of blackmail can never be contradicted. It is here inserted, marked "U":

BEECHER TO MOULTON.

"MY DEAR FRANK : I looked for you Saturday and received your *note* this morning—Monday.

"Howard writes that T. T. has sent to Mr. Halliday a note announcing that he did not consider himself for two years a member of the church.

"There is also a movement to let the other party [meaning Bowen] go to trial, and also to give him an avoidance of trial by some form of letter, I don't know what. I have not been consulted. I do not mean to meddle. It is *vacation*. Governor Claflin and wife, of Mass., will be here this week. I am getting at my writing again—at work on my book. I despaired of finishing it. I am more encouraged now. For a thousand encouragements—for service that no one can appreciate who has not been as sore-hearted as I have been, for your honorable delicacy, for confidence and affection—I owe you so much that I can neither express nor pay it. Not the least has been the great-hearted kindness and trust which your noble wife has shown, and which have lifted me out of despondencies often, though sometimes her clear truthfulness has laid me pretty flat.

"I mean to run down some day. Will let you know beforehand, that I may not *miss* you, for to tell the truth I am a little heart-hungry to see you ; not now because I am *pressed*, but because I love you, and will ever be faithfully yours,
" HENRY WARD BEECHER.

"Peekskill, July 14, 1873."

This shows how utterly and confidingly Mr. Beecher trusted me, and yet he now states that I had been blackmailing him for years and that Tilton had been a co-conspirator with me. And yet this letter recites that Tilton had written a note to the assistant-pastor of the church that he had not considered himself a member for two years.

Again, the letter shows that as to "the other party," Bowen, his church was colloguing together to give him an avoidance of a trial by some form of letter for the slanders of Bowen, lest Beecher should be injured. I say the church was colloguing, because Beecher says he had not been consulted and did not mean to meddle.

Mark, I call attention again, to emphasize it, to this letter, in order that there may be no mistake as to what Beecher's opinion was of the man who he now says he felt was blackmailing him at the time ; to the phrases : "For a thousand encouragements, for service that no one can appreciate who has not been as sore-hearted as I have been, for your honorable delicacy "—what, delicate blackmailing ?—"for confidence and affection, I owe you so much that I can neither express nor pay it."

Again, mark his promised visit to the blackmailer in these words : "To tell the truth, I am a little heart-hungry to see you, not because I am *pressed*, but because I love you, and will ever be faithfully yours."

I think I may be pardoned for lingering over this letter, for in it is my vindication from a black charge, to which Henry Ward Beecher is driven, to save himself, to make against me. Not only was I serving him at this time, but my wife—who knew all and knows all that I know—was saving him from despondencies and threatened suicide, and this letter gives the thanks he felt for her efforts, "although," he says, "sometimes her clear truthfulness has laid me pretty flat." I have already given one of those exhibitions of her truthfulness when she advised him to confess his sin, and ask forgiveness of man as he expected forgiveness of God.

Again I produce a letter of October 3, 1873, five months after the time when, he says in his statement, he believed that I was blackmailing him and "felt dissatisfied with himself " that he permitted it. It is marked " V ":

BEECHER TO MOULTON.

" FRIDAY NOON, October 3, 1873.

" MY DEAR FRANK : I have this morning got back, sound and fresh, and want to send my love to you and yours. I should see you to-morrow, but shall be out of town till evening. God bless you, my dear old fellow !

" H. W. BEECHER."

Let all the lawyers search all the annals of the crime of blackmailing, overhaul every police report, and produce another instance where, five months after it was known to the victim, he addresses his blackmailer with a "God bless you, my dear old fellow !"

It will be observed that these letters which I have thus far produced upon this question were *subsequent* to the time he learned that he was blackmailed. I now produce a letter of *previous* date, February 16, 1873, enclosing a check of that date, which is marked "W " :

BEECHER TO MOULTON.

" SUNDAY MORNING, February 16, 1873.

" MY DEAR FRANK : I have tried three times to see you this week, but the fates were against me. I wanted to store up a little courage and hopefulness before my three weeks' absence.

"I revisit my old home and haunts, and shall meet great cordiality.

"I enclose check subject to your discretion.

"Should any accident befall me, remember how deeply I feel your fidelity and friendship, your long-continued kindness and your affection.

"With kindest remembrances to Mrs. M., I remain always yours,

" H. W. BEECHER."

This discloses a still more singular transaction, because it shows that without being called upon the victim has tried three times to see me in one week, but failed. He was to be absent for three weeks, going to his old home, and wanted "to store up a little courage and hopefulness " for the occasion, although his old friends were to meet him with great cordiality. He says: "I enclose a check subject to your discretion;" that is, "Feed my lambs while I am away." Why don't Beecher produce the check of that date among those that he paraded before the Committee, and let us see how much of the $2,000 that made ? I wait for his reply before I speak further, lest "other hearts ache." Not content with expressions of gratitude while leaving, the note shows that he makes a will. He leaves it as a legacy to me in case of accidental death, that he died with the memory in his heart of my fidelity, friendship, and long-continued affection.

Is it necessary to my vindication that I should pursue this miserable afterthought of a charge of blackmail further?

If to obtain advantage to one's self by using the unfortunate situation of another is blackmail, then Beecher himself will come fully within that description. Beecher protected himself from Bowen by using the power that Tilton had over Bowen to get the tripartite covenant out of him, and yet he puts the fact in exactly the contrary light :

"The domestic offence which he [Tilton] alleged was very quietly and easily put aside, but yet in such a way as to keep my feelings stirred up, in order that I might, through my friends, be used to extract from Mr. Bowen $7,000, the amount of a claim in dispute among them. The check for that sum in hand, Mr. Tilton signed an agreement of peace and concord, not made by me, but accepted by me as sincere."

The precise contrary of this is true. Mr. Bowen had made certain charges against Beecher, and thereby caused Tilton to write a letter on the 26th of December, 1870, requiring Beecher to leave his church and city, which Bowen carried to Beecher. Why should Tilton have selected Bowen to be the bearer of such a letter if Bowen had not made the statements which Tilton recites in his letter to him were made, when Oliver Johnson was present, of five different acts and specifications of adulterous intercourse with five different women?

That letter was read by Beecher, and the dreadful accusations made by Bowen were fully known to him; and as this matter was contemporaneous with the accusations made by Tilton as to his own wife, Beecher desired that I should endeavor to protect him from these also, and insisted that I should agree to a reference to an arbitration, of which his friend and present committeeman, Mr. H. B. Claflin, was chairman, and submit Tilton's claim for damages for breach of contract by Bowen to that arbitration. And after a full hearing, in which all these so grave charges by Bowen to Tilton against Beecher—one of which was no less than rape—were stated in Bowen's and their presence, the arbitration unanimously agreed, first, that Bowen should pay Tilton $7,000 for a breach of his contract, and it was also made a condition that Bowen and Tilton should sign a covenant that they would not thereafterwards repeat accusations which were annexed to the paper; a majority of Bowen's friends on that arbitration—who had been agreed to by me because they were Beecher's friends—insisting upon Bowen and Tilton signing such a covenant in behalf of Beecher before Bowen and Tilton could have their money accounts settled; all of which was done at the same day and date.. So that Beecher in fact used Tilton's position with Bowen to extort from Bowen a certificate of good character, and that, too, after he had agreed to give Bowen three business advantages, and had also given him a certificate of good character and conduct in the church, in February, 1870, which he renewed at this time in these words:

"I deeply regret the causes of suspicion, jealousy, and estrangement which have come between us. It is a joy for me to have my old regard for Henry C. Bowen and Theodore Tilton restored, and a happiness to me to resume the old relations of love, respect, and reliance to each and both of them."

How could Beecher, if innocent, have signed such a certificate as that to Bowen upon a simple withdrawal of the charges, one of which described a brutal rape, without any averment that they were untrue, Bowen merely saying that he did not "*know*" anything of them?" And yet, without even the withdrawal of those charges privately a year before, after these statements had been made by Bowen and after the accusations were well known to Beecher, "after hours of conference, everything was adjusted and we shook hands;" and Beecher stated the fact of the reconciliation in Plymouth Church, and spoke highly of his Christian brother Bowen, and a new adjustment was obtained again in the manner I have stated at the time of the tripartite covenant. I do not republish the documents which show all this under Beecher's own hand, as they are already published in my former statement, and lithographed.

I agree that these facts are so unusual, so strange, so more startling than anything in fiction, that if I should state them upon my bare word I should challenge discredit everywhere except among those who know me well. But that they probably were well known to Mr. H. B. Claflin, one of Beecher's Committee, will appear from a letter heretofore published from Beecher to me, which I reproduce, as follows:

"MONDAY.

"MY DEAR FRIEND :—I called last evening as agreed. but you had stepped out. On the way to church last evening I met Claflin. He says B. [Bowen] *denies* any such treacherous whisperings, and is in a right state. I mentioned my proposed letter. He liked the idea. I read him the draft of it (in lecture-room). He drew back and said better not send it. I asked him if B. had ever made him a statement of the very *bottom* [sic] facts ; if there were any charges I did not know. He evaded, and intimated that if he had he hardly would be right in telling me. I think he would be right in telling *you*—ought to. I have not sent any note, and have destroyed that prepared. The real point to avoid is an appeal to the church, and then to a council. It would be a' conflagration, and give every possible chance for *parties*, for hidings and evasions, and increase an hundred-fold this scandal without healing anything. I shall see you as soon as I return. Meantime I confide everything to your wisdom, as I always have, and with such success hitherto that I have full trust for future. Don't fail to see C. [Claflin] and have a full and confidential talk. Yours ever."

It will be seen from this note that it was not Tilton's accusations that I then had in charge, but Bowen's, and the real point to avoid was " an appeal to the church and then to a council," and with such an appeal it would be a " conflagration."

In obedience to that letter I had a confidential talk with Claflin, and told him of the "treacherous whisperings" of Bowen, and also gave him the name of the party to whom Bowen had said that it was true that Beecher had made confession to him; and, as nearly as I can remember, that Bowen had not and did not intend to retract the charges which he had made against Beecher. Mr. Claflin deemed this so serious that he thought it best to call on Bowen with me, and we went, accompanied by the gentleman who had reported Bowen's conversation to me, and he repeated to Mr. Bowen in the presence of us all exactly what Bowen had said to him, "and," said he to Bowen, "if you say to the contrary you utter a falsehood."

Now, to conceal these "bottom facts," known to me if not to Claflin, Beecher had influenced Claflin to require, as arbitrator, the tripartite covenant—to which all Bowen's charges as set forth in Tilton's letter of January 1, 1871, were annexed—as a condition of the settlement of money matters between Tilton and Bowen, which alone were referred to that arbitration. What were those "bottom facts?" So far as Mr. Beecher is concerned, I have his full liberty to disclose all that I may know, as put in his public statement, and the public will now be in position to judge whether he really meant that I should:

"Q. Has Moulton any secret of yours in paper, in document, or in knowledge of any act of yours that you would not have see the light this hour? A. Not that I am aware of.

"Q. Have you any doubt? A. I have none.

"Q. Do you now call upon him to produce all he has and tell all he knows? A. I do."

(The compiler omits a passage in reference to a lady whose name was not mentioned elsewhere in the case. This passage appeared in the summons and complaint in the suit of Miss Edna Dean Proctor against Mr. Francis D. Moulton, printed below.)

I submit that if I had been inclined to blackmail Henry Ward Beecher either for myself or Tilton, Beecher knew, and the public now knows, in a degree, that I had much more cogent and all-powerful facts in my possession to strip him of his fortune to purchase my silence than the case of Mr. Tilton, and that if I had been, as he alleges, untrue to him, or if I had been, as is alleged in the report of his Committee, a "coadjutor with Tilton," "secretly from the beginning," to extort money from Beecher through a series of years, instead of standing as a shield to him, protecting him any and everywhere against the consequences of his own wicked acts, and only receiving money from him to aid in so shielding him—first, to support and educate the girl Bessie, lest she might injure him by prattling in the church under the influences of Mrs. Tilton's mother, Mrs. Morse, who, Bessie says, in her letter in a former statement, promised her dresses to tell lies, which fact she relates under her own hand—and only otherwise to aid him in some degree to repair the wrong which he admitted and now admits he had done to Tilton in breaking up his business, so that the temptation of poverty and want might not come to him as an inducement to turn upon Beecher, the author of his misfortunes;—I say if I had been inclined to extort money from him, either Tilton or myself might to-day have been the recipients of all the salary, earnings, and emoluments of Henry Ward Beecher, except enough only for a reasonably economical living for himself and family.

In view of these terrible revelations, the question will, indeed, well be asked, as it has been: "How could you, Mr. Moulton, sustain Beecher, knowing all these things, so monstrous, horrible, and revolting?" To this question, urgently springing from the facts, I answer that I did not know them all at once, as the public now know them. I began in the interest of a friend. I met another man of brilliant genius and high standing, older than I, who asked my friendship, which I promised him, and who trusted me implicitly; and as disclosure came after disclosure, as fact piled on fact, I could only stagger along under the load. These acts of guilt had already been done, many of them, years before, and at the time he promised me most faithfully and with sincere sorrow, tears rolling down his cheek, that all that was past, and his future should be bright and holy, as his past had been deemed to be by those who knew him not. However much I might cease to respect or love any party in the controversy, yet there were other hearts to ache. There were innocent children to be destroyed, families—more than one or three—to be separated, and a blight put upon Christianity and a shock to the moral sense of the community such as it never before received, if I threw down my burden; and therefore I have borne it as best I could, and now only speak in defense of my own honor, which I have endeavored to keep untarnished, so that those who come after me may not be overwhelmed in this maelstrom of vice and wickedness, in which I have nearly been submerged.

It is also objected to me that when I have been questioned in regard to these facts I have made a denial of them; and Mr. Beecher himself, or his lawyers, have had the temerity to publish in his statement a letter of mine to him of June 1, 1873, in answer to his despairing one of same date, telling me how he had lost all hope, and intimating to me in writing, as he had frequently before in words, that his only refuge was suicide.

Having made an allusion to Beecher's suicide, it may be well for me to state here the full circumstances of his confession concerning his proposed design. He told me—and repeated to another in my presence—that he had within reach in his own study a poison, which he would take if the story of his crime with Elizabeth should ever come to the public. He told me of a visit which he had made to a photographer's gallery, where he learned that one of the employes had mistaken a glass of poison for a glass of water, and, having taken and drunken it had fallen dead, with scarcely time to drop the glass. Beecher said that was what he wanted for himself; and, under plea of making some photographic experiments, he procured some of this same poison from the photographer, which he told me he intended to use if the revelation of his crime should be made. "And then," he said, "it would be simply reported that Beecher died of apoplexy; but God, and you, and I will know what caused my death." If those who blame me could have looked into his grief-stricken face and listened to the tones of his voice in the great emergencies in which he said there was no refuge for him but in death, they would have felt impelled, as I was, to as generous, as open-hearted a service as I practiced toward him. It would have taken a harder heart than mine, being witness of his sorrows, not to forget his sins.

"I have [he writes] a strong feeling upon me, and it brings great peace with it, that I am spending my *last Sunday*, and preaching my last sermon." I did, indeed, write to him, "you can stand if the whole case were published to-morrow." I did believe that, if he had made, as he was advised to make, a full and frank confession of the whole truth, as he had done to me, accompanied by such expressions of contrition and repentance as he had made to me, his church and the world would have forgiven him, and he would have stood. How much more, then, must I believe it now, when he can stand before the public preaching the gospel of Jesus Christ with all the facts made known, and I am driven, by blows and assaults of his people, from that which should be the house of God, wherein his adulteries and hypocrisies have been condoned by an admiring church?

For all this, I would not blame the deceived and worshipping Christians of that church, knowing how grossly they have been misled by those who have undertaken to exculpate Beecher at all hazards. They will at some time know. And when they do, they will pardon the strength of my language when I denounced in their presence their orator, who was addressing them, by the name of "liar." He stood before them vouching for the innocence of Beecher, and told them that he was the only one, besides the lawyers, who knew all the facts. Poor, deluded, young man! When he reads the following letter from Beecher, dated December 2, 1873, he will find that Beecher purposely kept him from knowing all the facts, and only introduced him to me that he might tell to me what was going on in the church. It is as follows, marked "X":

BEECHER TO MOULTON.

"LITTLE FALLS, N. Y., December 2, 1873.

"MY DEAR FRANK: I send you two letters for Banfield—to choose from,—the one extended, the other short and crisp. I hope that light is not far ahead; the night passes—the morning comes!

"I shall hear nothing from home of the progress of my affairs till I return.

"I introduced you to young Raymond because he is a personal friend, acute, and safe *should you need*. Of course I have never exchanged a word with him as I have with you—and he represents me only in church action.

"I hope you thought to see Woodruff about the matter I spoke of—lending money, &c.

"Would not Robinson, who stands strong in the Society of Pilgrims, be able to strike down in some degree the folly, and hold back that folly of running headlong after such malignants as Buck, Johnson, &c.? I only suggest.

"Give my love to the mother, and my earnest hopes that she is rapidly recovering.

"Ever truly yours, H. W. BEECHER."

And when he reads Beecher's letter of February 5, 1872: "If you [Moulton], too, cease to trust me and love me, I am alone. I have not another person in the world to whom I can go;" and again, in his testimony, where he says: "For he was the only man on the globe I could talk with on this subject; I was shut up to every human being; I could not go to my wife; I could not go to my children, and I could not go to my brothers and sisters; I could not go to my church; he was the only one person to whom I could talk; and when I got that rebuff from him, it seemed as though it would kill me, and the letter was the product of that mood into which I was thrown"—will "young Raymond" really think that he was ever the confidant of Beecher? He certainly never was a confidant of mine, for, measuring him at a glance, I never had an interview with him after Beecher introduced him to me. Which will Plymouth Church believe, their pastor's statement that Raymond did and could know nothing of the facts in this case, or believe young Raymond when he says he knows all?

Nay, even more, Beecher's Committee rest his exculpation upon my interview with the Rev. Mr. Halliday, in which, in language guarded, but intended to mislead that simple, confiding agent of Beecher, his assistant, I spoke to him what Beecher desired and instructed me to say when even that simple-minded old man's suspicions had been aroused by conferences with Tilton and others; and for that speech, by which I admit Halliday was misled, I received from Beecher the following letter, heretofore published, sent me on the Lord's day by a Christian minister, giving his thanks for my prevarication in his behalf to his assistant:

"SUNDAY, A. M.

"MY DEAR FRIEND: Halliday called last night. T.'s interview with him did not satisfy, but disturbed. It was the same with Bell, who was present. It tended directly to unsettling. Your interview last night was *very beneficial* and gave confidence. This must be looked after. It is vain to build if the foundation sinks under every effort. I shall see you at 10:30 to-morrow—if you return by way of 49 Remsen."

It has been held honorable for men who had had amours with a reputable woman to deny, even under oath, those amours, to protect from exposure the fair fame and name which had been confided to their keeping. Not by any means intending to set up any such standard of morality, but which is sustained in Beecher by a portion of the press, which says he ought to stand by the woman, under how much more temptation was I acting when in my charge had been placed, without any guilt on my part, the honor of women of fair name and high station, the welfare of a church, the upholding of the fame and reputation of the foremost preacher of the world, the well-being of Christianity itself, and the morals of the community—all, and more, involved in my failure to hold the facts concealed from every mortal eye! The silent "volcano" on which he says he was walking, might have been at any time caused to burst forth by my imprudent answers to scandal-loving, curiously-prying men and women, or ministers of the Gospel who were engaged in endeavoring to find out; and my silence when their questions were put to me, stating supposed facts, would have been at once deemed assent.

But if there was any wrong in my concealment of these facts from the world let Plymouth Church labor with Mr. Bowen, one of its leading members, who concealed them from the church in consideration of the publication of his pastor's letters and sermons in the *Independent*. Let Mr. Claflin, Beecher's chosen committeeman, who presumably, had been told the "very bottom facts," be dealt with; and, indeed, let him who is without sin among them all in that regard, first cast a stone.

I do not review or animadvert upon the report of the Committee, because every one has expected the result of its labors from the beginning. No disclosures were made to them, and they took care not to call before them any witnesses who knew the facts except the parties implicated, and have clearly shown that it was a partizan tribunal, organized to acquit—as Beecher confessed to me on the 5th of July last it was. By thinking men no weight will be given to its unsupported opinions, however speciously argued in a report which is but a rehash of the statements of the accused criminals, both written in whole or in part by his lawyers.

I was quite aware that I was to be struck down in case I did not side with Beecher, if "I did not choose between Tilton's statement and mine," as he states he asked me to do. My friends put before me the consequences of my standing firm in what I knew to be the truth and the right; that I must incur the enmity, as I have felt the assaults of Plymouth Church; that great financial interests were involved in the standing of that church, whereby much gain comes, in money, if from nothing else, to some favored members thereof; and I feel that I have a right to say that if I could have been swerved from my sense of duty to myself and to justice, every outside inducement urged me to stand by "Beecher's statement." Of course I discerned that any statement I should make must be ruinous to Mr. Beecher, and if I made it I must be taken as siding with the falling cause of my nearly ruined friend, Theodore Tilton. And I appeal to the fair judgment of all men, what motive could I have in making myself his ally and the enemy of Mr. Beecher, except impelled by integrity of purpose and all that makes up the word "duty," to stand by the right as I knew the right to be.

I have, however, the consolation of knowing that I only suffer as everybody else suffers who has dared to say a word for the truth against Beecher. Each and all in turn have been assailed by every form of obloquy and detraction as the new phases of the case required for the exculpation of the accused. First, it was heard through the press that the letters which Tilton put in his sworn statement were forgeries, when it was supposed that the originals would not be forthcoming. Then, Tilton was insane, and a labored analysis of all the maladies of his family was paraded before the public to show that he was insane ; but the "method in his madness" exploded that theory. And then, the last refuge was that all that he had done was for the purpose of blackmailing Beecher, and as all that was done was through my hand, of course I must be destroyed, or the new theory of a conspiracy of four years' duration would come to nought. Everybody who should come forward to say a single word upon the subject unfavorable to the accused has received the same treatment. Mr. Carpenter is placarded to the world through Beecher's statement as "a kind of genial, good-natured fool," and Mr. Beecher's sister, the amiable, intelligent, enthusiastic, and clear-headed Mrs. Hooker, now, happily for her peace, abroad, who had become the recipient of the knowledge of the facts of Beecher's guilt, was placarded as insane ; and when she had advised him to make a clear and full confession, in the interest of truth and justice, to rescue a woman from jail whom Mrs. Hooker believed was incarcerated for having told simply the truth, and threatened to disclose the truth from his pulpit if Beecher would not, by Beecher's authority, and under his advice, conveyed through me with his approbation, Tilton went to poor Mrs. Hooker and broached the slander that she, too, was charged with being guilty of adultery from the same source as his wife was, and when Mr. Beecher was told that his sister sunk down in tears and gave up under such a gross accusation, he chuckled at the success of the "device." Whatever " devices" were used to protect Henry Ward Beecher to save himself, it was not one of mine to defile the fair fame of his sister. And, until it was ascertained what part she would take in the controversy, his wife, Mrs. Beecher herself, was struck at in his behalf by his elder brother, Rev.

William Beecher, in an interview published in a Western paper, from which I extract the following, the correctness of which has not been, so far as I know, denied :

"I believe he [Beecher] looks upon the marriage relation as sacredly as any one. In fact I know he has suffered great trouble on account of his wife, and has endeavored to be faithful to her, notwithstanding the sore trials she has cost him. It has separated him from his kindred, from his brothers and sisters, who were prevented from coming to the house on her account. Yet he bore with her, and in every way endeavored to arrange matters so that they might visit him. Still I think she loved him and was faithful to him."

Notwithstanding this, Beecher appeals in his statement to "his happy home" as one of the reasons why he could not have been unfaithful to his marriage vow.

Again, it is paraded in the newspapers that Mrs. Beecher produced before the Committee all Mrs. Tilton's letters, having opened them before Beecher had had an opportunity to read them, as she did all of his other letters, and this report gains credence from the fact that he wrote to Elizabeth after he declares he had stopped all intimacy, as he had promised to do, "that she was now permitted to write to him because he was living alone with his sister," and in another letter takes care to inform her of the fact that his wife had sailed for Havana and Florida. And Mrs. Tilton, too, after having said and unsaid everything in order to save Beecher, after having falsified and stultified herself in every possible way for his salvation, and so become useless hereafter as a witness or "refreshment," only remains in his mind "under a divided consciousness" that "she was a saint and chief of sinners." And she is thrown aside like a worthless weed in this cruel paragraph of the report of his Committee :

"It is not for the Committee to defend the course of Mrs. Tilton. Her conduct upon human responsibility is indefensible."

All these attacks were before me, and I knew I should not escape, and I have not, although all the blessings of heaven were called down upon me by Beecher in every note he ever wrote me, all of which breathed the fullest confidence in me up to the 4th of August, nine days before he made his statement, wherein he charges me with a most contemptible crime because I refused to give up the papers to him which I knew were my only protection against him ; for I had learned to know the selfishness and cruelty of the man who sacrifices all for himself.

And yet, in view of our relations for the past four years, I can scarcely realize the fact that he turned upon me, even when at his request I was keeping silent for his sake ; and now, with all that he has put upon me, it is with difficulty that I summon sufficient resolution, in anguish of spirit, to enable me to put forth the statement that I am now compelled to do. For I here aver that I never have made public what was the nature of Beecher's offense, or what was the evidence in my possession to prove it, until I did so in my former statement prepared for the Committee, although statements were made in the newspapers to that effect which may have inflamed the mind of Beecher against me. I had pledged my honor to silence except I was attacked, and I have redeemed that pledge at whatever violence to my feelings and sense of justice. Nor have I ever made public the facts in this subsequent statement until they now appear, and yet there has been a newspaper report publishing what purports to be a portion of them, but which was gathered from others and not from me. On the contrary, I have taken every and all means that I could to conceal and keep them out of sight, driven even to answer many men who asked me in regard to them in such a way as to mislead them without stating to them any absolute falsehood, although I have no doubt some of them, remembering the impression they got from me, thought that I have stated to them what has since been contradicted by my published statement of what has actually been known to me, and the reasons of which I have heretofore explained.

All the present necessary facts to form a correct judgment of Henry Ward Beecher, and my own course and character are now before the public, and I submit to the candor and judgment of all good men and women whether, under all the emergencies in which I have been placed, I have not endeavored to do that which seemed to me to be right and proper, faithfully and loyally to those whose interests I had in charge, and especially to Beecher himself, pleading guilty to everything of want of judgment and unwisdom in trying to master the almost insurmountable difficulties which surrounded me, which can rightly be imputed to me.

If the true interests of the Christian church are promoted, under the light of existing and known facts, by sustaining Beecher, as the foremost man in it, it is a matter of concern to Christian people, in which my judgment will not be consulted. But let them remember as they do so the teachings of the Master from the Mount :

"Ye have heard that it was said by them of old time, Thou shalt not commit adultery.

"But I say unto you, whosoever looketh on a woman to lust after her, hath committed adultery with her already in his heart.

"And if thy right eye offend thee, pluck it out and cast it from thee, for it is profitable for thee that one of thy members should perish, and not that thy whole body should be cast into hell."

FRANCIS D. MOULTON.

PROCTOR VERSUS MOULTON.

, THE following is the text of the papers in the suit for damages of Miss Edna Dean Proctor against Mr. Francis D. Moulton, for the writing and publishing an alleged libel. The lady claims damages in $100,000. The papers were published on September 17, but owing to the absence of Mr. Moulton from Brooklyn on that date, they were not then served. The papers consist of a "precipe," a "capias ad respondendum," a "complaint," and an "affidavit." They are as follows in their order:

THE PRECIPE.

CIRCUIT COURT OF THE UNITED STATES, EASTERN DISTRICT OF NEW YORK.—Edna Dean Proctor *versus* Francis D. Moulton.

CITY OF BROOKLYN, September 17, 1874.

SIR: Please issue a process out of the District Court of the United States for the Eastern District of New York, pursuant to directions given below.

TRACY, CATLIN & BRODHEAD.

To the Clerk of the United States District Court for the Eastern District of New York:

Plaintiff—Edna Dean Proctor.
Defendant—Francis D. Moulton.
Form of process—Capias ad respondendum.
On what brought—Action on the case for libel.
Amount of claim—$100,000.
Date of process—September 17, 1874.
Costs.
When served—September 17, 1874.
When returnable—(Date).

Upon this a *capias* is issued which reads as follows:

CAPIAS AD RESPONDENDUM.

The President of the United States to the Marshal of the Eastern District of New York, Greeting:

We command you that you take Francis D. Moulton, if he shall be found in your district, and him safely keep, so that you may have his body before the Judge of the Circuit Court of the United States of America, for the Eastern District of New York, to be held at 168 Montague street, in the City of Brooklyn, in the said Eastern District, on the first Wednesday of October, to answer said Edna Dean Proctor, plaintiff, in a plea of trespass, in this case for libel ; and also to a certain bill of said plaintiff against said defendant for composing and publishing a false and malicious libel of and concerning the said plaintiff, Edna Dean Proctor, to her damage of $100,000, according to the custom of said Court, before the said Judge, then and there to be established, and that you have then and there this writ.

Witness, the Honorable Morrison R. Waite, Chief Justice U. S. Supreme Court of the United States, at the City of Brooklyn, the 17th day of September, in the year one thousand eight hundred and seventy-four. B. L. BENEDICT, Clerk,

E. B. HUSTED, Deputy Clerk.

Tracy, Catlin & Brodhead, Att'ys of Miss Proctor.

THE COMPLAINT READS AS FOLLOWS :

U. S. CIRCUIT COURT FOR THE EASTERN DISTRICT OF NEW YORK.—Edna Dean Proctor, plaintiff, against Francis D. Moulton, defendant.—Eastern District of New York, to wit: Edna D. Proctor complains of Francis D. Moulton and alleges

That whereas the said Edna Dean Proctor, at the time of the libel hereinafter mentioned and long before did use and exercise the business and employment of author and editor of books and literary works, and thereby acquired considerable gains, profits and advantages ; and that the said Edna Dean

Proctor, in, about and concerning said employment and said books and literary works, and concerning questions and disputes arising out of and relating thereto did write and sign the paper or document set forth without signature, dated January 10, 1871.

That said Edna Dean Proctor now, is a good, true, honest, just, and chaste person, and as such has always behaved and conducted herself, and until the committing of the grievances by the said Francis D. Moulton in publishing said libel as hereinafter mentioned, was always respected, esteemed, and accepted by and among all her neighbors and other good and worthy persons, to whom she was in anywise known, to be a person of good name, fame and credit.

That the said Edna Dean Proctor hath not ever been justly, or until the time of the publishing of the said libel by the said Francis D. Moulton, as hereinafter mentioned, been suspected to have been unchaste or to have had sensual connection with any man, by ravishment or otherwise.

By means of which premises the said Edna Dean Proctor before the publication of said libels by said Francis D. Moulton, as hereinafter mentioned, had deservedly obtained the good opinion and credit of all her neighbors, and other good and worthy persons to whom she was in anywise known.

That the said Francis D. Moulton, defendant herein, well knowing the premises but greatly envying the happy state and condition of the said Edna Dean Proctor, and contriving, and wickedly and maliciously intending to injure the said Edna Dean Proctor, and her said good name and credit, and her business, and employment, as aforesaid, and to bring her into public scandal, infamy, and disgrace, with and among her neighbors and other good and worthy persons, and to cause her to be suspected and believed that she, the said Edna Dean Proctor, had been and was unchasted and had had sexual connection with the Rev. Henry Ward Beecher, a minister of the Gospel, by ravishment, fornication, or otherwise ; and to vex, harass, oppress, impoverish and wholly ruin the said Edna Dean Proctor heretofore about the 11th day of September, 1874, said defendant, Francis D. Moulton, did compose and publish, and cause and procure to be published, of and concerning this plaintiff, the said Edna Dean Proctor, in a printed newspaper called the *New York Daily Graphic*, published in New York City, a certain false, scandalous, defamatory and libelous matter, following, to wit :

I showed to Mr. Beecher the letter of Tilton to Bowen bearing date January 1, 1871, containing charges alleged to have been made by Bowen in the presence of Tilton and Oliver Johnson, and he (Beecher) deemed it necessary to tell me the truth concerning the adultery with the woman [meaning the plaintiff] to whom he supposed Bowen referred in that interview, although the charge gave no names.* According to Tilton's letter Bowen charged Beecher with the rape of a virgin. Beecher said he was in ——'s house, told me for what purpose he was there, and mentioned the name of the woman [meaning the plaintiff], who, he said, when he was leaving, gave him what he strangely termed a "paroxysmal kiss"—(I never heard that word before, which causes me to remember it vividly)—and that, being tempted by the woman, he had sexual intercourse with her. He said : "I knew she was not a virgin," and described to me his means of knowing that fact, the precise language of the description of which I trust his friends will excuse me from repeating. He said that she immediately retired from the room, went up-stairs, and came down very much fluttered, saying : "Oh, I am covered with blood !" He said he knew she lied, and was surprised at her, feeling convinced that she had had other and previous experiences of the same sort.

Having myself had knowledge of the facility with which he could obtain from his women [meaning unchaste women] a retraction of such charges and denial of the fact, as in the case of Mrs. Tilton of the confessed adulteries by her, on the 30th of December—twelve days before—I said to him. "It will be necessary for you, if you are on friendly terms with that woman [meaning the plaintiff], to get from her a retraction. Otherwise you may find yourself some day at Bowen's mercy." He went to get a

---

* Before this sentence the following paragraphs appear in Moulton's "Vindication" :

Passing by the more indefinite charges of Bowen, "the many adulteries committed by Beecher," let us take the crime, the exact language of which in my former statement I felt called upon to omit in the interest of public decency. But in order that the charge of Bowen, which was twice reconciled and condoned by Beecher, using this word both in its legal and literal sense, because if not true there can be no more outrageous libel, which is a crime—I feel compelled, in the cause of public justice, to give the very words as they originally appeared in Tilton's private letter to Bowen, of January 1, 1871, and as they are annexed to the covenant of reconciliation:

"You [Bowen] related to me the case of a woman whom you said (as nearly as I can recall your words) Mr. Beecher took in his arms by force, threw down upon a sofa, accomplished his deviltry upon her, and left her flowing with blood."

Could an innocent clergyman have allowed such a charge to be made and more than once reiterated, however guardedly, by a leading member of his church, and rest content until his innocence was fully and clearly established, if in no other way, in a court of justice? Bowen, I was informed, claimed to have the details of this transaction from the woman's own lips. And it was to avoid the investigation of this charge among others, that Beecher says in his letter that "the real point to avoid is an appeal to the church and then to a council," and upon that he advised with me.

I feel it due to myself, however, before proceeding further in this narrative, to make this explanation. In my former statement to the public, prepared for the Committee, I endeavored in all matters to state the facts with as much delicacy as their wickedness would allow, the consequence of which was, that my very reticence and suppression of the exact language in which Beecher's confessions were conveyed to me were by his friends made a ground of accusation that I had either mistaken the purport of what he said, or that, if I were telling the truth, I would give his words. Therefore I am now compelled, in narrating this most shameful affair, to violate the bounds which I set myself in my former statement, in order that no such like accusation may be reiterated against me. And if that is published which ought not to be published, it is not my fault, but the necessity made by Beecher and his friends for my own vindication.

retraction from her, and on the 10th of January, 1871, brought back the paper I here insert, which he so obtained :

"Some ten years ago, when under great grief and excitement, I said things injurious to Mr. Beecher to Mr. Bowen. I always speak strongly, and then I was nearly beside myself and used unmeasured terms, which represented rather my feeling than my judgment.

"I afterwards became convinced that in many things I was mistaken. I became satisfied that Mr. Beecher's course toward me was meant to be kind and honorable.

"From that day to this our relations have been cordial and friendly. —— —— ——.

"January 10, 1871."

A casual glance at this document shows that Mr. Beecher was not as successful in this retraction, which he evidently did not dictate, as in the case of Mrs. Tilton; and the retraction itself, in its cautious wording, was so much more damaging as evidence than a direct charge of the woman that might be contradicted would be, that it was thought best that it should not see the light of day, and it has not until now.

The question was, Did he ravish this person ? He admitted to me the connection, but insisted that he used no force, only dalliance. That accusation had been repeated by Bowen, and the best Mr. Beecher could get from her was that she had "told Bowen things injurious" to Beecher; that she "always speaks strongly," and was "nearly beside herself and used unmeasured terms, which represented rather my feeling than my judgment."

But what was desired to get denied was the fact itself, and that fact the criminal connection, which was neither matter of "feeling" nor "judgment" in the sense in which the words are used in the retraction. But whether done by force or dalliance is a question of both feeling and judgment, and so much is retracted ; and knowing the relations between this woman and Beecher to have been not only "cordial and friendly," but thereafterwards very intimate, I gave credit to this version of his intercourse, and particularly because Mr. Beecher, to confirm his statement that he had not ravished her, brought to me several letters from her to him, which I still hold, showing the continuance of friendly relations with her. I do not give the lady's name, and withhold the photo-lithograph of her letter, because I do not wish needlessly to involve a reputation which has thus far escaped public mention by any of the parties to this controversy. If the facts stated here should identify the person [meaning the plaintiff] concerned with him and if those who are interested in her feel aggrieved, let them avenge that grief, if upon any one, upon the pastor of Plymouth Church, and not upon me, as I have heard threatened it would be if I ventured to state the facts of Beecher's guilt in this case [meaning that he committed adultery with this plaintiff].*

Said defendant, meaning and intending that this plaintiff was the author or writer of the paper or document dated January 10, 1871, and that this plaintiff is the woman concerning whom said communications and confessions were made, and that said libelous and defamatory matter which said defendant alleges was communicated to and confessed to him by said Beecher was as a matter of fact true.

By the means of publishing of which said libel by the said defendant, Francis D. Moulton aforesaid the plaintiff, the said Edna Dean Proctor, hath been and is greatly injured and damaged in her business and employment, namely in the sum of $100,000, and hath been and is greatly injured in her said good name, fame, credit and brought into public scandal, infamy and disgrace.

That the defendant, Francis D. Moulton is, and at the time of the said libel was, a resident of the City of Brooklyn. in the State of New York.

That now and at the time of the publication of said libel, this plaintiff, said Edna Dean Proctor, is and was not a resident of New York, but a resident of South Framingham, in the Commonwealth of Massachusetts, and therefore she brings her suit, etc.

Wherefore this plaintiff demands judgment against said defendant, Francis D. Moulton, for the sum or $100,000, together with the costs of this action.   TRACY, CATLIN & BRODHEAD,
Attorneys for Plaintiff, 189 Montague street, Brooklyn.

MISS PROCTOR'S AFFIDAVIT READS THUS:

UNITED STATES OF AMERICA, EASTERN DISTRICT OF NEW YORK, *ss.*:

Edna Dean Proctor, being duly sworn, doth say that she is the plaintiff in the above entitled action, that the foregoing complaint and declaration is true of her own knowledge.

[Signed]   EDNA DEAN PROCTOR.

Sworn to before me, this seventeenth day of September, 1874.

[Signed]   SAMUEL B. CALDWELL,
Notary Public Kings County, N. Y.

---

* The following sentence closes the paragraph as it appeared originally in Moulton's "Vindication":

I have felt the blows of Plymouth Church already because I have told the exact truth about their pastor. I have been threatened with more if I shall continue to do so. But unawed by threats, and, as far as I may be, unbiased by wrong, injustice, and false accusations, the facts shall be stated as they are known to me—and known to God ; and only adding that this last terrible narrative of crime was given me by Beecher in the presence of a witness, I dismiss this tragic episode to the main controversy.

TILTON ON BEECHER.

A COMPLETE STATEMENT OF THE CASE AGAINST THE PLYMOUTH PASTOR.

On Friday, Sept. 18, the following final and complete Statement of Mr. Theodore Tilton's case against Mr. Henry Ward Beecher was published:

Throughout the country, if I rightly interpret the public press, a majority of candid minds admit the truth of my indictment against the Rev. Henry Ward Beecher. But many fair-minded persons, animated by a charitable doubt, have asked me for some further confirmation of the one chief allegation in this controversy. My Sworn Statement, published in the Brooklyn *Argus* of July 20, was not written for publication, otherwise I would have cited in it a greater number of facts and proofs. The only use which I designed for that Statement was simply to read it to the Investigating Committee, before whom I expected to confirm its charges by such additional testimony as the investigators (if such they could be called) should require. But the Committee, consisting of six trusted friends of the accused, appointed by him for the sole purpose, not of discovering his guilt, but of pronouncing his acquittal, resented my accusation against their popular favorite, and, to punish me for making it, converted their tribunal into a star chamber for trying, not him, but me. The questions which they asked me were mostly irrelevant to the case, and the only part of my testimony that bore directly on Mr. Beecher's adultery they cancelled from their report of my examination. One of the Committee's attorneys said to me, "If Mr. Beecher is guilty, I prefer not to know it." The whole Committee acted on this predetermined plan. The chief witnesses who could testify against Mr. Beecher—notably Francis D. Moulton, Joseph H. Richards, Martha B. Bradshaw, Susan B. Anthony, Francis B. Carpenter, Emma R. Moulton, Henry C. Bowen, Thomas Kinsella, and others—were either not willing to testify, or their testimony was set aside as not being officially before a tribunal that did not wish to receive it.

Accordingly, my indictment against Mr. Beecher was left by the Committee to stand without other proof than that which my statement of July 20 afforded, unassisted by other witnesses. When the Committee asked me if the statement contained my whole case, I answered no; for it was simply a succinct narrative, giving only such dates and documents as I thought sufficient for the Committee's private inquiry, and yet more than sufficient to put an impartial Committee on the right road to the whole truth. Since the date of its publication several counter-statements have appeared, including Mr. Beecher's denial, closely followed by Mrs. Tilton's—both of which were untrue; then by the Committee's numerous publications of one-sided testimony, and last of all by a verdict based solely on these untruthful denials, to the neglect of all the positive allegations on the other side ; so that the Committee accepted the silly fictions of Bessie Turner, but rejected the serious facts of Mr. Moulton, nor did they even invite Mr. Bowen to appear before them ; all which unfair proceedings and uncandid publications require of me, for the sake of some hesitant minds, a reply which the larger portion of the community have already made for themselves. I therefore submit the following facts and evidences, arranged as far as convenient in chronological order, and making a narrative which, as it progresses step by step, will aim to correct and counteract, one by one, the untrue denials of Mr. Beecher and Mrs. Tilton, and the unjust deductions of the Committee.

I. I will begin by showing the kindly nature of my personal relations with the Rev. Henry Ward Beecher down to July 3, 1870, the date of Mrs. Tilton's confession of their criminal intimacy; disproving by authentic documents the charge that I was animated towards him by vindictiveness or any other hostile feeling.

First. During his absence in England, Mr. Beecher sent to me, under date of Sunday, October 18, 1863, the long and memorable letter which Mrs. Stowe afterwards incorporated in her biography of him. In this letter he says:

"MY DEAR THEODORE: * * * Should I die on sea or land, I wanted to say to *you who have been so near and dear* to me, etc."

The single phrase which I have italicised is sufficient to show that Mr. Beecher, while traveling in a foreign land, having left behind him a greater multitude of friends than most men could have claimed, and seeking to choose from all these one to be the custodian of his special and secret thoughts, chose *me*. And his affectionate reason for so doing is stated by himself to be that I was "*near and dear to him.*"

Second. Two years later, on the arising of political differences between Mr. Beecher and me, resulting in my publicly criticising his course, I addressed to him a private letter, November 30, 1865, containing my heartfelt assurances that these differences did not becloud my love for him. In this letter I said :

"If *I* should die leaving *you* alive, I ask you to love my children for their father's sake, who has taught them *to reverence you and to regard you as the man of men.*"

The above tribute derives the greater force because I paid it to Mr. Beecher when we were at political variance and in public antagonism.

Third. Three years later he sent to me a gift copy of "Norwood," inscribed by his own hand with the following affectionate words :

"To
THEODORE TILTON—
who greatly encouraged the author to begin and persevere—with the affectionate regards of
HENRY WARD BEECHER.

"March 18, 1868."

I distinctly recall several warm allusions which Mr. Beecher, in conversations with me at that period, made to the good cheer with which he said I inspired him during the composition of that book.

Fourth. A year later such was the respect in which I held Mr. Beecher that I spent more money than I could afford in order to possess his portrait, painted by the first artist of our day. The following money receipt will speak for itself :

"Received from Theodore Tilton, by draft from Aurora, Illinois, dated February 25, 1869, five hundred dollars, being payment in full for portrait of Rev. Henry Ward Beecher.   WM. PAGE.
"April 1, 1869."
    [Stamp cancelled.]

Mr. Beecher acknowledges that he sat *fifty times for this portrait at my request*—a fact which puts to flight the charge that either he or Mrs. Tilton regarded me as his enemy, or as anything but his admiring friend.

Fifth. In the winter of 1869-70 I published a volume called "Sanctum Sanctorum," which contained numerous affectionate references to Mr. Beecher, of which the following, taken from an editorial of mine in the *Independent*, is a sufficient specimen—one of many :

"With grateful pride we look back to our joint connection with that good man in this journal as a golden period in our life and labor."

Such words as the above are the unmistakable tribute of a friend to a friend.

Sixth. Coming down still later, I received from William Lloyd Garrison a letter dated Roxbury, April 6, 1870, from which I quote the following lines :

"You say of Mr. Beecher that he would honor the presidency of any society."

This brief extract shows that I not only honored Mr. Beecher myself, but sought to make my friends honor him likewise.

Seventh. On the 11th of May, 1870, a public and fraternal correspondence passed between Mr. Beecher and me in our capacity as presidents of two suffrage societies holding their public meetings simultaneously in New York, and I still possess his autograph letter sent to me on that kindly occasion.

I have given the above brief extracts (which I might multiply) to show the uniform friendliness of my feeling towards Mr. Beecher down to the time when the discovery was made to me of his fatal assaults on the honor of my house. These evidences disprove Mrs. Tilton's extraordinary and fictitious charge, wherein—speaking of what she calls "the last ten years," "whose stings and pains she daily schooled herself to bury and forgive,"—she said that one of these "stings and pains" was the fact that her husband made an "almost daily threat that he lived to crush out Mr. Beecher; that he [Mr. T.] had always been Mr. Beecher's superior, and that all that lay in his path—wife, children, and reputation if need be—should fall before this purpose." This charge by Mrs. Tilton of malice on my part towards Mr. Beecher was a pure invention. She might with equal truth have accused me of entertaining during the same period a secret and daily hostility towards Horace Greeley or Charles Sumner. The Committee accepting Mrs. Tilton's false statement, incorporated it into their verdict, and thereby falsely charge me with exhibiting towards Mr. Beecher what they called "a heated and malicious mind," an accusation which has never been true of me towards any human being, and which even at the present hour is not true of me towards the Rev. Henry Ward Beecher. In so far, therefore, as the Committee's verdict bases itself on this supposed fact—which is not a fact but a falsehood—the report for lack of foundation falls to the ground.

II. I ought next to show, by similar documentary evidences, the harmony and affection existing between Mrs. Tilton and myself to July 3, 1870. But this argument has been so fully made by the publication of the voluminous private correspondence between myself and wife, filling several pages of the

Chicago *Tribune*, of August 13, 1874, that I need here only point to that great sheaf of letters, and to pluck merely a few straws from them—just enough to remind the reader of their general scope and tone:

MRS. TILTON TO HER HUSBAND.

April 16, 1866.—"I know not how I could live without your precious daily letter."
December 28, 1866.—"Above all you rise grandest, highest, best."
January 7, 1867.—"What a delicious way you have of rebuking and teaching me—pretending, always, that you think I am the loveliest and best of little wives."
January 11, 1867.—"When I look at you I say, 'Yes, my soul is satisfied; our union is perfect.'"
January 20, 1867.—"Your letter expressing great patience toward me in reference to my finances, came yesterday, and I thank you with all my heart; you are magnanimous and generous beyond all men."
February 5, 1867.—"The inspiration of my daily life now is the thought of looking upon your dear face again."
February 11, 1867.—"God bless you for the confession of your perfect love for me."
February 1, 1868.—"The supreme place is yours forever."
February 7, 1868.—"Oh, you are truly and nobly loved in your home."
February 18, 1868.—The idea of a faithful, true marriage will be lost out of the world—certainly out of the literary and refined world—unless *we* revive it."
March 15, 1868.—"If the *thought* of seeing you is so delicious, what will be the *reality?*"
February 4, 1869.—"My darling, I must believe that this beautiful home which you have made for us must have given you a greater amount of satisfaction than we generally secure from earthly labors."
February 7, 1869.—"I consecrate myself to you so long as I shall live."
February 11, 1869.—"You will find a worn and weary woman thoroughly satisfied when once again she may rest in your bosom."
February 28, 1869.—"Among the terrible changes of many hearths God has kept us steadfast with a glowing love, admiration, and respect for each other."
March 20, 1869.—"I am nearly beside myself thinking that in *one week* I am yours and you are mine again."
August 18, 1869.—"I have taken your sentence in large letters,'*With Love Unbounded*,' and hung it over my mantel-piece."
January 3, 1870.—"I am in a neat little hotel where the hostess reads the *Independant*, and wishes more to see its editor than any other living man. Such a sentiment from this simple-hearted woman was like wine to my tired body and soul."

MR. TILTON (DURING THE SAME TIME) TO HIS WIFE.

January 9, 1865.—"My sweet love, I begin to see, as never before, that the center of the world, to an honorable man, is his own family, his wife's sitting-room, his children's play-places, his HOME."
October 25, 1865.—"Nothing is more deeply rooted in my conviction than that I owe more to your pure love and wifely example than to all the world beside."
March 28, 1866.—"But, whichever wind blows, I find in a little while that you, my dearest, are my sheet-anchor."
December 6, 1866.—"If you should ever appear to me anything less than the ideal woman—the Christian saint that I know you to be—I shall not care to live a day longer."
December 12, 1866.—"More and more you grow into the picture of the perfect wife."
December 14, 1866.—"I see you as the noblest of women."
December 18, 1866.—"I believe that if you were not on the earth, but in heaven, I could not help writing to you a letter every day."
January 3, 1867.—"If we should have achieved nothing besides a perfect union of two loving hearts, we shall have wrought out for ourselves a heaven on earth, and perhaps afterwards the heaven above the earth."
January 21, 1867.—Not a day passes over my head but I have some rare, high, and beautiful transfiguration of yourself before my soul, by which I see an image that fills me with love, reverence, and humility."
February 15, 1867.—I count your love for me as the chief reward and pleasure of my life."
January 10, 1868.—"I think sometimes that I have the sweetest family that God ever gave to a man."
March 13, 1868.—"Every letter which you have sent has been like a buoy under me, helping me to swim in a sea of troubles."
March 4, 1869.—"My chief title to self-respect is that I have won and kept the unblemished love of the best and truest woman whom I have ever known."
January 30, 1870.—"I shall feel like a sailor tossed on the sea until I get to my final haven of rest in my own house:—there is but one home."
April 6, 1870.—"Accept my undivided and ever-growing love, and kiss the children for their father's sake."

Let it be borne in mind that the above correspondence between Mrs. Tilton and myself covers the long period which her testimony assigns to my feigned ill-treatment of her, namely, "the ten years of sorrow, filled with stings and pains," including my alleged locking her in a room for days together, and depriving her of food and fire!

To throw a side-light on the happy domestic relations which the above correspondence portrays, I will add here a brief letter, without year, received by me while on my lecturing travels from my then office-associate in the *Independent* and Mr. Beecher's present editor of the *Christian Union:*

OLIVER JOHNSON TO THEODORE TILTON.

"INDEPENDENT OFFICE, December 12.
"MY DEAR THEODORE: I wonder what you would give for a chance to kiss the little woman who only an hour since kissed me!

"Ah, my dear fellow, it is a great sacrifice you make in leaving such a home as yours.

"I was delighted this morning on receiving a visit from your wife, and hearing her say what beautiful love-letters she gets from you. She seemed well, and smiled on me through her tears as she spoke of you and the long season of separation that is before you. * * * Yours lovingly,

"OLIVER JOHNSON."

Mr. Beecher himself strikes a similar blow at Mrs. Tilton's pretence of my ill-treatment of her :

"She seemed to me [Mr. Beecher says] an affectionate and devoted wife, *looking up to her husband as one far above the common race of men.*"

Mrs. Tilton's charge of ill-treatment is already so universally discredited that I need not answer it further. Nevertheless, I take a just pride in mentioning that my venerated mother, who recently made a journey from her country home to visit me in Brooklyn, did me the sweet honor to declare that both she and my father, in lately looking back over my nearly forty years of life, were unable to recollect that I ever spoke to either of my parents a single harsh word, whether as child, youth, or man. My own children could testify that never one of them has received from me a solitary stroke from whip or rod, nor ever once a blow of the hand in corporal punishment. I have had offers from some of my past associates both in the *Independent* and the *Golden Age* to testify that during the years of my daily association with them they never once saw me in anger. Many of the former inmates of my house, including relatives, friends, and domestics, stand ready to testify to my uniform gentleness towards Mrs. Tilton and towards all other persons in my home. As God is my witness, I solemnly aver that I never laid my hand on my wife save in the way of caress, nor did I ever threaten her with violence, nor subject her to privation. Furthermore, she has at all times possessed herself of all my means and resources, it being well known to my family that my earnings were spent always for the beautifying of my home, and never for purposes in which my wife and children had not an equal share with myself.

I will insert here the following extract from a written statement signed jointly by my father and mother.

"KEYPORT, N. J., August 30. 1874.

. . . "Also we further testify that we never heard of any ill-feeling between our son Theodore and his wife, or any complaint of ill-treatment by him towards her, until we lately heard of it for the first time in Elizabeth's published testimony, which we believe to be untrue.

(Signed)

"SILAS TILTON.
"EUSELIA TILTON."

III. Having thus (in section I.) disposed of my alleged vindictiveness towards Mr. Beecher, and (in section II.) of my imaginary brutality towards Mrs. Tilton, I now come to Mrs. Tilton's confession, July 3, 1870, wherein she narrated the story of her seduction by her pastor, the Rev. Henry Ward Beecher. It is a requirement of truth that I should state explicitly the circumstances out of which this confession sprang, and the substance of the confession itself.

During several weeks previous to July 3, 1870, Mrs. Tilton had been in the country, having gone thither in a spirit of alienation. I had recently detected in her, to my grief, a tendency to deceit and falsehood foreign to her normal and pure nature. Accordingly a cloud was on her spirit at parting. But I neither knew nor suspected that her depression had its root in her relations with Mr. Beecher.

During her absence I wrote to her that she would forfeit my respect the moment she ceased to tell the truth—a letter which she afterwards reminded me of, saying that "it had pierced her very soul."

After her absence had been prolonged for several weeks, during which only a slight correspondence passed between us, she came unexpectedly to Brooklyn, reaching home about nine o'clock in the evening of July 3. I expressed my surprise at seeing her, greeted her with cordiality, and marked her improved health and rosy look.

Within an hour after her arrival, sitting in her favorite chamber, wherein her infant son Paul had died two years before, she made a tender allusion to his death, and then said that she had come to tell me a secret which she had long kept in her heart in connection with that event—a secret which she had several months before, while on a sick-bed, resolved to tell me, but lacked the courage. Since then the tone of her mind, she said, had improved with her health, and, having prayed for strength to tell me the truth without fear, she had now come on purpose to clear her mind of a burden which, if longer concealed, she felt would by and by grow too great for her to bear.

What the secret was which she was about to disclose I could not conjecture.

Before disclosing it she exacted from me a solemn pledge that I would not injure the person of whom she was about to speak nor communicate to him the fact of her making such a revelation, for she wanted to inform him in her own way that she had divulged to me the facts in the case.

After exacting these conditions, to which I pledged myself, she narrated with modesty and diffidence, yet without shamefacedness or sense of guilt, a detailed history of her long acquaintance with Mr. Beecher—of a growing friendship between them—of a passionate fondness which he at length began to exhibit towards her—of the inadequacy of his home life and his consequent need that some other woman than Mrs. Beecher should act the part of a wife to him—of the great treasure which he found in Mrs. Tilton's sweet and tender affection—of his protestation of a greater homage for her than for any other woman—of her duty to minister to his mind and body—and of the many precious arguments by which he commended these views to her, in order to overcome her Puritan repugnance to them ; and she said that finally, in an interview between herself and Mr. Beecher at his house, not long after her little Paul's death, and as a recompense for the sympathy which her pastor had shown her during that bereavement, she then and there yielded her person to his sexual embrace.

This event, she stated, occurred October 10, 1868, during my absence in New England, and she showed me a memorandum in her diary marked at that date with the words, "A day memorable."

She further said that on the next Saturday evening (while I was still absent) Mr. Beecher visited her at her home in Livingston street and consummated with her another act of sexual intimacy.

She further confessed that at intervals during the ensuing fall and winter, and in the spring following, she repeated with him certain acts of criminal intercourse, yielding to him seldom though solicited often.

Furthermore, with great particularity, she mentioned the several places of these interviews, which I cannot bring myself to chronicle here.

This confession was made by Mrs. Tilton voluntarily, and not in response to any accusation by me, for I had never accused her of guilt either with Mr. Beecher or with any other person, nor had I ever suspected her of such wrong-doing. Neither was her confession made in sickness, but in unusual health. It was the free act of a sound mind under an accumulating pressure of conscience no longer to be resisted; her sin, as she described it to me, consisting not so much of her adultery as of the deceit which she was thereby compelled to practice towards her husband.

In Mrs. Tilton's published statement of July 24, 1874, she admits that she made to me in July, 1870, a "confession." She says:

"A like confession with hers (namely, Catherine Gaunt's) I had made to Mr. Tilton in telling of my love to my friend and pastor one year before."

So, too, the Committee's report concedes that Mrs. Tilton made a "confession." The report says:

"It now appears that Mrs. Tilton became strongly attached to Mr. Beecher, and in July, 1870, confessed to her husband an overshadowing affection for her pastor."

The above acknowledgments—the first by Mrs. Tilton and the second by the Committee—are true so far as they go. Mrs. Tilton did confess her love for her friend and pastor, but she also confessed not only her love for him, but his love for her; and still further she confessed (and this was the chief burden of her confession) that this love resulted in a sexual intimacy extending during fifteen or sixteen months.

This confession, stripped of its details but including its principal fact, was made by Mrs. Tilton, not only to me, but to several other persons, including Mr. Moulton and his wife; and a similar confession was made by Mr. Beecher, not only to me, but to Mr. Moulton and his wife.

Some of the confidants to whom Mrs. Tilton intrusted this secret were lady-friends of hers, whose names I am not willing to be the first to drag into this unhappy controversy. But as one of these persons has been already quoted by the public press (I refer to Miss Susan B. Anthony, to whom Mrs. Tilton told her story in the autumn of 1870), I here adduce a portion of a letter from Miss Anthony to Mr. Beecher's sister, Mrs. Hooker, of Hartford. It will be seen from the date that the letter was written just a fortnight after the publication of the Woodhull tale—two years ago :

SUSAN B. ANTHONY TO MRS. HOOKER.

"ROCHESTER, November 16, 1872.
* * * "The reply of your brother to you is not more startling, not so open a falsehood, as that to Mr. Watters [a newspaper reporter] : 'Of course, Mr. Beecher, this is a fraud from beginning to end ?' 'Entirely.'

"Wouldn't you think if God ever did strike any one dead for telling a lie, He would have struck then ?

"I feel the deepest sympathy with all the parties involved, but most of all for poor, dear, trembling Mrs. Tilton. My heart bleeds for her every hour. I would fain take her in my arms, with her precious comforts—all she has on earth—her children—and hide her away from the wicked gaze of men.
* * * * * * * *
"For a cultivated man, at whose feet the whole world of men as well as of women sits in love and reverence, whose moral, intellectual, social resources are without limit—for such a man, so blest, so overflowing with soul food ;—for him to ask or accept the body of one or a dozen of his reverent and revering devotees. I tell you he is the sinner—if it be a sin—and who shall say it is not ?

"My pen has faltered and staggered ; it would not write you for these three days : and now, seven P. M., Saturday, comes a letter from Mrs. Stanton, in reply to mine, asking how could she make that denial in the Lewiston Telegram [Referring to a report of Mrs. S.'s having denied the Woodhull story]. She says : 'Dear Susan, I had supposed you knew enough of papers to trust a friend of twenty years' knowledge before them. I never made nor authorized the statement made in the Lewiston paper. I simply said I never used the language Mrs. Woodhull put in my mouth ; that whatever I said was clothed in refined language, at least, however disgusting the subject. I have said many times since the denouement that if my testimony of what I did know would save Victoria from prison I should feel compelled to give it. You do not monopolize, dear Susan, all the honor there is among womankind. I shall not run before I am sent, but when the time comes I shall prove myself as true as you. No, no ! I do not propose to shelter a man's liberty at a woman's liberty is at stake.'

"Now, my dear Mrs. Hooker, I wish you were with me to-night to rejoice with me that Mrs. Stanton is determined to stand firm to truth. I ought not to have believed the Telegram true. I feel ashamed of my doubts, or rather of my beliefs. Mrs. Stanton says her daughter Hattie heard all she said to the two clergymen, and said to her : ' Why, mother, you might as well have told them the whole thing was true.'

* * * * * * * * * *

" No, Mrs. Hooker ; I cannot now, any more than last winter, comply with your request to reveal Mrs. T's whole story.

* * * * * * * * * * *

"Your brother will yet see his way out ! and let us hope he will be able to prove himself above the willingness that others shall suffer for weakness or wickedness of his.

"If he has no new theories, then he will surely be compelled to admit either that he has failed to live or to preach those he has ; and, whichever horn of the dilemma he may choose, will acknowledge either weakness or wickedness, or both. Affectionately yours,

"SUSAN B. ANTHONY."

The above letter from Miss Anthony not only indicates that Mrs. Tilton confessed her sexual intimacy with Mr. Beecher, but shows also that this intimacy was brought about, not because (as Mr. Beecher dishonorably charges in his statement), Mrs. Tilton " *thrust her affection on him unsought*," but because he himself was the aggressor upon her love, honor, and good name. I know full well from Mrs. Tilton's truthful story—told me at a time when she could have had no possible motive to deceive —that Mr. Beecher made the advances, which she for a long time repelled. It was he, not she, who instigated and achieved the criminality between them. It was he, the revered pastor, who sought out his trustful parishioner and craftily spread his toils about her, ensnaring her virtue and accomplishing her seduction. Mrs. Tilton was always too much of a lady to thrust her affection upon Mr. Beecher or any other man " unsought." And yet Mr. Beecher, after having possessed himself of a woman at whose feet he had knelt for years before her surrender, has finally turned upon her with the false accusation that *she* was *his* tempter, not *he hers ;*—for which act on his part I brand him as a coward of uncommon baseness, whom all manly men, both good and bad, should equally despise. I shall never permit him to put the blame on this woman. " She is guiltless," he said in his apology. He shall never take back that word. He well knew that the motive to guilt did not come from this gentle lady's pure and cleanly mind. I repeat here what I said before the Committee—and what I shall believe to the end of my life—that Elizabeth Tilton is a woman of pure heart and mind, sinned against rather than sinning, yielding only to a strong man's triumph over her conscience and will, and through no wantonness or forwardness of her own.

I have been told that I endanger my success in the battle which I am now fighting by making this concession to my wife's goodness of motive. But I am determined in all this controversy to speak the exact truth in all points ; and I know that no indelicacy in Mrs. Tilton's behavior ever proceeded from her own voluntary impulse or suggestion ; but that, on the contrary, her highly emotional religious nature was made by her pastor, the means whereby he accomplished the ruin of his confiding victim.

I take the liberty to quote here a passage from a letter by Mrs. Elizabeth Cady Stanton to Mr. Moulton, as follows :

MRS. STANTON TO MR. MOULTON.

"TENAFLY, N. J., September 2, 1874.

" *Francis D. Moulton.*

"DEAR FRIEND : In your forthcoming statement, whatever you say or fail to say, do not forget as a brave knight to bring your steel on the head of " The Great Preacher" *for his base charge that Elizabeth Tilton thrust her love on him unsought.*

" *You* know, better than Susan or *I* do, the time and arguments by which he achieved his purpose.

" Alas ! alas ! how little charity, to say nothing of common justice, has been shown woman in this tragedy. * * *
Sincerely yours,

"ELIZABETH CADY STANTON."

One of Mrs. Tilton's friends—a lady to whom she long ago made her full confession—an intimate to whom she says in one of her letters, " Dear ——, I am as nearly open before you as before God; " and in another, " I love you as no other woman I ever knew; " and in still another, " You remain to me, darling, the chief of human friends; "—this lady has received many letters from Elizabeth, some of which contain allusions to Mr. Beecher, not by name, but by the pronoun *he* or *him*, with an underscoring. In Mrs. Tilton's behalf (not in mine) I have been shown one of these letters, putting an end to the idea that Mrs. Tilton imposed her affection upon Mr. Beecher " unsought." The letter opens thus :

MRS. TILTON TO MRS. ——.

" JULY 31, 1872.

" MY DEAR AND GOOD ——: ' Does not your heart prompt you to say a few words to your ——, or is it all on *her* side—this longing to put herself in communication with you ?'

" This extract from your sweet note of to-day I answer rather strangely, perhaps, but with all tenderness. I do not yearn, nor did I ever yearn for *him*, because yours [*i. e.*, your love], like his, was so unexpected, a perpetual surprise, a gift ever new, too high for me to appropriate."

The above letter utterly annihilates the idea that Mrs. Tilton " *thrust her affection on him unsought ;*" and no man who ever sued for and obtained a woman's love, however wrongfully rendered to him, could make such an accusation without proving himself capable of a baseness which few men,' I believe, entertain towards women.

If any further proof were needed that it was Mr. Beecher who solicited Mrs. Tilton's affection, and not she who thrust hers upon him—which he says many women in Plymouth Church do—this proof will be found in the letters which he wrote and in the gifts which he made to this ever grateful but never obtrusive woman. Touching these letters the Committee's verdict contains the following extraordinary statement:

"There is no proof (they say) of clandestine correspondence, nor attempts in that direction. Mr.. Beecher's letters were, as a rule, opened, arranged, and read by his wife."

In reply to the above (as a single illustration of its untruth) I need only say that after Mrs. Tilton deserted her home I found in a locked closet, hidden away beyond the chance of detection, a collection of clandestine letters from Mr. Beecher to Mrs. Tilton; some of them unaddressed to *her* name and unsigned by *his*, revealing their designation only by the envelopes, and their authorship only by the handwriting. In one of these letters, printed in Mr. Moulton's recent statement, Mr. Beecher says:

"My wife takes boat for Havana and Florida on Thursday."

In another he asks Mrs. Tilton to write to him, for he says:

"It would be safe. I am now at home here with my sister, and it is *permitted* to you."

A man who—taking prompt advantage of the departure of a lynx-eyed wife who, "as a rule, opens and arranges and reads his letters"—makes haste to send this information to another lady from whom he solicits letters, saying it will be safe now for her to write them—such a man cannot accuse this lady of "thrusting her affections upon him unsought."

In like manner, just as the Committee have denied Mr. Beecher's clandestine letters, he himself has denied his clandestine gifts. He says that the only gift-tokens which he ever made to Mrs. Tilton were a "brooch" and "a copy of books." I do not understand what he means by "a copy of books." Is it a copy of the English edition of "Norwood," in three volumes? He made her such a gift. But since her recent desertion of her home I have found a great number of books given to her by Mr. Beecher, sufficient to make a small library of themselves—a collection which I never saw before, nor did I know that he had given them to her. A few of these books—mainly his own productions—contain, in his own handwriting, inscriptions addressed to her expressive of his regard and esteem. I transcribe the following:

MR. BEECHER'S GIFT BOOKS TO MRS. TILTON.

ROYAL TRUTHS. Edition, Ticknor & Fields, 1865. Inscription:
"Mrs. Theodore Tilton, with the regards of the author."
THE SERMONS of Henry Ward Beecher. Edition, J. B. Ford & Co., 1869. First and second series, two volumes. Inscription in each volume:
"Mrs. Elizabeth Tilton, with the regards of Henry Ward Beecher.
"February 8, 1870."
THE OVERTURE OF ANGELS. Illustrated. Edition, J. B. Ford & Co., 1870. Inscription:
"Mrs. Elizabeth Tilton, from her friend and pastor, H. W. Beecher.
"February 8, '70."
LECTURE-ROOM TALKS. J. B. Ford & Co., 1870. Inscription:
"Mrs. Elizabeth Tilton, from H. W. Beecher.
"April 9, 1870."
LIFE OF JESUS THE CHRIST. Illustrated. Edition, J. B. Ford & Co., 1871. Inscription:
"Mrs. Elizabeth R. Tilton, with the respects and affections of her friend, Henry Ward Beecher.
"Brooklyn, N. Y., October 13, 1871."

Among his other gifts to her—one of the few which she did not secrete from my knowledge—was a large water-color painting of a trailing arbutus, done from nature by a well-known New England artist, and inscribed as follows:

"For MRS. ELIZABETH TILTON,
"From her friend,
"H. W. BEECHER.
"October 18, 1866."

The inkstand from which she wrote her letters to her husband was, as I have learned, a gift from Mr. Beecher. I have also learned that during my absence on lecturing tours he kept her constantly supplied with flowers. To these he added some flower-vases to hold them, of various patterns. He gave her perfumes, fancy soaps, note-paper, and envelopes. Moreover, hidden away in the same closet to which I have alluded, I found a collection of photographs of his face and figure in various postures. Another of his gifts to her, which I have found since her desertion, was a packet wrapped in a white cloth like a winding-sheet, which, on being opened, contained a religious picture marked in his handwriting, "July 29, 1866," representing a design of the Virgin Mary holding the dead Christ. I would not here particularize these clandestine letters and surreptitious gifts except that the Committee have boldly denied the letters and Mr. Beecher the gifts, and both Mr. Beecher and the Committee have attempted to deceive the public by the base defence that this misguided but always modest lady was guilty of an unwomanly boldness—foreign to her nature and impossible in her action—of " thrusting her affections upon him unsought."

IV. Immediately after Mrs. Tilton's confession and her retirement into the country, in the summer of 1870, the tone of her letters to her husband underwent a striking change. These letters were no longer shining links in a golden chain of daily messages of love and good will, like the series published in the Chicago *Tribune*. Every letter or note was now shaded by some allusion to the shipwreck which had been wrought in her life and her home.

These missives, thus freighted with the burden of her grief, I destroyed as soon as I received them, for fear they might be lost and found, and thus become tell-tales of the writer's secret. So far as I now remember, I destroyed every letter which I received from her during the summer and fall of 1870, and it is only by accident that I now possess a single one belonging to that period. This was written to her mother, and contained a copy of one written by my wife to me. Before producing this remarkable letter—or double letter—I must refer somewhat unfavorably to Mrs. Tilton's mother, the Hon. Mrs. N. B. Morse.

This eccentric lady has for years past been animated by violent hatreds and an uncontrollable temper, resulting often in hysterical fits. In one of these she clutched her husband by the throat and strangled him till he grew black in the face ; after which the venerable man called the family together and enacted a legal separation from her, which he maintains to this day. She has twice thrust her parasol like a rapier, into my breast, breaking off the handle in her violence. Often and often she has sent me notes avowing her intention of taking my life. Her stormy peculiarities are well known to our family, and are partly excused on the ground that she is not wholly responsible for her conduct;— a view of her case which led her physician, the late Dr. Barker, of Brooklyn, to recommend her for treatment to an asylum for the insane.

One evening in the summer of 1870, Mrs. Morse (before she received from Elizabeth her confession, though this confession had already been made to me) spoke calumniously of a lady who was then, and is now, Mrs. Tilton's most intimate and honored friend. Mrs. Morse's calumny was that this lady had permitted a *liaison* with myself. I said to Mrs. Morse in Mrs. Tilton's presence : " Madam, either you must retire from this house, or else speak more respectfully of its master and his guests ; and for your good behavior in this respect I shall hold your daughter responsible." Mrs. Morse instantly and in rage interpreted this as a counter-accusation against Mrs. Tilton, and turning towards her, cried fiercely : " Elizabeth, have you been doing wrong ? " There was something in the suddenness of the question which struck Elizabeth mute and dumb : whereupon Mrs. Morse fell upon her with another question : " Is it Mr. Beecher ? " Mrs. Tilton suddenly left the room, Mrs. Morse following her, repeating her question until Elizabeth bowed her head in assent. Mrs. Morse then wrung her hands and exclaimed, " Oh, my God ! my God ! "

During the several days immediately ensuing, Mrs. Morse, who had been made ill by the disclosure, held a few conversations with me, in which she begged me to be gentle with her daughter, who, she said, had never before committed any sin in her life.

So violent was Mrs. Morse's feeling against Mr. Beecher at this period, that she threatened to cut to pieces the oil-portrait of him which Page had painted for me ; in consequence of which threat I removed this work of art to Mr. Moulton's house, where it remains to this day.

Then, for a short time, Mrs. Morse showed me love and respect. With her hands on my head she gave me her blessing, and said that if I could forgive the wrong which her daughter had done me, I would receive the mother's affection so long as I lived. She said she was heart-broken and could henceforth look only to my leniency towards Elizabeth for any future comfort for either of them in this world.

This disposition towards me in my mother-in-law was of short duration. She soon became seized with the conviction that I would follow the common custom of men in similar situations, and would sue for a divorce, to the ruin of her daughter's name.

Finding that I took no such measure, yet expecting me to take it at any moment, she resolved upon a plan to thwart me in it. With great cunning, and with a gift for diplomacy amounting to genius, she conceived the idea of defeating my imaginary lawsuit for a divorce by inventing false tales against me, and hiring and bribing the young maid, Bessie, to propagate them. These are the tales which Bessie referred to four years ago when, in a letter to Mrs. Tilton, she said :

" Your mother, Mrs. Morse, has repeatedly attempted to *hire* me, by offering me dresses and presents, to go to certain persons and tell them *stories* injurious to the character of your husband."

The object for which these tales were told is thus described by Mrs. Tilton in a letter to a lady friend, dated January 13, 1874:

" *My husband has suffered much with me in a cruel conspiracy made by my poor, suffering mother, with an energy worthy of a better cause, to divorce us, etc.*"

The stories which Mrs. Morse propagated in the carrying out of this conspiracy, are mentioned by Mrs. Tilton in a letter to Mr. Moulton, as follows:

" *The story that I wanted a separation was a deliberate falsehood coined by my poor mother, who said she would take the responsibility of this and other statements she might make, etc.*"

The above extracts from familiar documents illustrate the machinations of Mrs. Morse, yet too faintly portray the incessant ingenuity of a woman who has been for years the cause of unhappiness to her husband, to her son, to her daughter, to all her family and relations, and especially to me.

The plan which Mrs. Morse devised for thwarting my supposed proceedings for divorce was carried forward by her during Mrs. Tilton's absence in Ohio, in the fall of 1870. Mrs. Morse was the more unchecked in prosecuting this scheme because she was at that time acting as my housekeeper and pretending to be my friend. But her experiment of housekeeping and friendship did not prosper long. After a few weeks of calm behavior, she gave me strange insults and threats. She provoked a quarrel with our servant Nora, and sent her away. She had a violent altercation with our other servant, Mary, necessitating the calling of a policeman. As I did not side with Mrs. Morse in this conflict she approached me with a carving-knife, and said she would like to cut my heart out. Unable to endure this treatment with equanimity, I ordered her to quit my house, which she did.

Mrs. Tilton being still absent in the West, Mrs. Morse's vacant place was taken by an elderly lady, Miss Sarah Ellen Dennis, who had been a friend of our family for twenty-five years, a good and upright woman, now in her grave. I am able to fix the time of Miss Dennis's coming, because my daughter Florence then wrote from Brooklyn to her mother in Ohio, October 26, 1870, as follows :

"Grandma is going to take charge of Mr. Bates's house. Father has gone to see if he can get Cousin Ellen to come here. I hope she *will* come, for I like her very much."

As a point has been made by Mrs. Tilton and Mr. Beecher of the alleged indignities which this high-minded and grave housekeeper practised toward Mrs. Tilton on the latter's return from the West, and as a malicious accusation of an improper intimacy between this good woman and myself has been concocted by Mrs. Morse, I am constrained to say, in behalf of the dead, that all who knew the late Miss Dennis will bear testimony to her gravity of character, her devotion to her duties, and her sober experience of years ; and I am outraged—as her relatives and friends justly are—that her honored memory should thus be insulted over her dust. Her only offense consisted in a kindly attempt to counteract with wise tact some of the extraordinary mischiefs which Mrs. Morse was preparing for the future ruin of my home. Miss Dennis, shortly after the publication of the Wood-hull tale, wrote to me a note, dated December 3, 1872, in which she said :

"Take the advice of a *true* friend. As you have waited so long, don't rush into the papers about this horrible Woodhull story. *If you deny it and put Mrs. Woodhull down, then Mrs. Morse will rise up. She tells these same tales herself, and then quotes you as the author of them.* This is the reward you get for defending Lib so manfully. *The more you try to do the more her mother will undo.*

After Mrs. Morse's retirement as my housekeeper, to be succeeded (at my daughter's request) by Miss Dennis, I received from my mother-in-law an almost daily letter of abuse. From these letters I will make a few extracts to show the spirit and temper of a woman with whom I believe no man could possibly dwell long at peace. These extracts will moreover serve to show how well Mrs. Morse understood her daughter's criminal intimacy with Mr. Beecher. I have hitherto shrank from making my wife's mother testify against her own daughter, but since these twain have united to wage against me a pitiless war of falsehood and obloquy, I am forced in self-defense to exhibit these extracts from Mrs. Morse's letters :

ELEGANT EXTRACTS FROM MRS. MORSE TO MR. TILTON.

—"You infernal villain ! This night you should be in jail. * * * Why your treacherous tongue has not ere this been taken out by the roots is a wonder."

—"Your slimy, polluted brawny hand curses everything you touch. A perfect type of Uriah Heep. This is not original. It is well understood why I have been turned out of your rotten house."

—"I have said you were not worth the time and paper, and I would never waste either on you; but the hypocrisy and villainy of your course has of late been so apparent, and the sight of your base and perfidious person so revolting, I can tell you my opinion better this than any other way."

—"I can with the stroke of my pen bring you to your knees and brand you for life. * * * The world would be better for the riddance of such a villain, and think no more of putting you aside than killing the meanest cur which runs the street. You diabolical, infernal, I would have killed you," etc., etc., etc.

—"You told Caroll I hit you. You poor deluded fool! Caroll knew you deserved it."

—"Retributive justice has partially overtaken you. Woman's rights have killed you. The remark I made three years ago last summer: If you had gone for your family instead of looking after woman's rights meetings, you would not be obliged to look up your lost trunk. For this I was told to leave the house and never enter it. For this you were made a beggar suddenly. Just as I predicted. And this I call retributive justice."

—"If you have given her [Miss Dennis] the privilege of going to people and insinuating her dark and damning facts regarding your wife and children, it is a poor rule which won't work both ways."

—"I *never* associated my child's name in the most *distant* manner with B. [Mr. Beecher.] The nearest I ever came was when Joseph [Mrs. Morse's son] questioned me how much I knew of the matter—if I thought B. was implicated. I said, 'All I can say is, I will tell you all my darling told me—*she bowed her head,*' just as she did on that '*dark and dreadful night*' when you, with your fist in her face, compelled her to acknowledge this *sacred secret.* And that act, with all its sickening details, will haunt me to my dying day."

—"My poor, dear child never answered your bestial want—too religious by nature and grace for such as you, and this want *he* answered. Till this hour I can swear that the only comfort I have taken has been in the fact that he *was* a comfort and *did* sympathize with her."

"Mr. M. * * * knows all, and it has been the sorrow of his life, and he now in a small measure understands my suffering."

—"Do you suppose after your vile tongue has been permitted to wag to E. D. that *I* would be silent? No, I will not. My poor, distracted child said, not a week since, 'Ma, I fear Ellen Dennis will ruin me and my children forever.'

—"*You retaliate by exposing the only deed which my martyred child ever did which was not God-like, and this was brought about by the love and sympathy* THAT *man had for her wretchedness; and how she ever came to expose him or herself to one she knew so well could not be trusted, eternity will not be long enough to reveal the mystery.*"

I will not garnish this narrative with further writings from Mrs. Morse, except to add two brief notes of hers—one to Mr. Bowen, the other to myself. Shortly after my retirement from the Brooklyn *Union*, one of Mr. Bowen's clerks, thinking to give me an illustration of public sentiment touching my removal, sent me the following anonymous scrap, which I discovered at a glance to be in the familiar handwriting of my affectionate mother-in-law Mrs. Morse :

"MR. BOWEN : I congratulate you upon being rid of an Infidel, Liar, Hypocrite, Unbeliever, Freelover, A Tyrant, Knave, and FOOL.
"January 20, 1871. SUBSCRIBER."

The latest communication received by me from the author of the above letters was at the beginning of the present year, contains the following confession and proposition :

"CLINTON PLACE, January 29, 1874.
"THEODORE : * * * I am more than willing to agree to this compact. It is this: If you from this day will agree to do all in your power to make the remainder of her life [Mrs. Tilton's] peaceful and happy *(as far as the fearful past is concerned), shield her from reproach, giving her the feeling of safety,* etc. * * I will for my part from this hour speak well of you." etc.

Not to amplify needless illustrations of the character of Mrs. Morse, I will add only one more, consisting of a letter I had occasion to address to Judge Morse, her husband, two years ago concerning her behavior in my house :

MR. TILTON TO JUDGE MORSE.

"174 LIVINGSTON STREET, December 6, 1872.
"*Hon. N. B. Morse.*
"MY DEAR FRIEND: I regret to trouble you with any new facts concerning your trials or mine growing out of the temper or mania of Mrs. Morse, but I need your advise.

"Mrs. Morse had not been in my house for two years or thereabouts (to the best of my recollection), when suddenly a few days ago she first sent me a violent and insulting letter, threatening my life, and followed this with entering the house and insisting on her right to stay in it. I had an interview with her on her first appearance, treating her with kindness and expressing gladness at seeing her. They were the first words which we had exchanged for many months. But she soon afterwards exhibited the old traits, and in an aggravated degree, with insults and outrages to my feelings of a character which self-respect does not permit me here to quote.

"I have made no reply to her except to request her to leave the house ; then, afterward, on her refusing to do so, positively to demand that she should go as soon as possible.

"She, therefore, asserts her claim to live in the house against my will, proposing to take the third story front room, to keep the key to it, and to encamp herself as a member of the family, having her meals sent to her in order that she may not be annoyed with sitting at the table.

"What I want to ask you is, is there any legal measure to which I can quietly resort, so as to save her from a public exposure of her eccentricities, and at the same time to protect myself in my own house?

"I will say still further that she does not hesitate to criminate her daughter in the most glaring way : to say that the only pleasure she now takes in the world is in looking back on the time when (as she says) Elizabeth had the solace of a paramour ; that she hopes she will have five hundred others, and that she is determined to have what she terms the family secret known and proven to the world.
"Yours, with more sorrow than patience,
"THEODORE TILTON."

The eccentric, uncontrollable, and mischief-making woman whose peculiarities are sufficiently set forth in the above extracts, devised a plan in 1870, as I have already said, to divorce Elizabeth from me in order to prevent my supposed design to divorce myself from her. In furtherance of this plan, Mrs. Morse, during Mrs. Tilton's absence in the West, not only circulated among my neighbors atrocious tales about me—such as kicking my wife while pregnant, knocking her with my fist to the floor, coming home drunk at night, etc.—but she furthermore undertook to win Elizabeth to this plan of divorce by plying her with letters filled with other equally false reports of my behavior—for example, that I was holding orgies in my house with strange women, making myself a —— —— and uttering drunken accusations against my wife, by vilifying her with Mr. Beecher as one of his many mistresses, etc.

Elizabeth, although she was needful to Mrs. Morse's design of divorce, could not be converted to it. Nevertheless, under the powerful influence of her mother's slanders concerning me, my wife became alarmed at the prospect of my using *her* ruin as a prelude to my *own*. She seemed to reflect her mother's idea that I was taking a sudden plunge to perdition, drinking to drown my sorrows, filling my hard-working daily life with more sins than I had time to commit, hoping for my wife's speedy death, and threatening to publish her infamy to the world as soon as she should be under the sod !

Accordingly, Mrs. Tilton wrote me an earnest letter, full of allusions to her own previously-confessed criminality with Mr. Beecher, begging me to be merciful to her in her brokenness of spirit, and remonstrating with me for the bad state of mind into which Mrs. Morse had described me to have fallen.

This letter I received at the office of the Brooklyn *Union* in November, 1870. I well remember reading it twice over, and then destroying it on the spot. I have since come into possession of a copy of it which Mrs. Tilton made at the time, incorporating it in a letter to her mother. This is the double letter to which I have previously alluded. It was written from Marietta, Ohio, to chide me for the supposed recklessness into which she had been informed by her mother that I had lapsed ever since the time of Mrs. Tilton's confession of adultery. The letter is as follows:

MRS. TILTON TO MRS. MORSE.

[Written from Marietta, Ohio, to Brooklyn.]

"NOVEMBER, 1870.

"I feel my duty now and love to you, my dear mother, impels me to send to you a copy which I this morning have written to Theodore, which I insist that you destroy, and use not in conversation with him. This—because of my trust in you—*you will do I'm sure.*"

"FRIDAY MORNING.

"Oh, Theodore, Theodore ! what shall I say to you ? My tongue and pen are dumb and powerless, but I must force my aching heart to protest against your cruelty. I do not willingly chide. *I* suffer most when I discover to you my feelings.

"Do you not know that yôu are fulfilling your threat—that 'I shall no longer be considered the saint ?'

"My life is before you. I have aspired to nothing save to do, through manifold infirmities, *my best*, and that not for human praise, but for the grateful love I feel towards Jesus Christ, my God.

"Do you not know, also, that when in any circle you blacken Mr. B's name—and soon after couple mine with it—you blacken mine as well ?

"When, by your threats, my mother cried out in agony to me, 'Why, what have *you* done Elizabeth, my child !' her worst suspicions were aroused, and I laid bare my heart then—that from *my* lips and not yours she might receive the dagger into her heart ! Did not my dead child [Florence] learn enough by insinuations, that her sweet, pure soul agonized in secret, till she broke out with the *dreadful question ?* I know not but it hath been her death blow."

"When you say to my beloved brother—' Mr. B. preaches to forty of his m——s every Sunday,' then follow with the remark that after *my* death you have a dreadful secret to reveal, need he be told any more ere the sword pass into *his* soul.

"After this 'you are my indignant champion,' are you ? It is now too late ; you have blackened my character, and it is for my loved ones that I suffer ; yea, for the agony which the revelation has caused *you*, my cries ascend to Heaven night and day that upon mine own head all the anguish may fall.

"Believe you that I would thrust a like dart into your sister's or mother's heart were there occasion? No, no, I would not, indeed.

"So after my death you will, to the bereaved hearts of those who love me, add the poisoned balm ? In heathen lands the sins of our beloved are buried, and only their virtues are remembered !

"Theodore, *your* past is safe with me, rolled up, put away never to be opened—though it is big with stains of various hues—unless you force me for the sake of my children and friends to discover it, in self-defence or their defence.

"Would *you* suffer were I to cast a shadow on any lady whom you love ? Certainly if you have any manliness you would. Even so every word, look, or intimation against Mr. B., though I be in no wise brought in, is an agony beyond the piercing of myself a hundred times. His position and his good name are dear to me ; and even thus do I agonize—yea, agony is the word—for *your* good name, and if you will only value it yourself to *keep it good*, I am and always will be your helper.

"Once again I implore you for your children's sake, to whom you have a duty in this matter, that *my past* be buried—left with me and my God. He is merciful. Will you, his son, be like Him ?

"Do not be alarmed about mother ; you are not responsible for *her* revelations. Do not think or say any more that my ill-health is on account of my sin and its discovery. It is not true, indeed. My sins and my life's record I have carried to my Saviour, and his delicacy and tenderness towards me passeth even a mother's love or the 'love of women.' *I rest in him, I trust in him*, and though the way is darker than death, I do hear 'the still small voice' which brings to me a peace life's experience has never before brought me. No, my prostration is owing to the suffering I have caused *you*, and will cause to those I love in the future if the spirit of forgiveness does not exorcise the spirit of hate. And add to this, the revelations you have made of your *fallen condition*, witness of which I am daily ! This it is that breaks my heart. How can I but 'linger at my praying' at thought of you ?

"Oh, do avoid all stimulating drinks, my darling. *I know* many a heart-ache would have been saved, only you knew not what or how the cruel word was said ! I have failed in my duty to you from lack of courage to speak of these things. Allow me to advise with you now, my dearly beloved, for surely I am your best friend, and for the sake of our precious born and unborn. I tell you that since I have *been conscious* of wronging you I needed only to *know* that, and always in everything I utterly forsake the wrong, repent before God alone, and strive to bring forth fruit worthy of repentance. Will you for the added reason of your soul's sake *do the same ?*

"I feel that you are not in the condition of mind to lead the 'woman's suffrage' movement, and I implore you to break away from your friends Susan, Mrs. Stanton, and everything that helps to make a conflict with your responsibilities as husband and father. My life is still spared ; my heart never yearned over you more in sorrowing love than now. But there must be a turning to God that will lead you to forsake forbidden ways, so that the sources and springs of your life be renewed, ere I shall feel it my duty to return.

"I have gained a little, and with this small addition of strength my first impulse is to fly to,you and comfort you in these new distractions which come to you through your business and its threatening changes. I have long felt, dear husband, you did not fill up your responsibilities towards the *Independent* as its religious chief and head. Oh, that you could be made to see and feel the amount of good you might do for Christ from that pulpit ! Oh, my babe would leap in my womb for joy did your soul but awake to love God, and serve him with the fervor of the early days.

" As I look out from my retirement here these are my thoughts and desires.

" I shall mourn if there seemeth to your aching heart a harsh word. I will pray God's spirit to follow the written line, and so it will not, cannot offend.

" I do not hesitate to return to Brooklyn and renew my home-work. Far be it from me to shirk my duty ; on the contrary, to have again the privilege of being with my entire family is the ambition I feel to gain in health here. Forgive the long letter. Good night.

" YOUR DEAR WIFE."

POSTSCRIPT.

" Dear mother, I will now add a line to you. I should mourn greatly if my life was to be made yet known to father ; his head would be bowed indeed to the grave. I love him very much, and it would soothe my heart could you be restored to him. I was greatly touched by his saying to you that ' you were still his wife.''

" Would not his sympathizing heart comfort you in your great sorrow?

" Both your letter and Theodore's came together, concerning your interviews with Joseph.

" You will see that by reading or showing this letter to any one you discover my secret. It is because I trust you, dear mother, that I send you this, that you may know my spirit completely toward you both.

" I have been told, Confide not in your mother ; but I reply, To whom on earth can I confide?

" I think it pre-eminently wise for us to destroy our letters respecting this subject, lest Florry or some one should pick them up.

" DARLING."

What a letter!

The brief confession which Mrs. Tilton wrote of her criminal intimacy with Mr. Beecher, and which was referred to by Mr. Moulton as held by him until I procured it from him and returned to her to be destroyed, has been falsely called a confession wrung from a wife at her husband's command. But no such accusation can hold against the above letter, which a daughter wrote to her mother, and which contains as plain a confession of Mrs. Tilton's intimacy with Mr. Beecher as language can express ; a confession all the more veritable because made without design, and in the absence of any other controlling influences upon the writer save the pressure of her own conscience and sorrow, as evinced in her melancholy contemplation of the calamity which had fallen upon honor and her home.

In view of Mrs. Tilton's truthful confession in the above letter four years ago, of what avail are her recent denials to the Committee ?

The Committee themselves have practically impugned the testimony which their own attorneys prompted Mrs. Tilton to make to them; and Mr. Beecher's own journal, the *Christian Union*, soon after the rendering of the verdict, published a conspicuous editorial article on purpose to put forth, under the stamp of Mr. Beecher's name, the following official rejection of Mrs Tilton's evidence by the Beecher party. The *Christian Union* says:

" *This poor woman has been shown to be so weak, so wholly subject to the strongest outside influence at the moment, that the general public can give but little weight to her testimony, either for or against Mr. Beecher.*"

The above extract from the *Christian Union* invalidating Mrs. Tilton's testimony necessarily blots out from Mr. Beecher's defence all Mrs. Tilton's recent denials of their criminality, and leaves him to be convicted by Mrs. Tilton's original, honest, dispassionate confession of their mutual sin, recorded in the above-quoted letter to her mother!

This letter, therefore, effectually disposes of two principal points of the Committee's verdict. One of these points the Committee state as follows :

" Tilton's allegation that she (Mrs. T.) confessed to her mother, Mrs. Morse, *is pronounced false by the mother*, who testified before the Committee."

Mrs. Tilton's letter, above given, together with the extracts from Mrs. Morse's letters, show that Mrs. Morse, in denying to the Committee that her daughter had ever made to her a confession of adultery, *was a deliberate falsehood*—half pardonable, perhaps, because uttered by a mother to save her daughter. The Committee, in relying on Mrs. Morse's testimony, relied on a false basis, which now sinks and carries down with it the Committee's verdict into an unfathomed depth.

The other point in the verdict which the above letter effectually settles, is the following :

" ' She,' (Mrs. Tilton) says the Committee, ' has always denied the charge *when free from the dominating influence of her husband.*' "

Mrs. Tilton's above letter to her mother was written "*free from the dominating influence of her husband.*" It was written 578 miles from her husband's presence. It was written not at request, but for his condemnation. It was written to reproduce to him the feelings excited in his wife's mind by the contemplation of her wrong-doing, and to appeal to him, from such a basis, against the moral recklessness which she then believed that her fall had produced upon his religious views and daily life. It was written before Mr. Beecher knew that she had betrayed him, and, of course, before he had indited his own equally agonizing "letter of contrition." It was written before Mrs. Tilton had any idea of future public proceedings by a church committee who would ask her to deny the truth in order to save Mr. Beecher. It was written before Mrs. Morse expected to be called upon to add her own falsehoods to her daughter's for this same purpose. It was written with no suspicion that these joint falsehoods of mother and daughter were thus to be exploded by the counter-records of their own correspondence !

On both these points the Committee's own witnesses falsify the Committee's own verdict.

Candor now requires me to state that the Committee are correct in one point. Their report says :

"This unhappy woman (Mrs. Tilton) has been the plastic victim of extorted falsehoods."

The Committee are correct in this view. Mrs. Tilton has indeed been "the plastic victim of extorted falsehoods." These are the falsehoods extorted from her during her cross-examination :— "extorted falsehoods" which the Committee reproduce in their verdict as true, namely : that she was a victim to my "ill-treatment," including deprivation of "food and fire," "imprisonment under lock and key," and other hardships from which she "fled for peace to the graves of her children ; "— "extorted falsehoods" never prompted by Mrs. Tilton's own mind (if she still remains the kindly and tender-hearted woman whom I knew), but extorted from her as the "plastic victim" of Mr. Beecher's attorneys, who having first used her for Mr. Beecher's defense, have since repudiated the very testimony which they thus extorted from her, pronouncing it worthless even for the base purpose for which it was thus extorted from this "plastic victim."

V. I now call attention to the difference of tone between Mrs. Tilton's letter to me written *before* her confession of July 3, 1870, and those written *after* it—as will be seen by comparing the extracts quoted (in section II.) from the correspondence published in the Chicago *Tribune*, with my wife's letter from Marietta, Ohio, to her mother in Brooklyn. This same difference is seen in all Mrs. Tilton's correspondence subsequent to her confession. All her letters written from Schoharie in the summer of 1871—of which the Catherine Gaunt letter and other penitential specimens have been heretofore published—exhibit a different woman from that whose portrait is unconsciously portrayed by her own hand in the correspondence published in the Chicago *Tribune*. The early sunshine of her life, which made golden every touch of her pen in those happier years, took a permanent shade at the date of her confession in July, 1870, and has since been never free from a cloud. It is impossible, for instance, to imagine such a letter as the following to have been written to me by Mrs. Tilton as one of the series in the Chicago *Tribune*, ending July 3, 1870 :

MRS. TILTON TO HER HUSBAND.

"July 29, 1871.

"Your lines sent to me in Flory's letter I respond to from my soul's depths.
"So you do not *hate*

"Your ——."

Nor in all that early period would she have written thus, dated Schoharie, June 20, 1871 :

"My mind no longer insists upon a lonely, daily wandering through my PAST."

Nor would she then have said, as she does in the last quoted letter :

"The romantic love of the sexes doth not satisfy."

Nor would she have cried out as follows, dated July 4, 1871 :

" *Oh, my dear husband, may you never need the discipline of being misled by a good woman, as I have been by a good man.*"

Nor could she have in happier days penned this, of the same date with the preceding :

" *I thank you for the sufferings of the past year. You have been my deliverer.*"

As a further illustration of Mrs. Tilton's prevailing state of mind, induced by her criminal intimacy with Mr. Beecher, by her confession thereof to her husband, and by the shadowy memories that followed these sad facts, I will mention an incident : One day in October, 1871, during a wearisome railroad ride, I beguiled myself with the composition of a little poem, which I sent in lead-pencil to the *Golden Age*, and which appeared in that paper under the title of "Sir Marmaduke's Musings," containing the following stanza :

"I clasped a woman's breast,
As if her heart I knew,
Or fancied, would be true,—
Who proved—alas, she, too !—
False like the rest."

On my return home after publishing the above, I was piteously assailed by Mrs. Tilton, who, with tears in her eyes, reproached me, saying : "O, Theodore, you might as well have called me by name." Meanwhile, I had not been conscious of any offense against my wife in the above publication, *because no public allusion had yet connected Mrs. Tilton's name with Mr. Beecher's.* The Woodhull story, which first did this, did not appear till more than a year afterward, namely, November 2, 1872!

In still further illustration of the excitable state of Mrs. Tilton's mind at any public allusion, friendly or otherwise, to the scandal which Mrs. Woodhull published, I may mention that shortly after that publication I prepared for the press the card known as the letter to "MY COMPLAINING FRIEND." I wrote it in my wife's presence, and submitted it to her judgment. She approved the card, and seemed pleased and satisfied. It was designed to throw a shield of protection over her against Mrs. Woodhull's attack. Although that card has been extensively published, I beg the favor of reproducing it here in order that its kindly phraseology towards my wife may be carefully weighed, and in order also that the comment which she subsequently made upon it may be understood. The card was as follows:

THE "COMPLAINING FRIEND" CARD.

"No. 174 LIVINGSTON STREET, }
"BROOKLYN, December 27, 1872. }

"MY COMPLAINING FRIEND: Thanks for your good letter of bad advice. You say, 'How easy to give the lie to the wicked story, and thus end it forever!' But stop and consider. The story is a whole library of statements—a hundred or more—and it would be strange if some of them were not correct, though I doubt if any are. To give a general denial to such an encyclopedia of assertion would be as vague and irrelevant as to take up the *Police Gazette*, with its twenty-four pages of illustrations, and say, 'This is all a lie.' So extensive a libel requires, if answered at all, a special denial of its several parts; and, furthermore, it requires, in this particular case, not only a denial of things misstated, but a truthful explanation of the things that remain unstated and in mystery. In other words, the false story, if met at all, should be confronted and confounded by the true one. Now, my friend, you urge me to speak; but, when the truth is a sword, God's mercy sometimes commands it sheathed. If you think I do not burn to defend my wife and little ones, you know not the fiery spirit within me. *But my wife's heart is more a fountain of charity, and quenches all resentments. She says: 'Let there be no suffering save to ourselves alone,' and forbids a vindication to the injury of others. From the beginning she has stood with her hand on my lips, saying, 'Hush!' So, when you prompt me to speak for her you countervail her more Christian mandate of silence.* Moreover, after all, the chief victim of the public displeasure is myself alone, and so long as this is happily the case, I shall try with patience to keep my answer within my own breast, lest it shoot forth like a thunderbolt through other hearts. Yours truly,
"THEODORE TILTON."

The above card—which was an attempt on my part, with my wife's knowledge and approval, to avoid telling a lie, and yet at the same time to avoid telling the truth—I published solely for the sake of the comfort which I thought its publication would bring to Mrs. Tilton by showing to the public that she and I were of one mind, and that inferentially, therefore, the scandalous story was false. To say that the card was *hostile* to Mrs. Tilton is to make a misuse of words. It was full of *friendliness* to her. She had approved it in manuscript. But no sooner had the card appeared in the Brooklyn *Eagle*, accompanied with some disparaging editorial comments, than Mrs. Tilton, although she herself had been a party to the publication, wrote and left on my desk the following bitter and reproachful note—the italics being her own:

MRS. TILTON TO HER HUSBAND.

"DECEMBER 28, 1872.

"THEODORE: I have had one of my selfish days. They are rare indeed. But your note in the *Eagle* of last night was so heartless. I did not hear when you read it—only realized it on seeing it in print.

"You should have sheltered me (a noble man would) *all the more* because the truth.

"*Innocence demanded nothing from you.*

"To you I owe this great injustice of exposure, such as has never before befallen a woman.

"Blow after blow, cea-cless and unrelenting these three years!

"O cruel spirit born of the devil of anger and revenge!

"*You know what I am.*

"Yet now that exposure has come, my whole nature revolts to join with you or standing with you."

As a further illustration of Mrs. Tilton's extreme feverishness of mind at any public allusion to the scandal, I will mention the following: The tripartite covenant, which was signed April 2, 1872, was published May 31, 1873: and its publication drew forth a few days afterward the appended card from Mr. Beecher in the Brooklyn *Eagle*, June 2, 1873:

MR. BEECHER'S CARD EXONERATING MR. TILTON.

"JUNE 2, 1873.

"*To the Editor of the Brooklyn Eagle:*

"DEAR SIR: I have maintained silence respecting the slanders which have for some time past followed me. I should not speak now but for the sake of relieving another of unjust imputation. The document that was recently published bearing my name, with others, was published without consultation either with me or with Mr. Tilton, nor with any authorization from us. If that document should lead the public to regard Theodore Tilton as the author of the calumnies to which it alludes it will do him great injustice. I am unwilling that he should even seem to be responsible for injurious statements whose force was derived wholly from others.

"H. W. BEECHER."

The agitation of Mr. Beecher's mind, out of which the above card grew, I well remember; and some traces of it appear in Mr. Beecher's reminiscences which he gave to the Committee during his examination; but the equally great distress of Mrs. Tilton at the same time has not yet been made public, and will appear in the following letter written by her to a friend who had rebuked her for imputing to me the publication of that covenant, although the bad business of publishing it was done by my friend, critic, and freely forgiven calumniator, Mr. Samuel Wilkeson, Mr. Beecher's Hotspur of a partner :

MRS. TILTON TO MRS. ——

"WEDNESDAY, June 4, 1873.

"MY DEARLY BELOVED: The terrible days of Saturday and Sunday last, resulting in the evil condition of soul wherein you found me yesterday, have utterly overcome me. I feel sick all over my body to-day. Indeed I cannot afford to be ugly and wicked.

"That you came, I bless God; for I vomited forth all the wickedness into your safe care—*and I am relieved, though profoundly ashamed, that I should judge and injure T. as I did ; yet in certain states of mind there are roused in me demons, which fill me with horror that they exist. Surely with so bad a heart as mine I cannot judge him !*

"*I sincerely hope he has had his last blow from* ME.—By-bye,   E——."

I have given the preceding letters and extracts to show how heavily Mrs. Tilton's guilty secret pressed on her heart, particularly in exigencies when she feared exposure; and there is much in her agonized expressions to remind the reader of Mr. Beecher's similar strains of woe over the same cause.

VI. Having thus considered Mrs. Tilton's confession of July 3, 1870, together with the various facts which cluster more closely about this than any other single branch of this case, I shall now take opportunity, before coming to my dealings face to face with Mr. Beecher, to refer to Mr. Henry C. Bowen. I must do this with some explicitness, because the key-note of Mr. Beecher's attack on me is that my accusation against him originated in my business troubles with Mr. Bowen. In Mr. Beecher's elaborate statement, the first proposition which he lays down, and which forms the basis of his ensuing argument, is in these words:

"*Four years ago, Theodore Tilton fell from one of the proudest editorial chairs in America.*"

I shall show that the above statement, together with the whole argument that Mr. Beecher bases upon it, is so wholly untrue that I might almost say that the language could not be put to a falser use.

From the beginning of 1856 to the close of 1870—a period of fifteen years—I was in Mr. Bowen's employ in the *Independent* in various characters, from subordinate to chief. How well I served my employer he himself publicly attested at the end of fourteen years of my service, when, in publishing an illuminated edition of the *Independent*, in commemoration of the twenty-first year of its age—which was the year before I left—he published over his own signature a special eulogy of my labors. In this article, which states that it was written "to do justice to its present editor, Theodore Tilton," Mr. Bowen looks back through my fourteen years of service and records himself as "approving his (Mr. Tilton's) every movement and suggestion," &c. I could not have wished higher praise from my employer, particularly as covering so long a period of service.

During the following year, 1870—which was the last of my connection with the *Independent*—I became temporarily the editor also of the Brooklyn daily *Union*. I have a letter from Mr. Bowen, dated as late as August 11, 1870, concerning my labors in the *Union*, which the writer begins in the following extravagant style :

"WOODSTOCK, CT.

"MY DEAR MR. TILTON : If I had a seventy-four pounder I would fire it among these hills and set them reverberating in honor of your last leader on politics."

The above is a fair specimen of the cordial way in which Mr. Bowen, during fifteen years, was prompt to approve my course—a degree of appreciation on his part which, in spite of my subsequent disagreement with him, I always looked back upon gratefully. My first difference with Mr. Bowen—a trifling one—occurred shortly after he wrote the above letter. He had meanwhile come to Brooklyn and taken a strong interest in the election of certain local candidates whom I had opposed. Moreover, he was a supporter of President Grant, whom he entertained at Woodstock, and whom I criticised in the *Independent*. After the Brooklyn election was over Mr. Bowen and I, in a friendly conversation, reviewed these differences, and other differences growing out of my increasing heterodoxy of religious belief. After two or three friendly interchanges, he expressed a desire to become himself sole editor of the *Independent*, just as he was its sole owner. To this end he wanted me to transfer my pen to the first page of that paper as its special contributor, while at the same time he wanted me to sign a contract to edit the Brooklyn *Union* for the ensuing five years. The pecuniary inducements which he held out to commend this proposed change to my mind were flattering, consisting of an income of about $14,000 a year and upwards. This arrangement took legal and binding form by the signing of two contracts between Mr. Bowen and myself about the 20th of December, 1870. Two days afterwards, in pursuance of these arrangements, the *Independent*, in publishing my valedictory, accompanied it with the following eulogy on its retiring editor :

MR BOWEN'S TRIBUTE TO MR. TILTON.

[*From the Independent, December 22, 1870.*]

"The proprietor and publisher, and hereafter editor of the *Independent*, in view of the discontinuance of Mr. Tilton's editorial relations to this paper, as indicated in the above valedictory, is happy to announce to the public that this change is not the fruit of any misunderstanding between Mr.

Tilton and himself. His retirement, though involving many regrets to both parties and sundering an official tie which has always been marked with the largest mutual confidence, is based on reasons in the wisdom and propriety of which both are alike agreed.

"Mr. Tilton has for the last seven years ably and successfully filled the editorial chair of the *Independent*, doing a great and good work for the country and the world, and uniformly writing the leader in the editorial column.

"If the paper has been a power among the people ; if its utterances have affected the policy of the nation during the bitter years of our war, and during the process of civil reconstruction ; or if a spirit of broader Christian charity has grown upon our readers ; all this has been due in no small degree to the genius of Mr. Tilton.

"Perhaps no other man in the country combines so many qualities that were needed to give us the position we have gained. Bold, uncompromising, a master among men ; crisp, direct, earnest ; brilliant, imaginative, poetic ; keen as a Damascus blade, and true as the needle to its pole in his sympathies with the needs of man, he was surely designed by Providence for the profession he has chosen.

"Our readers who have so long enjoyed the benefit of his racy and gifted pen will be glad to know that they will have an opportunity of meeting him weekly in our columns as a special contributor under his own name. He has consented to perform this service in addition to his labors as editor of the Brooklyn daily *Union*.

"Cordially welcoming him in his new character, and gratified in being able to say that his editorial connection with the *Independent* terminates only with honor and with most perfect satisfaction to himself, we shall in our next issue announce our plans for the future, etc., etc. * * *

"HENRY C. BOWEN"

Mr. Bowen, in addition to his published encomium of me above quoted, gave me a gold watch of a reputed value of $500 ; and Oliver Johnson, then the managing editor of the *Independent*, to whom I had made a similar gift, sent me the following note, December 29, 1870 :

"DEAR THEODORE :—Don't buy a chain for your new watch, for I have ordered one which I want you to accept as a New Year's present from me."

The above particulars of my retirement from the *Independent's* editorial chair—a retirement which Mr. Bowen said was to my honor, and which I believed was to my profit—I have thus been compelled to give at tedious length, in order that the exact facts may confront Mr. Beecher's false description of the same event, when he said as above quoted: "Four years ago Theodore Tilton *fell from one of the proudest editorial chairs in America.*"

The preceding record, from the *Independent's* own columns and by its own editors, touching the circumstances of my retirement from that editorial chair, show how I "fell:"—and I may add that I would be happy to experience another such fall.

As soon as I had completed the above-mentioned arrangements with Mr. Bowen, and they had been announced as above quoted, he urged me to make a more prominent figure of Plymouth Church in the daily *Union*, and remarked on my non-attendance at the church meetings.

This led me to reply that I had a good reason for not going to Plymouth Church, and that I should never again sit under Mr. Beecher's ministry.

On Mr. Bowen's urging me to give this reason, I reminded him first of his own oft-repeated charges against Mr. Beecher as a clergyman given to loose behavior with women, and dangerous to the families of his congregation. I said that I had in past times given little credence to these accusations, being slow to believe ill of my pastor and friend ; but that I had been informed by Mrs. Tilton, a few months previously, of improper behavior by Mr. Beecher towards her, and that I should never again attend Plymouth Church.

Mr. Bowen instantly pressed me to know the exact nature of what Mrs. Tilton had told me, but I declined to put him in possession of anything further than that Mr. Beecher had assaulted the honor of my house.

This announcement fanned Mr. Bowen to a flame of anger against Mr. Beecher. All his own past grievances against his pastor seemed to be rekindled into sudden heat. He walked up and down his library, denouncing Mr. Beecher as a man guilty of many adulteries, dating from his Western pastorate and running down through all the succeeding years. Mr. Bowen declared that Mr. Beecher had, in the preceding month of February, 1870, confessed to him certain of these adulteries, and Mr. Bowen pointed out to me the exact spot in his library whereon Mr. Beecher, with tears and humbleness, had (as Mr. Bowen said) acknowledged to him his guilt.

Mr. Bowen in this interview declared that he and I owed a duty to society in this matter, and that I ought to join him in a just demand on Mr. Beecher to retire from the ministry, to quit the city, and to betake himself beyond the reach of the families whose homes he was invading like a destroyer.

Mr. Bowen challenged me to write such a demand, and begged for an opportunity to bear it to Mr. Beecher in person, saying that he would support it by a great volume of evidence, and would compel its enforcement. I wrote on the spot the note mentioned in Mr. Moulton's Statement, and which seemed to please Mr. Bowen greatly. Just as I was leaving his house, his last word to me was, "Henry Ward Beecher is a wolf in the fold, and I know it; he ought never to preach another sermon nor write another word in a religious newspaper; he endangers families and disgraces religion; he should be blotted out."

This interview with Mr. Bowen occurred on the 26th of December, 1870, and was partly in the presence of Oliver Johnson, who retired before it was ended.

On that same day I informed Mr. Moulton of this interview, as he has noticed in his narrative.

I also informed Mrs. Tilton, who, as she was just recovering from a recent miscarriage, received the intelligence with great distress. She spoke alarmingly of Mr. Bowen's long hatred of Mr. Beecher, which now seemed to her to be about to break forth afresh, and said that if Mr. Bowen and I should thus combine against Mr. Beecher she would run a risk of an exposure of her own secret. She wept, and reminded me of the pledge which I had given her, six months before, to do her pastor no wrong. She said, moreover, that Mr. Beecher might not altogether understand my letter to him demanding his retirement " for reasons which he explicitly knew," because she had not yet informed him that she had made her confession to me. I was surprised at this intelligence, for in the previous August she told me that she had communicated to Mr. Beecher the fact that she had told me the story of their sexual association. She went on picturing to me the heart-break which she would suffer if, in the coming collision between Mr. Bowen and Mr. Beecher, her secret should be divulged. I well remember the pitiful accents in which, for the children's sake and her own, she pleaded her cause with me, and begged me to be gentle with Mr. Beecher, and to protect him from Mr. Bowen's anger ; also, to quench my own.

Lying on her bed sick, she said that unless I could stop the battle which seemed about to open, and could make peace between Mr. Bowen and Mr. Beecher—if not for *their* sakes at least for *hers*— and could myself become reconciled to the man who had wronged me, she would pray God that she might die. She then begged me to send for Mr. Beecher, desiring me to see him in her presence, to speak to him without malice when he came, and to assure him that I would not proceed in the matter of his expulsion from the pulpit. I declined such an interview as not comely for a sick woman's chamber, nor was I willing to subject her to the mortification of conferring with her paramour in the presence of her husband.

After this conversation with Mrs. Tilton, I notified Mr. Bowen that I intended to see Mr. Beecher face to face. In response to this intelligence, Mr. Bowen came into my editorial room at the *Union* office, and without asking or giving me any explanation, but exhibiting a passion such as I had never witnessed in him before, and speaking like one who was in fear and desperation, he exclaimed in a high key that if I divulged to Mr. Beecher the story of his numerous adulteries as he (Mr. Bowen) had narrated them, he (Mr. Bowen) would interdict me from ever again entering his office or his house. He then suddenly retired.

This unexpected exhibition on Mr. Bowen's part I could not comprehend : for I did not dream that Mr. Bowen, who was so determined an enemy of Mr. Beecher, had meanwhile entered into sudden league with the object of his hate, in order to overthrow, not Mr. Beecher, but myself !

I informed Elizabeth at once of Mr. Bowen's excited interview. She believed that his excitement was only a further evidence of his ancient malice against Mr. Beecher. She said that Mr. Beecher had often told her how greatly he feared Mr. Bowen. She was now appalled at the prospect of Mr. Bowen's violent assault on her pastor. She renewed her entreaty to me that I would prevent the coming conflict between the two men. Elizabeth's distress, in view of this expected conflict, it would be impossible to exaggerate, as it was heightened by her still enfeebled condition. She begged me to see Mr. Beecher without delay, and for *her* sake, to put him on his guard against Mr. Bowen, and to explain to him that, though I had written the letter demanding his retirement from the pulpit, yet that I had afterwards listened to my wife's entreaty, and had promised her that I would not press the demand to execution.

At her own suggestion she wrote a note to Mr. Beecher, and gave it to me, stating therein that she was distressed at the prospect of trouble, and begged, as the best mode of avoiding it, that a reconciliation might be had between Mr. Beecher and myself. She informed him in this letter that she had made to me a confession, six months before, of her sexual intimacy with him, and that she had hitherto deceived her husband into believing that her pastor knew of this confession having been made. She said she was distracted at having caused so much misery, and prayed that Mr. Beecher and her husband might instantly unite to prevent Mr. Bowen from doing the damage which he had threatened in instigating Mr. Beecher's retirement from the church.

This letter of Mrs. Tilton's was written on the 29th of December, 1870. I carried it in my pocket during the remainder of that day and all the next until evening, and then resolved that I would accede to my wife's request, and for her sake would prevent the threatened exposure of Mr. Beecher by Mr. Bowen.

I accordingly went to Mr. Moulton, as he has stated, and put into his hands my wife's letter, which conveyed to him his first knowledge of her adultery. He then, as he has described, brought Mr. Beecher to me, on Friday evening, December 30, through a violent winter storm, which Mr. Beecher referred to on the way as appropriate to the disturbed hour.

VII. The interview which followed between Mr. Beecher and me I shall relate somewhat in detail, because his recent distorted description of it is mainly a pretense, and not the truth. Mr. Beecher fills his false account with invented particulars of what he calls my complaint to him of my " business troubles," " loss of place and salary," and the like, with cognate complaints against him for his supposed agency in bringing about these results, whereas he forgets that I had *not yet lost* my " place and salary," and *had not yet come* into my "business troubles," nor did I then dream that he had conspired with Mr. Bowen to displace me from the *Independent* or the *Union*, or that any such disaster was then pending over my head, particularly as I had only a few days before signed two new contracts securing to me a lucrative connection with those two journals for years to come.

It was not because I had first "lost my place " that I held this interview with Mr. Beecher, for I did not "lose my place" until after this interview was held. Mr. Beecher confesses to an "imperfect memory of dates." This imperfection of memory has betrayed him here. My interview with him, as he acknowledges, was on Friday evening, December 30, 1870. This is correct. But it was not until Saturday evening, December 31, at nine o'clock at night, during the closing hours of the year, that my notification of dismissal came from Mr. Bowen. See *The Daily Graphic's* fac-simile of my letter to Mr. Bowen, January 1, 1871, in which I said:

I received *last evening* [that is, not December 30. but 31] your sudden notice breaking my two contracts, one with the *Independent*, the other with the Brooklyn *Union*.

It is thus plainly proven, as by mathematics, that my interview with Mr. Beecher—which he says occurred on account of my having "lost my place and salary"—occurred *before* I "lost my place and salary," and before I imagined that my two contracts—since both were new and fresh, and hardly a week old !—were to be summarily broken.

Indeed, even when I received, on the night after my interview with Mr. Beecher, Mr. Bowen's notice of their fracture I had no suspicion *then* that Mr. Beecher had meanwhile been using what he now admits to have been "his decisive influence to overthrow me," and to entail upon me "loss of place and salary." On the contrary, I still supposed that Mr. Bowen was more the enemy of Mr. Beecher than me, for he had given me abundant reason to believe so. It was not until after Mr. Beecher's written apology to me that I learned from his own humble and dust-covered lips that he had been guilty not only of ruining my home, but of displacing me from my public trusts.

Let me refer a little more in detail to this interview with Mr. Beecher, December 30, 1870, to show how thoroughly he has misrepresented it.

Mr. Beecher describes me as opening to him on that occasion a budget of particulars touching three points : that I accused him of procuring my "downfall"—whereas my downfall had not yet come ; next, that he had advised my wife to separate from me—a story of which I never heard until I heard it in the Investigating Committee ; and third, that I charged him with improper proposals to Elizabeth—which was indeed true, but only half the truth, for I informed him in detail of Elizabeth's confession of their adultery.

I must be repetitiously explicit on each of these points, so that neither of them shall escape the reader's mind.

First, then, touching my "downfall," or "business difficulties," or "loss of place and salary," I repeat that I had not yet suffered any of these losses, nor did I then suppose that such disasters were in store for me.

Next, as to his alleged "advice to my wife to separate from me," I solemnly aver that Mrs. Tilton has never to this day informed me that Mr. Beecher ever gave her any such advice, nor did she so inform the Committee ; that Mr. Moulton, like myself, never heard of such advice having been given until we both heard of it, to our surprise, during the present inquiry ; and that the only persons who had, as I supposed, advised Mrs. Tilton to leave me were Mrs. Morse and Mrs. Beecher, but not Mr. Beecher.

What evidence does Mr. Beecher now give to show that he ever advised Mrs. Tilton to separate from her husband ?

"I asked permission [he says] to bring my wife to see them (that is to see Mrs. Morse and Mrs. Tilton). * * * My wife [he continues] was extremely indignant towards Mr. Tilton. * * * I felt as strongly as she did, *but hesitated, as I always do, at giving advice in favor of separation.* It was agreed that my wife should give her (Mrs. Tilton) final advice at another visit. The next day, when ready to go, she wished a final word, but there was company and the children were present, and so I wrote on a scrap of paper : 'I incline to think that your view is right, and that a separation and a settlement of support will be wisest.' "

Admitting for the argument's sake that Mr. Beecher may have written such a scrap of paper (though I do not believe he did), the testimony of Mrs. Tilton makes no mention of having received such advice from her pastor. The only advice to this effect which she mentions she accords to her mother and to her pastor's wife, but not to Mr. Beecher. Furthermore, if Mr. Beecher had given the advice which he pretends to have given, Mrs. Morse would have known of it, would have eagerly made use of it, and would have urged (perhaps forced) her daughter to act upon it. Now, Mrs. Morse gives explicit testimony over her own hand that Mr. Beecher never gave any such advice; on the contrary she shows that the only advice which Mr. Beecher gave concerning the proposed separation was that Mrs. Tilton should not separate from her husband! I refer to Mrs. Morse's letter to Mr. Beecher, endorsed in his own handwriting as having been received from her by him January 27, 1871, only a few weeks after his apology. Mrs. Morse speaks in that letter complainingly to Mr. Beecher as follows :

"*You* or any one else *who advises her* (Mrs. Tilton), *to live with him* (Mr. Tilton), when he is doing all he can to kill her by slow torture, *is anything but a friend,.*"

It will be seen from the above that at the very time when Mr. Beecher pretends to have been suddenly thrown into remorse and despair for having given Elizabeth bad advice—namely, to separate from me—Elizabeth's mother was writing to Mr. Beecher to chide him because he had given, not that advice, but just the opposite! Mrs. Morse's letter accuses me of "killing her daughter by slow torture," and accuses him at the same time of advising her against a separation from such a brute.

In the presence of this letter of Mrs. Morse—who of all persons in the world was most solicitous to procure Elizabeth's separation, and who would be most likely to know on which side of the question Mr. Beecher had advised—I respectfully submit that Mr. Beecher's recent and pretended claim to have given such advice, and that this advice was the key-note to his four years of subsequent remorse and letter-writing, is blown to the winds—and the Committee report is whisked away with it.

Third, Mr. Beecher's statement that at this interview of December 30, 1870, I charged him with making impure proposals to Mrs. Tilton is (as I have said) true so far as it goes, but is only a part of the truth, for I charged him with adultery. It was this last topic, namely, his criminal relations with Mrs. Tilton, and not at all my financial troubles, since these had not yet come upon me; nor his advice to my wife to separate from me, of which I had not then heard—it was his criminal association with Mrs. Tilton—this, and this only—that constituted the basis of my interview with him on that memorable night. This interview, I repeat, was held at Mrs. Tilton's request, and my object in holding it was to quiet her apprehension concerning the possible exposure of their secret through what both she and I then supposed to be an imminent assault upon Mr. Beecher by Mr. Bowen. To this end I informed Mr. Beecher of the confession which Mrs. Tilton had made to me six months before, and which it had become necessary for her peace—perhaps even for her life—that Mr. Beecher should receive from my lips in order that he should so manage his case with Mr. Bowen that no danger would arise therefrom of Mrs. Tilton's exposure to the world. This was my purpose, and my only purpose, in that interview, as Mrs. Tilton and Mr. Beecher knew right well.

Now, in the light of these facts, thus proved, note Mr. Beecher's false statement of them as follows:

"It was not until Mr. Tilton [he says] had fallen into disgrace and lost his salary, that he thought it necessary to assail me with charges which he pretended to have had in mind for six months."

Against the above fallacious assertion I have set the counter testimony of incontrovertible facts, which I will recapitulate, namely: When I resolved to meet Mr. Beecher on Friday, December 30, 1870, I had just made two new contracts with Mr. Bowen, signing them only a few days previous, from which I looked forward to an income as large as the salary of the pastor of Plymouth Church. When I sat waiting for Mr. Beecher on that night I was in independent circumstances, and expected to be increasingly so for years to come. When Mr. Moulton brought him to me that night I had no thought—not the remotest—of "financial difficulties" or "business troubles" or "loss of place," for I had not yet come to these disasters, nor did I then foresee them. When I, as he said, "talked calmly" to him on that night, it was because I had previously demanded his retirement from the pulpit, and because this demand had well-nigh broken my wife's heart; for whose sake alone, and for no other reason, I agreed with her to meet him face to face in order to inform him that I knew of his intimacy with her, and to say to him that, for the sake of this suffering woman and her children, I would withdraw the demand upon him to quit the pulpit and flee the city, and that Mr. Bowen should have no ally in me in his proposed war against his pastor.

As God is my judge, I solemnly aver that that interview did not descend to points of finance, but, on the contrary, touched only two points: first, Mrs. Tilton's ruin, which had come through Mr. Beecher; and, second, Mrs. Tilton's safety, which must come through Mr. Beecher and myself.

In that interview, from a little memorandum in my hand, giving dates and places, I recited to Mr. Beecher Mrs. Tilton's long story as she had given it to me in the previous July, and which she had, on the previous day, reauthenticated in her note of December 29, which I had put into Mr. Moulton's hands to be the basis of his summons to Mr. Beecher to meet me for the conference. No extraneous subject did I introduce into that single-minded recital; for only one theme was in my thoughts; and in order that no intruder should interrupt me, or that Mr. Beecher should retire from hearing me, I locked the door and put the key in my pocket.

After I delivered my message, I unlocked the door and said to Mr. Beecher, "Now that we understand each other, you are free to go. If any harm or disgrace comes to Elizabeth or the children I shall hold you responsible. For her sake I spare you, but if you turn upon her, I will smite your name dead before the whole world."

When I ceased speaking, he hesitated to leave his chair, but sat with bowed head, and with eyes riveted to the floor. At length looking up into my face, he said: "Theodore, I am in a dream—I am in Dante's Inferno."

I pointed to the door, and said again, "You are free to retire."

In going out he stopped on the threshold, turned, looked me in the face, and asked with quivering lip whether or not I would permit him to see Elizabeth once more for the last time. I was about to answer, "No, never," but remembering my wife's grief and her expressed wish that this interview could have taken place in her presence, I felt that she would be better satisfied if I gave him the permission he asked, and so I said, "Yes, you may go at once, but you shall not chide Elizabeth for confessing the truth to her husband. Remember what I say ; if you reproach that sick woman for her confession, or utter to her a word to weigh heavily upon her broken heart for betraying you, I will visit you with vengeance. I have spared your life during the last six months and am able to spare it again ; but I am able also to destroy it. Mark me," I added, "Elizabeth is prostrate with grief—she must hear no word of blame or reproach."

"Oh, Theodore," he said, "I am in a wild whirl!"

After these words he retired from the room, and almost immediately (as Mr. Moulton has narrated), accompanied that gentleman to my house, where (as Mr. Beecher admits), he fell upon Elizabeth with "strong language," that is, full of reproach, and procured from her a retraction which he dictated to her, and which she wrote at his command—her tremor and fear being plainly visible in her handwriting, as shown in THE DAILY GRAPHIC'S fac-simile.

On my return home that evening, I found my wife far from being in the condition Mr. Beecher described when he styled her a marble statue or carved monument ; but on the contrary she was full of tears and misery, saying that he had called upon her, had reproached her in violent terms, had declared that she had "struck him dead," and that unless she would give him a writing for his protection, he would be "tried by a council of ministers."

She described to me his manner as full of mingled anger and grief, in consequence of which she was at one moment so terrified by the look on his face that she thought he would kill her.

. She grew nearly distracted at the thought that her womanly and charitable effort to make peace had only resulted in making Mr. Beecher *her* enemy and *mine*. I believe that if he had entered a second time into her presence that night she would have shuddered and fainted at his approach. Her narrative to me of the agony which he expressed to her, of the reproaches which he heaped upon her, and of the bitterness with which he denounced her for betraying her pastor to her husband—all this tale still lingers in my mind like a remembered horror.

The above plain statement of facts, fortified by documentary evidence proving that my interview with Mr. Beecher occurred *before* and not *after* my "loss of place and salary," effectually puts an end to the following passage in the committee's verdict—a passage which constitutes one of the principal findings of that strange tribunal. The committee say:

"It is clear that on the 29th of December, when the so-called memorandum of confession was procured from Mrs. Tilton, the chief inciting cause of that step on Tilton's part was his belief that Mr. Beecher had caused him his loss of place, business, and repute."

The above conclusion, drawn by the committee from the false facts which I have exploded, must be delivered over to the limbo of those remarkable insurance policies touching which Mr. Beecher swore to being in profound and perfect health, while at the same time he was on the daily edge of death from a hypochondria inherited from his grandfather, and from a remorse consequent upon giving bad advice.

VIII.—About one-half of the Committee's verdict is based on another equally remarkable falsehood, which I shall so completely expose that I believe the authors of it will receive the ridicule of a community whom they have attempted to deceive. The chief argument by the Committee is that my real charge against Mr. Beecher was simply "improper proposals," not "adultery ;" that they never heard of my charging him with "adultery" until I trumped up this latter accusation as part of a conspiracy which Mr. Moulton and I were prosecuting against Mr. Beecher with slow patience and for greed of gain! Without this argument, which comprises one-half the Committee's report, they would never have been able to make a report at all. But I shall rip this argument so completely out of the report that that document will at one stroke be torn in twain, and the half which is devoted to this fabrication will be cast aside as waste paper.

First, to do no injustice to the Committee, let me give them the chance of stating their argument in their own words, as follows :

"We believe (say they), and propose to show, from the evidence, that the original charge was improper advances, and that as time passed and the conspiracy deepened it was enlarged into adultery. The importance of this is apparent, because if the charge has been so changed then both Tilton and Moulton are conspirators and convicted of a vile fraud, which necessarily ends their influence in this controversy. What is the proof (they add) that the charge in the first instance was adultery ?"

I cannot understand, except on one ground, how Mr. Beecher's lawyers (since they are attendants at his church and acquainted with its proceedings) should have had the boldness to assume such a position as the above, since they must have known that I could disprove their fallacious statement by the official records of Plymouth Church itself. The one ground on which I presume they based their daring assertion was their supposition that I possessed no official copy of the papers in a certain famous proceeding in Plymouth Church which Mr. Beecher, with a rare hypocrisy, describes as his "attempt to keep me from public trial by the church." Perhaps Mr. Beecher and his Committee thought that in this case, too, "the papers had been burned." But I shall not allow him to escape "so as by fire."

Let me explain :

A few weeks after Mrs. Tilton's confession in July, 1870, and several months before Mr. Beecher's apology, I communicated the fact of their criminal intimacy to a grave and discreet friend of our family, Mrs. Martha B. Bradshaw, of Brooklyn, one of the best known and most honored members of Plymouth Church. The same information was subsequently given to Mrs. Bradshaw by Mrs. Tilton herself. On the basis of this information in the possession of Mrs. Bradshaw, Mr. William F. West, a member of Plymouth Church, relying on Mrs. Bradshaw to be a witness, indicted me before the church for circulating scandalous reports against the Rev. Henry Ward Beecher. Mr. West's charges and specifications, although a matter of notoriety at the time, have never yet been published. I herewith commit them to print for the purpose of showing that the verdict of Mr. Beecher's Committee stands disproved in its chief and central allegation by the official records of Plymouth Church itself. Mr. Beecher's six committeemen, like Mr. Beecher himself, have "bad memories." Let me not attempt to portray the mortification of this Committee and their attorneys at reading the following correct copy of official papers adopted by Plymouth Church, of which the originals are in my possession :

MR. TALLMADGE TO MR. TILTON.

"BROOKLYN, October 17, 1873.

" *Mr. Theodore Tilton,*
"DEAR SIR : At a meeting of the Examining Committee of Plymouth Church, held this evening, the clerk of the committee was instructed to forward to you a copy of the complaint and specifications made against you by Mr. William F. West, and was requested to notify you that any answer to the charges that you might desire to offer to the committee may be sent to the clerk on or before Thursday, October 23, 1873.

"Enclosed I hand you a copy of the charges and specifications referred to.
"Yours very respectfully,
" 393 Bridge street. D. W. TALLMADGE, Clerk.

COPY

" *Of the charges and specifications made by William F. West against Theodore Tilton :*
"I charg Theodore Tilton, a member of this Church, with having circulated and promoted scandals derogatory to the Christian integrity of our pastor, and injurious to the reputation of this church.

" *Specifications.*

" *First*—In an interview between Theodore Tilton and the Rev. E. L. L. Taylor, D.D., at the office of the Brooklyn *Union,* in the spring of 1871, the said Theodore Tilton stated that the Rev. Henry Ward Beecher preached to several (seven or eight) of his mistresses every Sunday evening. Upon being rebuked by Dr. Taylor, he reiterated the charge, and said that he would make it in Mr. Beecher's presence if desired.
" Witness
REV. E. L. L. TAYLOR, D.D.

" *Second*—In conversation with Mr. Andrew Bradshaw, in the latter part of November, 1873, Theodore Tilton requested Mr. Bradshaw not to repeat certain statements which had previously been made to him by Mr. Tilton, adding that he retracted none of the accusations which he had formerly made against Mr. Beecher, but that he wished to hush the scandal on Mr. Beecher's account ; that Mr. Beecher was a bad man, and not a safe person to be allowed to visit the families of his church ; that if this scandal ever were cleared up he (Tilton) would be the only one of the three involved who would be unhurt by it ; and that he was silently suffering for Mr. Beecher's sake.
" Witness :
ANDREW BRADSHAW.
" *Third*—At an interview with Mrs. Andrew Bradshaw, in Thompson's dining-rooms on Clinton street, on or about the 3d day of August, 1870, Theodore Tilton stated that he had discovered that *a criminal intimacy* existed between his wife and Mr. Beecher. Afterward, in November, 1872, referring to the above conversation, Mr. Tilton said to Mrs. Bradshaw that he retracted none of the accusations which he had formerly made against Mr. Beecher.
" Witness :
MRS. ANDREW BRADSHAW.

It will be seen from the third specification in the above document that I was indicted by Plymouth Church, and that an attempt was made to bring me to trial *because I had said on the 3d of August, 1870, that I had discovered* A CRIMINAL INTIMACY *between Mr. Beecher and Mrs. Tilton.* The date mentioned in this specification, namely, the 3d of August, 1870, *was only* THIRTY DAYS *after Mrs. Tilton's confession of July 3d of that year!* What shall be thought of the report of a so-called Investigating Committee of Plymouth Church which, in order to maintain and uphold the pastor's false denial of my true charge against him, is compelled, in his defense, to falsify the records of his own church ? The Committee's question, " What is the proof that the charge in the first instance was adultery ?" meets in the above official document by Plymouth Church so point-blank an answer that I am almost tempted to return to these six gentlemen the epithets they have put upon Mr. Moulton and me, and to say that for their own verdict, judged by their own church records, they stand " convicted of a vile fraud."

The above church record completely nullifies one-half—more than one-half—of the Committee's report !

IX.—In order that I may not need to refer again to Mr. West's charge and specifications, I may as well append in this place my proper comment on Mr. Beecher's extraordinary claim that I owe him gratitude for having kept me, as he says, from a " public trial by the church."

Why did Mr. Beecher keep me from a public trial by the church ? It was to save, not me, but himself. It was not I, but he, who feard to be tried, and who put forth the labors of a Hercules to prevent a trial. And with good reason: for, unless Mr. Beecher's case in that perilous hour had been conducted by the present Committee of six, on their novel plan of acquitting at all hazards, the trial would have proven him guilty. With wise sagacity, therefore, Mr. Beecher sought to keep me from that trial in order to save himself from that ruin. I well remember how, at that time, he spoke of his anxious and sleepless nights, full of fear and apprehension at the possible failure of his cunning attempt to prevent the coming on of a trial which, at the same time, he had to pretend to invite !

Furthermore, Mr. Beecher, evidently sharing the conviction of the Committee that I possessed no official copy of Mr. West's charges and specifications, ventured to speak of Mr. West's fearful indictment as follows, namely, that it—

"Presented no square issues upon which his (Mr. Beecher's) guilt or innocence could be tried."

And yet what issue could be more pointed and direct? If a clergyman is openly accused of adultery, and the indictment gives specifications, names, dates, and witnesses, does not the case present a square issue? I know whereof I affirm when I say that Mr. Beecher feared and dreaded the prospect of that trial, not because the "issues were not square," but, on the contrary, because the issues were so sharp and clear-cut that he dared not cast himself on their "rough and ragged edge."

Let me in this connection notice another point. The Committee have a singular way of arguing that the original charge could not have been "adultery," because (as they say) Mrs. Tilton's written retraction indicated only "improper proposals." With an extraordinary inconsistency of reasoning, the verdict has the following remarks :

"It is said, further, that Mr. Beecher confessed the act of adultery. Such alleged confession is not consistent with the retraction he received that evening from Mrs. Tilton. Is it likely, if the main offense had been charged, Mr. Beecher would have been satisfied with anything short of a retraction of that?"

The logic of the above is most pitiable. A clergyman is charged with adultery. He goes to the guilty woman and demands that she shall give him a written retraction. He carries to her bedside paper, pen, and ink, and compels her to phrase this retraction to suit him exactly. What does he make her say? Merely that there was no adultery? No, he makes her say still more than this—that there has been not even an attempt at such. Having appealed to her fears, having (as he admits) "used strong language to her," in other words, having intimidated her to do his bidding, he compels her to declare, not only that there was no "adultery," but that there was not even an "impure proposal." Is not this the most comprehensive retraction possible of the original charge? Suppose I—Mr. Beecher's accuser—had given to him a certificate that he had never made to my wife an "impure proposal?" Would he not plead such a certificate as abundantly—aye, superabundantly—acquitting him of the charge of "adultery." The Committee know well enough that the retraction of a charge of "impure proposals" covers—and more than covers—the charge of "adultery." The logic of the verdict is unworthy of the name of reasoning.

The same may be said of another paragraph in this sapient verdict—a statement of theirs which I am loath to charge upon these six gentlemen as a willful misrepresentation, and yet it seems as if they had here misrepresented me purposely and not by accident. The Committee quote from their own garbled report of my examination a mention made by me of the fact that Mr. Beecher, on the day after sending me his apology through Mr. Moulton, visited me at Mr. Moulton's house. The Committee quote from their report of my remarks the following words :

"He (Mr. Beecher) burst out in an expression of great sorrow to me, and said he hoped the communication which he had sent to me by Mr. Moulton was satisfactory to me. He then and there told Mr. Moulton he had done wrong ; not so much as some others had (referring to his wife, who had made statements to Mr. Bowen that ought to be unmade), and he there volunteered to write a letter to Mr. Bowen concerning the facts which he had misstated."

Now notice the captious use which the Committee make of the above quotation. They say :

"If the wrong to which Mr. Beecher refers was adultery, how could these words be used in reference to it, 'He had done wrong; not so much as some others.' The absurdity of such a claim is clear."

The above *comment* which the Committee make on my words, as anybody will see by looking carefully at the words themselves, has no application whatever to my *words*. When Mr. Beecher said that "he had·done me wrong, but not so much as some others had done," he was referring, as the report itself shows, not to his crime of adultery, but "to his wife, who had made statements to Mr. Bowen which ought to be unmade." The Committee devote a laborious paragraph to show that if Mr. Beecher had done less wrong than others, this "wrong" could not have been "adultery." The Committee themselves, if they had carefully read their own quotation from their own report of my examination, would have seen that Mr. Beecher, in the above-named interview with me, spoke first of the crime for which he had written me the apology of the night before, and that he then made a totally distinct and separate reference to an additional wrong which he had come that morning to undo—namely, the wrong of having given slanderous reports to Mr. Bowen concerning myself ; a wrong which, Mr.

Beecher said to me, he had not committed to so great an extent as his wife and Mrs. Morse had done. Promptly on the publication of the Committee's report of my examination, I published a card saying that this report had been garbled and was incorrect at many points. Among the points which I designated to several members of the press, who called upon me at the time, was the bungling manner in which the above interview between Mr. Beecher and myself was described. Nevertheless, even this bungling report, which the Committee's lawyers compressed into a shape to please them best, shows, even as it stands, that the matter concerning which Mr. Beecher said he had done less wrong than his wife was not adultery, since that would have been an imputation by Mr. Beecher of criminality on the part of his wife, but had sole reference, as the report itself states, to communications which Mr. Beecher and his wife had jointly made to Mr. Bowen against me, but in which Mr. Beecher had taken a less share than his wife. And yet, on the filmy basis of the above misrepresentation of my words, the Committee have belied their function as judicial inquirers by founding an argument to accuse me of conspiracy against a man who was himself a conspirator against *me*, and whose conspiring had already accomplished the ruin of my wife and the breaking up of my home.

The Committee say further:

"In the written statement of the offense shown to Dr. Storrs by Tilton and Carpenter, which was made in Mrs. Tilton's handwriting, under the demand of her husband, who says he dictated the precise words characterizing the offense, the charge was an improper proposal."

I will once again give the Committee a direct negative to this statement, as I did during my examination. The letter above referred to, in Mrs. Tilton's handwriting, is as follows:

"DECEMBER 16, 1872.

"In July, 1870, prompted by my duty, I informed my husband that Rev. H. W. Beecher, my friend and pastor, had solicited me to be a wife to him, together with all that this implies."

The entire letter, of which the above is the first sentence, was composed by Mrs. Tilton, except only the above sentence, which was mine. I suggested the above form of expression to her, because she was at that time in a delicate mood of conscience, and desired to confess the whole truth to Dr. Storrs, in hope thereby to end the troubles. She said she had grown tired of telling falsehoods, and if Dr. Storrs was to give wise counsel he ought to know the whole case. It was no unusual thing for her to be in the state of mind which she exhibited on that occasion. There was always an undercurrent of conscience running through all her thoughts, and she frequently lamented to me her sad fate to be condemned to "live a lie." Accordingly, she sought in the above letter to Dr. Storrs to tell the whole truth—not a part of it. I was unwilling that she should make such a damaging confession. She insisted that she must cease her falsehood at some time, and that that was a proper time. It was to meet this demand of her conscience that I framed for her the sentence above quoted—a sentence not inconsistent with the exact truth, because the words "*together with all that this implies*" might be as readily taken to imply that she had *yielded* to Mr. Beecher's solicitation as that she had *rejected* it. Dr. Storrs, in reading the above letter, seemed to take for granted from its terms that Mrs. Tilton had *not* yielded to this solicitation, and I did not undeceive him. I repeat that the opening sentence of the letter was framed by me expressly to satisfy Mrs. Tilton's desire to confess the whole truth—a desire on her part which I contemplated with pain and apprehension, and from which I sought to shield her by the above form of words. The Committee are guilty of little less than sharp practice in commenting on this phraseology as they have done in their verdict, for I was explicit to give them the exact explanation which I have given here.

But nothing is so astounding to me in the Committee's report as the following statement bearing on this same point:

"The further fact [they say] that Tilton treated the matter during four years *as an offense which could properly be apologized for and forgiven*, is wholly inconsistent with the charge in its present form."

The Committee express the same idea in a still more specious phraseology, as follows:

"If Moulton [say they] understood the charge to be adultery, then he is entitled to the credit of the invention or discovery that this crime can be the subject of an apology."

The above sentiment, thus put forth by the Committee, may possibly represent the club-house code of morals and of honor, and it seems to me that a church committee is bound to hold that no crime or wrong-doing should be beyond the Christian forgiveness of those against whom it is committed, and, in particular, that the crime in the present case should have reminded a churchly tribunal of the immortal maxim of Him who said of the woman taken in adultery, "Neither do I condemn thee."

X. Since, however, the Plymouth Church Committee abandons the Christian code of morality on this subject, and substitutes a more popular and cruel opinion—which I think should be tempered with greater lenity towards women who err—I will convict Mr. Beecher by the world's code of honor in such cases. It is a prime law of conduct among what are called "men of the world," that if a man has received a lady's extreme gift he is bound to protect her reputation and to shield her against any and every hazard of exposure. What, then, in view of this law, is the just measure of obloquy which "men of the world," according to their own etiquette of behavior, should visit upon Mr. Beecher, who, after having subdued a lady to his sexual uses for a period of more than a year, at last, in a spirit of bravado and desperation, publicly appoints a committee of six men, with two attorneys, to inquire into the facts of her guilt, involving her inevitable exposure and ruin ? Even Mr. Beecher's worldly-minded champion, Mr. Kinsella, though accused of the same kind of seduction, has proved more forbearing to his victim.

XI. Mr. Beecher, after giving his lifetime (according to his sister, Mrs. Hooker) to the study of the free-love philosophy; after having surreptitiously practiced free love in my own house, in the corruption of a Christian wife and mother; after having confessed to Mr. Moulton and me more adulterous alliances than this one;—after all that, Mr. Beecher goes back in his fictitious defense to the closing years of my connection with the *Independent*, and speaks of me in the following terms:

"His (Mr. Tilton's) loose notions of marriage and divorce begin to be shadowed editorially."

To this I make two replies—one general, the other specific.

In general, I say that I have never entertained loose notions of marriage. My notions of marriage are those which are common throughout Christendom. But I rejoice to say that my notions of divorce are at variance with the laws of my own State, and are expressed in the statutes of Wisconsin. I have strenuously urged the abrogation of the New York code of divorce (which is for one cause alone), and have asked for the substitution of the more liberal legislation of New England and the West.

Next, I reply in particular that the first article which I wrote in the *Independent* that elicited any criticism for what Mr. Beecher now calls my "loose notions of marriage and divorce," was a defense of Mrs. Richardson in the McFarland trial. But if I was wrong in my estimate of that case, Mr. Beecher was far more wrong than I, for he went to the Astor House and at Richardson's dying bed performed a marriage ceremony between that bleeding sufferer and a lady who was then the divorced (or undivorced) wife of the assassin. Mr. Beecher cannot condemn me for anything that I said growing out of that case without still more severely condemning himself. In proof of this statement I cite the testimony of Mr. William O. Bartlett, now one of Mr. Beecher's lawyers, defending Mr. Beecher for a far more unpardonable seduction than that whereof Mr. Richardson was accused. Mr. Bartlett published in the New York *Sun* on the day after Mr. Beecher's performance of the Astor House marriage the following biting characterization of Mr. Beecher's conduct on that occasion :

WHAT MR. BEECHER'S CHIEF ATTORNEY THINKS OF HIM.

[*From the New York Sun, December 2, 1869.*]

"The Astor House in this city was the scene on Tuesday afternoon of a ceremony which seems to us to set at defiance all those sentiments respecting the relation of marriage which regard it as anything intrinsically superior to prostitution. *The high priest of this occasion was Henry Ward Beecher.* * * * As the great and eloquent John Whipple said : 'He who enters the dwelling of a friend and, under the protection of friendship and hospitality, corrupts the integrity of his wife or daughter, by the common consent of mankind ought to be consigned to an immediate gallows.' * * * Consider, married men of New York! husbands and fathers! by what frail and bitter tenure your homes are yours. If you fail in business—and it is said that ninety-five out of one hundred business men fail—then your neighbor may charm away your wife, and the Rev. Henry Ward Beecher stands ready to marry her to the first libertine who will pay—not in affection, but in gold and greenbacks—the price of her frail charms. * * * Yes, it is the pious, the popular, the admired, the reverend Henry Ward Beecher, who comes boldly and even proudly forward, holding by the hand and leading Lust to her triumph over Religion ! Who can read the narrative and not wish that Plymouth Church were not sunk into the ground until the peak of its gable should be beneath the surface of the earth ?"

The above was the judgment of Mr. Beecher's present chief counselor touching Mr. Beecher's action in the celebrated case concerning which, for some comments of mine in the *Independent*, Mr. Beecher has now the effrontery to accuse me of having, in 1869, "shadowed " in my editorials "loose notions of marriage and divorce."

XII.—Mr. Beecher with equal inconsistency seeks to becloud me with the odium which attaches to Mrs. Woodhull's name. I am justly entitled to a severe—perhaps to an unsparing—criticism, by the public, for having linked my name with that woman, and particularly for having lent my pen to the portrayal of her life in the exaggerated colors in which I once painted it in a biographical sketch. But among all my critics who have stamped this *brochure* with their just opprobrium, I have never yet found any one who has denounced me for it half so severely as I have condemned myself. Nobody shall have my consent to defend me for having written that sketch. I refuse to be defended.

But having made this explicit statement against myself—which justice requires—I am entitled to tell the precise story of my relations with Mrs. Woodhull, and to compare these with Mr. Beecher's relations with the same woman, at the same time, and to the same end.

About a year after Mrs. Tilton's confession to me, and about a half a year after Mr. Beecher's apology, and after Mr. Moulton had put forth the many strenuous efforts to which Mr. Beecher's letters written during this period bear witness, a new and sudden enemy of our safety appeared before the public in the person of Victoria C. Woodhull, who published in the *World* and the *Times* the card quoted in my Sworn Statement, saying that a "distinguished clergyman in a neighboring city was living in concubinage with the wife of another public teacher in the same city."

On the publication of this card Mrs. Woodhull—to whom I was then a stranger—sent for me and informed me that this card referred to Mr. Beecher and Mrs. Tilton. I was stunned by the intelligence, for I instantly felt that the guilty secret which Mr. Moulton was trying to suppress was in danger of coming to the surface. Taking advantage of my surprise on that occasion Mrs. Woodhull poured forth in vehement speech the hundred or more particulars (most of which were untrue) that afterwards constituted the scandalous tale of November 2, 1872.

Meanwhile the fact that she possessed such knowledge, and had the audacity to fling it into my very face, led me to seek Mr. Moulton at once for counsel. We felt that some influence must be brought to bear upon this strange woman to induce her to suppress the dangerous tale. We thought that kindness was the best influence that we could use. Mr. Beecher concurred with us in this view, and we all joined in the policy of rendering her such services as would naturally (so we supposed) put the person who received them under obligations to the doers.

In carrying out this policy Mr. Beecher joined with us and approved our course. He made Mrs. Woodhull's personal acquaintance, and strove by his kindly interest in her to maintain and increase her good-will. He says that he saw her but three times, but his "memory of dates and details is bad;" and I myself have been in her presence with him more times than that. He took uncommon pains to impress upon her his respectful consideration, and though I never heard them discuss each other's views to any prolonged extent, I once heard him say to her that the time might come when the rules by which thoroughbred animals are brought to perfection would govern the relations of men and women.

I declare explicitly that Mr. Beecher fostered the acquaintance which Mr. Moulton and I made with Mrs. Woodhull. He urged us to maintain it, and begged us not to lose our hold upon her; he constantly inquired of us as to the ascendency which we held over her, and always said that he looked as much to our influence with Mrs. Woodhull to keep back the scandal from publication as to any other possible means of future safety, both for *my* family and *his.*

When Mrs. Stowe made an elaborate attack on Mrs. Woodhull in the *Christian Union,* Mr. Beecher, who had not seen the proof-sheets before publication, was in great distress until Mr. Moulton and I reported to him that we had seen Col. Blood (Mrs. Woodhull's husband), and had urged him to publish a kindly instead of a revengeful reply to Mrs. Stowe's attack. Mr. Beecher's gratification, which he expressed at this evidence of our power with Mrs. Woodhull and her husband to prevent mischief, was of no ordinary kind. Mr. Beecher said to me on that occasion that every service which I could render to *her* was a service to *him.*

Among the services which I thus rendered—for *his* sake, because for Mrs. Tilton's—was the writing of an elaborate pamphlet on woman suffrage, which cost me a week of hard labor. Another service was the biographical sketch to which I have already alluded, and which, so far as I was concerned, was the work of only a single day, for my task consisted only in the rewriting of a sketch already prepared by her husband, the original manuscript of which I still possess. The third and last public service which I rendered to her was to preside at Steinway Hall on an occasion when I had some expectation that Mr. Beecher himself would fill the chair.

My entire acquaintance with Mrs. Woodhull was comprised between the month of May, 1871, and the month of April, 1872—less than a year—and during a great part of that time I was absent from the city on a lecturing tour. During my whole acquaintance with her I never heard from her lips an unladylike word nor noted in her behavior an unchaste act. Whatever she may have since become (and I know not), she was then high in the esteem of Lucretia Mott, Elizabeth Cady Stanton, Isabella Beecher Hooker, and other persons whose judgment of what constitutes a good woman I took to be sound and final. The story of any ill-behavior between Mrs. Woodhull and me, she herself has done me the justice—unasked by me—to deny with the proper indignation which belongs to an outrage against the truth. I broke with her suddenly in the spring of 1872, because she threatened to attack several of the lady advocates of the woman suffrage cause, whom I knew and honored. In a frank conversation which I had with her at that time, full of vehemence on my part, I denounced her proposed course, washed my hands of all responsibility for *it* and *her,* and have never seen her since.

But in thus voluntarily breaking my acquaintance and co-operation with Mrs. Woodhull, I did not have the approval either of Mrs. Tilton or Mr. Beecher, both of whom felt that I had acted unwisely in parting from her so suddenly. Mr. Beecher, in particular, feared that the future would not be secure if Mrs. Woodhull were left unrestrained by Mr. Moulton or myself. Mrs. Tilton, though she grew to have a personal antipathy towards Mrs. Woodhull, nevertheless took several occasions to show friendliness towards her, and once sent her a gift-book inscribed with the words:

"To my friend, Victoria C. Woodhull.   ELIZABETH R. TILTON."

Moreover, Mrs. Tilton wrote to me from Schoharie, June 29, 1871, expressing her satisfaction with an article which I had written in the *Golden Age,* the object of which was to give to Mrs. Woodhull an honorable place in the woman suffrage movement. This article was entitled "A Legend of Good

Women," and the women whom I named in it were Lucretia Mott, Elizabeth Cady Stanton, Julia Ward Howe, Mary A. Livermore, Lucy Stone, Paulina Wright Davis, Victoria C. Woodhull, and Isabella Beecher Hooker. In this article I spoke of all those persons in such complimentary terms as I then thought their lives and labors deserved. The article was dated June 20, 1871. Mrs. Tilton's letter approving it contained the following words:

"The 'Legend' seems an ingenious stroke of policy to control and hold together the fractions elements of that noble band."

In view of such a letter, with such a date—namely, a year after Mrs. Tilton's confession, and a half a year after Mr. Beecher's apology—I need not comment on the pretense that one of the causes of the trouble which led to the scenes of December, 1870, ending with Mr. Beecher's apology, was my relations with Mrs. Woodhull—whom I never saw till half a year afterwards, and whom Mrs. Tilton herself was complimenting at a still later period as one of "a noble band."

Mr. Beecher's extraordinary statement that he besought me to part from Mrs. Woodhull is not only wholly untrue, but even after I had parted from her, which I did in the spring of 1872, he wanted me to renew my good-will towards her for the sake of the influence which he thought I could exert over her plans and purposes—an influence for the suppression of the scandal and for his personal safety.

It was not until after the publication of her malicious story, November 2, 1872, that Mr. Beecher besought me to print a card publicly disavowing Mrs. Woodhull; but his sole object in then wishing me to do so was that my disavowal would be a denial of Mrs. Woodhull's charge incriminating his character.

I have thus given an exact history of my personal relationship with Mrs. Woodhull, and of the motive which inspired my services towards her. Now that I look back upon those days and sacrifices, my only marvel is that I did not commit acts of greater folly for the sake of preventing the exposure of my family secret. I ought to have known that such efforts could not, by their very nature, be successful, except for a short time. We do not learn everything in a day. But, however much I am to blame for my association during a few months with Mrs. Woodhull, the Rev. Henry Ward Beecher is not the man to criticise me for it, for he participated in it, urged it forward, was the first person to express to me his regret at its discontinuance, and never asked me to "disavow" that dangerous woman until she published a story which he wanted me to deny for his own sake.

I will simply add that my relations with Mrs. Woodhull differed in no kind, almost in no degree, from Mr. Beecher's relations with her, except, that I saw her more frequently than he, and was less smooth-spoken to her face, and less insulting behind her back; nor can Mr. Beecher now throw over me the shadow of Mrs. Woodhull's darkened name, without also covering his own with the same cloud.

XIII—In my Sworn Statement I made oath to the fact that Mr. Beecher confessed to me his criminal intimacy with Mrs. Tilton. I will state the substance of this confession, which was often renewed and repeated.

On the night of December 30, 1870, during my interview with him at Mr. Moulton's house, he received my accusation without denial, and confessed it by his assenting manner and grief.

In the apology written January 1, 1871, which he sent me through Mr. Moulton, his contrition was based on the fact that both Mr. Moulton and I had become acquainted with his guilt.

During the subsequent personal interview which took place between Mr. Beecher and myself at Mr. Moulton's house a few mornings afterward, Mr. Beecher in set terms spoke to Mr. Moulton and myself of the agony and remorse which he had suffered within the past few days at having brought ruin and blight upon Elizabeth and her family. He buried his face in his hands and wept, saying that *he* ought to bear the whole blame, because from his ripe age and sacred office he was unpardonably culpable in leading her astray. He assured me that during the earlier years of his friendship for Elizabeth he and she had no sexual commerce with each other, and that the latter feature of their intimacy had been maintained between them not much over a year and less than a year and a half.

He said to me that I must do with him what I would—he would not resist me—but that if I could possibly restore Elizabeth to my love and respect he would feel the keen edge of his remorse dulled a little into less pain. He asked me if I would permit the coming pew-renting to proceed, and that if I insisted on his resignation he would write it forthwith. He reminded me that his wife was my bitter enemy, and would easily become his own and begged that she might not be informed of his conduct. He said that he had meditated suicide, and could not live to face exposure. He implored me to give him my word that if circumstances should ever compel me to disclose his secret, I would give him notice in advance, so that he might take some measure, either by death or flight, to hide himself from the world's gaze. He said that he had wakened as from a sleep, and likened himself to one sitting dizzy and distracted on the yawning edge of hell. He said that he would pray night and day for Elizabeth, that her heart might not be utterly broken, and that God would inspire me to restore her to her lost place in my home and esteem.

All this, and more like it, took place in the interview of which I speak, including his voluntary proposition to mend certain ill work which he had done in giving to Mr. Bowen false reports about me.

Shortly afterward, I sent for Mr. Beecher to come to my house to hold an interview with me on a subject which I shrink from mentioning here, yet which the truth compels me to state. In June, 1869, a child had been born to Elizabeth R. Tilton. In view of Mrs. Tilton's subsequent disclosures to me, made July 3, 1870—namely, that sexual relations between Mr. Beecher and herself had begun October 10, 1868—I wished to question Mr. Beecher as to the authenticity of that date, in order to settle the doubtful paternity of the child. This interview he held with me in my study, and during a portion of it Mrs. Tilton was present. They both agreed on the date at which their sexual commerce had begun—namely, October 10, 1868, Mrs. Tilton herself being the authority, and referring again, as she had done before, to her diary.

Certain facts which Mr. Beecher gave me on that occasion, concerning his criminal connection with Mrs. Tilton—the times, the places, the frequency, together with other particulars which I feel a repugnance to name—I must pass over ; but I cannot forbear to mention again, as I have stated heretofore, that Mr. Beecher always took the blame to himself, never imputing it to Elizabeth ; and never till he came before the Investigating Committee did he put forth the unmanly pretext that Mrs. Tilton had "thrust her affections on him unsought."

On numerous occasions, from the winter of 1871 to the spring of 1874, Mr. Beecher frequently made to me allusions, in Mr. Moulton's presence, to the abiding grief, which, he said, God would never lift from his soul for having corrupted so pure-minded a woman as Elizabeth Tilton to her loss of honor, and also for having violated the chastity of friendship towards myself as his early and trusting friend.

Never have I seen such grief and contrition manifested on a human countenance as I have often seen it on Henry Ward Beecher in his self-reproaches for having accomplished Elizabeth's ruin. The fact that he suffered so greatly from constant fear of an exposure of his crime made me sometimes almost forget the wrong he had done me, and filled my breast with a fervid desire to see him restored again to peace with himself. At every effort which I made in conjunction with Mr. Moulton to suppress inquiry into scandal, Mr. Beecher used to thank me with a gratitude that was burdensome to receive. He always put himself before me in so dejected, humble and conscience-stricken a mood, that if I had been a tenfold harder man than I was I could not have had the heart to strike him. When I wrote the letter to the church declining to appear for trial, on the ground that I had not been for four years a member, he met me the next day at Mr. Moulton's house, and, catching my right hand in both of his, said with great feeling, "Theodore, God himself inspired you to write that letter."

When, at a later period, in the same house, he gave me the first intimation of the coming Council, he said : "Theodore, if you will not turn upon me, Dr. Storrs cannot harm me, and I shall owe my life once again to your kindness."

I could record many different expressions and acts of Mr. Beecher like those which I have above given, to show his perpetual and never-relieved distress of mind through fear of the exposure of his adultery, accompanied by a constant and growing fear that I could not really forgive him, and must sooner or later bring him to punishment.

I ought to say that I sometimes half suspected that Mr. Beecher's exhibitions to me of profound dejection and heart-break were not real but feigned, being of the nature of appeals to my sympathies, which (he knew) were always readily aroused at the sight of distress. But Mr. Moulton never admitted any doubt of Mr. Beecher's real penitence, and this was one of the reasons why Mr. Moulton sought so zealously to shield this sorrowful man from the consequences of his sin.

I close this section by declaring, with a solemn sense of the meaning of my words, that Mr. Beecher's recent denial under oath that he committed adultery with Mrs. Tilton is known to him, to her, to Mr. Moulton, to me, and to several other persons to be an act of perjury.

XIV. Perhaps there is no single touch of hypocrisy in Mr. Beecher's statement that exceeds his following allusion to his domestic happiness :

"His (Mr. Tilton's) affairs at home [says Mr. Beecher] did not promise that sympathy and strength which makes one's house, *as mine has been*, in times of adversity, a refuge from the storm and a tower of defense."

In no ordinary controversy would I be justified in taking up such an allusion as this of Mr. Beecher to his own home in contrast with mine, as mine once was. But the truth constrains me to do so now. Mr. Beecher's purpose, thus adroitly expressed, is to set himself before the public in the light of a man who has so happy a home of his own that he does not need to covet his neighbor's wife.

But, on the contrary, as Mrs. Tilton has repeatedly assured me, and as she has assured confidential friends to whom her confessions have been made, Mr. Beecher had a house which was not a home—a wife who was not a mate ; and hence he sought and found a more wifely companion. He often pictured to Mrs. Tilton the hungry needs of his heart, which he said Mrs. Beecher did not supply ; and he made his poverty and barrenness at home the ground of his application to Mrs. Tilton to afford him the solace of a supplemental love.

In the days when I was confidential with Mr. Beecher, he used to pour in my ears unending complaints against his wife, spoken never with bitterness, but always with pain. He said to me one day, "O Theodore, God might strip all other gifts from me if He would only give me a wife like Elizabeth and a home like yours." One day he walked the streets with me saying, "I dread to go back to my own house ; I wish the earth would open and swallow me up." He told me that when his daughter was married, Mrs. Beecher's behavior on that occasion was such as to wring his heart ; and when he described her unwifely actions during that scene he burst into tears, and clenched his hands in an agony which I feared would take the form of a revenge. He has told me repeatedly of acts of cruelty by Mrs. Beecher towards his late venerable father, saying to me once that she had virtually driven that aged man out of doors. A catalogue of the complaints which Henry Ward Beecher has made to me against his wife would be a chapter of miseries such as I will not depict upon this page.

Many of his relatives stand in fear of this woman, and some of them have not entered her house for years—as one of Mr. Beecher's brothers lately testified in a public print. I have seen from one of his sisters a private letter concerning the marital relations of Mr. and Mrs. Beecher which it would be scandalous to reproduce here. And yet this man, in order to give to the ignorant public one of human nature's most plausible reasons why a man should not invade another's house, paints a false picture of the sweet refuge of his so-called happy home.

I know that my allusion to Mr. Beecher's home-life is rough and harsh, but I know also that it is true; for as I pen it down there rises in my mind a vivid recollection of the many years of my daily association with Mr. Beecher during which he taught me to sympathize with him for the very reason that his house, instead of being what he now calls it, "a refuge from the storm," was more often the storm itself, from which he sought refuge in mine.

Mr. Beecher has charged me with blackmail. This charge wore a cold and keen point for a single morning, but soon melted away like an icicle in the sun. The angry indictment had so brief a vitality that the life was all gone from it before the Committee wrote their verdict. In that verdict the Committee did not repeat that charge, knowing that it could not be sustained. They made only the faintest possible allusion to the subject, by suggesting that "innocent men have sometimes been blackmailed," but they even neglected to mention that Mr. Beecher was one of these.

Now, although the Committee have dismissed the subject of blackmail as too tenuous to be made a part of their special pleadings, I am not willing that this outrageous pretense shall be allowed to pass into swift and easy oblivion. I will do what the Committee had not the courage to do—I will revive Mr. Beecher's charge of blackmail, in order that I may take apart, piece by piece, the ingenious but fallacious argument which he put forth to sustain this visionary indictment.

In the first place, before Mr. Beecher ventured on such an extravagant accusation he prepared the way for it by misrepresenting me as a man reduced to such poverty and desperation that I would be likely to resort to blackmail. As a preliminary requisite for the coming charge Mrs. Tilton was instructed to say that I had deprived her of food and fire—a statement showing a condition of distress not only on her part, but on mine ; a distress so great that (as hunger is said to break through stone walls) would presumably tempt me to commit murder, highway robbery, or blackmail.

But it so happens that at the very time when (according to this description) I was without the means to furnish food and fire to my family, namely, the winter of 1870-71, *I had several thousands of dollars in cash* to my account on the books of an eminent commercial house in New York—a larger sum than I ever had at any one time in loose money even in my most prosperous days ! *And Mr. Beecher knew of this fact at the time,* because when Mrs. Morse wrote to him the letter in which she falsely and impudently said that if my honest debts were paid I would not be worth a cent, Mr. Beecher was then informed by one of the custodians of my money, first, that I had no debts unpaid, and next that I had several thousands of dollars in cash to my account.

I distinctly declare, therefore, that the story put into Mrs. Tilton's mouth by the persons who advised her to say that she had not the means wherewith to feed and warm herself and family, was a fabricated statement put forth to be one of the necessary preliminaries to the subsequent charge of blackmail.

After thus falsely misrepresenting me as passing the winter of 1870-71 without food and fire, Mr. Beecher's second preliminary to the intended charge of blackmail consisted in his saying that in the following winter of 1871-72 I was driven in disgrace from the public platform, and that my lecturing engagements were brought to naught. In vivid language he portrays my supposed distress at this time thus :

"The winter following (1871-72), Mr. Tilton [he says] *returned from the lecturing field in despair. Engagements had been canceled, invitations withdrawn, and he spoke of the prejudice and repugnance with which he was everywhere met as indescribable.*"

The above statement is not only the direct opposite of the truth, but when I first came upon it in the midst of Mr. Beecher's defense, and before I saw the end to which it pointed—namely, that it was a step in the argument to prove me a man in sufficient desperation to resort to blackmail—I could not understand the mysterious purpose of his coining such an unnecessary fiction ; but soon afterwards I saw that, as Mrs. Tilton's invention of her privations of food and fuel came first in order, so next came Mr. Beecher's equally fanciful invention of my lecturing losses and disgrace. Both of these alleged events—one occurring one winter, the other in the next—were to create the desperate determination of mind on my part which was to turn me into a blackmailer.

Mrs. Tilton's falsities (I call them hers, always remembering that they were not of her own prompting) have already been sufficiently answered. I need only to answer Mr. Beecher's. And if he does not blush for his statement above quoted when he reads the following refutation of it, then he must be lost to a proper regard for that strict truth which should form the basis of any and every accusation which one man brings against another.

NOTE FROM MR. TILTON'S LECTURE AGENT.

"COOPER INSTITUTE, NEW YORK, }
"September 1, 1874. }

"DEAR SIR : In reference to our books, I find that *you filled more lecture engagements during the season of 1871-72 than any other of the one hundred or more lecturers, readers, &c., on our list, save one.*

"Only three of your engagements were canceled, and two of these were in the West, where the great Chicago fire had almost paralyzed the lecture business. All lecturers in the West that season suffered from canceled engagements. In seven places you were called to give a second lecture, and in one place a third.   Very truly yours,

"American Literary Bureau,
"CHARLES MUMFORD, Vice President.

"Theodore Tilton, Esq."

Mrs. Tilton, who accompanied me at my request during a portion of the above-named lecturing trip (for I thought that if she were thus seen traveling with me, the stories against her would receive in that way a most effectual rebuff), wrote home the following :

MRS. TILTON TO MRS. '——.

"WATERTOWN, MASS., March 1, 1872.
"MY SWEET FRIEND : * * * Theodore has about twenty engagements remaining, which will bring us home the last week in March. We have met with exceedingly nice people, *and always Theodore reinstates himself against the prejudices grown up the past year.* * * *
"YOUR DEAR ELIZABETH."

It will thus be seen that Mr. Beecher's declaration that I had lost my lecturing engagements, and was heaping up prejudices against myself wherever I went is flatly contradicted by Mr. Mumford, my lecturing agent, who says that of his hundred lecturers and readers I had more engagements than any other person save *one;* and Mrs. Tilton testifies that instead of my giving rise to prejudices against myself I was everywhere clearing them away!

What becomes of Mr. Beecher's case when its principal statements are thus, one after another, seen to be utterly baseless, and therefore utterly base ?

Mr. Beecher—after first instigating Mrs. Tilton to say that in the winter of 1870-71 our house was a hovel of privations, and then permitting himself to declare that in the following winter of 1871-72 I was hunted from the public rostrum and deprived of my livelihood—had by these two misrepresentations plausibly reduced me, in his statement, to the condition of a man whose next alternative would be to levy blackmail.

After these progressive preparations for his intended indictment, Mr. Beecher next exhibits the same cat-footed care in presenting his successive charges.

Thus he cautiously pretends, before directly preferring his main accusation of blackmail, that I made use of him to extort from Mr. Bowen the sum of $7,000.

There is something to provoke a smile in this insinuation, for I have yet to hear of any man, living or dead, who has been able to extort from Mr. Bowen a cent of money not justly due.

What is the story of the $7,000 which I received from Mr. Bowen ? It was a just debt which Mr. Bowen owed me and paid me, and that was the whole matter; but he did not pay me through Mr. Beecher's influence, nor through any other influence save the necessary obligation devolving on a man who owes money to pay it. The transaction was as follows : According to the contracts made between Mr. Bowen and myself in the latter part of December, 1870, I was to edit the Brooklyn *Union* for five years, at an annual salary of $5,200, together with ten per cent. of the profits ; and I was to furnish to the *Independent* a weekly article at an annual salary of $5,200, making, from these two sources, a yearly income estimated by Mr. Bowen at $14,000 and upwards. These two contracts contained the following provisions, namely : They could be annulled by the death of either party, or by the consent of both parties, or by one party giving to the other half a year's notice of intention to do so, or at once by either party paying to the other a forfeit equal to half a year's income, say about $7,000. Mr. Bowen, through Mr. Beecher's influence (as Mr. Beecher admits), chose to terminate these contracts *at once.* He had a perfect right to do this on paying the stipulated forfeit of $7,000. If these contracts had been terminated in this manner by me instead of by Mr. Bowen, I would have been legally bound to pay Mr. Bowen a half year's income, or $7,000. In like manner, the contracts having been terminated by Mr. Bowen, he was bound to pay the same amount to me. The contracts showed on their face exactly what they meant. and were as peremptory as a note of hand. The only possible doubt as to the precise amount of money due under them was, How much did ten per cent. of the *Union's* profits amount to? Mr. Bowen, who has a clever business faculty for submitting all money claims to arbitration, on the economical ground that arbitrators usually compromise by cutting the disputed claim in two, like a knife through a peach—giving each party half—sagaciously urged me to arbitrate. This proposition I first declined, fearing that my just claim would be cut in two like the peach. This declinature I made by the advice of Mr. Moulton, who was not willing that I should lose a penny of my just due. Meanwhile Mr. Bowen, who knew something but not everything of Mr. Beecher's relations with Mrs. Tilton, naturally felt that I would be sensitive about collecting my claim through a lawyer and in a court, from my unwillingness to involve Mr. Beecher and thereby compromise my family. Accordingly Mr. Bowen felt safe in dilly-dallying concerning the payment beyond my point of patience. At length I instructed Mr. F. A. Ward, of the law firm of Reynolds & Ward, of Brooklyn, to stop Mr. Bowen's sharp practice and collect my claim at once in court. About the same time, but wholly unconnected with this affair, I wrote an article for the *Golden Age*, correcting, in behalf of my Western readers (among whom I had just been traveling as a lecturer), some unfounded reports that my retirement from the editorial chair of the *Independent* had not been (as Mr. Bowen publicly said it was in December, 1870) "to my honor," but was from some cause not honorable to myself. The proof-sheet of this article I showed in advance to Mr. Moulton, who, seeing that it disagreeably introduced the name of Mr. Beecher, begged me on that account to suppress it. He showed it to Mr. Beecher, who shrank from the prospect of its publication because it contained Mr. Bowen's charges against him. Mr. Moulton, finding Mr. Beecher greatly concerned and full of trepidation, conferred, at Mr. Beecher's request, with Mr. Horace B. Claflin, who, having some mysterious influence over Mr. Bowen (which I am not able to this day to understand), advised Mr. Bowen to settle my claim at once and not permit me to put it into the courts, since legal proceedings would reflect equally on Mr. Bowen and Mr. Beecher by exhibiting their mutual grievances in a glaring light to the public.

It was wholly in Mr. Beecher's interest and not in mine that Mr. Moulton and my legal advisers withheld my claim of $7,000 from a public court, and handed it over to private arbitration. The following letters will prove this point to a demonstration:

MR. MOULTON TO MR. CLAFLIN.

"BROOKLYN, April 1, 1872.

"MY DEAR MR. CLAFLIN; After full consideration of all interests, *other than Theodore's*, I have advised him to arbitrate, etc. * * * Cordially yours,

"FRANCIS D. MOULTON."

JUDGE REYNOLDS TO MR TILTON.

"LAW OFFICES OF REYNOLDS & WARD,
"April 1. 1872.

"MY DEAR MR. TILTON: On strictly legal grounds I should strenuously advise you against any submittance to arbitration of your differences with Mr. Bowen. I consider your case so clear in law that there is no reason, *so far as you are concerned*, for diverting its prosecution from the regular course.

"But there are weighty moral considerations arising out of the fact that *other parties* might be seriously involved, which lead me to hope you may secure your rights through the proposed arbitration.

"You can only do so, however. by obtaining not only the money due you but a personal vindication at the hands of Bowen. A trial of the case in a public court would afford such vindication, and if you forego that Mr. Bowen must expect to clear you himself from the imputations which his conduct has cast upon you. Yours very truly,

"GEORGE G. REYNOLDS."

MR. WARD TO MR. TILTON.

"LAW OFFICES OF REYNOLDS & WARD,
"April 2. 1872.

"MY DEAR SIR: I fully share in the reluctance which I believe Judge Reynolds has expressed, that this matter should be left to arbitration.

"The case is as clear as daylight, and the arbitration is entirely in the interest of a *third* party, not yourself.

"I am acting of course as your *legal* adviser: if *you* are acting as the counsel of a *third* party I have nothing to say.

"Personally I would not consent to the arbitration unless Bowen would pay the full amount due under the contract and give a full justification besides of your integrity.

"In other words there is no possible object in arbitration, as all your rights can be clearly established in a court of law. Very truly yours,

"F. A. WARD."

The "third party" mentioned in the above letters was none other than the Rev. Henry Ward Beecher. It was for Mr. Beecher's sake—for his alone, not mine—that my just claim against Mr. Bowen was held in abeyance for a year and a half, and was then finally kept out of court and settled privately through Mr. Moulton's fear that a public lawsuit. which Mr. Bowen seemed at one time to invite for the sake of the mischief which it promised to disclose against Mr. Beecher, would result in irretrievable damage to Mr. Beecher's name. Mr. Moulton's special apprehension was that Mr. Bowen, cherishing a secret hostility to his pastor, was tempting me to carry the case into court for the purpose of involving Mr. Beecher in a public scandal.

When, therefore, Mr. Beecher says that I made use of him to extort $7,000 from Mr. Bowen, he speaks what is not true. The truth is, that my just claim of $7,000 would have been paid long before it was except for Mr. Moulton's reluctance to give Mr. Bowen an opportunity to use legal proceedings as an indirect means of gratifying his supposed revengeful feelings against Mr. Beecher.

It was Mr. Claflin who persuaded Mr. Bowen to withhold the case from Court and submit it to arbitration. The three arbitrators were Horace B. Claflin, James Freeland, and Charles Storrs. They met at the house of Mr. Moulton, who was present during the interview. Mr. Bowen and I appeared before them. I made no claim for a specific amount, but simply laid my two contracts on the table and said, "Here are two contracts which Mr. Bowen and I mutually signed. Read them and judge for yourselves how much money is due me." Mr. Claflin then took out his lead-pencil, asked how much the profits of the *Union* were, footed up the figures, requested Mr. Bowen and myself to retire into the front parlor for a few minutes, summoned us back shortly afterward, and announced that the arbitrators, after having read the contracts, had unanimously decided that Mr. Bowen owed me $7,000. Mr. Bowen thereupon took from his pocket a blank check, filled it out on the spot for $7,000, and handed it to me, saying that the next week's *Independent* should contain a handsome tribute to me at the head of the editorial columns.

Before this proposed tribute was printed I had meanwhile sent to Mr. Bowen a note asking him to correct certain false reports concerning my retirement from the *Independent*. In reply to this note he sent me privately the following:

MR. BOWEN TO MR. TILTON.

"*Mr. Theodore Tilton.*

"Sir: I shall publish with great pleasure in the *Independent* your letter to me, followed by such editorial remarks as, I trust, will please you and your numerous friends.

"We have been bound together as co-workers for many years, and I now most solemnly declare to you that never for one moment have I entertained a single unfriendly feeling towards you.

"To-day I rejoice that we may meet and clasp hands as friends.

"If I have done you any wrong in the past I most sincerely regret it, and ask you to overlook and forget it. Henceforth let us have peace and goodwill between us, each doing his own work in his own way as it seemeth best in the sight of God.

"We shall meet now as friends, and I hope as Christian friends ; and no act of mine shall disturb our friendly relations.

"With many good wishes for you and yours, I am, truly your friend,

          "HENRY C. BOWEN."

In addition to the above letter, Mr. Bowen sent me, within a day or two, the following :

MR. BOWEN TO MR. TILTON.

"*Mr. Theodore Tilton.*

"Sir : I authorize you to say at any time, at your discretion, and on my authority, that your retirement from the *Independent* and daily *Union* was for no unfriendly reasons or any desire on my part to reflect on your character or standing ; and furthermore, that whatever tales or rumors may exist to your injury, I most sincerely regret and condemn.

"With a sincere desire for your best present and future welfare and prosperity, and that of your respected family, I remain your friend,

          "HENRY C. BOWEN.

"BROOKLYN, April 3, 1872."

Simultaneously with the receipt of the above private letters from Mr. Bowen came the *Independent*, containing at the head of its editorial columns a very handsome personal tribute to myself, which, as Mr. Moulton quoted it in substance, I need not reproduce here. In this article Mr. Bowen referred to what he was pleased to style "my long and brilliant services to the *Independent*," and he said in it :

"We have felt too kindly towards him to allow the *Independent* to countenance the abuse heaped upon him by some other papers."

Furthermore, as if expressly to furnish me in advance with the best possible material for answering Mr. Beecher's charge that I had extorted money from Mr. Bowen, he (Mr. Bowen) spoke particularly as follows :

"Our disagreement with him on some religious and other questions does not prevent our recognizing his honest purposes, and his chivalrous defense of what he believes to be *true*, as well as those qualities of heart which make him dear to those who know him best."

I have thus quoted Mr. Bowen's effectual answer to the charge that I had wronged him in any way ; but I am happily able to quote Mr. Beecher's own answer to it, which will be still more triumphant ! Mr. Beecher was so gratified at my settlement with Mr. Bowen and the encomium of me in the *Independent*, that he copied it into the next week's *Christian Union*, with an added eulogy of his own, as follows :

MR. BEECHER PRAISES MR. TILTON.

[*From Mr. Beecher's Article in the Christian Union, April* 17, 1872.]

"This honorable testimony from Mr. Bowen [says Mr. Beecher] ought to clear away the misconceptions which have shaded the path of this brilliant young writer. *We have never parted with our faith that time would reconquer for Theodore Tilton the place in Journalism, literature, and reform to which his talents and past services entitle him.* * * * Upon this testimony of the estimation in which his principles and character are held by a wise and strong man, who was closely associated with him for fifteen years in the conduct of the *Independent* the public must needs put aside prejudices of judgment which they have permitted to cloud this young orator and writer. Those who know him best are the most sure that he is *honest in his convictions, as he is fearless in their utterance, and that he is manly and straightforward in the ways in which he works for what seems to him best for man and for society.*

"We trust that the gold in the *Golden Age* will not grow dim, but that, dropping its drops in the refining fires, it will shine with the luster of gold seven times refined and purified."

I leave the above article by Mr. Beecher, written two years ago by his own pen, in his own journal, touching the settlement of this very disputed claim with Mr. Bowen concerning the identical $7,000 now in question—I leave this article by Mr. Beecher to confute Mr. Beecher's recent pretense that I used him to extort this money from Mr. Bowen !

Mr. Beecher's next step in the fanciful argument to prove me a blackmailer is his mention of the payment to Mr. Moulton of certain sums of money amounting to $2,000. I had nothing to do with this money or any part of it. But I happen to know that it went, either in whole or in part, to pay the girl Bessie's school-bills at the Steubenville Seminary, Ohio. (See receipt signed by the principal.)

This child came to my house a dozen years ago as a waif, bearing the name of McDermott, knowing neither father nor mother, nor relative, nor circumstances of her birth, nor her age, concerning all whom and which she remained in total ignorance for years until, after many efforts, I traced her parentage, and learned that her true name was Turner, which she has since borne.

This unfortunate child, when she lived in my family, was afflicted frequently with strange glooms, so that she sometimes passed days together in sullen silence without speaking to any one in the house, then bursting gayly into an incessant noise ; and at night she would often fall into a species of nightmare which would control her so powerfully that her moans and cries would alarm the house.

Miss Anthony, who knew her well, describes her (though I think a little too roughly) as a "half-idiot, into whose head it was impossible to instill principles of truth."

My father and mother in their joint card, from which I have already quoted, dated Keyport, N. J., August 30, 1874, refer to this child as follows :

"The girl Bessie, before she was sent to boarding-school at the West, was often an inmate of our house, and we were well acquainted with her character at that time. We grieve to say that this girl was guilty of such ill-conduct in our family, including falsehoods and insults to us, that in 1870, when she went from our house, we forbid her entering it again."

My wife's letters used to contain frequent allusions to her troubles with Bessie, which were of so vexing a kind that Mrs. Tilton often doubted the rightfulness of keeping such an eccentric child in the house, for fear of her evil influence on our children. For instance, Mrs. Tilton, in a letter to me dated February 6, 1867, speaks of this troublesome girl as follows :

"Libby [says Mrs. Tilton] continues to be the only disturber of the peace of our household. Saturday and Sunday are the time usual for her moods, and as the little girls grow older she wins them less and less to herself, owing to her unfortunate disposition. They do not love her nor get along pleasantly. I am perplexed lest my children grow irritable through her influence over them."

The above expresses a frequent complaint of Mrs. Tilton against Bessie ; and yet as my wife was a kind-hearted and self-sacrificing woman—especially zealous to do good to lowly and unfortunate persons—she could never permit herself to dismiss Bessie, and send her forth helpless into the wide world. A thousand times over has Bessie expressed her gratitude to Mrs. Tilton and me for having rescued her from some horrible fate which she used to fancy would have been hers had not our family given her a home. Nor do I believe that she would have proved an ingrate to me had she not been made a tool in Mrs. Morse's ingenious hands for working out her scheme of a divorce for Elizabeth by breaking down my reputation. It will be remembered that Bessie wrote to Mrs. Tilton, January 20, 1870, saying :

"Mrs. Morse has repeatedly *attempted to hire me by offering me dresses and presents* to go to certain persons and tell them stories injurious to the character of your husband."

The young girl whom Mrs. Morse "bribed," Mrs. Tilton "deceived," as is seen by Mrs. Tilton's letter to Mrs. P., dated November 8, 1872, as follows :

"*I have mistakenly felt obliged to deceive Bessie these two years* that my husband had made false accusations against me, which he never has to her nor any one."

The young girl—"bribed" by Mrs. Morse and "deceived" by Mrs. Tilton, and always the easy instrument of either—became suddenly one day the terror of both, for she overheard a conversation between Mrs. Tilton and myself, in which allusion was made to Mrs. Tilton's sexual intimacy with Mr. Beecher. The Committee, in their verdict, admit that the girl overheard this remark, for they quote her as using the following words :

"*He* (Mr. Tilton) said she (Mrs. Tilton) *had confessed to him that she had been criminally inti-mate with Mr. Beecher.* She identified the date at which she overheard the remark. The question was put to her, 'When was that?' and the Committee received her answer, 'This all occurred on the day that we went back in the fall of 1870.'"

After overhearing this remark, the young tell-tale went to several members of the family and re-ported it with her prattling tongue. She also went to Mr. Beecher and did the same. Mr. Beecher, in his statement, *acknowledges that Bessie came to him;* but, with that disregard of the truth which characterizes his entire defense, he changes the story which she came to him to tell, and makes it appear that her disclosure was not what the Committee admit, namely, that she had heard of Mr. Beecher's criminal relations with Mrs. Tilton, but quite another tale. The same reluctance which Mr. Beecher has since had to put the true story of Bessie's errand into Bessie's recent testimony, he long ago manifested at having her tell it to our friends and relatives. Such a tell-tale tongue was danger-ous to Mr. Beecher's peace. Accordingly, no sooner had Mr. Moulton undertaken the task of organ-izing Mr. Beecher's safety, than one of the first necessary "devices" to this end was the removal of Bessie to a safe distance from Brooklyn. So she was housed at Mr. Beecher's expense in a Western boarding-school for a term of years. The money which Mr. Beecher paid for Bessie is all the money which I ever heard (until recently) of his paying either directly or indirectly in consequence of his association with my family or with this scandal.

After Bessie was put to school, one of her first acts—and this wholly destroys the false statement that I ever sought to injure her—was to write me a letter of thanks and gratitude for her school priv-iliges, on the supposition that *I* was her benefactor. This letter I did not answer, because I thought it not prudent to undeceive the child as to her pecuniary relationship to Mr. Beecher, believing that her knowledge of this fact (if she should learn it) would only increase the very mischief which we all sought to hide. Moreover, I did not wish to take to myself an expression of thanks for benefactions which another man had made. Accordingly, I sent Bessie no answer to her letter.

Some time afterwards, however, a proposition was made to Bessie by a lady in Marietta, Ohio, one of Mr. Beecher's friends, to the effect that a young hunchback in that town, who had money enough to support a wife, but who found it difficult to find a girl who would marry him, was willing to take Bessie out of school and marry her. The moment I heard of this "device" I wrote to Bessie, giving her such good counsel as I thought the occasion demanded, warning her against marrying any one whom she did not know or respect or love. In reply to this letter she wrote me seven or eight school-girlish pages, which I still possess, dated, "Steubenville, January 13, 1873," beginning : "Mr. Tilton, my dear friend," acknowledging my letter and the admonitions which it contained; describ-ing to me her astonishment at Mrs. ——'s proposal to her to marry the deformed stranger; express-ing her repugnance to marry such a disfigured person; and ending her long letter to me as follows :

"I should have written you many times [she says] and told you how much I enjoyed and appre-ciated being here at school, but as I had written you one letter and you had not answered it, I dreamed you did not care to hear how I was getting along."

In Bessie's letters to my wife, with whom she corresponded regularly, she often addressed to me kindly messages, and on one occasion spoke of sending one of her schoolmates on purpose to be in-troduced to me.

I mention these trifles to relieve this foolish girl in part from the odium which attaches to her of having spoken with falsehood and ingratitude of a man who never showed her anything but kindness, and of whom I know she would never have thought of saying an ungrateful word until taught, four years ago, to do so by Mrs. Morse, who then invented for a bad purpose the tales which the young tale-bearer has since been instructed to repeat for a worse.

The habit of story-telling which Mrs. Morse instilled into this maid's mind is still further illus-trated in the false statement which Bessie made to the editor of the Pittsburg *Leader,* a marked copy of which journal, of August 21, 1874, has been sent to me, containing a statement made by Bessie in that city, as follows :

"Her tuition and board," she said, "were paid out of her own money, and that Mr. Tilton held $1,000 as her guardian."

I never was her guardian, nor had she ever any money of her own, nor did I ever hold any in trust for her.

This story—so wholly unnecessary and apparently without any purpose—is of a piece with the other shallow and false tales which this partly irresponsible girl has since promulgated concerning Mrs. Stanton, Miss Anthony, and myself.

It is not strange, however, that Bessie, under the influence of the deception habitually practiced upon her by Mrs. Tilton, and under the inspiration of her own native and unfortunate instinct in the same direction, and having long ago fallen into the snare of Mrs. Morse, and more recently into the manipulation of Mr. Beecher's lawyers—it is not strange, I say, that through all these influences she should have been easily fashioned into a willing tool in their hands for the reproduction of the false testimony which Mrs. Morse long ago fabricated, and which Mrs. Morse's own regard for consistency has required that Bessie should repeat afresh in the same old form.

My regret is that this shallow-minded girl, in permitting herself to be used by these people to my discredit, finds *her* name brought into the general ruin in which they have involved their *own*.

How much of Mr. Beecher's $2,000 has been spent on Bessie Turner, I do not know; but I do know that almost every letter which Bessie has written to Mrs. Tilton for the last three or four years has asked for money; I know, also, that this money came through Mr. Moulton from Henry Ward Beecher; and I know still further that the sole purpose of Mr. Beecher's paying this money, and the sole purpose of Mrs. Tilton's keeping Bessie "deceived," was because this girl accidentally overheard four years ago the remark which she repeated to the Committee, and which the Committee admit, namely, a disclosure of the criminal intimacy between Mrs. Tilton and Mr. Beecher.

I must therefore put upon Bessie the burden of blackmail, so far at least as the school-bills go, say the whole or a large part of the aforesaid $2,000.

The next step in Mr. Beecher's untruthful indictment against me brings me to the mortgage.

On the 1st of May, 1873, Mr. Beecher deceived his wife by obtaining her signature to a mortgage on his house; and he has since attempted to deceive the public by saying that the $5,000 which she thus helped him raise from a Brooklyn bank was an extortion by Mr. Moulton for blackmail in my behalf. If Mr. Beecher had succeeded in proving (which he did not) that I had used him to extort $7,000 from Mr. Bowen, and that I then had levied on him (as he likewise charged) successive assessments amounting to $2,000, he might reasonably have expected, on the basis of these two robberies of him by me, to prove me guilty, through Mr. Moulton, of a third.

Before Mr. Beecher made this charge Mr. Moulton, with a straightforward honesty which does not belong to a blackmailer, had already set forth a plain and business-like acknowledgment or receipt of $5,000 from Mr. Beecher in May, 1873—being a sum contributed by Mr. Beecher unbeknown to me, through Mr. Moulton, for the *Golden Age.* This is not all the money which Mr. Moulton contributed to the *Golden Age,* but it is all which he derived in any way from Mr. Beecher for that purpose. I never knew or dreamed that Mr. Beecher had made through Mr. Moulton such a contribution until I first learned of it, as the general public did, two months after I had ceased to be the owner of that journal.

In June last, a quarter of a year before Mr. Moulton gave to me or to the public this intelligence of the $5,000, the *Golden Age,* with its good-will, subscription list, office fixtures, and debts, together with Mr. Beecher's unknown share of contributed capital, was sold by me for a nominal sum. I have thus been saved the mortification of feeling myself at any time, even for a day or an hour, the conscious possessor of Mr. Beecher's money. I have pride enough to say that were I clothed in the rags of beggary and perishing with hunger, I would not accept a penny from Mr. Beecher for food or raiment. Had I known of this man's surreptitious gift to the *Golden Age* I would have returned it to him, saying, "Thy money perish with thee!"

Mr. Beecher trifles with the truth and is merely playing a bravado's part when he says I tinkled his gold in my pocket, and sent him in return a mock message of good-will. I sent him that message, not in mockery, but in earnest, one day last summer, shortly after the publication of the tripartite covenant, followed as that was by the pressing of Mr. West's threatening charges, and these in turn by the rumors of a future council. Mr. Beecher was reported to me to be in a state of profound depression, bordering on despair. Mr. Moulton begged me to speak some word to the stricken man to prevent him from sinking into hopeless gloom. I remembered a favorite text with Mr. Beecher, which I often heard him use years ago, and I sent it to him one Sunday morning, written on a scrap of paper, thus:

"H. W. B.—Grace, mercy, and peace.   T. T."

The next time I saw him he told me that this line, greeting him in his pulpit, had shone like a sunbeam through his mind during all that morning's service, and that I would never know how greatly it had cheered him. He added also that the least word of kindness from me always had the power to reanimate him like wine. This message of mine to Mr. Beecher has since been held up to ridicule by his attorneys, but when Mr. Beecher thanked me for sending it he was in no mood of ridicule, but only of gratitude. I told the Committee that I had sent to him at other times of his despondency other messages of like import; and I hope that so long as I live I shall always be able to do the same in similar circumstances, even to an enemy. Little did I suspect that in sending such a message to Mr. Beecher—like a straw to a drowning man—I was thereby furnishing him with materials out of which he would construct a future charge against me of blackmail.

I must not forbear to mention that the suggestion that Mr. Beecher should contribute money to the *Golden Age* came, not from Mr. Moulton but from Mr. Thomas Kinsella, editor of the Brooklyn *Eagle,* who, having made a similar offer of a larger sum to the husband of a wife whom he seduced, naturally felt, perhaps, that all men who have committed similar crimes have no alternative of safety except to purchase with money their exemption from exposure.

I have asked myself the question whether Mr. Beecher and Mr. Kinsella deliberately sought by such gifts to entangle me in their toils, and perhaps I would be rash if I were to acquit them of such a charge; for the appearances are against them in one particular, namely: both Mr. Beecher and Mr.

Kinsella are simultaneously to be tried in court as seducers, and both have meanwhile simultaneously accused me of blackmail. The joint attack which these two gentlemen thus made upon me, constrains me to relate the following circumstances:

On the Saturday before my sworn statement was read to the Committee, and while the public were expecting it with much anxiety, Mr. Kinsella called at my house, and in a long and earnest interview with me, in which he expressed in warm terms his appreciation of what he called my high intellectual and moral character, begged me to withhold from the Committee my forthcoming statement. He said to me emphatically : "Mr. Tilton, I know the justice of your case; Mr. Beecher has himself admitted to me his guilt; he has wronged you most foully; I acknowledge it all. But remember that he is an old man; his career is nearly ended, and yours has only just begun. If you will withhold your forthcoming statement, and spare this old man the blow which you are about to strike him, I will see that you and your family shall never want for anything in the world."

I declined Mr. Kinsella's polite proposition.

A few weeks afterward, while the public was similarly expecting Mr. Moulton's statement, Mr. Kinsella's business partner, Mr. William C. Kingsley, sought and obtained an interview with me, in which he urged me to use my influence with Mr. Moulton to secure the suppression of *his* statement, as Mr. Kinsella had sought the suppression of *mine*. Mr. Kingsley freely admitted to me Mr. Beecher's guilt, not from personal knowledge, but only from assured belief, derived (as I understood) from Mr. Kinsella. Mr. Kingsley's argument with me was that if Mr. Moulton's statement were added to mine Mr. Beecher would be "struck dead." "What then," asked Mr. Kingsley, "will happen to Mr. Moulton and yourself? Be assured," he said, "the world will never forgive either of you for your agency in destroying Henry Ward Beecher." At the close of this interview Mr. Kingsley expressed his sympathy with me for the pecuniary losses which he said he knew I must have sustained, growing out of the calamity which Mr. Beecher had brought upon my name and popularity, after which, feeling that I was perhaps a man to be dealt with like a member of the Legislature, Mr. Kingsley benignantly said to me—and he repeated it in Mr. Moulton's presence—that " I needed only to give him (Mr. K.) twenty-four hours' notice and he would be happy to make me a friendly token of his appreciation in the shape of $5,000."

Now, when it is remembered that Mr. Kinsella first suggested the idea that Mr. Beecher should contribute money to the *Golden Age*, and that Mr. Kingsley, Mr. Kinsella's co-proprietor of the *Eagle*, made to me a direct offer of money to purchase the suppression of the truth against Mr. Beecher, I think the public at large will put a new construction on the joint charge which Mr. Beecher and the *Eagle* have made against me of blackmail!

If it be thought strange that the editor of the Brooklyn *Eagle* should privately admit Mr. Beecher's adultery (as Mr. Kinsella has often done at club-houses and card-tables), and that he should at the same time publicly proclaim in his newspaper Mr. Beecher's innocence, let it be remembered that Mr. Kinsella is not the only editor in this neighborhood who, on this question, expresses one opinion in private, and another in public : Mr. Kinsella shares this prerogative with the editor of the New York *Tribune*.

"Finally," says Mr. Beecher, adding the cap-sheaf to his argument, "a square demand and threat was made to one of my confidential friends that if $5,000 more was not paid, Tilton's charges would be laid before the public."

Mr. Beecher's weapon, which he draws in these words, is struck at one of the most honest and truthful of men—Mr. Francis B. Carpenter. As soon as Mr. Carpenter heard this accusation in his summer camping-ground in the woods of Lewis County, in this State, twenty-five miles from a post-office, he sent to New York the following message :

"This charge against me is a lie, concocted since Mr. Tilton's statement."

Mr. Beecher, in order to communicate the impression that Mr. Carpenter is a man capable of machinations (though, on the contrary, his character is of uncommon guilelessness and simplicity), made the following singular statement concerning Mr. Carpenter :

"I recollect [says Mr. Beecher] but one interview with him that had any peculiar significance. He came to see me once when the council was in session and our document was published. There was a phase introduced in it that Tilton thought pointed to him, and that night was in a bonfire flame and walked up and down the street with Moulton. I was at Freeland's, and in comes Carpenter, with his dark and mysterious eyes. He sat down on the sofa, and, in a kind of sepulchral whisper, told me of some matters. Says I : 'That is all nonsense ; that it meant * * * and * * * and Carpenter was rejoiced to hear it, and then went out.'"

Mr. Beecher's bugaboo paragraph about Mr. Carpenter, with its ominous stars and blanks, shall be explained ; and the explanation will prove little to the credit of a clergyman who condescends to tell not only great falsehoods but small. I had read in that evening's Brooklyn *Union* the document sent by Plymouth Church to the council. There was an allusion in that document, as there printed, which prompted me to send to Mr. Beecher, through Mr. Carpenter, the following message:

MR. TILTON TO MR. CARPENTER.

"No. 174 Livingston Street,
March 25, 1874.

" *Mr. Francis B. Carpenter:*

"My Dear Sir : As you are a friend both to Mr. Beecher and myself, I request you to call his attention to the following paragraph which occurs in an official paper adopted by his church this morning, and reported in the Brooklyn *Union* this evening:

" 'It was not given to us always to be indifferent when Sanballat and Tobias mocked—still less when our own familiar friends, in whom we trusted, which did eat of our bread, lifted up the heel against us.'

"You will do me the favor to ask Mr. Beecher whether or not the above allusion to Sanballat or Tobias was pointed directly or indirectly at myself. Furthermore, please say to him, in my behalf, that I will give him the opportunity to undo such an impression, if he wishes to embrace it. If not, I shall feel at liberty to take such notice of it as I think my own self-respect requires. Truly yours,

"Theo. Tilton."

Mr. Carpenter, on bearing the above message to Mr. Beecher, received from him, in reply, the statement : "No, I did not refer to Theodore ; for Sanballat and Tobias are Storrs and Buddington."

Before Mr. Carpenter came away, Mr. Beecher, apparently forgetting that he had already made one answer, wrote another to be sent to me, as follows :

MR. BEECHER TO MR. CARPENTER.

"My Dear Mr. Carpenter : The paragraph which appeared in the *Union* respecting Sanballat and Tobias was *not* in the copy read to the council, nor in the printed copy distributed, as you will see by the copy given you herewith.

"A number of things in the original draft were stricken out as having too much *feeling* towards our antagonists. This was among them. It was directed to *Buck and Dwight Johnson.* But I protested against it and thought it was struck out before going to the printer. When the 'revise' came this morning I had it struck out of the ten or twelve copies—and the regular edition does not have it. But nothing was further from the mind of the writer, and nothing further from the thought of the committee, and certainly from *my* thought, than that it referred to Mr. Tilton.

"Yours cordially,	H. W. Beecher."

I have little respect for any man, and particularly for a clergyman, who can trifle with the truth in the manner indicated by the two different answers which Mr. Beecher gave to Mr. Carpenter within the same hour.

Mr. Beecher's whole charge against Mr. Carpenter is as false as the spirit of the above note.

Nor can I understand how Mr. Henry M. Cleveland, who has visited my office many times in company with Mr. Carpenter, and has always professed to be a warm friend to both Mr. Carpenter and myself, could consent to be referred to by Mr. Beecher as having received from Mr. Carpenter a proposition of blackmail. My associates in the *Golden Age* will testify that during the last year or more, whenever Mr. Cleveland has called to see me (as he has frequently done) he has always expressed a cordial interest in my welfare, and evinced an esteem for me of a more than ordinary kind. He has repeatedly referred to the pleasure which he professed to take in my society, at his country residence. Moreover, only a few months ago, being one of the proprietors of the *Christian Union*, and finding that that paper was in need of one hundred thousand dollars to carry it forward, he intimated to me his intention to quit Mr. Beecher as "a sinking ship." About the time of my publishing the Bacon letter, Mr. Cleveland called on me, and, taking from his pocket a letter from his wife, said that if he felt at liberty to read it to me, which he did not, I would be glad to hear that that good lady sympathized with my side of the controversy as thus far developed. During the session of the present Committee, Mrs. Tilton came home on the night of her first meeting with it, and quoted to me a remark which Mr. Cleveland had made to her, in the presence of the whole Committee, in these words: "Mrs. Tilton, you don't know how much I love your husband." And yet this is the gentleman who—having a pecuniary interest in Mr. Beecher as his business partner—undertakes, for the furtherance of a desperate defense, to accuse his intimate friend, Mr. Carpenter, of being a conspirator, with me, another friend, in the heinous crime of blackmail ! I do not wonder that neither Mr. Cleveland nor any of his five associates in the Committee had the courage, in making up their verdict, to perpetuate a charge of which they grew so quickly ashamed.

Let me adduce a few further particulars touching this charge of blackmail ; for it is not enough that the Committee have abandoned it—they ought never to have entertained it.

Mr. Beecher, after mortgaging his house, May 1, 1873, "mentioned that fact," he says, "to Oliver Johnson."

This statement leads me to refer to a striking evidence of the profound effect which this information—namely, my conspiring in a scheme of blackmail—must have produced on Mr. Johnson's mind. Among my souvenirs is a beautiful little book, printed on tinted paper, entitled "In Memoriam," containing a funeral tribute spoken by me at the bier of Mrs. Mary A. Johnson, wife of Oliver Johnson, on June 10, 1872. It was about a year afterward—May 1, 1873—that Mr. Beecher mortgaged his house, and "mentioned the matter to Oliver Johnson." On the ensuing June 4th of that year, when the mortgage must have been a fresh and recent topic of reflection by all who had been informed of it as a blackmailing operation, Mr. Johnson wrote me an affectionate letter, from which I make the following quotation:

"MY DEAR THEODORE: * * * I have often thought that when I should be dead I should wish you to speak words of comfort to those who love me, and pay a tribute to my memory. Yours lovingly,

"OLIVER JOHNSON."

Mr. Johnson omitted a good opportunity in the above note to accuse me of blackmail, if he then believed me guilty of it.

Moreover, a few months afterwards, Mr. Beecher neglected a striking opportunity to expose me, when, on the 31st of October, 1873, just about six months after the mortgage, I ascended the platform in Plymouth Church, and asked if the pastor had any charges to make against me, and he replied in a most conspicuous manner as follows:

"Mr. Tilton asks me if I have any charges to make. *I have none.*"

If Mr. Beecher then knew me to be a blackmailer, who had extorted a mortgage from him of $5,000, why did he not brand me for it on the spot, and have me mobbed at once, as the same congregation afterwards mobbed Mr. Moulton?

It will not be forgotten that during the proceedings of the Congregational Council, held in the spring of 1874, a year after my alleged extortion of money from Mr. Beecher through Mr. Moulton, Mr. Beecher wrote a letter to Mr. Moulton, in which, while denouncing so good a man as the Rev. Dr. Storrs, he at the same time took occasion to pay a tribute to myself in these words:

Theodore, who has borne so much, etc.

These are Mr. Beecher's words, written a year after the mortgage! Against all Mr. Beecher's present pleadings and pretences these words, "Theodore, who has borne so much," show that when Mr. Beecher thought of me in private he thought of my forbearance, which gives the lie to his public pretense of my extortion.

It only remains for me to say further touching the charge of blackmail—a charge impossible to attach for a day to a man like Mr. Moulton, whose honor is above such infamy, and whose wealth is above such temptation—that this charge is the false defense of a desperate man who, in thus basely pretending that his best friend blackmailed him, thereby unconsciously confesses the guilt which would have made blackmailing possible.

Wherefore, as the Committee dismissed the charge of blackmail from their verdict, so I dismiss it here.

XV.—Mr. Beecher says that I have "garbled his letters." I presented in my Sworn Statement brief extracts from his letters, simply because I had not access to the letters complete. But the letters complete bear more severely against him than the fragments which I quoted. I now ask the public to judge him by his complete letters, not by my extracts, for he will thus fall into far greater condemnation. When in my Bacon letter I quoted a few lines of Mr. Beecher's apology, it was said that if I had added the remainder of that apology the second part would have explained away the first. But it was found afterwards that the entire apology, when printed, was tenfold weightier than the few lines in my first extract. In like manner the brief phrases and paragraphs which I gave in my Sworn Statement from his letters were not afterward softened, but intensified, by the publication of the letters in full. The brief extracts were the wind—the complete letters were the whirlwind. I no more garbled Mr. Beecher's letters by making from them the extracts which I did, than I would garble the decalogue by quoting to him from it the single commandment,

"Thou shalt not commit adultery."

Nevertheless, it *is* true, as Mr. Beecher says, that his letters have been "garbled." He goes so far as to say that they have been "wickedly garbled;" and this, too, cannot be denied. But it is not I who have garbled Mr. Beecher's letters; it is Mr. Beecher himself. For I maintain that the pretended explanations which he has given of them—against their plain meaning—against what he knows to be the facts to which they refer—and against the common sense of an intelligent public; all this is garbling of a heinous kind. Mr. Beecher is the man who has garbled his letters. It is he who has tried to take out of them their manifest meaning. It is he who has perverted their plain phrases into doubtful interpretation.

Mr. Beecher saw at a glance that his letters, on being read in a straightforward manner by the public, convicted him of adultery. He knew that unless these letters could be explained into something which they did not mean he would stand self-condemned—put to death by the point of his own pen. It is the part of a brave man when he speaks to abide by his words. Mr. Beecher's behavior towards his own letters proves him to be that most pitiable of all cowards—a man who dares not face his own handwriting.

His defense is that these letters were written to express his remorse for having given to Mrs. Tilton bad advice. I have already proven by the written testimony of Mrs. Tilton's mother that Mr. Beecher never gave any such advice to Elizabeth, but gave just the opposite. But even had he given such advice—namely, that Mrs. Tilton should separate from her husband—I hold that such advice, given on the theory that her husband had deprived her of food, fuel, and personal liberty, would not have been bad, but good; and the giver of such advice would never need to have repented of giving it.

But I will go further and say that, granting such advice to have been given, and to have been bad, yet since Mrs. Tilton did not accept this advice, but rejected it—since she did not separate from her husband and home, but remained with her family as before—in other words, since Mr. Beecher's bad advice was not followed by ill consequences, but no harm whatever came of it ;—it is a mockery of human reason to say that he spent four years of remorse in contemplating the giving of bad advice which was never taken and which produced no effect of harm or ill !

Such an explanation of Mr. Beecher's letters is "garbling" indeed !

Had Mr. Beecher's alleged advice ever been given, as I believe it was not ; had this advice been followed by Mrs. Tilton's separation from her husband at that time, though no such separation then ensued ; had a permanent sundering actually taken place between husband and wife, induced without other cause than simply a clergyman's bad advice—involving the scattering of a family of children, made fatherless and motherless by that worst of all orphanage which comes by the divorce of parents ; had Mr. Beecher seen all this during the past four years as he will see it during the next four, he might well have had occasion to mourn the giving of such advice ; but I repeat that the advice which he pretends to have given was not followed ; and there is the best evidence that he never gave any such advice at all, nor ever wrote one of his letters for any such reason.

It is he, then, who has garbled away the meaning from his letters.

Mr. Beecher's adroit effort to persuade the public to accept a false interpretation of these letters is vain. They have a plain meaning which no counter-explanation can ever blot out. They are all based on one central fact, a criminal intimacy between himself and Mrs. Tilton, which had been confessed by both parties to her husband and to Mr. Moulton. This simple fact is the key which unlocks all the mysteries of these letters—if mysteries they contain. All the letters, notes, and memoranda refer to the crime of adultery, to the fear of disclosure, and to the consequent "devices" for the safety of the participants.

When Mrs. Tilton made to me her confession of July 3, 1870, it was a confession of adultery. When in her note of December 30, following, she said, "I gave a letter implicating my friend, Henry Ward Beecher," it was an implication of adultery. When in her second note of the same evening she said that Mr. Beecher had visited her bedside and reproached her for having "struck him dead," it was because she had disclosed his adultery. When Mr. Beecher cast himself upon Mr. Moulton's strong and faithful protection, it was because the wretched man had been detected in his adultery. When, during the four years that followed the 1st of January, 1871, hardly a month or week passed which did not witness Mr. Beecher in some consultation with Mr. Moulton, either by letter or in person, it was to concoct measures for concealing this adultery. When Mr. Beecher, conscious of his guilt and fearing detection, fell often into hopeless gloom at the prospect of disclosure, it was because the crime to be disclosed was adultery. When from the beginning to the end of Mr. Moulton's relationship with Mr. Beecher, those two men pursued a common plan—in which I, too, participated—this plan was to guard two families of children from the consequences of this adultery. When Mr. Beecher wrote to me his letter of contrition, it was because he sought to placate me into forgiveness of his adultery. When he asked me to remember "all the other hearts that would ache," it was because of the misery which two households and their wide connections would suffer by the discovery of his adultery. When he wrote to Mrs. Tilton that Mr. Moulton had "tied up the storm which was ready to burst upon their heads," it was because Mr. Moulton had skillfully held back Mr. Bowen's meditated proceedings against Mr. Beecher for adultery. When Mr. Beecher wrote that it would "kill him if Mr. Moulton were not a friend to Mrs. Tilton's honor," he meant that this lady's "honor," like every other "lady's honor," was her reputation for chastity, and he relied on Mr. Moulton to keep the world from knowing that this lady's pastor had soiled her "honor" by adultery. When Mr. Beecher requested Mrs. Morse to call him her "son," which she did, and when she begged him to come and see her, pledging herself not to allude to her "daughter's secret," it was because this mother knew that this "son" and daughter had committed adultery. When this mother gave this "son" the troublesome information that "twelve persons" had been put in possession of this secret, it was the guilty and perilous secret of adultery. When Mr. Beecher shuddered at the likelihood that Mr. Bowen had communicated to Mr. Claflin "the bottom facts," it was because the chief fact lying at the bottom of all was adultery. When Mr. Beecher said to Mr. Moulton, "Can't we hit upon some plan to break the force of my letter to Tilton ?" it was because the letter whose force he wished to break was his letter of contrition for his adultery. When in his despair he wrote, "Would to God, Theodore, Elizabeth and I could be friends again—Theodore would have the hardest task in such a case," it was because this "hardest task" would consist of forgiving a wife and her paramour for their adultery. When Mrs. Tilton wrote imploringly both to Mr. Moulton and to Mr. Beecher that "the papers should be destroyed," it was because those papers were records of adultery. When in brokenness of spirit Mrs. Tilton wrote to ask her seducer's forgiveness, it was because of her womanly distress at having betrayed him for his adultery. When in one of her clandestine notes to him she referred to her "nest-hiding," it was a means of more pleasantly reminding him of his own poetic expression for their adultery. When her destroyer wrote to Mr. Moulton, February 5, 1872, saying, "I would not believe that any one could have passed through my experience and be alive or sane," he confessed the agony of living on the verge of public punishment for adultery. When he said to Mr. Moulton, "You are literally all my stay and comfort," it was because this brave and tender friend was the barrier between the public and the knowledge of a clergyman's adultery. When Mr. Beecher, who was never tired of sending to his friend such love-letters as a man seldom writes to a man, said to him, "I would have fallen on the way but for the courage with which you inspired me," it was his ever grateful acknowledgment to one who was saving him from the faith which punishes clergymen for adultery. When he bewailed the "keen suspicions with which he was pressed," these were the dangerous suspicions of a congregation to whom public rumor had carried a horrible hint of their pastor's adultery. When he feared an "appeal to the church, and then a council," and prognosticated thereby a "conflagration," it was because he foresaw how the public mind would be influenced by the knowledge of his adultery. When he portrayed himself as standing in daily dread of those personal friends who were making a "ruinous defence" of him, it was because he feared that their clamorous statements of his innocence would blunderingly lead to the detection of his adultery. When he cried out that he was "suffering the torments of the damned," he was pouring out his heart's anguish to the only man to whom he had liberty to unburden his remorse for his adultery. When he said that he could not carry this burden to his wife and children, it was because he was ashamed to acknowledge to them his adultery. When he wrote to Moulton, saying, "Sacrifice me without hesitation if you can clearly see your way to his (Mr. Tilton's) safety and happiness thereby," he alluded to the sacrifice of his good name in expiation of his adultery. When he said of himself, "I should be destroyed, but he (Mr. Tilton) would not be saved," it was because all that was needed for his destruction was simply that the world should be told of his adultery. When he said "Elizabeth and her children would have their future clouded," he saw hanging over this ruined mother and her brood the black and awful cloud which hangs over every matron guilty of adultery. When he wrote "Life would be pleasant if I could see that rebuilt which is shattered," he referred to the moral impossibility of reconstructing a home once broken by adultery. When he compared himself to "Esau who sold his birthright and found no place for repentance, though he sought it carefully with tears," it was because the unpardonable crime which this minister had committed was adultery. When he spoke in eulogy of Mr. Moulton's wife as reviving "his waning faith in womanhood," it was because his thoughts were then of another and weaker woman, whose moral nature he had overcome, and who afterwards had betrayed him for his adultery. When the strong woman who had thus restored "his waning faith in womanhood" counselled him to make "a frank and manly confession of his sin, asking man's forgiveness for it, as he expected God's," and when he afterwards wrote that "her clear truthfulness laid him flat"—all this shows how he quailed before a virtuous woman's rebuke for his adultery. When he said to me that I "would have been a better man than he in such circumstances," he meant that I would have disdained to stoop to the crime of seducing the wife of an intimate friend, or of using the power of a clergyman to corrupt a trusting parishioner into adultery. When he said of me that I had "condoned my wife's fault," pointing me to this condonation as constituting on my part a pledge of forgiveness towards him, he wrote in that word "condone" the plainest possible confession of his adultery. In like manner all Mr. Beecher's letters, when read in view of the one sad and guilty fact which is the key-note to their tragic meaning, constitute a four years' history of a mind afflicted with "anxiety, remorse, fear and despair"—all in consequence of a discovered adultery.

If I have been thus explicit in reiterating Mr. Beecher's crime, it is not for the sake of proving it from his letters, for I have sufficiently proved it without help from these, but only to show that I did not *garble* these letters when I pointed to them as proofs of adultery; and I repeat that, if Beecher's letters have been (as he says) "wickedly garbled," it is he who has garbled them. It is I who have restored them to their true meaning.

XVI. I revert now to a letter of my own—the Bacon letter. Why did I write it? Let the facts speak. I wish to be candidly judged by the following statement:

"Ever since 1870 when I quitted Plymouth Church because of its pastor's crime against my family, I had been year after year persecuted by certain members and officers of that church—a persecution which its pastor might and ought to have prevented, and for which I always held him responsible; a persecution including the introduction of charges against me for slandering him, whereas the so-called slanders, instead of being false, where true: a persecution including the dropping of my name from the roll in a manner craftily designed to cast opprobrium upon me, under an appearance of official fairness by the church; a persecution involving a public insult to my family by Mr. T. G. Shearman, Clerk of the church, for which he was compelled to apologize; a persecution including the presentation to the Brooklyn Council of a document in which Mr. Beecher and his church defended themselves before that tribunal on the ground that I had been dropped for "bringing dishonor on the Christian name," whereas I had been dropped because Mr. Beecher himself was the man who had "brought dishonor on the Christian name;" a persecution culminating at last in a public implication cast upon me by the moderator of that council, the Rev. Leonard Bacon, D.D., who, after carefully studying the records of Plymouth Church in my case, decided from these that I was proven a "knave and dog," and that Mr. Beecher's behaviour towards me showed him to be "the most magnanimous of men."

This accumulation of wrongs I resolved no longer to bear. I announced this to Mr. Beecher, and told him that either he or I must correct Dr. Bacon's misrepresentations of my conduct, since these would ruin me before the world. I provided an easy way by which Mr. Beecher, without a confession of his guilt, and even without a humiliation to his feelings, could assure Dr. Bacon—and Dr. Bacon the public—that I had acted towards Mr. Beecher the part of a fair and honorable man.

I waited three months for Mr. Beecher to put this plan (or some other) into effect. But he did not choose to embrace the opportunity. He neglected—perhaps disdained it.

I then resolved—against Mr. Moulton's expostulations, but at the dictate of my self-respect—to rescue myself from the false position in which Plymouth Church and its pastor had placed me, and to make a struggle to regain my good name which I had done nothing to forfeit.

The best method of vindication which suggested itself to me was to write a public letter to Dr. Bacon giving the true reason of my retirement from Plymouth Church, which was that a wrong had been committed against me by the pastor, in evidence of which I quoted a few lines from his apology.

I well knew that I could thus make the world see at a glance (which it did) that I was less the creature of Mr. Beecher's magnanimity than *he* was of *mine*. I sought and accomplished this purpose, and this only, by the Bacon letter, and did it solely in self-defence.

Now, in so doing, I not only had no wish to compromise my wife, but, on the contrary, I sought, while rectifying *my* position, to do the same by *hers*. To this end I introduced into the Bacon letter Mr. Shearman's apology to Mrs. Tilton, together with a eulogistic reference to her in my own words, as "a lady of devout religious faith and life." The Bacon letter was thus a tribute to, not an attack upon, Mrs. Tilton.

Mr. Beecher saw by this tribute (and by others which I habitually paid to my wife) that, however willing I might be to cope with *him*, I was never willing to endanger *her*. No other man in the world knew so well as Mr. Beecher did how strong an affection I have always held—and shall always hold—for my wife. He had seen, by long observation of my sympathy for her, that his safest protection against any possible resentment of mine was always in my unwillingness to compromise this tender and wounded woman.

Accordingly, on the appearance of the Bacon letter, Mr. Beecher, after contriving various methods of meeting it (which Mr. Moulton has described), finally adopted the bold and wicked expedient of appointing a committee to inquire into the acts of a lady whom he first led into adultery, and whom he then delivered up to a tribunal for examination into her crime! Never can I forget my sickening astonishment, on her account, on the day when, by public proclamation from Mr. Beecher's pen, and amid the published clamor of his partisans, he called all the world to witness that he had commissioned six committeemen *to inquire into his offence*—his offence being also *hers*, so that an inquiry into it also involved equally the ruin of both—but especially (as in all such cases) the woman, albeit the lesser offender. On that ominous morning I shuddered for the fate of the woman whom Mr. Beecher was thus ruthlessly exposing to the hazard of public shame.

Mr. Beecher's design in this public inquiry into his "offence" and "apology" was to make a bold pretence that he had never committed any "offence" nor ever offered any "apology."

To make this pretence of innocence the more plausible to the public, his agents had previously arranged that on this same day Mrs. Tilton should take flight from her home to join Beecher in his attack on me; and she has never recrossed my threshold since that hour.

Distinctly should it be borne in mind that Mr. Beecher's publication of his challenge, and Mrs. Tilton's desertion to him to sustain it, occurred on the same morning, namely, July 11, 1874. On that morning at six o'clock she quitted the house, not to return to it; and an hour afterwards the daily papers were furnished to me, containing, under flaming head-lines, Mr. Beecher's commission to his Committee of Investigation.

These two acts—one by Mrs. Tilton, the other by Mr. Beecher—were parts of one and the same event; a joint attack on me—the two assailants striking their opening blows at the same moment.

Mr. Beecher's assault was the more public of the two, for it reached me through all the newspapers on that first morning; but in order that Mrs. Tilton's act towards me might lose no force through lack of prompt publicity, Mr. Ovington hastened to publish a card in the Brooklyn *Argus* announcing that Mrs. Tilton, on the previous Saturday, had "parted from her husband forever."

That eventful Saturday morning, the 11th of July, found me in the strangest situation of my whole life—a situation which I had not foreseen, and which I could with difficulty realize—a situation consisting of the following elements: First, I had been publicly challenged by Mr. Beecher to divulge to a church committee the story of his criminality with Mrs. Tilton; and, second, Mrs. Tilton herself, by her open desertion to her paramour, had publicly seconded him in this audacious demand.

What should I do? After two days of reflection—the most agonizing which I ever endured—I felt it my duty to accept this challenge; and in one week afterwards I laid the facts before the Committee in a document now known as my Sworn Statement.

It will thus be seen that my Sworn Statement was not given to the Committee until the ninth day after Mrs. Tilton's desertion from her husband, and after her publicly joining his enemies, who were seeking by their powerful ecclesiastical enginery to crush out his little remnant of a broken name.

Had Mrs. Tilton remained with me, my Sworn Statement would never have been made ; nor did the thought of making such a statement enter my mind until after her desertion ; but at last, when Mr. Beecher and Mrs. Tilton publicly turned upon me and demanded that I should expose them, I had no course open to me but to state the plain truth and to let all the parties abide by the consequences.

Mr. Moulton has shown how great was my desire, during the earlier sessions of the Committee, to shield my wife ; in other words, how little I demanded from the Committee in my *own* behalf and how much in *hers*. My proposed form for their report (as quoted by Mr. Moulton) concluded as follows :

"The Committee cannot forbear to state that the Rev. Henry Ward Beecher, Mr. Theodore Tilton, and Mrs. Tilton (*and in an especial manner the latter*) merit and should receive the sympathy and respect of Plymouth Church and congregation."

It was on the very next morning after I wrote the above proposed kindly and charitable report for the Committee to adopt, and showed it to my wife, who not only approved it, but expressed with tears her marvel that I should have demanded more for *her* good name than I had done for *mine ;* it was, I say, on the very next morning after my writing that very report that Mrs. Tilton, in obedience to Mr. Beecher's advisers, deserted the home to which she has never since returned.

I repeat ; therefore, that the exposure which I made to the Committee and to the public was no suggestion of mine, but was brought about by Mr. Beecher and Mrs. Tilton, who united in demanding it at my hands, and who, by this demand, left me no alternative but to comply or to refuse ; my compliance being ruin to *them ;* my refusal, ruin to *myself*. Forced to make choice between these two alternatives—both almost equally horrible to my feelings—I at last determined not to be thus browbeaten by two persons who, having received my past pardon and my continuous forbearance, seemed at last attacking my very life.

I ask the public, therefore, to weigh the one fact which I have thus set forth, namely, that the responsibility for the revelations which I have made rests, not on me, but on Mr. Beecher and Mrs. Tilton. I wash my hands of it.

XVI. This rehearsal of events will now enable me to answer two points which have been made against me. One is this—I am asked frequently : "Mr. Tilton, how could you, after condoning your wife's fault four years ago, proclaim it at so late a day ?" My answer has been just foreshadowed, and it is this : I made this exposure, not of my free will, but from compulsion ; I made it because Mr. Beecher and Mrs. Tilton compelled me to make it. I did not volunteer it. I would gladly have continued to shield both parties for the sake of one. But when Mr. Beecher and Mrs. Tilton made a public league against me, and in the face of the whole community defied me to tell the facts, I was either forced to accept their joint challenge, or, by declining it to deserve the contempt of mankind. That is my answer and candid men and women will acknowledge it to be just.

Next, I have an equally plain answer to those critics who condemn me for having committed, as they say, a blunder in condoning my wife's fault at first.

And my answer is : I am perfectly willing to accept this condemnation from all who choose to offer it—whether from foes or friends. Before God I hold that I did right and not wrong, in forgiving an erring woman who went astray through a powerful temptation. No regret beclouds my mind for this forgiveness of my wife—which, I am sure, I shall look back to from my dying bed with pleasure, not with pain. I forgave this gentle woman because I loved her ; I forgave her for her children's sake ; I forgave her because I despise the public sentiment which condones such faults in men, and then compels men to punish them in women ; I forgave her because, even after her grievous error, she still remained a woman loving right rather than wrong, and seeking good rather than evil ; I forgave her because I tenderly remembered that Christ himself forgave a similar fault in a more wicked woman—and who was I to scorn the law of His great example ? No criticism of my forgiveness of Mrs. Tilton can prick me with any pang. If all the acts of my life had been as righteous as this good deed of charity—albeit towards a woman who has since but poorly requited me for it—I would now be a better man than I am.

XVII. I have only to add that I know no words of measured moderation in which to characterize fitly Mr. Beecher's recent treatment of this broken-hearted lady, whom he has flung against the wall of Plymouth Church and dashed to pieces. First, he instituted a public committee to inquire into her adultery with him, whereas he ought to have protected her against this exposure ; then he beckoned her away from her husband's house, making her very flight bear witness to her guilt ; then he suborned her to give false testimony against her husband, with a view to destroy him before the world ; then, with unparalleled baseness, he turned upon the companion of his crime, and accused her of having been the tempter rather than the tempted—declaring that she had "thrust her affections upon him unsought ;" then he variously indicted her for what he called "her needless treachery to her friend and pastor," expressing his doubts whether to call her (as he says) "a saint or the chief of sinners," arguing (as he says again) that she must be either "corrupted to deceit or so broken in mind as to be irresponsible," debating with himself (as he says still further) whether he should not "pour out his indignation upon her and hold her up to contempt ;" and then, after making all these contemptuous references to her in his published statement, he prompted his Committee to render a verdict against her in which they declare her conduct towards Mr. Beecher, even on their own theory of her innocence, to be "utterly indefensible ;" and last of all he permitted his own journal, the *Christian Union*, to stigmatize her as a "poor, weak woman," whose testimony was of no value either for or against the man who had tempted her to utter her falsehoods in his own behalf !

All this base and brutal conduct by Mr. Beecher towards Mrs. Tilton prompts me to speak of him in fierce and burning words. But I forbear. "Vengeance is mine, I will repay, saith the Lord." I have become so used to sorrows in my life that I cannot wish for their infliction upon another man, not even on my worst enemy. I will not ask the public to visit upon Mr. Beecher any greater condemnation than for the desolation which he has brought upon those who loved, trusted, and served him, than I have in past times seen him suffer from his own self-inflicted tortures in contemplation of the very crime for which he has now been exposed to the scorn and pity of the world. I know well enough how his own thoughts have bowed him in agony to the dust ; and this is enough. Wherefore in contemplating my empty house, my scattered children, and my broken home, I thank Heaven that my heart is spared the pang of this man's remorse for having wrought a ruin which not even Almighty God can repair.

Brooklyn, September 16, 1874.   THEODORE TILTON.

www.ingramcontent.com/pod-product-compliance
Lightning Source LLC
Chambersburg PA
CBHW021711110726
47902CB00005B/1151